Battle Goddess Productions Presents

Bulfinch's Mythology

Thomas Bulfinch, 1796-1867

Initially Revised by Rev. E. E. Hale

Revised by Valerie Willis

Published By: Accomplishing Innovation Press an imprint of 4 Horsemen Publications, Inc.

Accomplishing Innovation Press
℅ 4 Horsemen Publications, Inc.
PO Box 419
Sylva, NC 28779
4horsemenpublications.com
info@4horsemenpublications.com

Artwork from cover: FRONT "Udine in Flood" by Arthur Rackham, Border from Howard Pyle; SPINE: Flower border by Howard Pyle; BACK: "Mermaid" by Warwick Goble, Border by Howard Pyle;

Artwork from title page from top to bottom: "Wagner's Ring Cycle" by Arthur Rackham, Photo of Thomas Bulfinch by Unknown Photographer, and Raven Logo by Valerie Willis.

Author: Thomas Bulfinch, 1796-1867
Initially Revised by: Rev. E. E. Hale
First published in 1859
Designed by: Valerie Willis
Interior Illustrations: Various Artists, Public Domain, many acquired from oldbookillustrations.com and Wikimedia Commons

Black and White Paperback ISBN-13: 978-1-64450-124-5
Colored Hardcover ISBN-13: 978-1-64450-233-4
Ebook ISBN-13: 978-1-64450-234-1

About This Book

Welcome to the Battle Goddess Edition of "Bulfinch's Mythology" by Thomas Bulfinch as revised by Rev. E. E. Hale. This is a cornerstone piece for anyone wanting to dive deeper into mythology of various kinds. Mr. Bulfinch does a wonderful job in making a collective account of stories for most of the entities he covers, including several excerpts from poets, historians, Milton, Homer, including his own brother, and many more. Traversing from Greek to Roman to Hindu to Celtic and beyond, this is a great book for any mythology lover. If this wasn't enticing enough, we added in the volumes of "King Arthur and His Knights" and even "Legends of Charlemagne" to give you an unforgettable resource and collection.

This book and its contents were created in the late 1800's and thus, the wording and spelling of many of the deities, places, and beyond are vastly different from their modern versions. In an attempt to bring this up to speed, while maintaining its original state, Battle Goddess Productions has replaced the spellings that may hinder someone's ability to discover more research on the stories and mythology found within. This includes the spelling of names, such as but not limited to, Corea – Korea, Thibet – Tibet, or in some cases we added the alternative spelling "Halcyone/Alcyone" in order not to lose the original grip it holds. Another change we did was break out the dialogue and excerpts so that they may stand out clearly and be easier read or found. Hope these extra efforts involving the textual content make this a more pleasant experience for discovering mythology.

The artwork found within is a collection of work from a mixture of artists from over a hundred years ago and older. A listing of artists can be found in the back matter so you may search for more of their work within our edition. Not all of the public domain images had the artist labelled, but we felt the "unknown" deserved to be shown off right along with the more well-known artists. The collective was known for illustrating fairy tales, mythology, or even prior versions of Bulfinch's own publications including Arthur Rackham, who is a personal favorite. Please note there will be two editions, a Black and White interior and a more pricey Colored version (due to added cost for coloration and paper). We wanted to make the paperback affordable, but also wanted to still provide the colored edition for those seeking something extraordinary.

If you have ever wondered where and how so many authors tie mythology into their work, then this may be the key you were looking for. Within this piece are many stories both familiar and lesser known. There will be information discovered in here that may shed light on modern retellings and inspired work like "American Gods" by Neil Gaiman to our very own "Cedric the Demonic Knight" by Valerie Willis.

By no means is this a complete collection of all things mythology, worldly, or monsters. Though, as a complete geek for mythology, it is a must-have as part of your at home collection. There are several other up to date sources, but there is a flavor you will not, cannot, find. If you wish to research these further, seek out other books such as J.A. Coleman's "Dictionary of Mythology," "The Encyclopedia of Celtic Mythology and Folklore" by Patricia Monaghan, "Norse Mythology A to Z" by Kathleen N. Daly and even Carol Rose's "Giants, Monsters, and Dragons" – all of these are found in our very own arsenal of go-to books for research.

Foreword From Battle Goddess Productions

Prepare to dive into the Rabbit Hole of Research. It's a dangerous yet precious place which often takes me to the past in unique ways. Information found within these hundred-year-old, if not older, tomes may not be accurate and do not reflect new findings in our present-day set. This is where you must be vigilant and check what you find here with other resources. Regardless, some of my best findings or at least clues have been found in older books such as this one.

I now invite you to enjoy this refreshing edition we have compiled. Inside is a layout meant to make it easier to read and a piece one can show off to friends and fellow research savvy geeks. Illustrations may not be what originally came with the content and not every book we "make pretty" had illustrations to include. For a nostalgic old-world look, we have added these treats to help the imagination and support the content in a visual manner.

Please be aware this is a Public Domain piece. This means you can find ALL the information within these pages for FREE in several areas on the internet. You should also be able to find many of these titles at your local library and even on their digital archives. Battle Goddess is responsible for the fresh look, layout, and many aesthetics that have transformed the old into a unique look for our readers' pleasure.

Beware of being consumed by the Research or falling into a place of no return!

Thank you to all our volunteer proofers:

Aisha Hall
Amy Copeland
Andretta Schellinger
Angelique M Keppler Bochnak
Annmarie O'dooley
April Allen
Arielle Haughee
Chris Coad Taylor
Cynthia Hennemann Bingham
Gene Stiles
Jen J. Schultz
Jennifer Kotick
Jennifer Sweet
Kara Tate Schilling
Karen Webster
Kathy Twigg
Kerry Tastinger
Kim Plasket
Mika Tamika
Niki Mattes
Ryan Bonner
Sett Avri Knight
Steve Harper
Tamye Davis Whitener
Vanessa Valiente

Valerie Willis

Figure 1: "Battles" by Adolf Ehrhardt

Table of Contents

The Mabinogion

Legends of Charlemagne

Original Publisher's Preface

No new edition of Bulfinch's classic work can be considered complete without some notice of the American scholar to whose wide erudition and painstaking care it stands as a perpetual monument. "The Age of Fable" has come to be ranked with older books like "Pilgrim's Progress," "Gulliver's Travels," "The Arabian Nights," "Robinson Crusoe," and five or six other productions of world-wide renown as a work with which every one must claim some acquaintance before his education can be called really complete. Many readers of the present edition will probably recall coming in contact with the work as children, and, it may be added, will no doubt discover from a fresh perusal the source of numerous bits of knowledge that have remained stored in their minds since those early years. Yet to the majority of this great circle of readers and students the name Bulfinch in itself has no significance.

Thomas Bulfinch was a native of Boston, Mass., where he was born in 1796. His boyhood was spent in that city, and he prepared for college in the Boston schools. He finished his scholastic training at Harvard College, and after taking his degree was for a period a teacher in his home city. For a long time later in life he was employed as an accountant in the Boston Merchants' Bank. His leisure time he used for further pursuit of the classical studies which he had begun at Harvard, and his chief pleasure in life lay in writing out the results of his reading, in simple, condensed form for young or busy readers. The plan he followed in this work, to give it the greatest possible usefulness, is set forth in the Author's Preface.

- "Age of Fable," First Edition, 1855;
- "The Age of Chivalry," 1858;
- "The Boy Inventor," 1860;
- "Legends of Charlemagne, or Romance of the Middle Ages," 1863;
- "Poetry of the Age of Fable," 1863;
- "Oregon and Eldorado, or Romance of the Rivers,"1860.

In this complete edition of his mythological and legendary lore "The Age of Fable," "The Age of Chivalry," and "Legends of Charlemagne" are included. Scrupulous care has been taken to follow the original text of Bulfinch, but attention should be called to some additional sections which have been inserted to add to the rounded completeness of the work, and which the publishers believe would meet with the sanction of the author himself, as in no way intruding upon his original plan but simply carrying it out in more complete detail. The section on Northern Mythology has been enlarged by a retelling of the epic of the "Nibelungen Lied," together with a summary of Wagner's version of the legend in his series of music-dramas. Under the head of "Hero Myths of the British Race" have been included outlines of the stories of Beowulf, Cuchulain, Hereward the Wake, and Robin Hood. Of the verse extracts which occur throughout the text, thirty or more have been added from literature which has appeared since Bulfinch's time, extracts that he would have been likely to quote had he personally supervised the new edition.

Finally, the index has been thoroughly overhauled and, indeed, remade. All the proper names in the work have been entered, with references to the pages where they occur, and a concise explanation or definition of each has been given. Thus what was a mere list of names in the original has been enlarged into a small classical and mythological dictionary, which it is hoped will prove valuable for reference purposes not necessarily connected with "The Age of Fable."

Acknowledgments are due the writings of Dr. Oliver Huckel for information on the point of Wagner's rendering of the Nibelungen legend, and M. I. Ebbutt's authoritative volume on "Hero Myths and Legends of the British Race," from which much of the information concerning the British heroes has been obtained

Original Author's Preface

If no other knowledge deserves to be called useful but that which helps to enlarge our possessions or to raise our station in society, then Mythology has no claim to the appellation. But if that which tends to make us happier and better can be called useful, then we claim that epithet for our subject. For Mythology is the handmaid of literature; and literature is one of the best allies of virtue and promoters of happiness.

Without a knowledge of mythology much of the elegant literature of our own language cannot be understood and appreciated. When Byron calls Rome "the Niobe of nations," or says of Venice, "She looks a Sea-Cybele fresh from ocean," he calls up to the mind of one familiar with our subject, illustrations more vivid and striking than the pencil could furnish, but which are lost to the reader ignorant of mythology. Milton abounds in similar allusions. The short poem "Comus" contains more than thirty such, and the ode "On the Morning of the Nativity" half as many. Through "Paradise Lost" they are scattered profusely. This is one reason why we often hear persons by no means illiterate say that they cannot enjoy Milton. But were these persons to add to their more solid acquirements the easy learning of this little volume, much of the poetry of Milton which has appeared to them "harsh and crabbed" would be found "musical as is Apollo's lute." Our citations, taken from more than twenty-five poets, from Spenser to Longfellow, will show how general has been the practice of borrowing illustrations from mythology.

The prose writers also avail themselves of the same source of elegant and suggestive illustration. One can hardly take up a number of the "Edinburgh" or "Quarterly Review" without meeting with instances. In Macaulay's article on Milton there are twenty such.

But how is mythology to be taught to one who does not learn it through the medium of the languages of Greece and Rome? To devote study to a species of learning which relates wholly to false marvels and obsolete faiths is not to be expected of the general reader in a practical age like this. The time even of the young is claimed by so many sciences of facts and things that little can be spared for set treatises on a science of mere fancy.

But may not the requisite knowledge of the subject be acquired by reading the ancient poets in translations? We reply, the field is too extensive for a preparatory course; and these very translations require some previous knowledge of the subject to make them intelligible. Let any one who doubts it read the first page of the "Aeneid," and see what he can make of "the hatred of Juno," the "decree of the Parcae," the "judgment of Paris," and the "honors of Ganymede," without this knowledge.

Shall we be told that answers to such queries may be found in notes, or by a reference to the Classical Dictionary? We reply, the interruption of one's reading by either process is so annoying that most readers prefer to let an allusion pass unapprehended rather than submit to it. Moreover, such sources give us only the dry facts without any of the charm of the original narrative; and what is a poetical myth when stripped of its poetry? The story of Ceyx and Halcyone, which fills a chapter in our book, occupies but eight lines in the best (Smith's) Classical Dictionary; and so of others.

Our work is an attempt to solve this problem, by telling the stories of mythology in such a manner as to make them a source of amusement. We have endeavored to tell them correctly, according to the ancient authorities, so that when the reader finds them referred to he may not be at a loss to recognize the reference. Thus we hope to teach mythology not as a study, but as a relaxation from study; to give our work the charm of a story-book, yet by means of it to impart a knowledge of an important branch of education. The index at the end will adapt it to the purposes of reference, and make it a Classical Dictionary for the parlor.

Most of the classical legends in "Stories of Gods and Heroes" are derived from Ovid and Virgil. They are not literally translated, for, in the author's opinion, poetry translated into literal prose is very unattractive reading. Neither are they in verse, as well for other reasons as from a conviction that to translate faithfully under all the embarrassments of rhyme and measure is impossible. The attempt has been made to tell the stories in prose, preserving so much of the poetry as resides in the thoughts and is separable from the language itself, and omitting those amplifications which are not suited to the altered form.

The Northern mythological stories are copied with some abridgment from Mallet's "Northern Antiquities." These chapters, with those on Oriental and Egyptian mythology, seemed necessary to complete the subject, though it is believed these topics have not usually been presented in the same volume with the classical fables.

The poetical citations so freely introduced are expected to answer several valuable purposes. They will tend to fix in memory the leading fact of each story, they will help to the attainment of a correct pronunciation of the proper names, and they will enrich the memory with many gems of poetry, some of them such as are most frequently quoted or alluded to in reading and conversation.

Having chosen mythology as connected with literature for our province, we have endeavored to omit nothing which the reader of elegant literature is likely to find occasion for. Such stories and parts of stories as are offensive to pure taste and good morals are not given. But such stories are not often referred to, and if they occasionally should be, the English reader need feel no mortification in confessing his ignorance of them.

Our work is not for the learned, nor for the theologian, nor for the philosopher, but for the reader of English literature, of either sex, who wishes to comprehend the allusions so frequently made by public speakers, lecturers, essayists, and poets, and those which occur in polite conversation.

In the "Stories of Gods and Heroes" the compiler has endeavored to impart the pleasures of classical learning to the English reader, by presenting the stories of Pagan mythology in a form adapted to modern taste. In "King Arthur and His Knights" and "The Mabinogeon" the attempt has been made to treat in the same way the stories of the second "age of fable," the age which witnessed the dawn of the several states of Modern Europe.

It is believed that this presentation of a literature which held unrivalled sway over the imaginations of our ancestors, for many centuries, will not be without benefit to the reader, in addition to the amusement it may afford. The tales, though not to be trusted for their facts, are worthy of all credit as pictures of manners; and it is beginning to be held that the manners and modes of thinking of an age are a more important part of its history than the conflicts of its peoples, generally leading to no result. Besides this, the literature of romance is a treasure-house of poetical material, to which modern poets frequently resort. The Italian poets, Dante and Ariosto, the English, Spenser, Scott, and Tennyson, and our own Longfellow and Lowell, are examples of this.

These legends are so connected with each other, so consistently adapted to a group of characters strongly individualized in Arthur, Launcelot, and their compeers, and so lighted up by the fires of imagination and invention, that they seem as well adapted to the poet's purpose as the legends of the Greek and Roman mythology. And if every well-educated young person is expected to know the story of the Golden Fleece, why is the quest of the Sangreal less worthy of his acquaintance? Or if an allusion to the shield of Achilles ought not to pass unapprehended, why should one to Excalibar, the famous sword of Arthur?—

"Of Arthur, who, to upper light restored,
With that terrific sword,
Which yet he brandishes for future war,
Shall lift his country's fame above the polar star."

[Footnote: Wordsworth]

It is an additional recommendation of our subject, that it tends to cherish in our minds the idea of the source from which we sprung. We are entitled to our full share in the glories and recollections of the land of our forefathers, down to the time of colonization thence. The associations which spring from this source must be fruitful of good influences;

among which not the least valuable is the increased enjoyment which such associations afford to the American traveller when he visits England, and sets his foot upon any of her renowned localities.

The legends of Charlemagne and his peers are necessary to complete the subject.

In an age when intellectual darkness enveloped Western Europe, a constellation of brilliant writers arose in Italy. Of these, Pulci (born in 1432), Boiardo (1434), and Ariosto (1474) took for their subjects the romantic fables which had for many ages been transmitted in the lays of bards and the legends of monkish chroniclers. These fables they arranged in order, adorned with the embellishments of fancy, amplified from their own invention, and stamped with immortality. It may safely be asserted that as long as civilization shall endure these productions will retain their place among the most cherished creations of human genius.

In "Stories of Gods and Heroes," "King Arthur and His Knights" and "The Mabinogeon" the aim has been to supply to the modern reader such knowledge of the fables of classical and mediaeval literature as is needed to render intelligible the allusions which occur in reading and conversation. The "Legends of Charlemagne" is intended to carry out the same design. Like the earlier portions of the work, it aspires to a higher character than that of a piece of mere amusement. It claims to be useful, in acquainting its readers with the subjects of the productions of the great poets of Italy. Some knowledge of these is expected of every well-educated young person.

In reading these romances, we cannot fail to observe how the primitive inventions have been used, again and again, by successive generations of fabulists. The Siren of Ulysses is the prototype of the Siren of Orlando, and the character of Circe reappears in Alcina. The fountains of Love and Hatred may be traced to the story of Cupid and Psyche; and similar effects produced by a magic draught appear in the tale of Tristram and Isoude, and, substituting a flower for the draught, in Shakspeare's "Midsummer Night's Dream." There are many other instances of the same kind which the reader will recognize without our assistance.

The sources whence we derive these stories are, first, the Italian poets named above; next, the "Romans de Chevalerie" of the Comte de Tressan; lastly, certain German collections of popular tales. Some chapters have been borrowed from Leigh Hunt's Translations from the Italian Poets. It seemed unnecessary to do over again what he had already done so well; yet, on the other hand, those stories could not be omitted from the series without leaving it incomplete.

THOMAS BULFINCH.

The Age of Fable

Chapter 1

INTRODUCTION

The literature of our time, as of all the centuries of Christendom, is full of allusions to the gods and goddesses of the Greeks and Romans. Occasionally, and, in modern days, more often, it contains allusions to the worship and the superstitions of the northern nations of Europe. The object of this book is to teach readers who are not yet familiar with the writers of Greece and Rome, or the ballads or legends of the Scandinavians, enough of the stories which form what is called their mythology, to make those allusions intelligible which one meets every day, even in the authors of our own time.

The Greeks and Romans both belong to the same race or stock. It is generally known in our time as the Aryan family of mankind; and so far, as we know its history, the Greeks and Romans descended from the tribes which emigrated from the high table- lands of Northern India. Other tribes emigrated in different directions from the same center, so that traces of the Aryan language are found in the islands of the Pacific Ocean.

The people of this race, who moved westward, seem to have had a special fondness for open air nature, and a willingness to personify the powers of nature. They were glad to live in the open air, and they specially encouraged the virtues which an open-air people prize. Thus, no Roman was thought manly who could not swim, and every Greek exercised in the athletic sports of the palaestra.

The Romans and Grecian and German divisions of this great race are those with which we have most to do in history and in literature. Our own English language is made up of the dialects of different tribes, many of whom agreed in their use of words which they had derived from our Aryan ancestry. Thus, our substantive verb I AM appears in the original Sanscrit of the Aryans as ESMI, and m for ME (MOI), or the first person singular, is found in all the verbal inflections. The Greek form of the same verb was ESMI, which became ASMI, and in Latin the first and last vowels have disappeared, the verb is SUM. Similar relationships are traced in the numerals, and throughout all the languages of these nations.

The Romans, like the Etruscans who came before them, were neither poetical nor imaginative in temperament. Their activity ran in practical directions. They therefore invented few, if any stories, of the gods whom they worshipped with fixed rites. Mr. Macaulay speaks of these gods as "the sober abstractions of the Roman pantheon." We owe most of the stories of the ancient mythology to the wit and fancy of the Greeks, more playful and imaginative, who seized from Egypt and from the East such legends as pleased them, and adapted them in their own way. It often happens that such stories, resembling each other in their foundation, are found in the Greek and Roman authors in several different forms.

To understand these stories, we will here first acquaint ourselves with the ideas of the structure of the universe, which the poets and others held, and which will form the scenery, so to speak, of the narratives.

The Greek poets believed the earth to be flat and circular, their own country occupying the middle of it, the central point being either Mount Olympus, the abode of the gods, or Delphi, so famous for its oracle.

The circular disk of the earth was crossed from west to east, and divided into two equal parts by the SEA, as they called the Mediterranean, and its continuation the Euxine.

Around the earth flowed the RIVER OCEAN, its course being from south to north on the western side of the earth, and in a contrary direction on the eastern side. It flowed in a steady, equable current, unvexed by storm or tempest. The sea, and all the rivers on earth, received their waters from it.

The northern portion of the earth was supposed to be inhabited by a happy race named the Hyperboreans [this word means "who live beyond the north" from the word "hyper," beyond, and boreas, the north wind], dwelling in everlasting bliss and spring beyond the lofty mountains whose caverns were supposed to send forth the piercing blasts of the north wind, which chilled the people of Hellas (Greece). Their country was inaccessible by land or sea. They lived exempt from disease or old age, from toils and warfare. Moore has given us the "Song of a Hyperborean," beginning:

"I come from a land in the sun-bright deep,
Where golden gardens glow,
Where the winds of the north, becalmed in sleep,
Their conch-shells never blow."

On the south side of the earth, close to the stream of Ocean, dwelt a people happy and virtuous as the Hyperboreans. They were named the Æthiopians. The gods favored them so highly that they were wont to leave at times their Olympian abodes, and go to share their sacrifices and banquets.

On the western margin of the earth, by the stream of Ocean, lay a happy place named the Elysian Plain, whither mortals favored by the gods were transported without tasting of death, to enjoy an immortality of bliss. This happy region was also called the "fortunate fields," and the "Isles of the Blessed."

We thus see that the Greeks of the early ages knew little of any real people except those to the east and south of their own country, or near the coast of the Mediterranean. Their imagination meantime peopled the western portion of this sea with giants, monsters, and enchantresses; while they placed around the disk of the earth, which they probably regarded as of no great width, nations enjoying the peculiar favor of the gods, and blessed with happiness and longevity.

The Dawn, the Sun, and the Moon were supposed to rise out of the Ocean, on the western side, and to drive through the air, giving light to gods and men. The stars also, except those forming Charles' Wain or Bear, and others near them, rose out of and sank into the stream of Ocean. There the sun-god embarked in a winged boat, which conveyed him round by the northern part of the earth, back to his place of rising in the east. Milton alludes to this in his "Commmus":

"Now the gilded car of day
His golden axle doth allay
In the steep Atlantic stream,
And the slope sun his upward beam
Shoots against the dusky pole,
Pacing towards the other goal
Of his chamber in the east."

The abode of the gods was on the summit of Mount Olympus, in Thessaly. A gate of clouds, kept by the goddesses named the Seasons, opened to permit the passage of the Celestials to earth, and to receive them on their return. The gods had their separate dwellings; but all, when summoned, repaired to the palace of Jupiter [Or Zeus. The relation of these names to each other will be explained on the next page], as did also those deities whose usual abode was the earth, the waters, or the underworld. It was also in the great hall of the palace of the Olympian king that the gods feasted each day on ambrosia and nectar, their food and drink, the latter being handed round by the lovely goddess Hebe. Here they conversed of the affairs of heaven and earth; and as they quaffed their nectar, Apollo, the god of music, delighted them with the tones of his lyre, to which the muses sang in responsive strains. When the sun was set, the gods retired to sleep in their respective dwellings.

The following lines from the Odyssey will show how Homer conceived of Olympus:

"So saying, Minerva, goddess azure-eyed,
Rose to Olympus, the reputed seat
Eternal of the gods, which never storms
Disturb, rains drench, or snow invades, but calm
The expanse and cloudless shines with purest day.
T here the inhabitants divine rejoice
Forever.:" – Cowper

Such were the abodes of the gods as the Greeks conceived them. The Romans, before they knew the Greek poetry, seem to have had no definite imagination of such an assembly of gods. But the Roman and Etruscan races were by no means irreligious. They venerated their departed ancestors, and in each family the worship of these ancestors was an important duty. The images of the ancestors were kept in a sacred place, each family observed, at fixed times, memorial rites in their honor, and for these and other religious observances the family hearth was consecrated. The earliest rites of Roman worship are supposed to be connected with such family devotions.

As the Greeks and Romans became acquainted with other nations, they imported their habits of worship, even in early times. It will be remembered that as late as St. Paul's time, he found an altar at Athens "to an unknown god." Greeks and Romans alike were willing to receive from other nations the legends regarding their gods, and to incorporate them as well as they could with their own. It is thus that in the poetical mythology of those nations, which we are now to study, we frequently find a Latin and a Greek name for one imagined divinity. Thus Zeus, of the Greeks, becomes in Latin with the addition of the word pater (a father) [The reader will observe that father is one of the words derived from an Ayan root. Let p and t become rough, as the grammarians say, let p become ph, and t th, and you have phather or father], Jupiter Kronos of the Greeks appears as "Vulcanus" of the Latins, "Ares" of the Greeks is "Mars" or Mavors of the Latins, "Poseidon" of the Greeks is "Neptunus" of the Latins, "Aphrodite" of the Greeks is "Venus" of the Latins. This variation is not to be confounded with a mere translation, as where "Paulos" of the Greek becomes "Paulus" in Latin, or "Odysseus" becomes "Ulysses," or as when "Pierre" of the French becomes "Peter" in English. What really happened was, that as the Romans, more cultivated than their fathers, found in Greek literature a god of fire and smithery, they transferred his name "Hephaistos" to their own old god "Vulcanus," who had the same duties, and in their after literature the Latin name was used for the stories of Greek and Latin origin.

As the English literature came into being largely on French and Latin models, and as French is but a degraded Latin and retains Latin roots largely, in our older English poets the Latin forms of these names are generally used. In our own generation, with the precision now so much courted, a fashion has come in, of designating Mars by his Greek name of "Ares," Venus by her name of "Aphrodite," and so on. But in this book, as our object is to make familiar the stores of general English literature which refer to such subjects, we shall retain, in general, the Latin names, only calling the attention of the reader to the Greek names, as they appear in Greek authors, and in many writers of the more recent English schools.

The real monarch of the heavens in the mythology of both Greece and Rome is Jupiter (Zeus-pater, father-Jove) [Jove appears to be a word derived from the same root as Zeus, and it appears in the root dev of the Sanscrit, where devas are gods of different forms. Our English word devil probably comes from the French diable, Italian diavolo, Latin diabolus, one who makes division,- - literally one who separates balls, or throws balls about,— instead of throwing them frankly and truly at the batsman. It is not to be traced to the Sanscrit deva.]

In the mythological system we are tracing Zeus is himself the father of many of the gods, and he is often spoken of as father of gods and men. He is the father of Vulcan [In Greek Hephaistos], of Venus [in Greek Aphrodite], of Minerva [in Greek Pallas Athene, or either name separately], of Apollo [of Phoebus], Diana [in Greek Artemis], and of Mercury [in Greek Hermes], who are ranked among the twelve superior gods, and of many inferior deities. But Jupiter himself is not the original deity in these systems. He is the son of Saturnus, as in the Greek Zeus is the son of Kronos. Still the inevitable question would occur where did Saturnus or Kronos come from. And, in forms and statements more and more vague, the answer was that he was born from Uranus or Ouranos, which is the name of the Heaven over all which seemed to embrace all things. The Greek name of Saturn was spelled Kronos. The Greek name of Time was spelled Chronos. A similarity between the two was imagined. And the whole statement, when reduced to rationalistic language, would be that from Uranus, the infinite, was born Chronos, Time,— that from Time, Zeus or Jupiter was born, and that he is the only child of Time who has complete sway over mortals and immortals.

"The will of Jove I own,
Who mortals and immortals rules alone." – Homer, II.xii

Jupiter was son of Saturn (Kronos) [The names included in parentheses are the Greek, the others being the Roman or Latin names] and Ops (Rhea in Greek, sometimes confounded with the Phrygian Cybele).

Saturn and Rhea were of the race of Titans, who were the children of Earth and Heaven, which sprang from Chaos, of which we shall give a further account in our next chapter.

In allusion to the dethronement of Ouranos by Kronos, and of Kronos or Saturnus by Zeus or Jupiter, Prometheus says in Æschylus's tragedy:

"You may deem
Its towers impregnable; but have I not
already seen two monarchs hurled from them."

There is another cosmogony, or account of the creation, according to which Earth, Erebus, and Love were the first of beings. Love (Eros)_ issued from the egg of Night, which floated on Chaos. By his arrows and torch he pierced and vivified all things, producing life and joy.

Saturn and Rhea were not the only Titans. There were others, whose names were Oceanus, Hyperion, Iapetus, and Ophion, males; and Themis, Mnemosyne, Eurynome, females. They are spoken of as the elder gods, whose dominion was afterwards transferred to others. Saturn yielded to Jupiter, Oceanus to Neptune, Hyperion to Apollo. Hyperion was the father of the Sun, Moon, and Dawn. He is therefore the original sun-god, and is painted with the splendor and beauty which were afterwards bestowed on Apollo.

"Hyperion's curls, the front of Jove himself." – Shakespeare

Ophion and Eurynome ruled over Olympus till they were dethroned by Saturn and Rhea. Milton alludes to them in Paradise Lost. He says the heathen seem to have had some knowledge of the temptation and fall of man:

"And fabled how the serpent, whom they called
Ophion, with Eurynome (the wide-
Encroaching Eve perhaps), had first the rule
Of high Olympus, thence by Saturn driven."

The representations given of Saturn are not very consistent, for on the one hand his reign is said to have been the golden age of innocence and purity, and on the other he is described as a monster who devoured his own children [This inconsistency arises from considering the Saturn of the Romans the same with the Grecian deity Chronos (Time), which, as it brings an end to all things which have had a beginning, may be said to devour its own offspring.] Jupiter, however, escaped this fate, and when grown up espoused Metis (Prudence), who administered a draught to Saturn which caused him to disgorge his children. Jupiter, with his brothers and sisters, now rebelled against their father Saturn, and his brothers the Titans; vanquished them, and imprisoned some of them in Tartarus, inflicting other penalties on others. Atlas was condemned to bear up the heavens on his shoulders.

On the dethronement of Saturn, Jupiter with his brothers Neptune (Poseidon) and Pluto (Dis) divided his dominions. Jupiter's portion was the heavens, Neptune's the ocean, and Pluto's the realms of the dead. Earth and Olympus were common property. Jupiter was king of gods and men. The thunder was his weapon, and he bore a shield called Ægis, made for him by Vulcan. The eagle was his favorite bird, and bore his thunderbolts.

Juno (Hera)[pronounce He-re, in two syllables] was the wife of Jupiter, and queen of the gods. Iris, the goddess of the rainbow, was her attendant and messenger. The peacock was her favorite bird.

Vulcan (Hephaistos), the celestial artist, was the son of Jupiter and Juno. He was born lame, and his mother was so displeased at the sight of him that she flung him out of heaven. Other accounts say that Jupiter kicked him out for taking part with his mother, in a quarrel which occurred between them. Vulcan's lameness, according to this account, was the consequence of his fall. He was a whole day falling, and at last alighted in the island of Lemnos, which was thenceforth sacred to him. Milton alludes to this story in Paradise lost, Book I:

"From morn
To noon he fell, from noon to dewy eve,
A summer's day; and with the setting sun
Dropped from the zenith, like a falling star,
On Lemnos, the Ǣgean isle."

Mars (Ares), the god of war, was the son of Jupiter and Juno. Phoebus Apollo [this is a Greek name of a Greek divinity, who seems to have had no Roman resemblance], the god of archery, prophecy, and music, was the son of Jupiter and Latona, and brother of Diana (Artemis). He was god of the sun, as Diana, his sister, was the goddess of the moon.

Venus (Aphrodite), the goddess of love and beauty, was the daughter of Jupiter and Dione. Others say that Venus sprang from the foam of the sea. The zephyr wafted her along the waves to the Isle of Cyprus, where she was received and attired by the Seasons, and then led to the assembly of the gods. All were charmed with her beauty, and each one demanded her for his wife. Jupiter gave her to Vulcan, in gratitude for the service he had rendered in forging thunderbolts. So, the most beautiful of the goddesses became the wife of the most ill-favored of the gods. Venus possessed an embroidered girdle called the Cestus, which had the power of inspiring love. Her favorite birds were swans and doves, and the plants sacred to her were the rose and the myrtle.

Cupid (Eros), the god of love, was the son of Venus. He was her constant companion; and, armed with bow and arrows, he shot the darts of desire into the bosoms of both gods and men. There was a deity named Anteros, who was sometimes represented as the avenger of slighted love, and sometimes as the symbol of reciprocal affection. The following legend is told of him:

Venus, complaining to Themis that her son Eros continued always a child, was told by her that it was because he was solitary, and that if he had a brother he would grow apace. Anteros was soon afterwards born, and Eros immediately was seen to increase rapidly in size and strength.

Minerva (Pallas Athene), the goddess of wisdom, was the offspring of Jupiter, without a mother. She sprang from his head, completely armed. Her favorite bird was the owl, and the plant sacred to her the olive.

Byron, in "Childe Harold," alludes to the birth of Minerva thus:

"Can tyrants but by tyrants conquered be,
And freedom find no champion and no child,
Such as Columbia saw arise, when she
Sprang forth a Pallas, armed and undefiled?
Or must such minds be nourished in the wild,
Deep in the unpruned forest, 'midst the roar
Of Cataracts, where nursing Nature smiled
On infant Washington? Has earth no more
Such seeds within her breast, or Europe no such shore?"

Mercury (Hermes), was the son of Jupiter and Maia. He presided over commerce, wrestling and other gymnastic exercises; even over thieving, and everything, in short, which required skill and dexterity. He was the messenger of Jupiter, and wore a winged cap and winged shoes. He bore in his hand a rod entwined with two serpents, called the Caduceus.

Mercury is said to have invented the lyre. Four hours after his birth he found the shell of a tortoise, made holes in the opposite edges of it, and drew cords of linen through

Figure 2: "Bewitched Bosom" by William Heath Robinson

them, and the instrument was complete [From this origin of the instrument, the word "shell" is often used as synonymous with :"lyre," and figuratively for music and poetry. Thus Gray, in his ode on the "Progress of Poesy," says,— "O Sovereign of the willing soul, Parent of sweet and solemn-breathing airs, Enchanting shell! The sullen Cares And Frantic Passions hear thy soft control."] The cords were nine, in honor of the nine Muses. Mercury gave the lyre to Apollo, and received from him in exchange the caduceus.

Ceres (Demeter), was the daughter of Saturn and Rhea. She had a daughter named Proserpine (Persephone), who became the wife of Pluto, and queen of the realms of the dead. Ceres presided over agriculture.

Bacchus (Dionysus), the god of wine, was the son of Jupiter and Semele. He represents not only the intoxicating power of wine, but its social and beneficent influences likewise; so that he is viewed as the promoter of civilization, and a lawgiver and lover of peace.

The muses were the daughters of Jupiter and Mnemosyne (Memory). They presided over song, and prompted the memory. They were nine in number, to each of whom was assigned the presidency over some particular department of literature, art, or science. Calliope was the muse of epic poetry, Clio of history, Euterpe of lyric poetry, Melpomene of tragedy, Terpischore of choral dance and song, Erato of love-poetry, Polyhymnia of sacred poetry, Urania of astronomy, Thalia [Pronounced Tha-lei-a, with the emphasis on the second syllable] of comedy.

Spenser described the office of the Graces thus:

"These three on men all gracious gifts bestow
Which deck the body or adorn the mind,
To make them lovely or well-favored show;
As comely carriage, entertainment kind,
Sweet semblance, friendly offices that bind,
And all the compliments of courtesy;
They teach us how to each degree and kind
We should ourselves demean, to low, to high.
To friends, to foes; which skill men call Civility."

The Fates were also three Clotho, Lachesis, and Atropos. Their office was to spin the thread of human destiny, and they were armed with shears, with which they cut it off when they pleased. They were the daughters of Themis (Law), who sits by Jove on his throne to give him counsel.

The Erinnyes, or Furies, were three goddesses who punished crimes by their secret stings. The heads of the Furies were wreathed with serpents, and their whole appearance was terrific and appalling. Their names were Alecto, Tisiphone, and Megaera. They were also called Eumenides.

Nemesis was also an avenging goddess. She represents the righteous anger of the gods, particularly towards the proud and insolent.

Pan [the name Pan means everything, and he is sometimes spoken of as the god of all nature] was the god of flocks and shepherds. His favorite residence, as the Greeks describe him, was in Arcadia.

The Satyrs were deities of the woods and fields. They were conceived to be covered with bristly hair, their heads decorated with short, sprouting horns, and their feet like goats' feet.

Momus was the god of laughter, and Plutus the god of wealth.

ROMAN DIVINITIES

The preceding are Grecian divinities, though received also by the Romans. Those which follow are peculiar to Roman mythology.

Saturn was an ancient Italian deity. The Roman poets tried to identify him with the Grecian god Kronos, and fabled that after his dethronement by Jupiter, he fled to Italy, where he reigned during what was called the Golden Age. In memory of his beneficent dominion, the feast of Saturnalia was held every year in the winter season. Then all public business was suspended, declarations of war and criminal executions were postponed, friends made presents to one another, and the slaves were indulged with great liberties. A feast was given them at which they sat at table, while their masters served them, to show the natural equality of men, and that all things belonged equally to all, in the reign of Saturn.

Faunus, or Fauna [there was also a goddess called Fauna, or], the grandson of Saturn, was worshipped as the god of fields and shepherds, and also as a prophetic god. His name in the plural, Fauns, expressed a class of gamesome deities, like the Satyrs of the Greeks.

Quirinus was a war god, said to be no other than Romulus the founder of Rome, exalted after his death to a place among the gods.

Bellona, a war goddess.

Terminus, the god of landmarks. His statue was a rude stone or post, set in the ground to mark the boundaries of fields.

Pales, the goddess presiding over cattle and pastures.

Pomona presided over fruit trees.

Flora, the goddess of flowers.

Lucina, the goddess of childbirth.

Vesta (the Hestia of the Greeks) was a deity presiding over the public and private hearth. A sacred fire, tended by six virgin priestesses called Vestals, flamed in her temple. As the safety of the city was held to be connected

Figure 3: "Venus and Anchises" by William Blake Richmond

with its conservation, the neglect of the virgins, if they let it go out, was severely punished, and the fire was rekindled from the rays of the sun.

Liber is another Latin name of Bacchus; and Mulciber of Vulcan.

Janus was the porter of heaven. He opens the year, the first month being named after him. He is the guardian deity of gates, on which account he is commonly represented with two heads, because every door looks two ways. His temples at Rome were numerous. In war time the gates of the principal one were always open. In peace they were closed; but they were shut only once between the reign of Numa and that of Augustus.

The Penates were the gods who were supposed to attend to the welfare and prosperity of the family. Their name is derived from Penus, the pantry, which was sacred to them. Every master of a family was the priest to the Penates of his own house.

The Lares, or Lars, were also household gods, but differed from the Penates in being regarded as the deified spirits of mortals. The family Lars were held to be the souls of the ancestors, who watched over and protected their descendants. The words Lemur and Larva more nearly correspond to our word Ghost.

The Romans believed that every man had his Genius, and every woman her Juno; that is, a spirit who had given them being, and was regarded as a protector through life. On birthdays men made offerings to their Genius, women to their Juno.

Macaulay thus alludes to some of the Roman gods:

"Pomona loves the orchard,
And Liber loves the vine,
And Pales loves the straw-built shed
Warm with the breath of kine;
And Venus loves the whisper
Of plighted youth and maid
In April's ivory moonlight,
Beneath the Chestnut shade."
"Prophecy of Capys."
N.B.

It is to be observed that in proper names the final e and es are to be sounded. Thus, Cybele and Penates are words of three syllables. But Proserpine and Thebes have been so long used as English words, that they may be regarded as exceptions, to be pronounced as if English. Hecate is sometimes pronounced by the poets as a dissylable. In the Index at the close of the volume, we shall mark the accented syllable, in all words which appear to require it.

Chapter 2

PROMETHEUS AND PANDORA

The Roman poet Ovid gives us a connected narrative of creation. Before the earth and sea and the all-covering heaven, one aspect, which we call Chaos, covered all the face of Nature,— a rough heap of inert weight and discordant beginnings of things clashing together. As yet no sun gave light to the world, nor did the moon renew her slender horn month by month,— neither did the earth hang in the surrounding air, poised by its own weight, — nor did the sea stretch its long arms around the earth. Wherever there was earth, there was also sea and air. So the earth was not solid nor was the water fluid, neither was the air transparent.

God and Nature at last interposed and put an end to this discord, separating earth from sea, and heaven from both. The fiery part, being the lightest, sprang up, and formed the skies; the air was next in weight and place. The earth, being heavier, sank below, and the water took the lowest place and buoyed up the earth.

Here some god, no man knows who, arranged and divided the land. He placed the rivers and bays, raised mountains and dug out valleys and distributed woods, fountains, fertile fields and stony plains. Now that the air was clear the stars shone out, the fishes swam the sea and birds flew in the air, while the four-footed beasts roamed around the earth. But a nobler animal was needed, and man was made in the image of the gods with an upright stature [The two Greek words for man have the root an, "up"], so that while all other animals turn their faces downward and look to the earth, he raises his face to heaven and gazes on the stars [Every reader will be interested in comparing this narrative with that in the beginning of Genesis. It seems clear that so many Jews were in Rome in Ovid's days, many of whom were people of consideration among those with whom he lived, that he may have heard the account in the Hebrew Scriptures translated. Compare JUDAISM by Prof. Frederic Huidekoper.]

To Prometheus the Titan and to his brother Epimetheus was committed the task of making man and all other animals, and of endowing them with all needful faculties. This Epimetheus did, and his brother overlooked the work. Epimetheus then gave to the different animals their several gifts of courage, strength, swiftness and sagacity. He gave wings to one, claws to another, a shelly covering to the third. Man, superior to all other animals, came last. But for man Epimetheus had nothing,— he had bestowed all his gifts elsewhere. He came to his brother for help, and Prometheus, with the aid of Minerva, went up to heaven, lighted his torch at the chariot of the sun, and brought down fire to man. With this, man was more than equal to all other animals. Fire enabled him to make weapons to subdue wild beasts, tools with which to till the earth. With fire he warmed his dwelling and bid defiance to the cold.

Woman was not yet made. The story is, that Jupiter made her, and sent her to Prometheus and his brother, to punish them for their presumption in stealing fire from heaven; and man, for accepting the gift. The first woman was named Pandora. She was made in heaven, every god contributing something to perfect her. Venus gave her beauty, Mercury persuasion, Apollo music. Thus equipped, she was conveyed to earth, and presented to Epimetheus, who gladly accepted her, though cautioned by his brother to beware of Jupiter and his gifts.

Epimetheus had in his house a jar, in which were kept certain noxious articles, for which, in fitting man for his new abode, he had had no occasion. Pandora was seized with an eager curiosity to know what this jar contained; and one day she slipped off the cover and looked in. Forthwith there escaped a multitude of plagues for hapless man,— such as gout, rheumatism, and colic for his body, and envy, spite, and revenge for his mind,— and scattered themselves far and wide. Pandora hastened to replace the lid; but, alas! The whole contents of the jar had escaped, one thing only excepted, which lay at the bottom, and that was HOPE. So we see at this day, whatever evils are abroad, hope never entirely leaves us; and while we have THAT, no amount of other ills can make us completely wretched.

Another story is, that Pandora was sent in good faith, by Jupiter, to bless man; that she was furnished with a box, containing her marriage presents, into which every god had put some blessing. She opened the box incautiously, and the blessings all escaped, HOPE only excepted. This story seems more consistent than the former; for how could HOPE, so precious a jewel as it is, have been kept in a jar full of all manner of evils?

The world being thus furnished with inhabitants, the first age was an age of innocence and happiness, called the GOLDEN AGE. Truth and right prevailed, though not enforced by law, nor was there any magistrate to threaten or punish. The forest had not yet been robbed of its trees to furnish timbers for vessels, nor had men built fortifications round their towns. There were no such things as swords, spears, or helmets. The earth brought forth all things necessary for man, without his labor in ploughing or sowing. Perpetual spring reigned, flowers sprang up without seed, the rivers flowed with milk and wine, and yellow honey distilled from the oaks.

"But when good Saturn, banished from above,
Was driven to hell, the world was under Jove.
Succeeding times a Silver Age behold,
Excelling brass, but more excelled by gold.
Then summer, autumn, winter did appear,
And spring was but a season of the year.
The sun his annual course obliquely made,
Good days contracted and enlarged the bad,
Then air, with sultry heats, began to glow;
The wings of winds were clogged with ice and sno
And shivering mortals into houses driven,
Sought shelter from the inclemency of heaven.
Those houses then were caves, or homely sheds;
With twining osiers fenced; and moss their beds.
Then ploughs, for seed, the fruitful furrows broke,
And oxen labored first beneath the yoke.
To this came next in course the Brazen Age:
A warlike offspring, prompt to bloody rage,
Not impious yet! . .
. . . Hard Steel succeeded then;
And stubborn as the metal were the men."
Ovid's Metam, Book I. Dryden's Translation.

Crime burst in like a flood; modesty, truth, and honor fled. In their places came fraud and cunning, violence, and the wicked love of gain. Then seamen spread sails to the wind, and the trees were torn from the mountains to serve for keels to ships, and vex the face of ocean. The earth, which till now had been cultivated in common, began to be divided off into possessions. Men were not satisfied with what the surface produced, but must dig into its bowels, and draw forth from thence the ores of metals. Mischievous IRON, and more mischievous GOLD, were produced. War sprang up, using both as weapons; the guest was not safe in his friend's house; and sons-in-law and fathers-in- law, brothers and sisters, husbands and wives, could not trust one another. Sons wished their fathers dead, that they might come to the inheritance; family love lay prostrate. The earth was wet with slaughter, and the gods abandoned it, one by one, till Astraea [the goddess of innocence and purity. After leaving earth, she was placed among the stars, where she became the constellation Virgo The Virgin. Themis (Justice) was the mother of Astraea. She is represented as holding aloft a pair of scales, in which she weighs the claims of opposing parties. It was a favorite idea of the old poets, that these goddesses would one day return, and bring back the Golden Age. Even in a Christian Hymn, the Messiah of Pope, this idea occurs.

"All crimes shall cease, and ancient fraud shall fail,
Returning Justice lift aloft her scale,
Peace o'er the world her olive wand extend,
And white-robed Innocence from heaven descend."

See, also, Milton's Hymn on the nativity, stanzas xiv, and xv]

---

alone was left, and finally she also took her departure.

Jupiter, seeing this state of things, burned with anger. He summoned the gods to council. They obeyed the call, and took The road to the palace of heaven. The road, which any one may see in a clear night, stretches across the face of the sky, and is called the Milky Way. Along the road stand the palaces of the illustrious gods; the common people of the skies live apart, on either side. Jupiter addressed the assembly. He set forth the frightful condition of things on the earth, and closed by announcing his intention to destroy the whole of its inhabitants, and provide a new race, unlike the first, who would be more worthy of life, and much better worshippers of the gods. So saying he took a thunderbolt, and was about to launch it at the world, and destroy it by burning it; but recollecting the danger that such a conflagration might set heaven itself on fire, he changed his plan, and resolved to drown the world. Aquilo, the north wind, which scatters the clouds, was chained up; Notus, the south, was sent out, and soon covered all the face of heaven with a cloak of pitchy darkness. The clouds, driven together, resound with a crash; torrents of rain fall; the crops are laid low; the year's labor of the husbandman perishes in an hour. Jupiter, not satisfied with his own waters, calls on his brother Neptune to aid him with his. He lets loose the rivers, and pours them over the land. At the same time, he heaves the land with an earthquake, and brings in the reflux of the ocean over the shores. Flocks, herds, men, and houses are swept away, and temples, with their sacred enclosures, profaned. If any edifice remained standing, it was overwhelmed, and its turrets lay hid beneath the waves. Now all was sea; sea without shore. Here and there some one remained on a projecting hill-top, and a few, in boats, pulled the oar where they had lately driven the plough. The fishes swim among the tree-tops; the anchor is let down into a garden. Where the graceful lambs played but now, unwieldy sea-calves gambol. The wolf swims among the sheep; the yellow lions and tigers struggle in the water. The strength of the wild boar serves him not, nor his swiftness the stag. The birds fall with weary wing into the water, having found no land for a resting place. Those living beings whom the water spared fell a prey to hunger.

Parnassus alone, of all the mountains, overtopped the waves; and there Deucalion and his wife Pyrrha, of the race of Prometheus, found refuge he a just man, and she a faithful worshipper of the gods. Jupiter, when he saw none left alive but this pair, and remembered their harmless lives and pious demeanor, ordered the north winds to drive away the clouds, and disclose the skies to earth, and earth to the skies. Neptune also directed Triton to blow on his shell, and sound a retreat to the waters. The waters obeyed, and the sea returned to its shores, and the rivers to their channels. Then Deucalion thus addressed Pyrrha: "O wife, only surviving woman, joined to me first by the ties of kindred and marriage, and now by a common danger, would that we possessed the power of our ancestor Prometheus, and could renew the race as he at first made it! But as we cannot, let us seek yonder temple, and inquire of the gods what remains for us to do." They entered the temple, deformed as it was with slime, and approached the altar, where no fire burned. There they fell prostrate on the earth, and prayed the goddess to inform them how they might retrieve their miserable affairs. The oracle answered, "Depart from the temple with head veiled and garments unbound, and cast behind you the bones of your mother." They heard the words with astonishment. Pyrrha first broke silence: "We cannot obey; we dare not profane the remains of our parents." They sought the thickest shades of the wood, and revolved the oracle in their minds. At length Deucalion spoke: "Either my sagacity deceives me, or the command is one we may obey without impiety. The earth is the great parent of all; the stones are her bones; these we may cast behind us; and I think this is what the oracle means. At least, it will do no harm to try." They veiled their faces, unbound their garments, and picked up stones, and cast them behind them. The stones (wonderful to relate) began to grow soft, and assume shape. By degrees, they put on a rude resemblance to the human form, like a block half-finished in the hands of the sculptor. The moisture and slime that were about them became flesh; the stony part became bones; the veins remained veins, retaining their name, only changing their use. Those thrown by the hand of the man became men, and those by the woman became women. It was a hard race, and well adapted to labor, as we find ourselves to be at this day, giving plain indications of our origin.

The comparison of Eve to Pandora is too obvious to have escaped Milton, who introduces it in Book IV, of Paradise Lost:

"More lovely than Pandora, whom the gods
Endowed with all their gifts; and O, too like
In sad event, when to the unwiser son
Of Jupiter, brought by Hermes, she ensnared
Mankind with her fair looks, to be avenged
On him who had stole Jove's authentic fire."

Prometheus and Epimetheus were sons of Iapetus, which Milton changes to Japhet.

Prometheus, the Titan son of Iapetus and Themis, is a favorite subject with the poets. Æschylus wrote three tragedies on the subjects of his confinement, his release, and his worship at Athens. Of these only the first is preserved, the Prometheus Bound. Prometheus was the only one in the council of the gods who favored man. He alone was kind to the human race, and taught and protected them.

"I formed his mind,
And through the cloud of barbarous ignorance

Diffused the beams of knowledge . . . .
They saw indeed, they heard, but what availed
Or sight or hearing, all things round them rolling,
Like the unreal imagery of dreams
In wild confusion mixed! The lightsome wall
Of finer masonry, the raftered roof
They knew not; but like ants still buried, delved
Deep in the earth and scooped their sunless caves.
Unmarked the seasons ranged, the biting winter,
The flower-perfumed spring, the ripening summer
Fertile of fruits. At random all their works
Till I instructed them to mark the stars,
Their rising, and, a harder science yet,
Their setting. The rich train of marshalled numbers
I taught them, and the meet array of letters.
To impress these precepts on their hearts I sent
Memory, the active mother of all reason.
I taught the patient steer to bear the yoke,
In all his toils joint-laborer of man.
By me the harnessed steed was trained to whirl
The rapid car, and grace the pride of wealth.
The tall bark, lightly bounding o'er the waves,
I taught its course, and winged its flying sail.
To man I gave these arts."
Potter's Translation from the Prometheus Bound

Jupiter, angry at the insolence and presumption of Prometheus in taking upon himself to give all these blessings to man, condemned the Titan to perpetual imprisonment, bound on a rock on Mount Caucasus while a vulture should forever prey upon his liver. This state of torment might at any time have been brought to an end by Prometheus if he had been willing to submit to his oppressor. For Prometheus knew of a fatal marriage which Jove must make and by which he must come to ruin. Had Prometheus revealed this secret he would at once have been taken into favor. But this he disdained to do. He has therefore become the symbol of magnanimous endurance of unmerited suffering and strength of will resisting oppression.

Byron and Shelley have both treated this theme. The following are Byron's lines:

"Titan! To whose immortal eyes
The sufferings of mortality,
Seen in their sad reality,
Were not as things that gods despise,
What was thy pity's recompense?
A silent suffering, and intense;
The rock, the vulture, and the chain;
All that the proud can feel of pain;
The agony they do not show;
The suffocating sense of woe.

"Thy godlike crime was to be kind;
To render with thy precepts less
The sum of human wretchedness,
And strengthen man with his own mind.
And, baffled as thou wert from high,
Still, in thy patient energy,
In the endurance and repulse,
Of thine impenetrable spirit,
Which earth and heaven could not convulse,
A mighty lesson we inherit."

PYTHON

The slime with which the earth was covered by the waters of the flood, produced an excessive fertility, which called forth every variety of production, both bad and good. Among the rest, Python, an enormous serpent, crept forth, the terror of the people, and lurked in the caves of Mount Parnassus. Apollo slew him with his arrows weapons which he had not before used against any but feeble animals, hares, wild goats, and such game. In commemoration of this illustrious conquest he instituted the Pythian games, in which the victor in feats of strength, swiftness of foot, or in the chariot race, was crowned with a wreath of beech leaves; for the laurel was not yet adopted by Apollo as his own tree. And here Apollo founded his oracle at Delphi, the only oracle "that was not exclusively national, for it was consulted by many outside nations, and, in fact, was held in the highest repute all over the world. In obedience to its decrees, the laws of Lycurgus were introduced, and the earliest Greek colonies founded. No cities were built without first consulting the Delphic oracle, for it was believed that Apollo took special delight in the founding of cities, the first stone of which he laid in person; nor was any enterprise ever undertaken without inquiry at this sacred fane as to its probable success" [From Beren's Myths and Legends of Greece and Rome.]

The famous statue of Apollo called the Belvedere [From the Belvedere of the Vatican palace where it stands] represents the god after his victory over the serpent Python. To this Byron alludes in his Childe Harold, iv. 161:

"The lord of the unerring bow,
The god of life, and poetry, and light,
The Sun, in human limbs arrayed, and brow
All radiant from his triumph in the fight.
The shaft has just been shot; the arrow bright
With an immortal's vengeance; in his eye
And nostril, beautiful disdain, and might,
And majesty flash their full lightnings by,
Developing in that one glance the Deity."

Figure 4: "Daphne Root Bound" by Arthur Rackham

APOLLO AND DAPHNE

Daphne was Apollo's first love. It was not brought about by accident, but by the malice of Cupid. Apollo saw the boy playing with his bow and arrows; and being himself elated with his recent victory over Python, he said to him, "What have you to do with warlike weapons, saucy boy? Leave them for hands worthy of them. Behold the conquest I have won by means of them over the vast serpent who stretched his poisonous body over acres of the plain! Be content with your torch, child, and kindle up your flames, as you call them, where you will, but presume not to meddle with my weapons."

Venus's boy heard these words, and rejoined,": Your arrows may strike all things else, Apollo, but mine shall strike you.:" So saying, he took his stand on a rock of Parnassus, and drew from his quiver two arrows of different workmanship, one to excite love, the other to repel it. The former was of gold and sharp- pointed, the latter blunt and tipped with lead. With the leaden shaft he struck the nymph Daphne, the daughter of the river god Peneus, and with the golden one Apollo, through the heart. Forthwith the god was seized with love for the maiden, and she abhorred the thought of loving. Her delight was in woodland sports and in the spoils of the chase. Many lovers sought her, but she spurned them all, ranging the woods, and taking thought neither of Cupid nor of Hymen. Her father often said to her, "Daughter, you owe me a son-in-law; you owe me grandchildren." She, hating the thought of marriage as a crime, with her beautiful face tinged all over with blushes, threw her arms around her father's neck, and said, "Dearest father, grant me this favor, that I may always remain unmarried, like Diana." He consented, but at the same time said, "Your own face will forbid it."

Apollo loved her, and longed to obtain her; and he who gives oracles to all in the world was not wise enough to look into his own fortunes. He saw her hair flung loose over her shoulders, and said, "If so charming in disorder, what would it be if arranged?" He saw her eyes bright as stars; he saw her lips, and was not satisfied with only seeing them. He admired her hands and arms bared to the shoulder, and whatever was hidden from view he imagined more beautiful still. He followed her; she fled, swifter than the wind, and delayed not a moment at his entreaties. "Stay," said he, "daughter of Peneus; I am not a foe. Do not fly me as a lamb flies the wolf, or a dove the hawk. It is for love I pursue you. You make me miserable, for fear you should fall and hurt yourself on these stones, and I should be the cause. Pray run slower, and I will follow slower. I am no clown, no rude peasant. Jupiter is my father, and I am lord of Delphos and Tenedos, and know all things, present and future. I am the god of song and the lyre. My arrows fly true to the mark; but alas! An arrow more fatal than mine has pierced my heart! I am the god of medicine, and know the virtues of all healing plants. Alas! I suffer a malady that no balm can cure!"

The nymph continued her flight, and left his plea half uttered. And even as she fled she charmed him. The wind blew her garments, and her unbound hair streamed loose behind her. The god grew impatient to find his wooings thrown away, and, sped by Cupid, gained upon her in the race. It was like a hound pursuing a hare, with open jaws ready to seize, while the feebler animal darts forward, slipping from the very grasp. So, flew the god and the virgin he on the wings of love, and she on those of fear. The pursuer is the more rapid, however, and gains upon her, and his panting breath blows upon her hair. Now her strength begins to fail, and, ready to sink, she calls upon her father, the river god: "Help me, Peneus! Open the earth to enclose me, or change my form, which has brought me into this danger!"

Scarcely had she spoken, when a stiffness seized all her limbs; her bosom began to be enclosed in a tender bark; her hair became leaves; her arms became branches; her feet stuck fast in the ground, as roots; her face became a tree-top, retaining nothing of its former self but its beauty. Apollo stood amazed. He touched the stem, and felt the flesh tremble under the new bark. He embraced the branches, and lavished kisses on the wood. The branches shrank from his lips. "Since you cannot be my wife," said he, "you shall assuredly be my tree. I will wear you for my crown. With you I will decorate my harp and my quiver; and when the great Roman conquerors lead up the triumphal pomp to the Capitol, you shall be woven into wreaths for their brows. And, as eternal youth is mine, you also shall be always green, and your leaf know no decay." The nymph, now changed into a laurel tree, bowed its head in grateful acknowledgment.

Apollo was god of music and of poetry and also of medicine. For, as the poet Armstrong says, himself a physician:

"Music exalts each joy, allays each grief,
Expels disease, softens every pain;
And hence the wise of ancient days adored
One power of physic, melody, and song."

The story of Apollo and Daphne is often alluded to by the poets. Waller applies it to the case of one whose amatory verses, though they did not soften the heart of his mistress, yet won for the poet wide-spread fame.

"Yet what he sung in his immortal strain,
Though unsuccessful, was not sung in vain.
All but the nymph that should redress his wrong,
Attend his passion and approve his song.
Like Phoebus thus, acquiring unsought praise,
He caught at love and filled his arms with bays."

The following stanza from Shelley's Adonais alludes to Byron's early quarrel with the reviewers:

"The herded wolves, bold only to pursue;
The obscene ravens, clamorous o'er the dead;
The vultures, to the conqueror's banner true,
Who feed where Desolation first has fed.
And whose wings rain contagion; how they fled,
When like Apollo, from his golden bow,
The Pythian of the age one arrow sped
And smiled! The spoilers tempt no second blow;
They fawn on the proud feet that spurn them as they go."

PYRAMUS AND THISBE

Pyramus was the handsomest youth, and Thisbe the fairest maiden, in all Babylonia, where Semiramis reigned. Their parents occupied adjoining houses; and neighborhood brought the young people together, and acquaintance ripened into love. They would gladly have married, but their parents forbade. One thing, however, they could not forbid that love should glow with equal ardor in the bosoms of both. They conversed by signs and glances, and the fire burned more intensely for being covered up. In the wall that parted the two houses there was a crack, caused by some fault in the structure. No one had remarked it before, but the lovers discovered it. 'What will love not discover? It afforded a passage to the voice; and tender messages used to pass backward and forward through the gap. As they stood, Pyramus on this side, Thisbe on that, their breaths would mingle. "Cruel wall," they said, "why do you keep two lovers apart? But we will not be ungrateful. We owe you, we confess, the privilege of transmitting loving words to willing ears." Such words they uttered on different sides of the wall; and when night came and they must say farewell, they pressed their lips upon the wall, she on her side, he on his, as they could come no nearer.

One morning, when Aurora had put out the stars, and the sun had melted the frost from the grass, they met at the accustomed spot. Then, after lamenting their hard fate, they agreed that next night, when all was still, they would slip away from watchful eyes, leave their dwellings and walk out into the fields; and to insure a meeting, repair to a well-known edifice, standing without the city's bounds, called the tomb of Ninus, and that the one who came first should await the other at the foot of a certain tree. It was a white mulberry tree and stood near a cool spring. All was agreed on, and they waited impatiently for the sun to go down beneath the waters and night to rise up from them. Then cautiously Thisbe stole forth, unobserved by the family, her head covered with a veil, made her way to the monument and sat down under the tree. As she sat alone in the dim light of the evening she descried a lioness, her jaws reeking with recent slaughter, approaching the fountain to slake her thirst. Thisbe fled at the sight, and sought refuge in the hollow of a rock. As she fled she dropped her veil. The lioness, after drinking at the spring, turned to retreat to the woods, and seeing the veil on the ground, tossed and rent it with her bloody mouth.

Pyramus, having been delayed, now approached the place of meeting. He saw in the sand the footsteps of the lion, and the color fled from his cheeks at the sight. Presently he found the veil all rent and bloody. "Oh, hapless girl," said he, "I have been the cause of thy death! Thou, more worthy of life than I, hast fallen the first victim. I will follow. I am the guilty cause, in tempting thee forth to a place of such peril, and not being myself on the spot to guard thee. Come forth, ye lions, from the rocks, and tear this guilty body with your teeth" He took up the veil, carried it with him to the appointed tree, and covered it with kisses and with tears. "My blood also shall stain your texture," said he, and drawing his sword plunged it into his heart. The blood spurted from the wound, and tinged the white mulberries of the tree all red; and sinking into the earth reached the roots, so that the red color mounted through the trunk to the fruit.

By this time, Thisbe, still trembling with fear, yet wishing not to disappoint her lover, stepped cautiously forth, looking anxiously for the youth, eager to tell him the danger she had escaped. When she came to the spot and saw the changed color of the mulberries she doubted whether it was the same place. While she hesitated she saw the form of one struggling in the agonies of death. She started back, a shudder ran through her frame as a ripple on the face of the still water when a sudden breeze sweeps over it. But as soon as she recognized her lover, she screamed and beat her breast; embracing the lifeless body, pouring tears into its wounds, and imprinting kisses on the cold lips. "Oh, Pyramus," she cried, "what has done this? Answer me, Pyramus; it is your own Thisbe that speaks. Hear me, dearest, and lift that drooping head!" At the name of Thisbe, Pyramus opened his eyes, then closed them again. She saw her veil stained with blood and the scabbard empty of its sword. "Thy own hand has slain thee, and for my sake," she said. "I too can be brave for once, and my love is as strong as thine. I will follow thee in death, for I have been the cause; and death, which alone could part us, shall not prevent my joining thee. And ye, unhappy parents of us both, deny us not our united request. As love and death have joined us, let one tomb contain us. And thou, tree, retain the marks of slaughter. Let thy berries still serve for memorials of our blood." So saying, she plunged the sword into her breast. Her parents acceded to her wish; the gods also ratified it. The two bodies were buried in one sepulchre, and the tree ever after brought forth purple berries, as it does to this day.

Moore, in the Sylph's Ball, speaking of Davy's Safety Lamp, is reminded of the wall that separated Thisbe and her lover:

"O for that lamp's metallic gauze,
That curtain of protecting wire,
Which Davy delicately draws
Around illicit, dangerous fire!

"The wall he sets 'twixt Flame and Air,
(Like that which barred young Thisbe's bliss),
Through whose small holes this dangerous pair
May see each other, but not kiss."

In Mickle's translation of the Lusiad occurs the following allusion to the story of Pyramus and Thisbe, and the metamorphosis of the mulberries. The poet is describing the Island of Love.

"here each gift Pomona's hand bestows
In cultured garden, free uncultured flows,
The flavor sweeter and the hue more fair
Than e'er was fostered by the hand of care.
The cherry here in shining crimson glows,
And stained with lover's blood, in pendent rows,
The mulberries o'erload the bending boughs."

If any of our young readers can be so hard-hearted as to enjoy a laugh at the expense of poor Pyramus and Thisbe, they may find an opportunity by turning to Shakespeare's play of Midsummer Night's Dream, where it is most amusingly burlesqued.

Here is the description of the play and the characters by the Prologue.

"Gentles, perchance you wonder at this show;
But wonder on, till truth makes all things plain.
This man is Pyramus, if you would know;
This lovely lady Thisby is certain.

This man with lime and roughcast, doth present
Wall, that vile Wall, which did these lovers sunder;
And through Wall's chink, poor souls, they are content
To whisper. At the which let no man wonder.
This man, with lanthorn, dog and bush of thorn,
Presenteth Moonshine; for, if you will know,
By Moonshine did these lovers think no scorn
To meet at Ninus' tomb, there, there to woo.
This grisly beast, which by name Lion hight.
The trusty Thisby, coming first by night,
Did scare away, or rather did affright;
And, as she fled, her mantle she did fall,
Which Lion vile with bloody mouth did stain.

Anon comes Pyramus, sweet youth and tall,
And finds his trusty Thisby's mantle slain;
Whereat with blade, with bloody blameful blade,
He bravely broached his boiling bloody breast;
And, Thisby, tarrying in mulberry shade,
His dagger drew and died."
Midsummer Night's Dream, v.1,128, et seq.

Figure 5: "A Midsummer Night's Dream" by Arthur Rackham

CEPHALUS AND PROCRIS

Cephalus was a beautiful youth and fond of manly sports. He would rise before the dawn to pursue the chase. Aurora saw him when she first looked forth, fell in love with him, and stole him away. But Cephalus was just married to a charming wife whom he loved devotedly. Her name was Procris. She was a favorite of Diana, the goddess of hunting, who had given her a dog which could outrun every rival, and a javelin which would never fail of its mark; and Procris gave these presents to her husband. Cephalus was so happy in his wife that he resisted all the entreaties of Aurora, and she finally dismissed him in displeasure, saying, "Go, ungrateful mortal, keep your wife, whom, if I am not much mistaken, you will one day be very sorry you ever saw again."

Cephalus returned, and was as happy as ever in his wife and his woodland sports. Now it happened some angry deity had sent a ravenous fox to annoy the country; and the hunters turned out in great strength to capture it. Their efforts were all in vain; no dog could run it down; and at last they came to Cephalus to borrow his famous dog, whose name was Lelaps. No sooner was the dog let loose than he darted off, quicker than their eye could follow him. If they had not seen his footprints in the sand they would have thought he flew. Cephalus and others stood on a hill and saw the race. The fox tried every art; he ran in a circle and turned on his track, the dog close upon him, with open jaws, snapping at his heels, but biting only the air. Cephalus was about to use his javelin, when suddenly he saw both dog and game stop instantly. The heavenly powers who had given both, were not willing that either should conquer. In the very attitude of life and action they were turned into stone. So lifelike and natural did they look, you would have thought, as you looked at them, that one was going to bark, the other to leap forward.

Cephalus, though he had lost his dog, still continued to take delight in the chase. He would go out at early morning, ranging the woods and hills unaccompanied by any one, needing no help, for his javelin was a sure weapon in all cases. Fatigued with hunting, when the sun got high he would seek a shady nook where a cool stream flowed, and, stretched on the grass with his garments thrown aside, would enjoy the breeze. Sometimes he would say aloud, "Come, sweet breeze, come and fan my breast, come and allay the heat that burns me." Some one passing by one day heard him talking in this way to the air, and, foolishly believing that he was talking to some maiden, went and told the secret to Procris, Cephalus's wife. Love is credulous. Procris, at the sudden shock, fainted away. Presently recovering, she said, "It cannot be true; I will not believe it unless I myself am a witness to it." So she waited, with anxious heart, till the next morning, when Cephalus went to hunt as usual. Then she stole out after him, and concealed herself in the place where the informer directed her. Cephalus came as he was wont when tired with sport, and stretched himself on the green bank, saying, "Come, sweet breeze, come and fan me; you know how I love you! You make the groves and my solitary rambles delightful." He was running on in this way when he heard, or thought he heard, a sound as of a sob in the bushes. Supposing it some wild animal, he threw hie javelin at the spot. A cry from his beloved Procris told him that the weapon had too surely met its mark. He rushed to the place, and found her bleeding and with sinking strength endeavoring to draw forth from the wound the javelin, her own gift. Cephalus raised her from the earth, strove to stanch the blood, and called her to revive and not to leave him miserable, to reproach himself with her death. She opened her feeble eyes, and forced herself to utter these few words: "I implore you, if you have ever loved me, if I have ever deserved kindness at your hands, my husband, grant me this last request; do not marry that odious Breeze!" This disclosed the whole mystery; but alas! What advantage to disclose it now? She died; but her face wore a calm expression, and she looked pityingly and forgivingly on her husband when he made her understand the truth.

In Shakespeare's play just quoted, there is an allusion to Cephalus and Procris, although rather badly spelt.

Pyramus says, "Not Shafalus to Procrus was so true."
Thisbe. "As Shafalus to Procrus, I to you."

Moore, in his Legendary Ballads, has one on Cephalus and Procris, beginning thus:

"A hunter once in a grove reclined,
To shun the noon's bright eye,
And oft he wooed the wandering wind
To cool his brow with its sigh.
While mute lay even the wild bee's hum,
Nor breath could stir the aspen's hair,
His song was still, 'Sweet Air, O come!'
While Echo answered, 'Come, sweet Air!'"

Chapter 3

IO AND CALLISTO. DIANA AND ACTAEON. THE STORY OF PHAETON

Jupiter and Juno, although husband and wife, did not live together very happily. Jupiter did not love his wife very much, and Juno distrusted her husband, and was always accusing him of unfaithfulness. One day she perceived that it suddenly grew dark, and immediately suspected that her husband had raised a cloud to hide some of his doings that would not bear the light. She brushed away the cloud, and saw her husband, on the banks of a glassy river, with a beautiful heifer standing near him. Juno suspected that the heifer's form concealed some fair nymph of mortal mould. This was indeed the case; for it was Io, the daughter of the river god Inachus, whom Jupiter had been flirting with, and, when he became aware of the approach of his wife, had changed into that form.

Juno joined her husband, and noticing the heifer, praised its beauty, and asked whose it was, and of what herd. Jupiter, to stop questions, replied that it was a fresh creation from the earth. Juno asked to have it as a gift. What could Jupiter do? He was loth to give his mistress to his wife; yet how refuse so trifling a present as a simple heifer? He could not, without arousing suspicion; so he consented. The goddess was not yet relieved of her suspicions; and she delivered the heifer to Argus, to be strictly watched.

Now Argus had a hundred eyes in his head, and never went to sleep with more than two at a time, so that he kept watch of Io constantly. He suffered her to feed through the day, and at night tied her up with a vile rope round her neck. She would have stretched out her arms to implore freedom of Argus, but she had no arms to stretch out, and her voice was a bellow that frightened even herself. She saw her father and her sisters, went near them, and suffered them to pat her back, and heard them admire her beauty. Her father reached her a tuft o grass, and she licked the outstretched hand. She longed to make herself known to him, and would have uttered her wish; but, alas! words were wanting. At length she bethought herself of writing, and inscribed her name it was a short one with her hoof on the sand. Inachus recognized it, and discovering that his daughter, whom he had long sought in vain, was hidden under this disguise, mourned over her, and, embracing her white neck, exclaimed, "Alas! My daughter, it would have been a less grief to have lost you altogether!" While he thus lamented, Argus, observing, came and drove her away, and took his seat on a high bank, whence he could see in every direction.

Jupiter was troubled at beholding the sufferings of his mistress, and calling Mercury, told him to go and dispatch Argus. Mercury made haste, put his winged slippers on his feet, and cap on his head, took his sleep-producing wand, and leaped down from the heavenly towers to the earth. There he laid aside his wings, and kept only his wand, with which he presented himself as a shepherd driving his flock. As he strolled on he blew upon his pipes. These were what are called the Syrinx or Pandean pipes. Argus listened with delight, for he had never heard the instrument before. "Young man," said he, "come and take a seat by me on this stone. There is no better place for your flock to graze in than hereabouts, and here is a pleasant shade such as shepherds love." Mercury sat down, talked, and told stories until it grew late, and played upon his pipes his most soothing strains, hoping to lull the watchful eyes to sleep, but all in vain; for Argus still contrived to keep some of his eyes open, though he shut the rest.

Among other stories, Mercury told him how the instrument on which he played was invented. "There was a certain nymph, whose name was Syrinx, who was much beloved by the satyrs and spirits of the wood; but she would have none of them, but was a faithful worshipper of Diana, and followed the chase. You would have thought it was Diana herself, had you seen her in her hunting dress, only that her bow was of horn and Diana's of silver. One day, as she was returning from the chase, Pan met her, told her just this, and added more of the same sort. She ran away, without stopping to hear his compliments, and he pursued till she came to the bank of the river, where he overtook her, and she had only time to call for help on her friends, the water nymphs. They heard and consented. Pan threw his arms around what he supposed to be the form of the nymph, and found he embraced only a tuft of reeds! As he breathed a sigh, the air sounded through the reeds, and produced a plaintive melody. The god, charmed with the novelty and with the sweetness of the music, said 'Thus, then, at least, you shall be mine.' And he took some of the reeds, and placing them together, of unequal lengths, side by side, made an instrument which he called Syrinx, in honor of the nymph." Before Mercury had finished his story, he saw Argus's eyes all asleep. As his head nodded forward on his breast, Mercury with one stroke cut his neck through, and tumbled his head down the rocks. O hapless Argus! The light of your hundred eyes is quenched at once! Juno took them and put them as ornaments on the tail of her peacock, where they remain to this day.

But the vengeance of Juno was not yet satiated. She sent a gadfly to torment Io, who fled over the whole world from its pursuit. She swam through the Ionian Sea, which derived its name from her, then roamed over the plains of Illyria, ascended Mount Haemus, and crossed the Thracian strait, thence named the Bosphorus (cow-bearer), rambled on through Scythia and the country of the Cimmerians, and arrived at last on the banks of the Nile. At length Jupiter interceded for her, and, upon his promising not to pay her any more attentions, Juno consented to restore her to her form. It was curious to see her gradually recover her former self. The coarse hairs fell from her body, her horns shrunk up, her eyes grew narrower, her mouth shorter; hands and fingers came instead of hoofs to her forefeet; in fine, there was nothing left of the heifer except her beauty. At first she was afraid to speak for fear she should low, but gradually she recovered her confidence, and was restored to her father and sisters.

In a poem dedicated to Leigh Hunt, by Keats, the following allusion to the story of Pan and Syrinx occurs:

"So did he feel who pulled the boughs aside,
That we might look into a forest wide,
* * * * * * * *
Telling us how fair trembling Syrinx fled
Arcadian Pan, with such a fearful dread.
Poor nymph poor Pan how he did weep to find
Nought but a lovely sighing of the wind
Along the reedy stream; a half-heard strain,
Full of sweet desolation, balmy pain."

CALLISTO

Callisto was another maiden who excited the jealousy of Juno, and the goddess changed her into a bear. "I will take away," said she, :"that beauty with which you have captivated my husband." Down fell Callisto on her hands and knees; she tried to stretch out her arms in supplication,— they were already beginning to be covered with black hair. Her hands grew rounded, became armed with crooked claws, and served for feet; her mouth, which Jove used to praise for its beauty, became a horrid pair of jaws; her voice, which if unchanged would have moved the heart to pity, became a growl, more fit to inspire terror. Yet her former disposition remained, and, with continued groaning, she bemoaned her fate, and stood upright as well as she could, lifting up her paws to beg for mercy; and felt that Jove was unkind, though she could not tell him so. Ah, how often, afraid to stay in the woods all night alone, she wandered about the neighborhood of her former haunts; how often, frightened by the dogs, did she, so lately a huntress, fly in terror from the hunters! Often she fled from the wild beasts, forgetting that she was now a wild beast herself; and, bear as she was, was afraid of the bears.

One day a youth espied her as he was hunting. She saw him and recognized him as her own son, now grown a young man. She stopped, and felt inclined to embrace him. As she was about to approach, he, alarmed, raised his hunting spear, and was on the point of transfixing her, when Jupiter, beholding, arrested the crime, and, snatching away both of them, placed them in the heavens as the Great and Little Bear.

Juno was in a rage to see her rival so set in honor, and hastened to ancient Tethys and Oceanus, the powers of ocean, and, in answer to their inquiries, thus told the cause of her coming; "Do you ask why I, the queen of the gods, have left the heavenly plains and sought your depths. Learn that I am supplanted in heaven,— my place is given to another. You will hardly believe me; but look when night darkens the world, and you shall see the two, of whom I have so much reason to complain, exalted to the heavens, in that part where the circle is the smallest, in the neighborhood of the pole. Why should any one hereafter tremble at the thought of offending Juno, when such rewards are the consequence of my displeasure! See what I have been able to effect! I forbade her to wear the human form,— she is placed among the stars! So do my punishments result,— such is the extent of my power! Better that she should have resumed her former shape, as I permitted Io to do. Perhaps he means to marry her, and put me away! But you, my foster parents, if you feel for me, and see with displeasure this unworthy treatment of me, show it, I beseech you, by forbidding this guilty couple from coming into your waters." The powers of the ocean assented, and consequently the two constellations of the Great and Little Bear move round and round in heaven, but never sink, as the other stars do, beneath the ocean.

Milton alludes to the fact that the constellation of the Bear never sets, when he says,

"Let my lamp at midnight hour
Be seen in some high lonely tower,
Where I may oft outwatch the Bear."
Il Penseroso

And Prometheus, in James Russell Lowell's poem, says,

"One after one the stars have risen and set,
Sparkling upon the hoar-frost of my chain;
The Bear that prowled all night about the fold
Of the North Star, hath shrunk into his den,
Scared by the blithsome footsteps of the dawn."

The last star in the tail of the Little Bear is the Pole star, called also the Cynosure. Milton says,

"Straight mine eye hath caught new pleasures
While the landscape round it measures.
* * * * * * * *
Towers and battlements it sees
Bosomed high in tufted trees,
Where perhaps some beauty lies
The Cynosure of neighboring eyes."
L'Allegro.

The reference here is both to the Pole-star as the guide of mariners, and to the magnetic attraction of the North. He calls it also the "Star of Aready," because Callisto's boy was named Arcas, and they lived in Arcadia. In Milton's Comus, the elder brother, benighted in the woods, says,

"Some gentle taper!
Through a rush candle, from
the wicker hole
Of some clay habitation,
visit us
With thy long levelled rule
of streaming light,
And thou shalt be our star of Aready,
Or Tyrian Chynsure."

DIANA AND ACTAEON

It was midday, and the sun stood equally distant from either goal, when young Actaeon, son of King Cadmus, thus addressed the youths who with him were hunting the stag in the mountains:

"Friends, our nets and our weapons are wet with the blood of our victims; we have had sport enough for one day, and tomorrow we can renew our labors. Now, while Phoebus parches the earth, let us put by our instruments and indulge ourselves with rest."

There was a valley thickly enclosed with cypresses and pines, sacred to the huntress-queen, Diana. In the extremity of the valley was a cave, not adorned with art, but nature had counterfeited art in its construction, for she had turned the arch of its roof with stones as delicately fitted as if by the hand of man. A fountain burst out from one side, whose open basin was bounded by a grassy rim. Here the goddess of the woods used to come when weary with hunting and lave her virgin limbs in the sparkling water.

One day, having repaired thither with her nymphs, she handed her javelin, her quiver, and her bow to one, her robe to another, while a third unbound the sandals from her feet. Then Crocale, the most skillful of them, arranged her hair, and Nephele, Hyale, and the rest drew water in capacious urns. While the goddess was thus employed in the labors of the toilet, behold, Actaeon, having quitted his companions, and rambling without any especial object, came to the place, led thither by his destiny. As he presented himself at the entrance of the cave, the nymphs, seeing a man, screamed and rushed towards the goddess to hide her with their bodies. But she was taller than the

Figure 6: "Huntress Dian" by Arthur Rackham

rest, and overtopped them all by a head. Such a color as tinges the clouds at sunset or at dawn came over the countenance of Diana thus taken by surprise. Surrounded as she was by her nymphs, she yet turned half away, and sought with a sudden impulse for her arrows. As they were not at hand, she dashed the water into the face of the intruder, adding these words: "Now go and tell, if you can, that you have seen Diana unapparelled." Immediately a pair of branching stag's horns grew out of his head, his neck gained in length, his ears grew sharp-pointed, his hands became feet, his arms long legs, his body was covered with a hairy spotted hide. Fear took the place of his former boldness, and the hero fled. He could not but admire his own speed; but when he saw his horns in the water, "Ah, wretched me!: he would have said, but no sound followed the effort. He groaned, and tears flowed down the face that had taken the place of his own. Yet his consciousness remained. What shall he do? Go home to seek the palace, or lie hid in the woods? The latter he was afraid, the former he was ashamed, to do. While he hesitated, the dogs saw him. First Melampus, a Spartan dog, gave the signal with his bark, then Pamphagus, Dorceus, Lelaps, Theron, Nape, Tigris, and all the rest, rushed after him swifter than the wind. Over rocks and cliffs, through mountain gorges that seemed impracticable, he fled, and they followed. Where he had often chased the stag and cheered on his pack, his pack now chased him, cheered on by his own huntsmen. He longed to cry out, "I am Actaeon; recognize your master!" But the words came not at his will. The air resounded with the bark of the dogs. Presently one fastened on his back, another seized his shoulder. While they held their master, the rest of the pack came up and buried their teeth in his flesh. He groaned, not in a human voice, yet certainly not in a stag's, and, falling on his knees, raised his eyes, and would have raised his arms in supplication, if he had had them. His friends and fellow-huntsmen cheered on the dogs, and looked everywhere for Actaeon, calling on him to join the sport. At the sound of his name, he turned his head, and heard them regret that he should be away. He earnestly wished he was. He would have been well pleased to see the exploits of his dogs, but to feel them was too much. They were all around him, rending and tearing; and it was not till they had torn his life out that the anger of Diana was satisfied.

In the "Epic of Hades" there is a description of Actaeon and his change of form. Perhaps the most beautiful lines in it are when Actaeon, changed to a stag, first hears his own hounds and flees.

"But as I gazed, and careless turned and passed
Through the thick wood, forgetting what had been,
And thinking thoughts no longer, swift there came
A mortal terror; voices that I knew.
My own hounds' bayings that I loved before,
As with them often o'er the purple hills
I chased the flying hart from slope to slope,
Before the slow sun climbed the eastern peaks,
Until the swift sun smote the western plain;
Whom often I had cheered by voice and glance,
Whom often I had checked with hand and thong;
Grim followers, like the passions, firing me,
True servants, like the strong nerves, urging me
On many a fruitless chase, to find and take

Some too swift-fleeting beauty, faithful feet
And tongues, obedient always: these I knew
Clothed with a new-born force and vaster grown,
And stronger than their master; and I thought,
What if they tore me with their jaws, nor knew
That once I ruled them, brute pursuing brute,
And I the quarry? Then I turned and fled
If it was I indeed that feared and fled
Down the long glades, and through the tangled brakes,
Where scarce the sunlight pierced; fled on and on,
And panted, self-pursued. But evermore
The dissonant music which I knew so sweet,
When by the windy hills, the echoing vales
And whispering pines it rang; now far, now near
As from my rushing steed I leant and cheered
With voice and horn the chase; this brought to me
Fear of I knew not what, which bade me fly,
Fly always, fly; but when my heart stood still,
And all my limbs were stiffened as I fled,
Just as the white moon ghost-like climbed the sky,
Nearer they came and nearer, baying loud,
With bloodshot eyes and red jaws dripping foam;
And when I strove to check their savagery,
Speaking with words; no voice articulate came,
Only a dumb, low bleat. Then all the throng
Leapt swift upon me and tore me as I lay,
And left me man again."

In Shelley's poem Adonais is the following allusion to the story of Actaeon:

"Midst others of less note came one frail form,
A phantom among men; companionless
As the last cloud of an expiring storm,
Whose thunder is its knell; he, as I guess,
Had gazed on Nature's naked loveliness,
Actaeon-like, and now he fled astray
With feeble steps o'er the world's wilderness;
And his own Thoughts, along that rugged way,
Pursued like raging hounds their father and their prey."
Adonais, stanza 31.

The allusion is probably to Shelley himself.

LATONA AND THE RUSTICS

Some thought the goddess in this instance more severe than was just, while others praised her conduct as strictly consistent with her virgin dignity. As usual, the recent event brought older ones to mind, and one of the bystanders told this story. "Some countrymen of Lycia once insulted the goddess Latona, but not with impunity. When I was young, my father, who had grown too old for active labors, sent me to Lycia to drive thence some choice oxen, and there I saw the very pond and marsh where the wonder happened. Nearby stood an ancient altar, black with the smoke of sacrifice and almost buried among the reeds. I inquired whose altar it might be, whether of Faunus or the Naiads or some god of the neighboring mountain, and one of the country people replied, 'No mountain or river god possesses this altar, but she whom royal Juno in her jealousy drove from land to land, denying her any spot of earth whereon to rear her twins. Bearing in her arms the infant deities, Latona reached this land, weary with her burden and parched with thirst. By chance she espied in the bottom of the valley this pond of clear water, where the country people were at work gathering willows and osiers. The goddess approached, and kneeling on the bank would have slaked her thirst in the cool stream, but the rustics forbade her. 'Why do you refuse me water?' said she; 'water is free to all. Nature allows no one to claim as property the sunshine, the air, or the water. I come to take my share of the common blessing. Yet I ask it of you as a favor. I have no intention of washing my limbs in it, weary though they be, but only to quench my thirst. My mouth is so dry that I can hardly speak. A draught of water would be nectar to me; it would revive me, and I would own myself indebted to you for life itself. Let these infants move your pity, who stretch out their little arms as if to plead for me'; and the children, as it happened, were stretching out their arms.

"Who would not have been moved with these gentle words of the goddess? But these clowns persisted in their rudeness; they even added jeers and threats of violence if she did not leave the place. Nor was this all. They waded into the pond and stirred up the mud with their feet, so as to make the water unfit to drink. Latona was so angry that she ceased to feel her thirst. She no longer supplicated the clowns, but lifting her hands to heaven exclaimed, 'May they never quit that pool, but pass their lives there!' And it came to pass accordingly. They now live in the water, sometimes totally submerged, then raising their heads above the surface, or swimming upon it. Sometimes they come out upon the bank, but soon leap back again into the water. They still use their base voices in railing, and though they have the water all to themselves, are not ashamed to croak in the midst of it. Their voices are harsh, their throats bloated, their mouths have become stretched by constant railing, their necks have shrunk up and disappeared, and their heads are joined to their bodies. Their backs are green, their disproportioned bellies white, and in short they are now frogs, and dwell in the slimy pool."

This story explains the allusion in one of Milton's sonnets, "On the detraction which followed upon his writing certain treatises."

"I did but prompt the age to quit their clogs
By the known laws of ancient liberty,.
When straight a barbarous noise environs me
Of owls and cuckoos, asses, apes and dogs.
As when those hinds that were transformed to frogs
Railed at Latona's twin-born progeny,
Which after held the sun and moon in fee."

The persecution which Latona experienced from Juno is alluded to in the story. The tradition was that the future mother of Apollo and Diana, flying from the wrath of Juno, besought all the islands of the Aegean to afford her a place of rest, but all feared too much the potent queen of heaven to assist her rival. Delos alone consented to become the birthplace of the future deities. Delos was then a floating island; but when Latona arrived there, Jupiter fastened it with adamantine chains to the bottom of the sea, that it might be a secure resting place for his beloved. Byron alludes to Delos in his Don Juan:

"The isles of Greece! The isles of Greece!
Where burning Sappho loved and sung,
Where grew the arts of war and peace,
Where Delos rose and Phoebus sprung!"

PHAETON

Epaphus was the son of Jupiter and Io. Phaeton, child of the Sun, was one day boasting to him of his high descent and of his father Phoebus. Epaphus could not bear it. "Foolish fellow," said he "you believe your mother in all things, and you are puffed up by your pride in a false father." Phaeton went in rage and shame and reported this to his mother, Clymene. "If," said he, "I am indeed of heavenly birth, give me, mother, some proof of it, and establish my claim to the honor." Clymene stretched forth her hands towards the skies, and said, "I call to witness the Sun which looks down upon us, that I have told you the truth. If I speak falsely, let this be the last time I behold his light. But it needs not much labor to go and inquire for yourself; the land whence the sun rises lies next to ours. Go and demand of him whether he will own you as a son" Phaeton heard with delight. He travelled to India, which lies directly in the regions of sunrise; and, full of hope and pride, approached the goal whence the Sun begins his course.

The palace of the Sun stood reared aloft on columns, glittering with gold and precious stones, while polished ivory formed the ceilings, and silver the doors. The workmanship surpassed the material; for upon the walls Vulcan had represented earth, sea and skies, with their inhabitants. In the sea were the nymphs, some sporting in the waves, some riding on the backs of fishes, while others sat upon the rocks and dried their sea-green hair. Their faces were not all alike, nor yet unlike, but such as sisters' ought to be. The earth had its towns and forests and rivers and rustic divinities. Over all was carved the likeness of the glorious heaven; and on the silver doors the twelve signs of the zodiac, six on each side.

Clymene's son advanced up the steep ascent, and entered the halls of his disputed father. He approached the paternal presence, but stopped at a distance, for the light was more than he could bear. Phoebus, arrayed in a purple vesture, sat on a throne which glittered as with diamonds. On his right hand and his left stood the Day, the Month, and the Year, and, at regular intervals, the Hours. Spring stood with her head crowned with flowers, and Summer, with garment cast aside, and a garland formed of spears of ripened grain, and Autumn, with his feet stained with grape juice, and icy Winter, with his hair stiffened with hoar frost. Surrounded by these attendants, the Sun, with the eye that sees every thing, beheld the youth dazzled with the novelty and splendor of the scene, and inquired the purpose of his errand. The youth replied, "Oh, light of the boundless world, Phoebus, my father, if you permit me to use that name, give me some proof, I beseech you, by which I may be known as yours." He ceased; and his father, laying aside the beams that shone all around his head, bade him approach, and embracing him, said, "My son, you deserve not to be disowned, and I confirm what your mother has told you. To put an end to your doubts, ask what you will, the gift shall be yours. I call to witness that dreadful lake, which I never saw, but which we gods swear by in our most solemn engagements." Phaeton immediately asked to be permitted for one day to drive the chariot of the sun. The father repented of his promise; thrice and four times he shook his radiant head in warning. "I have spoken rashly," said he; "only this request I would fain deny. I beg you to withdraw it. It is not a safe boon, nor one, my Phaeton, suited to your youth and strength. Your lot is mortal, and you ask what is beyond a mortal's power. In your ignorance you aspire to do that which not even the gods themselves may do. None but myself may drive the flaming car of day; not even Jupiter, whose terrible right arm hurls the thunder bolts. The first part of the way is steep, and such as the horses when fresh in the morning can hardly climb; the middle is high up in the heavens, whence I myself can scarcely, without alarm, look down and behold the earth and sea stretched beneath me. The last part of the road descends rapidly, and requires most careful driving. Tethys, who is waiting to receive me, often trembles for me lest I should fall headlong. Add to all this, the heaven is all the time turning round and carrying the stars with it. I have to be perpetually on my guard lest that movement, which sweeps everything else along, should hurry me also away. Suppose I should lend you the chariot, what would you do? Could you keep your course while the sphere was revolving under you? Perhaps you think that there are forests and cities, the abodes of gods, and palaces and temples on the way. On the contrary, the road is through the midst of frightful monsters. You pass by the horns of the Bull, in front of the Archer, and near the Lion's jaws, and where the Scorpion stretches its arms in one direction and the Crab in another. Nor will you find it easy to guide those horses, with their breasts full of fire which they breathe forth from their mouths and nostrils. I can scarcely govern them myself, when they are unruly and resist the reins. Beware, my son, lest I should give you a fatal gift; recall your request while yet you may. Do you ask me for proof that you are sprung from my blood? I give you a proof in my fears for you. Look at my face,— I would that you could look into my breast, you would there see all a father's anxiety. Finally," he continued, "look round the world and choose whatever you will of what earth or sea contains most precious, ask it and fear no refusal. This only I pray you not to urge. It is not honor, but destruction you seek. Why do you hang round my neck and still entreat me? You shall have it if you persist, the oath is sworn and must be kept, but I beg you to choose more wisely."

He ended; but the youth rejected all admonition, and held to his demand. So, having resisted as long as he could, Phoebus at last led the way to where stood the lofty chariot. It was of gold, the gift of Vulcan; the axle was of gold, the pole and wheels of gold, the spokes of silver. Along the seat were rows of chrysolites and diamonds, which reflected all around the brightness of the sun. While the daring youth gazed in admiration, the early Dawn threw open the purple doors of the east, and showed the pathway strewn with roses. The stars withdrew, marshalled by the Daystar, which last of all retired also. The father, when he saw the earth beginning to glow, and the Moon preparing to retire, ordered the Hours to harness up the horses. They obeyed, and led forth from the lofty stalls the steeds full fed with ambrosia, and attached the reins. Then the father bathed the face of his son with a powerful unguent, and made him capable of enduring the brightness of the flame. He set the rays on his head, and, with a foreboding sigh, said, "If, my son, you will in this at least heed my advice, spare the whip and hold tight the reins. They go fast enough of their own accord; the labor is to hold them in. You are not to take the straight road directly between the five circles, but turn off to the left. Keep within the limit of the middle zone, and avoid the northern and the southern alike. You will see the marks of the wheels, and they will serve to guide you. And, that the skies and the earth may each receive their due share of heat, go not too high, or you will burn the heavenly dwellings, nor too low, or you will set the earth on fire; the middle course is safest and best. And now I leave you to your chance, which I hope will plan better for you than you have done for yourself. Night is passing out of the western gates and we can delay no longer. Take the reins; but if at last your heart fails you, and you will benefit by my advice, stay where you are in safety, and suffer me to light and warm the earth." The agile youth sprang into the chariot, stood erect and grasped the reins with delight, pouring out thanks to his reluctant parent.

Meanwhile the horses fill the air with their snortings and fiery breath, and stamp the ground impatient. Now the bars are let down, and the boundless plain of the universe lies open before them. They dart forward and cleave the opposing clouds, and outrun the morning breezes which started from the same eastern goal. The steeds soon perceived that the load they drew was lighter than usual; and as a ship without ballast is tossed hither and thither on the sea, so the chariot, without its accustomed weight, was dashed about as if empty. They rush headlong and leave the travelled road. He is alarmed, and knows not how to guide them; nor, if he knew, has he the power. Then, for the first time, the Great and Little Bear were scorched with heat, and would fain, if it were possible, have plunged into the water; and the Serpent which lies coiled up round the north pole, torpid and harmless, grew warm, and with warmth felt its rage revive. Bootes, they say, fled away, though encumbered with his plough, and all unused to rapid motion.

When hapless Phaeton looked down upon the earth, now spreading in vast extent beneath him, he grew pale and his knees shook with terror. In spite of the glare all around him, the sight of his eyes grew dim. He wished he had never touched his father's horses, never learned his parentage, never prevailed in his request. He is borne along like a vessel that flies before a tempest, when the pilot can do no more and betakes himself to his prayers. What shall he do? Much of the heavenly road is left behind, but more remains before. He turns his eyes from one direction to the other; now to the goal whence he began his course, now to the realms of sunset which he is not destined to reach. He loses his self-command, and knows not what to do, whether to draw tight the reins or throw them loose; he forgets the names of the horses. He sees with terror the monstrous forms scattered over the surface of heaven. Here the Scorpion extended his two great arms, with his tail and crooked claws stretching over two signs of the zodiac. When the boy beheld him, reeking with poison and menacing with his fangs, his courage failed, and the reins fell from his hands. The horses, feeling the reins loose on their backs, dashed headlong, and unrestrained went off into unknown regions of the sky, in among the stars, hurling the chariot over pathless places, now up in high heaven, now down almost to the earth. The moon saw with astonishment her brother's chariot running beneath her own. The clouds begin to smoke, and the mountain tops take fire; the fields are parched with heat, the plants wither, the trees with their leafy branches burn, the harvest is ablaze! But these are small things. Great cities perished, with their walls and towers; whole nations with their people were consumed to ashes! The forest-clad mountains burned, Athos and Taurus and Tmolus and Œte; Ida, once celebrated for fountains, but now all dry; the Muses' mountain Helicon, and Haemus; Ǣtna, with fires within and without, and Parnassus, with his two peaks, and Rhodope, forced at last to part with his snowy crown. Her cold climate was no protection to Scythia, Caucasus burned, and Ossa and Pindus, and, greater than both, Olympus; the Alps high in air, and the Apennines crowned with clouds.

Then Phaeton beheld the world on fire, and felt the heat intolerable. The air he breathed was like the air of a furnace and full of burning ashes, and the smoke was of a pitchy darkness. He dashed forward he knew not whither. Then, it is believed, the people of Ǣthiopia became black by the blood being forced so suddenly to the surface, and the Libyan desert was dried up to the condition in which it remains to this day. The Nymphs of the fountains, with dishevelled hair, mourned their waters, nor were the rivers safe beneath their banks; Tanais smoked, and Caicus, Xanthus and Meander. Babylonian Euphrates and Ganges, Tagus with golden sands, and Caijster where the swans resort. Nile fled away and hid his head in the desert, and there it still remains concealed. Where he used to discharge his waters through seven mouths into the sea, there seven dry channels alone remained. The earth cracked open, and through the chinks light broke into Tartarus, and frightened the king of shadows and his queen. The sea shrank up. Where before was water, it became a dry plain; and the mountains that lie beneath the waves lifted up their heads and became islands. The fishes sought the lowest depths, and the dolphins no longer ventured as usual to sport on the surface. Even Nereus, and his wife Doris, with the Nereids, their daughters, sought the deepest caves for refuge. Thrice Neptune essayed to raise his head above the surface and thrice was driven back by the heat. Earth, surrounded as she was by waters, yet with head and shoulders bare, screening her face with her hand, looked up to heaven, and with a husky voice called on Jupiter.

Chapter 3: Phaeton

"O ruler of the gods, if I have deserved this treatment, and it is your will that I perish with fire, why withhold your thunderbolts? Let me at least fall by your hand. Is this the reward of my fertility, of my obedient service? Is it for this that I have supplied herbage for cattle, and fruits for men, and frankincense for your altars? But if I am unworthy of regard, what has my brother Ocean done to deserve such a fate? If neither of us can excite your pity, think, I pray you, of your own heaven, and behold how both the poles are smoking which sustain your palace, which must fall if they be destroyed. Atlas faints, and scarce holds up his burden. If sea, earth, and heaven perish, we fall into ancient Chaos. Save what yet remains to us from the devouring flame. Oh, take thought for our deliverance in this awful moment!"

Thus, spoke Earth, and overcome with heat and thirst, could say no more. Then Jupiter Omnipotent, calling to witness all the gods, including him who had lent the chariot, and showing them that all was lost unless some speedy remedy were applied, mounted the lofty tower from whence he diffuses clouds over the earth, and hurls the forked lightnings. But at that time not a cloud was to be found to interpose for a screen to earth, nor was a shower remaining unexhausted. He thundered, and brandishing a lightning-bolt in his right hand launched it against the charioteer, and struck him at the same moment from his seat and from existence! Phaeton, with his hair on fire, fell headlong, like a shooting star which marks the heavens with its brightness as it falls, and Eridanus, the great river, received him and cooled his burning frame. The Italian Naiads reared a tomb for him, and inscribed these words upon the stone:

"Driver of Phoebus' chariot, Phaeton,
Struck by Jove's thunder, rests beneath this stone.
He could not rule his father's car of fire,
Yet was it much so nobly to aspire."

His sisters, the Heliades, as they lamented his fate were turned into poplar trees, on the banks of the river, and their tears, which continued to flow, became amber as they dropped into the stream.

One of Prior's best remembered poems is that on the Female Phaeton, from which we quote the last verse.

Kitty has been imploring her mother to allow her to go out into the world as her friends have done, if only for once.

"Fondness prevailed, mamma gave way;
Kitty, at heart's desire,
Obtained the chariot for a day,
And set the world on fire."

Milman, in his poem of Samor, makes the following allusion to Phaeton's story:

"As when the palsied universe aghast
Lay .... mute and still,
When drove, so poets sing, the sun-born youth
Devious through Heaven's affrighted signs his sire's
Ill-granted chariot. Him the Thunderer hurled
From th'empyrean headlong to the gulf
Of the half-parched Eridanus, where weep
Even now the sister trees their amber tears
O 'er Phaeton untimely dead."

In the beautiful lines of Walter Savage Lando describing the sea- shell, there is an allusion to the sun's palace and chariot. The water-nymph says,

---

"I have sinuous shells of pearly hue
Within, and things that lustre have imbibed
In the sun's palace porch, where when unyoked
His chariot-wheel stands midway in the wave.
Shake one and it awakens; then apply
Its polished lip to your attentive car,
And it remembers its August abodes,
And murmurs as the ocean murmurs there."
Gebir, Book 1

Chapter 4

MIDAS. BAUCIS AND PHILEMON. PLUTO AND PROSERPINE.

Bacchus, on a certain occasion, found his old school master and foster father, Silenus, missing. The old man had been drinking, and in that state had wandered away, and was found by some peasants, who carried him to their king, Midas. Midas recognized him, and treated him hospitably, entertaining him for ten days and nights with an unceasing round of jollity. On the eleventh day he brought Silenus back, and restored him in safety to his pupil. Whereupon Bacchus offered Midas his choice of whatever reward he might wish. He asked that whatever he might touch should be changed into GOLD. Bacchus consented, though sorry that he had not made a better choice. Midas went his way, rejoicing in his newly acquired power, which he hastened to put to the test. He could scarce believe his eyes when he found that a twig of an oak, which he plucked from the branch, became gold in his hand. He took up a stone it changed to gold. He touched a sod it did the same. He took an apple from the tree you would have thought he had robbed the garden of the Hesperides. His joy knew no bounds, and as soon as he got home, he ordered the servants to set a splendid repast on the table. Then he found to his dismay that whether he touched bread, it hardened in his hand; or put a morsel to his lips, it defied his teeth. He took a glass of wine, but it flowed down his throat like melted gold.

In consternation at the unprecedented affliction, he strove to divest himself of his power; he hated the gift he had lately coveted. But all in vain; starvation seemed to await him. He raised his arms, all shining with gold, in prayer to Bacchus, begging to be delivered from his glittering destruction. Bacchus, merciful deity, heard and consented. "Go," said he, "to the river Pactolus, trace the stream to its fountain-head, there plunge in your head and body and wash away your fault and its punishment." He did so, and scarce had he touched the waters before the gold-creating power passed into them, and the river sands became changed into GOLD, as they remain to this day.

Thenceforth Midas, hating wealth and splendor, dwelt in the country, and became a worshipper of Pan, the god of the fields. On a certain occasion Pan had the temerity to compare his music with that of Apollo, and to challenge the god of the lyre to a trial of skill. The challenge was accepted, and Tmolus, the mountain-god, was chosen umpire. Tmolus took his seat and cleared away the trees from his ears to listen. At a given signal Pan blew on his pipes, and with his rustic melody gave great satisfaction to himself and his faithful follower, Midas, who happened to be present. Then Tmolus turned his head toward the sun-god, and all his trees turned with him. Apollo rose, his brow wreathed with Parnassian laurel, while his robe of Tyrian purple swept the ground. In his left hand he held the lyre, and with his right hand struck the strings. Ravished with the harmony, Tmolus at once awarded the victory to the god of the lyre, and all but Midas acquiesced in the judgment. He dissented, and questioned the justice of the award. Apollo would not suffer such a depraved pair of ears any longer to wear the human form, but caused them to increase in length, grow hairy, within and without, and to become movable, on their roots; in short, to be on the perfect pattern of those of an ass.

Mortified enough was King Midas at this mishap; but he consoled himself with the thought that it was possible to hide his misfortune, which he attempted to do by means of an ample turban or headdress. But his hairdresser of course knew the secret. He was charged not to mention it, and threatened with dire punishment if he presumed to disobey. But he found it too much for his discretion to keep such a secret; so he went out into the meadow, dug a hole in the ground, and stooping down, whispered the story, and covered it up. Before long a thick bed of reeds sprang up in the meadow, and as soon as it had gained its growth, began whispering the story, and has continued to do so, from that day to this, with every breeze which passes over the place.

The story of King Midas has been told by others with some variations. Dryden, in the Wife of Bath's Tale, makes Midas' queen the betrayer of the secret.

"This Midas knew, and durst communicate
To none but to his wife his ears of state."

Midas was king of Phrygia. He was the son of Gordius, a poor countryman, who was taken by the people and made king, in obedience to the command of the oracle, which had said that their future king should come in a wagon. While the people were deliberating, Gordius with his wife and son came driving his wagon into the public square.

Gordius, being made king, dedicated his wagon to the deity of the oracle, and tied it up in its place with a fast knot. This was the celebrated GORDIAN KNOT, of which, in after times it was said, that whoever should untie it should become lord of all Asia. Many tried to untie it, but none succeeded, till Alexander the Great, in his career of conquest, came to Phrygia. He tried his skill with as ill success as the others, till growing impatient he drew his sword and cut the knot. When he afterwards succeeded in subjecting all Asia to his sway, people began to think that he had complied with the terms of the oracle according to its true meaning.

BAUCIS AND PHILEMON

On a certain hill in Phrygia stand a linden tree and an oak, enclosed by a low wall. Not far from the spot is a marsh, formerly good habitable land, but now indented with pools, the resort of fen-birds and cormorants. Once on a time, Jupiter, in human shape, visited this country, and with him his son Mercury (he of the caduceus), without his wings. They presented themselves at many a door as weary travellers, seeking rest and shelter, but found all closed, for it was late, and the inhospitable inhabitants would not rouse themselves to open for their reception. At last a humble mansion received them, a small thatched cottage, where Baucis, a pious old dame, and her husband Philemon, united when young, had grown old together. Not ashamed of their poverty, they made it endurable by moderate desires and kind dispositions. One need not look there for master or for servant; they two were the whole household, master and servant alike. When the two heavenly guests crossed the humble threshold, and bowed their heads to pass under the low door, the old man placed a seat, on which Baucis, bustling and attentive, spread a cloth, and begged them to sit down. Then she raked out the coals from the ashes, kindled up a fire, and fed it with leaves and dry bark, and with her scanty breath blew it into a flame. She brought out of a corner split sticks and dry branches, broke them up, and placed them under the small kettle. Her husband collected some pot-herbs in the garden, and she shred them from the stalks, and prepared them for the pot He reached down with a forked stick a flitch of bacon hanging in the chimney, cut a small piece, and put it in the pot to boil with the herbs, setting away the rest for another time. A beechen bowl was filled with warm water that their guests might wash. While all was doing they beguiled the time with conversation.

On the bench designed for the guests was laid a cushion stuffed with sea-weed; and a cloth, only produced on great occasions, but old and coarse enough, was spread over that. The old woman, with her apron on, with trembling hand set the table. One leg was shorter than the rest, but a shell put under restored the level. When fixed, she rubbed the table down with some sweet-smelling herbs. Upon it she set some olives, Minerva's-fruit, some cornel-berries preserved in vinegar, and added radishes and cheese, with eggs lightly cooked in the ashes. All were served in earthen dishes, and an earthenware pitcher, with wooden cups, stood beside them. When all was ready, the stew, smoking hot, was set on the table. Some wine, not of the oldest, was added; and for dessert, apples and wild honey; and over and above all, friendly faces, and simple but hearty welcome.

Now while the repast proceeded, the old folks were astonished to see that the wine, as fast as it was poured out, renewed itself in the pitcher, of its own accord. Struck with terror, Baucis and Philemon recognized their heavenly guests, fell on their knees, and with clasped hands implored forgiveness for their poor entertainment. There was an old goose, which they kept as the guardian of their humble cottage; and they bethought them to make this a sacrifice in honor of their guests. But the goose, too nimble for the old folks, eluded their pursuit with the aid of feet and wings, and at last took shelter between the gods themselves. They forbade it to be slain; and spoke in these words: "We are gods. This inhospitable village shall pay the penalty of its impiety; you alone shall go free from the chastisement. Quit your house, and come with us to the top of yonder hill." They hastened to obey, and staff in hand, labored up the steep ascent. They had come within an arrow's flight of the top, when turning their eyes below, they beheld all the country sunk in a lake, only their own house left standing. While they gazed with wonder at the sight, and lamented the fate of their neighbors, that old house of theirs was changed into a TEMPLE. Columns took the place of the corner-posts, the thatch grew yellow and appeared a gilded roof, the floors became marble, the doors were enriched with carving and ornaments of gold. Then spoke Jupiter in benignant accents: "Excellent old man, and woman worthy of such a husband, speak, tell us your wishes; what favor have you to ask of us?" Philemon took counsel with Baucis a few moments; then declared to the gods their united wish. "We ask to be priests and guardians of this your temple; and since here we have passed our lives in love and concord, we wish that one and the same hour may take us both from life, that I may not live to see her grave, nor be laid in my own by her." Their prayer was granted. They were the keepers of the temple as long as they lived. When grown very old, as they stood one day before the steps of the sacred edifice, and were telling the story of the place, Baucis saw Philemon begin to put forth leaves, and old Philemon saw Baucis changing in like manner. And now a leafy crown had grown over their heads, while exchanging parting words, as long as they could speak. "Farewell, dear spouse," they said, together, and at the same moment the bark closed over their mouths. The Tyanean shepherd long showed the two trees, standing side by side, made out of the two good old people.

The story of Baucis and Philemon has been imitated by Swift, in a burlesque style, the actors in the change being two wandering saints and the house being changed into a church, of which Philemon is made the parson The following may serve as a specimen:

"They scarce had spoke when, fair and soft,
The roof began to mount aloft;
Aloft rose every beam and rafter;
The heavy wall climbed slowly after.
The chimney widened and grew higher,
Became a steeple with a spire.
The kettle to the top was hoist,
And there stood fastened to a joist,
But with the upside down, to show
Its inclination for below;
In vain, for a superior force,
Applied at bottom, stops its course;
Doomed ever in suspense to dwell,
'Tis now no kettle, but a bell.
A wooden jack, which had almost
Lost by disuse the art to roast,
A sudden alteration feels,
Increased by new intestine wheels;
And, what exalts the wonder more,
The number made the motion slower;
The flier, though 't had leaden feet,
Turned round so quick you scarce could see 't:
But slackened by some secret power,
Now hardly moves an inch an hour.
The jack and chimney, near allied,
Had never left each other's side.
The chimney to a steeple grown,
The jack would not be left alone;
But up against the steeple reared,
Became a clock, and still adhered;
And still its love to household cares
By a shrill voice at noon declares.
Warning the cook-maid not to burn
That roast meat which it cannot turn.
The groaning chair began to crawl,
Like a huge snail, along the wall;
There stuck aloft in public view,
And, with small change, a pulpit grew.
A bedstead of the antique mode,
Compact of timber many a load,
Such as our ancestors did use,
Was metamorphosed into pews,
Which still their ancient nature keep
By lodging folks disposed to sleep."

PROSEPINE, OR PERSEPHONE, OR CORA, OR KORE

Under the island of Aetna lies Typhoeus the Titan, in punishment for his share in the rebellion of the giants against Jupiter. Two mountains press down the one his right and the other his left hand while Aetna lies over his head. As Typhoeus moves, the earth shakes; as he breathes, smoke and ashes come up from Aetna. Pluto is terrified at the rocking of the earth, and fears that his kingdom will be laid open to the light of day. He mounts his chariot with the four black horses and comes up to earth and looks around. While he is thus engaged, Venus, sitting on Mount Eryx playing with her boy Cupid, sees him and says: "My son, take your darts with which you conquer all, even Jove himself, and send one into the breast of yonder dark monarch, who rules the realm of Tartarus. Why should he alone escape? Seize the opportunity to extend your empire and mine. Do you not see that even in heaven some despise our power? Minerva the wise, and Diana the huntress, defy us; and there is that daughter of Ceres, who threatens to follow their example. Now do you, if you have any regard for your own interest or mine, join these two in one." The boy unbound his quiver, and selected his sharpest and truest arrow; then, straining the bow against his knee, he attached the string, and, having made ready, shot the arrow with its barbed point right into the heart of Pluto.

In the vale of Enna there is a lake embowered in woods, which screen it from the fervid rays of the sun, while the moist ground is covered with flowers, and spring reigns perpetual. Here Proserpine was playing with her companions, gathering lilies and violets, and filling her basket and her apron with them, when Pluto saw her from his chariot, loved her, and carried her off. She screamed for help to her mother and her companions; and when in her fright she dropped the corners of her apron and let the flowers fall, childlike, she felt the loss of them as an addition to her grief. The ravisher urged on his steeds, calling them each by name, and throwing loose over their heads and necks his iron-colored reins. When he reached the River Cyane, and it opposed his passage, he struck the river bank with his trident, and the earth opened and gave him a passage to Tartarus.

Ceres sought her daughter all the world over. Bright-haired Aurora, when she came forth in the morning, and Hesperus, when he led out the stars in the evening, found her still busy in the search. But it was all unavailing. At length, weary and sad, she sat down upon a stone and continued sitting nine days and nights, in the open air, under the sunlight and moonlight and falling showers. It was where now stands the city of Eleusis, then the home of an old man named Celeus. He was out in the field, gathering acorns and blackberries, and sticks for his fire. His little girl was driving home their two goats, and as she passed the goddess, who appeared in the guise of an old woman, she said to her, "Mother," and the name was sweet to the ears of Ceres, "why do you sit here alone upon the rocks?" The old man also stopped, though his load was heavy, and begged her to come into his cottage, such as it was. She declined, and he urged her. "Go in peace," she replied, "and be happy in your daughter; I have lost mine." As she spoke, tears or something like tears, for the gods never weep fell down her cheeks upon her bosom. The compassionate old man and his child wept with her. Then said he, "Come with us, and despise not our humble roof; so may your daughter be restored to you in safety." "Lead on," said she, "I cannot resist that appeal!" So, she rose from the stone and went with them. As they walked he told her that his only son, a little boy, lay very sick, feverish and sleepless. She stooped and gathered some poppies. As they entered the cottage they found all in great distress, for the boy seemed past hope of recovery. Metanira, his mother, received her kindly, and the goddess stooped and kissed the lips of the sick child. Instantly the paleness left his face, and healthy vigor returned to his body. The whole family were delighted that is, the father, mother, and little girl, for they were all; they had no servants. They spread the table, and put upon it curds and cream, apples, and honey in the comb. While they ate, Ceres mingled poppy juice in the milk of the boy. When night came and all was still, she arose, and taking the sleeping boy, moulded his limbs with her hands, and uttered over him three times a solemn charm, then went and laid him in the ashes. His mother, who had been watching what her guest was doing, sprang forward with a cry and snatched the child from the fire. Then Ceres assumed her own form, and a divine splendor shone all around. While they were overcome with astonishment, she said, "Mother, you have been cruel in your fondness to your son. I would have made him immortal, but you have frustrated my attempt. Nevertheless, he shall be great and useful. He shall teach men the use of the plough, and the rewards which labor can win from the cultivated soil." So saying, she wrapped a cloud about her, and mounting her chariot rode away.

Ceres continued her search for her daughter, passing from land to land, and across seas and rivers, till at length she returned to Sicily, whence she at first set out, and stood by the banks of the River Cyane, where Pluto made himself a passage with his prize to his own dominions.

The river-nymph would have told the goddess all she had witnessed, but dared not, for fear of Pluto; so she only ventured to take up the girdle which Proserpine had dropped in her flight, and waft it to the feet of the mother. Ceres, seeing this, was no longer in doubt of her loss, but she did not yet know the cause, and laid the blame on the innocent land. "Ungrateful soil," said she, "which I have endowed with fertility and clothed with herbage and nourishing grain, No more shall you enjoy my favors" Then the cattle died, the plough broke in the furrow, the seed failed to come up; there was too much sun, there was too much rain; the birds stole the seeds, thistles and brambles were the only growth. Seeing this, the fountain Arethusa interceded for the land. "Goddess," said she, "blame not the land; it opened unwillingly to yield a passage to your daughter. I can tell you of her fate, for I have seen her. This is not my native country; I came hither from Elis. I was a woodland nymph, and delighted in the chase. They praised my beauty, but I cared nothing for it, and rather boasted of my hunting exploits. One day I was returning from the wood, heated with exercise, when I came to a stream silently flowing, so clear that you might count the pebbles on the bottom. The willows shaded it, and the grassy bank sloped down to the water's edge. I approached, I touched the water with my foot. I stepped in knee-deep, and not content with that, I laid my garments on the willows and went in. While I sported in the water, I heard an indistinct murmur coming up as out of the depths of the stream; and made haste to escape to the nearest bank. The voice said, 'Why do you fly, Arethusa? I am Alpheus, the god of this stream.' I ran, he pursued; he was not more swift than I, but he was stronger, and gained upon me, as my strength failed. At last, exhausted, I cried for help to Diana. 'Help me, goddess! Help your votary!' The goddess heard, and wrapped me suddenly in a thick cloud. The river-god looked now this way and now that, and twice came close to me, but could not find me. 'Arethusa! Arethusa!' he cried. Oh, how I trembled, like a lamb that hears the wolf growling outside the fold. A cold sweat came over me, my hair flowed down in streams; where my foot stood there was a pool. In short, in less time than it takes to tell it I became a fountain. But in this form Alpheus knew me, and attempted to mingle his stream with mine. Diana cleft the ground, and I, endeavoring to escape him, plunged into the cavern, and through the bowels of the earth came out here in Sicily. While I passed through the lower parts of the earth, I saw your Proserpine. She was sad, but no longer showing alarm in her countenance. Her look was such as became a queen, the queen of Erebus; the powerful bride of the monarch of the realms of the dead."

When Ceres heard this, she stood for a while like one stupefied; then turned her chariot towards heaven, and hastened to present herself before the throne of Jove. She told the story of her bereavement, and implored Jupiter to interfere to procure the restitution of her daughter. Jupiter consented on one condition, namely, that Proserpine should not during her stay in the lower world have taken any food; otherwise, the Fates forbade her release. Accordingly, Mercury was sent, accompanied by Spring, to demand Proserpine of Pluto. The wily monarch consented; but alas! the maiden had taken a pomegranate which Pluto offered her, and had sucked the sweet pulp from a few of the seeds. This was enough to prevent her complete release; but a compromise was made, by which she was to pass half the time with her mother, and the rest with her husband Pluto.

Ceres allowed herself to be pacified with this arrangement, and restored the earth to her favor. Now she remembered Celeus and his family, and her promise to his infant son Triptolemus. When the boy grew up, she taught him the use of the plough, and how to sow the seed. She took him in her chariot, drawn by winged dragons, through all the countries of the earth, imparting to mankind valuable grains, and the knowledge of agriculture. After his return, Triptolemus build a magnificent temple to Ceres in Eleusis, and established the worship of the goddess, under the name of the Eleusinian mysteries, which, in the splendor and solemnity of their observance, surpassed all other religious celebrations among the Greeks.

There can be little doubt but that this story of Ceres and Proserpine is an allegory. Proserpine signifies the seedcorn, which, when cast into the ground, lies there concealed, that is, she is carried off by the god of the underworld; it reappears, that is, Proserpine is restored to her mother. Spring leads her back to the light of day.

Milton alludes to the story of Proserpine in Paradise lost, Book IV.:

"Not that fair field
Of Enna where Proserpine gathering flowers,
Herself a fairer flower, by gloomy Dis (a name for Pluto)
Was gathered, which cost Ceres all that pain
To seek her through the world,
might with this Paradise
Of Eden strive."

Hood, in his Ode to Melancholy, uses the same allusion very beautifully:

"Forgive, if somewhile I forget,
In woe to come the present bliss;
As frightened Proserpine let fall
Her flowers at the sight of Dis."

The River Alpheus does in fact disappear under ground, in part of its course, finding its way through subterranean channels, till it again appears on the surface. It was said that the Sicilian fountain Arethusa was the same stream, which, after passing under the sea, came up again in Sicily. Hence the story ran that a cup thrown into the Alpheus appeared again in Arethusa. It is this fable of the underground course of Alpheus that Coleridge alludes to in his poem of Kubla Khan:

"In Xanadu did Kubla Khan
A stately pleasure-dome decree,
Where Alph, the sacred river, ran
Through caverns measureless to man,
Down to a sunless sea."

In one of Moore's juvenile poems he alludes to the same story, and to the practice of throwing garlands, or other light objects on the stream to be carried downward by it, and afterwards thrown out when the river comes again to light.

"Oh, my beloved, how divinely sweet
Is the pure joy when kindred spirits meet!
Like him the river-god, whose waters flow,
With love their only light, through caves below,
Wafting in triumph all the flowery braids
And festal rings, with which Olympic maids
Have decked his current, as an offering meet
To lay at Arethusa's shining feet.
Think, when he meets at last his fountain bride,
What perfect love must thrill the blended tide!
Each lost in each, till mingling into one,
Their lot the same for shadow or for sun,
A type of true love, to the deep they run."

The following extract from Moore's Rhymes on the Road gives an account of a celebrated picture by Albano at Milan, called a Dance of Loves:

"'Tis for the theft of Enna's flower from earth
These urchins celebrate their dance of mirth,
Round the green tree, like fays upon a heath,
Those that are nearest linked in order bright,
Cheek after cheek, like rosebuds in a wreath;
And those more distant showing from beneath
The others' wings their little eyes of light.
While see! Among the clouds, their eldest brother,
But just flown up, tells with a smile of bliss,
This prank of Pluto to his charmed mother,
Who turns to greet the tidings with a kiss."

GLAUCUS AND SCYLLA

Glaucus was a fisherman. One day he had drawn his nets to land, and had taken a great many fishes of various kinds. So he emptied his net, and proceeded to sort the fishes on the grass. The place where he stood was a beautiful island in the river, a solitary spot, uninhabited, and not used for pasturage of cattle, nor ever visited by any but himself. On a sudden, the fishes, which had been laid on the grass, began to revive and move their fins as if they were in the water; and while he looked on astonished, they one and all moved off to the water, plunged in and swam away. He did not know what to make of this, whether some god had done it, or some secret power in the herbage. "What herb has such a power?" he exclaimed; and gathering some, he tasted it. Scarce had the juices of the plant reached his palate when he found himself agitated with a longing desire for the water. He could no longer restrain himself, but bidding farewell to earth, he plunged into the stream. The gods of the water received him graciously, and admitted him to the honor of their society. They obtained the consent of Oceanus and Tethys, the sovereigns of the sea, that all that was mortal in him should be washed away. A hundred rivers poured their waters over him. Then he lost all sense of his former nature and all consciousness. When he recovered, he found himself changed in form and mind. His hair was sea-green, and trailed behind him on the water; his shoulders grew broad, and what had been thighs and legs assumed the form of a fish's tail. The seagods complimented him on the change of his appearance, and he himself was pleased with his looks.

One day Glaucus saw the beautiful maiden Scylla, the favorite of the water-nymphs, rambling on the shore, and when she had found a sheltered nook, laving her limbs in the clear water. He fell in love with her, and showing himself on the surface, spoke to her, saying such things as he thought most likely to win her to stay; for she turned to run immediately on sight of him and ran till she had gained a cliff overlooking the sea. Here she stopped and turned round to see whether it was a god or a sea-animal, and observed with wonder his shape and color. Glaucus, partly emerging from the water, and supporting himself against a rock, said, "Maiden, I am no monster, nor a sea-animal, but a god; and neither Proteus nor Triton ranks higher than I. Once I was a mortal, and followed the sea for a living; but now I belong wholly to it." Then he told the story of his metamorphosis and how he had been promoted to his present dignity, and added, "But what avails all this if it fails to move your heart?" He was going on in this strain, but Scylla turned and hastened away.

Glaucus was in despair, but it occurred to him to consult the enchantress, Circe. Accordingly he repaired to her island, the same where afterwards Ulysses landed, as we shall see in another story. After mutual salutations, he said, "Goddess, I entreat your pity; you alone can relieve the pain I suffer. The power of herbs I know as well as any one, for it is to them I owe my change of form I love Scylla. I am ashamed to tell you how I have sued and promised to her, and how scornfully she has treated me. I beseech you to use your incantations, or potent herbs, if they are more prevailing, not to cure me of my love, for that I do not wish, but to make her share it and yield me a like return." To which Circe replied, for she was not insensible to the attractions of the sea-green deity, "You had better pursue a willing object; you are worthy to be sought, instead of having to seek in vain. Be not diffident, know your own worth. I protest to you that even I, goddess though I be, and learned in the virtues of plants and spells, should not know how to refuse you If she scorns you, scorn her; meet one who is ready to meet you half way, and thus make a due return to both at once." To these words Glaucus replied, "Sooner shall trees grow at the bottom of the ocean, and seaweed on the top of the mountains, than I will cease to love Scylla, and her alone."

The goddess was indignant, but she could not punish him, neither did she wish to do so, for she liked him too well; so she turned all her wrath against her rival, poor Scylla. She took plants of poisonous powers and mixed them together, with incantations and charms. Then she passed through the crowd of gambolling beasts, the victims of her art, and proceeded to the coast of Sicily, where Scylla lived. There was a little bay on the shore to which Scylla used to resort, in the heat of the day, to breathe the air of the sea, and to bathe in its waters. Here the goddess poured her poisonous mixture, and muttered over it incantations of mighty power. Scylla came as usual and plunged into the water up to her waist. What was her horror to perceive a brood of serpents and barking monsters surrounding her! At first she could not imagine they were a part of herself, and tried to run from them, and to drive them away; but as she ran she carried them with her, and when she tried to touch her limbs, she found her hands touch only the yawning jaws of monsters. Scylla remained rooted to the spot. Her temper grew as ugly as her form, and she took pleasure in devouring hapless mariners who came within her grasp. Thus she destroyed six of the companions of Ulysses, and tried to wreck the ships of Aeneas, till at last she was turned into a rock, and as such still continues to be a terror to mariners.

The following is Glaucus's account of his feelings after his "sea-change":

"I plunged for life or death. To interknit
One's senses with so dense a breathing stuff
Might seem a work of pain; so not enough
Can I admire how crystal-smooth it felt,
And buoyant round my limbs. At first I dwelt
Whole days and days in sheer astonishment;
Forgetful utterly of self-intent,
Moving but with the mighty ebb and flow.
Then like a new-fledged bird that first doth show
His spreaded feathers to the morrow chill,
I tried in fear the pinions of my well.
"Twas freedom! And at once I visited
The ceaseless wonders of this ocean-bed."
Keats.

Chapter 5

PYGMALION. DRYOPE. VENUS AND ADONIS. APOLLO AND HYACINTHUS. CEYX AND HALCYONE/ALCYONE.

Pygmalion saw so much to blame in women that he came at last to abhor the sex, and resolved to live unmarried. He was a sculptor, and had made with wonderful skill a statue of ivory, so beautiful that no living woman could be compared to it in beauty. It was indeed the perfect semblance of a maiden that seemed to be alive, and only prevented from moving by modesty. His art was so perfect that it concealed itself, and its product looked like the workmanship of nature. Pygmalion admired his own work, and at last fell in love with the counterfeit creation. Oftentimes he laid his hand upon it, as if to assure himself whether it were living or not, and could not even then believe that it was only ivory. He caressed it, and gave it presents such as young girls love, bright shells and polished stones, little birds and flowers of various hues, beads and amber. He put raiment on its limbs, and jewels on its fingers, and a necklace about its neck. To the ears he hung earrings and strings of pearls upon the breast. Her dress became her, and she looked not less charming than when unattired. He laid her on a couch spread with cloths of Tyrian dye, and called her his wife, and put her head upon a pillow of the softest feathers, as if she could enjoy their softness.

The festival of Venus was at hand, a festival celebrated with great pomp at Cyprus. Victims were offered, the altars smoked, and the odor of incense filled the air. When Pygmalion had performed his part in the solemnities, he stood before the altar and timidly said, "Ye gods, who can do all things, give me, I pray you, for my wife" he dared not say "my ivory virgin," but said instead "one like my ivory virgin." Venus, who was present at the festival, heard him and knew the thought he would have uttered; and, as an omen of her favor, caused the flame on the altar to shoot up thrice in a fiery point into the air. When he returned home, he went to see his statue, and, leaning over the couch, gave a kiss to the mouth. It seemed to be warm. He pressed its lips again, he laid his hand upon the limbs; the ivory felt soft to his touch, and yielded to his fingers like the wax of Hymettus. While he stands astonished and glad, though doubting, and fears he may be mistaken, again and again with a lover's ardor he touches the object of his hopes. It was indeed alive! The veins when pressed yielded to the finger and then resumed their roundness. Then at last the votary of Venus found words to thank the goddess, and pressed his lips upon lips as real as his own. The virgin felt the kisses and blushed, and, opening her timid eyes to the light, fixed them at the same moment on her lover. Venus blessed the nuptials she had formed, and from this union Paphos was born, from whom the city, sacred to Venus, received its name.

Schiller, in his poem, the Ideals, applies this tale of Pygmalion to the love of nature in a youthful heart. In Schiller's version, as in William Morris's, the statue is of marble.

"As once with prayers in passion flowing,
Pygmalion embraced the stone,
Till from the frozen marble glowing,
The light of feeling o'er him shone,
So did I clasp with young devotion
Bright Nature to a poet's heart;
Till breath and warmth and vital motion
Seemed through the statue form to dart.

"And then in all my ardor sharing,
The silent form expression found;
Returned my kiss of youthful daring,
And understood my heart's quick sound.
Then lived for me the bright creation.
The silver rill with song was rife;
The trees, the roses shared sensation,
An echo of my boundless life."
Rev. A. G. Bulfinch (brother of the author).

Morris tells the story of Pygmalion and the Image in some of the most beautiful verses of the Earthly Paradise.

This is Galatea's description of her metamorphosis:

"'My sweet,' she said, 'as yet I am not wise,
Or stored with words aright the tale to tell,

But listen: when I opened first mine eyes
I stood within the niche thou knowest well,
And from my hand a heavy thing there fell
Carved like these flowers, nor could I see things clear,
But with a strange confused noise could hear.

"'At last mine eyes could see a woman fair,
But awful as this round white moon o'erhead,So that I trembled when I saw her there,
For with my life was born some touch of dread,
And therewithal I heard her voice that said,
"Come down and learn to love and be alive,
For thee, a well-prized gift, today I give."'"

DRYOPE

Dryope and Iole were sisters. The former was the wife of Andraemon, beloved by her husband, and happy in the birth of her first child. One day the sisters strolled to the bank of a stream that sloped gradually down to the water's edge, while the upland was overgrown with myrtles. They were intending to gather flowers for forming garlands for the altars of the nymphs, and Dryope carried her child at her bosom, a precious burden, and nursed him as she walked. Near the water grew a lotus plant, full of purple flowers. Dryope gathered some and offered them to the baby, and Iole was about to do the same, when she perceived blood dropping from the places where her sister had broken them off the stem. The plant was no other than the Nymph Lotis, who, running from a base pursuer, had been changed into this form. This they learned from the country people when it was too late.

Dryope, horror-struck when she perceived what she had done, would gladly have hastened from the spot, but found her feet rooted to the ground. She tried to pull them away, but moved nothing but her arms. The woodiness crept upward, and by degrees invested her body. In anguish she attempted to tear her hair, but found her hands filled with leaves. The infant felt his mother's bosom begin to harden, and the milk cease to flow. Iole looked on at the sad fate of her sister, and could render no assistance. She embraced the growing trunk, as if she would hold back the advancing wood, and would gladly have been enveloped

Figure 7: "Dryope" from Les Metamorphoses d'Ovide

in the same bark. At this moment Andraemon, the husband of Dryope, with her father, approached; and when they asked for Dryope, Iole pointed them to the new-formed lotus. They embraced the trunk of the yet warm tree, and showered their kisses on its leaves.

Now there was nothing left of Dryope but her face. Her tears still flowed and fell on her leaves, and while she could she spoke. "I am not guilty. I deserve not this fate. I have injured no one. If I speak falsely, may my foliage perish with drought and my trunk be cut down and burned. Take this infant and give him to a nurse. Let him often be brought and nursed under my branches, and play in my shade; and when he is old enough to talk, let him be taught to call me mother, and to say with sadness, 'My mother lies hid under this bark' But bid him be careful of river banks, and beware how he plucks flowers, remembering that every bush he sees may be a goddess in disguise. Farewell, dear husband, and sister, and father. If you retain any love for me, let not the axe wound me, nor the flocks bite and tear my branches. Since I cannot stoop to you, climb up hither and kiss me; and while my lips continue to feel, lift up my child that I may kiss him. I can speak no more, for already the bark advances up my neck, and will soon shoot over me. You need not close my eyes; the bark will close them without your aid." Then the lips ceased to move, and life was extinct; but the branches retained, for some time longer the vital heat.

Keats, in Endymion, alludes to Dryope thus:

"She took a lute from which there pulsing came
A lively prelude, fashioning the way
In which her voice should wander. 'Twas a lay
More subtle-cadenced, more forest-wild
Than Dryope's lone lulling of her child."

VENUS AND ADONIS

Venus, playing one day with her boy Cupid, wounded her bosom with one of his arrows. She pushed him away, but the wound was deeper than she thought. Before it healed she beheld Adonis, and was captivated with him. She no longer took any interest in her favorite resorts, Paphos, and Cnidos, and Amathos, rich in metals. She absented herself even from Olympus, for Adonis was dearer to her than heaven. Him she followed and bore him company. She who used to love to recline in the shade, with no care but to cultivate her charms, now rambled through the woods and over the hills, dressed like the huntress Diana. She called her dogs, and chased hares and stags, or other game that it is safe to hunt, but kept clear of the wolves and bears, reeking with the slaughter of the herd. She charged Adonis, too, to beware of such dangerous animals. "Be brave towards the timid," said she; "courage against the courageous is not safe. Beware how you expose yourself to danger, and put my happiness to risk. Attack not the beasts that Nature has armed with weapons. I do not value your glory so highly as to consent to purchase it by such exposure. Your youth, and the beauty that charms Venus, will not touch the hearts of lions and bristly boars. Think of their terrible claws and prodigious strength! I hate the whole race of them. Do you ask why?" Then she told him the story of Atalanta and Hippomenes, who were changed into lions for their ingratitude to her.

Having given him this warning, she mounted her chariot drawn by swans, and drove away through the air. But Adonis was too noble to heed such counsels. The dogs had roused a wild boar from his lair, and the youth threw his spear and wounded the animal with a sidelong stroke. The beast drew out the weapon with his jaws, and rushed after Adonis, who turned and ran; but the boar overtook him, and buried his tusks in his side, and stretched him dying upon the plain.

Venus, in her swan-drawn chariot, had not yet reached Cyprus, when she heard coming up through midair the groans of her beloved, and turned her white-winged coursers back to earth. As she drew near and saw from on high his lifeless body bathed in blood, she alighted, and bending over it beat her breast and tore her hair. Reproaching the Fates, she said, "Yet theirs shall be but a partial triumph; memorials of my grief shall endure, and the spectacle of your death, my Adonis, and of my lamentation shall be annually renewed. Your blood shall be changed into a flower; that consolation none can envy me." Thus speaking, she sprinkled nectar on the blood; and as they mingled, bubbles rose as in a pool on which raindrops fall, and in an hour's time there sprang up a flower of bloody hue like that of a pomegranate. But it is short-lived. It is said the wind blows the blossoms open, and afterwards blows the petals away; so it is called Anemone, or wind Flower, from the cause which assists equally in its production and its decay.

Milton alludes to the story of Venus and Adonis in his Comus:

"Beds of hyacinth and roses
Where young Adonis oft reposes,
Waxing well of his deep wound
In slumber soft, and on the ground
Sadly sits th'Assyrian queen."

And Morris also in Atalanta's Race:

"There by his horn the Dryads well might know
His thrust against the bear's heart had been true,
And there Adonis bane his javelin slew"

APOLLO AND HYACINTHUS

Apollo was passionately fond of a youth named Hyacinthus. He accompanied him in his sports, carried the nets when he went fishing, led the dogs when he went to hunt, followed him in his excursions in the mountains, and neglected for him his lyre and his arrows. One day they played a game of quoits together, and Apollo, heaving aloft the discus, with strength mingled with skill, sent it high and far. Hyacinthus watched it as it flew, and excited with the sport ran forward to seize it, eager to make his throw, when the quoit bounded from the earth and struck him in the forehead. He fainted and fell. The god, as pale as himself, raised him and tried all his art to stanch the wound and retain the flitting life, but all in vain; the hurt was past the power of medicine. As, when one has broken the stem of a lily in the garden, it hangs its head and turns its flowers to the earth, so the head of the dying boy, as if too heavy for his neck, fell over on his shoulder. "Thou diest, Hyacinth," so spoke Phoebus, "robbed of thy youth by me. Thine is the suffering, mine the crime. Would that I could die for thee! But since that may not be thou shalt live with me in memory and in song. My lyre shall celebrate thee, my song shall tell thy fate, and thou shalt become a flower inscribed with my regrets." While Apollo spoke, behold the blood which had flowed on the ground and stained the herbage, ceased to be blood; but a flower of hue more beautiful than the Tyrian sprang up, resembling the lily, if it were not that this is purple and that silvery white (it is evidently not our modern hyacinth that is here described. It is perhaps some species of iris, or perhaps of larkspur, or of pansy.) And this was not enough for Phoebus; but to confer still grater honor, he marked the petals with his sorrow, and inscribed "Ah! Ah!" upon them, as we see to this day. The flower bears the name of Hyacinthus, and with every returning spring revives the memory of his fate.

It was said that Zephyrus (the West-wind), who was also fond of Hyacinthus and jealous of his preference of Apollo, blew the quoit out of its course to make it strike Hyacinthus. Keats alludes to this in his Endymion, where he describes the lookers- on at the game of quoits:

"Or they might watch the quoit-pitchers, intent
On either side, pitying the sad death
Of Hyacinthus, when the cruel breath
Of Zephyr slew him; Zephyr penitent,
Who now ere Phoebus mounts the firmament,
Fondles the flower amid the sobbing rain."

An allusion to Hyacinthus will also be recognized in Milton's Lycidas:

"Like to that sanguine flower inscribed with woe."

CEXY AND HALCYONE: OR, THE HALCYON BIRDS. ALCYONE.

Ceyx was King of Thessaly, where he reigned in peace without violence or wrong. He was son of Hesperus, the Day-star, and the glow of his beauty reminded one of his father. Halcyone, the daughter of Aeolus, was his wife, and devotedly attached to him. Now Ceyx was in deep affliction for the loss of his brother, and direful prodigies following his brother's death made him feel as if the gods were hostile to him. He thought best therefore to make a voyage to Claros in Ionia, to consult the oracle of Apollo. But as soon as he disclosed his intention to his wife Halcyone, a shudder ran through her frame, and her face grew deadly pale. "What fault of mine, dearest husband, has turned your affection from me? Where is that love of me that used to be uppermost in your thoughts? Have you learned to feel easy in the absence of Halcyone? Would you rather have me away?" She also endeavored to discourage him, by describing the violence of the winds, which she had known familiarly when she lived at home in her father's house, Aeolus being the god of the winds, and having as much as he could do to restrain them. "They rush together," said she, "with such fury that fire flashes from the conflict. But if you must go," she added, "dear husband, let me go with you, Otherwise I shall suffer, not only the real evils which you must encounter, but those also which my fears suggest."

These words weighed heavily on the mind of king Ceyx, and it was no less his own wish than hers to take her with him, but he could not bear to expose her to the dangers of the sea. He answered, therefore, consoling her as well as he could, and finished with these words: "I promise, by the rays of my father the Day-star, that if fate permits I will return before the moon shall have twice rounded her orb." When he had thus spoken he ordered the vessel to be drawn out of the ship-house, and the oars and sails to be put aboard. When Halcyone saw these preparations she shuddered, as if with a presentiment of evil. With tears and sobs she said farewell, and then fell senseless to the ground.

Ceyx would still have lingered, but now the young men grasped their oars and pulled vigorously through the waves, with long and measured strokes. Halcyone raised her streaming eyes, and saw her husband standing on the deck, waving his hand to her. She answered his signal till the vessel had receded so far that she could no longer distinguish his form from the rest. When the vessel itself could no more be seen, she strained her eyes to catch the last glimmer of the sail, till that too disappeared. Then, retiring to her chamber, she threw herself on her solitary couch.

Meanwhile they glide out of the harbor, and the breeze plays among the ropes. The seamen draw in their oars, and hoist their sails. When half or less of their course was passed, as night drew on, the sea began to whiten with swelling waves, and the east wind to blow a gale. The master gives the word to take in sail, but the storm forbids obedience, for such is the roar of the winds and waves that his orders are unheard. The men, of their own accord, busy themselves to secure the oars, to strengthen the ship, to reef the sail. While they thus do what to each one seems best, the storm increases. The shouting of the men, the rattling of the shrouds, and the dashing of the waves, mingle with the roar of the thunder. The swelling sea seems lifted up to the heavens, to scatter its foam among the clouds; then sinking away to the bottom assumes the color of the shoal, a Stygian blackness.

The vessel obeys all these changes. It seems like a wild beast that rushes on the spears of the hunters. Rain falls in torrents, as if the skies were coming down to unite with the sea. When the lightning ceases for a moment, the night seems to add its own darkness to that of the storm; then comes the flash, rending the darkness asunder, and lighting up all with a glare. Skill fails, courage sinks, and death seems to come on every wave. The men are stupefied with terror. The thought of parents, and kindred, and pledges left at home, comes over their minds. Ceyx thinks of Halcyone. No name but hers is on his lips, and while he yearns for her, he yet rejoices in her absence. Presently the mast is shattered by a stroke of lightning, the rudder broken, and the triumphant surge curling over looks down upon the wreck, then falls, and crushes it to fragments. Some of the seamen, stunned by the stroke, sink, and rise no more; others cling to fragments of the wreck. Ceyx, with the hand that used to grasp the sceptre, holds fast to a plank, calling for help, alas, in vain, upon his father and his father-in-law. But oftenest on his lips was the name of Halcyone. His thoughts cling to her. He prays that the waves may bear his body to her sight, and that it may receive burial at her hands. At length the waters overwhelm him, and he sinks. The Day-star looked dim that night. Since it could not leave the heavens, it shrouded its face with clouds.

Figure 8: "What Seest Thou Else in the Dark Backward and Abysm Time" by Edmund Dulac

In the mean while Halcyone, ignorant of all these horrors, counted the days till her husband's promised return. Now she gets ready the garments which he shall put on, and now what she shall wear when he arrives. To all the gods she offers frequent incense but more than all to Juno. For her husband, who was no more, she prayed incessantly; that he might be safe; that he might come home; that he might not, in his absence, see any one that he would love better than her. But of all these prayers, the last was the only one destined to be granted. The goddess, at length, could not bear any longer to be pleaded with for one already dead, and to have hands raised to her altars, that ought rather to be offering funeral rites. So, calling Iris, she said, "Iris, my faithful messenger, go to the drowsy dwelling of Somnus, and tell him to send a vision to Halcyone, in the form of Ceyx, to make known to her the event."

Iris puts on her robe of many colors, and tingeing the sky with her bow, seeks the palace of the King of Sleep. Near the Cimmerian country, a mountain cave is the abode of the dull god, Somnus, Here Phoebus dares not come, either rising, or at midday, or setting. Clouds and shadows are exhaled from the ground, and the light glimmers faintly. The bird of dawn, with crested head, never calls aloud there to Aurora, nor watchful dog, nor more sagacious goose disturbs the silence. (This comparison of the dog and the goose is a reference by Ovid to a passage in Roman history.) No wild beast, nor cattle, nor branch moved with the wind, nor sound of human conversation, breaks the stillness. Silence reigns there; and from the bottom of the rock the River Lethe flows, and by its murmur invites to sleep. Poppies grow abundantly before the door of the cave, and other herbs, from whose juices Night collects slumbers, which she scatters over the darkened earth. There is no gate to the mansion, to creak on its hinges, nor any watchman; but in the midst, a couch of black ebony, adorned with black plumes and black curtains. There the god reclines, his limbs relaxed with sleep. Around him lie dreams, resembling all various forms, as many as the harvest bears stalks, or the forest leaves, or the seashore grains of sand.

As soon as the goddess entered and brushed away the dreams that hovered around her, her brightness lit up all the cave. The god, scarce opening his eyes, and ever and anon dropping his beard upon his breast, at last shook himself free from himself, and leaning on his arm, inquired her errand, for he knew who she was. She answered, "Somnus, gentlest of the gods, tranquillizer of minds and soother of careworn hearts, Juno sends you her commands that you dispatch a dream to Halcyone, in the city of Trachinae, representing her lost husband and all the events of the wreck."

Having delivered her message, Iris hasted away, for she could not longer endure the stagnant air, and as she felt drowsiness creeping over her, she made her escape, and returned by her bow the way she came. Then Somnus called one of his numerous sons, Morpheus, the most expert at counterfeiting forms, and in imitating the walk, the countenance, and mode of speaking, even the clothes and attitudes most characteristic of each. But he only imitates men, leaving it to another to personate birds, beasts, and serpents. Him they call Icelos; and Phantasos is a third, who turns himself into rocks, waters, woods, and other things without life. These wait upon kings and great personages in their sleeping hours, while others move among the common people. Somnus chose, from all the brothers, Morpheus, to perform the command of Iris; then laid his head on his pillow and yielded himself to grateful repose.

Morpheus flew, making no noise with his wings, and soon came to the Haemonian city, where, laying aside his wings, he assumed the form of Ceyx. Under that form, but pale like a dead man, naked, he stood before the couch of the wretched wife. His beard seemed soaked with water, and water trickled from his drowned locks. Leaning over the bed, tears streaming from his eyes, he said, "Do you recognize your Ceyx, unhappy wife, or has death too much changed my visage? Behold me, know me, your husband's shade, instead of himself. Your prayers, Halcyone, availed me nothing. I am dead. No more deceive yourself with vain hopes of my return. The stormy winds sunk my ship in the Aegean Sea; waves filled my mouth while it called aloud on you. No uncertain messenger tells you this, no vague rumor brings it to your ears. I come in person, a shipwrecked man, to tell you my fate. Arise! Give me tears, give me lamentations, let me not go down to Tartarus unwept." To these words Morpheus added the voice which seemed to be that of her husband; he seemed to pour forth genuine tears; his hands had the gestures of Ceyx.

Halcyone, weeping, groaned, and stretched out her arms in her sleep, striving to embrace his body, but grasping only the air. "Stay!" she cried; "whither do you fly? Let us go together." Her own voice awakened her. Starting up, she gazed eagerly around, to see if he was still present, for the servants, alarmed by her cries, had brought a light. When she found him not, she smote her breast and rent her garments. She cares not to unbind her hair, but tears it wildly. Her nurse asks what is the cause of her grief. "Halcyone is no more," she answers; "she perished with her Ceyx. Utter not words of comfort, he is shipwrecked and dead. I have seen him. I have recognized him. I stretched out my hands to seize him and detain him. His shade vanished, but it was the true shade of my husband. Not with the accustomed features, not with the beauty that was his, but pale, naked, and with his hair wet with sea-water, he appeared to wretched me. Here, in this very spot, the sad vision stood," and she looked to find the mark of his footsteps. "This it was, this that my presaging mind foreboded, when I implored him not to leave me to trust himself to the waves. O, how I wish, since thou wouldst go, that thou hadst taken me with thee! It would have been far better. Then I should have had no remnant of life to spend without thee, nor a separate death to die. If I could bear to live and struggle to endure, I should be more cruel to myself than the sea has been to me. But I will not struggle. I will not be separated from thee, unhappy husband. This time, at least I will keep thee company. In death, if one tomb may not include us, one epitaph shall; if I may not lay my ashes with thine, my name, at least, shall not be separated." Her grief forbade more words, and these were broken with tears and sobs.

It was now morning. She went to the sea-shore, and sought the spot where she last saw him, on his departure. "Here he lingered and cast off his tacklings and gave me his last kiss." While she reviews every moment, and strives to recall every incident, looking out over the sea, she descries an indistinct object floating in the water. At first she was in doubt what it was, but by degrees the waves bore it nearer, and it was plainly the body of a man. Though unknowing of whom, yet, as it was of some shipwrecked one, she was deeply moved, and gave it her tears, saying, "Alas! Unhappy one, and unhappy, if such there be, thy wife!" Borne by the waves, it came nearer. As she more and more nearly views it, she trembles more and more. Now, now it approaches the shore. Now marks that she recognizes appear. It is her husband! Stretching out her trembling hands towards it, she exclaims, "O, dearest husband, is it thus you return to me?"

There was built out from the shore a mole, constructed to break the assaults of the sea, and stem its violent ingress. She leaped upon this barrier and (it was wonderful she could do so) she flew, and striking the air with wings produced on the instant, skimmed along the surface of the water, an unhappy bird. As she flew, her throat poured forth sounds full of grief, and like the voice of one lamenting. When she touched the mute and bloodless body, she enfolded its beloved limbs with her new- formed wings, and tried to give kisses with her horny beak. Whether Ceyx felt it, or whether it was only the action of the waves, those who looked on doubted, but the body seemed to raise its head. But indeed he did feel it, and by the pitying gods both of them were changed into birds. They mate and have their young ones. For seven placid days, in winter time, Halcyone broods over her nest, which floats upon the sea. Then the way is safe to seamen. Aeolus guards the winds, and keeps them from disturbing the deep. The sea is given up, for the time, to his grandchildren.

The following lines from Byron's Bride of Abydos might seem borrowed from the concluding part of this description, if it were not stated that the author derived the suggestion from observing the motion of a floating corpse.

"As shaken on his restless pillow,
His head heaves with the heaving billow;
That hand, whose motion is not life,
Yet feebly seems to menace strife,
Flung by the tossing tide on high,.
Then levelled with the wave "

Milton, in his Hymn for the Nativity, thus alludes to the fable of the Halcyon:

"But peaceful was the night
Wherein the Prince of light
His reign of peace upon the earth began;
The winds with wonder whist,
Smoothly the waters kist,
Whispering new joys to the mild ocean
Who now hath quite forgot to rave
While birds of calm sit brooding on the charmed wave."

Keats, also, in Endymion, says:

"O magic sleep! O comfortable bird
That broodest o'er the troubled sea of the mind
Till it is hushed and smooth."

Chapter 6

VERTUMNUS AND POMONA. CUPID AND PSYCHE

The Hamadryads were Wood-nymphs. Among them was Pomona, and no one excelled her in love of the garden and the culture of fruit. She cared not for forests and rivers, but loved the cultivated country and trees that bear delicious apples. Her right hand bore for its weapon not a javelin, but a pruning knife. Armed with this, she worked at one time, to repress the too luxuriant growths, and curtail the branches that straggled out of place; at another, to split the twig and insert therein a graft, making the branch adopt a nursling not its own. She took care, too, that her favorites should not suffer from drought, and led streams of water by them that the thirsty roots might drink. This occupation was her pursuit, her passion; and she was free from that which Venus inspires. She was not without fear of the country people, and kept her orchard locked, and allowed not men to enter. The Fauns and Satyrs would have given all they possessed to win her, and so would old Sylvanus, who looks young for his years, and Pan, who wears a garland of pine leaves around his head. But Vertumnus loved her best of all; yet he sped no better than the rest. Oh, how often, in the disguise of a reaper, did he bring her corn in a basket, and looked the very image of a reaper! With a hay-band tied round him, one would think he had just come from turning over the grass. Sometimes he would have an ox-goad in his hand, and you would have said he had just unyoked his weary oxen. Now he bore a pruning-hook, and personated a vine-dresser; and again with a ladder on his shoulder, he seemed as if he was going to gather apples. Sometimes he trudged along as a discharged soldier, and again he bore a fishing-rod as if going to fish. In this way, he gained admission to her, again and again, and fed his passion with the sight of her.

One day he came in the guise of an old woman, her gray hair surmounted with a cap, and a staff in her hand. She entered the garden and admired the fruit. "It does you credit, my dear," she said, and kissed Pomona, not exactly with an old woman's kiss. She sat down on a bank, and looked up at the branches laden with fruit which hung over her. Opposite was an elm entwined with a vine loaded with swelling grapes. She praised the tree and its associated vine, equally. "But," said Vertumnus, "if the tree stood alone, and had no vine clinging to it, it would lie prostrate on the ground. Why will you not take a lesson from the tree and the vine, and consent to unite yourself with some one? I wish you would. Helen herself had not more numerous suitors, nor Penelope, the wife of shrewd Ulysses. Even while you spurn them, they court you rural deities and others of every kind that frequent these mountains. But if you are prudent and want to make a good alliance, and will let an old woman advise you, who loves you better than you have any idea of, dismiss all the rest and accept Vertumnus, on my recommendation. I know him as well as he knows himself. He is not a wandering deity, but belongs to these mountains. Nor is he like too many of the lovers nowadays, who love any one they happen to see; he loves you, and you only. Add to this, he is young and handsome, and has the art of assuming any shape he pleases, and can make himself just what you command him. Moreover, he loves the same things that you do, delights in gardening, and handles your apples with admiration. But NOW he cares nothing for fruits, nor flowers, nor anything else, but only yourself. Take pity on him, and fancy him speaking now with my mouth. Remember that the gods punish cruelty, and that Venus hates a hard heart, and will visit such offenses sooner or later. To prove this, let me tell you a story, which is well known in Cyprus to be a fact; and I hope it will have the effect to make you more merciful.

"Iphis was a young man of humble parentage, who saw and loved Anaxarete, a noble lady of the ancient family of Teucer. He struggled long with his passion, but when he found he could not subdue it, he came a suppliant to her mansion. First he told his passion to her nurse, and begged her as she loved her foster- child to favor his suit. And then he tried to win her domestics to his side. Sometimes he committed his vows to written tablets, and often hung at her door garlands which he had moistened with his tears. He stretched himself on her threshold, and uttered his complaints to the cruel bolts and bars. She was deafer than the surges which rise in the November gale; harder than steel from the German forges, or a rock that still clings to its native cliff. She mocked and laughed at him, adding cruel words to her ungentle treatment, and gave not the slightest gleam of hope.

"Iphis could not any longer endure the torments of hopeless love, and standing before her doors, he spake these last words: 'Anaxarete, you have conquered, and shall no longer have to bear my importunities. Enjoy your triumph! Sing songs of joy, and bind your forehead with laurel, you have conquered! I die; stony heart, rejoice! This at least I can do to gratify you, and force you to praise me; and thus shall I prove that the love of you left me but with life. Nor will I leave it to rumor to tell you of my death. I will come myself, and you shall see me die, and feast your eyes on the spectacle. Yet, Oh, ye gods, who look down on mortal woes, observe my fate! I ask but this! Let me be remembered in coming ages, and add those years to my name which you have reft from my life.' Thus he said, and, turning his pale face and weeping eyes towards her mansion, he fastened a rope to the gate-post, on which he had hung garlands, and putting his head into the noose, he murmured, 'This garland at least will please you, cruel girl!' And falling, hung suspended with his neck broken. As he fell he struck against the gate, and the sound was as the sound of a groan. The servants opened the door and found him dead, and with exclamations of pity raised him and carried him home to his mother, for his father was not living. She received the dead body of her son, and folded the cold form to her bosom; while she poured forth the sad words which bereaved mothers utter. The mournful funeral passed through the town, and the pale corpse was borne on a bier to the place of the funeral pile. By chance the home of Anaxarete was on the street where the procession passed, and the lamentations of the mourners met the ears of her whom the avenging deity had already marked for punishment.

"'Let us see this sad procession,' said she, and mounted to a turret, whence through an open window she looked upon the funeral. Scarce had her eyes rested upon the form of Iphis stretched on the bier, when they began to stiffen, and the warm blood in her body to become cold. Endeavoring to step back, she found she could not move her feet; trying to turn away her face, she tried in vain; and by degrees all her limbs became stony like her heart. That you may not doubt the fact, the statue still remains, and stands in the temple of Venus at Salamis, in the exact form of the lady. Now think of these things, my dear, and lay aside your scorn and your delays, and accept a lover. So may neither the vernal frosts blight your young fruits, nor furious winds scatter your blossoms!"

When Vertumnus had spoken thus, he dropped the disguise of an old woman, and stood before her in his proper person, as a comely youth. It appeared to her like the sun bursting through a cloud. He would have renewed his entreaties, but there was no need; his arguments and the sight of his true form prevailed, and the Nymph no longer resisted, but owned a mutual flame.

Pomona was the especial patroness of the apple-orchard, and as such she was invoked by Phillips, the author of a poem on Cider, in blank verse, in the following lines:

"What soil the apple loves, what care is due
To orchats, timeliest when to press the fruits,
Thy gift, Pomona, in Miltonian verse
Adventurous I presume to sing."

Thomson, in the Seasons, alludes to Phillips:

"Phillips, Pomona's bard, the second thou
Who nobly durst, in rhyme-unfettered verse,
With British freedom, sing the British song."

It will be seen that Thomson refers to the poet's reference to Milton, but it is not true that Phillips is only the second writer of English blank verse. Many other poets beside Milton had used it long before Phillips' time.

But Pomona was also regarded as presiding over other fruits, and, as such, is invoked by Thomson:

"Bear me, Pomona, to thy citron groves,
To where the lemon and the piercing lime,
With the deep orange, glowing through the green,
Their lighter glories blend. Lay me reclined
Beneath the spreading tamarind, that shakes,
Fanned by the breeze, its fever-cooling fruit."

CUPID AND PSYCHE

A certain king had three daughters. (This seems to be one of the latest fables of the Greek mythology. It has not been found earlier than the close of the second century of the Christian era. It bears marks of the higher religious notions of that time.) The two elder were charming girls, but the beauty of the youngest was so wonderful that language is too poor to express its due praise. The fame of her beauty was so great that strangers from neighboring countries came in crowds to enjoy the sight, and looked on her with amazement, paying her that homage which is due only to Venus herself. In fact, Venus found her altars deserted, while men turned their devotion to this young virgin. As she passed along, the people sang her praises, and strewed her way with chaplets and flowers.

This perversion to a mortal of the homage due only to the immortal powers gave great offence to the real Venus. Shaking her ambrosial locks with indignation, she exclaimed, "Am I then to be eclipsed in my honors by a mortal girl? In vain then did that royal shepherd, whose judgment was approved by Jove himself, give me the palm of beauty over my illustrious rivals, Pallas and June. But she shall not so quietly usurp my honors. I will give her cause to repent of so unlawful a beauty."

Thereupon she calls her winged son Cupid, mischievous enough in his own nature, and rouses and provokes him yet more by her complaints. She points out Psyche to him, and says, "My dear son, punish that contumacious beauty; give thy mother a revenge as sweet as her injuries are great; infuse into the bosom of that haughty girl a passion for some low, mean, unworthy being, so that she may reap a mortification as great as her present exultation and triumph."

Cupid prepared to obey the commands of his mother. There are two fountains in Venus's garden, one of sweet waters, the other of bitter. Cupid filled two amber vases, one from each fountain, and suspending them from the top of his quiver, hastened to the chamber of Psyche, whom he found asleep. He shed a few drops from the bitter fountain over her lips, though the sight of her almost moved him to pity; then touched her side with the point of his arrow. At the touch she awoke, and opened eyes upon Cupid (himself invisible) which so startled him that in his confusion he wounded himself with his own arrow. Heedless of his wound his whole thought now was to repair the mischief he had done, and he poured the balmy drops of joy over all her silken ringlets.

Psyche, henceforth frowned upon by Venus, derived no benefit from all her charms. True, all eyes were cast eagerly upon her, and every mouth spoke her praises; but neither king, royal youth, nor plebeian presented himself to demand her in marriage. Her two elder sisters of moderate charms had now long been married to two royal princes; but Psyche, in her lonely apartment, deplored her solitude, sick of that beauty, which, while it procured abundance of flattery, had failed to awaken love.

Her parents, afraid that they had unwittingly incurred the anger of the gods, consulted the oracle of Apollo, and received this answer: "The virgin is destined for the bride of no mortal lover. Her future husband awaits her on the top of the mountain. He is a monster whom neither gods nor men can resist."

This dreadful decree of the oracle filled all the people with dismay, and her parents abandoned themselves to grief. But Psyche said, "Why, my dear parents, do you now lament me? You should rather have grieved when the people showered upon me undeserved honors, and with one voice called me a Venus. I now perceive that I am a victim to that name. I submit. Lead me to that rock to which my unhappy fate has destined me." Accordingly, all things being prepared, the royal maid took her place in the procession, which more resembled a funeral than a nuptial pomp, and with her parents, amid the lamentations of the people, ascended the mountain, on the summit of which they left her alone, and with sorrowful hearts returned home.

While Psyche stood on the ridge of the mountain, panting with fear and with eyes full of tears, the gentle Zephyr raised her from the earth and bore her with an easy motion into a flowery dale. By degrees her mind became composed, and she laid herself down on the grassy bank to sleep. When she awoke, refreshed with sleep, she looked round and beheld nearby a pleasant grove of tall and stately trees. She entered it, and in the midst discovered a fountain, sending forth clear and crystal waters, and hard by, a magnificent palace whose August front impressed the spectator that it was not the work of mortal hands, but the happy retreat of some god. Drawn by admiration and wonder, she approached the building and ventured to enter. Every object she met filled her with pleasure and amazement. Golden pillars supported the vaulted roof, and the walls were enriched with carvings and paintings representing beasts of the chase and rural scenes, adapted to delight the eye of the beholder. Proceeding onward she perceived that besides the apartments of state there were others, filled with all manner of treasures, and beautiful and precious productions of nature and art.

While her eyes were thus occupied, a voice addressed her, though she saw no one, uttering these words: "Sovereign lady, all that you see is yours. We whose voices you hear are your servants, and shall obey all your commands with our utmost care and diligence. Retire therefore to your chamber and repose on your bed of down, and when you see fit repair to the bath. Supper will await you in the adjoining alcove when it pleases you to take your seat there."

Psyche gave ear to the admonitions of her vocal attendants, and after repose and the refreshment of the bath, seated herself in the alcove, where a table immediately presented itself, without any visible aid from waiters or servants, and covered with the greatest delicacies of food and the most nectareous wines. Her ears too were feasted with music from invisible performers; of whom one sang, another played on the lute, and all closed in the wonderful harmony of a full chorus.

She had not yet seen her destined husband. He came only in the hours of darkness, and fled before the dawn of morning, but his accents were full of love, and inspired a like passion in her. She often begged him to stay and let her behold him, but he would not consent. On the contrary, he charged her to make no attempt to see him, for it was his pleasure, for the best of reasons, to keep concealed. "Why should you wish to behold me?" he said. "Have you any doubt of my love? Have you any wish ungratified? If you saw me, perhaps you would fear me, perhaps adore me, but all I ask of you is to love me. I would rather you would love me as an equal than adore me as a god."

This reasoning somewhat quieted Psyche for a time, and while the novelty lasted she felt quite happy. But at length the thought of her parents, left in ignorance of her fate, and of her sisters, precluded from sharing with her the delights of her situation, preyed on her mind and made her begin to feel her palace as but a splendid prison. When her husband came one night, she told him her distress, and at last drew from him an unwilling consent that her sisters should be brought to see her. So calling Zephyr, she acquainted him with her husband's commands, and he, promptly obedient, soon brought them across the mountain down to their sister's valley. They embraced her and she returned their caresses. "Come," said Psyche, "enter with me my house and refresh yourselves with whatever your sister has to offer." Then taking their hands she led them into her golden palace, and committed them to the care of her numerous train of attendant voices, to refresh them in her baths and at her table, and to show them all her treasures. The view of these celestial delights caused envy to enter their bosoms, at seeing their young sister possessed of such state and splendor, so much exceeding their own.

They asked her numberless questions, among others what sort of a person her husband was. Psyche replied that he was a beautiful youth, who generally spent the daytime in hunting upon the mountains. The sisters, not satisfied with this reply, soon made her confess that she had never seen him. Then they proceeded to fill her bosom with dark suspicions. "Call to mind," they said, "the Pythian oracle that declared you destined to marry a direful and tremendous monster. The inhabitants of this valley say that your husband is a terrible and monstrous serpent, who nourishes you for a while with dainties that he may by and by devour you. Take our advice. Provide yourself with a lamp and a sharp knife; put them in concealment that your husband may not discover them, and when he is sound asleep, slip out of bed bring forth your lamp and see for yourself whether what they say is true or not. If it is, hesitate not to cut off the monster's head, and thereby recover your liberty."

Psyche resisted these persuasions as well as she could, but they did not fail to have their effect on her mind, and when her sisters were gone, their words and her own curiosity were too strong for her to resist. So she prepared her lamp and a sharp knife, and hid them out of sight of her husband. When he had fallen into his first sleep, she silently rose and uncovering her lamp beheld not a hideous monster, but the most beautiful and charming of the gods, with his golden ringlets wandering over his snowy neck and crimson cheek, with two dewy wings on his shoulders, whiter than snow, and with shining feathers like the tender blossoms of spring. As she leaned the lamp over to have a nearer view of his face a drop of burning oil fell on the shoulder of the god, startled with which he opened his eyes and fixed them full upon her; then, without saying one word, he spread his white wings and flew out of the window. Psyche, in vain endeavoring to follow him, fell from the window to the ground. Cupid, beholding her as she lay in the dust, stopped his flight for an instant and said, "O foolish Psyche, is it thus you repay my love? After having disobeyed my mother's commands and made you my wife, will you think me a monster and cut off my head? But go; return to your sisters, whose advice you seem to think preferable to mine. I inflict no other punishment on you than to leave you forever. Love cannot dwell with suspicion." So saying he fled away, leaving poor Psyche prostrate on the ground, filling the place with mournful lamentations.

When she had recovered some degree of composure she looked around her, but the palace and gardens had vanished, and she found herself in the open field not far from the city where her sisters dwelt. She repaired thither and told them the whole story of her misfortunes, at which, pretending to grieve, those spiteful creatures inwardly rejoiced; "for now," said they, "he will perhaps choose one of us." With this idea, without saying a word of her intentions, each of them rose early the next morning and ascended the mountain, and having reached the top, called upon Zephyr to receive her and bear her to his lord; then leaping up, and not being sustained by Zephyr, fell down the precipice and was dashed to pieces.

Psyche meanwhile wandered day and night, without food or repose, in search of her husband. Casting her eyes on a lofty mountain having on its brow a magnificent temple, she sighed and said to herself, "Perhaps my love, my lord, inhabits there," and directed her steps thither.

She had no sooner entered than she saw heaps of corn, some in loose ears and some in sheaves, with mingled ears of barley. Scattered about lay sickles and rakes, and all the instruments of harvest, without order, as if thrown carelessly out of the weary reapers' hands in the sultry hours of the day.

This unseemly confusion the pious Psyche put an end to, by separating and sorting every thing to its proper place and kind, believing that she ought to neglect none of the gods, but endeavor by her piety to engage them all in her behalf. The holy Ceres, whose temple it was, finding her so religiously employed, thus spoke to her: "O Psyche, truly worthy of our pity, though I cannot shield you from the frowns of Venus, yet I can teach you how best to allay her displeasure. Go then, voluntarily surrender yourself to your lady and sovereign, and try by modesty and submission to win her forgiveness; perhaps her favor will restore you the husband you have lost."

Psyche obeyed the commands of Ceres and took her way to the temple of Venus, endeavoring to fortify her mind and thinking of what she should say and how she should best propitiate the angry goddess, feeling that the issue was doubtful and perhaps fatal.

Venus received her with angry countenance. "Most undutiful and faithless of servants," said she, "do you at last remember that you really have a mistress? Or have you rather come to see your sick husband, yet suffering from the wound given him by his loving wife? You are so ill-favored and disagreeable that the only way you can merit your lover must be by dint of industry and diligence. I will make trial of your housewifery." Then she ordered Psyche to be led to the storehouse of her temple, where was laid up a great quantity of wheat, barley, millet, vetches, beans, and lentils prepared for food for her doves, and said, "Take and separate all these grains, putting all of the same kind in a parcel by themselves, and see that you get it done before evening." Then Venus departed and left her to her task.

But Psyche, in perfect consternation at the enormous work, sat stupid and silent, without moving a finger to the inextricable heap.

While she sat despairing, Cupid stirred up the little ant, a native of the fields, to take compassion on her. The leader of the ant-hill, followed by whole hosts of his six-legged subjects, approached the heap, and with the utmost diligence taking grain by grain, they separated the pile, sorting each kind to its parcel; and when it was all done, they vanished out of sight in a moment.

Venus at the approach of twilight returned from the banquet of the gods, breathing odors and crowned with roses. Seeing the task done she exclaimed, "This is no work of yours wicked one, but his, whom to your own and his misfortune you have enticed." So saying, she threw her a piece of black bread for her supper and went away.

Next morning Venus ordered Psyche to be called, and said to her, "Behold yonder grove which stretches along the margin of the water. There you will find sheep feeding without a shepherd, with golden-shining fleeces on their backs. Go, fetch me a sample of that precious wool gathered from every one of their fleeces.

Psyche obediently went to the river-side, prepared to do her best to execute the command. But the river-god inspired the reeds with harmonious murmurs, which seemed to say, "O maiden, severely tried, tempt not the dangerous flood, nor venture among the formidable rams on the other side, for as long as they are under the influence of the rising sun, they burn with a cruel rage to destroy mortals with their sharp horns or rude teeth. But when the noontide sun has driven the flock to the shade, and the serene spirit of the flood has lulled them to rest, you may then cross in safety, and you will find the woolly gold sticking to the bushes and the trunks of the trees."

Thus the compassionate river-god gave Psyche instructions how to accomplish her task, and by observing his directions she soon returned to Venus with her arms full of the golden fleece; but she received not the approbation of her implacable mistress, who said, "I know very well it is by none of your own doings that you have succeeded in this task, and I am not satisfied yet that you have any capacity to make yourself useful. But I have another task for you. Here, take this box, and go your way to the infernal shades, and give this box to Proserpine, and say, 'My mistress Venus desires you to send her a little of your beauty, for in tending her sick son she has lost some of her own.' Be not too long on your errand, for I must paint myself with it to appear at the circle of the gods and goddesses this evening."

Psyche was now satisfied that her destruction was at hand, being obliged to go with her own feet directly down to Erebus. Wherefore, to make no delay of what was not to be avoided, she goes to the top of a high tower to precipitate herself headlong, thus to descend the shortest way to the shades below. But a voice from the tower said to her, "Why, poor unlucky girl, dost thou design to put an end to thy days in so dreadful a manner? And what cowardice makes thee sink under this last danger, who hast been so miraculously supported in all thy former?" Then the voice told her how by a certain cave she might reach the realms of Pluto, and how to avoid all the dangers of the road, to pass by Cerberus, the three-headed dog, and prevail on Charon, the ferryman, to take her across the black river and bring her back again. But the voice added, "When Proserpine has given you the box, filled with her beauty, of all things this is chiefly to be observed by you, that you never once open or look into the box nor allow your curiosity to pry into the treasure of the beauty of the goddesses.

Psyche encouraged by this advice obeyed it in all things, and taking heed to her ways travelled safely to the kingdom of Pluto. She was admitted to the palace of Proserpine, and without accepting the delicate seat or delicious banquet that was offered her, but contented with coarse bread for her food, she delivered her message from Venus. Presently the box was returned to her, shut and filled with the precious commodity. Then she returned the way she came, and glad was she to come out once more into the light of day.

But having got so far successfully through her dangerous task a longing desire seized her to examine the contents of the box. "What," said she, "shall I, the carrier of this divine beauty, not take the least bit to put on my cheeks to appear to more advantage in the eyes of my beloved husband!:" So she carefully opened the box, but found nothing there of any beauty at all, but an infernal and truly Stygian sleep, which being thus set free from its prison, took possession of her, and she fell down in the midst of the road, a sleepy corpse without sense or motion.

But Cupid being now recovered from his wound, and not able longer to bear the absence of his beloved Psyche, slipping through the smallest crack of the window of his chamber which happened to be left open, flew to the spot where Psyche lay, and gathering up the sleep from her body closed it again in the box, and waked Psyche with a light touch of one of his arrows. "Again," said he, "hast thou almost perished by the same curiosity. But now perform exactly the task imposed on you by my mother, and I will take care of the rest."

Then Cupid, as swift as lightning penetrating the heights of heaven, presented himself before Jupiter with his supplication. Jupiter lent a favoring ear, and pleaded the cause of the lovers so earnestly with Venus that he won her consent. On this he sent Mercury to bring Psyche up to the heavenly assembly, and when she arrived, handing her a cup of ambrosia, he said, "Drink this, Psyche, and be immortal; nor shall Cupid ever break away from the knot in which he is tied, but these nuptials shall be perpetual."

Thus Psyche became at last united to Cupid, and in due time they had a daughter born to them whose name was Pleasure.

The fable of Cupid and Psyche is usually considered allegorical. The Greek name for a butterfly is Psyche, and the same word means the soul. There is no illustration of the immortality of the soul so striking and beautiful as the butterfly, bursting on brilliant wings from the tomb in which it has lain, after a dull, groveling caterpillar existence, to flutter in the blaze of day and feed on the most fragrant and delicate productions of the spring. Psyche, then, is the human soul, which is purified by sufferings and misfortunes, and is thus prepared for the enjoyment of true and pure happiness.

In works of art Psyche is represented as a maiden with the wings of a butterfly, alone or with Cupid, in the different situations described in the allegory.

Milton alludes to the story of Cupid and Psyche in the conclusion of his Comus:

"Celestial Cupid, her famed son, advanced,
Holds his dear Psyche sweet entranced,
After her wandering labors long,
Till free consent the gods among
Make her his eternal bride;
And from her fair unspotted side
T wo blissful twins are to be born,
Youth and Joy; so Jove hath sworn."

The allegory of the story of Cupid and Psyche is well presented in the beautiful lines of T. K. Hervey:

"They wove bright fables in the days of old
When reason borrowed fancy's painted wings;
When truth's clear river flowed o'er sands of gold,
And told in song its high and mystic things!
And such the sweet and solemn tale of her
The pilgrim-heart, to whom a dream was given.
That led her through the world, Love's worshipper,
To seek on earth for him whose home was heaven!

"In the full city, by the haunted fount,
Through the dim grotto's tracery of spars,
'Mid the pine temples, on the moonlit mount,
Where silence sits to listen to the stars;
In the deep glade where dwells the brooding dove,
The painted valley, and the scented air,
She heard far echoes of the voice of Love,
And found his footsteps' traces everywhere.

"But never more they met! Since doubts and fears,
Those phantom-shapes that haunt and blight the earth,
Had come 'twixt her, a child of sin and tears,
And that bright spirit of immortal birth;
Until her pining soul and weeping eyes
Had learned to seek him only in the skies;
Till wings unto the weary heart were given,
And she became Love's angel bride in heaven!"

The story of Cupid and Psyche first appears in the works of Apuleius, a writer of the second century of our era. It is therefore of much more recent date than most of the legends of the Age of Fable. It is this that Keats alludes to in his Ode to Psyche.

"O latest born and loveliest vision far
Of all Olympus' faded hierarchy!
Fairer than Phoebe's sapphire-regioned star
Or Vesper, amorous glow-worm of the sky;
Fairer than these, though temple thou hast none,
Nor altar heaped with flowers;
Nor virgin-choir to make delicious moan
Upon the midnight hours;
No voice, no lute, no pipe, no incense sweet,
From chain-swung censer teeming;
No shrine, no grove, no oracle, no heat
Of Pale-mouthed prophet dreaming."

In Moore's Summer Fete, a fancy ball is described, in which one of the characters personated is Psyche.

"not in dark disguise to-night
Hath our young heroine veiled her light;
For see, she walks the earth, Love's own.
His wedded bride, by holiest vow
Pledged in Olympus, and made known
To mortals by the type which now
Hangs glittering on her snowy brow,
That butterfly, mysterious trinket,
Which means the soul (though few would think it),
And sparkling thus on brow so white,
Tells us we've Psyche here to-night."

Chapter 7

CADMUS. THE MYRMIDONS.

Jupiter, under the disguise of a bull, had carried away to the island of Crete, Europa, the daughter of Agenor king of Phoenicia. Agenor commanded his son Cadmus to go in search of his sister, and not to return without her. Cadmus went and sought long and far for his sister, but could not find her, and not daring to return unsuccessful, consulted the oracle of Apollo to know what country he should settle in. The oracle informed him that he should find a cow in the field, and should follow her wherever she might wander, and where she stopped, should build a city and call it Thebes. Cadmus had hardly left the Castalian cave, from which the oracle was delivered, when he saw a young cow slowly walking before him. He followed her close, offering at the same time his prayers to Phoebus. The cow went on till she passed the shallow channel of Cephisus and came out into the plain of Panope. There she stood still, and raising her broad forehead to the sky, filled the air with her lowings. Cadmus gave thanks, and stooping down kissed the foreign soil, then lifting his eyes, greeted the surrounding mountains. Wishing to offer a sacrifice to Jupiter, he sent his servants to seek pure water for a libation. Nearby there stood an ancient grove which had never been profaned by the axe, in the midst of which was a cave, thick covered with the growth of bushes, its roof forming a low arch, from beneath which burst forth a fountain of purest water. In the cave lurked a horrid serpent with a crested head and scales glittering like gold. His eyes shone like fire, his body was swollen with venom, he vibrated a triple tongue, and showed a triple row of teeth. No sooner had the Tyrians (Cadmus and his companions came from Tyre, the chief city of Phoenicia) dipped their pitchers in the fountain, and the ingushing waters made a sound, than the glittering serpent raised his head out of the cave and uttered a fearful hiss. The vessels fell from their hands, the blood left their cheeks, they trembled in every limb. The serpent, twisting his scaly body in a huge coil, raised his head so as to overtop the tallest trees, and while the Tyrians from terror could neither fight nor fly, slew some with his fangs, others in his folds, and others with his poisonous breath.

Cadmus having waited for the return of his men till midday, went in search of them. His covering was a lion's hide, and besides his javelin he carried in his hand a lance, and in his breast a bold heart, a surer reliance than either. When he entered the wood and saw the lifeless bodies of his men, and the monster with his bloody jaws, he exclaimed, "O faithful friends, I will avenge you, or share your death." So saying he lifted a huge stone and threw it with all his force at the serpent. Such a block would have shaken the wall of a fortress, but it made no impression on the monster. Cadmus next threw his javelin, which met with better success, for it penetrated the serpent's scales, and pierced through to his entrails. Fierce with pain the monster turned back his head to view the wound, and attempted to draw out the weapon with his mouth, but broke it off, leaving the iron point rankling in his flesh. His neck swelled with rage, bloody foam covered his jaws, and the breath of his nostrils poisoned the air around. Now he twisted himself into a circle, then stretched himself out on the ground like the trunk of a fallen tree. As he moved onward, Cadmus retreated before him, holding his spear opposite to the monster's opened jaws. The serpent snapped at the weapon and attempted to bite its iron point. At last Cadmus, watching his chance, thrust the spear at a moment when the animal's thrown back came against the trunk of a tree, and so succeeded in pinning him to its side. His weight bent the tree as he struggled in the agonies of death.

While Cadmus stood over his conquered foe, contemplating its vast size, a voice was heard (from whence he knew not, but he heard it distinctly), commanding him to take the dragon's teeth and sow them in the earth. He obeyed. He made a furrow in the ground, and planted the teeth, destined to produce a crop of men. Scarce had he done so when the clods began to move, and the points of spears to appear above the surface. Next helmets, with their nodding plumes, came up, and next, the shoulders and breasts and limbs of men with weapons, and in time a harvest of armed warriors. Cadmus, alarmed, prepared to encounter a new enemy, but one of them said to him, "Meddle not with our civil war." With that he who had spoken smote one of his earth-born brothers with a sword, and he himself fell pierced with an arrow from another. The latter fell victim to a fourth, and in like manner the whole crowd dealt with each other till all fell slain with mutual wounds except five survivors. One of

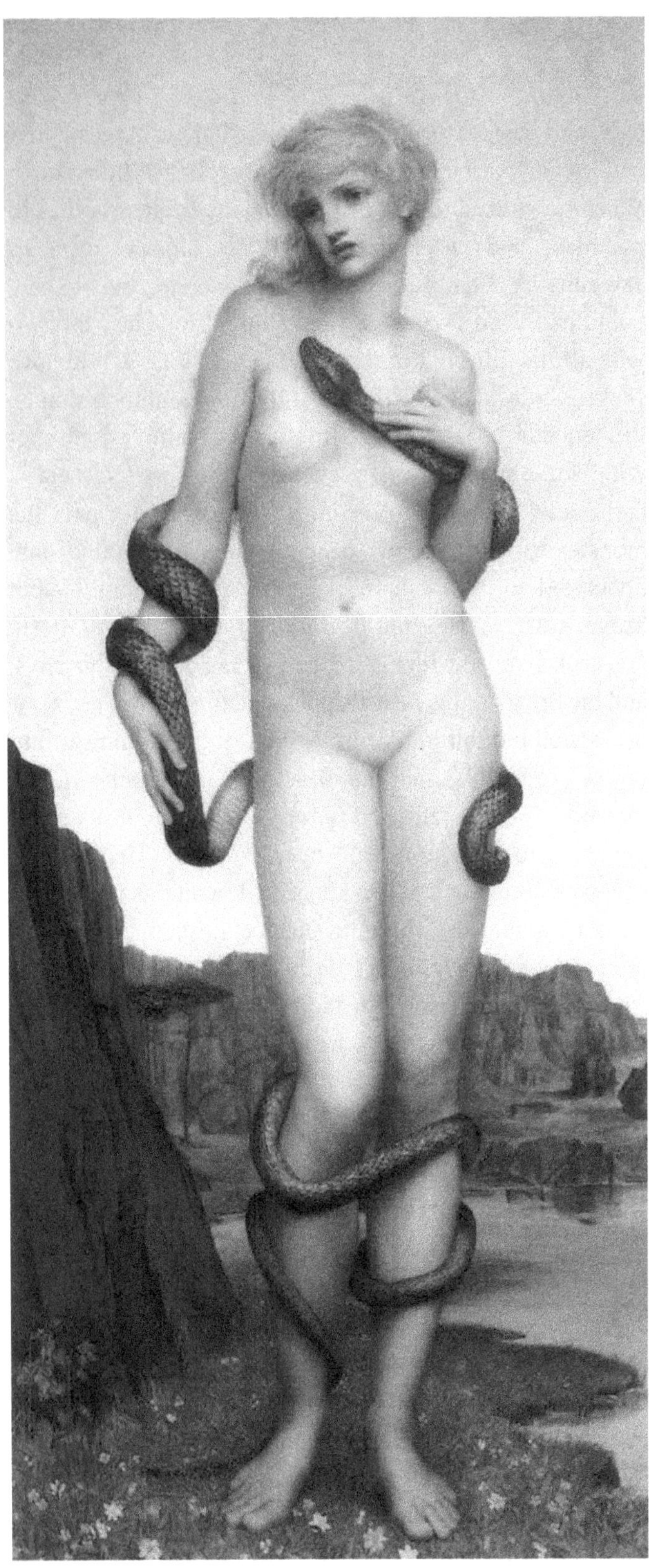

Figure 9: "Cadmus Harmonia" by Evelyn De Morgan

these cast away his weapons and said, "Brothers, let us live in peace!" These five joined with Cadmus in building his city, to which they gave the name of Thebes.

Cadmus obtained in marriage Harmonia, the daughter of Venus. The gods left Olympus to honor the occasion with their presence, and Vulcan presented the bride with a necklace of surpassing brilliancy, his own workmanship. But a fatality hung over the family of Cadmus in consequence of his killing the serpent sacred to Mars. Semele and Ino, his daughters, and Actaeon and Pentheius, his grandchildren, all perished unhappily; and Cadmus and Harmonia quitted Thebes, now grown odious to them, and emigrated to the country of the Enchelians, who received them with honor and made Cadmus their king. But the misfortunes of their children still weighed upon their minds; and one day Cadmus exclaimed, "If a serpent's life is so dear to the gods, I would I were myself a serpent." No sooner had he uttered the words than he began to change his form. Harmonia beheld it, and prayed to the gods to let her share his fate. Both became serpents. They lie in the woods, but mindful of their origin they neither avoid the presence of man nor do they ever injure any one.

There is a tradition that Cadmus introduced into Greece the letters of the alphabet which were invented by the Phoenicians. This is alluded to by Byron, where, addressing the modern Greeks, he says:

"You have the letters Cadmus gave,
Think you he meant them for a slave?"

Milton, describing the serpent which tempted Eve, is reminded of the serpents of the classical stories, and says,

"——pleasing was his shape, And lovely; never since of serpent kind Lovelier; not those that in Illyria changed Hermione and Cadmus, nor the god in Epidaurus."

The "god in Epidaurus" was Æsculapius. Serpents were held sacred to him.

THE MYRMIDONS

The Myrmidons were the soldiers of Achilles in the Trojan war. From them all zealous and unscrupulous followers of a political chief are called by that name down to this day. But the origin of the Myrmidons would not give one the idea of a fierce and bloody race, but rather of a laborious and peaceful one.

Cephalus, king of Athens, arrived in the island of Ægina to seek assistance of his old friend and ally Æacus, the king, in his wars with Minos, king of Crete. Cephalus was kindly received, and the desired assistance readily promised. "I have people enough," said Æacus, "to protect myself and spare you such a force as you need." "I rejoice to see it," replied Cephalus, "and my wonder has been raised, I confess, to find such a host of youths as I see around me, all apparently of about the same age. Yet there are many individuals whom I previously knew that I look for now in vain. What has become of them?" Æacus groaned, and replied with a voice of sadness, "I have been intending to tell you, and will now do so without more delay, that you may see how from the saddest beginning a happy result sometimes flows. Those whom you formerly knew are now dust and ashes! A plague sent by angry Juno devastated the land. She hated it because it bore the name of one of her husband's female favorites. While the disease appeared to spring from natural causes we resisted it as we best might by natural remedies; but it soon appeared that the pestilence was too powerful for our efforts, and we yielded. At the beginning the sky seemed to settle down upon the earth, and thick clouds shut in the heated air. For four months together a deadly south wind prevailed. The disorder affected the wells and springs; thousands of snakes crept over the land and shed their poison in the fountains. The force of the disease was first spent on the lower animals; dogs, cattle, sheep, and birds. The luckless ploughman wondered to see his oxen fall in the midst of their work, and lie helpless in the unfinished furrow. The wool fell from the bleating sheep, and their bodies pined away. The horse, once foremost in the race, contested the palm no more, but groaned at his stall, and died an inglorious death. The wild boar forgot his rage, the stag his swiftness, the bears no longer attacked the herds. Everything languished; dead bodies lay in the roads, the fields, and the woods; the air was poisoned by them. I tell you what is hardly credible, but neither dogs nor birds would touch them, nor starving wolves. Their decay spread the infection. Next the disease attacked the country people, and then the dwellers in the city. At first the cheek was flushed, and the breath drawn with difficulty. The tongue grew rough and swelled, and the dry mouth stood open with its veins enlarged and gasped for the air. Men could not bear the heat of their clothes or their beds, but preferred to lie on the bare ground; and the ground did not cool them, but on the contrary, they heated the spot where they lay. Nor could the physicians help, for the disease attacked them also, and the contact of the sick gave them infection, so that the most faithful were the first victims. At last all hope of relief vanished and men learned to look upon death as the only deliverer from disease. Then they gave way to every inclination, and cared not to ask what was expedient, for nothing was expedient. All restraint laid aside, they crowded around the wells and fountains, and drank till they died, without quenching thirst. Many had not strength to get away from the water, but died in the midst of the stream, and others would drink of it notwithstanding. Such was their weariness of their sick-beds that some would creep forth, and if not strong enough to stand, would die on the ground. They seemed to hate their friends, and got away from their homes, as if, not knowing the cause of their sickness, they charged it on the place of their abode. Some were seen tottering along the road, as long as they could stand, while others sank on the earth, and turned their dying eyes around to take a last look, then closed them in death.

Figure 10: "The Rage of Achilles" by Giovanni Battista Tiepolo

"What heart had I left me, during all this, or what ought I to have had, except to hate life and wish to be with my dead subjects? On all sides lay my people strewn like over-ripened apples beneath the tree, or acorns under the storm-shaken oak. You see yonder a temple on the height. It is sacred to Jupiter. Oh, how many offered prayers there; husbands for wives, fathers for sons, and died in the very act of supplication! How often, while the priest made ready for sacrifice, the victim fell, struck down by disease without waiting for the blow. At length all reverence for sacred things was lost. Bodies were thrown out unburied, wood was wanting for funeral piles, men fought with one another for the possession of them. Finally, there were none left to mourn; sons and husbands, old men and youths, perished alike unlamented.

"Standing before the altar I raised my eyes to heaven. 'Oh, Jupiter,' I said, 'if thou art indeed my father, and art not ashamed of thy offspring, give me back my people, or take me also away!' At these words a clap of thunder was heard. 'I accept the omen,' I cried; 'oh, may it be a sign of a favorable disposition towards me!' By chance there grew by the place where I stood an oak with wide-spreading branches, sacred to Jupiter. I observed a troop of ants busy with their labor, carrying minute grains in their mouths and following one another in a line up the trunk of the tree. Observing their numbers with admiration, I said, 'Give me, oh father, citizens as numerous as these, and replenish my empty city.' The tree shook and gave a rustling sound with its branches though no wind agitated them. I trembled in every limb, yet I kissed the earth and the tree. I would not confess to myself that I hoped, yet I did hope. Night came on and sleep took possession of my frame oppressed with cares. The tree stood before me in my dreams, with its numerous branches all covered with living, moving creatures. It seemed to shake its limbs and throw down over the ground a multitude of those industrious grain-gathering animals, which appeared to gain in size, and grow larger, and by-and-by to stand erect, lay aside their superfluous legs and their black color, and finally to assume the human form. Then I awoke, and my first impulse was to chide the gods who had robbed me of a sweet vision and given me no reality in its place. Being still in the temple my attention was caught by the sound of many voices without; a sound of late unusual to my ears. While I began to think I was yet dreaming, Telamon, my son, throwing open the temple-gates, exclaimed, 'Father, approach, and behold things surpassing even your hopes!' I went forth; I saw a multitude of men, such as I had seen in my dream, and they were passing in procession in the same manner. While I gazed with wonder and delight they approached, and kneeling, hailed me as their king. I paid my vows to Jove, and proceeded to allot the vacant city to the new-born race, and to parcel out the fields among them. I called them Myrmidons from the ant (myrmex), from which they sprang. You have seen these persons; their dispositions resemble those which they had in their former shape. They are a diligent and industrious race, eager to gain, and tenacious of their gains. Among them you may recruit your forces. They will follow you to the war, young in years and bold in heart."

This description of the plague is copied by Ovid from the account which Thucydides, the Greek historian, gives of the plague of Athens. The historian drew from life, and all the poets and writers of fiction since his day, when they have had occasion to describe a similar scene, have borrowed their details from him.

Figure 11: "Education of Achilles by Chiron" by Jean-Baptiste Regnault

Chapter 8

NISUS AND SCYLLA. ECHO AND NARCISSUS. CLYTIE. HERO AND LEANDER

Minos, king of Crete, made war upon Megara. Nisus was king of Megara, and Scylla was his daughter. The siege had now lasted six months, and the city still held out, for it was decreed by fate that it should not be taken so long as a certain purple lock, which glittered among the hair of King Nisus, remained on his head. There was a tower on the city walls, which overlooked the plain where Minos and his army were encamped. To this tower Scylla used to repair, and look abroad over the tents of the hostile army. The siege had lasted so long that she had learned to distinguish the persons of the leaders. Minos, in particular, excited her admiration. She admired his graceful deportment; if he threw his javelin, skill seemed combined with force in the discharge; if he drew his bow, Apollo himself could not have done it more gracefully. But when he laid aside his helmet, and in his purple robes bestrode his white horse with its gay caparisons, and reined in its foaming mouth, the daughter of Nisus was hardly mistress of herself; she was almost frantic with admiration. She envied the weapon that he grasped, the reins that he held. She felt as if she could, if it were possible, go to him through the hostile ranks; she felt an impulse to cast herself down from the tower into the midst of his camp, or to open the gates to him, or do anything else, so only it might gratify Minos. As she sat in the tower, she talked thus with herself: "I know not whether to rejoice or grieve at this sad war. I grieve that Minos is our enemy; but I rejoice at any cause that brings him to my sight. Perhaps he would be willing to grant us peace, and receive me as a hostage. I would fly down, if I could, and alight in his camp, and tell him that we yield ourselves to his mercy. But, then, to betray my father! No! Rather would I never see Minos again. And yet no doubt it is sometimes the best thing for a city to be conquered when the conqueror is clement and generous. Minos certainly has right on his side. I think we shall be conquered; and if that must be the end of it, why should not love unbar the gates to him, instead of leaving it to be done by war? Better spare delay and slaughter if we can. And, oh, if any one should wound or kill Minos! No one surely would have the heart to do it; yet ignorantly, not knowing him, one might. I will, I will surrender myself to him, with my country as a dowry, and so put an end to the war. But how? The gates are guarded, and my father keeps the keys; he only stands in my way. Oh, that it might please the gods to take him away! But why ask the gods to do it? Another woman, loving as I do, would remove with her own hands whatever stood in the way of her love. And can any other woman dare more than I? I would encounter fire and sword to gain my object; but here there is no need of fire and sword. I only need my father's purple lock. More precious than gold to me, that will give me all I wish."

While she thus reasoned night came on, and soon the whole palace was buried in sleep. She entered her father's bedchamber and cut off the fatal lock; then passed out of the city and entered the enemy's camp. She demanded to be led to the king, and thus addressed him: "I am Scylla, the daughter of Nisus. I surrender to you my country and my father's house. I ask no reward but yourself; for love of you I have done it. See here the purple lock! With this I give you my father and his kingdom." She held out her hand with the fatal spoil. Minos shrunk back and refused to touch it. "The gods destroy thee, infamous woman," he exclaimed; "disgrace of our time! May neither earth nor sea yield thee a resting place! Surely, my Crete, where Jove himself was cradled, shall not be polluted with such a monster!" Thus he said, and gave orders that equitable terms should be allowed to the conquered city, and that the fleet should immediately sail from the island.

Scylla was frantic. "Ungrateful man," she exclaimed, "is it thus you leave me? Me who have given you victory, who have sacrificed for you parent and country! I am guilty, I confess, and deserve to die, by not by your hand." As the ships left the shore, she leaped into the water, and seizing the rudder of the one which carried Minos, she was borne along an unwelcome companion of their course. A sea-eagle soaring aloft, it was her father who had been changed into that form, seeing her, pounced down upon her, and struck her with his beak and claws. In terror she let go the ship, and would have fallen into the water, but some pitying deity changed her into a bird. The sea- eagle still cherishes the old animosity; and whenever he espies her in his lofty flight, you may see him dart down upon her, with beak and claws, to take vengeance for the ancient crime.

ECHO AND NARCISSUS

Echo was a beautiful nymph, fond of the woods and hills, where she devoted herself to woodland sports. She was a favorite of Diana, and attended her in the chase. But Echo had one failing; she was fond of talking, and whether in chat or argument would have the last word. One day Juno was seeking her husband, who, she had reason to fear, was amusing himself among the nymphs. Echo by her talk contrived to detain the goddess till the nymphs made their escape. When Juno discovered it, she passed sentence upon Echo in these words: "You shall forfeit the use of that tongue with which you have cheated me, except for that one purpose you are so fond of REPLY. You shall still have the last word, but no power to speak first."

This nymph saw Narcissus, a beautiful youth, as he pursued the chase upon the mountains. She loved him, and followed his footsteps. Oh, how she longed to address him in the softest accents, and win him to converse, but it was not in her power. She waited with impatience for him to speak first, and had her answer ready. One day the youth, being separated from his companions, shouted aloud, "Who's here?" Echo replied, "Here." Narcissus looked around, but seeing no one, called out, "Come." Echo answered, "Come." As no one came, Narcissus called again, "Why do you shun me?" Echo asked the same question. "Let us join one another," said the youth. The maid answered with all her heart in the same words, and hastened to the spot, ready to throw her arms about his neck. He started back, exclaiming, "Hands off! I would rather die than you should have me." "Have me," said she; but it was all in vain. He left her, and she went to hide her blushes in the recesses of the woods. From that time forth she lived in caves and among mountain cliffs. Her form faded with grief, till at last all her flesh shrank away. Her bones were changed into rocks, and there was nothing left of her but her voice. With that she is still ready to reply to any one who calls her, and keeps up her old habit of having the last word.

Narcissus was cruel not in this case alone. He shunned all the rest of the nymphs as he had done poor Echo. One day a maiden, who had in vain endeavored to attract him, uttered a prayer that he might some time or other feel what it was to love and meet no return of affection. The avenging goddess heard and granted the prayer.

There was a clear fountain, with water like silver, to which the shepherds never drove their flocks. Nor did the mountain goats resort to it, nor any of the beasts of the forest; neither was it defaced with fallen leaves or branches; but the grass grew fresh around it, and the rocks sheltered it from the sun. Hither came one day the youth fatigued with hunting, heated and thirsty. He stooped down to drink, and saw his own image in the water; he thought it was some beautiful water=spirit living in the fountain. He stood gazing with admiration at those bright eyes, those locks curled like the locks of Bacchus or Apollo, the rounded cheeks, the ivory neck, the parted lips, and the glow of health and exercise over all. He fell in love with himself. He brought his lips near to take a kiss; he plunged his arms in to embrace the beloved object. It fled at the touch, but returned again after a moment and renewed the fascination. He could not tear himself away; he lost all thought of food or rest, while he hovered over the brink of the fountain gazing upon his own image. He talked with the supposed spirit: "Why, beautiful being, do you shun me? Surely my face is not one to repel you. The nymphs love me, and you yourself look not indifferent upon me. When I stretch forth my arms you do the same; and you smile upon me and answer my beckonings with the like." His tears fell into the water and disturbed the image. As he saw it depart, he exclaimed, "Stay, I entreat you! Let me at least gaze upon you, if I may not touch you." With this, and much more of the same kind, he cherished the flame that consumed him, so that by degrees he lost his color, his vigor, and the beauty which formerly had so charmed the nymph Echo. She kept near him, however, and when he exclaimed, "Alas! Alas!" she answered him with the same words. He pined away and died; and when his shade passed the Stygian river, it leaned over the boat to catch a look of itself in the waters. The nymphs mourned for him, especially the water-nymphs; and when they smote their breasts, Echo smote hers also. They prepared a funeral pile, and would have burned the body, but it was nowhere to be found; but in its place a flower, purple within, and surrounded with white leaves, which bears the name and preserves the memory of Narcissus.

Milton alludes to the story of Echo and Narcissus in the Lady's song in Comus. She is seeking her brothers in the forest, and sings to attract their attention.

"Sweet Echo, sweetest nymph, that liv'st unseen
Within thy aery shell
By slow Meander's margent green.
And in the violet-embroidered vale,
Where the love-lorn nightingale
Nightly to thee her sad song mourneth well;
Canst thou not tell me of a gentle pair
That likes thy Narcissus are?
Oh, if thou have
Hid them in some flowery cave,
Tell me but where,
Sweet queen of parly, daughter of the sphere,
So may'st thou be translated to the skies,
And give resounding grace to all heaven's harmonies."

Milton has imitated the story of Narcissus in the account which he makes Eve give of the first sight of herself reflected in the fountain:

"That day I oft remember when from sleep
I first awaked, and found myself reposed
Under a shade on flowers, much wondering where
And what I was, whence thither brought, and how
Not distant far from thence a murmuring sound
Of waters issued from a cave, and spread
Into a liquid plain, then stood unmoved
Pure as the expanse of heaven; I thither went
With unexperienced thought, and laid me down
On the green bank, to look into the clear
Smooth lake that to me seemed another sky.
As I bent down to look, just opposite
A shape within the watery gleam appeared,
Bending to look on me. I started back;
It started back; but pleased I soon returned,
Pleased it returned as soon with answering looks
Of sympathy and love. There had I fixed
Mine eyes till now, and pined with vain desire,
Had not a voice thus warned me: 'What thou seest,
What there thou seest, fair creature, is thyself.'"
Paradise Lost, Book IV

The fable of Narcissus is often alluded to by the poets. Here are two epigrams which treat it in different ways. The first is by Goldsmith:

"ON A BEAUTIFUL YOUTH STRUCK BLIND BY LIGHTNING:
"Sure 'twas by Providence designed,
Rather in pity than in hate,
That he should be like Cupid blind,
To save him from Narcissus' fate"

The other is by Cowper:

"ON AN UGLY FELLOW
"Beware, my friend, of crystal brook
Or fountain, lest that hideous hook.
Thy nose, thou chance to see;
Narcissus' fate would then be thine,
And self-detested thou would'st pine,
As self-enamored he."

CLYTIE

Clytie was a water-nymph and in love with Apollo, who made her no return. So she pined away, sitting all day long upon the cold ground, with her unbound tresses streaming over her shoulders. Nine days she sat and tasted neither food nor drink, her own tears and the chilly dew her only food. She gazed on the sun when he rose, and as he passed through his daily course to his setting; she saw no other object, her face turned constantly on him. At last, they say, her limbs rooted in the ground, her face became a sunflower, which turns on its stem so as always to face the sun throughout its daily course; for it retains to that extent the feeling of the nymph from whom it sprang.

One of the best known of the marble busts discovered in our own time, generally bears the name of Clytie. It has been very frequently copied in plaster. It represents the head of a young girl looking down, the neck and shoulders being supported in the cup of a large flower, which by a little effort of imagination can be made into a giant sunflower. The latest supposition, however, is that this bust represented not Clytie, but Isis.

Hood in his Flowers thus alludes to Clytie:

"I will not have the mad Clytie,
Whose head is turned by the sun;
The tulip is a courtly quean,
Whom therefore I will shun;
The cowslip is a country wench,
The violet is a nun;
But I will woo the dainty rose,
The queen of every one."

The sunflower is a favorite emblem of constancy. Thus, Moore uses it:

"The heart that has truly loved never forgets,
But as truly loves on to the close;
As the sunflower turns on her god when he sets
The same look that she turned when he rose."

It is only for convenience that the modern poets translate the Latin word HELIOTROPIUM, by the English sunflower. The sunflower, which was known to the ancients, was called in Greek, helianthos, from HELIOS, the sun; and ANTHOS a flower, and in Latin, helianthus. It derives its name from its resemblance to the sun; but, as any one may see, at sunset, it does not "turn to the God when he sets the same look that it turned when he rose."

The Heliotrope of the fable of Clytie is called Turnsole in old English books, and such a plant is known in England. It is not the sweet heliotrope of modern gardens, which is a South American plant. The true classical heliotrope is probably to be found in the heliotrope of southern France, a weed not known in America. The reader who is curious may examine the careful account of it in Larousse's large dictionary.

HERO AND LEANDER

Leander was a youth of Abydos, a town of the Asian side of the strait which separates Asia and Europe. On the opposite shore in the town of Sestos lived the maiden Hero, a priestess of Venus. Leander loved her, and used to swim the strait nightly to enjoy the company of his mistress, guided by a torch which she reared upon the tower, for the purpose. But one night a tempest arose and the sea was rough; his strength failed, and he was drowned. The waves bore his body to the European shore, where Hero became aware of his death, and in her despair cast herself down from the tower into the sea and perished.

The following sonnet is by Keats:

"ON A PICTURE OF LEANDER
"Come hither, all sweet maidens, soberly,
Down looking aye, and with a chasten'd light,
Hid in the fringes of your eyelids white,
And meekly let your fair hands joined be,
As if so gentle that ye could not see,
Untouch'd, a victim of your beauty bright,
Sinking away to his young spirit's night,
Sinking bewilder'd 'mid the dreary sea.
'Tis young Leander toiling to his death.
Nigh swooning, he doth purse his weary lips
For Hero's cheek, and smiles against her smile.
Oh, horrid dream! See how his body dips
Dead-heavy; arms and shoulders gleam awhile;
He's gone; up bubbles all his amorous breath!"

The story of Leander's swimming the Hellespont was looked upon as fabulous, and the feat considered impossible, till Lord Byron proved its possibility by performing it himself. In the Bride of Abydos he says,

---

"These limbs that buoyant wave hath borne."

The distance in the narrowest part is almost a mile, and there is a constant current setting out from the Sea of Marmora into the Archipelago. Since Byron's time the feat has been achieved by others; but it yet remains a test of strength and skill in the art of swimming sufficient to give a wide and lasting celebrity to any one of our readers who may dare to make the attempt and succeed in accomplishing it.

In the beginning of the second canto of the same poem, Byron alludes to this story:

"The winds are high on Helle's wave,
As on that night of stormiest water,
When Love, who sent, forgot to save

The young, the beautiful, the brave,
The lonely hope of Sestos' daughter.
Oh, when alone along the sky
The turret-torch was blazing high,
Though rising gale and breaking foam,
And shrieking sea-birds warned him home;
And clouds aloft and tides below,
With signs and sounds forbade to go,
He could not see, he would not hear
Or sound or sight foreboding fear.
His eye but saw that light of love,
The only star it hailed above;
His ear but rang with Hero's song,
'Ye waves, divide not lovers long.'
That tale is old, but love anew
May nerve young hearts to prove as true."

The subject has been a favorite one with sculptors.

Schiller has made one of his finest ballads from the tragic fate of the two lovers. The following verses are a translation from the latter part of the ballad:

"Upon Hellespont's broad currents
Night broods black, and rain in torrents
From the cloud's full bosom pours;
Lightnings in the sky are flashing,
All the storms below are dashing
On the crag-piled shores.
Awful chasms gaping widely,
Separate the mountain waves;
Ocean yawning as to open
Downward e'en to Pluto's caves."

After the storm has arisen, Hero sees the danger, and cries,

"Woe, ah! Woe; great Jove have pity,
Listen to my sad entreaty,
Yet for what can Hero pray?
Should the gods in pity listen,
He, e'en now the false abyss in,
Struggles with the tempest's spray.
All the birds that skim the wave
In hasty flight are hieing home;
T the lee of safer haven
All the storm-tossed vessels come.

"Ah! I know he laughs at danger,
Dares again the frequent venture,
Lured by an almighty power;
For he swore it when we parted,
With the vow which binds true-hearted
Lovers to the latest hour.
Yes! Even as this moment hastens
Battles he the wave-crests rude,
And to their unfathomed chasms
Dags him down the angry flood.

"Pontus false! Thy sunny smile
Was the lying traitor's guile,
Like a mirror flashing there:
All thy ripples gently playing
Til they triumphed in betraying
Him into thy lying snare.
Now in thy mid-current yonder,
Onward still his course he urges,
Thou the false, on him the fated
Pouring loose thy terror-surges.
Waxes high the tempest's danger,
Waves to mountains rise in anger,
Oceans swell, and breakers dash,
Foaming, over cliffs of rock
Where even navies, stiff with oak,
Could not bear the crash.
In the gale her torch is blasted,
Beacon of the hoped-for strand;
Horror broods above the waters,
Horror broods above the land.

Prays she Venus to assuage
The hurricane's increasing rage,
And to sooth the billows' scorn.
And as gale on gale arises,
Vows to each as sacrifices
Spotless steer with gilded horn.
To all the goddesses below,
To "all the gods in heaven that be,"

Figure 12: "Hero Holding the Beacon for Leander" by Evelyn De Morgan

She prays that oil of peace may flow
Softly on the storm-tossed sea.

Blest Leucothea, befriend me!
From cerulean halls attend me;
Hear my prayer of agony.
In the ocean desert's raving,
Storm-tossed seamen, succor craving,
Find in thee their helper nigh.
Wrap him in thy charmed veil,
Secret spun and secret wove,
Certain from the deepest wave
To lift him to its crests above."

Now the tempests wild are sleeping,
And from the horizon creeping
Rays of morning streak the skies,
Peaceful as it lay before
The placid sea reflects the shore,
Skies kiss waves and waves the skies.
Little ripples, lightly plashing,
Break upon the rock-bound strand,
And they trickle, lightly playing
O'er a corpse upon the sand.

Yes, 'tis he! Although he perished,
Still his sacred troth he cherished,
An instant's glance tells all to her;
Not a tear her eye lets slip
Not a murmur leaves her lip;
Down she looks in cold despair;
Gazes round the desert sea,
Trustless gazes round the sky,
Flashes then of noble fire
Through her pallid visage fly!

"Yes, I know, ye mighty powers,
Ye have drawn the fated hours
Pitiless and cruel on.
Early full my course is over.
Such a course with such a lover;
Such a share of joy I've known.
Venus, queen, within thy temple,
Thou hast known me vowed as thine,
Now accept thy willing priestess
As an offering at thy shrine."

Downward then, while all in vain her
Fluttering robes would still sustain her,
Springs she into Pontus' wave;
Grasping him and her, the god
Whirls them in his deepest flood,
And, himself, becomes their grave.
With his prizes then contented,
Peaceful bids his waters glide,
From the unexhausted vessels,
Whence there streams an endless tide.

Chapter 9

MINERVA AND ARACHNE. NIOBE. THE STORY OF PERSEUS

Minerva, the goddess of wisdom, was the daughter of Jupiter. She, they say, sprang forth from his brain full grown and clad in complete armor. She presided over the useful and ornamental arts, both those of men, such as agriculture and navigation, and those of women, spinning, weaving, and needle-work. She was also a warlike divinity; but a lover of defensive war only. She had no sympathy with Mars's savage love of violence and bloodshed. Athens was her chosen seat, her own city, awarded to her as the prize of a contest with Neptune, who also aspired to it. The tale ran that in the reign of Cecrops, the first king of Athens, the two deities contended for the possession of the city. The gods decreed that it should be awarded to that one who produced the gift most useful to mortals. Neptune gave the horse; Minerva produced the olive. The gods gave judgment that the olive was the more useful of the two, and awarded the city to the goddess; and it was named after her, Athens, her name in Greek being Athene.

In another contest, a mortal dared to come in competition with Minerva. That mortal was Arachne, a maiden who had attained such skill in the arts of weaving and embroidery that the nymphs themselves would leave their groves and fountains to come and gaze upon her work. It was not only beautiful when it was done, but beautiful also in the doing. To watch her, as she took the wool in its rude state and formed it into rolls, or separated it with her fingers and carded it till it looked as light and soft as a cloud, or twirled the spindle with skilful touch, or wove the web, or, when woven, adorned it with her needle, one would have said that Minerva herself had taught her. But this she denied, and could not bear to be thought a pupil even of a goddess. "Let Minerva try her skill with mine," said she; "if beaten, I will pay the penalty." Minerva heard this and was displeased. Assuming the form of an old woman, she went and gave Arachne some friendly advice. "I have had much experience,: said she, "and I hope you will not despise my counsel. Challenge your fellow-mortals as you will, but do not compete with a goddess. On the contrary, I advise you to ask her forgiveness for what you have said, and, as she is merciful, perhaps she will pardon you." Arachne stopped her spinning, and looked at the old dame with anger in her countenance. "Keep your counsel," said she, "for your daughters or handmaids; for my part, I know what I say, and I stand to it. I am not afraid of the goddess; let her try her skill, if she dare venture." "She comes," said Minerva; and dropping her disguise, stood confessed. The nymphs bent low in homage, and all the bystanders paid reverence. Arachne alone was unterrified. She blushed, indeed; a sudden color dyed her cheek, and then she grew pale. But she stood to her resolve, and with a foolish conceit of her own skill rushed on her fate. Minerva forbore no longer, nor interposed any further advice. They proceed to the contest. Each takes her station and attaches the web to the beam. Then the slender shuttle is passed in and out among the threads. The reed with its fine teeth strikes up the woof into its place and compacts the web. Both work with speed; their skilful hands move rapidly, and the excitement of the contest makes the labor light. Wool of Tyrian dye is contrasted with that of other colors, shaded off into one another so adroitly that the joining deceives the eye. Like the bow, whose long arch tinges the heavens, formed by sunbeams reflected from the shower (this description of the rainbow is literally translated rom Ovid), in which, where the colors meet they seem as one, but at a little distance from the point of contact are wholly different.

Minerva wrought on her web the scene of her contest with Neptune. Twelve of the heavenly powers are represented, Jupiter, with August gravity, sitting in the midst. Neptune, the ruler of the sea, holds his trident, and appears to have just smitten the earth, from which a horse has leaped forth. Minerva depicted herself with helmed head, her Ægis covering her breast. Such was the central circle; and in the four corners were represented incidents illustrating the displeasure of the gods at such presumptuous mortals as had dared to contend with them. These were meant as warnings to her rival to give up the contest before it was too late.

Arachne filled her web with subjects designedly chosen to exhibit the failings and errors of the gods. One scene represented Leda caressing the swan, under which form Jupiter had disguised himself; and another, Danae, in the brazen tower in which her father had imprisoned her, but where the god effected his entrance in the form of a shower of gold. Still another depicted Europa deceived by Jupiter under the disguise of a bull. Encouraged by the tameness of the animal, Europa ventured to mount his back, whereupon Jupiter advanced into the sea, and swam with her to Crete. You would have thought it was a real bull so naturally was it wrought, and so natural was the water in which it swam. She seemed to look with longing eyes back upon the shore she was leaving, and to call to her companions for help. She appeared to shudder with terror at the sight of the heaving waves, and to draw back her feet from the water.

Arachne filled her canvas with these and like subjects, wonderfully well done, but strongly marking her presumption and impiety. Minerva could not forbear to admire, yet felt indignant at the insult. She struck the web with her shuttle, and rent it in pieces; she then touched the forehead of Arachne, and made her feel her guilt and shame. She could not endure it, and went and hanged herself. Minerva pitied her as she saw her hanging by a rope. "Live, guilty woman," said she; " and that you may preserve the memory of this lesson, continue to hang, you and your descendants, to all future times." She sprinkled her with the juices of aconite, and immediately her hair came off, and her nose and ears likewise. Her form shrank up, and her head grew smaller yet; her fingers grew to her side, and served for legs. All the rest of her is body, out of which she spins her thread, often hanging suspended by it, in the same attitude as when Minerva touched her and transformed her into a spider.

Spenser tells the story of Arachne in his Muiopotmos, adhering very closely to his master Ovid, but improving upon him in the conclusion of the story. The two stanzas which follow tell what was done after the goddess had depicted her creation of the olive tree:

"Amongst these leaves she made a Butterfly,
With excellent device and wondrous slight,
Fluttering among the olives wantonly,
That seemed to live, so like it was in sight;
The velvet nap which on his wings doth lie,
The silken down with which his back is dight,
His broad outstretched horns, his hairy thighs,
His glorious colors, and his glistening eyes."

"Which when Arachne saw, as overlaid
And mastered with workmanship so rare.
She stood astonished long, ne aught gainsaid;
And with fast-fixed eyes on her did stare,
And by her silence, sign of one dismayed,
The victory did yield her as her share;
Yet did she inly fret and felly burn,
And all her blood to poisonous rancor turn."

And so the metamorphosis is caused by Arachne's own mortification and vexation, and not by any direct act of the goddess.

The following specimen of old-fashioned gallantry is by Garrick:

UPON A LADY'S EMBROIDERY
"Arachne once, as poets tell,
A goddess at her art defied,
And soon the daring mortal fell
The hapless victim of her pride.

"Oh, then, beware Arachne's fate;
Be prudent, Chloe, and submit,
For you'll most surely meet her hate,
Who rival both her art and wit."

Tennyson, in his Palace of Art, describing the works of art with which the palace was adorned, thus alludes to Europa:

"—— sweet Europa's mantle blew unclasped
From off her shoulder, backward borne,
From one hand drooped a crocus, one hand grasped
The mild bull's golden horn."

In his Princess there is this allusion to Danae:

"Now lies the earth all Danae to the stars,
And all thy heart lies open unto me."

NIOBE

The fate of Arachne was noised abroad through all the country, and served as a warning to all presumptuous mortals not to compare themselves with the divinities. But one, and she a matron too, failed to learn the lesson of humility. It was Niobe, the queen of Thebes. She had indeed much to be proud of; but it was not her husband's fame, nor her own beauty, nor their great descent, nor the power of their kingdom that elated her. It was her children; and truly the happiest of mothers would Niobe have been, if only she had not claimed to be so. It was on occasion of the annual celebration in honor of Latona and her offspring, Apollo and Diana, when the people of Thebes were assembled, their brows crowned with laurel, bearing frankincense to the altars and paying their vows, that Niobe appeared among the crowd. Her attire was splendid with gold and gems, and her face as beautiful as the face of an angry woman can be. She stood and surveyed the people with haughty looks. "What folly," said she, "is this! to prefer beings whom you never saw to those who stand before your eyes! Why should Latona be honored with worship rather than I? My father was Tantalus, who was received as a guest at the table of the gods; my mother was a goddess. My husband built and rules this city, Thebes; and Phrygia is my paternal inheritance. Wherever I turn my eyes I survey the elements of my power; nor is my form and presence unworthy of a goddess. To all this let me add, I have seven sons and seven daughters, and look for sons-in-law and daughters-in- law of pretensions worthy of my alliance. Have I not cause for pride? Will you prefer to me this Latona, the Titan's daughter, with her two children? I have seven times as many. Fortunate indeed am I, and fortunate I shall remain! Will any one deny this? My abundance is my security. I feel myself too strong for Fortune to subdue. She may take from me much; I shall still have much left. Were I to lose some of my children, I should hardly be left as poor as Latona with her two only. Away with you from these solemnities, put off the laurel from your brows, have done with this worship!" The people obeyed, and left the sacred services uncompleted.

The goddess was indignant. On top of Mount Cynthus where she dwelt, she thus addressed her son and daughter: "My children, I who have been so proud of you both, and have been used to hold myself second to none of the goddesses except Juno alone, begin now to doubt whether I am indeed a goddess. I shall be deprived of my worship altogether unless you protect me." She was proceeding in this strain, but Apollo interrupted her. "Say no more," said he; "speech only delays punishment." So said Diana also. Darting through the air, veiled in clouds, they alighted on the towers of the city. Spread out before the gates was a broad plain, where the youth of the city pursued their warlike sports. The sons of Niobe were there among the rest, some mounted on spirited horses richly caparisoned, some driving gay chariots. Ismenos, the first-born, as he guided his foaming steeds, struck with an arrow from above, cried out, "Ah, me!" dropped the reins and fell lifeless. Another, hearing the sound of the bow, like a boatman who sees the storm gathering and makes all sail for the port, gave the rein to his horses and attempted to escape. The inevitable arrow overtook him as he fled. Two others, younger boys, just from their tasks, had gone to the playground to have a game of wrestling. As they stood breast to breast, one arrow pierced them both. They uttered a cry together, together cast a parting look around them, and together breathed their last. Alphenor, an elder brother, seeing them fall, hastened to the spot to render them assistance, and fell stricken in the act of brotherly duty. One only was left, Ilioneus. He raised his arms to heaven to try whether prayer might not avail. "Spare me, ye gods!" he cried, addressing all, in his ignorance that all needed not his intercession; and Apollo would have spared him, but the arrow had already left the string, and it was too late.

The terror of the people and grief of the attendants soon made Niobe acquainted with what had taken place. She could hardly think it possible; she was indignant that the gods had dared and amazed that they had been able to do it. Her husband, Amphion, overwhelmed with the blow, destroyed himself. Alas! How different was this Niobe from her who had so lately driven away the people from the sacred rites, and held her stately course through the city, the envy of her friends, now the pity even of her foes! She knelt over the lifeless bodies, and kissed, now one, now another of her dead sons. Raising her pallid arms to heaven, "Cruel Latona," said she, "feed full your rage with my anguish! Satiate your hard heart, while I follow to the grave my seven sons. Yet where is your triumph? Bereaved as I am, I am still richer than you, my conqueror. Scarce had she spoken when the bow sounded and struck terror into all hearts except Niobe's alone. She was brave from excess of grief. The sisters stood in garments of mourning over the biers of their dead brothers. One fell, struck by an arrow, and died on the corpse she was bewailing. Another, attempting to console her mother, suddenly ceased to speak, and sank lifeless to the earth. A third tried to escape by flight, a fourth by concealment, another stood trembling, uncertain what course to take. Six were now dead, and only one remained, whom the mother held clasped in her arms, and covered as it were with her whole body.

"Spare me one, and that the youngest! Oh, spare me one of so many?!" she cried; and while she spoke, that one fell dead. Desolate she sat, among sons, daughters, husband, all dead, and seemed torpid with grief. The breeze moved not her hair, nor color was on her cheek, her eyes glared fixed and immovable, there was no sign of life about her. Her very tongue clave to the roof of her mouth, and her veins ceased to convey the tide of life. Her neck bent not, her arms made no gesture, her foot no step. She was changed to stone, within and without. Yet tears continued to flow; and, borne on a whirlwind to her native mountain, she still remains, a mass of rock, from which a trickling stream flows, the tribute of her never-ending grief.

The story of Niobe has furnished Byron with a fine illustration of the fallen condition of modern Rome:

"The Niobe of nations! There she stands,
Childless and crownless in her voiceless woe;
An empty urn within her withered hands,
Whose holy dust was scattered long ago;
The Scipios' tomb contains no ashes now;
The very sepulchres lie tenantless
Of their heroic dwellers; dost thou flow,
Old Tiber! Through a marble wilderness?
Rise with thy yellow waves, and mantle her distress."
Childe Harold, IV.79

The slaughter of the children of Niobe by Apollo, alludes to the Greek belief that pestilence and illness were sent by Apollo, and one dying by sickness was said to be struck by Apollo's arrow.

It is to this that Morris alludes in the Earthly Paradise:

"While from the freshness of his blue abode,
Glad his death-bearing arrows to forget,
The broad sun blazed, nor scattered plagues as yet."

Our illustration of this story is a copy of a celebrated statue in the imperial gallery of Florence. It is the principal figure of a group supposed to have been originally arranged in the pediment of a temple. The figure of the mother clasped by the arm of her terrified child, is one of the most admired of the ancient statues. It ranks with the Laocoon and the Apollo among the masterpieces of art. The following is a translation of a Greek epigram supposed to relate to this statue:

"To stone the gods have changed her, but in vain;
The sculptor's art has made her breathe again."
Tragic as is the story of Niobe we cannot forbear to smile at the use Moore has made of it in Rhymes on the Road:
"'Twas in his carriage the sublime
Sir Richard Blackmore used to rhyme,
And, if the wits don't do him wrong,
'Twixt death and epics passed his time,
Scribbling and killing all day long;
Like Phoebus in his car at ease,
Now warbling forth a lofty song,
Now murdering the young Niobes."

Sir Richard Blackmore was a physician, and at the same time a very prolific and very tasteless poet, whose works are now forgotten, unless when recalled to mind by some wit like Moore for the sake of a joke.

THE GRAEAE AND GORGONS

The Graeae were three sisters who were gray-haired from their birth, whence their name. The Gorgons were monstrous females with huge teeth like those of swine, brazen claws, and snaky hair. They also were three in number, two of them immortal, but the other, Medusa, mortal. None of these beings make much figure in mythology except Medusa, the Gorgon, whose story we shall next advert to. We mention them chiefly to introduce an ingenious theory of some modern writers, namely, that the Gorgons and Graeae were only personifications of the terrors of the sea, the former denoting the STRONG billows of the wide open main, and the latter the WHITE-crested waves that dash against the rocks of the coast. Their names in Greek signify the above epithets.

PERSEUS AND MEDUSA

Acrisius was the king who ruled in Argos. To him had an oracle declared that he should be slain by the child of his daughter Danae. Therefore the cruel king, thinking it better that Danae should have no children than that he should be slain, ordered a tower of brass to be made, and in this tower he confined his daughter away from all men.

But who can withstand Jupiter? He saw Danae, loved her, and changing his form to a shower of gold, he shone into the apartment of the captive girl.

Perseus was the child of Jupiter and Danae. Acrisius, finding that his precautions had come to nought, and yet hardly daring to kill his own daughter and her young child, placed them both in a chest and sent the chest floating on the sea. It floated away and was finally entangled in the net of Dicte, a fisherman in the island of Seriphus. He brought them to his house and treated them kindly, and in the house of Dicte, Perseus grew up. When Perseus was grown up, Polydectes, king of that country, wishing to send Perseus to his death, bade him go in quest of the head of Medusa. Medusa had once been a beautiful maiden, whose hair was her chief glory, but as she dared to vie in beauty with Minerva, the goddess deprived her of her charms and changed her beautiful ringlets into hissing serpents. She became a cruel monster of so frightful an aspect that no living thing could behold her without being turned into stone. All around the cavern where she dwelt might be seen the stony figures of men and beasts which had chanced to catch a glimpse of her and had been petrified with the sight. Minerva and Mercury aided Perseus. From Minerva, Perseus borrowed her shield, and from Mercury the winged shoes and the harpe or crooked sword. After having flown all over the earth Perseus espied in the bright shield the image of Medusa and her two immortal sisters. Flying down carefully he cut at her with his harpe and severed her head. Putting the trophy in his pouch he flew away just as the two immortal sisters were awakened by the hissings of their snaky locks.

PERSEUS AND ATLAS

After the slaughter of Medusa, Perseus, bearing with him the head of the Gorgon, flew far and wide, over land and sea. As night came on, he reached the western limit of the earth, where the sun goes down. Here he would gladly have rested till morning. It was the realm of King Atlas, whose bulk surpassed that of all other men. He was rich in flocks and herds and had no neighbor or rival to dispute his state. But his chief pride was in his gardens, whose fruit was of gold, hanging from golden branches, half hid with golden leaves. Perseus said to him, "I come as a guest. If you honor illustrious descent, I claim Jupiter for my father; if mighty deeds, I plead the conquest of the Gorgon. I seek rest and food." But Atlas remembered that an ancient prophecy had warned him that a son of Jove should one day rob him of his golden apples. So he answered, "Begone! Or neither your false claims of glory nor of parentage shall protect you;" and he attempted to thrust him out. Perseus, finding the giant too strong for him, said, "Since you value my friendship so little, deign to accept a present;" and turning his face away, he held up the Gorgon's head. Atlas, with all his bulk, was changed into stone. His beard and hair became forests, his arms and shoulders cliffs, his head a summit, and his bones rocks. Each part increased in bulk till he became a mountain, and (such was the pleasure of the gods) heaven with all its stars rests upon his shoulders.

And all in vain was Atlas turned to a mountain, for the oracle did not mean Perseus, but the hero Hercules, who should come long afterwards to get the golden apples for his cousin Eurystheus.

Perseus, continuing his flight, arrived at the country of the Æthiopians, of which Cepheus was king. Cassiopeia, his queen, proud of her beauty, had dared to compare herself to the Sea- Nymphs, which roused their indignation to such a degree that they sent a prodigious sea-monster to ravage the coast. To appease the deities, Cepheus was directed by the oracle to expose his daughter Andromeda to be devoured by the monster. As Perseus looked down from his aerial height he beheld the virgin chained to a rock, and waiting the approach of the serpent. She was so pale and motionless that if it had not been for her flowing tears and her hair that moved in the breeze, he

Figure 13: "Atlas Turned to Stone" by Edward Burne-Jones

would have taken her for a marble statue. He was so startled at the sight that he almost forgot to wave his wings. As he hovered over her he said, "O virgin, undeserving of those chains, but rather of such as bind fond lovers together, tell me, I beseech you, your name and the name of your country, and why you are thus bound." At first she was silent from modesty, and, if she could, would have hid her face with her hands; but when he repeated his questions, for fear she might be thought guilty of some fault which she dared not tell, she disclosed her name and that of her country, and her mother's pride of beauty. Before she had done speaking, a sound was heard off upon the water, and the sea-monster appeared, with his head raised above the surface, cleaving the waves with his broad breast. The virgin shrieked, the father and mother who had now arrived at the scene, wretched both, but the mother more justly so, stood by, not able to afford protection, but only to pour forth lamentations and to embrace the victim. Then spoke Perseus: "There will be time enough for tears; this hour is all we have for rescue. My rank as the son of Jove and my renown as the slayer of the Gorgon might make me acceptable as a suitor; but I will try to win her by services rendered, if the gods will only be propitious. If she be rescued by my valor, I demand that she be my reward." The parents' consent (how could they hesitate?) And promise a royal dowry with her.

And now the monster was within the range of a stone thrown by a skillful slinger, when with a sudden bound the youth soared into the air. As an eagle, when from his lofty flight he sees a serpent basking in the sun, pounces upon him and seizes him by the neck to prevent him from turning his head round and using his fangs, so the youth darted down upon the back of the monster and plunged his sword into its shoulder. Irritated by the wound the monster raised himself into the air, then plunged into the depth; then, like a wild boar surrounded by a pack of barking dogs, turned swiftly from side to side, while the youth eluded its attacks by means of his wings. Wherever he can find a passage for his sword between the scales he makes a wound, piercing now the side, now the flank, as it slopes towards the tail. The brute spouts from his nostrils water mixed with blood. The wings of the hero are wet with it, and he dares no longer trust to them. Alighting on a rock which rose above the waves, and holding on by a projecting fragment, as the monster floated near he gave him a death-stroke. The people who had gathered on the shore shouted so that the hills re-echoed to the sound. The parents, transported with joy, embraced their future son-in-law, calling him their deliverer and the savior of their house, and the virgin, both cause and reward of the contest, descended from the rock.

Cassiopeia was an Aethiopian, and consequently, in spite of her boasted beauty, black; at least so Milton seems to have thought, who alludes to this story in his Penseroso, where he addresses Melancholy as the:

"—— goddess, sage and holy,
Whose saintly visage is too bright
To hit the sense of human sight,
And, therefore, to our weaker view
O'erlaid with black, staid Wisdom's hue.
Black, but such as in esteem
Prince Memnon's sister might beseem,
Or that starred Aethiop queen that strove
To set her beauty's praise above
The Sea-nymphs, and their powers offended."

Cassiopeia is called "the starred Aethiop queen," because after her death she was placed among the stars, forming the constellation of that name. Though she attained this honor, yet the Sea-Nymphs, her old enemies, prevailed so far as to cause her to be placed in that part of the heaven near the pole, where every night she is half the time held with her head downward, to give her a lesson of humility.

"Prince Memnon" was the son of Aurora and Tithonus, of whom we shall hear later.

THE WEDDING FEAST

The joyful parents, with Perseus and Andromeda, repaired to the palace, where a banquet was spread for them, and all was joy and festivity. But suddenly a noise was heard of war-like clamor, and Phineus, the betrothed of the virgin, with a party of his adherents, burst in, demanding the maiden as his own. It was in vain that Cepheus remonstrated, "You should have claimed her when she lay bound to the rock, the monster's victim. The sentence of the gods dooming her to such a fate dissolved all engagements, as death itself would have done.:" Phineus made no reply, but hurled his javelin at Perseus, but it missed its mark and fell harmless. Perseus would have thrown his in turn, but the cowardly assailant ran and took shelter behind the altar. But his act was a signal for an onset by his band upon the guests of Cepheus. They defended themselves and a general conflict ensued, the old king retreating from the scene after fruitless expostulations, calling the gods to witness that he was guiltless of this outrage on the rights of hospitality.

Perseus and his friends maintained for some time the unequal contest; but the numbers of the assailants were too great for them, and destruction seemed inevitable, when a sudden thought struck Perseus: "I will make my enemy defend me." Then, with a loud voice he exclaimed, :If I have any friend here let him turn away his eyes!" and held aloft the Gorgon's head. "Seek not to frighten us with your jugglery," said Thescelus, and raised his javelin in act to throw, and became stone in the very attitude. Ampyx was about to plunge his sword into the body of a prostrate foe, but his arm stiffened and he could neither thrust forward nor withdraw it. Another, in the midst of a vociferous challenge, stopped, his mouth open, but no sound issuing. One of Perseus's friends, Aconteus, caught sight of the Gorgon and stiffened like the rest. Astyages struck him with his sword, but instead of wounding, it recoiled with a ringing noise.

Phineus beheld this dreadful result of his unjust aggression, and felt confounded. He called aloud to his friends, but got no answer; he touched them and found them stone. Falling on his knees and stretching out his hands to Perseus, but turning his head away, he begged for mercy. "Take all," said he, "give me but my life." "Base coward," said Perseus, "thus much I will grant you; no weapon shall touch you; moreover you shall be preserved in my house as a memorial of these events." So saying, he held the Gorgon's head to the side where Phineus was looking, and in the very form in which he knelt, with his hands outstretched and face averted, he became fixed immovably, a mass of stone!

The following allusion to Perseus is from Milman's Samor:

"As 'mid the fabled Libyan bridal stood
Perseus in stern tranquillity of wrath,
Half stood, half floated on his ankle-plumes
Out-swelling, while the bright face on his shield
Looked into stone the raging fray; so rose,
But with no magic arms, wearing alone
Th' appalling and control of his firm look,
The Briton Samor; at his rising awe
Went abroad, and the riotous hall was mute."

Then Perseus returned to Seriphus to King Polydectes and to his mother Danae and the fisherman Dicte. He marched up the tyrant's hall, where Polydectes and his guests were feasting. "Have you the head of Medusa?" exclaimed Polydectes. "Here it is," answered Perseus, and showed it to the king and to his guests.

The ancient prophecy which Acrisius had so much feared at last came to pass. For, as Perseus was passing through the country of Larissa, he entered into competition with the youths of the country at the game of hurling the discus. King Acrisius was among the spectators. The youths of Larissa threw first, and then Perseus. His discus went far beyond the others, and, seized by a breeze from the sea, fell upon the foot of Acrisius. The old king swooned with pain, and was carried away from the place only to die. Perseus, who had heard the story of his birth and parentage from Danae, when he learned who Acrisius was, filled with remorse and sorrow, went to the oracle at Delphi, and there was purified from the guilt of homicide.

Perseus gave the head of Medusa to Minerva, who had aided him so well to obtain it. Minerva took the head of her once beautiful rival and placed it in the middle of her Aegis.

Milton, in his Comus, thus alludes to the Aegis:

"What was that snaky-headed Gorgon-shield
That wise Minerva wore, unconquered virgin,
Wherewith she freezed her foes to congealed stone,
But rigid looks of chaste austerity,
And noble grace that dashed brute violence
With sudden adoration and blank awe!"

Armstrong, the poet of the Art of Preserving Health, thus describes the effect of frost upon the waters:

"Now blows the surly North and chills throughout
the stiffening regions, while by stronger charms
Than Circe e'er or fell Medea brewed,
Each brook that wont to prattle to its banks
Lies all bestilled and wedged betwixt its banks,
Nor moves the withered reeds. . . .
The surges baited by the fierce Northeast,
Tossing with fretful spleen their angry heads,
E'en in the foam of all their madness struck
To monumental ice.

* * * * *

Such execution,
So stern, so sudden, wrought the grisly aspect
Of terrible Medusa,
When wandering through the woods she turned to stone
Their savage tenants; just as the foaming lion
Sprang furious on his prey, her speedier power
Outran his haste,
And fixed in that fierce attitude he stands
Like Rage in marble!"
Imitations of Shakespeare

Of Atlas there is another story, which I like better than the one told. He was one of the Titans who warred against Jupiter like Typhoeus, Briareus, and others. After their defeat by the king of gods and men, Atlas was condemned to stand in the far western part of the earth, by the Pillars of Hercules, and to hold on his shoulders the weight of heaven and the stars.

The story runs that Perseus, flying by, asked and obtained rest and food. The next morning he asked what he could do to reward Atlas for his kindness. The best that giant could think of was that Perseus should show him the snaky head of Medusa, that he might be turned to stone and be at rest from his heavy load.

Chapter 10

MONSTERS. GIANTS. SPHINX. PEGASUS AND THE CHIMAERA. CENTAURS. GRIFFIN. PYGMIES

Monsters, in the language of mythology, were beings of unnatural proportions or parts, usually regarded with terror, as possessing immense strength and ferocity, which they employed for the injury and annoyance of men. Some of them were supposed to combine the members of different animals; such were the Sphinx and the Chimaera; and to these all the terrible qualities of wild beasts were attributed, together with human sagacity and faculties. Others, as the giants, differed from men chiefly in their size; and in this particular we must recognize a wide distinction among them. The human giants, if so they may be called, such as the Cyclopes, Antaeus, Orion, and others, must be supposed not to be altogether disproportioned to human beings, for they mingled in love and strife with them. But the superhuman giants, who warred with the gods, were of vastly larger dimensions. Tityus, we are told, when stretched on the plain, covered nine acres, and Enceladus required the whole of Mount Ætna to be laid upon him to keep him down.

Figure 14: "Saw Storks" by William Heath Robinson

We have already spoken of the war which the giants waged against the gods, and of its result. While this war lasted the giants proved a formidable enemy. Some of them, like Briareus, had a hundred arms; others, like Typhon, breathed out fire. At one time they put the gods to such fear that they fled into Egypt, and hid themselves under various forms. Jupiter took the form of a ram, whence he was afterwards worshipped in Egypt as the god Ammon, with curved horns. Apollo became a crow, Bacchus a goat, Diana a cat, Juno a cow, Venus a fish, Mercury a bird. At another time the giants attempted to climb up into heaven, and for that purpose took up the mountain Ossa and piled it on Pelion. They were at last subdued by thunderbolts, which Minerva invented, and taught Vulcan and his Cyclopes to make for Jupiter.

THE SPHINX

Laius, king of Thebes, was warned by an oracle that there was danger to his throne and life if his new-born son should be suffered to grow up. He therefore committed the child to the care of a herdsman, with orders to destroy him; but the herdsman, moved to pity, yet not daring entirely to disobey, tied up the child by the feet, and left him hanging to the branch of a tree. Here the infant was found by a herdsman of Polybus, king of Corinth, who was pasturing his flock upon Mount Cithaeron. Polybus and Merope, his wife, adopted the child, whom they called Œdipus, or Swollen-foot, for they had no children themselves, and in Corinth Œdipus grew up. But as Œdipus was at Delphi, the oracle prophesied to him that he should kill his father and marry his own mother. Fighting against Fate, Œdipus resolved to leave Corinth and his parents, for he thought that Polybus and Merope were meant by the oracle.

Soon afterwards, Laius being on his way to Delphi, accompanied only by one attendant, met in a narrow road a young man also driving in a chariot. On his refusal to leave the way at their command, the attendant killed one of his horses, and the stranger, filled with rage, slew both Laius and his attendant. The young man was Œdipus, who thus unknowingly became the slayer of his own father.

Shortly after this event the city of Thebes was afflicted with a monster which infested the high-road. It was called the Sphinx. It had the body of a lion, and the upper part of a woman. It lay crouched on the top of a rock, and stopped all travellers who came that way, proposing to them a riddle, with the condition that those who could solve it should pass safe, but those who failed should be killed. Not one had yet succeeded in solving it, and all had been slain. Œdipus was not daunted by these alarming accounts, but boldly advanced to the trial. The Sphinx asked him, "What animal is that which in the morning goes on four feet, at noon on two, and in the evening upon three?" Œdipus replied, "Man, who in childhood creeps on hands and knees, in manhood walks erect, and in old age with the aid of a staff." The Sphinx was so mortified at the solving of her riddle that she cast herself down from the rock and perished.

The gratitude of the people for their deliverance was so great that they made Œdipus their king, giving him in marriage their queen Jocasta. Œdipus, ignorant of his parentage, had already become the slayer of his father; in marrying the queen he became the husband of his mother. These horrors remained undiscovered, till at length Thebes was afflicted with famine and pestilence, and the oracle being consulted, the double crime of Œdipus came to light. Jocasta put an end to her own life, and Œdipus, seized with madness, tore out his eyes, and wandered away from Thebes, dreaded and abandoned by all except his daughters, who faithfully adhered to him; till after a tedious period of miserable wandering, he found the termination of his wretched life.

PEGASUS AND THE CHIMAERA, OR CHIMERA

When Perseus cut off Medusa's head, the blood sinking into the earth produced the winged horse Pegasus. Minerva caught and tamed him, and presented him to the Muses. The fountain Hippocrene, on the Muses' mountain Helicon, was opened by a kick from his hoof.

The Chimaera was a fearful monster, breathing fire. The fore part of its body was a compound of the lion and the goat, and the hind part a dragon's. It made great havoc in Lycia, so that the king Iobates sought for some hero to destroy it. At that time there arrived at his court a gallant young warrior, whose name was Bellerophon. He brought letters from Proetus, the son-in-law of Iobates, recommending Bellerophon in the warmest terms as an unconquerable hero, but added at the close a request to his father-in-law to put him to death. The reason was that Proetus was jealous of him, suspecting that his wife Antea looked with too much admiration on the young warrior. From this instance of Bellerophon being unconsciously the bearer of his own death- warrant, the expression "Bellerophontic letters" arose, to describe any species of communication which a person is made the bearer of, containing matter prejudicial to himself.

Iobates, on perusing the letters, was puzzled what to do, not willing to violate the claims of hospitality, yet wishing to oblige his son-in-law. A lucky thought occurred to him, to send Bellerophon to combat with the Chimaera. Bellerophon accepted the proposal, but before proceeding to the combat consulted the soothsayer Polyidus, who advised him to procure if possible the horse Pegasus for the conflict. For this purpose he directed him to pass the night in the temple of Minerva. He did so, and as he slept Minerva came to him and gave him a golden bridle. When he awoke the bridle remained in his hand. Minerva also showed him Pegasus drinking at the well of Pirene, and at sight of the bridle, the winged steed came willingly and suffered himself to be taken. Bellerophon mounting, rose with him into the air, and soon found the Chimaera, and gained an easy victory over the monster.

After the conquest of the Chimaera, Bellerophon was exposed to further trials and labors by his unfriendly host, but by the aid of Pegasus he triumphed in them all; till at length Iobates, seeing that the hero was a special favorite of the gods, gave him his daughter in marriage and made him his successor on the throne. At last Bellerophon by his pride and presumption drew upon himself the anger of the gods; it is said he even attempted to fly up into heaven on his winged steed; but Jupiter sent a gadfly which stung Pegasus and made him throw his rider, who became lame and blind in consequence. After this Bellerophon wandered lonely through the Aleian field, avoiding the paths of men, and died miserably.

Figure 15: "A Great Black Horse at Once Appeared" by Percy J. Billinghurst

Milton alludes to Bellerophon in the beginning of the seventh book of Paradise Lost:

"Descend from Heaven, Urania, by that name
If rightly thou art called, whose voice divine
Following above the Olympian hill I soar,
Above the flight of Pegasean wing,
Up-led by thee,
Into the Heaven of Heavens I have presumed,
An earthly guest, and drawn empyreal air,
(Thy tempering;) with like safety guided down
Return me to my native element;
Lest from this flying steed unreined, (as once
Bellerophon, though from a lower sphere,)
Dismounted on the Aleian field I fall,
Erroneous there to wander, and forlorn."

Young in his Night Thoughts, speaking of the skeptic, says,

"He whose blind thought futurity denies,
Unconscious bears, Bellerophon, like thee
His own indictment; he condemns himself,
Who reads his bosom reads immortal life,
Or nature there, imposing on her sons,
Has written fables; man was made a lie."
Vol. II.1,12.

Pegasus, being the horse of the Muses, has always been at the service of the poets. Schiller tells a pretty story of his having been sold by a needy poet, and put to the cart and the plough. He was not fit for such service, and his clownish master could make nothing of him. But a youth stepped forth and asked leave to try him. As soon as he was seated on his back, the horse, which had appeared at first vicious, and afterwards spirit-broken, rose kingly, a spirit, a god; unfolded the splendor of his wings and soared towards heaven. Our own poet Longfellow also records an adventure of this famous steed in his Pegasus in Pound.

Shakespeare alludes to Pegasus in Henry IV, where Vernon describes Prince Henry:

"I saw young Harry, with his beaver on,
His cuishes on his thighs, gallantly armed,
Rise from the ground like feathered Mercury,
And vaulted with such ease into his seat,
As if an angel dropped down from the clouds,
To turn and wind a fiery Pegasus,
And witch the world with noble horsemanship."

THE CENTAURS

The Greeks loved to people their woods and hills with strange wild people, half man, half beast. Such were the Satyrs men with goats' legs. But nobler and better were the Centaurs, men to the waist, while the rest was the form of a horse. The ancients were too fond of a horse to consider the union of his nature with man's as forming any very degraded compound, and accordingly the Centaur is the only one of the fancied monsters of antiquity to which any good traits are assigned. The Centaurs were admitted to the companionship of man, and at the marriage of Pirithous with Hippodamia, they were among the guests.

At the feast, Eurytion, one of the Centaurs, becoming intoxicated with the wine, attempted to offer violence to the bride; the other Centaurs followed his example, and a dreadful conflict arose in which several of them were slain. This is the celebrated battle of the Lapithae and Centaurs, a favorite subject with the sculptors and poets of antiquity.

But all the Centaurs were not like the rude guests of Pirithous. Chiron was instructed by Apollo and Diana, and was renowned for his skill in hunting, medicine, music, and the art of prophecy. The most distinguished heroes of Grecian story were his pupils. Among the rest the infant Aesculapius was intrusted to his charge, by Apollo, his father. When the sage returned to his home bearing the infant, his daughter Ocyroe came forth to meet him, and at sight of the child burst forth into a prophetic strain (for she was a prophetess), foretelling the glory that he was to achieve. Aesculapius, when grown up, became a renowned physician, and even in one instance succeeded in restoring the dead to life. Pluto resented this, and Jupiter, at his request, struck the bold physician with lightning and killed him, but after his death received him into the number of the gods.

Chiron was the wisest and justest of all the Centaurs, and at his death Jupiter placed him among the stars as the constellation Sagittarius.

THE PYGMIES

The Pygmies were a nation of dwarfs, so called from a Greek word which means the cubit (a cubit was a measure of about thirteen inches), which was said to be the height of these people. They lived near the sources of the Nile, or according to others, in India. Homer tells us that the cranes used to migrate every winter to the Pygmies' country, and their appearance was the signal of bloody warfare to the puny inhabitants, who had to take up arms to defend their cornfields against the rapacious strangers. The Pygmies and their enemies the cranes form the subject of several works of art.

Later writers tell of an army of Pygmies which finding Hercules asleep made preparations to attack him, as if they were about to attack a city. But the hero awaking laughed at the little warriors, wrapped some of them up in his lion's-skin, and carried them to Eurystheus.

Milton used the Pygmies for a simile, Paradise Lost, Book I:

"——like that Pygmaean race
Beyond the Indian mount, or fairy elves
Whose midnight revels by a forest side,
Or fountain, some belated peasant sees,
(Or dreams he sees), while overhead the moon
Sits artibress, and nearer to the earth
Wheels her pale course; they on their mirth and dance
Intent, with jocund music charm his ear.
At once with joy and fear his heart rebounds."

THE GRIFFIN, OR GRYPHON

The Griffin is a monster with the body of a lion, the head and wings of an eagle, and back covered with feathers. Like birds it builds its nest, and instead of an egg lays an agate therein. It has long claws and talons of such a size that the people of that country make them into drinking-cups. India was assigned as the native country of the Griffins. They found gold in the mountains and built their nests of it, for which reason their nests were very tempting to the hunters, and they were forced to keep vigilant guard over them. Their instinct led them to know where buried treasures lay, and they did their best to keep plunderers at a distance. The Arimaspians, among whom the Griffins flourished, were a one-eyed people of Scythia.

Milton borrows a simile from the Griffins, Paradise Lost, Book II.:

"As when a Gryphon through the wilderness,
With winged course, o'er hill and moory dale,
Pursues the Arimaspian who by stealth
Hath from his wakeful custody purloined
His guarded gold."

Chapter 11

THE GOLDEN FLEECE. MEDEA. THE CALYDONIAN HUNT

In very ancient times there lived in Thessaly a king and queen named Athamas and Nephele. They had two children, a boy and a girl. After a time Athamas grew indifferent to his wife, put her away, and took another. Nephele suspected danger to her children from the influence of the step-mother, and took measures to send them out of her reach. Mercury assisted her, and gave her a ram, with a GOLDEN FLEECE, on which she set the two children, trusting that the ram would convey them to a place of safety. The ram sprung into the air with the children on his back, taking his course to the east, till when crossing the strait that divides Europe and Asia, the girl, whose name was Helle, fell from his back into the sea, which from her was called the Hellespont, now the Dardanelles. The ram continued his career till he reached the kingdom of Colchis, on the eastern shore of the Black Sea, where he safely landed the boy Phyrxus, who was hospitably received by Æetes, the king of the country. Phryxus sacrificed the ram to Jupiter, and gave the golden fleece to Æetes, who placed it in a consecrated grove, under the care of a sleepless dragon.

There was another kingdom in Thessaly near to that of Athamas, and ruled over by a relative of his. The king Æson, being tired of the cares of government, surrendered his crown to his brother Pelias, on condition that he should hold it only during the minority of Jason, the son of Æson. When Jason was grown up and came to demand the crown from his uncle, Pelias pretended to be willing to yield it, but at the same time suggested to the young man the glorious adventure of going in quest of the golden fleece, which it was well known was in the kingdom of Colchis, and was, as Pelias pretended, the rightful property of their family. Jason was pleased with the thought, and forthwith made preparations for the expedition. At that time the only species of navigation known to the Greeks consisted of small boats or canoes hollowed out from trunks of trees, so that when Jason employed Argus to build him a vessel capable of containing fifty men, it was considered a gigantic undertaking. It was accomplished, however, and the vessel was named the Argo, from the name of the builder. Jason sent his invitation to all the adventurous young men of Greece, and soon found himself at the head of a band of bold youths, many of whom afterwards were renowned among the heroes and demigods of Greece. Hercules, Theseus, Orpheus, and Nestor were among them. They are called the Argonauts, from the name of their vessel.

The Argo with her crew of heroes left the shores of Thessaly and having touched at the Island of Lemnos, thence crossed to Mysia and thence to Thrace. Here they found the sage Phineus, and from him received instruction as to their future course. It seems the entrance of the Euxine Sea was impeded by two small rocky islands, which floated on the surface, and in their tossings and heavings occasionally came together, crushing and grinding to atoms any object that might be caught between them. They were called the Symplegades, or Clashing Islands. Phineus instructed the Argonauts how to pass this dangerous strait. When they reached the islands they let go a dove, which took her way between the rocks, and passed in safety, only losing some feathers of her tail. Jason and his men seized the favorable moment of the rebound, plied their oars with vigor, and passed safe through, though the islands closed behind them, and actually grazed their stern. They now rowed along the shore till they arrived at the eastern end of the sea, and landed at the kingdom of Colchis.

Jason made known his message to the Colchian king, Æetes, who consented to give up the golden fleece if Jason would yoke to the plough two fire-breathing bulls with brazen feet, and sow the teeth of the dragon, which Cadmus had slain, and from which it was well known that a crop of armed men would spring up, who would turn their weapons against their producer. Jason accepted the conditions, and a time was set for making the experiment. Previously, however, he found means to plead his cause to Medea, daughter of the king. He promised her marriage, and as they stood before the altar of Hecate, called the goddess to witness his oath. Medea yielded and by her aid, for she was a potent sorceress, he was furnished with a charm, by which he could encounter safely the breath of the fire-breathing bulls and the weapons of the armed men.

At the time appointed, the people assembled at the grove of Mars, and the king assumed his royal seat, while the multitude covered the hill-sides. The brazen-footed bulls rushed in, breathing fire from their nostrils, that burned up the herbage as they passed. The sound was like the roar of a furnace, and the smoke like that of water upon quick-lime. Jason advanced boldly to meet them. His friends, the chosen heroes of Greece, trembled to behold him. Regardless of the burning breath, he soothed their rage with his voice, patted their necks with fearless hands, and adroitly slipped over them the yoke, and compelled them to drag the plough. The Colchians were amazed; the Greeks shouted for joy. Jason next proceeded to sow the dragon's teeth and plough them in. And soon the crop of armed men sprang up, and wonderful to relate! no sooner had they reached the surface than they began to brandish their weapons and rush upon Jason. The Greeks trembled for their hero, and even she who had provided him a way of safety and taught him how to use it, Medea herself, grew pale with fear. Jason for a time kept his assailants at bay with his sword and shield, till finding their numbers overwhelming, he resorted to the charm which Medea had taught him, seized a stone and threw it in the midst of his foes. They immediately turned their arms against one another, and soon there was not one of the dragon's brood left alive. The Greeks embraced their hero, and Medea, if she dared, would have embraced him too.

Then Æetes promised the next day to give them the fleece, and the Greeks went joyfully down to the Argo with the hero Jason in their midst. But that night Medea came down to Jason, and bade him make haste and follow her, for that her father proposed the next morning to attack the Argonauts and to destroy their ship. They went together to the grove of Mars, where the golden fleece hung guarded by the dreadful dragon, who glared at the hero and his conductor with his great round eyes that never slept. But Medea was prepared, and began her magic songs and spells, and sprinkled over him a sleeping potion which she had prepared by her art. At the smell he relaxed his rage, stood for a moment motionless, then shut those great round eyes, that had never been known to shut before, and turned over on his side, fast asleep. Jason seized the fleece, and with his friends and Medea accompanying, hastened to their vessel, before ÆETES, the king, could arrest their departure, and made the best of their way back to Thessaly, where they arrived safe, and Jason delivered the fleece to Pelias, and dedicated the Argo to Neptune. What became of the fleece afterwards we do not know, but perhaps it was found, after all, like many other golden prizes, not worth the trouble it had cost to procure it.

This is one of those mythological tales, says a modern writer, in which there is reason to believe that a substratum of truth exists, though overlaid by a mass of fiction. It probably was the first important maritime expedition, and like the first attempts of the kind of all nations, as we know from history, was probably of a half piratical character. If rich spoils were the result, it was enough to give rise to the idea of the golden fleece.

Another suggestion of a learned mythologist, Bryant, is that it is a corrupt tradition of the story of Noah and the ark. The name Argo seems to countenance this, and the incident of the dove is another confirmation.

Pope, in his Ode on St. Cecelia's Day, thus celebrates the launching of the ship Argo, and the power of the music of Orpheus, whom he calls the Thracian:

"So when the first bold vessel dared the seas,
High on the stern the Thracian raised his strain,
While Argo saw her kindred trees
Descend from Pelion to the main.
Transported demigods stood round,
And men grew heroes at the sound."

In Dyer's poem of The Fleece there is an account of the ship Argo and her crew, which gives a good picture of this primitive maritime adventure:

"From every region of Aegea's shore
The brave assembled; those illustrious twins,
Castor and Pollux; Orpheus, tuneful bard;
Zetes and Calais, as the wind in speed;
Strong Hercules and many a chief renowned.
On deep Iolcos' sandy shore they thronged,
Gleaming in armor, ardent of exploits;
And soon, the laurel cord and the huge stone
Uplifting to the deck, unmoored the bark;
Whose keel of wondrous length the skilful hand
Of Argus fashioned for the proud attempt;
And in the extended keel a lofty mast
Upraised, and sails full swelling; to the chiefs
Unwonted objects. Now first, now they learned
Their bolder steerage over ocean wave,

Led by the golden stars, as Chiron's art
Had marked the sphere celestial."

Hercules left the expedition at Mysia, for Hylas, a youth beloved by him, having gone for water, was laid hold of and kept by the nymphs of the spring, who were fascinated by his beauty. Hercules went in quest of the lad, and while he was absent the Argo put to sea and left him. Moore, in one of his songs, makes a beautiful allusion to this incident:

"When Hylas was sent with his urn to the fount,
Through fields full of light and with heart full of play,
Light rambled the boy over meadow and mount,
And neglected his task for the flowers in the way.

"Thus many like me, who in youth should have tasted
The fountain that runs by Philosophy's shrine,
Their time with the flowers on the margin have wasted,
And left their light urns all as empty as mine."

But Hercules, as some say, went onward to Colchis by land, and there performed many mighty deeds, and wiped away the stain of cowardice which might have clung to him.

MEDEA AND ĀESON

Amid the rejoicings for the recovery of the golden Fleece, Jason felt that one thing was wanting, the presence of ǢSON, his father, who was prevented by his age and infirmities from taking part in them. Jason said to Medea, "My wife, I would that your arts, whose power I have seen so mighty for my aid, could do me one further service, and take some years from my life to add them to my father's." Medea replied, "Not at such a cost shall it be done, but if my art avails me, his life shall be lengthened without abridging yours." The next full moon she issued forth alone, while all creatures slept; not a breath stirred the foliage, and all was still. To the stars she addressed her incantations, and to the moon; to Hecate (Hecate was a mysterious divinity sometimes identified with Diana and sometimes with Proserpine. As Diana represents the moonlight splendor of night, so Hecate represents its darkness and terrors. She was the goddess of sorcery and witchcraft, and was believed to wander by night along the earth, seen only by the dogs whose barking told her approach.), the goddess of the underworld, and to Tellus, the goddess of the earth, by whose power plants potent for enchantments are produced. She invoked the gods of the woods and caverns, of mountains and valleys, of lakes and rivers, of winds and vapors. While she spoke the stars shone brighter, and presently a chariot descended through the air, drawn by flying serpents. She ascended it, and, borne aloft, made her way to distant regions, where potent plants grew which she knew how to select for her purpose. Nine nights she employed in her search, and during that time came not within the doors of her palace nor under any roof, and shunned all intercourse with mortals.

She next erected two altars, the one to Hecate, the other to Hebe, the goddess of youth, and sacrificed a black sheep, pouring libations of milk and wine. She implored Pluto and his stolen bride that they would not hasten to take the old man's life. Then she directed that ÆSON should be led forth, and having thrown him into a deep sleep by a charm, had him laid on a bed of herbs, like one dead. Jason and all others were kept away from the place, that no profane eyes might look upon her mysteries. Then, with streaming hair, she thrice moved round the altars, dipped flaming twigs in the blood, and laid them thereon to burn. Meanwhile the caldron with its contents was got ready. In it she put magic herbs, with seeds and flowers of acrid juice, stones from the distant East, and sand from the shore of all-surrounding ocean; hoar frost, gathered by moonlight, a screech-owl's head and wings, and the entrails of a wolf. She added fragments of the shells of tortoises, and the liver of stags, animals tenacious of life, and the head and beak of a crow, that outlives nine generations of men. These, with many other things without a name, she boiled together for her purposed work, stirring them up with a dry olive branch; and behold, the branch when taken out instantly became green, and before long was covered with leaves and a plentiful growth of young olives; and as the liquor boiled and bubbled, and sometimes ran over, the grass, wherever the sprinklings fell, shot forth with a verdure like that of spring.

Seeing that all was ready, Medea cut the throat of the old man and let out all his blood, and poured into his mouth and into his wound the juices of her caldron. As soon as he had completely imbibed them, his hair and beard laid by their whiteness and assumed the blackness of youth; his paleness and emaciation were gone; his veins were full of blood, his limbs of vigor and robustness. ÆSON is amazed at himself, and remembers that such as he now is he was in his youthful days, forty years before.

Medea used her arts here for a good purpose, but not so in another instance, where she made them the instruments of revenge. Pelias, our readers will recollect, was the usurping uncle of Jason, and had kept him out of his kingdom. Yet he must have had some good qualities, for his daughters loved him, and when they saw what Medea had done for ÆSON, they wished her to do the same for their father. Medea pretended to consent, and prepared her caldron as before. At her request an old sheep was brought and plunged into the caldron. Very soon a bleating was heard in the kettle, and, when the cover was removed, a lamb jumped forth and ran frisking away into the meadow. The daughters of Pelias saw the experiment with delight, and appointed a time for their father to undergo the same operation. But Medea prepared her caldron for him in a very different way. She put in only water and a few simple herbs. In the night she with the sisters entered the bed-chamber of the old king, while he and his guards slept soundly under the influence of a spell cast upon them by Medea. The daughters stood by the bedside with their weapons drawn, but hesitated to strike, till Medea child their irresolution. Then, turning away their faces and giving random blows, they smote him with their weapons. He, starting from his sleep, cried out, "My daughters, what are you doing? Will you kill your father?:" Their hearts failed them, and the weapons fell from their hands, but Medea struck him a fatal blow, and prevented his saying more.

Then they placed him in the caldron, and Medea hastened to depart in her serpent-drawn chariot before they discovered her treachery, for their vengeance would have been terrible. She escaped, however, but had little enjoyment of the fruits of her crime. Jason, for whom she had done so much, wishing to marry Creusa, princess of Corinth, put away Medea. She, enraged at his ingratitude, called on the gods for vengeance, sent a poisoned robe as a gift to the bride, and then killing her own children, and setting fire to the palace, mounted her serpent drawn chariot and fled to Athens, where she married King Ægeus, the father of Theseus; and we shall meet her again when we come to the adventures of that hero.

The incantations of Medea will remind the reader of those of the witches in Macbeth. The following lines are those which seem most strikingly to recall the ancient model:

"Round about the caldron go;
In the poisoned entrails throw.
* * * * * *
Fillet of a fenny snake
In the caldron boil and bake;
Eye of newt and toe of frog,
Wool of bat and tongue of dog.
Adder's fork and blind-worm's sting,
Lizard's leg and howlet's wing:
* * * * * *
Maw of ravening salt-sea shark,
Root of hemlock digged in the dark."
Macbeth, Act IV., Scene 1

And again:

Macbeth. What is't you do?
Witches. A deed without a name.

There is another story of Medea almost too revolting for record even of a sorceress, a class of persons to whom both ancient and modern poets have been accustomed to attribute every degree of atrocity. In her flight from Colchis she had taken her young brother Absyrtus with her. Finding the pursuing vessels of ÆETES gaining upon the Argonauts, she caused the lad to be killed and his limbs to be strewn over the sea. ÆETES on reaching the place found these sorrowful traces of his murdered son; but while he tarried to collect the scattered fragments and bestow upon them an honorable interment, the Argonauts escaped.

In the poems of Campbell will be found a translation of one of the choruses of the tragedy of Medea, where the poet Euripides has taken advantage of the occasion to pay a glowing tribute to Athens, his native city. It begins thus:

"Oh, haggard queen! To Athens dost thou guide
Thy glowing chariot, steeped in kindred gore;

Or seek to hide thy damned parricide
Where Peace and Justice dwell for evermore?"

THE CALYDONIAN HUNT. MELEAGER AND ATLANTA

The search for the Golden Fleece was undertaken by Jason, aided by heroes from all Greece, or Hellas as it was then called. It was the first of their common undertakings which made the Greeks feel that they were in truth one nation, though split up into many small kingdoms. Another of their great gatherings was for the Calydonian Hunt, and another, the greatest and most famous of all, for the Trojan War.

The hero of the quest for the golden Fleece was Jason. With the other heroes of the Greeks, he was present at the Calydonian Hunt. But the chief hero was Meleager, the son of Œneus, king of Calydon, and Althea, his queen.

Althea, when her son was born, beheld the three Destinies, who, as they spun their fatal thread, foretold that the life of the child should last no longer than a brand then burning upon the hearth. Althea seized and quenched the brand, and carefully preserved it for years, while Meleager grew to boyhood, youth, and manhood. It chanced, then, that Œneus, as he offered sacrifices to the gods, omitted to pay due honors to Diana, and she, indignant at the neglect, sent a wild boar of enormous size to lay waste the files of Calydon. Its eyes shone with blood and fire, its bristles stood like threatening spears, its tusks were like those of Indian elephants. The growing corn was trampled, the vines and olive trees laid waste, the flocks and herds were driven in wild confusion by the slaughtering foe. All common aid seemed vain; but Meleager called on the heroes of Greece to join in a bold hunt for the ravenous monster. Theseus and his friend Pirithous, Jason, Peleus afterwards the father of Achilles, Telamon the father of Ajax, Nestor, then a youth, but who in his age bore arms with Achilles and Ajax in the Trojan war, these and many more joined in the enterprise. With them came Atalanta, the daughter of Iasius, king of Arcadia. A buckle of polished gold confined her vest, an ivory quiver hung on her left shoulder, and her left hand bore the bow. Her face blent feminine beauty with the best graces of martial youth. Meleager saw and loved.

But now already they were near the monster's lair. They stretched strong nets from tree to tree; they uncoupled their dogs, they tried to find the footprints of their quarry in the grass. From the wood was a descent to marshy ground. Here the boar, as he lay among the reeds, heard the shouts of his pursuers, and rushed forth against them. One and another is thrown down and slain. Jason throws his spear with a prayer to Diana for success; and the favoring goddess allows the weapon to touch, but not to wound, removing the steel point of the spear even in its flight. Nestor, assailed, seeks and finds safety in the

Figure 16: "Meleager and Atlanta" by Stefano della Bella

branches of a tree. Telamon rushes on, but stumbling at a projecting root, falls prone. But an arrow from Atalanta at length for the first time tastes the monster's blood. It is a slight wound, but Meleager sees and joyfully proclaims it. Anceus, excited to envy by the praise given to a female, loudly proclaims his own valor, and defies alike the boar and the goddess who had sent it; but as he rushes on, the infuriated beast lays him low with a mortal wound. Theseus throws his lance, but it is turned aside by a projecting bough. The dart of Jason misses its object, and kills instead one of their own dogs. But Meleager, after one unsuccessful stroke, drives his spear into the monsters side, then rushes on and despatches him with repeated blows.

Then rose a shout from those around; they congratulated the conqueror, crowding to touch his hand. He, placing his foot upon the slain boar, turned to Atalanta and bestowed on her the head and the rough hide which were the trophies of his success. But at this, envy excited the rest to strife. Phlexippus and Toxeus, the uncles of Meleager and Althea's brothers, beyond the rest opposed the gift, and snatched from the maiden the trophy she had received. Meleager, kindling with rage at the wrong done to himself, and still more at the insult offered to her whom he loved, forgot the claims of kindred, and plunged his sword into the offenders' hearts.

As Althea bore gifts of thankfulness to the temples for the victory of her son, the bodies of her murdered brothers met her sight. She shrieks, and beats her breast, and hastens to change the garments of rejoicing for those of mourning. But when the author of the deed is known, grief gives way to the stern desire of vengeance on her son. The fatal brand, which once she rescued from the flames, the brand which the Destinies had linked with Meleager's life, she brings forth, and commands a fire to be prepared. Then four times she essays to place the brand upon the pile; four times draws back, shuddering at the thought of bringing destruction on her son. The feelings of the mother and the sister contend within her. Now she is pale at the thought of the purposed deed, now flushed again with anger at the act of her son. As a vessel, driven in one direction by the wind, and in the opposite by the tide, the mind of Althea hangs suspended in uncertainty. But now the sister prevails above the mother, and she begins as she holds the fatal wood: "Turn, ye Furies, goddesses of punishment! Turn to behold the sacrifice I bring! Crime must atone for crime. Shall Œneus rejoice in his victor son, while the house of Thestius (Thestius was father of Toxeus, Phlexippus and Althea) is desolate? But, alas! To what deed am I borne along? Brothers, forgive a mother's weakness! My hand fails me. He deserves death, but not that I should destroy him. But shall he then live, and triumph, and reign over Calydon, while you, my brothers, wander unavenged among the shades? No! Thou has lived by my gift; die, now, for thine own crime. Return the life which twice I gave thee, first at thy birth, again when I snatched this brand from the flames. O that thou hadst then died! Alas! Evil is the conquest; but, brothers, ye have conquered." And, turning away her face, she threw the fatal wood upon the burning pile.

It gave, or seemed to give, a deadly groan. Meleager, absent and unknowing of the cause, felt a sudden pang. He burns and only by courageous pride conquers the pain which destroys him. He mourns only that he perishes by a bloodless and unhonored death. With his last breath he calls upon his aged father, his brother, and his fond sisters, upon his beloved Atalanta, and upon his mother, the unknown cause of his fate. The flames increase, and with them the pain of the hero. Now both subside; now both are quenched. The brand is ashes and the life of Meleager is breathed forth to the wandering winds.

Althea, when the deed was done, laid violent hands upon herself. The sisters of Meleager mourned their brother with uncontrollable grief; till Diana, pitying the sorrows of the house that once had aroused her anger, turned them into birds.

ATLANTA

The innocent cause of so much sorrow was a maiden whose face you might truly say was boyish for a girl, yet too girlish for a boy. Her fortune had been told, and it was to this effect: "Atalanta, do not marry; marriage will be your ruin." Terrified by this oracle, she fled the society of men, and devoted herself to the sports of the chase. To all suitors (for she had many) she imposed a condition which was generally effectual in relieving her of their persecutions: "I will be the prize of him who shall conquer me in the race; but death must be the penalty of all who try and fail." In spite of this hard condition some would try. Hippomenes was to be judge of the race. "Can it be possible that any will be so rash as to risk so much for a wife?" said he. But when he saw her lay aside her robe for the race, he changed his mind, and said, "Pardon me, youths, I knew not the prize you were competing for." As he surveyed them he wished them all to be beaten, and swelled with envy of any one that seemed at all likely to win. While such were his thoughts, the virgin darted forward. As she ran, she looked more beautiful than ever. The breezes seemed to give wings to her feet; her hair flew over her shoulders, and the gay fringe of her garment fluttered behind her. A ruddy hue tinged the whiteness of her skin, such as a crimson curtain casts on a marble wall. All her competitors were distanced, and were put to death without mercy. Hippomenes, not daunted by this result, fixing his eyes on the virgin, said, "Why boast of beating those laggards? I offer myself for the contest." Atalanta looked at him with a pitying countenance, and hardly knew whether she would rather conquer him or not. "What god can tempt one so young and handsome to throw himself away? I pity him, not for his beauty (yet he is beautiful), but for his youth. I wish he would give up the race, or if he will be so mad, I hope he may outrun me." While she hesitates, revolving these thoughts, the spectators grow impatient for the race, and her father prompts her to prepare. Then Hippomenes addressed a prayer to Venus; "Help me, Venus, for you have led me on" Venus heard, and was propitious.

In the garden of her temple, in her own island of Cyprus, is a tree with yellow leaves and yellow branches, and golden fruit. Hence Venus gathered three golden apples, and, unseen by all else, gave them to Hippomenes, and told him how to use them. The signal is given; each starts from the goal, and skims over the sand. So light their tread, you would almost have thought they might run over the river surface or over the waving grain without sinking. The cries of the spectators cheered on Hippomenes: "Now, now do your best! Haste, haste! You gain on her! Relax not! One more effort!" It was doubtful whether the youth or the maiden heard these cries with the greater pleasure. But his breath began to fail him, his throat was dry, the goal yet far off. At that moment he threw down one of the golden apples. The virgin was all amazement. She stopped to pick it up. Hippomenes shot ahead. Shouts burst forth from all sides. She redoubled her efforts, and soon overtook him. Again he threw an apple. She stopped again, but again came up with him. The goal was near; one chance only remained. "Now, goddess," said he, "prosper your gift!" and threw the last apple off at one side. She looked at it, and hesitated; Venus impelled her to turn aside for it. She did so, and was vanquished. The youth carried off his prize.

But the lovers were so full of their own happiness that they forgot to pay due honor to Venus; and the goddess was provoked at their ingratitude. She caused them to give offence to Cybele. That powerful goddess was not to be insulted with impunity. She took from them their human form and turned them into animals of characters resembling their own: of the huntress-heroine, triumphing in the blood of her lovers, she made a lioness, and of her lord and master a lion, and yoked them to her ear, there they are still to be seen in all representations, in statuary or painting, of the goddess Cybele.

Cybele is the Latin name of the goddess called by the Greeks Rhea and Ops. She was the wife of Cronos and mother of Zeus. In works of art, she exhibits the matronly air which distinguishes Juno and Ceres. Sometimes she is veiled, and seated on a throne with lions at her side, at other times riding in a chariot drawn by lions. She sometimes wears a mural crown, that is, a crown whose rim is carved in the form of towers and battlements. Her priests were called Corybantes.

Byron in describing the city of Venice, which is built on a low island in the Adriatic Sea, borrows an illustration from Cybele:

"She looks a sea-Cybele fresh from ocean,
Rising with her tiara of proud towers
At airy distance, with majestic motion,
A ruler of the waters and their powers."
Childe Harold, IV

In Moore's Rhymes on the Road, the poet, speaking of Alpine scenery, alludes to the story of Atalanta and Hippomenes, thus:

"Even here, in this region of wonders, I find
That light-footed Fancy leaves Truth far behind,
Or at least, like Hippomenes, turns her astray
By the golden illusions he flings in her way."

Chapter 12

HERCULES. HEBE AND GANYMEDE

Hercules (in Greek, Heracles) was the son of Jupiter and Alemena. As Juno was always hostile to the offspring of her husband by mortal mothers, she declared war against Hercules from his birth. She sent two serpents to destroy him as he lay in his cradle, but the precocious infant strangled them with his own hands. (On this account the infant Hercules was made the type of infant America, by Dr. Franklin, and the French artists whom he employed in the American Revolution. Horatio Greenough has placed a bas- relief of the Infant Hercules on the pedestal of his statue of Washington, which stands in front of the Capitol.) He was however by the arts of Juno rendered subject to his cousin Eurystheus and compelled to perform all his commands. Eurystheus enjoined upon him a succession of desperate adventures, which are called the twelve "Labors of Hercules." The first was the fight with the Nemean lion. The valley of Nemea was infested by a terrible lion. Eurystheus ordered Hercules to bring him the skin of this monster. After using in vain his club and arrows against the lion, Hercules strangled the animal with his hands. He returned carrying the dead lion on his shoulders; but Eurystheus was so frightened at the sight of it and at this proof of the prodigious strength of the hero, that he ordered him to deliver the account of his exploits in future outside the town.

His next labor was to slaughter the Hydra. This monster ravaged the country of Argos, and dwelt in a swamp near the well of Amymone, of which the story is that when the country was suffering from drought, Neptune, who loved her, had permitted her to touch the rock with his trident, and a spring of three outlets burst forth. Here the Hydra took up his position, and Hercules was sent to destroy him. The Hydra had nine heads, of which the middle one was immortal. Hercules struck off its head with his club, but in the place of the head knocked off, two new ones grew forth each time. At length with the assistance of his faithful servant Iolaus, he burned away the heads of the Hydra, and buried the ninth or immortal one under a huge rock.

Another labor was the cleaning of the Augean stables. Augeas, king of Elis, had a herd of three thousand oxen, whose stalls had not been cleansed for thirty years. Hercules brought the rivers Alpheus and Peneus through them, and cleansed them thoroughly in one day.

His next labor was of a more delicate kind. Admeta, the daughter of Eurystheus, longed to obtain the girdle of the queen of the Amazons, and Eurystheus ordered Hercules to go and get it. The Amazons were a nation of women. They were very warlike and held several flourishing cities. It was their custom to bring up only the female children; the boys were either sent away to the neighboring nations or put to death. Hercules was accompanied by a number of volunteers, and after various adventures at last reached the country of the Amazons. Hippolyta, the queen, received him kindly, and consented to yield him her girdle; but Juno, taking the form of an Amazon, went among the other Amazons and persuaded them that the strangers were carrying off their queen. The Amazons instantly armed and came in great numbers down to the ship. Hercules, thinking that Hippolyta had acted treacherously, slew her, and taking her girdle, made sail homewards.

Another task enjoined him was to bring to Eurystheus the oxen of Geryon, a monster with three bodies who dwelt in the island Erytheia (the red), so called because it lay at the west, under the rays of the setting sun. This description is thought to apply to Spain, of which Geryon was said to be king. After traversing various countries, Hercules reached at length the frontiers of Libya and Europe, where he raised the two mountains of Calpe and Abyla, as monuments of his progress, or according to another account rent one mountain into two and left half on each side, forming the Straits of Gibraltar, the two mountains being called the Pillars of Hercules. The oxen were guarded by the giant Eurytion and his two-headed dog, but Hercules killed the giant and his dog and brought away the oxen in safety to Eurystheus.

The most difficult labor of all was bringing the , for Hercules did not know where to find them. These were the apples which Juno had received at her wedding from the goddess of the Earth, and which she had intrusted to the keeping of the daughters of Hesperis, assisted by a watchful dragon. After various adventures Hercules arrived at Mount Atlas in Africa. Atlas was one of the

Titans who had warred against the gods, and after they were subdued, Atlas was condemned to bear on his shoulders the weight of the heavens. He was the father of the Hesperides, and Hercules thought, might, if any one could, find the apples and bring them to him. But how to send Atlas away from his post, or bear up the heavens while he was gone? Hercules took the burden on his own shoulders, and sent Atlas to seek the apples. He returned with them, and though somewhat reluctantly, took his burden upon his shoulders again, and let Hercules return with the apples to Eurystheus. (Hercules was a descendant of Perseus. Perseus changed Atlas to stone. How could Hercules take his place? This is only one of the many anachronisms found in ancient mythology.)

Milton in his Comus makes the Hesperides the daughters of Hesperus, and nieces of Atlas:

"—— amidst the gardens fair
Of Hesperus and his daughters three,
That sing about the golden tree."

The poets, led by the analogy of the lovely appearance of the western sky at sunset, viewed the west as a region of brightness and glory. Hence they placed in it the Isles of the blest, the ruddy isle Erytheia, on which the bright oxen of Geryon were pastured, and the isle of the Hesperides. The apples are supposed by some to be the oranges of Spain, of which the Greeks had heard some obscure accounts.

A celebrated exploit of Hercules was his victory over Antaeus. Antaeus, the son of Terra (the Earth) was a mighty giant and wrestler, whose strength was invincible so long as he remained in contact with his mother Earth. He compelled all strangers who came to his country to wrestle with him, on condition that if conquered (as they all were), they should be put to death. Hercules encountered him, and finding that it was of no avail to throw him, for he always rose with renewed strength from every fall, he lifted him up from the earth and strangled him in the air.

Cacus was a huge giant, who inhabited a cave on Mount Aventine (one of the seven hills of Rome), and plundered the surrounding country. When Hercules was driving home the oxen of Geryon, Cacus stole part of the cattle, while the hero slept. That their foot-prints might not serve to show where they had been driven, he dragged them backward by their tails to his cave; so their tracks all seemed to show that they had gone in the opposite direction. Hercules was deceived by this stratagem, and would have failed to find his oxen, if it had not happened that in driving the remainder of the herd past the cave where the stolen ones were concealed, those within began to low, and were thus discovered. Cacus was slain by Hercules.

The last exploit we shall record was bringing Cerberus from the lower world. Hercules descended into Hades, accompanied by Mercury and Minerva. He obtained permission from Pluto to carry Cerberus to the upper air, provided he could do it without the use of weapons; and in spite of the monster's struggling he seized him, held him fast, and carried him to Eurystheus, and afterwards brought him back again. When he was in Hades he obtained the liberty of Theseus, his admirer and imitator, who had been detained a prisoner there for an unsuccessful attempt to carry off Proserpine.

Hercules in a fit of madness killed his friend Iphitus and was condemned for this offence to become the slave of Queen Omphale for three years. While in this service the hero's nature seemed changed. He lived effeminately, wearing at times the dress of a woman, and spinning wool with the handmaidens of Omphale, while the queen wore his lion's skin. When this service was ended he married Dejanira and lived in peace with her three years. On one occasion as he was travelling with his wife, they came to a river, across which the Centaur Nessus carried travellers for a stated fee. Hercules himself forded the river, but gave Dejanira to Nessus to be carried across. Nessus attempted to run away with her, but Hercules heard her cries, and shot an arrow into the heart of Nessus. The dying Centaur told Dejanira to take a portion of his blood and keep it, as it might be used as a charm to preserve the love of her husband.

Dejanira did so, and before long fancied she had occasion to use it. Hercules in one of his conquests had taken prisoner a fair maiden, named Iole, of whom he seemed more fond than Dejanira approved. When Hercules was about to offer sacrifices to the gods in honor of his victory, he sent to his wife for a white robe to use on the occasion. Dejanira, thinking it a good opportunity to try her love-spell, steeped the garment in the blood of Nessus. We are to suppose she took care to wash out all traces of it, but the magic power remained, and as soon as

Figure 17: "Hercules Killing the Lernean Hydra" by Cornelis Cort

the garment became warm on the body of Hercules, the poison penetrated into all his limbs and caused him the most intense agony. In his frenzy he seized Lichas, who had brought him the fatal robe, and hurled him into the sea. He wrenched off the garment, but it stuck to his flesh, and with it he tore away whole pieces of his body. In this state he embarked on board a ship and was conveyed home. Dejanira on seeing what she had unwittingly done, hung herself. Hercules, prepared to die, ascended Mount Œta, where he built a funeral pile of trees, gave his bow and arrows to Philoctetes, and laid himself down on the pile, his head resting on his club, and his lion's skin spread over him. With a countenance as serene as if he were taking his place at a festal board, he commanded Philoctetes to apply the torch. The flames spread apace and soon invested the whole mass.

Milton thus alludes to the frenzy of Hercules:

"As when Alcides (Alcides, a name of Hercules; the word means
"descendant of Alcaeus"), from OEchalia crowned
With conquest, felt the envenomed robe, and tore,
Through pain, up by the roots Thessalian pines
And Lichas from the top of Œta threw
Into the Euboic Sea."

The gods themselves felt troubled at seeing the champion of the earth so brought to his end; but Jupiter with cheerful countenance thus addressed them; "I am pleased to see your concern, my princes, and am gratified to perceive that I am the ruler of a loyal people, and that my son enjoys your favor. For although your interest in him arises from his noble deeds, yet it is not the less gratifying to me. But now I say to you, Fear not. He who conquered all else is not to be conquered by those flames which you see blazing on Mount Œta. Only his mother's share in him can perish; what he derived from me is immortal. I shall take him, dead to earth, to the heavenly shores, and I require of you all to receive him kindly. If any of you feel grieved at his attaining this honor, yet no one can deny that he has deserved it." The gods all gave their assent; Juno only heard the closing words with some displeasure that she should be so particularly pointed at, yet not enough to make her regret the determination of her husband. So when the flames had consumed the mother's share of Hercules, the diviner part, instead of being injured thereby, seemed to start forth with new vigor, to assume a more lofty port and a more awful dignity. Jupiter enveloped him in a cloud, and took him up in a four-horse chariot to dwell among the stars. As he took his place in heaven, Atlas felt the added weight.

Juno, now reconciled to him, gave him her daughter Hebe in marriage.

The poet Schiller, in one of his pieces called the Ideal and Life, illustrates the contrast between the practical and the imaginative in some beautiful stanzas, of which the last two may be thus translated:

"Deep degraded to a coward's slave,
Endless contests bore Alcides brave,
Through the thorny path of suffering led;
Slew the Hydra, crushed the lion's might,
Threw himself, to bring his friend to light,
Living, in the skiff that bears the dead.
All the torments, every toil of earth
Juno's hatred on him could impose,
Well he bore them, from his fated birth
To life's grandly mournful close.
Till the god, the earthly part forsaken,
From the man in flames asunder taken,
Drank the heavenly ether's purer breath.
Joyous in the new unwonted lightness,
Soared he upwards to celestial brightness,
Earth's dark heavy burden lost in death.
High Olympus gives harmonious greeting
To the hall where reigns his sire adored;
Youth's bright goddess, with a blush at meeting,
Gives the nectar to her lord."
S. G. Bulfinch

HEBE AND GANYMEDE

Hebe, the daughter of Juno, and goddess of youth, was cupbearer to the gods. The usual story is, that she resigned her office on becoming the wife of Hercules. But there is another statement which our countryman Crawford, the sculptor, has adopted in his group of Hebe and Ganymede, now in the gallery of the Boston Athenaeum. According to this, Hebe was dismissed from her office in consequence of a fall which she met with one day when in attendance on the gods. Her successor was Ganymede, a Trojan boy whom Jupiter, in the disguise of an eagle, seized and carried off from the midst of his playfellows on Mount Ida, bore up to heaven, and installed in the vacant place.

Tennyson, in his Palace of Art, describes among the decorations on the walls, a picture representing this legend:

"There, too, flushed Ganymede his rosy thigh
Half buried in the eagle's down,
Sole as a flying star shot through the sky
Above the pillared town."

And in Shelley's Prometheus, Jupiter calls to his cup-bearer thus:

"Pour forth heaven's wine, Idaean Ganymede,
And let it fill the Daedal cups like fire."

The beautiful legend of the Choice of Hercules may be found in the Tatler, No. 97. The same story is told in the Memorabilia of Xenophon.

Chapter 13

THESEUS. DAEDALUS. CASTOR AND POLLUX

Theseus was the son of Ǣgeus, king of Athens, and of Aethra, daughter of the king of Troezene. He was brought up at Troezene, and, when arrived at manhood, was to proceed to Athens and present himself to his father. Ǣgeus, on parting from Aethra, before the birth of his son, placed his sword and shoes under a large stone, and directed her to send his son to him when he became strong enough to roll away the stone and take them from under it. When she thought the time had come, his mother led Theseus to the stone, and he removed it with ease, and took the sword and shoes. As the roads were infested with robbers, his grandfather pressed him earnestly to take the shorter and safer way to his father's country, by sea; but the youth, feeling in himself the spirit and the soul of a hero, and eager to signalize himself like Hercules, with whose fame all Greece then rang, by destroying the evil-doers and monsters that oppressed the country, determined on the more perilous and adventurous journey by land.

His first day's journey brought him to Epidaurus, where dwelt a man named Periphetes, a son of Vulcan. This ferocious savage always went armed with a club of iron, and all travellers stood in terror of his violence. When he saw Theseus approach, he assailed him, but speedily fell beneath the blows of the young hero, who took possession of his club, and bore it ever afterwards as a memorial of his first victory.

Several similar contests with the petty tyrants and marauders of the country followed, in all of which Theseus was victorious. One of these evil-doers was called Procrustes, or the Stretcher. He had an iron bedstead, on which he used to tie all travellers who fell into his hands. If they were shorter than the bed, he stretched their limbs to make them fit it; if they were longer than the bed, he lopped off a portion. Theseus served him as he had served others.

Having overcome all the perils of the road, Theseus at length reached Athens, where new dangers awaited him. Medea, the sorceress, who had fled from Corinth after her separation from Jason, had become the wife of Ǣgeus, the father of Theseus. Knowing by her arts who he was, and fearing the loss of her influence with her husband, if Theseus should be acknowledged as his son, she filled the mind of Ǣgeus with suspicions of the young stranger, and induced him to present him a cup of poison; but at the moment when Theseus stepped forward to take it, the sight of the sword which he wore discovered to his father who he was, and prevented the fatal draught. Medea, detected in her arts, fled once more from deserved punishment, and arrived in Asia, where the country afterwards called Media received its name from her. Theseus was acknowledged by his father, and declared his successor.

The Athenians were at that time in deep affliction, on account of the tribute which they were forced to pay to Minos, king of Crete. This tribute consisted of seven youths and seven maidens, who were sent every year to be devoured by the Minotaur, a monster with a bull's body and a human head. It was exceedingly strong and fierce, and was kept in a labyrinth constructed by Daedalus, so artfully contrived that whoever was enclosed in it could by no means find his way out unassisted. Here the Minotaur roamed, and was fed with human victims.

Theseus resolved to deliver his countrymen from this calamity, or to die in the attempt. Accordingly, when the time of sending off the tribute came, and the youths and maidens were, according to custom, drawn by lot to be sent, he offered himself as one of the victims, in spite of the entreaties of his father. The ship departed under black sails, as usual, which Theseus promised his father to change for white, in case of his returning victorious. When they arrived in Crete, the youths and maidens were exhibited before Minos; and Ariadne, the daughter of the king, being present, became deeply enamored of Theseus, by whom her love was readily returned. She furnished him with a sword, with which to encounter the Minotaur, and with a clew of thread by which he might find his way out of the labyrinth. He was successful, slew the Minotaur, escaped from the labyrinth, and taking Ariadne as the companion of his way, with his rescued companions sailed for Athens. On their way they stopped at the island of Naxos, where Theseus abandoned Ariadne, leaving her asleep. For Minerva had appeared to Theseus in a dream, and warned him that Ariadne was destined to be the wife of Bacchus, the wine-god. (One of the finest pieces of sculpture in Italy, the recumbent Ariadne of the Vatican, represents this incident. A copy is in the Athenaeum gallery, Boston. The celebrated statue of Ariadne, by Danneker, represents her as riding on the tiger of Bacchus, at a somewhat later period of her story.)

On approaching the coast of Attica, Theseus, intent on Ariadne, forgot the signal appointed by his father, and neglected to raise the white sails, and the old king, thinking his son had perished, put an end to his own life. Theseus thus became king of Athens.

One of the most celebrated of the adventures of Theseus is his expedition against the Amazons. He assailed them before they had recovered from the attack of Hercules, and carried off their queen, Antiope. The Amazons in their turn invaded the country of Athens and penetrated into the city itself; and the final battle in which Theseus overcame them was fought in the very midst of the city. This battle was one of the favorite subjects of the ancient sculptors, and is commemorated in several works of art that are still extant.

The friendship between Theseus and Pirithous was of a most intimate nature, yet it originated in the midst of arms. Pirithous had made an irruption into the plain of Marathon, and carried off the herds of the king of Athens. Theseus went to repel the plunderers. The moment Pirithous beheld him, he was seized with admiration; he stretched out his hand as a token of peace, and cried, "Be judge thyself, what satisfaction dost thou require?" "Thy friendship," replied the Athenian, and they swore inviolable fidelity. Their deeds corresponded to their professions, and they ever continued true brothers in arms. Each of them aspired to espouse a daughter of Jupiter. Theseus fixed his choice on Helen, then but a child, afterwards so celebrated as the cause of the Trojan war, and with the aid of his friend he carried her off. Pirithous aspired to the wife of the monarch of Erebus; and Theseus, though aware of the danger, accompanied the ambitious lover in his descent to the underworld. But Pluto seized and set them on an enchanted rock at his palace gate, where they remained till Hercules arrived and liberated Theseus, leaving Pirithous to his fate.

After the death of Antiope, Theseus married Phaedra, daughter of Minos, king of Crete. Phaedra saw in Hippolytus, the son of Theseus, a youth endowed with all the graces and virtues of his father, and of an age corresponding to her own. She loved him, but he repulsed her advances, and her love was changed to hate. She used her influence over her infatuated husband to cause him to be jealous of his son, and he imprecated the vengeance of Neptune upon him. As Hippolytus was one day driving his chariot along the shore, a sea-monster raised himself above the waters, and frightened the horses so that they ran away and dashed the chariot to pieces. Hippolytus was killed, but by Diana's assistance Aesculapius restored him to life. Diana removed Hippolytus from the power of his deluded father and false stepmother, and placed him in Italy under the protection of the nymph Egeria.

Theseus at length lost the favor of his people, and retired to the court of Lycomedes, king of Scyros, who at first received him kindly, but afterwards treacherously slew him. In a later age the Athenian general Cimon discovered the place where his remains were laid, and caused them to be removed to Athens, where they were deposited in a temple called the Theseum, erected in honor of the hero.

The queen of the Amazons whom Theseus espoused is by some called Hippolyta. That is the name she bears in Shakespeare's Midsummer Night's Dream, the subject of which is the festivities attending the nuptials of Theseus and Hippolyta.

Mrs. Hemans has a poem on the ancient Greek tradition that the "Shade of Theseus" appeared strengthening his countrymen at the battle of Marathon.

Mr. Lewis Morris has a beautiful poem on Helen, in the Epic of Hades. In these lines Helen describes how she was seized by Theseus and his friend:

——"There came a night
When I lay longing for my love, and knew
Sudden the clang of hoofs, the broken doors,
The clash of swords, the shouts, the groans, the stain
Of red upon the marble, the fixed gaze
Of dead and dying eyes, that was the time
When first I looked on death, and when I woke
From my deep swoon, I felt the night air cool
Upon my brow, and the cold stars look down,
As swift we galloped o'er the darkling plain
And saw the chill sea-glimpses slowly wake,
With arms unknown around me. When the dawn
Broke swift, we panted on the pathless steeps,

And so by plain and mountain till we came
to Athens, ——."

Theseus is a semi-historical personage. It is recorded of him that he united the several tribes by whom the territory of Attica was then possessed into one state, of which Athens was the capital. In commemoration of this important event, he instituted the festival of Panathenaea, in honor of Minerva, the patron deity of Athens. This festival differed from the other Grecian games chiefly in two particulars. It was peculiar to the Athenians, and its chief feature was a solemn procession in which the Peplus or sacred robe of Minerva was carried to the Parthenon, and suspended before the statue of the goddess. The Peplus was covered with embroidery, worked by select virgins of the noblest families in Athens. The procession consisted of persons of all ages and both sexes. The old men carried olive- branches in their hands, and the young men bore arms. The young women carried baskets on their heads, containing the sacred utensils, cakes, and all things necessary for the sacrifices. The procession formed the subject of the bas-reliefs by Phidias which embellished the outside of the temple of the Parthenon. A considerable portion of these sculptures is now in the British museum among those known as the "Elgin marbles."

OLYMPIC AND OTHER GAMES

We may mention here the other celebrated national games of the Greeks. The first and most distinguished were the Olympic, founded, it was said , by Jupiter himself. They were celebrated at Olympia in Elis. Vast numbers of spectators flocked to them from every part of Greece, and from Asia, Africa, and Sicily. They were repeated every fifth year in midsummer, and continued five days. They gave rise to the custom of reckoning time and dating events by Olympiads. The first Olympiad is generally considered as corresponding with the year 776 B.C. The Pythian games were celebrated in the vicinity of Delphi, the Isthmian on the Corinthian isthmus, the Nemean at Nemea, a city of Argolis.

The exercises in these games were of five sorts: running, leaping, wrestling, throwing the quoit, and hurling the javelin, or boxing. Besides these exercises of bodily strength and agility, there were contests in music, poetry, and eloquence. Thus these games furnished poets, musicians, and authors the best opportunities to present their productions to the public, and the fame of the victors was diffused far and wide.

DAEDALUS

The labyrinth from which Theseus escaped by means of the clew of Ariadne, was built by Daedalus, a most skillful artificer. It was an edifice with numberless winding passages and turnings opening into one another, and seeming to have neither beginning nor end, like the river Maender, which returns on itself, and flows now onward, now backward, in its course to the sea. Daedalus built the labyrinth for King Minos, but afterwards lost the favor of the king, and was shut up in a tower. He contrived to make his escape from his prison, but could not leave the island by sea, as the king kept strict watch on all the vessels, and permitted none to sail without being carefully searched. "Minos may control the land and sea,:" said Daedalus, "but not the regions of the air. I will try that way." So he set to work to fabricate wings for himself and his young son Icarus. He wrought feathers together beginning with the smallest and adding larger, so as to form an increasing surface. The larger ones he secured with thread and the smaller with wax, and gave the whole a gentle curvature like the wings of a bird. Icarus, the boy, stood and looked on, sometimes running to gather up the feathers which the wind had blown away, and then handling the wax and working it over with his fingers, by his play impeding his father in his labors. When at last the work was done, the artist, waving his wings, found himself buoyed upward and hung suspended, poising himself on the beaten air. He next equipped his son in the same manner, and taught him how to fly, as a bird tempts her young ones from the lofty nest into the air. When all was prepared for flight, he said, "Icarus, my son, I charge you to keep at a moderate height, for if you fly too low the damp will clog your wings, and if too high the heat will melt them. Keep near me and you will be safe." While he gave him these instructions and fitted the wings to his shoulders, the face of the father was wet with tears, and his hands trembled. He kissed the boy, not knowing that it was for the last time. Then rising on his wings he flew off, encouraging him to follow, and looked back from his own flight to see how his son managed his wings. As they flew the ploughman stopped his work to gaze, and the shepherd learned on his staff and watched them, astonished at the sight, and thinking they were gods who could thus cleave the air.

They passed Samos and Delos on the left and Lebynthos on the right, when the boy, exulting in his career, began to leave the guidance of his companion and soar upward as if to reach heaven. The nearness of the blazing sun softened the wax which held the feathers together, and they came off. He fluttered with his arms, but no feathers remained to hold the air. While his mouth uttered cries to his father, it was submerged in the blue waters of the sea, which thenceforth was called by his name. His father cried, "Icarus, Icarus, where are you?" At last he saw the feathers floating on the water, and bitterly lamenting his own arts, he buried the body and called the land Icaria in memory of his child. Daedalus arrived safe in Sicily, where he built a temple to Apollo, and hung up his wings, an offering to the god.

Daedalus was so proud of his achievements that he could not bear the idea of a rival. His sister had placed her son Perdix under his charge to be taught the mechanical arts. He was an apt scholar and gave striking evidences of ingenuity. Walking on the seashore he picked up the spine of a fish. Imitating it, he took a piece of iron and notched it on the edge, and thus invented the SAW. He put two pieces of iron together, connecting them at one end with a rivet, and sharpening the other ends, and made a PAIR OF COMPASSES. Daedalus was so envious of his nephew's performances that he took an opportunity, when they were together one day on the top of a high tower, to push him off. But Minerva, who favors ingenuity, saw him falling, and arrested his fate by changing him into a bird called after his name, the Partridge. This bird does not build his next in the trees, nor take lofty flights, but nestles in the hedges, and mindful of his fall, avoids high places.

The death of Icarus is told in the following lines by Darwin:

"—— with melting wax and loosened strings
Sunk hapless Icarus on unfaithful wings;
Headlong he rushed through the affrighted air,
With limbs distorted and dishevelled hair;
His scattered plumage danced upon the wave,
And sorrowing Nereids decked his watery grave;
O'er his pale corse their pearly sea-flowers shed,
And strewed with crimson moss his marble bed;
Struck in their coral towers the passing bell,
And wide in ocean tolled his echoing knell."

CASTOR AND POLLUX

Castor and Pollux were the offspring of Leda and the Swan, under which disguise Jupiter had concealed himself. Leda gave birth to an egg, from which sprang the twins. Helen, so famous afterwards as the cause of the Trojan war, was their sister.

When Theseus and his friend Pirithous had carried off Helen from Sparta, the youthful heroes Castor and Pollux, with their followers, hasted to her rescue. Theseus was absent from Attica, and the brothers were successful in recovering their sister.

Castor was famous for taming and managing horses, and Pollux for skill in boxing. They were united by the warmest affection, and inseparable in all their enterprises. They accompanied the Argonautic expedition. During the voyage a storm arose, and Orpheus prayed to the Samothracian gods, and played on his harp, whereupon the storm ceased and stars appeared on the heads of the brothers. From this incident, Castor and Pollux came afterwards to be considered the patron deities of seamen and voyagers (One of the ships in which St. Paul sailed was named the Castor and Pollux. See Acts xxviii.II.), and the lambent flames, which in certain sates of the atmosphere play round the sails and masts of vessels, were called by their names.

After the Argonautic expedition, we find Castor and Pollux engaged in a war with Idas and Lynceus. Castor was slain, and Pollux, inconsolable for the loss of his brother, besought Jupiter to be permitted to give his own life as a ransom for him. Jupiter so far consented as to allow the two brothers to enjoy the boon of life alternately, passing one day under the earth and the next in the heavenly abodes. According to another form of the story, Jupiter rewarded the attachment of the brothers by placing them among the stars as Gemini, the Twins.

Figure 18: "Helene Delivered by Castor & Pollux" by Jean-Bruno Gassies

They received divine honors under the name of Dioscuri (sons of Jove). They were believed to have appeared occasionally in later times, taking part with one side or the other, in hard-fought fields, and were said on such occasions to be mounted on magnificent white steeds. Thus, in the early history of Rome, they are said to have assisted the Romans at the battle of Lake Regillus, and after the victory a temple was erected in their honor on the spot where they appeared.

Macaulay, in his Lays of Ancient Rome, thus alludes to the legend:

"So like they were, no mortal
Might one from other know;
White as snow their armor was,
Their steeds were white as snow.
Never on earthly anvil
Did such rare armor gleam,
And never did such gallant steeds
Drink of an earthly stream.

. . . .

"Back comes the chief in triumph
Who in the hour of fight
Hath seen the great Twin Brethren
In harness on his right.
Safe comes the ship to haven
Through billows and through gales,
If once the great Twin Brethren
Sit shining on the sails."

In the poem of Atalanta in Calydon Mr. Swinburne thus describes the little Helen and Clytemnestra, the sisters of Castor and Pollux:

MELEAGER
"Even such I saw their sisters, one swan white,
The little Helen, and less fair than she,
Fair Clytemnestra, grave as pasturing fawns,
Who feed and fear the arrow; but at whiles,
As one smitten with love or wrung with joy,
She laughs and lightens with her eyes, and then
Weeps; whereat Helen, having laughed, weeps too,
And the other chides her, and she being chid speaks naught,
But cheeks and lips and eyelids kisses her,
Laughing; so fare they, as in their blameless bud,
And full of unblown life, the blood of gods."
ALTHEA
"Sweet days before them, and good loves and lords,
And tender and temperate honors of the hearth;
Peace, and a perfect life and blameless bed"

Chapter 14

BACCHUS. ARIADNE

Bacchus was the son of Jupiter and Semele. Juno, to gratify her resentment against Semele, contrived a plan for her destruction. Assuming the form of Beroe, her aged nurse, she insinuated doubts whether it was indeed Jove himself who came as a lover. Heaving a sigh, she said, "I hope it will turn out so, but I can't help being afraid. People are not always what they pretend to be. If he is indeed Jove, make him give some proof of it. Ask him to come arrayed in all his splendors, such as he wears in heaven. That will put the matter beyond a doubt." Semele was persuaded to try the experiment. She asks a favor, without naming what it is. Jove gives his promise and confirms it with the irrevocable oath, attesting the river Styx, terrible to the gods themselves. Then she made know her request. The god would have stopped her as she spake, but she was too quick for him. The words escaped, and he could neither unsay his promise nor her request. In deep distress he left her and returned to the upper regions. There he clothed himself in his splendors, not putting on all his terrors, as when he overthrew the giants, but what is known among the gods as his lesser panoply. Arrayed in this he entered the chamber of Semele. Her mortal frame could not endure the splendors of the immortal radiance. She was consumed to ashes.

Jove took the infant Bacchus and gave him in charge to the Nysaean nymphs, who nourished his infancy and childhood, and for their care were rewarded by Jupiter by being placed, as the Hyades, among the stars. When Bacchus grew up he discovered the culture of the vine and the mode of extracting its precious juice; but Juno struck him with madness, and drove him forth a wanderer through various parts of the earth. In Phrygia the goddess Rhea cured him and taught him her religious rites, and he set out on a progress through Asia teaching the people the cultivation of the vine. The most famous part of his wanderings is his expedition to India, which is said to have lasted several years. Returning in triumph he undertook to introduce his worship into Greece, but was opposed by some princes who dreaded its introduction on account of the disorders and madness it brought with it.

As he approached his native city Thebes, Pentheus the king, who had no respect for the new worship, forbade its rites to be performed. But when it was known that Bacchus was advancing, men and women, but chiefly the latter, young and old poured forth to meet him and to join his triumphal march.

Mr. Longfellow in his Drinking Song thus describes the march of Bacchus:

"Fauns with youthful Bacchus follow;
Ivy crowns that brow, supernal
As the forehead of Apollo,
And possessing youth eternal.

"Round about him fair Bacchantes,
Bearing cymbals, flutes and thyrses,
Wild from Naxian groves or Zante's
Vineyards, sing delirious verses."

It was in vain Pentheus remonstrated, commanded, and threatened. "Go," said he to his attendants, "seize this vagabond leader of the rout and bring him to me. I will soon make him confess his false claim of heavenly parentage and renounce his counterfeit worship." It was in vain his nearest friends and wisest counselors remonstrated and begged him not to oppose the god. Their remonstrances only made him more violent.

But now the attendants returned whom he had despatched to seize Bacchus. They had been driven away by the Bacchanals, but had succeeded in taking one of them prisoner, whom, with his hands tied behind him, they brought before the king. Pentheus beholding him, with wrathful countenance said, "Fellow! You shall speedily be put to death, that your fate may be a warning to others; but though I grudge the delay of your punishment, speak, tell us who you are, and what are these new rites you presume to celebrate."

The prisoner unterrified responded, "My name is Acetes; my country is Maeonia; my parents were poor people, who had no fields or flocks to leave me, but they left me their fishing rods and nets and their fisherman's trade. This I followed for some time, till growing weary of remaining in one place, I learned the pilot's art and how to guide my course by the stars. It happened as I was sailing for Delos, we touched at the island of Dia and went ashore. Next morning I sent the men for fresh water and myself mounted the hill to observe the wind; when my men returned bringing with them a prize, as they thought, a boy of delicate appearance, whom they had found asleep. They judged he was a noble youth, perhaps a king's son, and they might get a liberal ransom for him. I observed his dress, his walk, his face. There was something in them which I felt sure was more than mortal. I said to my men, 'What god there is concealed in that form I know not, but some one there certainly is. Pardon us, gentle deity, for the violence we have done you, and give success to our undertakings.' Dictys, one of my best hands for climbing the mast and coming down by the ropes, and Melanthus, my steersman, and Epopeus the leader of the sailors' cry, one and all exclaimed, 'Spare your prayers for us.' So blind is the lust of gain! When they proceeded to put him on board I resisted them. 'This ship shall not be profaned by such impiety,' said I. 'I have a greater share in her than any of you.' But Lycabas, a turbulent fellow, seized me by the throat and attempted to throw me overboard, and I scarcely saved myself by clinging to the ropes. The rest approved the deed.

"Then Bacchus, for it was indeed he, as if shaking off his drowsiness, exclaimed, 'What are you doing with me? What is this fighting about? Who brought me here? Where are you going to carry me?' One of them replied, 'fear nothing; tell us where you wish to go and we will take you there.' ''Naxos is my home,' said Bacchus; 'take me there and you shall be well rewarded.' They promised so to do, and told me to pilot the ship to Naxos. Naxos lay to the right, and I was trimming the sails to carry us there, when some by signs and others by whispers signified to me their will that I should sail in the opposite direction, and take the boy to Egypt to sell him for a slave. I was confounded and said, 'Let someone else pilot the ship;' withdrawing myself from any further agency in their wickedness. They cursed me, and one of them exclaiming, 'Don't flatter yourself that we depend on you for our safety,' took my place as pilot, and bore away from Naxos.

"Then the god, pretending that he had just become aware of their treachery, looked out over the sea and said in a voice of weeping, 'Sailors, these are not the shores you promised to take me to; yonder island is not my home. What have I done that you should treat me so? It is small glory you will gain by cheating a poor boy.' I wept to hear him, but the crew laughed at both of us, and sped the vessel fast over the sea. All at once strange as it may seem, it is true the vessel stopped, in the mid sea, as fast as if it was fixed on the ground. The men, astonished, pulled at their oars, and spread more sail, trying to make progress by the aid of both, but all in vain. Ivy twined round the oars and hindered their motion, and clung with its heavy clusters of berries to the sails. A vine, laden with grapes, ran up the mast, and along the sides of the vessel. The sound of flutes was heard and the odor of fragrant wine spread all around. The god himself had a chaplet of vine leaves, and bore in his hand a spear wreathed with ivy. Tigers crouched at his feet, and lynxes and spotted panthers played around him. The sailors were seized with terror or madness; some leaped overboard; others, preparing to do the same, beheld their companions in the water undergoing a change, their bodies becoming flattened and ending in a crooked tail. One exclaimed, 'What miracle is this!' and as he spoke his mouth widened, his nostrils expanded, and scales covered all his body. Another endeavoring to pull the oar felt his hands shrink up, and presently to be no longer hands but fins; another trying to raise his arms to a rope found he had no arms, and curving his mutilated body, jumped into the sea. What had been his legs became the two ends of a crescent-shaped tail. The whole crew became dolphins and swam about the ship, now upon the surface, now under it, scattering the spray, and spouting the water from their broad nostrils. Of twenty men I alone was left. The god cheered me, as I trembled with fear. 'Fear not,' said he; 'steer toward Naxos.' I obeyed, and when we arrived there, I kindled the altars and celebrated the sacred rites of Bacchus."

Pentheus here exclaimed, "We have wasted time enough on this silly story. Take him away and have him executed without delay." Acetes was led away by the attendants and shut up fast in prison; but while they were getting ready the instruments of execution, the prison doors opened of their own accord and the chains fell from his limbs, and when the guards looked for him he was no where to be found.

Pentheus would take no warning, but instead of sending others, determined to go himself to the scene of the solemnities. The mountain Cithaeron was all alive with worshippers, and the cries of the Bacchanals resounded on every side. The noise roused the anger of Pentheus as the sound of a trumpet does the fire of a war-horse. He penetrated the wood and reached an open space where the wildest scene of the orgies met his eyes. At the same moment the women saw him; and first among them his own mother, Agave, blinded by the god, cried out, "See there the wild boar, the hugest monster that prowls in these woods! Come on, sisters! I will be the first to strike the wild boar." The whole band rushed upon him, and while he now talks less arrogantly, now excuses himself, and now confesses his crime and implores pardon, they press upon and wound him. In vain he cries to his aunts to protect him from his mother. Autonoe seized one arm, Ino the other, and between them he was torn to pieces, while his mother shouted, "Victory! Victory! We have done it; the glory is ours!"

So the worship of Bacchus was established in Greece.

There is an allusion to the story of Bacchus and the mariners in Milton's Comus, at line 46. The story of Circe will be found in Chapter 22.

"Bacchus that first from out the purple grape
Crushed the sweet poison of misused wine,
After the Tuscan mariners transformed,
Coasting the Tyrrhene shore as the winds listed
On Circe's island fell; (who knows not Circe,
The daughter of the Sun? Whose charmed cup
Whoever tasted lost his upright shape,
And downward fell into a grovelling swine.)"

ARIADNE

We have seen in the story of Theseus how Ariadne, the daughter of King Minos, after helping Theseus to escape from the labyrinth, was carried by him to the island of Naxos and was left there asleep, while Theseus pursued his way home without her. Ariadne, on waking and finding herself deserted, abandoned herself to grief. But Venus took pity on her, and consoled her with the promise that she should have an immortal lover, instead of the mortal one she had lost.

The island where Ariadne was left was the favorite island of Bacchus, the same that he wished the Tyrrhenian mariners to carry him to, when they so treacherously attempted to make prize of him. As Ariadne sat lamenting her fate, Bacchus found her, consoled her and made her his wife as Minerva had prophesied to Theseus. As a marriage present he gave her a golden crown, enriched with gems, and when she died, he took her crown and threw it up into the sky. As it mounted the gems grew brighter and were turned into stars, and preserving its form Ariadne's crown remains fixed in the heavens as a constellation, between the kneeling Hercules and the man who holds the serpent.

Spenser alludes to Ariadne's crown, though he has made some mistakes in his mythology. It was at the wedding of Pirithous, and not Theseus, that the Centaurs and Lapithae quarrelled.

"Look how the crown which Ariadne wore
Upon her ivory forehead that same day
That Theseus her unto his bridal bore,
When the bold Centaurs made that bloody fray
With the fierce Lapiths which did them dismay;
Being now placed in the firmament,
Through the bright heaven doth her beams display,
And is unto the stars an ornament,
Which round about her move in order excellent."

Figure 19: "Ariadne" by Herbert James Draper

Chapter 15

THE RURAL DEITIES. ERISICHTHON. RHOECUS. THE WATER DEITIES. CAMENAE. WINDS.

Pan, the god of woods and fields, of flocks and shepherds, dwelt in grottos, wandered on the mountains and in valleys, and amused himself with the chase or in leading the dances of the nymphs. He was fond of music, and, as we have seen, the inventor of the syrinx, or shepherd's pipe, which he himself played in a masterly manner. Pan, like other gods who dwelt in forests, was dreaded by those whose occupations caused them to pass through the woods by night, for the gloom and loneliness of such scenes dispose the mind to superstitious fears. Hence sudden fright without any visible cause was ascribed to Pan, and called a Panic terror.

As the name of the god signifies in Greek, ALL, Pan came to be considered a symbol of the universe and personification of Nature; and later still to be regarded as a representative of all the gods, and heathenism itself.

Sylvanus and Faunus were Latin divinities, whose characteristics are so nearly the same as those of Pan that we may safely consider them as the same personage under different names.

The wood-nymphs, Pan's partners in the dance, were but one of several classes of nymphs. There were beside them the Naiads, who presided over brooks and fountains, the Oreads, nymphs of mountains and grottos, and the Nereids, sea-nymphs. The three last named were immortal, but the wood-nymphs, called Dryads or Hamadryads, were believed to perish with the trees which had been their abode, and with which they had come into existence. It was therefore an impious act wantonly to destroy a tree, and in some aggravated cases was severely punished, as in the instance of Erisichthon, which we shall soon record.

Milton, in his glowing description of the early creation, thus alludes to Pan as the personification of Nature:

"Universal Pan,
Knit with the Graces and the Hours in dance,
Led on the eternal spring."

And describing Eve's abode:

"In shadier bower
More sacred or sequestered, though but feigned,
Pan or Sylvanus never slept, nor nymph
Nor Faunus haunted."
Paradise lost, B. IV.

It was a pleasing trait in the old Paganism that it loved to trace in every operation of nature the agency of deity. The imagination of the Greeks peopled all the regions of earth and sea with divinities, to whose agency it attributed those phenomena which our philosophy ascribes to the operation of the laws of nature. Sometimes in our poetical moods we feel disposed to regret the change, and to think that the heart has lost as much as the head has gained by the substitution. The poet Wordsworth thus strongly expresses this sentiment:

"Great God, I'd rather be
A Pagan, suckled in a creed outworn.
So might I, standing on this pleasant lea,
Have glimpses that would make me less forlorn;
Have sight of Proteus rising from th4e sea,
And hear old Tritou blow his wreathed horn."

Schiller, in his poem The Gods of Greece, expresses his regret for the overthrow of the beautiful mythology of ancient times in a way which has called forth an answer from a Christian poetess, Mrs. Browning, in her poem called The Dead Pan. The two following verses are a specimen:

"By your beauty which confesses
Some chief Beauty conquering you,
By our grand heroic guesses
Through your falsehood at the True,
We will weep NOT! Earth shall roll
Heir to each god's aureole,
And Pan is dead.

"Earth outgrows the mythic fancies
Sung beside her in her youth;

And those debonaire romances
Sound but dull beside the truth.
Phoebus' chariot course is run!
Look up poets, to the sun!
Pan, Pan is dead."

These lines are founded on an early Christian tradition that when the heavenly host told the shepherds at Bethlehem of the birth of Christ, a deep groan, heard through all the isles of Greece, told that the great Pan was dead, and that all the royalty of Olympus was dethroned, and the several deities were sent wandering in cold and darkness. So Milton, in his Hymn to the Nativity:

"The lonely mountains o'er,
And the resounding shore,
A voice of weeping heard and loud lament;
From haunted spring and dale,
Edged with poplar pale,
The parting genius is with sighing sent;
With flower-enwoven tresses torn,
The nymphs in twilight shade of tangled thickets mourn."

ERISICHTHON

Erisichthon was a profane person and a despiser of the gods. On one occasion he presumed to violate with the axe a grove sacred to Ceres. There stood in this grove a venerable oak, so large that it seemed a wood in itself, its ancient trunk towering aloft, whereon votive garlands were often hung and inscriptions carved expressing the gratitude of suppliants to the nymph of the tree. Often had the Dryads danced round it hand in hand. Its trunk measured fifteen cubits round, and it overtopped the other trees as they overtopped the shrubbery. But for all that, Erisichthon saw no reason why he should spare it, and he ordered his servants to cut it down. When he saw them hesitate, he snatched an axe from one, and thus impiously exclaimed, :"I care not whether it be a tree beloved of the Goddess or not; were it the goddess herself it should come down, if it stood in my way." So saying, he lifted the axe, and the oak seemed to shudder and utter a groan. When the first blow fell upon the trunk, blood flowed from the wound. All the bystanders were horror-struck, and one of them ventured to remonstrate and hold back the fatal axe. Erisichthon with a scornful look, said to him, "Receive the reward of your piety;" and turned against him the weapon which he had held aside from the tree, gashed his body with many wounds, and cut off his head. Then from the midst of the oak came a voice, "I who dwell in this tree am a nymph beloved of Ceres, and dying by your hands, forewarn you that punishment awaits you." He desisted not from his crime, and at last the tree, sundered by repeated blows and drawn by ropes, fell with a crash, and prostrated a great part of the grove in its fall.

The Dryads, in dismay at the loss of their companion, and at seeing the pride of the forest laid low, went in a body to Ceres, all clad in garments of mourning, and invoked punishment upon Erisichthon. She nodded her assent, and as she bowed her head the grain ripe for harvest in the laden fields bowed also. She planned a punishment so dire that one would pity him, if such a culprit as he could be pitied to deliver him over to Famine. As Ceres herself could not approach Famine, for the Fates have ordained that these two goddesses shall never come together, she called an Oread from her mountain and spoke to her in these words: "There is a place in the farthest part of ice-clad Scythia, a sad and sterile region without trees and without crops. Cold dwells there, and Fear, and Shuddering, and Famine. Go to Famine and tell her to take possession of the bowels of Erisichthon. Let not abundance subdue her, nor the power of my gifts drive her away. Be not alarmed at the distance," (for Famine dwells very far from Ceres,) "but take my chariot. The dragons are fleet and obey the rein, and will take you through the air in a short time." So she gave her the reins, and she drove away and soon reached Scythia. On arriving at Mount Caucasus she stopped the dragons and found Famine in a stony field, pulling up with teeth and claws the scanty herbage. Her hair was rough, her eyes sunk, her face pale, her lips blanched, her jaws covered with dust, and her skin drawn tight, so as to show all her bones. As the Oread saw her afar off (for she did not dare to come near) she delivered the commands of Ceres; and though she stopped as short a time as possible, and kept her distance as well as she could, yet she began to feel hungry, and turned the dragons' heads and drove back to Thessaly.

In obedience to the commands of Ceres, Famine sped through the air to the dwelling of Erisichthon, entered the bed-chamber of the guilty man, and found him asleep. She enfolded him with her wings and breathed herself into him, infusing her poison into his veins. Having discharged her task, she hastened to leave the land of plenty and returned to her accustomed haunts. Erisichthon still slept, and in his dreams craved food, and moved his jaws as if eating. When he awoke his hunger was raging. Without a moment's delay he would have food set before him, of whatever kind earth, sea, or air produces; and complained of hunger even while he ate. What would have sufficed for a city or a nation was not enough for him. The more he ate, the move he craved. His hunger was like the sea, which receives all the rivers, yet is never filled; or like fire that burns all the fuel that is heaped upon it, yet is still voracious for more.

His property rapidly diminished under the unceasing demands of his appetite, but his hunger continued unabated. At length he had spent all, and had only his daughter left, a daughter worthy of a better parent. HER TOO HE SOLD. She scorned to be the slave of a purchaser, and as she stood by the seaside, raised her hands in prayer to Neptune. He heard her prayer, and, though her new master was not far off, and had his eye upon her a moment before, Neptune changed her form, and made her assume that of a fisherman busy at his occupation. Her master, looking for her and seeing her in her altered form, addressed her and said, "Good fisherman, whither went the maiden whom I saw just now, with hair dishevelled and in humble garb, standing about where you stand? Tell me truly; so may your luck be good, and not a fish nibble at your hook and get away." She perceived that her prayer was answered, and rejoiced inwardly at hearing the question asked her of herself. She replied, "Pardon me, stranger, but I have been so intent upon my line, that I have seen nothing else; but I wish I may never catch another fish if I believe any woman or other person except myself to have been hereabouts for some time." He was deceived and went his way, thinking his slave had escaped. Then she resumed her own form. Her father was well pleased to find her still with him, and the money too that he got by the sale of her; so he sold her again. But she was changed by the favor of Neptune as often as she was sold, now into a horse, now a bird, now an ox, and now a stag, got away from her purchasers and came home. By this base method the starving father

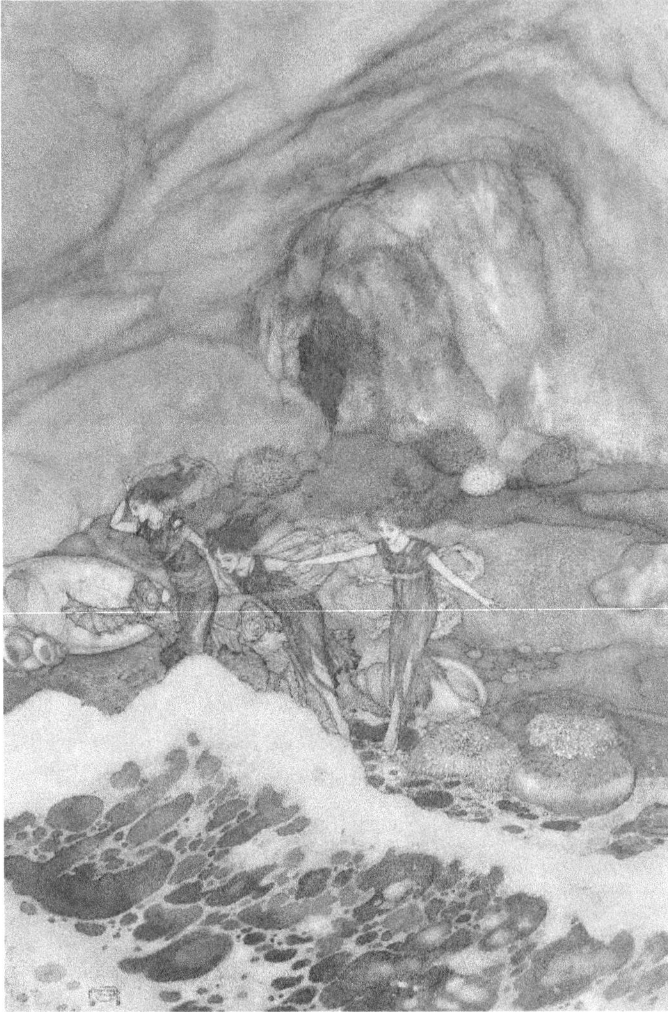

Figure 20: "Chasing the Ebbing Neptune" by Edmund Dulac

procured food; but not enough for his wants, and at last hunger compelled him to devour his limbs, and he strove to nourish his body by eating his body, till death relieved him from the vengeance of Ceres.

RHOECUS

The Hamadryads could appreciate services as well as punish injuries. The story of Rhoecus proves this. Rhoecus, happening to see an oak just ready to fall, ordered his servants to prop it up. The nymph, who had been on the point of perishing with the tree, came and expressed her gratitude to him for having saved her life, and bade him ask what reward he would have for it. Rhoecus boldly asked her love, and the nymph yielded to his desire. She at the same time charged him to be constant, and told him that a bee should be her messenger,

Figure 21: "Sea Nymphs Hourly Ring His Knell" by Warwick Goble

and let him know when she would admit his society. One time the bee came to Rhoecus when he was playing at draughts, and he carelessly brushed it away. This so incensed the nymph that she deprived him of sight.

Our countryman, James Russell Lowell, has taken this story for the subject of one of his shorter poems. He introduces it thus:

"Hear now this fairy legend of old Greece,
As full of freedom, youth and beauty still,
As the immortal freshness of that grace
Carved for all ages on some Attic frieze."

THE WATER DEITIES

Oceanus and Tethys were the Titans who ruled over the Sea. When Jove and his brothers overthrew the Titans and assumed their power, Neptune and Amphitrite succeeded to the dominion of the waters in place of Oceanus and Tethys.

NEPTUNE

Neptune was the chief of the water deities. The symbol of his power was the trident, or spear with three points, with which he used to shatter rocks, to call forth or subdue storms, to shake the shores, and the like. He created the horse, and was the patron of horse races. His own horses had brazen hoofs and golden manes. They drew his chariot over the sea, which became smooth before him, while the monsters of the deep gambolled about his path.

AMPHITRITE

Amphitrite was the wife of Neptune. She was the daughter of Nereus and Doris, and the mother of Triton. Neptune, to pay his court to Amphitrite, came riding on the dolphin. Having won her, he rewarded the dolphin by placing him among the stars.

NEREUS AND DORIS

Nereus and Doris were the parents of the Nereids, the most celebrated of whom were Amphitrite, Thetis, the mother of Achilles, and Galatea, who was loved by the Cyclops Polyphemus. Nereus was distinguished for his knowledge, and his love of truth and justice, and is described as the wise and unerring Old Man of the Sea. The gift of prophecy was also ascribed to him.

TRITON AND PROTEUS

Triton was the son of Neptune and Amphitrite, and the poets make him his father's trumpeter. Proteus was also a son of Neptune. He, like Nereus, is styled a sea-elder for his wisdom and knowledge of future events. His peculiar power was that of changing his shape at will.

THETIS

Thetis, the daughter of Nereus and Doris, was so beautiful that Jupiter himself sought her in marriage; but having learned from Prometheus the Titan, that Thetis should bear a son who should be greater than his father, Jupiter desisted from his suit and decreed that Thetis should be the wife of a mortal. By the aid of Chiron the Centaur, Peleus succeeded in winning the goddess for his bride, and their son was the renowned Achilles. In our chapter on the Trojan war it will appear that Thetis was a faithful mother to him, aiding him in all difficulties, and watching over his interests from the first to the last.

LEUCOTHEA AND PALAEMON

Ino, the daughter of Cadmus and wife of Athamas, flying from her frantic husband, with her little son Melicertes in her arms, sprang from a cliff into the sea. The gods, out of compassion, made her a goddess of the sea, under the name of Leucothea, and him a god under that of Palaemon. Both were held powerful to save from shipwreck, and were invoked by sailors. Palaemon was usually represented riding on a dolphin. The Isthmian games were celebrated in his honor. He was called Portumnus by the Romans, and believed to have jurisdiction of the ports and shores.

Milton alludes to all these deities in the song at the conclusion of Comus.

"Sabrina fair,
Listen and appear to us,
In name of great Oceanus;
By the earth-shaking Neptune's mace,
And Tethys' grave, majestic pace,
By hoary Nereus' wrinkled look,
And the Carpathian wizard's hook (Proteus)
By scaly Triton's winding shell,
And old soothsaying Glaucus; spell,
By Leucothea's lovely hands,
And her son who rules the strands,
By Thetis' tinsel-slippered feet,
And the songs of Sirens sweet."

Armstrong, the poet of the Art of preserving Health, under the inspiration of Hygeia, the goddess of health, thus celebrates the Naiads. Paeon is a name both of Apollo and Aesculapius.

"Come, ye Naiads! To the fountains lead!
Propitious maids! The task remains to sing
Your gifts (so Paeon, so the powers of health
Command), to praise your crystal element.
Oh, comfortable streams! With eager lips
And trembling hands the languid thirsty quaff
New life in you; fresh vigor fills their veins.
No warmer cups the rural ages knew,
None warmer sought the sires of humankind;
Happy in temperate peace their equal days
Felt not the alternate fits of feverish mirth
And sick dejection; still serene and pleased,
Blessed with divine immunity from ills,
Long centuries they lived; their only fate
Was ripe old age, and rather sleep than death."

THE CAMAENAE

By this name the Latins designated the Muses, but included under it also some other deities, principally nymphs of fountains. Egeria was one of them, whose fountain and grotto are still shown. It was said that Numa, the second king of Rome, was favored by this nymph with secret interviews, in which she taught him those lessons of wisdom and of law which he embodied in the institutions of his rising nation. After the death of Numa the nymph pined away and was changed into a fountain.

Byron, in Childe Harold, Canto IV., thus alludes to Egeria and her grotto:

"Here didst thou dwell in this enchanted cover,
Egeria! All thy heavenly bosom beating
For the far footsteps of thy mortal lover;
The purple midnight veiled that mystic meeting
With her most starry canopy."

Tennyson, also, in his Palace of Art, gives us a glimpse of the royal lover expecting the interview.

"Holding one hand against his ear,
To list a footfall ere he saw
The wood-nymph, stayed the Tuscan king to hear
Of wisdom and of law."

THE WINDS

When so many less active agencies were personified, it is not to be supposed that the winds failed to be so. They were Boreas or Aquilo, the north wind, Zephyrus or Favonius, the west, Notus or Auster, the south, and Eurus, the east. The first two have been chiefly celebrated by the poets, the former as the type of rudeness, the latter of gentleness. Boreas loved the nymph Orithyia, and tried to play the lover's part, but met with poor success. It was hard for him to breathe gently, and sighing was out of the question. Weary at last of fruitless endeavors, he acted out his true character, seized the maiden and carried her off. Their children were Zetes and Calais, winged warriors, who accompanied the Argonautic expedition, and did good service in an encounter with those monstrous birds the Harpies.

Zephyrus was the lover of Flora. Milton alludes to them in Paradise Lost, where he describes Adam waking and contemplating Eve still asleep:

"He on his side
Leaning half raised, with looks of cordial love
Hung over her enamored, and beheld
Beauty which, whether waking or asleep,
Shot forth peculiar graces; then with voice,
Mild as when Zephyrus on Flora breathes,
Her hand soft touching, whispered thus, 'Awake!
My fairest, my espoused, my latest found,
Heaven's last, best gift, my ever-new delight.'"

Dr. Young, the poet of the Night Thoughts, addressing the idle and luxurious, says:

"Ye delicate! Who nothing can support
(Yourselves most insupportable), for whom
The winter rose must blow, . .
. . . . And silky soft
Favonious breathe still softer or be chid!"

Fortuna is the Latin name for Tyche, the goddess of Fortune. The worship of Fortuna held a position of much higher importance at Rome than did the worship of Tyche among the Greeks. She was regarded at Rome as the goddess of good fortune only, and was usually represented holding the cornucopia.

Victoria, the Latin form for the goddess Nike, was highly honored among the conquest-loving Romans, and many temples were dedicated to her at Rome. There was a celebrated temple at Athens to the Greek goddess Nike Apteros, or Wingless Victory, of which remains still exist.

Figure 22: "Cupid Armed" by Arthur Rackham

Chapter 16

ACHELOUS AND HERCULES. ADMETUS AND ALCESTIS. ANTIGONE. PENELOPE

The river-god Achelous told the story of Erisichthon to Theseus and his companions, whom he was entertaining at his hospitable board, while they were delayed on their journey by the overflow of his waters. Having finished his story, he added, "But why should I tell of other persons' transformations, when I myself am an instance of the possession of this power. Sometimes I become a serpent, and sometimes a bull, with horns on my head. Or I should say, I once could do so; but now I have but one horn, having lost one." And here he groaned and was silent.

Theseus asked him the cause of his grief, and how he lost his horn. To which question the river-god replied as follows: "Who likes to tell of his defeats? Yet I will not hesitate to relate mine, comforting myself with the thought of the greatness of my conqueror, for it was Hercules. Perhaps you have heard of the fame of Dejanira, the fairest of maidens, whom a host of suitors strove to win. Hercules and myself were of the number, and the rest yielded to us two. He urged in his behalf his descent from Jove, and his labors by which he had exceeded the exactions of Juno, his step-mother. I, on the other hand, said to the father of the maiden, 'Behold me, the king of the waters that flow through your land. I am no stranger from a foreign shore, but belong to the country, a part of your realm. Let it not stand in my way that royal Juno owes me no enmity, nor punishes me with heavy tasks. As for this man, who boasts himself the son of Jove, it is either a false pretence, or disgraceful to him if true, for it cannot be true except by his mother's shame.' As I said this Hercules scowled upon me, and with difficulty restrained his rage. 'My hand will answer better than my tongue,' said he. 'I yield you the victory in words, but trust my cause to the strife of deeds. With that he advanced towards me, and I was ashamed, after what I had said, to yield. I threw off my green vesture, and presented myself for the struggle. He tried to throw me, now attacking my head, now my body. My bulk was my protection, and he assailed me in vain. For a time we stopped, then returned to the conflict. We each kept our position, determined not to yield, foot to foot, I bending over him, clinching his hands in mine, with my forehead almost touching his. Thrice Hercules tried to throw me off, and the fourth time he succeeded, brought me to the ground and himself upon my back. I tell you the truth, it was as if a mountain had fallen on me. I struggled to get my arms at liberty, panting and reeking with perspiration. He gave me no chance to recover, but seized my throat. My knees were on the earth and my mouth in the dust.

"Finding that I was no match for him in the warrior's art, I resorted to others, and glided away in the form of a serpent. I curled my body in a coil, and hissed at him with my forked tongue. He smiled scornfully at this, and said, 'It was the labor of my infancy to conquer snakes.' So saying he clasped my neck with his hands. I was almost choked, and struggled to get my neck out of his grasp. Vanquished in this form, I tried what alone remained to me, and assumed the form of a bull. He grasped my neck with his arm, and, dragging my head down to the ground, overthrew me on the sand. Nor was this enough. His ruthless hand rent my horn from my head. The Naiades took it, consecrated it, and filled it with fragrant flowers. Plenty adopted my horn, and made it her own, and called it Cornucopia.

The ancients were fond of finding a hidden meaning in their mythological tales. They explain this fight of Achelous with Hercules by saying Achelous was a river that in seasons of rain overflowed its banks. When the fable says that Achelous loved Dejanira, and sought a union with her, the meaning is, that the river in its windings flowed through part of Dejanira's kingdom. It was said to take the form of a snake because of its winding, and of a bull because it made a brawling or roaring in its course. When the river swelled, it made itself another channel. Thus, its head was horned. Hercules prevented the return of these periodical overflows, by embankments and canals; and therefore he was said to have vanquished the river-god and cut off his horn. Finally, the lands formerly subject to overflow, but now redeemed, became very fertile, and this is meant by the horn of plenty.

There is another account of the origin of the Cornucopia. Jupiter at his birth was committed by his mother Rhea to the care of the daughters of Melisseus, a Cretan king. They fed the infant deity with the milk of the goat Amalthea. Jupiter broke off one of the horns of the goat and gave it to his nurses, and endowed it with the wonderful power of becoming filled with whatever the possessor might wish.

The name of Amalthea is also given by some writers to the mother of Bacchus. It is thus used by Milton, Paradise Lost, Book IV.:

"That Nyseian isle,
Girt with the river Triton, where old Cham,
Whom Gentiles Ammon call, and Libyan Jove,
Hid Amalthea and her florid son,
Young Bacchus, from his stepdame Rhea's eye."

ADMETUS AND ALCESTIS

Aesculapius, the son of Apollo, was endowed by his father with such skill in the healing art that he even restored the dead to life. At this Pluto took alarm, and prevailed on Jupiter to launch a thunderbolt at Aesculapius. Apollo was indignant at the destruction of his son, and wreaked his vengeance on the innocent workmen who had made the thunderbolt. These were the Cyclopes, who have their workshop under Mount Aetna, from which the smoke and flames of their furnaces are constantly issuing. Apollo shot his arrows at the Cyclopes, which so incensed Jupiter that he condemned him as a punishment to become he servant of a mortal for the space of one year. Accordingly, Apollo went into the service of Admetus, king of Thessaly, and pastured his flocks for him on the verdant banks of the river Amphrysus.

Admetus was a suitor, with others, for the hand of Alcestis, the daughter of Pelias, who promised her to him who should come for her in a chariot drawn by lions and boars. This task Admetus performed by the assistance of his divine herdsman, and was made happy in the possession of Alcestis. But Admetus fell ill, and being near to death, Apollo prevailed on the Fates to spare him on condition that someone would consent to die in his stead. Admetus, in his joy at this reprieve, thought little of the ransom, and perhaps remembering the declarations of attachment which he had often heard from his courtiers and dependents, fancied that it would be easy to find a substitute. But it was not so. Brave warriors, who would willingly have perilled their lives for their prince, shrunk from the thought of dying for him on the bed of sickness; and old servants who had experienced his bounty and that of his house from their childhood up, were not willing to lay down the scanty remnant of their days to show their gratitude. Men asked, "Why does not one of his parents do it? They cannot in the course of nature live much longer, and who can feel like them the call to rescue the life they gave from an untimely end?" But the parents, distressed though they were at the thought of losing him, shrunk from the call. Then Alcestis, with a generous self-devotion, proffered herself as the substitute. Admetus, fond as he was of life, would not have submitted to receive it at such a cost; but there was no remedy. The condition imposed by the Fates had been met, and the decree was irrevocable. Alcestis sickened as Admetus revived, and she was rapidly sinking to the grave.

Just at this time Hercules arrived at the palace of Admetus, and found all the inmates in great distress for the impending loss of the devoted wife and beloved mistress. Hercules, to whom no labor was too arduous, resolved to attempt her rescue. He went and lay in wait at the door of the chamber of the dying queen, and when Death came for his prey, he seized him and forced him to resign his victim. Alcestis recovered, and was restored to her husband.

Milton alludes to the story of Alcestis in his Sonnet on his deceased wife.

"Methought I saw my late espoused saint,
Brought to me like Alcestis from the grave,
Whom Jove's great son to her glad husband gave,
Rescued from death by force, though pale and faint."

James Russell Lowell has chosen the "Shepherd of King Admetus" for the subject of a short poem. He makes that event the first introduction of poetry to men.

"Men called him but a shiftless youth,
In whom no good they saw,
And yet unwittingly, in truth,
They made his careless words their law.
And day by day more holy grew
Each spot where he had trod,
Till after poets only knew
Their first-born brother was a god."

In The Love of Alcestis, one of the poems in The Earthly Paradise, Mr. Morris thus tells the story of the taming of the lions:

"—— Rising up no more delay he made,
But took the staff and gained the palace-door
Where stood the beasts, whose mingled whine and roar
Had wrought his dream; there two and two they stood,
Thinking, it might be, of the tangled wood,
And all the joys of the food-hiding trees.
But harmless as their painted images
'Neath some dread spell; then, leaping up, he took
The reins in hand and the bossed leather shook,
And no delay the conquered beasts durst make,
But drew, not silent; and folk just awake,
When he went by as though a god they saw,
Fell on their knees, and maidens come to draw
Fresh water from the fount, sank trembling down,
And silence held the babbling, wakened town."

ANTIGONE

The poems and histories of legendary Greece often relate, as has been seen, to women and their lives. Antigone was as bright an example of filial and sisterly fidelity as was Alcestis of connubial devotion. She was the daughter of Œdipus and Jocasta, who, with all their descendants, were the victims of an unrelenting fate, dooming them to destruction. Œdipus in his madness had torn out his eyes, and was driven forth from his kingdom Thebes, dreaded and abandoned by all men, as an object of divine vengeance. Antigone, his daughter, alone shared his wanderings, and remained with him till he died, and then returned to Thebes.

Her brothers, Eteocles and Polynices, had agreed to share the kingdom between them, and reign alternately year by year. The first year fell to the lot of Eteocles, who, when his time expired, refused to surrender the kingdom to his brother. Polynices fled to Adrastus, king of Argos, who gave him his daughter in marriage, and aided him with an army to enforce his claim to the kingdom. This led to the celebrated expedition of the "Seven against Thebes," which furnished ample materials for the epic and tragic poets of Greece.

Amphiaraus, the brother-in-law of Adrastus, opposed the enterprise, for he was a soothsayer, and knew by his art that no one of the leaders except Adrastus would live to return. But Amphiaraus, on his marriage to Eriphyle, the king's sister, had agreed that whenever he and Adrastus should differ in opinion, the decision should be left to Eriphyle. Polynices, knowing this, gave Eriphyle the collar of Harmonia, and thereby gained her to his interest. This collar or necklace was a present which Vulcan had given to Harmonia on her marriage with Cadmus, and Polynices had taken it with him on his flight from Thebes. Eriphyle could not resist so tempting a bribe, and by her decision the war was resolved on, and Amphiaraus went to his certain fate. He bore his part bravely in the contest, but could not avert his destiny. Pursued by the enemy he fled along the river, when a thunderbolt launched by Jupiter opened the ground, and he, his chariot, and his charioteer, were swallowed up.

It would not be in place here to detail all the acts of heroism or atrocity which marked the contest; but we must not omit to record the fidelity of Evadne as an offset to the weakness of Eriphyle. Capaneus, the husband of Evadne, in the ardor of the fight, declared that he would force his way into the city in spite of Jove himself. Placing a ladder against the wall, he mounted, but Jupiter, offended at his impious language, struck him with a thunderbolt. When his obsequies were celebrated, Evadne cast herself on his funeral pile and perished.

Early in the contest Eteocles consulted the soothsayer Tiresias as to the issue. Tiresias, in his youth, had by chance seen Minerva bathing. The goddess in her wrath deprived him of his sight, but afterwards relenting gave him in compensation the knowledge of future events. When consulted by Eteocles, he declared that victory should fall to Thebes if Menoeceus, the son of Creon, gave himself a voluntary victim. The heroic youth, learning the response, threw away his life in the first encounter.

The siege continued long, with various success. At length both hosts agreed that the brothers should decide their quarrel by single combat. They fought and fell by each other's hands. The armies then renewed the fight, and at last the invaders were forced to yield, and fled, leaving their dead unburied. Creon, the uncle of the fallen princes,

Figure 23: "King Oedipus" by Emil Teschendorff

now become king, caused Eteocles to be buried with distinguished honor, but suffered the body of Polynices to lie where it fell, forbidding every one, on pain of death, to give it burial.

Antigone, the sister of Polynices, heard with indignation the revolting edict which consigned her brother's body to the dogs and vultures, depriving it of those rites which were considered essential to the repose of the dead. Unmoved by the dissuading counsel of an affectionate but timid sister, and unable to procure assistance, she determined to brave the hazard and to bury the body with her own hands. She was detected in the act, and Creon gave orders that she should be buried alive, as having deliberately set at nought the solemn edict of the city. Her love, Haemon, the son of Creon, unable to avert her fate, would not survive her, and fell by his own hand.

Antigone forms the subject of two fine tragedies of the Grecian poet Sophocles. Mrs. Jameson, in her Characteristics of Women, has compared her character with that of Cordelia, in Shakespeare's King Lear. The perusal of her remarks cannot fail to gratify our readers.

The following is the lamentation of Antigone over Œdipus, when death has at last relieved him from his sufferings:

"Alas! I only wished I might have died
With my poor father; wherefore should I ask
For longer life?
Oh, I was fond of misery with him;
E'en what was most unlovely grew beloved
When he was with me. Oh, my dearest father,
Beneath the earth now in deep darkness hid,
Worn as thou wert with age, to me thou still
Wast dear, and shalt be ever."
Francklin's Sophocles

PENELOPE

Penelope is another of those mythic heroines whose beauties were rather those of character and conduct than of person. She was the daughter of Icarius, a Spartan prince. Ulysses, king of Ithaca, sought her in marriage, and won her over all competitors. When the moment came for the bride to leave her father's house, Icarius, unable to bear the thoughts of parting with his daughter, tried to persuade her to remain with him, and not accompany her husband to Ithaca. Ulysses gave Penelope her choice, to stay or go with him. Penelope made no reply, but dropped her veil over her face. Icarius urged her no further, but when she was gone erected a statue to Modesty on the spot where they parted.

Ulysses and Penelope had not enjoyed their union more than a year when it was interrupted by the events which called Ulysses to the Trojan war. During his long absence, and when it was doubtful whether he still lived, and highly improbable that he would ever return, Penelope was importuned by numerous suitors, from whom there seemed no refuge but in choosing one of them for her husband. Penelope, however, employed every art to gain time, still hopping for Ulysses' return. One of her arts of delay was engaging in the preparation of a robe for the funeral canopy of Laertes, her husband's father. She pledged herself to make her choice among the suitors when the robe was finished. During the day she worked at the robe, but in the night she undid the work of the day. This is the famous Penelope's web, which is used as a proverbial expression for anything which is perpetually doing but never done. The rest of Penelope's history will be told when we give an account of her husband's adventures.

Chapter 17

ORPHEUS AND EURYDICE. ARTISTAEUS. AMPHION. LINUS. THAMYRIS. MARSYAS. MELAMPUS. MUSAEUS

Orpheus was the son of Apollo and the muse Calliope. He was presented by his father with a lyre and taught to play upon it, and he played to such perfection that nothing could withstand the charm of his music. Not only his fellow mortals, but wild beasts were softened by his strains, and gathering round him laid by their fierceness, and stood entranced with his lay. Nay, the very trees and rocks were sensible to the charm. The former crowded round him and the latter relaxed somewhat of their hardness, softened by his notes.

Hymen had been called to bless with his presence the nuptials of Orpheus with Eurydice; but though he attended, he brought no happy omens with him. His very torch smoked and brought tears into their eyes. In coincidence with such prognostics Eurydice, shortly after her marriage, while wandering with the nymphs, her companions, was seen by the shepherd Aristaeus, who was struck with her beauty, and made advances to her. She fled, and in flying trod upon a snake in the grass, was bitten in the foot and died. Orpheus sang his grief to all who breathed the upper air, both gods and men, and finding it all unavailing resolved to seek his wife in the regions of the dead. He descended by a cave situated on the side of the promontory of Taenarus and arrived at the Stygian realm. He passed through crowds of ghosts, and presented himself before the throne of Pluto and Proserpine. Accompanying the words with the lyre, he sung, "O deities of the underworld, to whom all we who live must come, hear my words, for they are true! I come not to spy out the secrets of Tartarus, nor to try my strength against the three-headed dog with snaky hair who guards the entrance. I come to seek my wife, whose opening years the poisonous viper's fang has brought to an untimely end. Love had led me here, Love, a god all powerful with us who dwell on the earth, and, if old traditions say true, not less so here. I implore you by these abodes full of terror, these realms of silence and uncreated things, unite again the thread of Eurydice's life. We all are destined to you, and sooner or later must pass to your domain. She too, when she shall have filled her term of life, will rightly be yours. But till then grant her to me, I beseech you. If you deny me, I cannot return alone; you shall triumph in the death of us both."

As he sang these tender strains, the very ghosts shed tears. Tantalus, in spite of his thirst, stopped for a moment his efforts for water, Ixion's wheel stood still, the vulture ceased to tear the giant's liver, the daughters of Danaus rested from their task of drawing water in a sieve, and Sisyphus sat on his rock to listen. Then for the first time, it is said, the cheeks of the Furies were wet with tears. Proserpine could not resist, and Pluto himself gave way. Eurydice was called. She came from among the new-arrived ghosts, limping with her wounded foot. Orpheus was permitted to take her away with him on one condition, that he should not turn round to look at her till they should have reached the upper air. Under this condition they proceeded on their way, he leading, she following, through passages dark and steep, in total silence, till they had nearly reached the outlet into the cheerful upper world, when Orpheus, in a moment of forgetfulness, to assure himself that she was still following, cast a glance behind him, when instantly she was borne away. Stretching out their arms to embrace one another they grasped only the air. Dying now a second time she yet cannot reproach her husband, for how can she blame his impatience to behold her? "Farewell," she said, "a last farewell," and was hurried away, so fast that the sound hardly reached his ears.

Orpheus endeavored to follow her, and besought permission to return and try once more for her release but the stern ferryman repulsed him and refused passage. Seven days he lingered about the brink, without food or sleep; then bitterly accusing of cruelty the powers of Erebus, he sang his complaints to the rocks and mountains, melting the hearts of tigers and moving the oaks from their stations. He held himself aloof from womankind, dwelling constantly on the recollection of his sad mischance. The Thracian maidens tried their best to captivate him, but he repulsed their advances. They bore with him as long as they could; but finding him insensible, one day, one of them, excited by the rites of Bacchus, exclaimed, "See yonder our despiser!" and threw at him her javelin. The weapon, as soon as it came within the sound of his lyre, fell harmless at his feet. So did also the stones that they threw at him. But the women raised a scream and drowned the voice of the music, and then the missiles reached him and soon were stained with his blood. The maniacs tore him limb from limb, and threw his head and his lyre into the river Hebrus, down which they floated, murmuring sad music, to which the shores responded a plaintive symphony. The Muses gathered up the fragments of his body and buried them at Libethra, where the nightingale is said to sing over his grave more sweetly than in any other part of Greece. His lyre was placed by Jupiter among the stars. His shade passed a second time to Tartarus, where he sought out his Eurydice and embraced her, with eager arms. They roam through those happy fields together now, sometimes he leads, sometimes she; and Orpheus gazes as much as he will upon her, no longer incurring a penalty for a thoughtless glance.

Figure 24: "Orpheus" by Arthur Rackham

The story of Orpheus has furnished Pope with an illustration of the power of music, for his Ode for St. Cecelia's Day. The following stanza relates the conclusion of the story:

"But soon, too soon the lover turns his eyes;
Again she falls, again she dies, she dies!
How wilt thou now the fatal sisters move?
No crime was thine, if 'tis no crime to love.
Now under hanging mountains,
Beside the falls of fountains,
Or where Hebrus wanders,
Rolling in meanders,
All alone,
He makes his moan,
And calls her ghost,
Forever, ever, ever lost!
Now with furies surrounded,
Despairing, confounded,
He trembles, he glows,
Amidst Rhodope's snows.
See, wild as the winds o'er the desert he flies;
Hark! Haemus resounds with the Bacchanals' cries.
Ah, see, he dies!
Yet even in death Eurydice he sung,
Eurydice still trembled on his tongue;
Eurydice the woods,
Eurydice the floods,
Eurydice the rocks and hollow mountains rung."

The superior melody of the nightingale's song over the grave of Orpheus, is alluded to by Southey in his Thalaba:

"Then on his ear what sounds
Of harmony arose!
Far music and the distance-mellowed song
From bowers of merriment;
The waterfall remote;
The murmuring of the leafy groves;
The single nightingale
Perched in the rosier by, so richly toned,

That never from that most melodious bird
Singing a love-song to his brooding mate,
Did Thracian shepherd by the grave
Of Orpheus hear a sweeter melody,
Though there the spirit of the sepulchre
All his own power infuse, to swell
The incense that he loves."

ARISTAEUS, THE BEE-KEEPER

Man avails himself of the instincts of the inferior animals for his own advantage. Hence sprang the art of keeping bees. Honey must first have been known as a wild product, the bees building their structures in hollow trees or holes in the rocks, or any similar cavity that chance offered. Thus occasionally the carcass of a dead animal would be occupied by the bees for that purpose. It was no doubt from some such incident that the superstition arose that the bees were engendered by the decaying flesh of the animal; and Virgil, in the following story (From the Georgies, Book IV.1.317), shows how this supposed fact may be turned to account for renewing the swarm when it has been lost by disease or accident.

The shepherd Aristaeus, who first taught the management of bees, was the son of the water-nymph Cyrene. His bees had perished, and he resorted for aid to his mother. He stood at the river side and thus addressed her: "Oh, mother, the pride of my life is taken from me! I have lost my precious bees. My care and skill have availed me nothing, and you, my mother, have not warded off from me the blow of misfortune." His mother heard these complaints as she sat in her palace at the bottom of the river with her attendant nymphs around her. They were engaged in female occupations, spinning and weaving, while one told stories to amuse the rest. The sad voice of Aristaeus interrupting their occupation, one of them put her head above the water and seeing him, returned and gave information to his mother, who ordered that he should be brought into her presence. The river at her command opened itself and let him pass in, while it stood curled like a mountain on either side. He descended to the region where the fountains of the great rivers lie; he saw the enormous receptacles of waters and was almost deafened with the roar, while he surveyed them hurrying off in various directions to water the face of the earth. Arriving at his mother's apartment he was hospitably received by Cyrene and her nymphs, who spread their table with the richest dainties. They first poured out libations to Neptune, then regaled themselves with the feast, and after that Cyrene thus addressed him: "There is an old prophet named Proteus, who dwells in the sea and is a favorite of Neptune, whose herd of sea-calves he pastures. We nymphs hold him in great respect, for he is a learned sage, and knows all things, past, present, and to come. He can tell you, my son, the cause of the mortality among your bees, and how you may remedy it. But he will not do it voluntarily, however you may entreat him. You must compel him by force. If you seize him and chain him, he will answer your questions in order to get released, for he cannot, by all his arts, get away if you hold fast the chains. I will carry you to his cave, where he comes at noon to take his midday repose. Then you may easily secure him. But when he finds himself captured, his resort is to a power he possesses of changing himself into various forms. He will become a wild boar or a fierce tiger, a scaly dragon, or lion with yellow mane. Or he will make a noise like the crackling of flames or the rush of water, so as to tempt you to let go the chain, when he will make his escape. But you have only to keep him fast bound, and at last when he finds all his arts unavailing, he will return to his own figure and obey your commands." So saying she sprinkled her son with fragrant nectar, the beverage of the gods, and immediately an unusual vigor filled his frame and courage his heart, while perfume breathed all around him.

The nymph led her son to the prophet's cave, and concealed him among the recesses of the rocks, while she herself took her place behind the clouds. Then noon came and the hour when men and herds retreat from the glaring sun to indulge in quiet slumber, Proteus issued from the water, followed by his herd of sea- calves, which spread themselves along the shore. He sat on the rock and counted his herd; then stretched himself on the floor of the cave and went to sleep. Aristaeus hardly allowed him to get fairly asleep before he fixed the fetters on him and shouted aloud. Proteus, waking and finding himself captured, immediately resorted to his arts, becoming first a fire, then a flood, then a horrible wild beast, in rapid succession. But trying all in vain, he at last resumed his own form and addressed the youth in angry accents: "Who are you, bold youth, who thus invade my abode, and what do you want with me?" Aristaeus replied, "Proteus, you know already, for it is needless for anyone to attempt to deceive you. And do you also cease your efforts to elude me. I am led hither by divine assistance, to know from you the cause of my misfortune and how to remedy it." At these words the prophet, fixing on him his gray eyes with a piercing look, thus spoke: "You received the merited reward of your deeds, by which Eurydice met her death, for in flying from you she trod upon a serpent, of whose bite she died. To avenge her death the nymphs, her companions, have sent this destruction bo your bees. You have to appease their anger, and thus it must be done: Select four bulls of perfect form and size, and four cows of equal beauty, build four altars to the nymphs, and sacrifice the animals, leaving their carcasses in the leafy grove. To Orpheus and Eurydice you shall pay such funeral honors as may allay their resentment. Returning after nine days you will examine the bodies of the cattle slain and see what will befall." Aristaeus faithfully obeyed these directions. He sacrificed the cattle, he left their bodies in the grove, he offered funeral honors to the shades of Orpheus and Eurydice; then returning on the ninth day he examined the bodies of the animals, and, wonderful to relate! A swarm of bees had taken possession of one of the carcasses, and were pursuing their labors there as in a hive.

In the Task, Cowper alludes to the story of Aristaeus, when speaking of the ice-palace built by the Empress Anne of Russia. He has been describing the fantastic forms which ice assumes in connection with waterfalls, etc."

"Less worthy of applause though more admired,
Because a novelty, the work of man,
Imperial mistress of the fur-clad Russ,
Thy most magnificent and mighty freak,
The wonder of the north. No forest fell
When thou wouldst build, no quarry sent its stores
T'enrich thy walls; but thou didst hew the floods
And make thy marble of the glassy wave.
In such a palace Aristaeus found
Cyrene, when he bore the plaintive tale
Of his lost bees to her maternal ear."

Milton also appears to have had Cyrene and her domestic scene in his mind when he describes to us Sabrina, the nymph of the river Severn, in the Guardian-spirit's Song in Comus:

"Sabrina fair!
Listen when thou art sitting
Under the glassy, cool, translucent wave
In twisted braids of lilies knitting
The loose train of thy amber-dropping hair;
Listen for dear honor's sake,
Goddess of the silver lake!
Listen and save."

The following are other celebrated mythical poets and musicians, some of whom were hardly inferior to Orpheus himself:

AMPHION

Amphion was the son of Jupiter and Antiope, queen of Thebes. With his twin brother Zethus he was exposed at birth on Mount Cithaeron, where they grew up among the shepherds, not knowing their parentage. Mercury gave Amphion a lyre, and taught him to play upon it, and his brother occupied himself in hunting and tending the flocks. Meanwhile Antiope, their mother, who had been treated with great cruelty by Lycus, the usurping king of Thebes, and by Dirce, his wife, found means to inform her children of their rights, and to summon them to her assistance. With a band of their fellow-herdsmen they attacked and slew Lycus, and tying Dirce by the hair of her head to a bull, let him drag her till she was dead (the punishment of Dirce is the subject of a celebrated group of statuary now in the Museum at Naples). Amphion, having become king of Thebes fortified the city with a wall. It is said that when he played on his lyre the stones moved of their own accord and took their places in the wall.

In Tennyson's poem of Amphion is an amusing use of this story:

"Oh, had I lived when song was great,
In days of old Amphion,
And ta'en my fiddle to the gate
Nor feared for reed or scion!

And had I lived when song was great,
And legs of trees were limber,
And ta'en my fiddle to the gate,
And fiddled to the timber!

"'Tis said he had a tuneful tongue,
Such happy intonation,
Wherever he sat down and sung
He left a small plantation;
Whenever in a lonely grove
He set up his forlorn pipes,
The gouty oak began to move
And flounder into hornpipes."

LINUS

Linus was the instructor of Hercules in music, but having one day reproved his pupil rather harshly, he roused the anger of Hercules, who struck him with his lyre and killed him.

THAMYRIS

An ancient Thracian bard, who in his presumption challenged the Muses to a trial of skill, and being overcome in the contest was deprived by them of his sight. Milton alludes to him with other blind bards, when speaking of his own blindness (Paradise Lost, Book III.35).

MARSYAS

Minerva invented the flute, and played upon it to the delight of all the celestial auditors; but the mischievous urchin Cupid having dared to laugh at the queer face which the goddess made while playing, Minerva threw the instrument indignantly away, and it fell down to earth, and was found by Marsyas. He blew upon it, and drew from it such ravishing sounds that he was tempted to challenge Apollo himself to a musical contest. The god of course triumphed, and punished Marsyas by flaying him alive.

MELAMPUS

Melampus was the first mortal endowed with prophetic powers. Before his house there stood an oak tree containing a serpent's nest. The old serpents were killed by the servants, but Melampus took care of the young ones and fed them carefully. One day when he was asleep under the oak, the serpents licked his ears with their tongues. On awaking he was astonished to find that he now understood the language of birds and creeping things. This knowledge enabled him to foretell future events, and he became a renowned soothsayer. At one time his enemies took him captive and kept him strictly imprisoned. Melampus in the silence of night heard the wood-worms in the timbers talking together, and found out by what they said that the timbers were nearly eaten through, and the roof would soon fall in. He told his captors and demanded to be let out, warning them also. They took his warning, and thus escaped destruction, and rewarded Malampus and held him in high honor.

MUSAEUS

A semi-mythological personage who was represented by one tradition to be the son of Orpheus. He is said to have written sacred poems and oracles. Milton couples his name with that of Orpheus in his Il Penseroso:

"But, oh, sad virgin, that thy power
Might raise Musaeus from his bower,
Or bed the soul of Orpheus sing
Such notes as warbled to the string,
Drew iron tears down Pluto's cheek,
And made Hell grant what love did seek."

Chapter 18

ARION. IBYCUS. SIMONIDES. SAPPHO

The poets whose adventures compose this chapter were real persons, some of whose works yet remain, and their influence on poets who succeeded them is yet more important than their poetical remains. The adventures recorded of them in the following stories rest on the same authority as other narratives of the Age of Fable, that is, that of the poets who have told them. In their present form, the first two are translated from the German, the story of Arion from Schlegel, and that of Ibycus from Schiller.

ARION

Arion was a famous musician, and dwelt at the court of Periander, king of Corinth, with whom he was a great favorite. There was to be a musical contest in Sicily, and Arion longed to compete for the prize. He told his wish to Periander, who besought him like a brother to give up the thought. "Pray stay with me," he said, "and be contented. He who strives to win may lose." Arion answered, "A wandering life best suits the free heart of a poet. The talent which a god bestowed on me, I would fain make a source of pleasure to others. And if I win the prize, how will the enjoyment of it be increased by the consciousness of my wide- spread fame!" He went, won the prize, and embarked with his wealth in a Corinthian ship for home. On the second morning after setting sail, the wind breathed mild and fair. "Oh, Periander," he exclaimed, "dismiss your fears! Soon shall you forget them in my embrace. With what lavish offerings will we display our gratitude to the gods, and how merry will we be at the festal board!" The wind and sea continued propitious. Not a cloud dimmed the firmament. He had not trusted too much to the ocean, but he had to man. He overheard the seamen exchanging hints with one another, and found they were plotting to possess themselves of his treasure. Presently they surrounded him loud and mutinous, and said, "Arion, you must die! If you would have a grave on shore, yield yourself to die on this spot; but if otherwise, cast yourself into the sea." "Will nothing satisfy you but my life?" said he. "Take my gold, and welcome. I willingly buy my life at that price." "No, no; we cannot spare you. Your life will be too dangerous to us. Where could we go to escape from Periander, if he should know that you had been robbed by us? Your gold would be of little use to us, if, on returning home, we could never more be free from fear." "Grant me, then," said he, "a last request, since nought will avail to save my life, that I may die as I have lived, as becomes a bard. When I shall have sung my death-song, and my harp-strings shall cease to vibrate, then I will bid farewell to life, and yield uncomplaining to my fate." This prayer, like the others, would have been unheeded, they thought only of their booty, but to hear so famous a musician, that moved their rude hearts. "Suffer me," he added, "to arrange my dress. Apollo will not favor me unless I be clad in my minstrel garb."

He clothed his well-proportioned limbs in gold and purple fair to see, his tunic fell around him in graceful folds, jewels adorned his arms, his brow was crowned with a golden wreath, and over his neck and shoulders flowed his hair perfumed with odors. His left hand held the lyre, his right the ivory wand with which he struck its chords. Like one inspired, he seemed to drink the morning air and glitter in the morning ray. The seamen gazed with admiration. He strode forward to the vessel's side and looked down into the blue sea. Addressing his lyre, he sang, "Companion of my voice, come with me to the realm of shades. Though Cerberus may growl, we know the power of song can tame his rage. Ye heroes of Elysium, who have passed the darkling flood, ye happy souls, soon shall I join your band. Yet can ye relieve my grief? Alas, I leave my friend behind me. Thou, who didst find thy Eurydice, and lose her again as soon as found; when she had vanished like a dream, how didst thou hate the cheerful light! I must away, but I will not fear. The gods look down upon us. Ye who slay me unoffending, when I am no more, your time of trembling shall come. Ye Nereids, receive your guest, who throws himself upon your mercy!" So saying, he sprang into the deep sea. The waves covered him, and the seamen held on their way, fancying themselves safe from all danger of detection.

But the strains of his music had drawn round him the inhabitants of the deep to listen, and dolphins followed the ship as if chained by a spell. While he struggled in the

Figure 25: "Arion on the Dolphin" by Francois Boucher

waves, a dolphin offered him his back, and carried him mounted thereon safe to shore. At the spot where he landed, a monument of brass was afterwards erected upon the rocky shore, to preserve the memory of the event.

When Arion and the dolphin parted, each to his own element, Arion thus poured forth his thanks. "Farewell, thou faithful, friendly fish! Would that I could reward thee; but thou canst not wend with me, nor I with thee. Companionship we may not have. May Galatea, queen of the deep, accord thee her favor, and thou, proud of the burden, draw her chariot over the smooth mirror of the deep."

Arion hastened from the shore, and soon saw before him the towers of Corinth. He journeyed on, harp in hand, singing as he went, full of love and happiness, forgetting his losses, and mindful only of what remained, his friend and his lyre. He entered the hospitable halls, and was soon clasped in the embrace of Periander. "I come back to thee, my friend," he said. "The talent which a god bestowed has been the delight of thousands, but false knaves have stripped me of my well-earned treasure; yet I retain the consciousness of wide-spread fame." Then he told Periander all the wonderful events that had befallen him, who heard him with amazement. "Shall such wickedness triumph?" said he. "Then in vain is power lodged in my hands. That we may discover the criminals, you must remain here in concealment, and so they will approach without suspicion." When the ship arrived in the harbor, he summoned the mariners before him. "Have you heard anything of Arion?" he inquired. "I anxiously look for his return." They replied, "We left him well and prosperous in Tarentum." As they said these words, Arion stepped forth and faced them. His well-proportioned limbs were arrayed in gold and purple fair to see, his tunic fell around him in graceful folds, jewels adorned his arms, his brow was crowned with a golden wreath, and over his neck and shoulders flowed his hair perfumed with odors; his left hand held the lyre, his right the ivory wand with which he struck its chords. They fell prostrate at his feet, as if a lightning bolt had struck them. "We meant to murder him, and he has become a god. O Earth, open and receive us!" Then Periander spoke. "He lives, the master of the lay! Kind Heaven protects the poet's life. As for you, I invoke not the spirit of vengeance; Arion wishes not your blood. Ye slaves of avarice, begone! Seek some barbarous land, and never may aught beautiful delight your souls!"

Spencer represents Arion, mounted on his dolphin, accompanying the train of Neptune and Amphitrite:

"Then was there heard a most celestial sound
Of dainty music which did next ensue,
And, on the floating waters as enthroned,
Arion with his harp unto him drew
The ears and hearts of all that goodly crew;
Even when as yet the dolphin which him bore
Through the Aegean Seas from pirates' view,
Stood still, by him astonished at his love,
And all the raging seas for joy forgot to roar."

Byron, in his Childe Harold, Canto II., alludes to the story of Arion, when, describing his voyage, he represents one of the seamen making music to entertain the rest:

"The moon is up; by Heaven, a lovely eve!
Long streams of light o'er dancing waves expand;
Now lads on shore may sigh and maids believe;
Such be our fate when we return to land!
Meantime some rude Arion's restless hand
Wakes the brisk harmony that sailors love;
A circle there of merry listeners stand,
Or to some well-known measure featly move
Thoughtless as if on shore they still were free to rove."

IBYCUS

In order to understand the story of Ibycus which follows, it is necessary to remember, first, that the theatres of the ancients were immense buildings providing seats for from ten to thirty thousand spectators, and as they were used only on festal occasions, and admission was free to all, they were usually filled. They were without roofs and open to the sky, and the performances were in the daytime. Secondly, the appalling representation of the Furies is not exaggerated in the story. It is recorded that Æschylus, the tragic poet, having on one occasion represented the Furies in a chorus of fifty performers, the terror of the spectators was such that many fainted and were thrown into convulsions, and the magistrates forbade a like representation for the future.

Ibycus, the pious poet, was on his way to the chariot races and musical competitions held at the Isthmus of Corinth, which attracted all of Grecian lineage. Apollo had bestowed on him the gift of song, the honeyed lips of the poet, and he pursued his way with lightsome step, full of the god. Already the towers of Corinth crowning the height appeared in view, and he had entered with pious awe the sacred grove of Neptune. No living object was in sight, only a flock of cranes flew overhead, taking the same course as himself in their migration to a southern clime. "Good luck to you, ye friendly squadrons," he exclaimed, "my companions from across the sea. I take your company for a good omen. We come from far, and fly in search of hospitality. May both of us meet that kind reception which shields the stranger guest from harm!"

He paced briskly on, and soon was in the middle of the wood. There suddenly, at a narrow pass, two robbers stepped forth and barred his way. He must yield or fight. But his hand, accustomed to the lyre and not to the strife of arms, sank powerless. He called for help on men and gods, but his cry reached no defender's ear. "Then here must I die," said he, "in a strange land, unlamented, cut off by the hand of outlaws, and see none to avenge my cause." Sore wounded he sank to the earth, when hoarse screamed the cranes overhead. "Take up my cause, ye cranes," he said, "since no voice but yours answers to my cry." So saying, he closed his eyes in death.

The body, despoiled and mangled, was found, and though disfigured with wounds, was recognized by the friend in Corinth who had expected him as a guest. "Is it thus I find you restored to me?" he exclaimed; "I who hoped to entwine your temples with the wreath of triumph in the strife of song!"

The guests assembled at the festival heard the tidings with dismay. All Greece felt the wound, every heart owned its loss. They crowded round the tribunal of the magistrates, and demanded vengeance on the murderers and expiation with their blood.

But what trace or mark shall point out the perpetrator from amidst the vast multitude attracted by the splendor of the feat? Did he fall by the hands of robbers, or did some private enemy slay him? The all-discerning sun alone can tell, for no other eye beheld it. Yet not improbably the murderer even now walks in the midst of the throng, and enjoys the fruits of his crime, while vengeance seeks for him in vain. Perhaps in their own temple's enclosure he defies the gods, mingling freely in this throng of men that now presses into the ampitheatre.

For now crowded together, row on row, the multitude fill the seats till it seems as if the very fabric would give way. The murmur of voices sounds like the roar of the sea, while the circles widening in their ascent rise, tier on tier, as if they would reach the sky.

And now the vast assemblage listens to the awful voice of the chorus personating the Furies, which in solemn guise advances with measured step, and moves around the circuit of the theatre. Can they be mortal women who compose that awful group, and can that vast concourse of silent forms be living beings!

The choristers, clad in black, bore in their fleshless hands torches blazing with a pitchy flame. Their cheeks were bloodless, and in place of hair, writing and swelling serpents curled around their brows. Forming a circle, these awful beings sang their hymn, rending the hearts of the guilty, and enchaining all their faculties. It rose and swelled, overpowering the sound of the instruments, stealing the judgment, palsying the heart, curdling the blood.

"Happy the man who keeps his heart pure from guilt and crime! Him we avengers touch not; he treads the path of life secure from us. But woe! Woe! To him who has done the deed of secret murder. We, the fearful family of Night, fasten ourselves upon his whole being. Thinks he by flight to escape us? We fly still faster in pursuit, twine our snakes around his feet and bring him to the ground. Unwearied we pursue; no pity checks our course; still on and on to the end of life, we give him no peace nor rest." Thus the Eumenides sang, and moved in solemn cadence, while stillness like the stillness of death sat over the whole assembly as if in the presence of superhuman beings; and then in solemn march completing the circuit of the theatre, they passed out at the back of the stage.

Every heart fluttered between illusion and reality, and every breast panted with undefined terror, quailing before the awful power that watches secret crimes and winds unseen the skein of destiny. At that moment a cry burst forth from one of the uppermost benches "Look! Look! Comrade, yonder are the cranes of Ibycus!" And suddenly there appeared sailing across the sky a dark object which a moment's inspection showed to be a flock of cranes flying directly over the theatre. "Of Ibycus! did he say?" The beloved name revived the sorrow in every breast. As wave follows wave over the face of the sea, so ran from mouth to mouth the words, "Of Ibycus! Him whom we all lament, with some murderer's hand laid low! What have the cranes to do with him?" And louder grew the swell of voices, while like a lightning's flash the thought sped through every heart, "Observe the power of the Eumenides! The pious poet shall be avenged! The murderer has informed against himself. Seize the man who uttered that cry and the other to whom he spoke!"

The culprit would gladly have recalled his words, but it was too late. The faces of the murderers pale with terror betrayed their guilt. The people took them before the judge, they confessed their crime and suffered the punishment they deserved.

SIMONIDES

Simonides was one of the most prolific of the early poets of Greece, but only a few fragments of his compositions have descended to us. He wrote hymns, triumphal odes, and elegies. In the last species of composition he particularly excelled. His genius was inclined to the pathetic, and none could touch with truer effect the chords of human sympathy. The Lamentation of Danae, the most important of the fragments which remain of his poetry is based upon the tradition that Danae and her infant son were confined by order of her father Acrisius in a chest and set adrift on the sea. The chest floated towards the island of Seriphus, where both were rescued by Dictys, a fisherman, and carried to Polydectes, king of the country, who received and protected them. The child Perseus when grown up became a famous hero, whose adventures have been recorded in a previous chapter.

Simonides passed much of his life at the courts of princes, and often employed his talents in panegyric and festal odes, receiving his reward from the munificence of those whose exploits he celebrated. This employment was not derogatory, but closely resembles that of the earliest bards, such as Demodocus, described by Homer, or of Homer himself as recorded by tradition.

On one occasion when residing at the court of Scopas, king of Thessaly, the prince desired him to prepare a poem in celebration of his exploits, to be recited at a banquet. In order to diversify his theme, Simonides, who was celebrated for his piety, introduced into his poem the exploits of Castor and Pollux. Such digressions were not unusual with the poets on similar occasions, and one might suppose an ordinary mortal might have been content to share the praises of the sons of Leda. But vanity is exacting; and as Scopas sat at his festal board among his courtiers and sycophants, he grudged every verse that did not rehearse his own praises. When Simonides approached to receive the promised reward Scopas bestowed but half the expected sum, saying, "Here is payment for my portion of the performance, Castor and Pollux will doubtless compensate thee for so much as relates to them." The disconcerted poet returned to his seat amidst the laughter which followed the great man's jest. In a little time he received a message that two young men on horseback were waiting without and anxious to see him. Simonides hastened to the door, but looked in vain for the visitors. Scarcely however had he left the banqueting-hall when the roof fell in with a loud crash, burying Scopas and all his guests beneath the ruins. On inquiring as to the appearance of the young men who had sent for him, Simonides was satisfied that they were no other than Castor and Pollux themselves.

SAPPHO

Sappho was a poetess who flourished in a very early age of Greek literature. Of her works few fragments remain, but they are enough to establish her claim to eminent poetical genius. The story of Sappho commonly alluded to is that she was passionately in love with a beautiful youth named Phaon, and failing to obtain a return of affection she threw herself from the promontory of Leucadia into the sea, under a superstition that those who should take that "Lover's-leap," would, if not destroyed, be cured of their love.

Byron alludes to the story of Sappho in Childe Harold, Canto II.:

Those who wish to know more of Sappho and her leap, are referred to the Spectator, Nos. 223 and 229, and also to Moore's Evenings in Greece.

Figure 26: "Sappho and Erinna in a Garden at Mytilene" by Simeon Solomon

Chapter 19

ENDYMION. ORION. AURORA AND TITHONUS. ACIS AND GALATEA

Endymion was a beautiful youth who fed his flock on Mount Latmos. One calm, clear night, Diana, the Moon, looked down and saw him sleeping. The cold heart of the virgin goddess was warmed by his surpassing beauty, and she came down to him, kissed him, and watched over him while he slept.

Another story was that Jupiter bestowed on him the gift of perpetual youth united with perpetual sleep. Of one so gifted we can have but few adventures to record. Diana, it was said, took care that his fortunes should not suffer by his inactive life, for she made his flock increase, and guarded his sheep and lambs from the wild beasts.

The story of Endymion has a peculiar charm from the human meaning which it so thinly veils. We see in Endymion the young poet, his fancy and his heart seeking in vain for that which can satisfy them, finding his favorite hour in the quiet moonlight, and nursing there beneath the beams of the bright and silent witness the melancholy and the ardor which consumes him. The story suggests aspiring and poetic love, a life spent more in dreams than in reality, and an early and welcome death. S. G. Bulfinch.

The Endymion of Keats is a wild and fanciful poem, containing some exquisite poetry, as this, to the moon:

"The sleeping kine
Couched in thy brightness dream of fields divine.
Innumerable mountains rise, and rise,
Ambitious for the hallowing of thine eyes,
And yet thy benediction passeth not
One obscure hiding place, one little spot
Where pleasure may be sent; the nested wren
Has thy fair face within its tranquil ken."

Dr. Young in the Night Thoughts alludes to Endymion thus:

"These thoughts, O Night, are thine;
From thee they came like lovers' secret sighs,
While others slept. So Cynthia, poets feign,
In shadows veiled, soft, sliding from her sphere,
Her shepherd cheered, of her enamored less
Than I of thee."

Fletcher, in the Faithful Shepherdess, tells,

"How the pale Phoebe, hunting in a grove,
First saw the boy Endymion, from whose eyes
She took eternal fire that never dies;
How she conveyed him softly in a sleep,
His temples bound with poppy, to the steep
Head of Old Latmos, where she stoops each night,
Gilding the mountain with her brother's light,
To kiss her sweetest."

ORION

Orion was the son of Neptune. He was a handsome giant and a mighty hunter. His father gave him the power of wading through the depths of the sea, or as others say, of walking on its surface.

Orion loved Merope, the daughter of Oenopion, king of Chios, and sought her in marriage. He cleared the island of wild beasts, and brought the spoils of the chase as presents to his beloved; but as Oenopion constantly deferred his consent, Orion attempted to gain possession of the maiden by violence. Her father, incensed at this conduct, having made Orion drunk, deprived him of his sight, and cast him out on the sea shore. The blinded hero followed the sound of the Cyclops' hammer till he reached Lemnos, and came to the forge of Vulcan, who, taking pity on him, gave him Kedalion, one of his men, to be his guide to the abode of the sun. Placing Kedalion on his shoulders, Orion proceeded to the east, and there meeting the sun-god, was restored to sight by his beam.

After this he dwelt as a hunter with Diana, with whom he was a favorite, and it is even said she was about to marry him. Her brother was highly displeased and often chide her, but to no purpose. One day, observing Orion wading through the sea with his head just above the water, Apollo pointed it out to his sister and maintained that she could not hit that black thing on the sea. The archer-goddess discharged a shaft with fatal aim. The waves rolled the dead body of Orion to the land, and bewailing her fatal error with many tears, Diana placed him among the stars, where he appears as a giant, with a girdle, sword, lion's skin, and club. Sirius, his dog, follows him, and the Pleiads fly before him.

The Pleiads were daughters of Atlas, and nymphs of Diana's train. One day Orion saw them, and became enamored, and pursued them. In their distress they prayed to the gods to change their form, and Jupiter in pity turned them into pigeons, and then made them a constellation in the sky. Though their numbers was seven, only six stars are visible, for Electra, one of them, it is said, left her place that she might not behold the ruin of Troy, for that city was founded by her son Dardanus. The sight had such an effect on her sisters that they have looked pale ever since.

Mr. Longfellow has a poem on the "Occultation of Orion." The following lines are those in which he alludes to the mythic story. We must premise that on the celestial globe Orion is represented as robed in a lion's skin and wielding a club. At the moment the stars of the constellation one by one were quenched in the light of the moon, the poet tells us,

---

"Down fell the red skin of the lion
Into the river at his feet.
His mighty club no longer beat
The forehead of the bull; but he
Reeled as of yore beside the sea,
When blinded by Oenopion
He sought the blacksmith at his forge,
And climbing up the narrow gorge,
Fixed his blank eyes upon the sun."

Tennyson has a different theory of the Pleiads:

"Many a night I saw the Pleiads, rising through the mellow shade,
Glitter like a swarm of fire-flies tangled in a silver braid."
Locksley Hall

Byron alludes to the lost Pleiad:

"Like the lost Pleiad seen no more below."

See also Mrs. Heman's verses on the same subject.

AURORA AND TITHONUS

Aurora, the goddess of the Dawn, like her sister the Moon, was at times inspired with the love of mortals. Her greatest favorite was Tithonus, son of Laomedon, king of Troy. She stole him away, and prevailed on Jupiter to grant him immortality; but forgetting to have youth joined in the gift, after some time she began to discern, to her great mortification, that he was growing old. When his hair was quite white she left his society; but he still had the range of her palace, lived on ambrosial food, and was clad in celestial raiment. At length he lost the power of using his limbs, and then she shut him up in his chamber, whence his feeble voice might at times be heard. Finally she turned him into a grasshopper.

Memnon was the son of aurora and Tithonus. He was king of the Ǣthiopians, and dwelt in the extreme east, on the shore of Ocean. He came with his warriors to assist the kindred of his father in the war of Troy. King Priam received him with great honors, and listened with admiration to his narrative of the wonders of the ocean shore.

The very day after his arrival, Memnon, impatient of repose, led his troops to the field. Antilochus, the brave son of Nestor, fell by his hand, and the Greeks were put to flight, when Achilles appeared and restored the battle. A long and doubtful contest ensued between him and the son of Aurora; at length victor declared for Achilles, Memnon fell, and the Trojans fled in dismay.

Aurora, who, from her station in the sky, had viewed with apprehension the danger of her son, when she saw him fall directed his brothers, the Winds, to convey his body to the banks of the river Esepus in Paphlagonia. In the evening Aurora came, accompanied by the Hours and the Pleiads, and wept and lamented over her son. Night, in sympathy with her grief, spread the heaven with clouds; all nature mourned for the offspring of the Dawn. The Aethiopians raised his tomb on the banks of the stream in the grove of the nymphs, and Jupiter caused the sparks and cinders of his funeral-pile to be turned into birds, which,

Figure 27: "Aurora Triumphans" by Evelyn De Morgan

dividing into two flocks, fought over the pile till they fell into the flame. Every year, at the anniversary of his death, they return and celebrate his obsequies in like manner. Aurora remains inconsolable for the loss of her son. Her tears still flow, and may be seen at early morning in the form of dew-drops on the grass.

Unlike most of the marvels of ancient mythology, there will exist some memorials of this. On the banks of the river Nile, in Egypt, are two colossal statues, one of which is said to be the statue of Memnon. Ancient writers record that when the first rays of the rising sun fall upon this statue, a sound is heard to issue from it which they compare to the snapping of a harp- string. There is some doubt about the identification of the existing statue with the one described by the ancients, and the mysterious sounds are still more doubtful. Yet there are not wanting some modern testimonies to their being still audible. It has been suggested that sounds produced by confined air making its escape from crevices or caverns in the rocks may have given some ground for the story. Sir Gardner Wilkinson, a late traveler, of the highest authority, examined the statue itself, and discovered that it was hollow, and that "in the lap of the statue is a stone, which, on being struck, emits a metallic sound, that might still be made use of to deceive a visitor who was predisposed to believe its powers."

The vocal statue of Memnon is a favorite subject of allusion with the poets. Darwin, in his Botanic Garden, says,

---

"So to the sacred Sun in Memnon's fane
Spontaneous concords choired the matin strain;
Touched by his orient beam responsive rings
The living lyre and vibrates all its strings;
Accordant aisles the tender tones prolong,
And holy echoes swell the adoring song."

ACIS AND GALATEA

Scylla was a fair virgin of Sicily, a favorite of the Sea-Nymphs. She had many suitors, but repelled them all, and would go to the grotto of Galatea, and tell her how she was persecuted. One day the goddess, while Scylla dressed her hair, listened to the story, and then replied, "Yet, maiden, your persecutors are of the not ungentle race of men, whom if you will you can repel; but I, the daughter of Nereus, and protected by such a band of sisters, found no escape from the passion of the Cyclops but in the depths of the sea;" and tears stopped her utterance, which when the pitying maiden had wiped away with her delicate finger, and soothed the goddess, "Tell me, dearest," said she, "the cause of your grief." Galatea then said, "Acis was the son of Faunus and a Naiad. His father and mother loved him dearly, but their love was not equal to mine. For the beautiful youth attached himself to me alone, and he was just sixteen years old, the down just beginning to darken his cheeks. As much as I sought his society, so much did the cyclops seek mine; and if you ask me whether my love for Acis or my hatred for Polyphemus was the stronger, I cannot tell you; they were in equal measure. Oh, Venus, how great is thy power! This fierce giant, the terror of the woods, whom no hapless stranger escaped unharmed, who defied even Jove himself, learned to feel what love was, and touched with a passion for me, forgot his flocks and his well-stored caverns. Then, for the first time, he began to take some care of his appearance, and to try to make himself agreeable; he harrowed those coarse locks of his with a comb, and mowed his beard with a sickle, looked at his harsh features in the water, and composed his countenance. His love of slaughter, his fierceness and thirst of blood prevailed no more, and ships that touched at his island went away in safety. He paced up and down the sea-shore, imprinting huge tracks with his heavy tread, and, when weary, lay tranquilly in his cave.

"There is a cliff which projects into the sea, which washes it on either side. Thither one day the huge Cyclops ascended, and sat down while his flocks spread themselves around. Laying down his staff which would have served for a mast to hold a vessel's sail, and taking his instrument, compacted of numerous pipes, he made the hills and the waters echo the music of his song. I lay hid under a rock, by the side of my beloved Acis, and listened to the distant strain. It was full of extravagant praises of my beauty, mingled with passionate reproaches of my coldness and cruelty.

"When he had finished he rose up, and like a raging bull, that cannot stand still, wandered off into the woods. Acis and I thought no more of him, till on a sudden he came to a spot which gave him a view of us as we sat. 'I see you,' he exclaimed, 'and I will make this the last of your love-meetings.' His voice was a roar such as an angry Cyclops alone could utter. Ǣtna trembled at the sound. I, overcome with terror, plunged into the water. Acis turned and fled, crying, 'Save me, Galatea, save me, my parents!" The Cyclops pursued him, and tearing a rock from the side of the mountain hurled it at him. Though only a corner of it touched him it overwhelmed him.

"All that fate left in my power I did for Acis. I endowed him with the honors of his grandfather the river-god. The purple blood flowed out from under the rock, but by degrees grew paler and looked like the stream of a river rendered turbid by rains, and in time it became clear. The rock cleaved open, and the water, as it gushed from the chasm, uttered a pleasing murmur."

Thus Acis was changed into a river, and the river retains the name of Acis.

Figure 28: "Acis and Galatea" by Alexandre Charles Guillemont

Chapter 20

THE TROJAN WAR

Minerva was the goddess of wisdom, but on one occasion she did a very foolish thing; she entered into competition with Juno and Venus for the prize of beauty. It happened thus. At the nuptials of Peleus and Thetis all the gods were invited with the exception of Eris, or Discord. Enraged at her exclusion, the goddess threw a golden apple among the guests with the inscription, "For the most beautiful." Thereupon Juno, Venus, and Minerva, each claimed the apple. Jupiter not willing to decide in so delicate a matter, sent the goddesses to Mount Ida, where the beautiful shepherd Paris was tending his flocks, and to him was committed the decision. The goddesses accordingly appeared before him. Juno promised him power and riches, Minerva glory and renown in war, and Venus the fairest of women for his wife, each attempting to bias his decision in her own favor. Paris decided in favor of Venus and gave her the golden apple, thus making the two other goddesses his enemies. Under the protection of Venus, Paris sailed to Greece, and was hospitably received by Menelaus, king of Sparta. Now Helen, the wife of Menelaus, was the very woman whom Venus had destined for Paris, the fairest of her sex. She had been sought as a bride by numerous suitors, and before her decision was made known, they all, at the suggestion of Ulysses, one of their number, took an oath that they would defend her from all injury and avenge her cause if necessary. She chose Menelaus, and was living with him happily when Paris became their guest. Paris, aided by Venus, persuaded her to elope with him, and carried her to Troy, whence arose the famous Trojan war, the theme of the greatest poems of antiquity, those of Homer and Virgil.

Menelaus called upon his brother chieftains of Greece to fulfil their pledge, and join him in his efforts to recover his wife. They generally came forward, but Ulysses, who had married Penelope and was very happy in his wife and child, had no disposition to embark in such a troublesome affair. He therefore hung back and Palamedes was sent to urge him. When Palamedes arrived at Ithaca, Ulysses pretended to be mad. He yoked an ass and an ox together to the plough and began to sow salt. Palamedes, to try him, placed the infant Telemachus before the plough, whereupon the father turned the plough aside, showing plainly that he was no madman, and after that could no longer refuse to fulfil his promise. Being now himself gained for the undertaking, he lent his aid to bring in other reluctant chiefs, especially Achilles. This hero was the son of that Thetis at whose marriage the apple of Discord had been thrown among the goddesses. Thetis was herself one of the immortals, a sea-nymph, and knowing that her son was fated to perish before Troy if he went on the expedition, she endeavored to prevent his going. She sent him away to the court of king Lycomedes, and induced him to conceal himself in the disguise of a maiden among the daughters of the king. Ulysses, hearing he was there, went disguised as a merchant to the palace and offered for sale female ornaments, among which he had placed some arms. While the king's daughters were engrossed with the other contents of the merchant's pack, Achilles handled the weapons and thereby betrayed himself to the keen eye of Ulysses, who found no great difficulty in persuading him to disregard his mother's prudent counsels and join his countrymen in the war.

Priam was king of Troy, and Paris, the shepherd and seducer of Helen, was his son. Paris had been brought up in obscurity, because there were certain ominous forebodings connected with him from his infancy that he would be the ruin of the state. These forebodings seemed at length likely to be realized, for the Grecian armament now in preparation was the greatest that had ever been fitted out. Agamemnon, king of Mycenae, and brother of the injured Menelaus, was chosen commander-in-chief. Achilles was their most illustrious warrior. After him ranked Ajax, gigantic in size and of great courage, but dull of intellect, Diomedes, second only to Achilles in all the qualities of a hero, Ulysses, famous for his sagacity, and Nestor, the oldest of the Grecian chiefs, and one to whom they all looked up for counsel. But Troy was no feeble enemy. Priam, the king, was now old, but he had been a wise prince and had strengthened his state by good government at home and numerous alliances with his neighbors. But the principal stay and support of his throne was his son Hector, one of the noblest characters painted by heathen antiquity. Hector felt, from the first, a presentiment of the fall of his country, but still persevered in his heroic resistance, yet by no means justified the wrong which brought this danger upon her. He was united in marriage with Andromache, and as a husband and father his character was not less admirable than as a warrior. The principal leaders on the side of the Trojans, besides Hector, were Aeneas and Deiphobus, Glaucus and Sarpedon.

After two years of preparation the Greek fleet and army assembled in the port of Aulis in Boeotia. Here Agamemnon in hunting killed a stag which was sacred to Diana, and the goddess in return visited the army with pestilence, and produced a calm which prevented the ships from leaving the port. Calchas the soothsayer thereupon announced that the wrath of the virgin goddess could only be appeased by the sacrifice of a virgin on her altar, and that none other but the daughter of the offender would be acceptable. Agamemnon, however reluctant, yielded his consent, and the maiden Iphigenia was sent for under the pretence that she was to be married to Achilles. When she was about to be sacrificed the goddess relented and snatched her away, leaving a hind in her place, and Iphigenia enveloped in a cloud was carried to Tauris, where Diana made her priestess of her temple.

Tennyson, in his Dream of Fair women, makes Iphigenia thus describe her feelings at the moment of sacrifice, the moment represented in our engraving:

"I was cut off from hope in that sad place,
Which yet to name my spirit loathes and fears;
My father held his hand upon his face;
I, blinded by my tears,

"Still strove to speak; my voice was thick with sighs,
As in a dream. Dimly I could descry
The stern black-bearded kings, with wolfish eyes,
Waiting to see me die.

"The tall masts quivered as they lay afloat,
The temples and the people and the shore;
One drew a sharp knife through my tender throat
Slowly, and nothing more."

The wind now proving fair the fleet made sail and brought the forces to the coast of Troy. The Trojans came to oppose their landing, and at the first onset Protesilaus fell by the hand of Hector. Protesilaus had left at home his wife Laodamia, who was most tenderly attached to him. When the news of his death reached her she implored the gods to be allowed to converse with him only three hours. The request was granted. Mercury led Protesilaus back to the upper world, and when he died a second time Laodamia died with him. There was a story that the nymphs panted elm trees round his grave which grew very well till they were high enough to command a view of Troy, and then withered away, while fresh branches sprang from the roots.

Wordsworth has taken the story of Protesilaus and Laodamia for the subject of a poem. It seems the oracle had declared that victory should be the lot of that party from which should fall the first victim to the war. The poet represents Protesilaus, on his brief return to earth, as relating to Laodamia the story of his fate:

"The wished-for wind was given; I then revolved
The oracle, upon the silent sea;
And if no worthier led the way, resolved
That of a thousand vessels mine should be
The foremost prow impressing to the strand,
Mine the first blood that tinged the Trojan sand.

"Yet bitter, ofttimes bitter was the pang
When of thy loss I thought, beloved wife!
On thee too fondly did my memory hang,
And on the joys we shared in mortal life,
The paths which we had trod, these fountains, flowers;
My new planned cities and unfinished towers.

"But should suspense permit the foe to cry,
'Behold they tremble! Haughty their array,
Yet of their number no one dares to die!'"
In soul I swept the indignity away;
Old frailties then recurred; but lofty thought
In act embodied my deliverance wrought.

. . . .

Upon the side
Of Hellespont (such faith was entertained)
A knot of spiry trees for ages grew
From out the tomb of him for whom she died;
And ever when such stature they had gained
That Ilium's walls were subject to their view,
The trees' tall summits withered at the sight,
A constant interchange of growth and blight!"

THE ILIAD

The war continued without decisive results for nine years. Then an event occurred which seemed likely to be fatal to the cause of the Greeks, and that was a quarrel between Achilles and Agamemnon. It is at this point that the great poem of Homer, the Iliad, begins. The Greeks, though unsuccessful against Troy, had taken the neighboring and allied cities, and in the division of the spoil a female captive, by name Chryseis, daughter of Chryses, priest of Apollo, had fallen to the share of Agamemnon. Chryses came bearing the sacred emblems of his office, and begged the release of his daughter. Agamemnon refused. Thereupon Chryses implored Apollo to afflict the Greeks till they should be forced to yield their prey. Apollo granted the prayer of his priest, and sent pestilence into the Grecian camp. Then a council was called to deliberate how to allay the wrath of the gods and avert the plague. Achilles boldly charged their misfortunes upon Agamemnon as caused by his withholding Chryseis. Agamemnon enraged, consented to relinquish his captive, but demanded that Achilles should yield to him in her stead Briseis, a maiden who had fallen to Achilles' share in the division of the spoil. Achilles submitted, but forthwith declared that he would take no further part in the war. He withdrew his forces from the general camp and openly avowed his intention of returning home to Greece.

The gods and goddesses interested themselves as much in this famous war as the parties themselves. It was well known to them that fate had decreed that Troy should fall, at last, if her enemies should persevere and not voluntarily abandon the enterprise. Yet there was room enough left for chance to excite by turns the hopes and fears of the powers above who took part with either side. Juno and Minerva, in consequence of the slight put upon their charms by Paris, were hostile to the Trojans; Venus for the opposite cause favored them. Venus enlisted her admirer Mars on the same side, but Neptune favored the Greeks. Apollo was neutral, sometimes taking one side, sometimes the other, and Jove himself, though he loved the good King Priam, yet exercised a degree of impartiality; not however without exceptions.

Thetis, the mother of Achilles, warmly resented the injury done to her son. She repaired immediately to Jove's palace, and besought him to make the Greeks repent of their injustice to Achilles by granting success to the Trojan arms. Jupiter consented; and in the battle which ensued the Trojans were completely successful. The Greeks were driven from the field, and took refuge in their ships. Then Agamemnon called a council of his wisest and bravest chiefs. Nestor advised that an embassy should be sent to Achilles to persuade him to return to the field; that Agamemnon should yield the maiden, the cause of the dispute, with ample gifts to atone for the wrong he had done. Agamemnon consented, and Ulysses, Ajax, and Phoenix were sent to carry to Achilles the penitent message. They performed that duty, but Achilles was deaf to their entreaties. He positively refused to return to the field, and persisted in his resolution to embark for Greece without delay. The Greeks had constructed a rampart around their ships, and now, instead of besieging Troy, they were in a manner besieged themselves within their rampart. The next day after the unsuccessful embassy to Achilles, a battle was fought, and the Trojans, favored by Jove, were successful, and succeeded in forcing a passage through the Grecian rampart, and were about to set fire to the ships. Neptune, seeing the Greeks so pressed, came to their rescue. He appeared in the form of Calchas the prophet, encouraged the warriors with his shouts, and appealed to each individually till he raised their ardor to such a pitch that they forced the Trojans to give way. Ajax performed prodigies of valor, and at length encountered Hector. Ajax shouted defiance, to which Hector replied, and hurled his lance at the huge warrior. It was well aimed, and struck Ajax where the belts that bore his sword and shield crossed each other on the breast. The double guard prevented its penetrating, and it fell harmless. Then Ajax, seeing a huge stone, one of those that served to prop the ships, hurled it at Hector. It struck him in the neck and stretched him on the plain. His followers instantly seized him, and bore him off stunned and wounded.

While Neptune was thus aiding the Greeks and driving back the Trojans, Jupiter saw nothing of what was going on, for his attention had been drawn from the field by the wiles of Juno. That goddess had arrayed herself in all her charms, and, to crown all, had borrowed of Venus her girdle called Cestus, which had the effect to heighten the wearer's charms to such a degree that they were quite irresistible. So prepared, Juno went to join her husband, who sat on Olympus watching the battle. When he beheld her she looked so charming that the fondness of his early love revived, and, forgetting the contending armies and all other affairs of state, he thought only of her and let the battle go as it would.

But this absorption did not continue long, and when, upon turning his eyes downward, he beheld Hector stretched on the plain almost lifeless from pain and bruises, he dismissed Juno in a rage, commanding her to send Iris and Apollo to him. When Iris came he sent her with a stern message to Neptune, ordering him instantly to quit the field. Apollo was dispatched to heal Hector's bruises and to inspirit his heart. These orders were obeyed with such speed that while the battle still raged, Hector returned to the field and Neptune betook himself to his own dominions.

An arrow from Paris's bow wounded Machaon, son of Aesculapius, who inherited his father's art of healing, and was therefore of great value to the Greeks as their surgeon, besides being one of their bravest warriors. Nestor took Machaon in his chariot and conveyed him from the field. As they passed the ships of Achilles, that hero, looking out over the field, saw the chariot of Nestor and recognized the old chief, but could not discern who the wounded chief was. So calling Patroclus, his companion and dearest friend, he sent him to Nestor's tent to inquire.

Patroclus, arriving at Nestor's tent, saw Machaon wounded, and having told the cause of his coming would have hastened away, but Nestor detained him, to tell him the extent of the Grecian calamities. He reminded him also how, at the time of departing for Troy, Achilles and himself had been charged by their respective fathers with different advice; Achilles to aspire to the highest pitch of glory, Patroclus, as the elder, to keep watch over his friend, and to guide his inexperience. "Now," said Nestor, "is the time for such influence. If the gods so please, thou mayest win him back to the common cause; but if not let him at least send his soldiers to the field, and come thou, Patroclus, clad in his armor, and perhaps the very sight of it may drive back the Trojans."

Patroclus was strongly moved with this address, and hastened back to Achilles, revolving in his mind all he had seen and heard. He told the prince the sad condition of affairs at the camp of their late associates; Diomedes, Ulysses, Agamemnon, Machaon, all wounded, the rampart broken down, the enemy among the ships preparing to burn them, and thus to cut off all means of return to Greece. While they spoke the flames burst forth

Figure 29: "Achilles Lamenting the Death of Patroclus" by Gavin Hamilton

from one of the ships. Achilles, at the sight, relented so far as to grant Patroclus his request to lead the Myrmidons (for so were Achilles' soldiers called) to the field, and to lend him his armor that he might thereby strike more terror into the minds of the Trojans. Without delay the soldiers were marshalled, Patroclus put on the radiant armor and mounted the chariot of Achilles, and led forth the men ardent for battle. But before he went, Achilles strictly charged him that he should be content with repelling the foe. "Seek not," said he, "to press the Trojans without me, lest thou add still more to the disgrace already mine." Then exhorting the troops to do their best he dismissed them full of ardor to the fight.

Patroclus and his Myrmidons at once plunged into the contest where it raged hottest; at the sight of which the joyful Grecians shouted and the ships reechoed the acclaim. The Trojans, at the sight of the well-known armor, struck with terror, looked everywhere for refuge. First those who had got possession of the ship and set it on fire left and allowed the Grecians to retake it and extinguish the flames. Then the rest of the Trojans fled in dismay. Ajax, Menelaus, and the two sons of Nestor performed prodigies of valor. Hector was forced to turn his horses' heads and retire from the enclosure, leaving his men entangled in the fosse to escape as they could. Patroclus drove them before him, slaying many, none daring to make a stand against him.

At last Sarpedon, son of Jove, ventured to oppose himself in fight to Patroclus. Jupiter looked down upon him and would have snatched him from the fate which awaited him, but Juno hinted that if he did so it would induce all others of the inhabitants of heaven to interpose in like manner whenever any of their offspring were endangered; to which reason Jove yielded. Sarpedon threw his spear but missed Patroclus, but Patroclus threw his with better success. It pierced Sarpedon's breast and he fell, and, calling to his friends to save his body from the foe, expired. Then a furious contest arose for the possession of the corpse. The Greeks succeeded and stripped Sarpedon of his armor; but Jove would not allow the remains of his son to be dishonored, and by his command Apollo snatched from the midst of the combatants the body of Sarpedon and committed it to the care of the twin brothers Death and Sleep, by whom it was transported to Lycia, the native land of Sarpedon, where it received due funeral rites.

Thus far Patroclus had succeeded to his utmost wish in repelling the Trojans and relieving his countrymen, but now came a change of fortune. Hector, borne in his chariot, confronted him. Patroclus threw a vast stone at Hector, which missed its aim, but smote Cebriones, the charioteer, and knocked him from the car. Hector leaped from the chariot to rescue his friend, and Patroclus also descended to complete his victory. Thus the two heroes met face to face. At this decisive moment the poet, as if reluctant to give Hector the glory, records that Phoebus took part against Patroclus. He struck the helmet from his head and the lance from his hand. At the same moment an obscure Trojan wounded him in the back, and Hector pressing forward pierced him with his spear. He fell mortally wounded.

Then arose a tremendous conflict for the body of Patroclus, but his armor was at once taken possession of by Hector, who, retiring a short distance, divested himself of his own armor and put on that of Achilles, then returned to the fight. Ajax and Menelaus defended the body, and Hector and his bravest warriors struggled to capture it. The battle raged with equal fortune, when Jove enveloped the whole face of heaven with a dark cloud. The lightning flashed, the thunder roared, and Ajax, looking round for some one whom he might dispatch to Achilles to tell him of the death of his friend and of the imminent danger that his remains would fall into the hands of the enemy, could see no suitable messenger. It was then that he exclaimed in those famous lines so often quoted,

---

"Father of heaven and earth! Deliver thou
Achaia's host from darkness; clear the skies;
Give day; and, since thy sovereign will is such,
Destruction with it; but, oh, give us day."
Cowper.

Or, as rendered by Pope,

"Lord of earth and air!
Oh, king! Oh, father! Hear my humble prayer!
Dispel this cloud, the light of heaven restore;
Give me to see and Ajax asks no more;
If Greece must perish we thy will obey
But let us perish in the face of day."

Jupiter heard the prayer and dispersed the clouds. Then Ajax sent Antilochus to Achilles with the intelligence of Patroclus's death, and of the conflict raging for his remains. The Greeks at last succeeded in bearing off the body to the ships, closely pursued by Hector and Aeneas and rest of the Trojans.

Achilles heard the fate of his friend with such distress that Antilochus feared for a while that he would destroy himself. His groans reached the ears of his mother, Thetis, far down in the deeps of ocean where she abode, and she hastened to him to inquire the cause. She found him overwhelmed with self-reproach that he had indulged his resentment so far, and suffered his friend to fall a victim to it. But his only consolation was the hope of revenge. He would fly instantly in search of Hector. But his mother reminded him that he was now without armor, and promised him, if he would but wait till the morrow, she would procure for him a suit of armor from Vulcan more than equal to that he had lost. He consented, and Thetis immediately repaired to Vulcan's palace. She found him busy at his forge making tripods for his own use, so artfully constructed that they moved forward of their own accord when wanted, and retired again when dismissed. On hearing the request of Thetis, Vulcan immediately laid aside his work and hastened to comply with her wishes. He fabricated a splendid suit of armor for Achilles, first a shield adorned with elaborate devices, then a helmet crested with gold, then a corslet and greaves of impenetrable temper, all perfectly adapted to his form, and of consummate workmanship. It was all done in one night, and Thetis, receiving it, descended with it to earth and laid it down at Achilles' feet at the dawn of day.

The first glow of pleasure that Achilles had felt since the death of Petroclus was at the sight of this splendid armor. And now arrayed in it, he went forth into the camp, calling all the chiefs to council. When they were all assembled he addressed them. Renouncing his displeasure against Agamemnon and bitterly lamenting the miseries that had resulted from it, he called on them to proceed at once to the field. Agamemnon made a suitable reply, laying all the blame on Ate, the goddess of discord, and thereupon complete reconcilement took place between the heroes. Then Achilles went forth to battle, inspired with a rage and thirst for vengeance that made him irresistible. The bravest warriors fled before him or fell by his lance. Hector, cautioned by Apollo, kept aloof, but the god, assuming the form of one of Priam's sons, Lycaon, urged Æneas to encounter the terrible warrior. Æneas, though he felt himself unequal, did not decline the combat. He hurled his spear with all his force against the shield, the work of Vulcan. It was formed of five metal plates; two were of brass, two of tin, and one of gold. The spear pierced two thicknesses, but was stopped in the third. Achilles threw his with better success. It pierced through the shield of Aeneas, but glanced near his shoulder and made no wound. Then Æneas seized a stone, such as two men of modern times could hardly lift, and was about to throw it, and Achilles, with sword drawn, was about to rush upon him, when Neptune, who looked out upon the contest, moved with pity for Æneas, who he saw would surely fall a victim if not speedily rescued, spread a cloud between the combatants, and lifting Æneas from the ground, bore him over the heads of warriors and steeds to the rear of the battle. Achilles, when the mist cleared away, looked round in vain for his adversary, and acknowledging the prodigy, turned his arms against other champions. But none dared stand before him, and Priam looking down from his city walls beheld his whole army in full flight towards the city. He gave command to open wide the gates to receive the fugitives, and to shut them as soon as the Trojans should have passed, lest the enemy should enter likewise. But Achilles was so close in pursuit that that would have been impossible if Apollo had not, in the form of Agenor, Priam's son, encountered Achilles for a while, then turned to fly, and taken the way apart from the city. Achilles pursued and had chased his supposed victim far from the walls, when Apollo disclosed himself, and Achilles, perceiving how he had been deluded, gave up the chase. But when the rest had escaped into the town Hector stood without, determined to await the combat. His old father called to him from the walls and begged him to retire nor tempt the encounter. His mother, Hecuba, also

besought him to the same effect, but all in vain. "How can I," said he to himself, "by whose command the people went to this day's contest, where so many have fallen, seek safety for myself against a single foe? But what if I offer him to yield up Helen and all her treasures and ample of our own beside? Ah no! It is too late. He would not even hear me through, but slay me while I spoke." While he thus ruminated, Achilles approached, terrible as Mars, his armor flashing lighting as he moved. At that sight Hector's

Figure 30: "Helen of Troy" by Evelyn De Morgan

heart failed him and he fled. Achilles swiftly pursued. They ran, still keeping near the walls, till they had thrice encircled the city. As often as Hector approached the walls Achilles intercepted him and forced him to keep out in a wider circle. But Apollo sustained Hector's strength, and would not let him sink in weariness. Then Pallas, assuming the form of Deiphobus, Hector's bravest brother, appeared suddenly at his side. Hector saw him with delight, and, thus strengthened, stopped his flight and turned to meet Achilles. Hector threw his spear, which struck the shield of Achilles and bounded back. He turned to receive another from the hand of Deiphobus, but Deiphobus was gone. Then Hector understood his doom and said, "Alas! It is plain this is my hour to die! I thought Deiphobus at hand, but Pallas deceived me, and he is still in Troy. But I will not fall inglorious." So saying, he drew his falchion from his side and rushed at once to combat. Achilles, secured behind his shield, waited the approach of Hector. When he came within reach of his spear, Achilles, choosing with his eye a vulnerable part where the armor leaves the neck uncovered, aimed his spear at that part, and Hector fell, death-wounded, and feebly said, "Spare my body! Let my parents ransom it, and let me receive funeral rites from the sons and daughters of Troy." To which Achilles replied, "Dog, name not ransom nor pity to me, on whom you have brought such dire distress. No! Trust me, nought shall save thy carcass from the dogs. Though twenty ransoms and thy weight in gold were offered, I would refuse it all."

So saying, he stripped the body of its armor, and fastening cords to the feet, tied them behind his chariot, leaving the body to trail along the ground. Then mounting the chariot he lashed the steeds, and so dragged the body to and fro before the city. What words can tell the grief of King Priam and Queen Hecuba at this sight! His people could scarce restrain the old king from rushing forth. He threw himself in the dust, and besought them each by name to give him way. Hecuba's distress was not less violent. The citizens stood round them weeping. The sound of the mourning reached the ears of Andromache, the wife of Hector, as she sat among her maidens at work, and anticipating evil she went forth to the wall. When she saw the sight there presented, she would have thrown herself headlong from the wall, but fainted and fell into the arms of her maidens. Recovering, she bewailed her fate, picturing to herself her country ruined, herself a captive, and her son dependent for his bread on the charity of strangers.

When Achilles and the Greeks had taken their revenge on the killer of Patroclus they busied themselves in paying due funeral rites to their friend. A pile was erected, and the body burned with due solemnity; and then ensued games of strength and skill, chariot races, wrestling, boxing, and archery. Then the chiefs sat down to the funeral banquet and after that retired to rest. But Achilles neither partook of the feast nor of sleep. The recollection of his lost friend kept him awake, remembering their companionship in toil and dangers, in battle or on the perilous deep. Before the earliest dawn he left his tent, and joining to his chariot his swift steeds, he fastened Hector's body to be dragged behind. Twice he dragged him round the tomb of Patroclus, leaving him at length stretched in the dust. But Apollo would not permit the body to be torn or disfigured with all this abuse, but preserved it free from all taint or defilement.

When Achilles indulged his wrath in thus disgracing brave Hector, Jupiter in pity summoned Thetis to his presence. He told her to go to her son and prevail on him to restore the body of Hector to his friends. Then Jupiter sent Iris to King Priam to encourage him to go to Achilles and beg the body of his son. Iris delivered her message, and Priam immediately prepared to obey. He opened his treasures and took out rich garments and cloths, with ten talents in gold and two splendid tripods and a golden cup of matchless workmanship. Then he called to his sons and bade them draw forth his litter and place in it the various articles designed for a ransom to Achilles.

When all was ready, the old king with a single companion, as aged as himself, the herald Idaeus, drove forth from the gates, parting there with Hecuba his queen, and all his friends, who lamented him as going to certain death.

But Jupiter, beholding with compassion the venerable king, sent Mercury to be his guide and protector. Mercury, assuming the form of a young warrior, presented himself to the aged couple, and while at the sight of him they hesitated whether to fly or yield, the god approached, and grasping Priam's hand, offered to be their guide to Achilles' tent. Priam gladly accepted his offered service, and he, mounting the carriage, assumed the reins and soon conveyed them to the tent of Achilles. Mercury's wand put to sleep all the guards, and without hindrance he introduced Priam into the tent where Achilles sat, attended by two of his warriors. The old king threw himself at the feet of Achilles and kissed those terrible hands which had destroyed so many of his sons. "Think, O Achilles," he said, "of thy own father, full of days like me, and trembling on the gloomy verge of life. Perhaps even now some neighbor chief oppresses him, and there is none at hand to succor him in his distress. Yet doubtless knowing that Achilles lives he still rejoices, hoping that one day he shall see thy face again. But no comfort cheers me, whose bravest sons, so late the flower of Ilium, all have fallen. Yet one I had, one more than all the rest the strength of my age, whom fighting for his country, thou hast slain. I come to redeem his body, bringing inestimable ransom with me. Achilles, reverence the gods! Recollect thy father! For his sake show compassion to me!" These words moved Achilles and he wept; remembering by turns his absent father and his lost friend. Moved with pity of Priam's silver locks and beard, he raised him from the earth and thus spake: "Priam, I know that thou has reached this place conducted by some god, for without divine aid no mortal even in the prime of youth had dared the attempt. I grant thy request; moved thereto by the evident will of Jove." So saying he arose, and went forth with his two friends, and unloaded of its charge the litter, leaving two mantles and a robe for the covering of the body, which they placed on the litter, and spread the garments over it, that not unveiled it should be borne back to Troy. Then Achilles dismissed the old king with his attendants, having first pledged himself to allow a truce of twelve days for the funeral solemnities.

As the litter approached the city and was descried from the walls, the people poured forth to gaze once more on the face of their hero. Foremost of all, the mother and the wife of Hector came, and at the sight of the lifeless body renewed their lamentations. The people all wept with them, and to the going down of the sun there was no pause or abatement of their grief.

The next day preparations were made for the funeral solemnities. For nine days the people brought wood and built the pile, and on the tenth they placed the body on the summit and applied the torch; while all Troy, thronging forth, encompassed the pile. When it had completely burned, they quenched the cinders with wine, collected the bones and placed them in a golden urn, which they buried in the earth, and reared a pile of stones over the spot.

"Such honors Ilium to her hero paid,
And peaceful slept the mighty Hector's shade."
Pope's Homer

Chapter 21

THE FALL OF TROY. RETURN OF THE GREEKS. ORESTES AND ELECTRA

The story of the Iliad ends with the death of Hector, and it is from the Odyssey and later poems that we learn the fate of the other heroes. After the death of Hector, Troy did not immediately fall, but receiving aid from new allies still continued its resistance. One of these allies was Memnon, the ÆTHIOPIAN prince, whose story we have already told. Another was Penthesilea, queen of the Amazons, who came with a band of female warriors. All the authorities attest their valor and the fearful effect of their war-cry. Penthesilea slew many of the bravest warriors, but was at last slain by Achilles. But when the hero bent over his fallen foe, and contemplated her beauty, youth and valor, he bitterly regretted his victory. Thersites, an insolent brawler and demagogue, ridiculed his grief, and was in consequence slain by the hero.

Achilles by chance had seen Polyxena, daughter of King Priam, perhaps on occasion of the truce which was allowed the Trojans for the burial of Hector. He was captivated with her charms, and to win her in marriage agreed to use his influence with the Greeks to grant peace to Troy. While in the temple of Apollo, negotiating the marriage, Paris discharged at him a poisoned arrow, which guided by Apollo, wounded Achilles in the heel, the only vulnerable part about him. For Thetis, his mother, had dipped him when an infant in the river Styx, which made every part of him invulnerable except the heel by which she held him. (The story of the invulnerability of Achilles is not found in Homer, and is inconsistent with his account. For how could Achilles require the aid of celestial armor if he were invulnerable?)

The body of Achilles, so treacherously slain, was rescued by Ajax and Ulysses. Thetis directed the Greeks to bestow her son's armor on the hero who, of all survivors, should be judged most deserving of it. Ajax and Ulysses were the only claimants; a select number of the other chiefs were appointed to award the prize. It was awarded to Ulysses, thus placing wisdom before valor; whereupon Ajax slew himself. On the spot where his blood sank into the earth a flower sprang up, called the hyacinth, bearing on its leaves the first two letters of the name of Ajax, Ai, the Greek for "woe." Thus, Ajax is a claimant with the boy Hyacinthus for the honor of giving birth to this flower. There is a species of Larkspur which represents the hyacinth of the poets in preserving the memory of this event, the Delphinium Ajacis Ajax's Larkspur.

It was now discovered that Troy could not be taken but by the arrows of Hercules. They were in possession of Philoctetes, the friend who had been with Hercules at the last, and lighted his funeral pyre. Philoctetes had joined the Grecian expedition against Troy, but had accidentally wounded his foot with one of the poisoned arrows, and the smell from his wound proved so offensive that his companions carried him to the Isle of Lemnos and left him there. Diomedes was now sent to induce him to rejoin the army. He succeeded. Philoctetes was cured of his wound by Machaon, and Paris was the first victim of the fatal arrows. In his distress Paris bethought him of one whom in his prosperity he had forgotten. This was the nymph Œnone, whom he had married when a youth, and had abandoned for the fatal beauty Helen. Œnone, remembering the wrongs she had suffered, refused to heal the wound, and Paris went back to Troy and died. Œnone quickly repented, and hastened after him with remedies, but came too late, and in her grief hung herself.

Tennyson has chosen Œnone as the subject of a short poem; but he has omitted the concluding part of the story, the return of Paris wounded, her cruelty and subsequent repentance.

"—— Hither came at noon
Mournful OENONE, wandering forlorn
Of Paris, once her playmate on the hills.
Her cheek had lost the rose, and round her neck
Floated her hair, or seemed to float in rest.
She, leaning on a fragment twined with vine,
Sang to the stillness, till the mountain-shade
Sloped downward to her seat from the upper cliff.

. . . .

"'O Mother Ida, many-fountain'd Ida,
Dear Mother Ida, hearken ere I die.
I waited underneath the dawning hills,
Aloft the mountain lawn was dewy-dark,
And dewy-dark aloft the mountain pine:

Beautiful Paris, evil-hearted Paris,
Leading a jet-black goat, white-horned, white-hooved,
Come up from reedy Simois, all alone.

"'O Mother Ida, hearken ere I die.
Far off the torrent called me from the cliff:
Far up the solitary morning smote
The streaks of virgin snow. With downdropt eyes
I sat alone: white-breasted like a star
Fronting the dawn he moved; a leopard-skin
Drooped from his shoulder, but his sunny hair
Clustered about his temples like a God's,
And his cheek brightened as the foambow brightens
When the wind blows the foam, and all my heart
Went forth to embrace him coming, ere he came.

"'Dear Mother Ida, hearken ere I die.
He smiled, and opening out his milk-white palm
Disclosed a fruit of pure Hesperian gold,
That smelt ambrosially, and while I looked
And listened, the full-flowing river of speech
Came down upon my heart.

"My own OENONE,
Beautiful-browed OENONE, my own soul,
Behold this fruit, whose gleaming rind ingraven
'For the most fair,' would seem award it thine
As lovelier than whatever Oread haunt
The knolls of Ida, loveliest in all grace
Of movement, and the charm of married brows."

"'Dear Mother Ida, hearken ere I die.
He prest the blossom of his lips to mine,
And added, "This was cast upon the board,
When all the full-faced presence of the gods
Hanged in the halls of Peleus; whereupon
Rose feud, with question unto whom 'twas due;
But light-foot Iris brought it yester-eve
Delivering, that to me, by common voice
Elected umpire, Her comes to-day,
Pallas and Aphrodite, claiming each
This meed of fairest. Thou within the cave
Beyond yon whispering tuft of oldest pine,
May'st well behold them unbeheld, unheard
Hear all, and see thy Paris judge of gods."'"

There was in Troy a celebrated statue of Minerva called the Palladium. It was said to have fallen from heaven, and the belief was that the city could not be taken so long as this statue remained within it. Ulysses and Diomedes entered the city in disguise, and succeeded in obtaining the Palladium, which they carried off to the Grecian camp.

But Troy still held out, and the Greeks began to despair of ever subduing it by force, and by advice of Ulysses resolved to resort to stratagem. They pretended to be making preparations to abandon the siege, and a portion of the ships were withdrawn, and lay hid behind a neighboring island. The Greeks then constructed an immense WOODEN HORSE, which they gave out was intended as a propitiatory offering to Minerva, but in fact was filled with armed men. The remaining Greeks then betook themselves to their ships and sailed away, as if for a final departure. The Trojans, seeing the encampment broken up and the fleet gone, concluded the enemy to have abandoned the siege. The gates were thrown open, and the whole population issued forth rejoicing at the long-prohibited liberty of passing freely over the scene of the late encampment. The great horse was the chief object of curiosity. All wondered what it could be for. Some recommended to take it into the city as a trophy; others felt afraid of it.

While they hesitate, Laocoon, the priest of Neptune, exclaims, "What madness, citizens, is this! Have you not learned enough of Grecian fraud to be on your guard against it? For my part I fear the Greeks even when they offer gifts." So saying he threw his lance at the horse's side. It struck, and a hollow sound reverberated like a groan. Then perhaps the people might have taken his advice and destroyed the fatal horse and all its contents; but just at that moment a group of people appeared dragging forward one who seemed a prisoner and a Greek. Stupefied with terror he was brought before the chiefs, who reassured him, promising that his life should be spared on condition of his returning true answers to the questions asked him. He informed them that he was a Greek, Sinon by name, and that in consequence of the malice of Ulysses he had been left behind by his countrymen at their departure. With regard to the wooden horse, he told them that it was a propitiatory offering to Minerva, and made so huge for the express purpose of preventing its being carried within the city; for Calchas the prophet had told them that if the Trojans took possession of it, they would assuredly triumph over the Greeks. This language turned the tide of the people's feelings, and they began to think how they might best secure the monstrous horse and the favorable auguries connected with it, when suddenly a prodigy occurred which left no room to doubt. There appeared advancing over the sea two immense serpents. They came upon the land, and the crowd fled in all directions. The serpents advanced directly to the spot where Laocoon stood with his two sons. They first attacked the children, winding round their bodies and breathing their pestilential breath in their faces. The father, attempting to rescue them, is next seized and involved in the serpents' coils. He struggles to tear them away, but they overpower all his efforts and strangle him and the children in their poisonous folds. This event was regarded as a clear indication of the displeasure of the gods at Laocoon's irreverent treatment of the wooden horse, which they no longer hesitated to regard as a sacred object and prepared to introduce with due solemnity into the city. This was done with songs and triumphal acclamations, and the day closed with festivity. In the night the armed men who were enclosed in the body of the horse, being led out by the traitor Sinon, opened the gates of the city to their friends who had returned under cover of the night. The city was set on fire; the people, overcome with feasting and sleep, put to the sword, and Troy completely subdued.

One of the most celebrated groups of statuary in existence is that of Laocoon and his children in the embrace of the serpents. "There is a cast of it in the Boston Athenaeum; the original is in the Vatican at Rome. The following lines are from the Childe Harold of Byron:

"Now turning to the Vatican go see
Laocoon's torture dignifying pain;
A father's love and mortal's agony
With as immortal's patience blending; vain
The struggle! Vain against the coiling strain
And gripe and deepening of the dragon's grasp
The old man's clinch; the long envenomed chain
Rivets the living links; the enormous asp
Enforces pang on pang and stifles gasp on gasp."

The comic poets will also occasionally borrow a classical allusion. The following is from Swift's description of a City Shower:

"Boxed in a chair the beau impatient sits,
While spouts run clattering o'er the roof by fits,
And over and anon with frightful din
The leather sounds; he trembles from within.
So when Troy chairmen bore the wooden steed
Pregnant with Greeks, impatient to be freed,
(Those bully Greeks, who, as the moderns do,
Instead of paying chairmen, run them through;)
Laocoon struck the outside with a spear,
And each imprisoned champion quaked with fear."

King Priam lived to see the downfall of his kingdom, and was slain at last on the fatal night when the Greeks took the city. He had armed himself and was about to mingle with the combatants, but was prevailed on by Hecuba, his aged queen, to take refuge with herself and his daughters as a suppliant at the altar of Jupiter. While there, his youngest son Polites, pursued by Pyrrhus (Pyrrhus's exclamation, "Not such aid nor such defenders does the time require," has become proverbial.), the son of Achilles, rushed in wounded, and expired at the feet of his father; whereupon Priam, overcome with indignation, hurled his spear with feeble hand against Pyrrhus, and was forthwith slain by him.

Queen Hecuba and her daughter Cassandra were carried captives to Greece. Cassandra had been loved by Apollo, and he gave her the gift of prophecy; but afterwards offended with her, he rendered the gift unavailing by ordaining that her predictions should never be believed. Polyxena, another daughter, who had been loved by Achilles, was demanded by the ghost of this warrior, and was sacrificed by the Greeks upon his tomb.

From Schiller's poem "Cassandra":

"And men my prophet wail deride!
The solemn sorrow dies in scorn;
And lonely in the waste, I hide
The tortured heart that would forewarn.
Amid the happy, unregarded,
Mock'd by their fearful joy, I trod;
Oh, dark to me the lot awarded,

Thou evil Pythian God!

"Thine oracle, in vain to be,
Oh, wherefore am I thus consigned,
With eyes that every truth must see,
Lone in the city of the blind?
Cursed with the anguish of a power
To view the fates I may not thrall,
The hovering tempest still must lower,
The horror must befall!

Boots it th veil to lift, and give
To sight the frowning fates beneath?
For error is the life we live,
And, oh, our knowledge is but death!
Take back the clear and awful mirror,
Shut from my eyes the blood-red glare;
Thy truth is but the gift of terror,
When mortal lips declare.

"My blindness give to me once more,
They gay dim senses that rejoice;
The past's delighted songs are o'er
For lips that speak a prophet's voice.
To me the future thou hast granted;
I miss the moment from the chain
The happy present hour enchanted!
Take back thy gift again!"
Sir Edw. L. Bulwer's translation

MENELAUS AND HELEN

Our readers will be anxious to know the fate of Helen, the fair but guilty occasion of so much slaughter. On the fall of Troy Menelaus recovered possession of his wife, who had not ceased to love him, though she had yielded to the might of Venus and deserted him for another. After the death of Paris she aided the Greeks secretly on several occasions, and in particular when Ulysses and Diomedes entered the city in disguise to carry off the Palladium. She saw and recognized Ulysses, but kept the secret, and even assisted them in obtaining the image. Thus she became reconciled to her husband, and they were among the first to leave the shores of Troy for their native land. But having incurred the displeasure of the gods they were driven by storms from shore to shore of the Mediterranean, visiting Cyprus, Phoenicia and Egypt. In Egypt they were kindly treated and presented with rich gifts, of which Helen's share was a golden spindle and a basket on wheels. The basket was to hold the wool and spools for the queen's work.

Dyer, in his poem of The Fleece, thus alludes to the incident:

"——many yet adhere
To the ancient distaff at the bosom fixed.
Casting the whirling spindle as they walk.
. . . .
This was of old, in no inglorious days,
The mode of spinning, when the Egyptian prince
A golden distaff gave that beauteous nymph,
Too beauteous Helen; no uncourtly gift."

Milton also alludes to a famous recipe for an invigorating draught, called Nepenthe, which the Egyptian queen gave to Helen:

"Not that Nepenthes which the wife of Thone
In Egypt gave to Jove-born Helena,
Is of such power to stir up joy as this,
To life so friendly or so cool to thirst."
Comus

Menelaus and Helen at length arrived in safety at Sparta, resumed their royal dignity, and lived and reigned in splendor; and when Telemachus, the son of Ulysses, in search of his father, arrived at Sparta, he found Menelaus and Helen celebrating the marriage of their daughter Hermione to Neoptolemus, son of Achilles.

In "the Victory Feast," Schiller thus reviews the return of the Greek heroes.

"The son of Atreus, king of men,
The muster of the hosts surveyed,
How dwindled from the thousands, when
Along Scamander first arrayed!
With sorrow and the cloudy thought,

Figure 31: "The Remorse of Orestes" by William-Adolphe Bouguereau

The great king's stately look grew dim,
Of all the hosts to Ilion brought,
How few to Greece return with him!
Still let the song to gladness call,
For those who yet their home shall greet!
For them the blooming life is sweet;
Return is not for all!

"Nor all who reach their native land
May long the joy of welcome feel;
Beside the household gods may stand
Grim Murder, with awaiting steel
And they who 'scape the foe, may die
Beneath the foul, familiar glaive.
Thus he to whom prophetic eye
Her light the wise Minerva gave;
'Ah! Bless'd, whose hearth, to memory true
The goddess keeps unstained and pure;
For woman's guile is deep and sure,
And falsehood loves the new!'

"The Spartan eyes his Helen's charms,
By the best blood of Greece recaptured;
Round that fair form his glowing arms
(A second bridal) wreath, enraptured.
Woe waits the work of evil birth,
Revenge to deeds unblessed is given!
For watchful o'er the things of earth,
The eternal council-halls of heaven.

Yes, ill shall never ill repay;
Jove to the impious hands that stain
The altar of man's heart,
Again the doomer's doom shall weigh!"
Sir Edw. L. Bulwer's translation

AGAMEMNON, ORESTES, AND ELECTRA

Agamemnon, the general-in-chief of the Greeks, the brother of Menelaus, who had been drawn into the quarrel to avenge another's wrongs, was not so fortunate in the issue as his brother. During his absence his wife Clytemnestra had been false to him, and when his return was expected, she, with her paramour, Ægisthus, laid a plan for his destruction, and at the banquet given to celebrate his return, murdered him.

The conspirators intended also to slay his son Orestes, a lad not yet old enough to be an object of apprehension, but from whom, if he should be suffered to grow up, there might be danger. Electra, the sister of Orestes, saved her brother's life by sending him secretly away to his uncle Strophius, king of Phocis. In the palace of Strophius, Orestes grew up with the king's son, Pylades, and formed with him that ardent friendship which has become proverbial. Electra frequently reminded her brother by messengers of the duty of avenging his father's death, and when grown up he consulted the oracle of Delphi, which confirmed him in his design. He therefore repaired in disguise to Argos, pretending to he a messenger from Strophius, who had come to announce the death of Orestes, and brought the ashes of the deceased in a funeral urn. After visiting his father's tomb and sacrificing upon it, according to the rites of the ancients, he made himself known to his sister Electra, and soon after slew both Ǣgisthus and Clytemnestra.

This revolting act, the slaughter of a mother by her son, though alleviated by the guilt of the victim and the express command of the gods, did not fail to awaken in the breasts of the ancients the same abhorrence that it does in ours. The Eumenides, avenging deities, seized upon Orestes, and drove him frantic from land to land. Pylades accompanied him in his wanderings, and watched over him. At length in answer to a second appeal to the oracle, he was directed to go to Tauris in Scythia, and to bring thence a statue of Diana which was believed to have fallen from heaven. Accordingly, Orestes and Pylades went to Tauris, where the barbarous people were accustomed to sacrifice to the goddess all strangers who fell into their hands. The two friends were seized and carried bound to the temple to be made victims. But the priestess of Diana was no other than Iphigenia, the sister of Orestes, who, our readers will remember, was snatched away by Diana, at the moment when she was about to be sacrificed. Ascertaining from the prisoners who they were, Iphigenia disclosed herself to them, and the three made their escape with the statue of the goddess, and returned to Mycenae.

But Orestes was not yet relieved from the vengeance of the Erinnyes. At length he took refuge with Minerva at Athens. The goddess afforded him protection, and appointed the court of Areopagus to decide his fate. The Erinnyes brought forward their accusation, and Orestes made the command of the Delphic oracle his excuse. When the court voted and the voices were equally divided, Orestes was acquitted by the command of Minerva.

Byron, in Childe Harold, Canto IV, alludes to the story of Orestes:

"O thou who never yet of human wrong
Left the unbalanced scale, great Nemesis!
Thou who didst call the Furies from the abyss,
And round Orestes bade them howl and hiss,
For that unnatural retribution, just,
Had it but been from hands less near, in this,
Thy former realm, I call thee from the dust!"

One of the most pathetic scenes in the ancient drama is that in which Sophocles represents the meeting of Orestes and Electra, on his return from Phocis. Orestes, mistaking Electra for one of the domestics, and desirous of keeping his arrival a secret till the hour of vengeance should arrive, produces the urn in which his ashes are supposed to rest. Electra, believing him to be really dead, takes the urn, and embracing it, pours forth her grief in language full of tenderness and despair.

Milton, in one of his sonnets, says:

"The repeated air
Of sad Electra's poet had the power
To save the Athenian walls from ruin bare."

This alludes to the story that when, on one occasion, the city of Athens was at the mercy of her Spartan foes, and it was proposed to destroy it, the thought was rejected upon the accidental quotation, by some one, of a chorus of Euripides.

TROY

After hearing so much about the city of Troy and its heroes, the reader will perhaps be surprised to learn that the exact site of that famous city is still a matter of dispute. There are some vestiges of tombs on the plain which most nearly answers to the description given by Homer and the ancient geographers, but no other evidence of the former existence of a great city. Byron thus describes the present appearance of the scene:

"The winds are high, and Helle's tide
Rolls darkly heaving to the main;
And night's descending shadows hide
That field with blood bedewed in vain,
The desert of old Priam's pride,
The tombs, sole relics of his reign,
All save immortal dreams that could beguile
The blind old man of Scio's rocky isle."
Bride of Abydos.

Chapter 22

ADVENTURES OF ULYSSES. THE LOTUS-EATERS. CYCLOPES. CIRCE. SIRENS. SCYLLA AND CHARYBDIS. CALYPSO

The romantic poem of the Odyssey is now to engage our attention. It narrates the wanderings of Ulysses (Odysseus in the Greek language) in his return from Troy to his own kingdom of Ithaca.

From Troy the vessels first made land at Ismarus, a city of the Ciconians, where, in a skirmish with the inhabitants, Ulysses lost six men from each ship. Sailing thence they were overtaken by a storm which drove them for nine days along the sea till they reached the country of the Lotus-eaters. Here, after watering, Ulysses sent three of his men to discover who the inhabitants were. These men on coming among the Lotus-eaters were kindly entertained by them, and were given some of their own food, the lotus-plant to eat. The effect of this food was such that those who partook of it lost all thoughts of home and wished to remain in that country. It was by main force that Ulysses dragged these men away, and he was even obliged to tie them under the benches of his ship. (Tennyson in the Lotus-eaters has charmingly expressed the dreamy languid feeling which the lotus-food is said to have produced:

"How sweet it were, hearing the downward stream
With half-shut eyes ever to seem
Falling asleep in a half-dream!
To dream and dream, like yonder amber light
Which will not leave the myrrh-bush on the height;
To hear each other's whispered speech;
Eating the lotus, day by day,
To watch the crisping ripples on the beach,
And tender curving lines of creamy spray;
To lend our hearts and spirits wholly
To the influence of mild-minded melancholy;
To muse and brood and live again in memory,
With those old faces of our infancy
Heaped over with a mound of grass,
Two handfuls of white dust, shut in an urn of brass.")

They next arrived at the country of the Cyclopes. The Cyclopes were giants, who inhabited an island of which they were the only possessors. The name means "round eye," and these giants were so called because they had but one eye, and that placed in the middle of the forehead. They dwelt in caves and fed on the wild productions of the island and on what their flocks yielded, for they were shepherds. Ulysses left the main body of his ships at anchor, and with one vessel went to the Cyclopes' island to explore for supplies. He landed with his companions, carrying with them a jar of wine for a present, and coming to a large cave they entered it, and finding no one within examined its contents. They found it stored with the riches of the flock, quantities of cheese, pails and bowls of milk, lambs and kids in their pens, all in nice order. Presently arrived the master of the cave, Polyphemus, bearing an immense bundle of firewood, which he threw down before the cavern's mouth. He then drove into the cave the sheep and goats to be milked, and, entering, rolled to the cave's mouth an enormous rock, that twenty oxen could not draw. Next he sat down and milked his ewes, preparing a part for cheese, and setting the rest aside for his customary drink. Then turning round his great eye he discerned the strangers, and growled out to them, demanding who they were, and where from. Ulysses replied most humbly, stating that they were Greeks, from the great expedition that had lately won so much glory in the conquest of Troy; that they were now on their way home, and finished by imploring his hospitality in the name of the gods. Polyphemus deigned no answer, but reaching out his hand, seized two of the Greeks, whom he hurled against the side of the cave, and dashed out their brains. He proceeded to devour them with great relish, and having made a hearty meal, stretched himself out on the floor to sleep. Ulysses was tempted to seize the opportunity and plunge his sword into him as he slept, but recollected that it would only expose them all to certain destruction, as the rock with which the giant had closed up the door was far beyond their power to remove, and they would therefore be in hopeless imprisonment. Next morning the giant seized two more of the Greeks, and dispatched them in the same manner as their companions, feasting on their flesh till no fragment was left. He then moved away the rock from the door, drove out his flocks, and went out, carefully replacing the barrier after him. When he was gone Ulysses planned how he might take vengeance for his murdered friends, and effect his escape with his surviving companions. He made his men prepare a massive bar of wood cut by the Cyclops for a staff, which they found in the cave. They sharpened the end of it and seasoned it in the fire, and hid it under the straw on the cavern floor. Then four of the boldest were selected, with whom Ulysses joined himself as a fifth. The Cyclops came home at evening, rolled away the stone and drove in his flock as usual. After milking them and making his arrangements as before, he seized two more of Ulysses' companions and dashed their brains out, and made his evening meal upon them as he had on the others. After he had supped, Ulysses, approaching him, handed him a bowl of wine, saying, "Cyclops, this is wine; taste and drink after thy meal of man's flesh." He took and drank it, and was hugely delighted with it, and called for more. Ulysses supplied him once and again, which pleased the giant so much that he promised him as a favor that he should be the last of the party devoured. He asked his name, to which Ulysses replied, "My name is Noman."

After his supper the giant lay down to repose, and was soon sound asleep. Then Ulysses with his four select friends thrust the end of the stake into the fire till it was all one burning coal, then poising it exactly above the giant's only eye, they buried it deeply into the socket, twirling it round and round as a carpenter does his auger. The howling monster filled the cavern with his outcry, and Ulysses with his aids nimbly got out of his way and concealed themselves in the cave. The Cyclops, bellowing, called aloud on all the Cyclopes dwelling in the caves around him, far and near. They on his cry flocked around the den, and inquired what grievous hurt had caused him to sound such an alarm and break their slumbers. He replied, "O friends, I die, and Noman gives the blow." They answered, "If no man hurts thee it is the stroke of Jove, and thou must bear it." So saying, they left him groaning.

Next morning the Cyclops rolled away the stone to let his flock out to pasture, but planted himself in the door of the cave to feel of all as they went out, that Ulysses and his men should not escape with them. But Ulysses had made his men harness the rams of the flock three abreast, with osiers which they found on the floor of the cave. To the middle ram of the three one of the Greeks suspended himself, so protected by the exterior rams on either side. As they passed, the giant felt of the animals' backs and sides, but never thought of their bellies; so the men all passed safe, Ulysses himself being on the last one that passed. When they had got a few paces from the cavern, Ulysses and his friends released themselves from their rams, and drove a good part of the flock down to the shore to their boat. They put them aboard with all haste, then pushed off from the shore, and when at a safe distance Ulysses shouted, "Cyclops, the gods have well requited thee for thy atrocious deeds. Know it is Ulysses to whom thou owest thy shameful loss of sight." The Cyclops, hearing this, seized a rock that projected from the side of the mountain, and rending it from its bed he lifted it high in the air, then exerting all his force, hurled it in the direction of the voice. Down came the mass, just clearing the vessel's stern. The ocean, at the plunge of the huge rock, heaved the ship towards the land, so that it barely escaped being swamped by the waves. When they had with the utmost difficulty pulled off shore, Ulysses was about to hail the giant again, but his friends besought him not to do so. He could not forbear, however, letting the giant know that they had escaped his missile, but waited till they had reached a safer distance than before, The giant answered them with curses, but Ulysses and his friends plied their oars vigorously, and soon regained their companions.

Ulysses next arrived at the island of Æolus. To this monarch Jupiter had intrusted the government of the winds, to send them forth or retain them at his will. He treated Ulysses hospitably, and at his departure gave him, tied up in a leathern bag with a silver string, such winds as might be hurtful and dangerous, commanding fair winds to blow the barks towards their country. Nine days they sped before the wind, and all that time Ulysses had stood at the helm, without sleep. At last quite exhausted he lay down to sleep. While he slept, the crew conferred together about the mysterious bag, and concluded it must contain treasures given by the hospitable King Æolus to their commander. Tempted to secure some portion for themselves they loosed the string, when immediately the winds rushed forth. The ships were driven far from their course, and back again to the island they had just left. Æolus was so indignant at their folly that he refused to assist them further, and they were obliged to labor over their course once more by means of their oars.

THE LAESTRYGONIANS

The next adventure was with the barbarous tribe of Laestrygonians. The vessels pushed into the harbor, tempted by the secure appearance of the cove, completely land-locked; Ulysses alone moored his vessel without. As soon as the Laestrygonians found the ships completely in their power they attacked them, having huge stones which broke and overturned them, and with their spears dispatched the seamen as they struggled in the water. All the vessels with their crews were destroyed, except Ulysses' own ship which had remained outside, and finding no safety but in flight, he exhorted his men to ply their oars vigorously, and they escaped.

With grief for their slain companions mixed with joy at their own escape, they pursued their way till they arrived at the Aeaean isle, where dwelt Circe, the daughter of the sun. Landing here Ulysses climbed a hill, and gazing round saw no signs of habitation except in one spot at the centre of the island, where he perceived a palace embowered with trees. He sent forward one- half of his crew, under the command of Eurylochus, to see what prospect of hospitality they might find. As they approached the palace, they found themselves surrounded by lions, tigers and wolves, not fierce, but tamed by Circe's art, for she was a powerful magician. All these animals had once been men, but had been changed by Circe's enchantments into the forms of beasts. The sounds of soft music were heard from within, and a sweet female voice singing. Eurylochus called aloud and the goddess came forth and invited them in. They all gladly entered except Eurylochus, who suspected danger. The goddess conducted her guests to a seat, and had them served with wine and other delicacies. When they had feasted heartily, she touched them one by one with her wand, and they became immediately changed into SWINE, in "head, body, voice and bristles," yet with their intellects as before. She shut them in her sties, and supplied them with acorns and such other things as swine love.

Eurylochus hurried back to the ship and told the tale. Ulysses thereupon determined to go himself, and try if by any means he might deliver his companions. As he strode onward alone, he met a youth who addressed him familiarly, appearing to be acquainted with his adventures. He announced himself as Mercury, and informed Ulysses of the arts of Circe, and of the danger of approaching her. As Ulysses was not to be dissuaded from his attempts, Mercury provided him with a sprig of the plant Moly, of wonderful power to resist sorceries, and instructed him how to act. Ulysses proceeded, and reaching the palace was courteously received by Circe, who entertained him as she had done his companions, and after he had eaten and drank, touched him with her wand, saying, "Hence seek the sty and wallow with thy friends." But he, instead of obeying, drew his sword and rushed upon her with fury in his countenance. She fell on her knees and begged for mercy. He dictated a solemn oath that she would release his companions and practise no further against him or them; and she repeated it, at the same time promising to dismiss them all in safety after hospitably entertaining them. She was as good as her word. The men were restored to their shapes, the rest of the crew summoned from the shore, and the whole magnificently entertained day after day, till Ulysses seemed to have forgotten his native land, and to have reconciled himself to an inglorious life of ease and pleasure.

At length his companions recalled him to nobler sentiments, and he received their admonition gratefully. Circe aided their departure, and instructed them how to pas safely by the coast of the Sirens. The Sirens were Seanymphs who had the power of charming by their song all who had heard them, so that the unhappy mariners were irresistibly impelled to cast themselves into the sea to their destruction. Circe directed Ulysses to fill the ears of his seamen with wax, so that they should not hear the strain; and to cause himself to be bound to the mast, and his people to be strictly enjoined, whatever he might say or do, by no means to release him till they should have passed the Sirens' island. Ulysses obeyed these directions. He filled the ears of his people with wax, and suffered them to bind him with cords firmly to the mast. As they approached the Sirens' island, the sea was calm, and over the waters came the notes of music so ravishing and attractive, that Ulysses struggled to get loose, and by cries and signs to his people, begged to be released; but they, obedient to his previous orders, sprang forward and bound him still faster. They held on their course, and the music grew fainter till it ceased to be heard, when with joy

Ulysses gave his companions the signal to unseal their ears, and they relieved him from his bonds.

The imagination of a modern poet, Keats, has discovered for us the thoughts that passed through the brains of the victims of Circe, after their transformation. In his Endymion he represents one of them, a monarch in the guise of an elephant, addressing the sorceress in human language thus:

"I sue not for my happy crown again;
I sue not for my phalanx on the plain;
I sue not for my lone, my widowed wife;
I sue not for my ruddy drops of life,
My children fair, my lovely girls and boys;
I will forget them; I will pass these joys,
Ask nought so heavenward; so too too high;
Only I pray, as fairest boon, to die;
To be delivered from this cumbrous flesh,
From this gross, detestable, filthy mesh,
And merely given to the cold, bleak air.
Have mercy, goddess! Circe, feel my prayer!"

SCYLLA AND CHARYBDIS

Ulysses had been warned by Circe of the two monsters Scylla and Charybdis. We have already met with Scylla in the story of Glaucus, and remember that she was once a beautiful maiden and was changed into a snakymonster by Circe. She dwelt in a cave high up on the cliff, from whence she was accustomed to thrust forth her long necks for she had six heads, and in each of her mouths to seize one of the crew of every vessel passing within reach. The other terror, Charybdis, was a gulf, nearly on a level with the water. Thrice each day the water rushed into a frightful chasm, and thrice was disgorged. Any vessel coming near the whirlpool when the tide was rushing in must inevitably by ingulfed; not Neptune himself could save it.

On approaching the haunt of the dread monsters, Ulysses kept strict watch to discover them. The roar of the waters as Charybdis ingulfed them, gave warning at a distance, but Scylla could nowhere be discerned. While Ulysses and his men watched with anxious eyes the dreadful whirlpool, they were not equally on their guard from the attack of Scylla, and the monster darting forth her snaky heads, caught six of his men, and bore them away shrieking to her den. It was the saddest sight Ulysses had yet seen; to behold his friends thus sacrificed and hear their cries, unable to afford them any assistance.

Circe had warned him of another danger. After passing Scylla and Charybdis, the next land he would make was Trinakria, an island whereon were pastured the cattle of Hyperion, the Sun, tended by his daughters Lampetia and Phaethusa. These flocks must not be violated, whatever the wants of the voyagers might be. If this injunction were transgressed, destruction was sure to fall on the offenders.

Ulysses would willingly have passed the island of the Sun without stopping, but his companions so urgently pleaded for the rest and refreshment that would be derived from anchoring and passing the night on shore, that Ulysses yielded. He bound them, however, with an oath that they would not touch one of the animals of the sacred flocks and herds, but content themselves with what provision they yet had left of the supply which Circe had put on board. So long as this supply lasted the people kept their oath, but contrary winds detained them at the island for a month, and after consuming all their stock of provisions, they were forced to rely upon the birds and fishes they could catch. Famine pressed them, and at length one day, in the absence of Ulysses, they slew some of the cattle, vainly attempting to make amends for the deed by offering from them a portion to the offended powers. Ulysses, on his return to the shore, was horror-struck at perceiving what they had done, and the more so on account of the portentous signs which followed. The skins crept on the ground, and the joints of meat lowed on the spits while roasting.

The wind becoming fair they sailed from the island. They had not gone far when the weather changed, and a storm of thunder and lightning ensued. A stroke of lightning shattered their mast, which in its fall killed the pilot. At last the vessel itself came to pieces. The keel and mast floating side by side, Ulysses formed of them a raft, to which he clung, and, the wind changing, the waves bore him to Calypso's island. All the rest of the crew perished.

The following allusion to the stories we have just been relating is from Milton's Comus, line 252:

"I have often heard
My mother Circe and the Sirens three,
Amidst the flowery-kirtled Naiades,
Culling their potent herbs and baneful drugs,
Who as they sung would take the prisoned soul
And lap it in Elysium. Scylla wept,
And chid her barking waves into attention.
And fell Charybdis murmured soft applause."

Scylla and Charybdis have become proverbial, to denote opposite dangers which beset one's course.

CALYPSO

Calypso was a sea-nymph. One of that numerous class of female divinities of lower rank than the gods, yet sharing many of their attributes. Calypso received Ulysses hospitably, entertained him magnificently, became enamored of him, and wished to retain him forever, conferring on him immortality. But he persisted in his resolution to return to his country and his wife and son. Calypso at last received a command from Jove to dismiss him. Mercury brought the message to her, and found her in her grotto, which is thus described by Homer:

"A garden vine, luxuriant on all sides,
Mantled the spacious cavern, cluster-hung
Profuse; four fountains of serenest lymph,
Their sinuous course pursuing side by side,
Strayed all around, and every where appeared
Meadows of softest verdure purpled o'er
With violets; it was a scene to fill
A god from heaven with wonder and delight."

Calypso with much reluctance proceeded to obey the commands of Jupiter. She supplied Ulysses with the means of constructing a raft, provisioned it well for him, and gave him a favoring gale. He sped on his course prosperously for many days, till at length, when in sight of land, a storm arose that broke his mast, and threatened to rend the raft asunder. In this crisis he was seen by a compassionate sea-nymph, who in the form of a cormorant alighted on the raft, and presented him a girdle, directing him to bind it beneath his breast, and if he should

Figure 32: "Nymph Calypso" by William Heath Robinson

be compelled to trust himself to the waves, it would buoy him up and enable him by swimming to reach the land.

Fenelon, in his romance of Telemachus, has given us the adventures of the son of Ulysses in search of his father. Among other places at which he arrived, following on his father's footsteps, was Calypso's isle, and, as in the former case, the goddess tried every art to keep him with her, and offered to share her immortality with him. But Minerva, who, in the shape of Mentor, accompanied him and governed all his movements, made him repel her allurements, and when no other means of escape could be found, the two friends leaped from a cliff into the sea, and swam to a vessel which lay becalmed off shore. Byron alludes to this leap of Telemachus and Mentor in the following stanza:

"But not in silence pass Calypso's isles,
The sister tenants of the middle deep;
There for the weary still a haven smiles,
Though the fair goddess long has ceased to weep,
And o'er her cliffs a fruitless watch to keep
For him who dared prefer a mortal bride.
Here too his boy essayed the dreadful leap,
Stern Mentor urged from high to yonder tide;
While thus of both bereft the nymph-queen doubly sighed."

Chapter 23

THE ODYSSEY (CONTINUED)

THE PHAECIANS

Ulysses clung to the raft while any of its timbers kept together, and when it no longer yielded him support, binding the girdle around him, he swam. Minerva smoothed the billows before him and sent him a wind that rolled the waves towards the shore. The surf beat high on the rocks and seemed to forbid approach; but at length finding calm water at the mouth of a gentle stream, he landed, spent with toil, breathless and speechless and almost dead. After some time reviving, he kissed the soil, rejoicing, yet at a loss what course to take. At a short distance he perceived a wood, to which he turned his steps. There finding a covert sheltered by intermingling branches alike from the sun and the rain, he collected a pile of leaves and formed a bed, on which he stretched himself, and heaping the leaves over him, fell asleep.

The land where he was thrown was Scheria, the country of the Phaecians. These people dwelt originally near the Cyclopes; but being oppressed by that savage race, they migrated to the isle of Scheria, under the conduct of Nausithous their king. They were, the poet tells us, a people akin to the gods, who appeared manifestly and feasted among them when they offered sacrifices, and did not conceal themselves from solitary wayfarers when they met them. They had abundance of wealth and lived in the enjoyment of it undisturbed by the alarms of war, for as they dwelt remote from gain-seeking man, no enemy ever approached their shores, and they did not even require to make use of bows and quivers. Their chief employment was navigation. Their ships, which went with the velocity of birds, were endued with intelligence; they knew every port and needed no pilot. Alcinous, the son of Nausithous, was now their king, a wise and just sovereign, beloved by his people. Now it happened that the very night on which Ulysses was cast ashore on the Phaeacian island, and while he lay sleeping on his bed of leaves, Nausicaa, the daughter of the king, had a dream sent by Minerva, reminding her that her wedding-day was not far distant, and that it would be but a prudent preparation for that event to have a general washing of the clothes of the family. This was no slight affair, for the fountains were at some distance and the garments must be carried thither. On awaking, the princess hastened to her parents to tell them what was on her mind; not alluding to her wedding-day, but finding other reasons equally good. Her father readily assented and ordered the grooms to furnish forth a wagon for the purpose. The clothes were put therein, and the queen mother placed in the wagon, likewise an abundant supply of food and wine. The princess took her seat and plied the lash, her attendant virgins following her on foot. Arrived at the river side they turned out the mules to graze, and unloading the carriage, bore the garments down to the water, and working with cheerfulness and alacrity soon dispatched their labor. Then having spread the garments on the shore to dry, and having themselves bathed, they sat down to enjoy their meal; after which they rose and amused themselves with a game of ball, the princess singing to them while they played. But when they had refolded the apparel and were about to resume their way to the town, Minerva caused the ball thrown by the princess to fall into the water, whereat they all screamed, and Ulysses awaked at the sound.

Now we must picture to ourselves Ulysses, a shipwrecked mariner, but just escaped from the waves, and utterly destitute of clothing, awaking and discovering that only a few bushes were interposed between him and a group of young maidens, whom, by their deportment and attire, he discovered to be not mere peasant girls, but of a higher class. Sadly needing help, how could he yet venture, naked as he was, to discover himself and make his wants known? It certainly was a case worthy of the interposition of his patron goddess Minerva, who never failed him at a crisis. Breaking off a leafy branch from a tree, he held it before him and stepped out from the thicket. The virgins, at sight of him, fled in all directions, Nausicaa alone excepted, for Minerva aided and endowed her with courage and discernment. Ulysses, standing respectfully aloof, told his sad case, and besought the fair object (whether queen or goddess he professed he knew not) for food and clothing. The princess replied courteously, promising present relief and her father's hospitality when he should become acquainted with the facts. She called back her scattered maidens, chiding their alarm, and reminding them that the Phaeacians had no enemies to fear. This man, she told them, was an unhappy wanderer, whom it was a duty to cherish, for the poor and stranger are from Jove. She bade them bring food and clothing, for some of her brothers' garments were among the contents of the wagon. When this was done, and Ulysses, retiring to a sheltered place, had washed his body free from the sea-foam, clothed and refreshed himself with food, Pallas dilated his form and diffused grace over his ample chest and manly brows.

The princess, seeing him, was filled with admiration, and scrupled not to say to her damsels that she wished the gods would send her such a husband. To Ulysses she recommended that he should repair to the city, following herself and train so far as the way lay through the fields; but when they should approach the city she desired that he would no longer be seen in her company, for she feared the remarks which rude and vulgar people might make on seeing her return accompanied by such a gallant stranger; to avoid which she directed him to stop at a grove adjoining the city, in which were a farm and garden belonging to the king. After allowing time for the princess and her companions to reach the city, he was then to pursue his way thither, and would be easily guided by any he might meet to the royal abode.

Ulysses obeyed the directions, and in due time proceeded to the city, on approaching which he met a young woman bearing a pitcher forth for water. It was Minerva, who had assumed that form. Ulysses accosted her, and desired to be directed to the palace of Alcinous the king. The maiden replied respectfully, offering to be his guide; for the palace, she informed him, stood near her father's dwelling. Under the guidance of the goddess, and by her power enveloped in a cloud which shielded him from observation, Ulysses passed among the busy crowd, and with wonder observed their harbor, their ships, their forum (the resort of heroes), and their battlements, till they came to the palace, where the goddess, having first given him some information of the country, king, and people he was about to meet, left him. Ulysses, before entering the courtyard of the palace, stood and surveyed the scene. Its splendor astonished him. Brazen walls stretched from the entrance to the interior house, of which the doors were gold, the door-posts silver, the lintels silver ornamented with gold. On either side were figures of mastiffs wrought in gold and silver, standing in rows as if to guard the approach. Along the walls were seats spread through all their length with mantles of finest texture, the work of Phaeacian maidens. On these seats the princes sat and feasted, while golden statues of graceful youths held in their hands lighted torches, which shed radiance over the scene. Full fifty female menials served in household offices, some employed to grind the corn, others to wind off the purple wool or ply the loom. For the Phaeacian women as far exceeded all other women in household arts as the mariners of that country did the rest of mankind in the management of ships. Without the court a spacious garden lay, in which grew many a lofty tree, pomegranate, pear, apple, fig, and olive. Neither winter's cold nor summer's drought arrested their growth, but they flourished in constant succession, some budding while others were maturing. The vineyard was equally prolific. In one quarter you might see the vines, some in blossom, some loaded with ripe grapes, and in another observe the vintagers treading the wine-press. On the garden's borders flowers of every hue bloomed all the year round, arranged with neatest art. In the midst two fountains poured forth their waters, one flowing by artificial channels over all the garden, the other conducted through the courtyard of the palace, whence every citizen might draw his supplies.

Ulysses stood gazing in admiration, unobserved himself, for the cloud which Minerva spread around him still shielded him. At length, having sufficiently observed the scene, he advanced with rapid step into the hall where the chiefs and senators were assembled, pouring libation to Mercury, whose worship followed the evening meal. Just then Minerva dissolved the cloud and disclosed him to the assembled chiefs. Advancing toward the queen, he knelt at her feet and implored her favor and assistance to enable him to return to his native country. Then withdrawing, he seated himself in the manner of suppliants, at the hearth- side.

For a time none spoke. At last an aged statesman, addressing the king, said, "It is not fit that a stranger who asks our hospitality should be kept waiting in suppliant guise, none welcoming him. Let him therefore be led to a seat among us and supplied with food and wine." At these words the king rising gave his hand to Ulysses and led him to a seat, displacing thence his own son to make room for the stranger. Food and wine were set before him and he ate and refreshed himself.

The king then dismissed his guests, notifying them that the next day he would call them to council to consider what had best be done for the stranger.

Chapter 23: The Phaeacians

When the guests had departed and Ulysses was left alone with the king and queen, the queen asked him who he was and whence he came, and (recognizing the clothes which he wore as those which her maidens and herself had made) from whom he received his garments. He told them of his residence in Calypso's isle and his departure thence; of the wreck of his raft, his escape by swimming, and of the relief afforded by the princess. The parents heard approvingly, and the king promised to furnish him a ship in which he might return to his own land.

The next day the assembled chiefs confirmed the promise of the king. A bark was prepared and a crew of stout rowers selected, and all betook themselves to the palace, where a bounteous repast was provided. After the feast the king proposed that the young men should show their guest their proficiency in manly sports, and all went forth to the arena for games of running, wrestling, and other exercises. After all had done their best, Ulysses being challenged to show what he could do, at first declined, but being taunted by one of the youths, seized a quoit of weight far heavier than any the Phaeacians had thrown, and sent it farther than the utmost throw of theirs. All were astonished, and viewed their guest with greatly increased respect.

After the games they returned to the hall, and the herald led in Demodocus, the blind bard,

"Dear to the Muse,
Who yet appointed him both good and ill,
Took from him sight, but gave him strains divine."

He took for his theme the wooden horse, by means of which the Greeks found entrance into Troy. Apollo inspired him, and he sang so feelingly of the terrors and the exploits of that eventful time that all were delighted, but Ulysses was moved to tears. Observing which, Alcinous, when the song was done, demanded of him why at the mention of troy his sorrows awaked. Had he lost there a father or brother, or any dear friend? Ulysses in reply announced himself by his true name, and at their request, recounted the adventures which had befallen him since his departure from Troy. This narrative raised the sympathy and admiration of the Phaeacians for their guest to the highest pitch. The king proposed that each chief should present him with a gift, himself setting the example. They obeyed, and vied with one another in loading the illustrious stranger with costly gifts.

The next day Ulysses set sail in the Phaeacian vessel, and in a short time arrived safe at Ithaca, his own island. When the vessel touched the strand he was asleep. The mariners, without waking him, carried him on shore, and landed with him the chest containing his presents, and then sailed away.

But Neptune was displeased at the conduct of the Phaeacians in thus rescuing Ulysses from his hands. In revenge, on the return of the vessel to port, he transformed it into a rock, right opposite the mouth of the harbor.

Homer's description of the ships of the Phaeacians has been thought to look like an anticipation of the wonders of modern steam navigation. Alcinous says to Ulysses,

"Say from what city, from what regions tossed,
And what inhabitants those regions boast?
So shalt thou quickly reach the realm assigned,
In wondrous ships, self-moved, instinct with mind;
No helm secures their course, no pilot guides;
Like man intelligent they plough the tides,
Conscious of every coast and every bay
That lies beneath the sun's all-seeing ray."
Odyssey, Book VIII

Lord Carlisle, in his Diary in the Turkish and Greek Waters, thus speaks of Corfu, which he considers to be the ancient Phaeacian island:

"The sites explain the Odyssey. The temple of the sea-god could not have been more fitly placed, upon a grassy platform of the most elastic turf, on the brow of a crag commanding harbor, and channel, and ocean. Just at the entrance of the inner harbor there is a picturesque rock with a small convent perched atop it, which by one legend is the transformed pinnace of Ulysses.

"Almost the only river in the island is just at the proper distance from the probable site of the city and palace of the king, to justify the princess Nausicaa having had resort to her chariot and to luncheon when she went with the maidens of the court to wash their garments."

FATE OF THE SUITORS

It was now twenty years that Ulysses had been away from Ithaca, and when he awoke he did not recognize his native land. But Minerva, appearing to him in the form of a young shepherd, informed him where he was, and told him the state of things at his palace. More than a hundred nobles of Ithaca and of the neighboring islands had been for years suing for the hand of Penelope, his wife, imagining him dead, and lording it over his palace and people, as if they were owners of both. That he might be able to take vengeance upon them, it was important that he should not be recognized. Minerva accordingly metamorphosed him into an unsightly beggar, and as such he was kindly received by Eumaeus, the swine-herd, a faithful servant of his house.

Telemachus, his son, was absent in quest of his father. He had gone to the courts of the other kings, who had returned from the Trojan expedition. While on the search, he received counsel from Minerva to return home. Arriving at Ithaca, he sought Eumaeus to learn something of the state of affairs at the palace before presenting himself among the suitors. Finding a stranger with Eumaeus, he treated him courteously, though in the garb of a beggar, and promised him assistance. Eumaeus was sent to the palace to inform Penelope privately of her son's arrival, for caution was necessary with regard to the suitors, who, as Telemachus had learned, were plotting to intercept and kill him. When Eumaeus was gone, Minerva presented herself to Ulysses, and directed him to make himself known to his son. At the same time she touched him, removed at once from him the appearance of age and penury, and gave him the aspect of vigorous manhood that belonged to him. Telemachus viewed him with astonishment, and at first thought he must be more than mortal. But Ulysses announced himself as his father, and accounted for the change of appearance by explaining that it was Minerva's doing.

"Then threw Telemachus
His arms around his father's neck and wept,
Desire intense of lamentation seized
On both; soft murmurs uttering, each indulged
His grief."

The father and son took counsel together how they should get the better of the suitors and punish them for their outrages. It was arranged that Telemachus should proceed to the palace and mingle with the suitors as formerly; that Ulysses should go also, as a beggar, a character which in the rude old times had different privileges from those we concede to it now. As traveler and story-teller, the beggar was admitted in the halls of chieftains, and often treated like a guest; though sometimes, also, no doubt, with contumely. Ulysses charged his son not to betray, by any display of unusual interest in him, that he knew him to be other than he seemed, and even if he saw him insulted, or beaten, not to interpose otherwise than he might do for any stranger.

At the palace they found the usual scene of feasting and riot going on. The suitors pretended to receive Telemachus with joy at his return, though secretly mortified at the failure of their plots to take his life. The old beggar was permitted to enter, and provided with a portion from the table. A touching incident occurred as Ulysses entered the court-yard of the palace. An old dog lay in the yard almost dead with age, and seeing a stranger enter, raised his head, with ears erect. It was Argus, Ulysses' own dog, that he had in other days often led to the chase.

"Soon he perceived
Long-lost Ulysses nigh, down fell his ears
Clapped close, and with his tail glad signs he gave
Of gratulation, impotent to rise,
And to approach his master as of old.
Ulysses, noting him, wiped off a tear
Unmarked.
. . . Then his destiny released
Old Argus, soon as he had lived to see
Ulysses in the twentieth year restored."

As Ulysses sat eating his portion in the hall, the suitors soon began to exhibit their insolence to him. When he mildly remonstrated, one of them raised a stool and with it gave him a blow. Telemachus had hard work to restrain his indignation at seeing his father so treated in his own hall, but remembering his father's injunctions, said no more than what became him as master of the house and protector of his guests.

Chapter 23: Fate of the Suitors

Penelope had protracted her decision in favor of any one of her suitors so long, that there seemed to be no further pretence for delay. The continued absence of her husband seemed to prove that his return was no longer to be expected. Meanwhile her son had grown up, and was able to manage his own affairs. She therefore consented to submit the question of her choice to a trial of skill among the suitors. The test selected was shooting with the bow. Twelve rings were arranged in a line, and he whose arrow was sent through the whole twelve, was to have the queen for his prize. A bow that one of his brother heroes had given to Ulysses in former times, was brought from the armory, and with its quiver full of arrows was laid in the hall. Telemachus had taken care that all other weapons should be removed, under pretence that in the heat of competition, there was danger, in some rash moment, of putting them to an improper use.

All things being prepared for the trial, the first thing to be done was to bend the bow in order to attach the string. Telemachus endeavored to do it, but found all his efforts fruitless; and modestly confessing that he had attempted a task beyond his strength, he yielded the bow to another. HE tried it with no better success, and, amidst the laughter and jeers of his companions, gave it up. Another tried it and another; they rubbed the bow with tallow, but all to no purpose; it would not bend. Then spoke Ulysses, humbly suggesting that he should be permitted to try; for, said he, "beggar as I am, I was once a soldier, and there is still some strength in these old limbs of mine." The suitors hooted with derision, and commanded to turn him out of the hall for his insolence. But Telemachus spoke up for him, and merely to gratify the old man, bade him try. Ulysses took the bow, and handled it with the hand of a master. With ease he adjusted the cord to its notch, then fitting an arrow to the bow he drew the string and sped the arrow unerring through the rings.

Without allowing them time to express their astonishment, he said, "Now for another mark!" and aimed direct at the most insolent one of the suitors. The arrow pierced through his throat and he fell dead. Telemachus, Eumaeus, and another faithful follower, well armed, now sprang to the side of Ulysses. The suitors, in amazement, looked round for arms but found none, neither was there any way of escape, for Eumaeus had secured the door. Ulysses left them not long in uncertainty; he announced himself as the long-lost chief, whose house they had invaded, whose substance they had squandered, whose wife and son they had persecuted for ten long years; and told them he meant to have ample vengeance. All the suitors were slain, except Phemius the bard and Medon the herald, and Ulysses was left master of his own palace and possessor of his kingdom and his wife.

Among Schiller's works is the following epigram on Ulysses:

"To gain his home all oceans he explored;
Here Scylla frowned, and there Charybdis roared;
Horror on sea, and horror on the land,
In hell's dark boat he sought the spectre land,
Till borne a slumberer to his native spot,
He woke, and sorrowing, knew his country not."
Sir Edward Bulwer"s translation

Tennyson's poem of Ulysses represents the old hero, after his dangers past and nothing left but to stay at home and be happy, growing tired of inaction and resolving to set forth again in quest of new adventures.

"Come my friends,
'Tis not too late to seek a newer world.
Push off, and sitting well in order smite
The sounding furrows; for my purpose holds
To sail beyond the sunset, and the baths
Of all the western stars, until I die.
It may be that the gulfs will wash us down;
It may be we shall touch the Happy Isles,
And see the great Achilles whom we knew,
Tho' much is taken, much abides; and tho'
We are not now that strength which in old days
Moved earth and heaven; that which we are, we are;
One equal temper of heroic hearts,
Made weak by time and fate, but strong in will
To strive, to seek, to find, and not to yield."

Chapter 24

ADVENTURES OF ÆNEAS THE HARPIES DIDO PALINURUS

We have followed one of the Grecian heroes, Ulysses, in his wanderings, on his return home from Troy, and now we propose to share the fortunes of the remnant of the conquered people, under their chief Æneas, in their search for a new home, after the ruin of their native city. On that fatal night when the wooden horse disgorged its contents of armed men, and the capture and conflagration of the city were the result, Aeneas made his escape from the scene of destruction with his father, and his wife, and young son. The father, Anchises, was woo old to walk with the speed required, and Æneas took him upon his shoulders. Thus burdened, leading his son and followed by his wife, he made the best of his way out of the burning city; but in the confusion, his wife was swept away and lost.

On arriving at the place of rendezvous, numerous fugitives, of both sexes, were found, who put themselves under the guidance of Aeneas. Some months were spent in preparation and at length they embarked. They first landed on the neighboring shores of Thrace, and were preparing to build a city, but Æneas was deterred by a prodigy. Preparing to offer sacrifice, he tore some twigs from one of the bushes. To his dismay the wounded part dropped blood. When he repeated the act, a voice from the ground cried out to him, "Spare me, Æneas; I am your kinsman, Polydore, here murdered with many arrows, from which a bush has grown, nourished with my blood." These words recalled to the recollection of Æneas that Polydore was a young prince of Troy, whom his father had sent with ample treasures to the neighboring land of Thrace, to be there brought up, at a distance from the horrors of war. The king to whom he was sent had murdered him, and seized his treasures. Æneas and his companions hastened away, considering the land to be accursed by the stain of such a crime.

They next landed on the island of Delos, which was once a floating island, till Jupiter fastened it by adamantine chains to the bottom of the sea. Apollo and Diana were born there, and the island was sacred to Apollo. Here Æneas consulted the oracle of Apollo, and received an answer, as ambiguous as usual "Seek your ancient mother; there the race of Æneas shall dwell, and reduce all other nations to their sway." The Trojans heard with joy, and immediately began to ask one another, "Where is the spot intended by the oracle?" Anchises remembered that there was a tradition that their forefathers came from Crete, and thither they resolved to steer. They arrived at Crete, and began to build their city, but sickness broke out among them, and the fields that they had planted failed to yield a crop. In this gloomy aspect of affairs, Æneas was warned in a dream to leave the country, and seek a western land, called Hesperia, whence Dardanus, the true founder of the Trojan race, had originally migrated. To Hesperia, now called Italy, therefore, they directed their future course, and not till after many adventures and the lapse of time sufficient to carry a modern navigator several times round the world, did they arrive there.

Their first landing was at the island of the Harpies:

"——The daughters of the earth and sea,
The dreadful snatchers, who like women were
Down to the breast, with scanty coarse black hair
About their heads, and dim eyes ringed with red,
And bestial mouths set round with lips of lead,
But from their gnarled necks there began to spring
Half hair, half feathers, and a sweeping wing
Grew out instead of arm on either side,
And thick plumes underneath the breast did hide
The place where joined the fearful natures twain.
Gray-feathered were they else, with many a stain
Of blood thereon, and on birds' claws they went.
Morris: Life and Death of Jason

The Harpies had been sent by the gods to torment a certain Phineus, whom Jupiter had deprived of his sight in punishment of his cruelty; and whenever a meal was placed before him, the Harpies darted down from the air and carried it off. They were driven away from Phineus by the heroes of the Argonautic expedition, and took refuge in the island where Æneas now found them.

When they entered the port the Trojans saw herds of cattle roaming over the plain. They slew as many as they wished, and prepared for a feast. But no sooner had they seated themselves at the table, than a horrible clamor was heard in the air, and a flock of odious Harpies came rushing down upon them, seizing in their talons the meat from the dishes, and flying away with it. Æneas and his companions drew their swords and dealt vigorous blows among the monsters, but to no purpose, for they were so nimble it was almost impossible to hit them, and their feathers were like armor impenetrable to steel. One of them, perched on a neighboring cliff, screamed out, "Is it thus, Trojans, you treat us innocent birds, first slaughter our cattle, and then make war on ourselves?" She then predicted dire sufferings to them in their future course, and having vented her wrath flew away. The Trojans made haste to leave the country, and next found themselves coasting along the shore of Epirus. Here they landed, and to their astonishment learned that certain Trojan exiles, who had been carried there as prisoners, had become rulers of the country. Andromache, the widow of Hector, became the wife of one of the victorious Grecian chiefs, to whom she bore a son. Her husband dying, she was left regent of the country, as guardian of her son, and had married a fellow-captive, Helenus, of the royal race of Troy. Helenus and Andromache treated the exiles with the utmost hospitality, and dismissed them loaded with gifts.

From hence Æneas coasted along the shore of Sicily, and passed the country of Cyclopes. Here they were hailed from the shore by a miserable object, whom by his garments, tattered as they were, they perceived to be a Greek. He told them he was one of Ulysses' companions, left behind by that chief in his hurried departure. He related the story of Ulysses' adventure with Polyphemus, and besought them to take him off with them, as he had no means of sustaining his existence where he was, but wild berries and roots, and lived in constant fear of the Cyclopes. While he spoke Polyphemus made his appearance; a terrible monster, shapeless, vast, whose only eye had been put out. He walked with cautious steps, feeling his way with a staff, down to the sea-side, to wash his eye-socket in the waves. When he reached the water, he waded out towards them, and his immense height enabled him to advance far into the sea, so that the Trojans, in terror, took to their oars to get out of his way. Hearing the oars, Polyphemus shouted after them, so that the shores resounded, and at the noise the other Cyclopes came forth from their caves and woods, and lined the shore, like a row of lofty pine trees. The Trojans plied their oars, and soon left them out of sight.

Æneas had been cautioned by Helenus to avoid the strait guarded by the monsters Scylla and Charybdis. There Ulysses, the reader will remember, had lost six of his men, seized by Scylla, while the navigators were wholly intent upon avoiding Charybdis. Æneas, following the advice of Helenus, shunned the dangerous pass and coasted along the island of Sicily.

Juno, seeing the Trojans speeding their way prosperously towards their destined shore, felt her old grudge against them revive, for she could not forget the slight that Paris had put upon her, in awarding the prize of beauty to another. In heavenly minds can such resentments dwell! Accordingly she hastened to Æolus, the ruler of the winds, the same who supplied Ulysses with favoring gales, giving him the contrary ones tied up in a bag. Æolus obeyed the goddess and sent forth his sons, Boreas, Typhon and the other winds, to toss the ocean. A terrible storm ensued, and the Trojan ships were driven out of their course towards the coast of Africa. They were in imminent danger of being wrecked, and were separated, so that Æneas thought that all were lost except his own.

At this crisis, Neptune, hearing the storm raging, and knowing that he had given no orders for one, raised his head above the waves, and saw the fleet of Æneas driving before the gale. Knowing the hostility of Juno, he was at no loss to account for it, but his anger was not the less at this interference in his province. He called the winds, and dismissed them with a severe reprimand. He then soothed the waves, and brushed away the clouds from before the face of the sun. Some of the ships which had got on the rocks he pried off with his own trident, while Triton and a sea-nymph, putting their shoulders under others, set them afloat again. The Trojans, when the sea became calm, sought the nearest shore, which was the coast of Carthage, where Æneas was so happy as to find that one by one the ships all arrived safe, though badly shaken.

Waller, in his Panegyric to the Lord Protector (Cromwell), alludes to this stilling of the storm by Neptune:

"Above the waves, as Neptune showed his face,
To chide the winds and save the Trojan race,
So has your Highness, raised above the rest,
Storms of ambition tossing us repressed.."

DIDO

Carthage, where the exiles had now arrived, was a spot on the coast of Africa opposite Sicily, where at that time a Tyrian colony under Dido their queen, were laying the foundations of a state destined in later ages to be the rival of Rome itself. Dido was the daughter of Belus, king of Tyre, and sister of Pygmalion who succeeded his father on the throne. Her husband was Sichaeus, a man of immense wealth, but Pygmalion, who coveted his treasures, caused him to be put to death. Dido, with a numerous body of followers, both men and women, succeeded in effecting their escape from Tyre in several vessels, carrying with them the treasures of Sichaeus. On arriving at the spot which they selected as the seat of their future home, they asked of the natives only so much land as they could enclose with a bull's hide. When this was readily granted, she caused the hide to be cut into strips, and with them enclosed a spot on which she built a citadel, and called it Byrsa (a hide). Around this fort the city of Carthage rose, and soon became a powerful and flourishing place.

Such was the state of affairs when Æneas with his Trojans arrived there. Dido received the illustrious exiles with friendliness and hospitality. "Not unacquainted with distress," she said, "I have learned to succor the unfortunate." The queen's hospitality displayed itself in festivities at which games of strength and skill were exhibited. The strangers contended for the palm with her own subjects on equal terms, the queen declaring that whether the victor were "Trojan or Tyrian should make no difference to her." At the feast which followed the games, Æneas gave at her request a recital of the closing events of the Trojan history and his own adventures after the fall of the city. Dido was charmed with his discourse and filled with admiration of his exploits. She conceived an ardent passion for him, and he for his part seemed well content to accept the fortunate chance which appeared to offer him at once a happy termination of his wanderings, a home, a kingdom, and a bride. Months rolled away in the enjoyment of pleasant intercourse, and it seemed as if Italy and the empire destined to be founded on its shores were alike forgotten. Seeing which, Jupiter dispatched Mercury with a message to Æneas recalling him to a sense of his high destiny, and commanding him to resume his voyage.

Figure 33: "Dido" by Henry Fuseli

Æneas, under this divine command, parted from Dido, though she tried every allurement and persuasion to detain him. The blow to her affection and her pride was too much for her to endure, and when she found that he was gone, she mounted a funeral-pile which she had caused to be prepared, and, having stabbed herself, was consumed with the pile. The flames rising over the city were seen by the departing Trojans, and, though the cause was unknown, gave to Æneas some intimation of the fatal event.

We find in "Elegant Extracts" the following epigram:

From the Latin

"Unhappy, Dido, was thy fate
In first and second married state!
One husband caused thy flight by dying,
Thy death the other caused by flying."

Dr. Johnson was once challenged to make an epigram on the syllables di,do,dum. He immediately replied in these lines:

"When Dido found Aeneas would not come,
She wept in silence, and was Dido dumb.

PALINURUS

After touching at the island of Sicily, where Acestes, a prince of Trojan lineage, bore sway, who gave them a hospitable reception, the Trojans re-embarked, and held on their course for Italy. Venus now interceded with Neptune to allow her son at last to attain the wished-for goal, and find an end of his perils on the deep. Neptune consented, stipulating only for one life as a ransom for the rest. The victim was Palinurus, the pilot. As he sat watching the stars, with his hand on the helm, Somnus, sent by Neptune, approached in the guise of Phorbas and said, "Palinurus, the breeze is fair, the water smooth, and the ship sails steadily on her course. Lie down a while and take needful rest. I will stand at the helm in your place." Palinurus replied, "Tell me not of smooth seas or favoring winds, me who have seen so much of their treachery. Shall I trust Æneas to the chances of the weather and winds?" And he continued to grasp the helm and to keep his eyes fixed on the stars. But Somnus waved over him a branch moistened with Lethaean dew, and his eyes closed in spite of all his efforts. Then Somnus pushed him overboard and he fell; but keeping his hold upon the helm it came away with him. Neptune was mindful of his promise, and kept the ship on her track without helm or pilot, till Aeneas discovered his loss, and, sorrowing deeply for his faithful steersman, took charge of the ship himself.

There is a beautiful allusion to the story of Palinurus in Scott's Marmion, Introduction to Canto I., where the poet, speaking of the recent death of William Pitt, says:

"Oh, think how, to his latest day,
When death just hovering claimed his prey,
With Palinure's unaltered mood,
Firm at his dangerous post he stood;
Each call for needful rest repelled,
With dying hand the rudder held,
Till in his fall, with fateful sway,
The steerage of the realm gave way."

The ships at last reached the shores of Italy, and joyfully did the adventurers leap to land. While his people were employed in making their encampment Æneas sought the abode of the Sibyl. It was a cave connected with a temple and grove, sacred to Apollo and Diana. While Aeneas contemplated the scene, the Sibyl accosted him. She seemed to know his errand, and under the influence of the deity of the place burst forth in a prophetic strain, giving dark intimations of labors and perils through which he was destined to make his way to final success. She closed with the encouraging words which have become proverbial: "Yield not to disasters, but press onward the more bravely." Æneas replied that he had prepared himself for whatever might await him. He had but one request to make. Having been directed in a dream to seek the abode of the dead in order to confer with his father Anchises to receive from him a revelation of his future fortunes and those of his race, he asked her assistance to enable him to accomplish the task. The Sibyl replied, "The descent to Avernus is easy; the gate of Pluto stands open night and day; but to retrace one's steps and return to the upper air, that is the toil, that the difficulty. She instructed him to seek in the forest a tree on which grew a golden branch. This branch was to be plucked off, to be borne as a gift to Proserpine, and if fate was propitious, it would yield to the hand and quit its parent trunk, but otherwise no force could rend it away. If torn away, another would succeed.

Æneas followed the directions of the Sibyl. His mother Venus sent two of her doves to fly before him and show him the way, and by their assistance he found the tree, plucked the branch, and hastened back with it to the Sibyl.

Figure 34: "Aeneas' Flight from Troy" by Federico Barocci

Chapter 25

THE INFERNAL REGIONS THE SIBYL

At the commencement of our series we have given the pagan account of the creation of the world, so as we approach its conclusion, we present a view of the regions of the dead, depicted by one of their most enlightened poets, who drew his doctrines from their most esteemed philosophers. The region where Virgil places the entrance into this abode, is perhaps the most strikingly adapted to excite ideas of the terrific and preternatural of any on the face of the earth. It is the volcanic region near Vesuvius, where the whole country is cleft with chasms from which sulphurous flames arise, while the ground is shaken with pent-up vapors, and mysterious sounds issue from the bowels of the earth. The lake Avernus is supposed to fill the crater of an extinct volcano. It is circular, half a mile wide, and very deep, surrounded by high banks, which in Virgil's time were covered with a gloomy forest. Mephitic vapors rise from its waters, so that no life is found on its banks, and no birds fly over it. Here, according to the poet, was the cave which afforded access to the infernal regions, and here Ǣneas offered sacrifices to the infernal deities, Proserpine, Hecate, and the Furies. Then a roaring was heard in the earth, the woods on the hill-tops were shaken, and the howling of dogs announced the approach of the deities. "Now," said the Sibyl, "summon up your courage, for you will need it." She descended into the cave, and Ǣneas followed. Before the threshold of Hades they passed through a group of beings who are Griefs and avenging Cares, pale Diseases and melancholy Age, Fear and Hunger that tempt to crime, Toil, Poverty, and Death, forms horrible to view. The Furies spread their couches there, and Discord, whose hair was of vipers tied up with a bloody fillet. Here also were the monsters, Briareus with his hundred arms, Hydras hissing, and Chimaeras breathing fire. Ǣneas shuddered at the sight, drew his sword and would have struck, had not the Sibyl restrained him. They then came to the black river Cocytus, where they found the ferryman, Charon, old and squalid, but strong and vigorous, who was receiving passengers of all kinds into his boat, high-souled heroes, boys and unmarried girls as numerous as the leaves that fall at autumn, or the flocks that fly southward at the approach of winter. They stood pressing for a passage, and longing to touch the opposite shore. But the stern ferryman took in only such as he chose, driving the rest back. Ǣneas, wondering at the sight, asked the Sibyl, "Why this discrimination?: She answered, "Those who are taken on board the bark are the souls of those who have received due burial rites; the host of others who have remained unburied, are not permitted to pass the flood, but wander a hundred years, and flit to and fro about the shore, till at last they are taken over." Ǣneas grieved at recollecting some of his own companions who had perished in the storm. At that moment he beheld Palinurus, his pilot, who fell overboard and was drowned. He addressed him and asked him the cause of his misfortune. Palinurus replied that the rudder was carried away, and he, clinging to it, was swept away with it. He besought Aeneas most urgently to extend to him his hand and take him in company to the opposite shore. But the Sibyl rebuked him for the wish thus to transgress the laws of Pluto, but consoled him by informing him that the people of the shore where his body had been wafted by the waves, should be stirred up by the prodigies to give it the burial, and that the promontory should bear the name of Cape Palinurus, which it does to this day. Leaving Palinurus consoled by these words, they approached the boat. Charon, fixing his eyes sternly upon the advancing warrior, demanded by what right he, living and armed, approached the shore. To which the Sibyl replied that they would commit no violence, that Ǣneas's only object was to see his father, and finally exhibited the golden branch, at sight of which Charon's wrath relaxed, and he made haste to turn his back to the shore, and receive them on board. The boat, adapted only to the light freight of bodiless spirits, groaned under the weight of the hero. They were soon conveyed to the opposite shore. There they were encountered by the three- headed dog Cerberus, with his necks bristling with snakes. He barked with all his three throats till the Sibyl threw him a medicated cake, which he eagerly devoured, and then stretched himself out in his den and fell asleep. Ǣneas and the Sibyl sprang to land. The first sound that struck their ears was the wailing of young children, who had died on the threshold of life, and near to these were they who had perished under false charges. Minos presides over them as judge, and examines the deeds of each. The next class was of those who had died by their own hand, hating life and seeking refuge in death. Oh, how willingly would they now endure poverty, labor, and any other infliction, if they might but return to life! Next were situated the regions of sadness, divided off into retired paths, leading through groves of myrtle. Here roamed those who had fallen victims to unrequited love, not freed from pain even by death itself. Among these, Æneas thought he descried the form of Dido, with a wound still recent. In the dim light he was for a moment uncertain, but approaching perceived it was indeed herself. Tears fell from his eyes, and he addressed her in the accents of love. "Unhappy Dido! Was then the rumor true that you had perished? And was I, alas! the cause! I call the gods to witness that my departure from you was reluctant, and in obedience to the commands of Jove; nor could I believe that my absence would have cost you so dear. Stop, I beseech you, and refuse me not a last farewell." She stood for a moment with averted countenance, and eyes fixed on the ground, and then silently passed on, as insensible to his pleadings as a rock. Æneas followed for some distance; then, with a heavy heart, rejoined his companion and resumed his route.

They next entered the fields where roam the heroes who have fallen in battle. Here they saw many shades of Grecian and Trojan warriors. The Trojans thronged around him, and could not be satisfied with the sight. They asked the cause of his coming, and plied him with innumerable questions. But the Greeks, at the sight of his armor glittering through the murky atmosphere, recognized the hero, and filled with terror turned their backs and fled, as they used to flee on the plains of Troy.

Æneas would have lingered long with his Trojan friends but the Sibyl hurried him away. They next came to a place where the road divided, the one leading to Elysium, the other to the regions of the condemned. Æneas beheld on one side the walls of a mighty city, around which Phlegethon rolled its fiery waters. Before him was the gate of adamant that neither gods nor men can break through. An iron tower stood by the gate, on which Tisiphone, the avenging Fury, kept guard. From the city were heard groans, and the sound of the scourge, the creaking of iron, and the clanking of chains. Æneas, horror-struck, inquired of his guide what crimes were those whose punishments produced the sounds he hear? The Sibyl answered, "Here is the judgment-hall of Rhadamanthus, who brings to light crimes done in life, which the perpetrator vainly thought impenetrably hid. Tisiphone applies her whip of scorpions, and delivers the offender over to her sister Furies. At this moment with horrid clang the brazen gates unfolded, and Æneas saw within, a Hydra with fifty heads, guarding the entrance. The Sibyl told him that the Gulf of Tartarus descended deep, so that its recesses were as far beneath their feet as heaven was high above their heads. In the bottom of this pit, the Titan race, who warred against the gods, lie prostrate; Salmoneus, also, who presumed to vie with Jupiter, and built a bridge of brass over which he drove his chariot that the sound might resemble thunder, launching flaming brands at his people in imitation of lightning, till Jupiter struck him with a real thunderbolt, and taught him the difference between mortal weapons and divine. Here, also, is Tityus, the giant, whose form is so immense that as he lies, he stretches over nine acres, while a vulture preys upon his liver, which as fast as it is devoured grows again, so that his punishment will have no end.

Æneas saw groups seated at tables loaded with dainties, while near by stood a Fury who snatched away the viands from their lips, as fast as they prepared to taste them. Others beheld suspended over their heads huge rocks, threatening to fall, keeping them in a state of constant alarm. These were they who had hated their brothers, or struck their parents, or defrauded the friends who trusted them, or who having grown rich, kept their money to themselves, and gave no share to others; the last being the most numerous class. Here also were those who had violated the marriage vow, or fought in a bad cause, or failed in fidelity to their employers. Here was one who had sold his country for gold, another who perverted the laws, making them say one thing today and another tomorrow.

Ixion was there fastened to the circumference of a wheel ceaselessly revolving; and Sisyphus, whose task was to roll a huge stone up to a hill-top, but when the steep was well-nigh gained, the rock, repulsed by some sudden force, rushed again headlong down to the plain. Again, he toiled at it, while the sweat bathed all his weary limbs, but all to no effect. There was Tantalus, who stood in a pool, his chin level with the water, yet he was parched with thirst, and found nothing to assuage it; for when he bowed his hoary head, eager to quaff, the water fled away, leaving the ground at his feet all dry. Tall trees laden with fruit stooped their heads to him, pears, pomegranates, apples and luscious figs; but when with a sudden grasp he tried to seize them, winds whirled them high above his reach.

The Sibyl now warned Æneas that it was time to turn from these melancholy regions and seek the city of the blessed. They passed through a middle tract of darkness, and came upon the Elysian fields, the groves where the happy reside. They breathed a freer air, and saw all objects clothed in a purple light. The region has a sun and stars of its own. The inhabitants were enjoying themselves in various ways, some in sports on the grassy turf, in games of strength or skill, others dancing or singing. Orpheus struck the chords of his lyre, and called forth ravishing sounds. Here Æneas saw the founders of the Trojan state, high-souled heroes who lived in happier times. He gazed with admiration on the war-chariots and glittering arms now reposing in disuse. Spears stood fixed in the ground, and the horses, unharnessed, roamed over the plain. The same pride in splendid armor and generous steeds which the old heroes felt in life, accompanied them here. He saw another group feasting, and listening to the strains of music. They were in a laurel grove, whence the great river Po has its origin, and flows out among men. Here dwelt those who fell by wounds received in their country's cause, holy priests, also, and poets who have uttered thoughts worthy of Apollo, and others who have contributed to cheer and adorn life by their discoveries in the useful arts, and have made their memory blessed by rendering service to mankind. They wore snow- white fillets about their brows. The Sibyl addressed a group of these, and inquired where Anchises was to be found. They were directed where to seek him, and soon found him in a verdant valley, where he was contemplating the ranks of his posterity, their destinies and worthy deeds to be achieved in coming times. When he recognized Æneas approaching, he stretched out both hands to him, while tears flowed freely. "Have you come at last," said he, "long expected and do I behold you after such perils past? O my son, how have I trembled for you as I have watched your career!" To which Æneas replied, O father! Your image was always before me to guide and guard me. Then he endeavored to enfold his father in his embrace, but his arms enclosed only an unsubstantial image.

Æneas perceived before him a spacious valley, with trees gently waving to the wind, a tranquil landscape, through which the river Lethe flowed. Along the banks of the stream wandered a countless multitude, numerous as insects in the summer air. Æneas, with surprise, inquired who were these. Anchises answered, "They are souls to which bodies are to be given in due time. Meanwhile they dwell on Lethe's bank, and drink oblivion of their former lives." "Oh, father!" said Æneas, "is it possible that any can be so in love with life, as to wish to leave these tranquil seats for the upper world?" Anchises replied by explaining the plan of creation. The Creator, he told him, originally made the material of which souls are composed, of the four elements, fire, air, earth, and water, all which, when united, took the form of the most excellent part, fire, and became FLAME. This material was scattered like seed among the heavenly bodies, the sun, moon, and stars. Of this seed the inferior gods created man and all other animals, mingling it with various proportions of earth, by which its purity was alloyed and reduced. Thus the more earth predominates in the composition, the less pure is the individual; and we see men and women with their full-grown bodies have not the purity of childhood. So in proportion to the time which the union of body and soul has lasted, is the impurity contracted by the spiritual part. This impurity must be purged away after death, which is done by ventilating the souls in the current of winds, or merging them in water, or burning out their impurities by fire. Some few, of whom Anchises intimates that he is one, are admitted at once to Elysium, there to remain. But the rest, after the impurities of earth are purged away, are sent back to life endowed with new bodies, having had the remembrance of their former lives effectually washed away by the waters of Lethe. Some, however, there still are, so thoroughly corrupted, that they are not fit to be entrusted with human bodies, and these are made into brute animals, lions, tigers, cats, dogs, monkeys, etc. This is what the ancients called Metempsychosis, or the transmigration of souls; a doctrine which is still held by the natives of India, who scruple to destroy the life, even of the most insignificant animal, not knowing but it may be one of their relations in an altered form.

Anchises, having explained so much, proceeded to point out to Æneas individuals of his race, who were hereafter to be born, and to relate to him the exploits they should perform in the world. After this he reverted to the present, and told his son of the events that remained to him to be accomplished before the complete establishment of himself and his followers in Italy. Wars were to be waged, battles fought, a bride to be won, and in the result a Trojan state founded, from which should rise the Roman power, to be in time the sovereign of the world.

Æneas and the Sybil then took leave of Anchises, and returned by some short cut, which the poet does not explain, to the upper world.

The Egyptian name of Hades was Amenti. In the Revision of the Scriptures the Revising Commission has substituted the word Hades where "hell" was used in the version of King James.

ELYSIUM

Virgil, we have seen, places his Elysium under the earth, and assigns it for a residence to the spirits of the blessed. But in Homer Elysium forms no part of the realms of the dead. He places it on the west of the earth, near Ocean, and described it as a happy land, where there is neither snow, nor cold, nor rain, and always fanned by the delightful breezes of Zephyrus. Hither favored heroes pass without dying, and live happy under the rule of Rhadamanthus. The Elysium of Hesiod and Pindar is in the Isles of the Blessed, or Fortunate Islands, in the Western Ocean. From these sprang the legend of the happy island Atlantis. This blissful region may have been wholly imaginary, but possibly may have sprung from the reports of some storm-driven mariners who had caught a glimpse of the coast of America.

James Russell Lowell, in one of his shorter poems, claims for the present age some of the privileges of that happy realm. Addressing the Past, he says,

"Whatever of true life there was in thee,
Leaps in our age's veins.

. . . . . .

"Here, 'mid the bleak waves of our strife and care,
Float the green 'Fortunate Isles,'
Where all thy hero-spirits dwell and share
Our martyrdoms and toils.
The present moves attended
With all of brave and excellent and fair
That made the old time splendid."

Milton alludes to the same fable in Paradise Lost, Book III., 1.568.

"Like those Hesperian gardens famed of old,
Fortunate fields and groves and flowery vales,
Thrice happy isles."

And in Book II. he characterizes the rivers of Erebus according to the meaning of their names in the Greek language:

"Abhorred Styx, the flood of deadly hate,
Sad Acheron of sorrow black and deep;
Cocytus named of lamentation loud
Heard on the rueful stream; fierce Phlegethon
Whose waves of torrent fire inflame with rage.
Far off from these a slow and silent stream.
Lethe, the river of oblivion, rolls
Her watery labyrinth, whereof who drinks
Forthwith his former state and being forgets,
Forgets both joy and grief, pleasure and pain."

THE SIBYL

As Æneas and the Sibyl pursued their way back to earth, he said to her, "Whether thou be a goddess or a mortal beloved by the gods, by me thou shalt always be held in reverence. When I reach the upper air, I will cause a temple to be built to thy honor, and will myself bring offerings." "I am no goddess," said the Sibyl; "I have no claim to sacrifice or offering. I am mortal; yet if I could have accepted the love of Apollo, I might have been immortal. He promised me the fulfilment of my wish, if I would consent to be his. I took a handful of sand, and holding it forth, said, 'Grant me to see as many birthdays as there are sand-grains in my hand.' Unluckily I forgot to ask for enduring youth. This also he would have granted, could I have accepted his love, but offended at my refusal, he allowed me to grow old. My youth and youthful strength fled long ago. I have lived seven hundred years, and to equal the number of the sand-grains, I have still to see three hundred springs and three hundred harvests. My body shrinks up as years increase, and in time, I shall be

Figure 35: "Aeneas and the Cumaean Sibyl" by Fracois Perrier

lost to sight, but my voice will remain, and future ages will respect my sayings."

These concluding words of the Sibyl alluded to her prophetic power. In her cave she was accustomed to inscribe on leaves gathered from the trees the names and fates of individuals. The leaves thus inscribed were arranged in order within the cave, and might be consulted by her votaries. But if perchance at the opening of the door the wind rushed in and dispersed the leaves, the Sibyl gave no aid to restoring them again, and the oracle was irreparably lost.

The following legend of the Sibyl is fixed at a later date. In the reign of one of the Tarquins there appeared before the king a woman who offered him nine books for sale. The king refused to purchase them, whereupon the woman went away and burned three of the books, and returning offered the remaining books for the same price she had asked for the nine. The king again rejected them; but when the woman, after burning three books more, returned and asked for the three remaining the same price which she had before asked for the nine, his curiosity was excited, and he purchased the books. They were found to contain the destinies of the Roman state. They were kept in the temple of Jupiter Capitolinus, preserved in a stone chest, and allowed to be inspected only by especial officers appointed for that duty, who on great occasions consulted them and interpreted their oracles to the people.

There were various Sibyls; but the Cumaean Sibyl, of whom Ovid and Virgil write, is the most celebrated of them. Ovid's story of her life protracted to one thousand years may be intended to represent the various Sibyls as being only reappearances of one and the same individual.

It is now believed that some of the most distinguished Sibyls took the inspiration of their oracles from the Jewish scripture. Readers interested in this subject will consult, "Judaism," by Prof. F. Huidekoper.

Young, in the Night Thoughts, alludes to the Sibyl. Speaking of worldly Wisdom, he says:

"If future fate she plans 'tis all in leaves,
Like Sibyl, unsubstantial, fleeting bliss;
At the first blast it vanishes in air.

. . . . .

As worldly schemes resemble Sibyl's leaves,
The good man's days to Sibyl's books compare,
The price still rising as in number less."

Chapter 26

CAMILLA EVANDER NISUS AND EURYALUS MEZENTIUS TURNUS

Æneas, having parted from the Sibyl and rejoined his fleet, coasted along the shores of Italy and cast anchor in the mouth of the Tiber. The poet Virgil, having brought his hero to this spot, the destined termination of his wanderings, invokes his Muse to tell him the situation of things at that eventful moment. Latinus, third in descent from Saturn, ruled the country. He was now old and had no male descendant, but had one charming daughter, Lavinia, who was sought in marriage by many neighboring chiefs, one of whom, Turnus, king of the Rutulians, was favored by the wishes of her parents. But Latinus had been warned in a dream by his father Faunus, that the destined husband of Lavinia should come from a foreign land. From that union should spring a race destined to subdue the world.

Our readers will remember that in the conflict with the Harpies, one of those half-human birds had threatened the Trojans with dire sufferings. In particular she predicted that before their wanderings ceased they should be pressed by hunger to devour their tables. This portent now came true; for as they took their scanty meal, seated on the grass, the men placed their hard biscuit on their laps, and put thereon whatever their gleanings in the woods supplied. Having dispatched the latter they finished by eating the crusts. Seeing which, the boy Iulus said playfully, "See, we are eating our tables." Æneas caught the words and accepted the omen. "All hail, promised land!" he exclaimed, "this is our home, this our country!" He then took measures to find out who were the present inhabitants of the land, and who their rulers. A hundred chosen men were sent to the village of Latinus, bearing presents and a request for friendship and alliance. They went and were favorably received. Latinus immediately concluded that the Trojan hero was no other than the promised son-in-law announced by the oracle. He cheerfully granted his alliance and sent back the messengers mounted on steeds from his stables, and loaded with gifts and friendly messages.

Juno, seeing things go thus prosperously for the Trojans, felt her old animosity revive, summoned the Fury Alecto from Erebus, and sent her to stir up discord. The Fury first took possession of the queen, Amata, and roused her to oppose in every way the new alliance. Alecto then sped to the city of Turnus, and assuming the form of an old priestess, informed him of the arrival of the foreigners and of the attempts of their prince to rob him of his bride. Next she turned her attention to the camp of the Trojans. There she saw the boy Iulus and his companions amusing themselves with hunting. She sharpened the scent of the dogs, and led them to rouse up from the thicket a tame stag, the favorite of Silvia, the daughter of Tyrrheus, the king's herdsman. A javelin from the hand of Iulus wounded the animal, and he had only strength left to run homewards, and died at his mistress' feet. Her cries and tears roused her brothers and the herdsmen, and they, seizing whatever weapons came to hand, furiously assaulted the hunting party. These were protected by their friends, and the herdsmen were finally driven back with the loss of two of their number.

These things were enough to rouse the storm of war, and the queen, Turnus, and the peasants, all urged the old king to drive the strangers from the country. He resisted as long as he could, but finding his opposition unavailing, finally gave way and retreated to his retirement.

OPENING THE GATES OF JANUS

It was the custom of the country, when war was to be undertaken, for the chief magistrate, clad in his robes of office, with solemn pomp to open the gates of the temple of Janus, which were kept shut as long as peace endured. His people now urged the old king to perform that solemn office, but he refused to do so. While they contested, Juno herself, descending from the skies, smote the doors with irresistible force and burst them open. Immediately the whole country was in a flame. The people rushed from every side breathing nothing but war.

Turnus was recognized by all as leader; others joined as allies, chief of whom was Mezentius, a brave and able soldier, but of detestable cruelty. He had been the chief of one of the neighboring cities, but his people drove him out. With him was joined his son Lausus, a generous youth worthy of a better sire.

CAMILLA

Camilla, the favorite of Diana, a huntress and warrior, after the fashion of the Amazons, came with her band of mounted followers, including a select number of her own sex, and ranged herself on the side of Turnus. This maiden had never accustomed her fingers to the distaff or the loom, but had learned to endure the toils of war, and in speed to outstrip the wind. It seemed as if she might run over the standing corn without crushing it, or over the surface of the water without dipping her feet. Camilla's history had been singular from the beginning. Her father, Metabus, driven from his city by civil discord, carried with him in his flight his infant daughter. As he fled through the woods, his enemies in hot pursuit, he reached the bank of the river Amazenus, which, swelled by rains, seemed to debar a passage. He paused for a moment, then decided what to do. He tied the infant to his lance with wrappers of bark, and, poising the weapon in his upraised hand, thus addressed Diana: "Goddess of the woods! I consecrate this maid to you;" then hurled the weapon with its burden to the opposite bank. The spear flew across the roaring water. His pursuers were already upon him, but he plunged into the river and swam across, and found the spear with the infant safe on the other side. Thenceforth he lived among the shepherds, and brought up his daughter in woodland arts. While a child she was taught to use the bow and throw the javelin. With her sling she could bring down the crane or the wild swan. Her dress was a tiger's skin. Many mothers sought her for a daughter-in-law, but she continued faithful to Diana, and repelled the thought of marriage.

There is an allusion to Camilla in those well-known lines of Pope, in which, illustrating the rule that "the sound should be an echo to the sense," he says,

---

"When Ajax strives some rock's vast weight to throw,
The line too labors and the words move slow.
Not so when swift Camilla scours the plain,
Flies o'er th'unbendng corn or skims along the main."
Essay on Criticism

EVANDER

Such were the formidable allies that ranged themselves against Æneas. It was night, and he lay stretched in sleep on the bank of the river, under the open heavens. The god of the stream, Father Tiber, seemed to raise his head above the willows, and to say, "O goddess-born, destined possessor of the Latin realms, this is the promised land, here is to be your home, here shall terminate the hostility of the heavenly powers, if only you faithfully persevere. There are friends not far distant. Prepare your boats and row up my stream; I will lead you to Evander the Arcadian chief. He has long been at strife with Turnus and the Rutulians, and is prepared to become an ally of yours. Rise! Offer your vows to Juno, and deprecate her anger. When you have achieved your victory then think of me." Æneas woke and paid immediate obedience to the friendly vision. He sacrificed to Juno, and invoked the god of the river and all its tributary fountains to lend their aid. Then, for the first time, a vessel filled with armed warriors floated on the stream of the Tiber. The river smoothed its waves and bade its current flow gently, while, impelled by the vigorous strokes of the rowers, the vessel shot rapidly up the stream.

About the middle of the day they came in sight of the scattered buildings of the infant town where in after times the proud city of Rome grew, whose glory reached the skies. By chance the old king, Evander, was that day celebrating annual solemnities in honor of Hercules and all the gods. Pallas, his son, and all the chiefs of the little commonwealth stood by. When they saw the tall ship gliding onward through the wood, they were alarmed at the sight, and rose from the tables. But Pallas forbade the solemnities to be interrupted, and seizing a weapon, stepped forward to the river's bank. He called aloud, demanding who they were and what was their object. Æneas, holding forth an olive- branch, replied, "We are Trojans, friends to you and enemies to the Rutulians. We seek Evander, and offer to join our arms with yours." Pallas, in amazement at the sound of so great a name, invited them to land, and when Æneas touched the shore he seized his hand and held it long in friendly grasp. Proceeding through the wood they joined the king and his

Chapter 26: Evander

Figure 36: "Camilla at War" by Giacomo del Po

party, and were most favorably received. Seats were provided for them at the tables, and the repast proceeded.

When the solemnities were ended all moved towards the city. The king, bending with age, walked between his son and Æneas, taking the arm of one or the other of them, and with much variety of pleasing talk shortening the way. Æneas looked and listened with delight, observing all the beauties of the scene, and learning much of heroes renowned in ancient times. Evander said, "These extensive groves were once inhabited by fauns and nymphs, and a rude race of men who sprang from the trees themselves, and had neither laws nor social culture. They knew not how to yoke the cattle nor raise a harvest, nor provide from present abundance for future want; but browsed like beasts upon the leafy boughs, or fed voraciously on their hunted prey. Such were they when Saturn, expelled from Olympus by his sons, came among them and drew together the fierce savages, formed them into society, and gave them laws. Such peace and plenty ensued that men ever since have called his reign the golden age; but by degrees far other times succeeded, and the thirst of gold and the thirst of blood prevailed. The land was a prey to successive tyrants, till fortune and resistless destiny brought me hither, an exile from my native land, Arcadia."

Having thus said, he showed him the Tarpeian rock, and the rude spot then overgrown with bushes where in after times the Capitol rose in all its magnificence. He next pointed to some dismantled walls, and said, "Here stood Janiculum, built by Janus, and there Saturnia, the town of Saturn." Such discourse brought them to the cottage of poor Evander, whence they saw the lowing herds roaming over the plain where now the proud and stately Forum stands. They entered, and a couch was spread for Æneas, well stuffed with leaves and covered with the skin of the Libyan bear.

Next morning, awakened by the dawn and the shrill song of birds beneath the eaves of his low mansion, old Evander rose. Clad in a tunic, and a panther's skin thrown over his shoulders, with sandals on his feet, and his good sword girded to his side, he went forth to seek his guest. Two mastiffs followed him, his whole retinue and body-guard. He round the hero attended by his faithful Achates, and, Pallas soon joining them, the old king spoke thus:

"Illustrious Trojan, it is but little we can do in so great a cause. Our state is feeble, hemmed in on one side by the river, on the other by the Rutulians. But I propose to ally you with a people numerous and rich, to whom fate has brought you at the propitious moment. The Etruscans hold the country beyond the river. Mezentius was their king, a monster of cruelty, who invented unheard-of torments to gratify his vengeance. He would fasten the dead to the living, hand to hand and face to face, and leave the wretched victims to die in that dreadful embrace. At length the people cast him out, him and his house. They burned his palace and slew his friends. He escaped and took refuge with Turnus, who protects him with arms. The Etruscans' demand that he shall be given up to deserved punishment, and would ere now have attempted to enforce their demand; but their priests restrain then, telling them that it is the will of heaven that no native of the land shall guide them to victory, and that their destined leader must come from across the sea. They have offered the crown to me, but I am too old to undertake such great affairs, and my son is native-born, which precludes him from the choice. You, equally by birth and time of life, and fame in arms, pointed out by the gods, have but to appear to be hailed as their leader. With you I will join Pallas, my son, my only hope and comfort. Under you he shall learn the art of war, and strive to emulate your great exploits."

Then the king ordered horses to be furnished for the Trojan chiefs, and Æneas, with a chosen band of followers and Pallas accompanying, mounted and took the way to the Etruscan city, having sent back the rest of his party in the ships. Æneas and his band safely arrived at the Etruscan camp and were received with open arms by Tarchon, the Etruscan leader, and his countrymen.

NISUS AND EURYALUS

In the meanwhile Turnus had collected his bands and made all necessary preparations for the war. Juno sent Iris to him with a message inciting him to take advantage of the absence of Æneas and surprise the Trojan camp. Accordingly the attempt was made, but the Trojans were found on their guard, and having received strict orders from Æneas not to fight in his absence, they lay still in their intrenchments, and resisted all the efforts of the Rutulians to draw them in to the field. Night coming on, the army of Turnus in high spirits at their fancied superiority, feasted and enjoyed themselves, and finally stretched themselves on the field and slept secure.

In the camp of the Trojans things were far otherwise. There all was watchfulness and anxiety, and impatience for Æneas's return. Nisus stood guard at the entrance of the camp, and Euryalus, a youth distinguished above all in the army for graces of person and fine qualities, was with him. These two were friends and brothers in arms. Nisus said to his friend, "Do you perceive what confidence and carelessness the enemy display? Their lights are few and dim, and the men seem all oppressed with wine or sleep. You know how anxiously our chiefs wish to send to Æneas, and to get intelligence from him. Now I am strongly moved to make my way through the enemy's camp and to go in search of our chief. If I succeed, the glory of the deed will be enough reward for me, and if they judge the service deserves anything more, let them pay it to you."

Euryalus, all on fire with the love of adventure, replied, "Would you then, Nisus, refuse to share your enterprise with me? And shall I let you go into such danger alone? Not so my brave father brought me up, nor so have I planned for myself when I joined the standard of Æneas, and resolved to hold my life cheap in comparison with honor." Nisus replied, "I doubt it not, my friend; but you know the uncertain event of such an undertaking, and whatever may happen to me, I wish you to be safe. You are younger than I and have more of life in prospect. Nor can I be the cause of such grief to your mother, who has chosen to be here in the camp with you rather than stay and live in peace with the other matrons in Acestes' city." Euryalus replied, "Say no more. In vain you seek arguments to dissuade me. I am fixed in the resolution to go with you. Let us lose no time." They called the guard, and committing the watch to them, sought the general's tent. They found the chief officers in consultation, deliberating how they should send notice to Æneas of their situation. The offer of the two friends was gladly accepted, they themselves were loaded with praises and promised the most liberal rewards in case of success. Iulus especially addressed Euryalus, assuring him of his lasting friendship. Euryalus replied, "I have but one boon to ask. My aged mother is with me in the camp. For me she left the Trojan soil, and would not stay behind with the other matrons at the city of Acestes. I go now without taking leave of her. I could not bear her tears nor set at nought he entreaties. But do thou, I beseech thee, comfort her in her distress. Promise me that, and I shall go more boldly into whatever dangers may present themselves." Iulus and the other chiefs were moved to tears, and promised to do all his request. "Your mother shall be mine," said Iulus, "and all that I have promised to you shall be made good to her, if you do not return to receive it."

The two friends left the camp and plunged at once into the midst of the enemy. They found no watch, no sentinels posted, but all about, the sleeping soldiers strewn on the grass and among the wagons. The laws of war at that early day did not forbid a brave man to slay a sleeping foe, and the two Trojans slew, as they passed, such of the enemy as they could without exciting alarm. In one tent Euryalus made prize of a helmet brilliant with gold and plumes. They had passed through the enemy's ranks without being discovered, but now suddenly appeared a troop directly in front of them, which, under Volscens, their leader, were approaching the camp. The glittering helmet of Euryalus caught their attention, and Volscens hailed the two, and demanded who and whence they were. They made no answer, but plunged into the wood. The horsemen scattered in all directions to intercept their flight. Nisus had eluded pursuit and was out of danger, but Euryalus being missing he turned back to seek him. He again entered the wood and soon came within sound of voices. Looking through the thicket he saw the whole band surrounding Euryalus with noisy questions. What should he do? How extricate the youth? Or would it be better to die with him?

Raising his eyes to the moon which now shone clear, he said, "Goddess! Favor my effort!" And aiming his javelin at one of the leaders of the troop, struck him in the back and stretched him on the plain with a deathblow. In the midst of their amazement another weapon flew, and another of the party fell dead. Volscens, the leader, ignorant whence the darts came, rushed sword in hand upon Euryalus. "You shall pay the penalty of both," he said, and would have plunged the sword into his bosom, when Nisus, who from his concealment saw the peril of his friend, rushed forward, exclaiming, "'Twas I, 'twas I; turn your swords against me, Rutulians; I did it; he only followed me as a friend." While he spoke the sword fell, and pierced the comely bosom of Euryalus. His head fell over on his shoulder, like a flower cut down by the plough. Nisus rushed upon Volscens and plunged his sword into his body, and was himself slain on the instant by numberless blows.

MEZENTIUS

Æneas, with his Etrurian allies, arrived on the scene of action in time to rescue his beleaguered camp; and now the two armies being nearly equal in strength, the war began in good earnest. We cannot find space for all the details, but must simply record the fate of the principal characters whom we have introduced to our readers. The tyrant Mezentius, finding himself engaged against his revolted subjects, raged like a wild beast. He slew all who dared to withstand him, and put the multitude to flight wherever he appeared. At last he encountered Æneas, and the armies stood still to see the issue. Mezentius threw his spear, which striking Æneas's shield glanced off and hit Anthor. He was a Grecian by birth, who had left Argos, his native city, and followed Evander into Italy. The poet says of him, with simple pathos which has made the words proverbial, "He fell, unhappy, by a wound intended for another, looked up to the skies, and dying remembered sweet Argos." Æneas now in turn hurled his lance. It pierced the shield of Mezentius, and wounded him in the thigh. Lausus, his son, could not bear the sight, but rushed forward and interposed himself, while the followers pressed round Mezentius and bore him away. Æneas held his sword suspended over Lausus and delayed to strike, but the furious youth pressed on and he was compelled to deal the fatal blow. Lausus fell, and Æneas bent over him in pity. "Hapless youth," he said, "what can I do for you worthy of your praise? Keep those arms in which you glory, and fear not but that your body shall be restored to your friends, and have due funeral honors." So saying, he called the timid followers, and delivered the body into their hands.

Mezentius meanwhile had been borne to the river-side, and washed his wound. Soon the news reached him of Lausus's death, and rage and despair supplied the place of strength. He mounted his horse and dashed into the thickest of the fight, seeking Æneas. Having found him, he rode round him in a circle, throwing one javelin after another, while Aeneas stood fenced with his shield, turning every way to meet them. At last, after Mezentius had three times made the circuit, Æneas threw his lance directly at the horse's head. It pierced his temples and he fell, while a shout from both armies rent the skies. Mezentius asked no mercy, but only that his body might be spared the insults of his revolted subjects, and be buried in the same grave with his son. He received the fatal stroke not unprepared, and poured out his life and his blood together.

While these things were doing in one part of the field, in another Turnus encountered the youthful Pallas. The contest between champions so unequally matched could not be doubtful. Pallas bore himself bravely, but fell by the lance of Turnus. The victor almost relented when he saw the brave youth lying dead at his feet, and spared to use the privilege of a conqueror in despoiling him of his arms. The belt only, adorned with studs and carvings of gold, he took and clasped round his own body. The rest he remitted to the friends of the slain.

After the battle there was a cessation of arms for some days to allow both armies to bury their dead. In this interval Æneas challenged Turnus to decide the contest by single combat, but Turnus evaded the challenge. Another battle ensued, in which Camilla, the virgin warrior, was chiefly conspicuous. Her deeds of valor surpassed those of the bravest warriors, and many Trojans and Etruscans fell pierced with her darts or struck down by her battle-axe. At last an Etruscan named Aruns, who had watched her long, seeking for some advantage, observed her pursuing a flying enemy whose splendid armor offered a tempting prize. Intent on the chase she observed not her danger, and the javelin of Aruns struck her and inflicted a fatal wound. She fell and breathed her last in the arms of her attendant maidens. But Diana, who beheld her fate, suffered not her slaughter to be unavenged. Aruns, as he stole away, glad but frightened, was struck by a secret arrow, launched by one of the nymphs of Diana's train, and died ignobly and unknown.

At length the final conflict took place between Æneas and Turnus. Turnus had avoided the contest as long as he could, but at last impelled by the ill success of his arms, and by the murmurs of his followers, he braced himself to the conflict. It could not be doubtful. On the side of Æneas were the expressed decree of destiny, the aid of his goddess-mother at every emergency, and impenetrable armor fabricated by Vulcan, at Venus' request, for her son. Turnus, on the other hand, was deserted by his celestial allies, Juno having been expressly forbidden by Jupiter to assist him any longer. Turnus threw his lance, but it recoiled harmless from the shield of Æneas. The Trojan hero then threw his, which penetrated the shield of Turnus, and pierced his thigh. Then Turnus' fortitude forsook him and he begged for mercy; and Æneas would have given him his life, but at the instant his eye fell on the belt of Pallas, which Turnus had taken from the slaughtered youth. Instantly his rage revived, and exclaiming, "Pallas immolates thee with this blow," he thrust him through with his sword.

Here the Æneid closes, but the story goes that Æneas, having triumphed over his foes, obtained Lavinia as his bride. His son Iulus founded the city of Alba Longa. He, and his descendants after him, reigned over the town for many years. At length Numitor and Amulius, two brothers, quarrelled about the kingdom. Amulius seized the crown by force, cast out Numitor, and made his daughter, Rhea Silvia, a Vestal Virgin. The Vestal Virgins, the priestesses of the goddess Vesta, were sworn to celibacy. But Rhea Silvia broke her vow, and gave birth, by the god Mars, to the twins, Romulus and Remus. For this offence she was buried alive, the usual punishment accorded to unfaithful Vestals, while the children were exposed on the river Tiber. Romulus and Remus, however, were rescued by a herdsman, and were educated among the shepherds in ignorance of their parentage. But chance revealed it to them. They collected a band of friends, and took revenge on their granduncle for the murder of their mother. Afterwards they founded, by the side of the river Tiber, where they had been exposed in infancy, the city of Rome.

Chapter 27

PYTHAGORAS. EGYPTIAN DEITIES. ORACLES

The teachings of Anchises to Æneas, respecting the nature of the human soul, were in conformity with the doctrines of the Pythagoreans. Pythagoras (born, perhaps, about five hundred and forty years B.C.) was a native of the island of Samos, but passed the chief portion of his life at Crotona in Italy. He is therefore sometimes called "the Samian," and sometimes "the philosopher of Crotona." When young he travelled extensively and is said to have visited Egypt, where he was instructed by the priests in all their learning, and afterwards journeyed to the East, and visited the Persian and Chaldean Magi, and the Brahmins of India.

But Pythagoras left no writings which have been preserved. His immediate disciples were under a pledge of secrecy. Though he is referred to by many writers, at times not far distant from his own, we have no biography of him written earlier than the end of the second century of our era. In the interval between his life and this time, every sort of fable collected around what was really known of his life and teaching.

At Crotona, where he finally established himself, it is said that his extraordinary qualities collected round him a great number of disciples. The inhabitants were notorious for luxury and licentiousness, but the good effects of his influence were soon visible. Sobriety and temperance succeeded. Six hundred of the inhabitants became his disciples and enrolled themselves in a society to aid each other in the pursuit of wisdom; uniting their property in one common stock, for the benefit of the whole. They were required to practise the greatest purity and simplicity of manners. The first lesson they learned was SILENCE; for a time they were required to be only hearers. "He (Pythagoras) said so," (Ipse dixit,) was to be held by them as sufficient, without any proof. It was only the advanced pupils, after years of patient submission, who were allowed to ask questions and to state objections.

Pythagoras is said to have considered NUMBERS as the essence and principle of all things, and attributed to them a real and distinct existence; so that, in his view, they were the elements out of which the universe was constructed. How he conceived this process has never been satisfactorily explained. He traced the various forms and phenomena of the world to numbers as their basis and essence. The "Monad," or UNIT, he regarded as the source of all numbers. The number TWO was imperfect, and the cause of increase and division. THREE was called the number of the whole, because it had a beginning, middle, and end; FOUR, representing the square, is in the highest degree perfect; and TEN, as it contains the sum of the first three prime numbers (2+3+5=10. ONE is not counted, as being rather the source of number than a number itself) comprehends all musical and arithmetical proportions, and denotes the system of the world.

As the numbers proceed from the Monad, so he regarded the pure and simple essence of the Deity as the source of all the forms of nature. Gods, demons, and heroes are emanations of the Supreme; and there is a fourth emanation, the human soul. This is immortal, and when freed from the fetters of the body, passes to the habitation of the dead, where it remains till it returns to the world to dwell in some other human or animal body, and at last, when sufficiently purified, it returns to the source from which it proceeded. This doctrine of the transmigration of souls (metempsychosis), which was first Indian and Egyptian, and connected with the doctrine of reward and punishment of human actions, was the chief cause why the Pythagoreans killed no animals. Ovid represents Pythagoras addressing his disciples in these words: "Souls never die, but always on quitting one abode pass to another. I myself can remember that in the time of the Trojan was I was Euphorbus, the son of Panthus, and fell by the spear of Menelaus. Lately, being in the temple of Juno, at Argos, I recognized my shield hung up there among the trophies. All things change, nothing perishes. The soul passes hither and thither, occupying now this body, now that, passing from the body of a beast into that of a man, and thence to a beast's again. As wax is stamped with certain figures, then melted, then stamped anew with others, yet is always the same wax, so the soul, being always the same, yet wears at different times different forms. Therefore, if the love of kindred is not extinct in your bosoms, forbear, I entreat you, to violate the life of those who may haply be your own relatives."

Shakespeare, in the Merchant of Venice, makes Gratiano allude to the metempsychosis, where he says to Shylock:

"Thou almost mak'st me waver in my faith,
To hold opinion with Pythagoras,
That souls of animals infuse themselves
Into the trunks of men; thy currish spirit
Governed a wolf; who hanged for human slaughter
Infused his soul in thee; for thy desires
Are wolfish, bloody, starved, and ravenous."

The relation of the notes of the musical scale to numbers, whereby harmony results from vibrations in equal times, and discord from the reverse, led Pythagoras to apply the word "harmony" to the visible creation, meaning by it the just adaptation of parts to each other. This is the idea which Dryden expresses in the beginning of his song for St. Cecilia's Day:

"From harmony, from heavenly harmony
This everlasting frame began;
From harmony to harmony
Through all the compass of the notes it ran,
The Diapason closing full in Man."

In the centre of the universe (as Pythagoras taught) there was a central fire, the principle of life. The central fire was surrounded by the earth, the moon, the sun, and the five planets. The distances of the various heavenly bodies from one another were conceived to correspond to the proportions of the musical scale. The heavenly bodies, with the gods who inhabited them, were supposed to perform a choral dance round the central fire, "not without song." It is this doctrine which Shakespeare alludes to when he makes Lorenzo teach astronomy to Jessica in this fashion:

"Sit, Jessica, look how the floor of heaven
Is thick inlaid with patines of bright gold!
There's not the smallest orb that thou behold'st
But in this motion like an angel sings,
Still quiring to the young-eyed cherubim;
Such harmony is in immortal souls!
But whilst this muddy vesture of decay
Doth grossly close it in we cannot hear it."

Merchant of Venice

The spheres were conceived to be crystalline or glassy fabrics arranged over one another like a nest of bowls reversed. In the substance of each sphere one or more of the heavenly bodies was supposed to be fixed, so as to move with it. As the spheres are transparent, we look through them, and see the heavenly bodies which they contain and carry round with them. But as these spheres cannot move on one another without friction, a sound is thereby produced which is of exquisite harmony, too fine for mortal ears to recognize. Milton, in his Hymn to the Nativity, thus alludes to the music of the spheres:

"Ring out, ye crystal spheres!
Once bless our human ears;
(If ye have power to charm our senses so);
And let your silver chime
Move in melodious time,
And let the base of Heaven's deep organ blow:
And with your nine-fold harmony
Make up full concert with the angelic symphony."

Pythagoras is said to have invented the lyre, of which other fables give the invention to Mercury. Our own poet, Longfellow, in Verses to a Child, thus relates the story:

"As great Pythagoras of yore,
Standing beside the blacksmith's door,
And hearing the hammers as they smote
The Anvils with a different note,
Stole from the varying tones that hung
Vibrant on every iron tongue,
The secret of the sounding wire,
A nd formed the seven-chorded lyre."
See also the same poet's Occultation of Orion:
"The Samian's great Æolian lyre."

SYBARIS AND CROTONA

Sybaris, a neighboring city to Crotona, was as celebrated for luxury and effeminacy as Crotona for the reverse. The name has become proverbial. Lowell uses it in this sense in his charming little poem To the Dandelion:

"Not in mild June the golden-cuirassed bee
Feels a more summer-like, warm ravishment
In the white lily's breezy tent,
(His conquered Sybaris) than I when first
From the dark green thy yellow circles burst."

A war arose between the two cities, and Sybaris was conquered and destroyed. Milo, the celebrated athlete, led the army of Crotona. Many stories are told of Milo's vast strength, such as his carrying a heifer of four years old upon his shoulders, and afterwards eating the whole of it in a single day. The mode of his death is thus related: As he was passing through a forest he saw the trunk of a tree which had been partially split open by woodcutters, and attempted to rend it further; but the wood closed upon his hands and held him fast, in which state he was attacked and devoured by wolves.

Byron, in his Ode to Napoleon Bonaparte, alludes to the story of Milo:

"He who of old would rend the oak
Deemed not of the rebound;
Chained by the trunk he vainly broke,
Alone, how looked he round!"

EGYPTIAN DEITIES

The remarkable discovery by which Champollion the younger (so called to distinguish him from his older brother, Champollion Figeac, who also studied the hieroglyphics)) first opened to modern times the secret of the Egyptian hieroglyphics, has been followed up by laborious studies, which tell us more of Egyptian worship and mythology, with more precision, than we know of any other ancient religion but that of the Hebrews. We have even great numbers of copies of the liturgies, or handbooks of worship, of funeral solemnities, and other rituals, which have been diligently translated. And we have a sufficient body of the literature written and used by the priesthood.

These discoveries give to writers of this generation a much fuller knowledge of the Egyptian religion, of its forms, and of the names of its gods, than they had before. It is impossible, and probably always will be, to state with precision the theology on which it rested. It is impossible, because that theology was different in one time and with one school from what it was at other times. Mr. S. Birch, of the British Museum, says, "The religion of the Egyptians consisted of an extended polytheism represented by a system of local groups." But Mr. Pierret says, "The polytheism of the monuments is but an outward show. The innumerable gods of the Pantheon are but manifestations of the One Being in his various capacities. Mariette Bey says, "The one result is that according to the Egyptians, the universe was God himself, and that Pantheism formed the foundation of their religion."

In this book it is not necessary to reconcile views so diverse, nor indeed to enter on studies so profound as those which should decide between them. For our purpose here it is enough to know that the Sun was the older object of worship, and in his various forms rising, midday, or setting was adored under different names. Frequently his being and these names were united to the types of other deities. Mr. Birch believes that the worship of Osiris prevailed largely beside the worship of the Sun, and is not to be confounded with it. To Osiris, Set, the Egyptian devil, was opposed.

The original God, the origin of all things, manifests himself to men, in lesser forms, according to this mythology, more and more human and less and less intangible. These forms are generally triads, and resolve themselves into a male deity, a female deity, and their child. Triad after triad brings the original Divinity into forms more and more earthly, till at last we find "that we have no longer to do with the infinite and intangible God of the earliest days, but rather with a God of flesh and blood, who lives upon earth, and has so abased himself as to be no more than a human king. It is no longer the God of whom no man knew either the form or the substance: it is Kneph at Esneh, Hathor at Durderah, Horus, king of the divine dynasty at Edfoo." These words are M. Maspero's.

The Greek and Latin poets and philosophers, as they made some very slight acquaintance with Egyptian worship, give Greek or Latin names to the divinities worshipped. Thus we sometimes hear Osiris spoken of as the Egyptian Hermes. But such changes of names are confusing, and are at best but fanciful (In the same way Plutarch, a Greek writer, says of the Jews' Feast of Tabernacles, "I know that their God is our Bacchus." This was merely from the vines, vine leaves and wine used in the ceremonies.) It would happen sometimes, in later times, that a fashion of religion would carry the worship of one God or Goddess to a distance. Thus the worship of Isis became fashionable in Rome in the time of Nero and Paul, as readers of Bulwer's Last Days of Pompeii will remember.

The latest modern literature occasionally uses the Egyptian names, as the last two centuries have disinterred them from the inscriptions on the monuments, and from the manuscripts in the tombs. Earlier English writers generally use the names like Osiris, Anubis, and others found in Latin and Greek writers.

The following statement as to these deities and their names is from Mr. Birch:

"The deities of ancient Egypt consist of celestial, terrestrial, and infernal gods, and of many inferior personages, either representatives of the greater gods or attendants on them. Most of the gods were connected with the sun, and represented that luminary through the upper hemisphere or Heaven and the lower hemisphere or Hades. To the deities of the solar cycle belonged the great gods of Thebes and Heliopolis. In the local worship of Egypt the deities were arranged in local triads; thus at Memphis, Ptah, his wife Merienptah, and their son Nefer Atum, formed a triad, to which was sometimes added the goddess Bast or Bubastis. At Abydos the local triad was Osiris, Isis, and Horus, with Nephthys; at Thebes, Amen Ra or Ammon, Mut and Chons, with Neith; at Elephantine, Kneph, Anuka, Sati, and Hak. In most instances the names of the gods are Egyptian; thus, Ptah meant 'the opener'; Amen, 'the concealed'; Ra, 'the sun or day'; Athor, 'the house of Horus';' but some few, especially of later times, were introduced from Semitic sources, as Bal or Baal, Astaruta or Astarte, Khen or Kiun, Respu or Reseph. Besides the principal gods, several inferior or parhedral gods, sometimes personifications of the faculties, senses, and other objects, are introduced into the religious system, and genii, spirits or personified souls of deities formed part of the same. At a period subsequent to their first introduction the gods were divided into three orders. The first or highest comprised eight deities, who were different in the Memphian and Theban systems. They were supposed to have reigned over Egypt before the time of mortals. The eight gods of the first order at Memphis were 1. Ptah; 2. Shu; 3. Tefnu; 4. Seb; 5. Nut; 6. Osiris; 7. Isis and Horus; 8. Athor. Those of Thebes were 1. Amen Ra; 2. Mentu; 3. Atum; 4. Shu and Tefnu; 5. Seb; 6. Osiris; 7. Set and Nepthys; 8. Horus and Athor. The gods of the second order were twelve in number, but the name of one only, an Egyptian Hercules, has been preserved. The third order is stated to have comprised Osiris, who, it will be seen, belonged to the first order." GUIDE TO THE FIRST AND SECOND EGYPTIAN ROOMS, BRITISH MUSEUM. S. Birch

Miss Edwards gives the following convenient register of the names most familiar among the Egyptian gods (in her very interesting book, "A Thousand Miles up the Nile").

PHTAH or PTAH: In form a mummy, holding the emblem called by some the Nilometer, by others the emblem of Stability, called "the father of the Beginning, the Creator of the Egg of the Sun and Moon," Chief Deity of Memphis.

KNEPH, KNOUM or KNOUPHIS: Ram-headed, called the Maker of gods and men, the Soul of the gods. Chief Deity of Elephantine and the Cataracts.

RA: Hawk-headed, and crowned with the sun-disc, encircled by an asp. The divine disposer and organizer of the world; adored throughout Egypt.

AMEN RA, or Amun Ra: Of human form, crowned with a flat-topped cap and two long, straight plumes; clothed in the schenti; his flesh sometimes painted blue. There are various forms of this god (there were almost as many varieties of Ammon in Egypt as there are varieties of the Madonna in Italy or Spain), but he is most generally described as King of the Gods, chief deity of Thebes.

KHEM: Of human form, mummified; wears head-dress of Amen Ra; his right hand uplifted, holding a flail. The god of productiveness and generation. Chief deity of Khemmis, or Ekhmeem.

OSIRIS: Of human form, mummified, crowned with a mitre, and holding the flail and crook. Called the Good; the Lord above all; the one lord. Was the god of the lower world; judge of the dead; and representative of the sun below the horizon. Adored through Egypt. Local deity of Abydos.

NEFER ATUM: Human-headed, and crowned with the pschent. This god represented the nocturnal sun, or the sun lighting the lower world. Local deity of Heliopolis.

THOTH: In form a man, ibis-headed, generally depicted with the pen and palette of a scribe. Was the god of the moon, and of letters. Local deity of Sesoon, or Hermopolit.

SEB: The "Father of the Gods," and deity of terrestrial vegetation. In form like a man with a goose upon his head.

SET: Represented by a symbolic animal, with a muzzle and ears like a jackal, the body of an ass, and an upright tail, like the tail of a lion. Was originally a warlike god, and became in later times the symbol of evil and the enemy of Osiris.

KHONS: Hawk-headed, crowned with the sun-disc and horns. Is sometimes represented as a youth with the side-lock, standing on a crocodile.

HORUS: Horus appears variously as Horus, Horus Aroeris, and Horus Harpakhrat (Hippocrates), or Horus the child. Is represented under the first two forms as a man, hawk-headed, wearing the double crown of Egypt; in the latter as a child with the side- lock. Local deity of Edfoo (Apollinopolis Magna).

MAUT: A woman draped, and crowned with the pschent (the pschent was a double crown, worn by the king at his coronation), representing a vulture. Adored at Thebes.

NEITH: A woman draped, holding sometimes a bow and arrows, crowned with the crown of Lower Egypt. She presided over war, and the loom. Worshipped at Thebes.

ISIS: A woman crowned with the sun-disc surmounted by a throne, and sometimes enclosed between horns. Adored at Abydos. Her soul resided in Sothis on the Dog-star.

NUT: A woman so bent that her hands touched the earth. She represents the vault of heaven, and is the mother of the gods.

HATHOR: Cow-headed, and crowned with the disc and plumes. Deity of Amenti, or the Egyptian Hades. Worshipped at Denderah.

PASHT: Pasht and Bast appear to be two forms of the same goddess. As Bast she is represented as a woman, lion-headed, with the disc and uroeus; as Pasht she is cat-headed, and holds a sistrum. Adored at Bubastis. Observe the syllable BAST.

The highest visible deity of the Egyptians was Amun Ra, or Amen Ra, the concealed sun; the word Ra signifying the sun. This name appears in the Greek and Latin writers as Zeus Ammon and Jupiter Ammon. When Amun manifests himself by his word, will or spirit, he is known as Nu, Num, Noub, Nef, Neph, or Kneph, and this word Kneph through the form Cnuphis is, perhaps, the Anubis of the Greek and Latin authors. That word has not been found earlier than the time of Augustus. Anubis was then worshipped as the guardian god, and represented with a dog's head.

The soul of Osiris was supposed to exist in some way in the sacred bull Apis, of which Serapis or Sarapis is probably another name. "Apis," says Herodotus, "is a young bull, whose hair is black, on his forehead a white triangle, — on his back an eagle, with a beetle under his tongue and with the hair of his tail double." Ovid says he is of various colors. Plutarch says he has a crescent on his right side. These superstitions varied from age to age. Apis was worshipped in Memphis.

It must be observed, in general, that the names in the Latin classics belong to a much later period of the Egyptian religion than the names found on most of the monuments. It will be found, that, as in the change from Nu to Anubis, it is difficult to trace the progress of a name from one to the other. In the cases where an ox, a ram, or a dog is worshipped with, or as a symbol of, a god, we probably have the survival of a very early local idolatry.

Horus or Harpocrates, named above, was the son of Osiris. He is sometimes represented, seated on a Lotusflower, with his finger on his lips, as the god of silence.

In one of Moore's Irish Melodies is an allusion to Harpocrates: -

---

"Thyself shall, under some rosy bower,
Sit mute, with thy finger on thy lip:
Like him, the boy, who born among
The flowers that on the Nile-stream blush,
Sits over thus, his only song
To Earth and Heaven, "Hush, all, hush!"

MYTH OF OSIRIS AND ISIS

Osiris and Isis were at one time induced to descend to the earth to bestow gifts and blessings on its inhabitants. Isis showed them first the use of wheat and barley, and Osiris made the instruments of agriculture and taught men the use of them, as well as how to harness the ox to the plough. He then gave men laws, the institution of marriage, a civil organization, and taught them how to worship the gods. After he had thus made the valley of the Nile a happy country, he assembled a host with which he went to bestow his blessings upon the rest of the world. He conquered the nations everywhere, but not with weapons, only with music and eloquence. His brother Typhon (Typhon is supposed to be the Seth of the monuments) saw this, and filled with envy and malice sought, during his absence, to usurp his throne. But Isis, who held the reins of government, frustrated his plans. Still more embittered, he now resolved to kill his brother. This he did in the following manner: Having organized a conspiracy of seventy-two members, he went with them to the feast which was celebrated in honor of the king's return. He then caused a box or chest to be brought in, which had been made to fit exactly the size of Osiris, and declared that he would give that chest of precious wood to whosoever could get into it. The rest tried in vain, but no sooner was Osiris in it than Typhon and his companions closed the lid and flung the chest into the Nile. When Isis heard of the cruel murder she wept and mourned, and then with her hair shorn, clothed in black and beating her breast, she sought diligently for the body of her husband. In this search she was assisted by Anubis, the son of Osiris and Nephthys. They sought in vain for some time; for when the chest, carried by the waves to the shores of Byblos, had become entangled in the reeds that grew at the edge of the water, the divine power that dwelt in the body of Osiris imparted such strength to the shrub that it grew into a mighty tree, enclosing in its trunk the coffin of the god. This tree, with its sacred deposit, was shortly afterward felled, and erected as a column in the palace of the king of Phoenicia. But at length, by the aid of Anubis and the sacred birds, Isis ascertained these facts, and then went to the royal city. There she offered herself at the palace as a servant, and being admitted, threw off her disguise and appeared as the goddess, surrounded with thunder and lightning. Striking the column with her wand, she caused it to split open and give up the sacred coffin. This she seized and returned with it, and concealed it in the depth of a forest, but Typhon discovered it, and cutting the body into fourteen pieces, scattered them hither and thither. After a tedious search, Isis found thirteen pieces, the fishes of the Nile having eaten the other. This she replaced by an imitation of sycamore wood, and buried the body at Philoe, which became ever after the great burying place of the nation, and the spot to which pilgrimages were made from all parts of the country. A temple of surpassing magnificence was also erected there in honor of the god, and at every place where one of his limbs had been found, minor temples and tombs were built to commemorate the event. Osiris became after that the tutelar deity of the Egyptians. His soul was supposed always to inhabit the body of the bull Apis, and at his death to transfer itself to his successor.

Apis, the Bull of Memphis, was worshipped with the greatest reverence by the Egyptians. As soon as a bull marked with the marks which have been described, was found by those sent in search of him, he was placed in a building facing the east, and was fed with milk for four months. At the expiration of this term the priests repaired at new moon with great pomp, to his habitation, and saluted him Apis. He was placed in a vessel magnificently decorated and conveyed down the Nile to Memphis, where a temple, with two chapels and a court for exercise, was assigned to him. Sacrifices were made to him, and once every year, about the time when the Nile began to rise, a golden cup was thrown into the river, and a grand festival was held to celebrate his birthday. The people believed that during this festival the crocodiles forgot their natural ferocity and became harmless. There was however one drawback to his happy lot; he was not permitted to live beyond a certain period; and if when he had attained the age of twenty-five years, he still survived, the priests drowned him in the sacred cistern, and then buried him in the temple of Serapis. On the death of this bull, whether it occurred in the course of nature or by violence, the whole land was filled with sorrow and lamentations, which lasted until his successor was found.

A new Apis was found as late as the reign of Hadrian. A mummy made from one of the Sacred Bulls may be seen in the Egyptian collection of the Historical Society, New York.

Milton, in his Hymn of the Nativity, alludes to the Egyptian deities, not as imaginary beings, but as real demons put to flight by the coming of Christ:

"The brutish gods of Nile as fast,
Isis and Horus and the dog Anubis haste.
Nor is Osiris seen
In Memphian grove or green
Trampling the unshowered grass with lowings loud;*
Nor can he be at rest
Within his sacred chest;
Nought but profoundest hell can be his shroud.
In vain with timbrel'd anthems dark
The sable-stoled sorcerers bear his worshipped ark."

*(There being no rain in Egypt, the grass is "unshowered," and the country depends for its fertility upon the overflowings of the Nile. The ark alluded to in the last line is shown by pictures still remaining on the walls of the Egyptian temples to have been borne by the priests in their religious processions. It probably represented the chest in which Osiris was placed.)

Isis was represented in statuary with the head veiled, a symbol of mystery. It is this which Tennyson alludes to in Maud, 0V.8

"For the drift of the Maker is dark, an Isis hid by the veil."

ORACLES

Oracle was the name used to denote the place where answers were supposed to be given by any of the divinities to those who consulted them respecting the future. The word was also used to signify the response which was given.

Figure 37: "Waterhouse Circe Invidiosa" by John William Waterhouse

The most ancient Grecian oracle was that of Jupiter at Dodona. According to one account it was established in the following manner. Two black doves took their flight from Thebes in Egypt. One flew to Dodona in Epirus and alighting in a grove of oaks, it proclaimed in human language to the inhabitants of the district that they must establish there an oracle of Jupiter. The other dove flew to the temple of Jupiter Ammon in the Libyan oasis, and delivered a similar command there. Another account is, that they were not doves, but priestesses, who were carried off from Thebes in Egypt by the Phoenicians, and set up oracles at Oasis and Dodona. The responses of the oracle were given from the trees, by the branches rustling in the wind, the sounds being interpreted by the priests.

But the most celebrated of the Grecian oracles was that of Apollo at Delphi, a city built on the slopes of Parnassus in Phocis.

It had been observed at a very early period that the goats feeding on Parnassus were thrown into convulsions when they approached a certain long deep cleft in the side of the mountain. This was owing to a peculiar vapor arising out of the cavern, and one of the goatherds was induced to try its effects upon himself. Inhaling the intoxicating air he was affected in the same manner as the cattle had been, and the inhabitants of the surrounding country, unable to explain the circumstance, imputed the convulsive ravings to which he gave utterance while under the power of the exhalations, to a divine inspiration. The fact was speedily circulated widely, and a temple was erected on the spot. The prophetic influence was at first variously attributed to the goddess Earth, to Neptune, Themis, and others, but it was at length assigned to Apollo, and to him alone. A priestess was appointed whose office it was to inhale the hallowed air, and who was named the Pythia. She was prepared for this duty by previous ablution at the fountain of Castalia, and being crowned with laurel was seated upon a tripod similarly adorned, which was placed over the chasm whence the divine afflatus proceeded. Her inspired words while thus situated were interpreted by the priests.

ORACLE OF TROPHONIUS

Besides the oracles of Jupiter and Apollo, at Dodona and Delphi, that of Trophonius in Boeotia was held in high estimation. Trophonius and Agamedes were brothers. They were distinguished architechts, and built the temple of Apollo at Delphi, and a treasury for King Hyrieus. In the wall of the treasury they placed a stone, in such a manner that it could be taken out; and by this means from time to time purloined the treasure. This amazed Hyrieus, for his locks and seals were untouched, and yet his wealth, continually diminished. At length he set a trap for the thief and Agamedes was caught. Trophonius unable to extricate him, and fearing that when found he would be compelled by torture to discover his accomplice, cut off his head. Trophonius himself is said to have been shortly afterwards swallowed up by the earth.

The oracle of Trophonius was at Lebadea in Boeotia. During a great drought the Boeotians, it is said, were directed by the god at Delphi to seek aid of Trophonius at Lebadea. They came thither, but could find no oracle. One of them, however, happening to see a swarm of bees, followed them to a chasm in the earth, which proved to be the place sought.

Peculiar ceremonies were to be performed by the person who came to consult the oracle. After these preliminaries, he descended into the cave by a narrow passage. This place could be entered only in the night. The person returned from the cave by the same narrow passage, but walking backwards. He appeared melancholy and dejected; and hence the proverb which was applied to a person low-spirited and gloomy, "He has been consulting the oracle of Trophonius."

ORACLE OF AESCULAPIUS

There were numerous oracles of Aesculapius, but the most celebrated one was at Epidaurus. Here the sick sought responses and the recovery of their health by sleeping in the temple. It has been inferred from the accounts that have come down to us, that the treatment of the sick resembled what is now called Animal Magnetism or Mesmerism.

Serpents were sacred to Aesculapius, probably because of a superstition that those animals have a faculty of renewing their youth by a change of skin. The worship of Aesculapius was introduced into Rome in a time of great sickness, and an embassy sent to the temple of Epidaurus to entreat the aid of the god. Aesculapius was propitious, and on the return of the ship accompanied it in the form of a serpent. Arriving in the river Tiber, the serpent glided from the vessel and took possession of an island in the river, and a temple was there erected to his honor.

ORACLE OF APIS

At Memphis the sacred bull Apis gave answer to those who consulted him, by the manner in which he received or rejected what was presented to him. If the bull refused food from the hand of the inquirer it was considered an unfavorable sign, and the contrary when he received it.

It has been a question whether oracular responses ought to be ascribed to mere human contrivance or to the agency of evil spirits. The latter opinion has been most general in past ages. A third theory has been advanced since the phenomena of Mesmerism have attracted attention, that something like the mesmeric trance was induced in the Pythoness, and the faculty of clairvoyance really called into action.

Another question is as to the time when the Pagan oracles ceased to give responses. Ancient Christian writers assert that they became silent at the birth of Christ, and were heard no more after that date. Milton adopts this view in his Hymn of the Nativity, and in lines of solemn and elevated beauty pictures the consternation of the heathen idols at the advent of the Saviour.

"The oracles are dumb;
No voice or hideous hum
Rings through the arched roof in words deceiving.
Apollo from his shrine
Can no more divine,
With hollow shriek the steep of Delphos leaving.
No nightly trance or breathed spell
Inspires the pale-eyed priest from the prophetic cell."

In Cowper's poem of Yardley Oak there are some beautiful mythological allusions. The former of the two following is to the fable of Castor and Pollux; the latter is more appropriate to our present subject. Addressing the acorn he says,

"Thou fell'st mature; and in the loamy clod,
Swelling with vegetative force instinct,
Didst burst thine egg, as theirs the fabled Twins
Now stars; two lobes protruding, paired exact;
A leaf succeeded and another leaf,
And, all the elements thy puny growth
Fostering propitious, thou becam'st a twig.
Who lived when thou was such? Oh, couldst thou speak
As in Dodona once thy kindred trees
Oracular, I would not curious ask
The future, best unknown, but at thy mouth
Inquisitive, the less ambiguous past."

Tennyson in his Talking Oak alludes to the oaks of Dodona in these lines:

"And I will work in prose and rhyme,
And praise thee more in both
Than bard has honored beech or lime,
Or that Thessalian growth
In which the swarthy ring-dove sat
And mystic sentence spoke."

Byron alludes to the oracle of Delphi where, speaking of Rousseau, whose writings he conceives did much to bring on the French revolution, he says,

"For then he was inspired, and from him came,
As from the Pythian's mystic cave of yore,
Those oracles which set the world in flame,
Nor ceased to burn till kingdoms were no more."

Figure 38: "Psyche Opening the Golden Box" by John William Waterhouse

Chapter 28

ORIGIN OF MYTHOLOGY STATUES OF GODS AND GODDESSES POETS OF MYTHOLOGY

Having reached the close of our series of stories of Pagan mythology, an inquiry suggests itself. "Whence came these stories? Have they a foundation in truth, or are they simply dreams of the imagination?" Philosophers have suggested various theories on the subject of which we shall give three or four.

1. The Scriptural theory; according to which all mythological legends are derived from the narratives of Scripture, though the real facts have been disguised and altered. Thus Deucalion is only another name for Noah, Hercules for Samson, Arion for Jonah, etc. Sir Walter Raleigh, in his History of the World, says, "Jubal, Tubal, and Tubal-Cain were Mercury, Vulcan, and Apollo, inventors of Pasturage, Smithing, and Music. The Dragon which kept the golden apples was the serpent that beguiled Eve. Nimrod's tower was the attempt of the Giants against Heaven. There are doubtless many curious coincidences like these, but the theory cannot without extravagance be pushed so far as to account for any great proportion of the stories.

2. The Historical theory; according to which all the persons mentioned in mythology were once real human beings, and the legends and fabulous traditions relating to them are merely the additions and embellishments of later times. Thus the story of Æolus, the king and god of the winds, is supposed to have risen from the fact that Æolus was the ruler of some islands in the Tyrrhenian Sea, where he reigned as a just and pious king, and taught the natives the use of sails for ships, and how to tell from the signs of the atmosphere the changes of the weather and the winds. Cadmus, who, the legend says, sowed the earth with dragon's teeth, from which sprang a crop of armed men, was in fact an emigrant from Phoenicia, and brought with him into Greece the knowledge of the letters of the alphabet, which he taught to the natives. From these rudiments of learning sprung civilization, which the poets have always been prone to describe as a deterioration of man's first estate, the Golden Age of innocence and simplicity.

3. The Allegorical theory supposes that all the myths of the ancients were allegorical and symbolical, and contained some moral, religious, or philosophical truth or historical fact, under the form of an allegory, but came in process of time to be understood literally. Thus Saturn, who devours his own children, is the same power whom the Greeks called Kronos (Time), which may truly be said to destroy whatever it has brought into existence. The story of Io is interpreted in a similar manner. Io is the moon, and Argus the starry sky, which, as it were, keeps sleepless watch over her. The fabulous wanderings of Io represent the continual revolutions of the moon, which also suggested to Milton the same idea.

"To behold the wandering moon
Riding near her highest noon,
Like one that had been led astray
In the heaven's wide, pathless way."
Il Penseroso

---

4. The Astronomical theory supposes that the different stories are corrupted versions of astronomical statements, of which the true meaning was forgotten. This theory is pushed to its extreme by Dupuis, in his treatise "Sur tous les cultes."

5. The Physical theory, according to which the elements of air, fire, and water, were originally the objects of religious adoration, and the principal deities were personifications of the powers of nature. The transition was easy from a personification of the elements to the notion of supernatural beings presiding over and governing the different objects of nature. The Greeks, whose imagination was lively, peopled all nature with invisible beings, and supposed that every object, from the sun and sea to the smallest fountain and rivulet, was under the care of some particular divinity. Wordsworth, in his Excursion, has beautifully developed this view of Grecian mythology.

"In that fair clime the lonely herdsman, stretched
On the soft grass through half a summer's day,
With music lulled his indolent repose;
And, in some fit of weariness, if he,

When his own breath was silent, chanced to hear
A distant strain far sweeter than the sounds
Which his poor skill could make, his fancy fetched
Even from the blazing chariot of the sun
A beardless youth who touched a golden lute,
And filled the illumined groves with ravishment.
The mighty hunter, lifting up his eyes
Toward the crescent Moon, with grateful heart
Called on the lovely Wanderer who bestowed
That timely light to share his joyous sport;
And hence a beaming goddess with her nymphs
Across the lawn and through the darksome grove
(Not unaccompanied with tuneful notes
By echo multiplied from rock or cave)
Swept in the storm of chase, as moon and stars
Glance rapidly along the clouded heaven
When winds are blowing strong. The traveler slaked
His thirst from rill or gushing fount, and thanked
The Naiad. Sunbeams upon distant hills
Gliding apace with shadows in their train,
Might with small help from fancy, be transformed
Into fleet Oreads sporting visibly.
The Zephyrs, fanning, as they passed, their wings,
Lacked not for love fair objects whom they wooed
With gentle whisper. Withered boughs grotesque,
Stripped of their leaves and twigs by hoary age,
From depth of shaggy covert peeping forth
In the low vale, or on steep mountain side;
And sometimes intermixed with stirring horns
Of the live deer, or goat's depending beard;
These were the lurking Satyrs, a wild brood
Of gamesome deities; or Pan himself,
The simple shepherd's awe-inspiring god."

All the theories which have bene mentioned are true to a certain extent. It would therefore be more correct to say that the mythology of a nation has sprung from all these sources combined than from any one in particular. We may add also that there are many myths which have risen from the desire of man to account for those natural phenomena which he cannot understand; and not a few have had their rise from a similar desire of giving a reason for the names of places and persons.

STATUES OF THE GODS

Adequately to represent to the eye the ideas intended to be conveyed to the mind under the several names of deities, was a task which called into exercise the highest powers of genius and art. Of the many attempts FOUR have been most celebrated, the first two known to us only by the descriptions of the ancients, and by copies on gems, which are still preserved; the other two still extant and the acknowledged masterpieces of the sculptor's art.

THE OLYMPIAN JUPITER

The statue of the Olympian Jupiter by Phidias was considered the highest achievement of this department of Grecian art. It was of colossal dimensions, and was what the ancients called "chryselephantine;" that is, composed of ivory and gold; the parts representing flesh being of ivory laid on a core of wood or stone, while the drapery and other ornaments were of gold. The height of the figure was forty feet, on a pedestal twelve feet high. The god was represented seated on this throne. His brows were crowned with a wreath of olive, and he held in his right hand a sceptre, and in his left a statue of Victory. The throne was of cedar, adorned with gold and precious stones.

The idea which the artist essayed to embody was that of the supreme deity of the Hellenic (Grecian) nation, enthroned as a conqueror, in perfect majesty and repose, and ruling with a nod the subject world. Phidias avowed that he took his idea from the representation which Homer gives in the first book of the Iliad, in the passage thus translated by Pope:

"He spoke and awful bends his sable brows,
Shakes his ambrosial curls and gives the nod,
The stamp of fate and sanction of the god.
High heaven with reverence the dread signal took,
A nd all Olympus to the centre shook."

(Cowper's version is less elegant, but truer to the original.

"He ceased, and under his dark brows the nod
Vouchsafed of confirmation. All around
The sovereign's everlasting head his curls
Ambrosial shook, and the huge mountain reeled."

It may interest our readers to see how this passage appears in another famous version, that which was issued under the name of Tickell, contemporaneously with Pope's, and which, being by many attributed to Addison, led to the quarrel which ensued between Addison and Pope.

"This said, his kingly brow the sire inclined;
The large black curls fell awful from behind,
Thick shadowing the stern forehead of the god;
Olympus trembled at the almighty nod.")

THE MINERVA OF THE PARTHENON

This was also the work of Phidias. It stood in the Parthenon, or temple of Minerva at Athens. The goddess was represented standing. In one hand she held a spear, in the other a statue of Victory. Her helmet, highly decorated, was surmounted by a Sphinx. The statue was forty feet in height, and, like the Jupiter, composed of ivory and gold. The eyes were of marble, and probably painted to represent the iris and pupil. The Parthenon in which this statue stood was also constructed under the direction and superintendence of Phidias. Its exterior was enriched with sculptures, many of them from the hand of Phidias. The Elgin marbles now in the British Museum are a part of them.

Figure 39: "Minerva and the Muses" by Jacques Stella

Both the Jupiter and Minerva of Phidias are lost, but there is good ground to believe that we have, in several extant statues and busts, the artist's conceptions of the countenances of both. They are characterized by grave and dignified beauty, and freedom from any transient expression, which in the language of art is called REPOSE.

THE VENUS DE'MEDICI

The Venus of the Medici is so called from its having been in the possession of the princes of that name in Rome when it first attracted attention, about two hundred years ago. An inscription on the base records it to be the work of Cleomenes, an Athenian sculptor of 200 B.C., but the authenticity of the inscription is doubtful. There is a story that the artist was employed by public authority to make a statue exhibiting the perfection of female beauty, and to aid him in his task, the most perfect forms the city could supply were furnished him for models. It is this which Thomson alludes to in his Summer.

"So stands the statue that enchants the world;
So bending tries to veil the matchless boast,
The mingled beauties of exulting Greece."

Byron also alludes to this statue. Speaking of the Florence Museum, he says:

"There too the goddess loves in stone, and fills
The air around with beauty;"

And in the next stanza,

"Blood, pulse, and breast confirm the Dardan shepherd's prize."

This last allusion is explained in Chapter XX.

THE APOLLOA BELVEDERE

The most highly esteemed of all the remains of ancient sculpture is the statue of Apollo, called the Belvedere, from the name of the apartment of the Pope's palace at Rome, in which it is placed. The artist is unknown. It is supposed to be a work of Roman art, of about the first century of our era. It is a standing figure, in marble, more than seven feet high, naked except for the cloak which is fastened around the neck and hangs over the extended left arm. It is supposed to represent the god in the moment when he has shot the arrow to destroy the monster Python (See Chapter II). The victorious divinity is in the act of stepping forward. The left arm which seems to have held the bow is outstretched, and the head is turned in the same direction. In attitude and proportion the graceful majesty of the figure is unsurpassed. The effect is completed by the countenance, where, on the perfection of youthful godlike beauty there dwells the consciousness of triumphant power.

THE DIANA A LA BICHE

The Diana of the hind, in the palace of the Louvre, may be considered the counterpart to the Apollo Belvedere. The attitude much resembles that of the Apollo, the sizes correspond and also the style of execution. It is a work of the highest order, though by no means equal to the Apollo. The attitude is that of hurried and eager motion, the face that of a huntress in the excitement of the chase. The left hand is extended over the forehead of the Hind which runs by her side, the right arm reaches backward over the shoulder to draw an arrow from the quiver.

THE VENUS OF MELOS

Of the Venus of Melos, perhaps the most famous of our statues of mythology, very little is known. There are many indeed who believe that it is not a statue of Venus at all.

It was found in the year 1820 in the Island of Melos by a peasant, who sold it to the French consul at the place.

Figure 40: "Emptying Bosom" by William Heath Robinson

The statue was standing in the theatre, which had been filled up with rubbish in the course of centuries, and when discovered was broken in several places, and some of the pieces were gone. These missing pieces, notably the two arms, have been restored in various ways by modern artists. As has been said above, there is a controversy as to whether the statue represents Venus or some other goddess. Much has been written on each side, but the question still remains unsettled. The general opinion of those who contend that it is not Venus is that it is a statue or Nike or Victory.

THE POETS OF MYTHOLOGY

Homer, from whose poems of the Iliad and Odyssey we have taken the chief part of our chapters of the Trojan war and the return of the Grecians, is almost as mythical a personage as the heroes he celebrates. The traditionary story is that he was a wandering minstrel, blind and old, who travelled from place to place singing his lays to the music of his harp, in the courts of princes or the cottages

Figure 41: "Flashing Chariot" by Carl Larsson

of peasants, and dependent upon the voluntary offerings of his hearers for support. Byron calls him "The blind old man of Scio's rocky isle," and a well-known epigram, alluding to the uncertainty of the fact of his birthplace, says,

"Seven wealthy towns contend for Homer dead,
Through which the living Homer begged his bread."

An older version is,

"Seven cities warred for Homer being dead,
Who living had no roof to shroud his head."

These lines are by Thomas Heywood; the others are ascribed to Thomas Seward.

These seven cities were Smyrna, Scio, Rhodes, Colophon, Salamis, Argos, and Athens.

Modern scholars have doubted whether the Homeric poems are the work of any single mind. This arises from the difficulty of believing that poems of such length could have been committed to writing at so early an age as that usually assigned to these, an age earlier than the date of any remaining inscriptions or coins, and when no materials, capable of containing such long productions were yet introduced into use. On the other hand it is asked how poems of such length could have been handed down from age to age by means of the memory alone. This is answered by the statement that there was a professional body of men, called Rhapsodists, who recited the poems of others, and whose business it was to commit to memory and rehearse for pay the national and patriotic legends.

The prevailing opinion of the learned, at this time, seems to be that the framework and much of the structure of the poems belong to Homer, but that there are numerous interpolations and additions by other hands.

The date assigned to Homer, on the authority of Herodotus, is 850 B.C., but a range of two or three centuries must be given for the various conjectures of critics.

VIRGIL

Virgil, called also by his surname, Maro, from whose poem of the Ǣneid we have taken the story of Ǣneas, was one of the great poets who made the reign of the Roman emperor, Augustus, so celebrated, under the name of the Augustan age. Virgil was born in Mantua in the year 70 B.C. His great poem is ranked next to those of Homer, in the highest class of poetical composition, the Epic. Virgil is far inferior to Homer in originality and invention, but superior to him in correctness and elegance. To critics of English lineage Milton alone of modern poets seems worthy to be classed with these illustrious ancients. His poem of Paradise Lost, from which we have borrowed so many illustrations, is in many respects equal, in some superior, to either of the great works of antiquity. The following epigram of Dryden characterizes the three poets with as much truth as it is usual to find in such pointed criticism:

ON MILTON

"Three poets in three different ages born.
Greece, Italy, and England did adorn.
The first in loftiness of soul surpassed,
The next in majesty, in both the last.
The force of nature could no further go;
To make a third she joined the other two."

From Cowper's Table Talk:

"Ages elapsed ere Homer's lamp appeared,
And ages ere the Mantuan swan was heard.
To carry nature lengths unknown before,
To give a Milton birth, asked ages more.
Thus genius rose and set at ordered times,
And shot a dayspring into distant climes,
Ennobling every region that he chose;
He sunk in Greece, in Italy he rose,
And, tedious years of Gothic darkness past,
Emerged all splendor in our isle at last.
Thus lovely halcyons dive into the main,
Then show far off their shining plumes again."

OVID

Often alluded to in poetry by his other name of Naso, was born in the year 43 B.C. He was educated for public life and held some offices of considerable dignity, but poetry was his delight, and he early resolved to devote himself to it. He accordingly sought the society of the contemporary poets, and was acquainted with Horace and saw Virgil, though the latter died when Ovid was yet too young and undistinguished to have formed his acquaintance. Ovid spent an easy life at Rome in the enjoyment of a competent income. He was intimate with the family of Augustus, the emperor, and it is supposed that some serious offence given to some member of that family was the cause of an event which reversed the poet's happy circumstances and clouded all the latter portion of his life. At the age of fifty he was banished from Rome, and ordered to betake himself to Tomi, on the borders of the Black Sea. Here, among the barbarous people and in a severe climate, the poet, who had been accustomed to all the pleasures of a luxurious capital and the society of his most distinguished contemporaries, spent the last ten years of his life, worn out with grief and anxiety. His only consolation in exile was to address his wife and absent friends, and his letters were all poetical. Though these poems (The Tristia and Letters from Pontus) have no other topic than the poet's sorrows, his exquisite taste and fruitful invention have redeemed them from the charge of being tedious, and they are read with pleasure and even with sympathy.

The two great works of Ovid are his Metamorphoses and his Fasti. They are both mythological poems, and from the former we have taken most of our stories of Grecian and Roman mythology. A late writer thus characterizes these poems:

"The rich mythology of Greece furnished Ovid, as it may still furnish the poet, the painter, and the sculptor, with materials for his art. With exquisite taste, simplicity, and pathos he has narrated the fabulous traditions of early ages, and given to them that appearance of reality which only a master-hand could impart. His pictures of nature are striking and true; he selects with care that which is appropriate; he rejects the superfluous; and when he has completed his work, it is neither defective nor redundant. The Metamorphoses are read with pleasure by youth, and are re-read in more advanced age with still greater delight. The poet ventured to predict that his poem would survive him, and be read wherever the Roman name was known."

The prediction above alluded to is contained in the closing lines of the Metamorphoses, of which we give a literal translation below:

"And now I close my work, which not the ire
Of Jove, nor tooth of time, nor sword, nor fire
Shall bring to nought. Come when it will that day
Which o'er the body, not the mind, has sway,
And snatch the remnant of my life away,
My better part above the stars shall soar,
And my renown endure for evermore.
Where'er the Roman arms and arts shall spread,
There by the people shall my book be read;
And, if aught true in poet's visions be,
My name and fame have immortality."

Chapter 29

MODERN MONSTERS: THE PHOENIX BASILISK UNICORN SALAMANDER

There is a set of imaginary beings which seem to have been the successors of the "Gorgons, Hydras, and Chimaeras dire" of the old superstitions, and, having no connection with the false gods of Paganism, to have continued to enjoy an existence in the popular belief after Paganism was superseded by Christianity. They are mentioned perhaps by the classical writers, but their chief popularity and currency seem to have been in more modern times. We seek our accounts of them not so much in the poetry of the ancients, as in the old natural history books and narrations of travellers. The accounts which we are about to give are taken chiefly from the Penny Cyclopedia.

THE PHOENIX

Ovid tells the story of the Phoenix as follows: "Most beings spring from other individuals; but there is a certain kind which reproduces itself. The Assyrians call it the Phoenix. It does not live on fruit or flowers, but on frankincense and odoriferous gums. When it has lived five hundred years, it builds itself a nest in the branches of an oak, or on the top of a palm-tree. In this it collects cinnamon, and spikenard, and myrrh, and of these materials builds a pile on which it deposits itself, and dying, breathes out its last breath amidst odors. From the body of the parent bird a young Phoenix issues forth, destined to live as long a life as its predecessor. When this has grown up and gained sufficient strength, it lifts its nest from the tree (its own cradle and its parent's sepulchre) and carries it to the city of Heliopolis in Egypt, and deposits it in the temple of the Sun."

Such is the account given by a poet. Now let us see that of a philosophic historian. Tacitus says, "In the consulship of Paulus Fabius (A.D. 34), the miraculous bird known to the world by the name of Phoenix, after disappearing for a series of ages, revisited Egypt. It was attended in its flight by a group of various birds, all attracted by the novelty, and gazing with wonder at so beautiful an appearance." He then gives an account of the bird, not varying materially from the preceding, but adding some details. "The first care of the young bird as soon as fledged and able to trust to his wings is to perform the obsequies of his father. But this duty is not undertaken rashly. He collects a quantity of myrrh, and to try his strength makes frequent excursions with a load on his back. When he has gained sufficient confidence in his own vigor, he takes up the body of his father and flies with it to the altar of the Sun, where he leaves it to be consumed in flames of fragrance." Other writers add a few particulars. The myrrh is compacted in the form of an egg, in which the dead Phoenix is enclosed. From the mouldering flesh of the dead bird a worm springs, and this worm, when grown large, is transformed into a bird. Herodotus DESCRIBES the bird, though he says, "I have not seen it myself, except in a picture. Part of his plumage is gold-colored, and part crimson; and he is for the most part very much like an eagle in outline and bulk."

The first writer who disclaimed a belief in the existence of the Phoenix was Sir Thomas Browne, in his Vulgar Errors, published in 1646. He was replied to a few years later by Alexander Ross, who says, in answer to the objection of the Phoenix so seldom making his appearance, "His instinct teaches him to keep out of the way of the tyrant of the creation, MAN, for if he were to be got at some wealthy glutton would surely devour him, though there were no more in the world."

Dryden, in one of his early poems, has this allusion to the Phoenix:

"So when the new-born Phoenix first is seen,
Her feathered subjects all adore their queen,
And while she makes her progress through the East,
From every grove her numerous train's increased;
Each poet of the air her glory sings,
And round him the pleased audience clap their wings."

Milton, in Paradise lost, Book V, compares the angel Raphael descending to earth to a Phoenix:

"Down thither, prone in flight

He speeds, and through the vast ethereal sky
Sails between worlds and worlds, with steady wing,
Now on the polar winds, then with quick fan
Winnows the buxom air; till within soar
Of towering eagles, to all the fowls he seems
A Phoenix, gazed by all; as that sole bird
When, to enshrine his relics in the Sun's
Bright temple, to Egyptian Thebes he flies."

THE COCKATRICE, OR BASILISK

This animal was called the king of the serpents. In confirmation of his royalty, he was said to be endowed with a crest or comb upon the head, constituting a crown. He was supposed to be produced from the egg of a cock hatched under toads or serpents. There were several species of this animal. One species burned up whatever they approached; a second were a kind of wandering Medusa's heads, and their look caused an instant horror, which was immediately followed by death. In Shakespeare's play of Richard the Third, Lady Anne, in answer to Richard's compliment on her eyes, says, "Would they were basilisk's, to strike thee dead!"

The basilisks were called kings of serpents because all other serpents and snakes, behaving like good subjects, and wisely not wishing to be burned up or struck dead, fled the moment they heard the distant hiss of their king, although they might be in full feed upon the most delicious prey, leaving the sole enjoyment of the banquet to the royal monster.

The Roman naturalist Pliny thus describes him: "He does not impel his body like other serpents, by a multiplied flexion, but advances lofty and upright. He kills the shrubs, not only by contact but by breathing on them, and splits the rocks, such power of evil is there in him. It was formally believed that if killed by a spear from on horseback the power of the poison conducted through the weapon killed not only the rider but the horse also. To this Lucan alludes in these lines:

"What though the Moor the basilisk hath slain,
And pinned him lifeless to the sandy plain,
Up through the spear the subtle venom flies,
The hand imbibes it, and the victor dies."

Such a prodigy was not likely to be passed over in the legends of the saints. Accordingly, we find it recorded that a certain holy man going to a fountain in the desert suddenly beheld a basilisk. He immediately raised his eyes to heaven, and with a pious appeal to the Deity, laid the monster dead at his feet.

These wonderful powers of the basilisk are attested by a host of learned persons, such as Galen, Avicenna, Scaliger, and others. Occasionally one would demur to some part of the tale while he admitted the rest. Jonston, a learned physician, sagely remarks, "I would scarcely believe that it kills with its look, for who could have seen it and lived to tell the story?" The worthy sage was not aware that those who went to hunt the basilisk of this sort, took with them a mirror, which reflected back the deadly glare upon its author, and by a kind of poetical justice slew the basilisk with his own weapon.

But what was to attack this terrible and unapproachable monster? There is an old saying that "everything has its enemy," and the cockatrice quailed before the weasel. The basilisk might look daggers, the weasel cared not, but advanced boldly to the conflict. When bitten, the weasel retired for a moment to eat some rue, which was the only plant the basilisks could not wither, returned with renewed strength and soundness to the charge, and never left the enemy till he was stretched dead on the plain. The monster, too, as if conscious of the irregular way in which he came into the world, was supposed to have a great antipathy to a cock; and well he might, for as soon as he heard the cock crow he expired.

The basilisk was of some use after death. Thus we read that its carcass was suspended in the temple of Apollo, and in private houses, as a sovereign remedy against spiders, and that it was also hung up in the temple of Diana, for which reason no swallow ever dared enter the sacred place.

The reader will, we apprehend, by this time have had enough of absurdities, but still he may be interested to know that these details come from the work of one who was considered in his time an able and valuable writer on Natural History. Ulysses Aldrovandus was a celebrated naturalist of the sixteenth century, and his work on natural history, in thirteen folio volumes, contains with much that is valuable a large proportion of fables and inutilities. In particular he is so ample on the subject of the cock and the bull, that from his practice all rambling, gossiping tales of doubtful credibility are called COCK AND BULL STORIES. Still he is to be remembered with respect as the founder of a botanic garden, and one of the leaders in the modern habit of making scientific collections for research and inquiry.

Shelley, in his Ode to Naples, full of the enthusiasm excited by the intelligence of the proclamation of a Constitutional Government at Naples, in 1820, thus uses an allusion to the basilisk:

"What though Cimmerian anarchs dare blaspheme
Freedom and thee? A new Actaeon's error
Shall theirs have been, devoured by their own bounds!
Be thou like the imperial basilisk,
Killing thy foe with unapparent wounds!
Gaze on oppression, till at that dread risk,
Aghast she pass from the earth's disk.
Fear not, but gaze, for freemen mightier grow,
And slaves more feeble, gazing on their foe."

Figure 42: "Brave Tailor" by Robert Anning Bell

THE UNICORN

Pliny, the Roman naturalist, out of whose account of the unicorn most of the modern unicorns have been described and figured, records it as "a very ferocious beast, similar in the rest of its body to a horse, with the head of a deer, the feet of an elephant, the tail of a boar, a deep bellowing voice, and a single black horn, two cubits in length, standing out in the middle of its forehead." He adds that "it cannot be taken alive;" and some such excuse may have been necessary in those days for not producing the living animal upon the arena of the amphitheatre.

The unicorn seems to have been a sad puzzle to the hunters, who hardly knew how to come at so valuable a piece of game. Some described the horn as moveable at the will of the animal, a kind of small sword in short, with which ho hunter who was not exceedingly cunning in fence could have a chance. Others maintained that all the animal's strength lay in its horn, and that when hard pressed in pursuit, it would throw itself from the pinnacle of the highest rocks horn foremost, so as to pitch upon it, and then quietly march off not a whit the worse for its fall.

But it seems they found out how to circumvent the poor unicorn at last. They discovered that it was a great lover of purity and innocence, so they took the field with a young VIRGIN, who was placed in the unsuspecting admirer's way. When the unicorn spied her, he approached with all reverence, couched beside her, and laying his head in her lap, fell asleep. The treacherous virgin then gave a signal, and the hunters made in and captured the simple beast.

Modern zoologists, disgusted as they well may be with such fables as these, disbelieve generally the existence of the unicorn. Yet there are animals bearing on their heads a bony protuberance more or less like a horn, which may have given rise to the story. The rhinoceros horn, as it is called, is such a protuberance, though it does not exceed a few inches in height, and is far from agreeing with the descriptions of the horn of the unicorn. The nearest approach to a horn in the middle of the forehead is exhibited in the bony protuberance on the forehead of the giraffe; but this also is short and blunt, and is not the only horn of the animal, but a third horn standing in front of the two others. In fine, though it would be presumptuous to deny the existence of a one-horned quadruped other than the rhinoceros, it may be safely stated that the insertion of a long and solid horn in the living forehead of a horse-like or deer-like animal, is as near an impossibility as any thing can be.

THE SALAMANDER

The following is from the Life of Benvenuto Cellini, an Italian artist of the sixteenth century, written by himself, "When I was about five years of age, my father happening to be in a little room in which they had been washing, and where there was a good fire of oak burning, looked into the flames and saw a little animal resembling a lizard, which could live in the hottest part of that element. Instantly perceiving what it was he called for my sister and me, and after he had shown us the creature, he gave me a box on the ear. I fell a crying, while he, soothing me with caresses, spoke these words: 'My dear child, I do not give you that blow for any fault you have committed, but that you may recollect that the little creature you see in the fire is a salamander; such a one as never was beheld before to my knowledge.' So saying he embraced me, and gave me some money."

It seems unreasonable to doubt a story of which signor Cellini was both an eye and ear witness. Add to which the authority of numerous sage philosophers, at the head of whom are Aristotle and Pliny, affirms this power of the salamander. According to them, the animal not only resists fire, but extinguishes it, and when he sees the flame, charges it as an enemy which he well knows how to vanquish.

That the skin of an animal which could resist the action of fire should be considered proof against that element, is not to be wondered at. We accordingly find that a cloth made of the skins of salamanders (for there really is such an animal, a kind of lizard) was incombustible, and very valuable for wrapping up such articles as were too precious to be intrusted to any other envelopes. These fire-proof cloths were actually produced, said to be made of salamander's wool, though the knowing ones detected that the substance of which they were composed was Asbestos, a mineral, which is in fine filaments capable of being woven into a flexible cloth.

The foundation of the above fables is supposed to be the fact that the salamander really does secrete from the pores of his body a milky juice, which, when he is irritated, is produced in considerable quantity, and would doubtless, for a few moments, defend the body from fire. Then it is a hibernating animal, and in winter retires to some hollow tree or other cavity, where it coils itself up and remains in a torpid state till the spring again calls it forth. It may therefore sometimes be carried with the fuel to the fire, and wake up only time enough to put forth all its faculties for its defence. Its viscous juice would do good service, and all who profess to have seen it acknowledge that it got out of the fire as fast as its legs could carry it; indeed too fast for them ever to make prize of one, except in one instance, and in that one, the animal's feet and some parts of its body were badly burned.

Dr. Young, in the Night Thoughts, with more quaintness than good taste, compares the sceptic who can remain unmoved in the contemplation of the starry heavens, to a salamander unwarmed in the fire:

"An undevout astronomer is mad!
* * * * * *
Oh, what a genius must inform the skies!
And is Lorenzo's salamander-heart
Cold and untouched amid these sacred fires?"

Figure 43: "Satyr with Ram's Head" by Arthur Rackham

Chapter 30

EASTERN MYTHOLOGY ZOROASTER HINDU MYTHOLOGY CASTES BUDDHA GRAND LAMA

During the last fifty years new attention has been paid to the systems of religion of the Eastern world, especially to that of Zoroaster among the Persians, and that which is called Brahmanism and the rival system known as Buddhism in the nations farther east. Especial interest belongs to these inquiries for us, because these religions are religions of the great Aryan race to which we belong. The people among whom they were introduced all used some dialect of the family of language to which our own belongs. Even young readers will take an interest in such books as Clarke's Great Religions and Johnson's Oriental Religions, which are devoted to careful studies of them.

Our knowledge of the religion of the ancient Persians is principally derived from the Zendavesta, or sacred books of that people. Zoroaster was the founder of their religion, or rather the reformer of the religion which preceded him. The time when he lived is doubtful, but it is certain that his system became the dominant religion of Western Asia from the time of Cyrus (550 B.C.) to the conquest of Persia by Alexander the Great. Under the Macedonian monarchy the doctrines of Zoroaster appear to have been considerably corrupted by the introduction of foreign opinions, but they afterwards recovered their ascendancy.

Zoroaster taught the existence of a supreme being, who created two other mighty beings, and imparted to them so much of his own nature as seemed good to him. Of these, Ormuzd (called by the Greeks Oromasdes) remained faithful to his creator, and was regarded as the source of all good, while Ahriman (Arimanes) rebelled, and became the author of all evil upon the earth. Ormuzd created man, and supplied him with all the materials of happiness; but Ahriman marred this happiness by introducing evil into the world, and creating savage beasts and poisonous reptiles and plants. In consequence of this, evil and good are now mingled together in every part of the world, and the followers of good and evil the adherents of Ormuzd and Ahriman carry on incessant war. But this state of things will not last forever. The time will come when the adherents of Ormuzd shall everywhere be victorious, and Ahriman and his followers be consigned to darkness forever.

The religious rites of the ancient Persians were exceedingly simple. They used neither temples, altars, nor statues, and performed their sacrifices on the tops of mountains. They adored fire, light, and the sun, as emblems of Ormuzd, the source of all light and purity, but did not regard them as independent deities. The religious rites and ceremonies were regulated by the priests, who were called Magi. The learning of the Magi was connected with astrology and enchantment, in which they were so celebrated that their name was applied to all orders of magicians and enchanters.

"As to the age of the books of the Zendavesta, and the period at which Zoroaster lived, there is the greatest difference of opinion. He is mentioned by Plato, who speaks of 'the magic (or religious doctrines) of Zoroaster the Ormazdian.' As Plato speaks of his religion as something established in the form of Magism, or the system of the Medes in West Iran, which the Avesta appears to have originated in Bactria, or East Iran, this already carries the age of Zoroaster back to at least the sixth or seventh century before Christ.

* * * * * * * * * * * *

"Professor Whitney of New Haven places the epoch of Zoroaster at 'least B.C. 1000,' and adds that all attempts to reconstruct Persian chronology or history prior to the reign of the first Sassanid have been relinquished as futile. Dollinger thinks he may have been 'somewhat later than Moses, perhaps about B.C. 1300,' but says 'it is impossible to fix precisely' when he lived. Rawlinson merely remarks that Berosus places him anterior to B.C. 2234. Haug is inclined to date the Gathas, the oldest songs of the Avesta, as early as the time of Moses. Rapp, after a thorough comparison of ancient writers, concludes that Zoroaster lived B.C. 1200 or 1300. In this he agrees with Duncker, who, as we have seen, decided upon the same date. It is not far from the period given by the oldest Greek writer who speaks of Zoroaster, Xanthus of Sardis, a contemporary of Darius. It is the period given by Cephalion, a writer of the second century, who takes it from three independent sources. We have no sources now open to us which enable us to come nearer than this to the time in which he lived.

"Nor is anything known with certainty of the place where he lived, or the events of his life. Most modern writers suppose that he resided in Bactria. Haug maintains that the language of the Zend books is Bactrian. A highly mythological and fabulous life of Zoroaster, translated by Anquetil du Perron, called the Zartrisht-Namah, describes him as going to Iran in his thirtieth year, spending twenty years in the desert, working miracles during ten years, and giving lessons of philosophy in Babylon, with Pythagoras as his pupil. All this is based on the theory (now proved to be false) of his living in the time of Darius. 'The language of the Avesta,' says Max Muller, 'is so much more primitive than the inscriptions of Darius, that many centuries must have passed between the two periods represented by these two strata of language. These inscriptions are in the Achaemenian dialect, which is the Zend in a later stage of linguistic growth.;"

J. Freeman Clarke - Ten Great Religions

Wordsworth thus alludes to the worship of the Persians:

"the Persian, zealous to reject
Altar and Image, and the inclusive walls
And roofs of temples built by human hands,
The loftiest heights ascending from their tops,
With myrtle-wreathed Tiara on his brows,
Presented sacrifice to Moon and Stars
And to the Winds and mother Elements,
And the whole circle of the Heavens, for him
A sensitive existence and a God."
Excursion, Book IV

In Childe Harold, Byron speaks thus of the Persian worship:

"Not gainly did the early Persian make
His altar the high places and the peak
Of earth o'ergazing mountains, and thus take
A fit and unwalled temple, there to seek
The Spirit, in whose honor shrines are weak,
Upreared of human hands. Come and compare
Columns and idol-dwellings, Goth or Greek,
With Nature's realms of worship, earth and air,
Nor fix on fond abodes to circumscribe thy prayer."
III., 91.

The religion of Zoroaster continued to flourish even after the introduction of Christianity, and in the third century was the dominant faith of the East, till the rise of the Mahometan power and the conquest of Persia by the Arabs in the seventh century, who compelled the greater number of the Persians to renounce their ancient faith. Those who refused to abandon the religion of their ancestors fled to the deserts of Kerman and to Hindustan, where they still exist under the name of Parsees, a name derived from Pars, the ancient name of Persia. The Arabs call them Guebers, from an Arabic word signifying unbelievers. At Bombay the Parsees are at this day a very active, intelligent, and wealthy class. For purity of life, honesty, and conciliatory manners, they are favorably distinguished. They have numerous temples to Fire, which they adore as the symbol of the divinity.

The Persian religion makes the subject of the finest tale in Moore's Lalla Rookh, the Fire Worshippers. The Gueber chief says:

"Yes! I am of that impious race,
Those slaves of Fire, that moan and even
Hail their creator's dwelling place
Among the living lights of heaven;
Yes! I am of that outcast crew
To lean and to vengeance true,
Who curse the hour your Arabs came
To desecrate our shrines of flame,
And swear before God's burning eye,
To break our country's chains or die."

HINDU MYTHOLOGY

The religion of the Hindus is professedly founded on the Vedas. To these books of their scripture they attach the greatest sanctity, and state that Brahma himself composed them at the creation. But the present arrangement of the Vedas is attributed to the sage Vyasa, about five thousand years ago.

The Vedas undoubtedly teach the belief of one supreme God. The name of this deity is Brahma. His attributes are represented by the three personified powers of CREATION, PRESERVATION, and DESTRUCTION, which, under the respective names of Brahma, Vishnu, and Siva, form the TRIMURTI or triad of principal Hindu gods. Of the inferior gods the most important are, 1. Indra, the god of heaven, of thunder, lightning, storm, and rain; 2. Agni, the god of fire; 3. Yana, the god of the infernal regions; 4. Surya, the god of the sun.

Brahma is the creator of the universe, and the source from which all the individual deities have sprung, and into which all will ultimately be absorbed. "As milk changes to curd, and water to ice, so is Brahma variously transformed and diversified, without aid of exterior means of any sort. The human soul, according to the Vedas, is a portion of the supreme ruler, as a spark is of the fire.

"BRAHMA, at first a word meaning prayer and devotion, becomes in the laws of Manu the primal God, firstborn of the creation, from the self-existent being, in the form of a golden egg. He became the creator of all things by the power of prayer. In the struggle for ascendancy, which took place between the priests and the warriors, Brahma naturally became the deity of the former. But, meantime, as we have seen, the worship or Vishnu had been extending itself in one region, and that of Siva in another. Then took place those mysterious wars between the kings of the Solar and Lunar races, of which the great epics contain all that we know. And at the close of these wars a compromise was apparently accepted, by which Brahma, Vishnu, and Siva were united in one supreme God, as creator, preserver, and destroyer, all in one.

It is almost certain that this Hindoo Triad was the result of an ingenious and successful attempt, on the part of the Brahmans, to unite all classes of worshippers in India against the Buddhists. In this sense the Brahmans edited anew the Mahabharata, inserting in that epic passages extolling Vishnu in the form of Krishna. The Greek accounts of India which followed the invasion of Alexander speak of the worship of Hercules as prevalent in the East, and by Hercules they apparently mean the god Krishna. The struggle between the Brahmans and Buddhists lasted during nine centuries (from A.D. 500 to A.D. 1400), ending with the total expulsion of Buddhism and the triumphant establishment of the Triad as the worship of India.

"Before this Triad or Trimurti (of Brahma, Vishnu, and Siva) there seems to have been another, consisting of Agni, Indra, and Surya. This may have given the hint of the second Triad, which distributed among the three gods the attributes or Creation, Destruction, and Renovation. Of these Brahma, the creator, ceased soon to be popular, and the worship of Siva and Vishnu as Krishna remain as the popular religion of India. . . ..

"But all the efforts of Brahmanism could not arrest the natural development of the system. It passed on into polytheism and idolatry. The worship of India for many centuries has been divided into a multitude of sects. While the majority of the Brahmans still profess to recognize the equal divinity of Brahma, Vishnu, and Siva, the mass of the people worship Krishna, Rama, the Singam, and many other gods and idols. There are Hindoo Atheists, who revile the Vedas; there are the Kabirs, who are a sort of Hindoo Quakers, and oppose all worship; the RAMANUJAS, an ancient sect of Vishnu worshippers; the RAMAVATS, living in monasteries; the PANTHIS, who oppose all austerities; the MAHARAJAS, whose religion consists with great licentiousness. Most of these are worshippers of Vishnu or of Siva, for Brahma-worship has wholly disappeared." J. Freeman Clarke. TEN GREAT RELIGIONS.

VISHNU

Vishnu occupies the second place in the triad of the Hindus, and is the personification of the preserving principle. To protect the world in various epochs of danger, Vishnu descended to the earth in different incarnations, or bodily forms, which descents are called Avatars. They are very numerous, but ten are more particularly specified. The first Avatar was as Matsya, the Fish, under which form Vishnu preserved Manu, the ancestor of the human race, during a universal deluge. The second Avatar was in the form of a Tortoise, which form he assumed to support the earth when the gods were churning the sea for the beverage of immortality, Amrita.

We may omit the other Avatars, which were of the same general character, that is, interpositions to protect the right or to punish wrong-doers, and come to the ninth, which is the most celebrated of the Avatars of Vishnu, in which he appeared in the human form of Krishna, an invincible warrior, who by his exploits relieved the earth from the tyrants who oppressed it.

Buddha is by the followers of the Brahmanical religion regarded as a delusive incarnation of Vishnu, assumed by him in order to induce the Asuras, opponents of the gods, to abandon the sacred ordinances of the Vedas, by which means they lost their strength and supremacy.

Kalki is the name of the TENTH Avatar, in which Vishnu will appear at the end of the present age of the world to destroy all vice and wickedness, and to restore mankind to virtue and purity.

SIVA, OR SHIVA

Siva is the third person of the Hindu triad. He is the personification of the destroying principle. Though the third named, he is, in respect to the number of his worshippers and the extension of his worship, before either of the others. In the Puranas (the scriptures of the modern Hindu religion) no allusion is made to the original power of this god as a destroyer; as that power is not to be called into exercise till after the expiration of twelve millions of years, or when the universe will come to an end; and Mahadeva (another name for Siva) is rather the representative of regeneration than of destruction.

The worshippers of Vishnu and Siva form two sects, each of which proclaims the superiority of its favorite deity, denying the claims of the other, and Brahma, the creator, having finished his work, seems to be regarded as no longer active, and has now only one temple in India, while Mahadeva and Vishnu have many. The worshippers of Vishnu are generally distinguished by a greater tenderness for life and consequent abstinence from animal food, and a worship less cruel than that of the followers of Siva.

JUGGERNAUT

Whether the worshippers of Juggernaut are to be reckoned among the followers of Vishnu or Siva, our authorities differ. The temple stands near the shore, about three hundred miles southwest of Calcutta. The idol is a carved block of wood, with a hideous face, painted black, and a distended blood-red mouth. On festival days the throne of the image is placed on a tower sixty feet high, moving on wheels. Six long ropes are attached to the tower, by which the people draw it along. The priests and their attendants stand round the throne on the tower, and occasionally turn to the worshippers with songs and gestures. While the tower moves along numbers of the devout worshippers throw themselves on the ground, in order to be crushed by the wheels, and the multitude shout in approbation of the act, as a pleasing sacrifice to the idol. Every year, particularly at two great festivals in March and July, pilgrims flock in crowds to the temple. Not less than seventy or eighty thousand people are said to visit the place on these occasions, when all castes eat together.

CASTES

The division of the Hindus into classes or castes, with fixed occupations, existed from the earliest times. It is supposed by some to have been founded upon conquest, the first three castes being composed of a foreign race, who subdued the natives of the country and reduced them to an inferior caste. Others trace it to the fondness of perpetuating, by descent from father to son, certain offices or occupations.

The Hindu tradition gives the following account of the origin of the various castes. At the creation Brahma resolved to give the earth inhabitants who should be direct emanations from his own body. Accordingly from his mouth came forth the eldest born, Brahma (the priest), to whom he confided the four Vedas; from his right arm issued Shatriya (the warrior), and from his left, the warrior's wife. His thighs produced Vaissyas, male and female (agriculturists and traders), and lastly from his feet sprang Sudras (mechanics and laborers).

The four sons of Brahma, so significantly brought into the world, became the fathers of the human race, and heads of their respective castes. They were commanded to regard the four Vedas as containing all the rules of their faith, and all that was necessary to guide them in their religious ceremonies. They were also commanded to take rank in the order of their birth, the Brahmans uppermost, as having sprung from the head of Brahma.

A strong line of demarcation is drawn between the first three castes and the Sudras. The former are allowed to receive instruction from the Vedas, which is not permitted to the Sudras. The Brahmans possess the privilege of teaching the Vedas, and were in former times in exclusive possession of all knowledge. Though the sovereign of the country was chosen from the Shatriya class, also called Rajputs, the Brahmans possessed the real power, and were the royal counsellors, the judges and magistrates of the country; their persons and property were inviolable; and though they committed the greatest crimes, they could only be banished from the kingdom. They were to be treated by sovereigns with the greatest respect, for "a Brahman, whether learned or ignorant, is a powerful divinity."

When the Brahman arrives at years of maturity it becomes his duty to marry. He ought to be supported by the contributions of the rich, and not to be obliged to gain his subsistence by any laborious or productive occupation. But as all the Brahmans could not he maintained by the working classes of the community, it was found necessary to allow them to engage in productive employments.

We need say little of the two intermediate classes, whose rank and privileges may be readily inferred from their occupations. The Sudras or fourth class are bound to servile attendance on the higher classes, especially the Brahmans, but they may follow mechanical occupations and practical arts, as painting and writing, or become traders or husbandmen. Consequently, they sometimes grow rich, and it will also sometimes happen that Brahmans become poor. That fact works its usual consequence, and rich Sudras sometimes employ poor Brahmans in menial occupations.

There is another class lower even than the Sudras, for it is not one of the original pure classes, but springs from an unauthorized union of individuals of different castes. These are the Pariahs, who are employed in the lowest services and treated with the utmost severity. They are compelled to do what no one else can do without pollution. They are not only considered unclean themselves, but they render unclean everything they touch. They are deprived of all civil rights, and stigmatized by particular laws, regulating their mode of life, their houses and their furniture. They are not allowed to visit the pagodas or temples of the other castes, but have their own pagodas and religious exercises. They are not suffered to enter the houses of the other castes; if it is done incautiously or from necessity, the place must be purified by religious ceremonies. They must not appear at public markets, and are confined to the use of particular wells, which they are obliged to surround with bones of animals, to warn others against using them. They dwell in miserable hovels, distant from cities and villages, and are under no restrictions in regard to food, which last is not a privilege, but a mark of ignominy, as if they were so degraded that nothing could pollute them. The three higher castes are prohibited entirely the use of flesh. The fourth is allowed to eat all kinds except beef, but only the lowest caste is allowed every kind of food without restrictions.

BUDDHA

Buddha, whom the Vedas represent as a delusive incarnation of Vishnu, is said by his followers to have been a mortal sage, whose name was Gautama, called also by the complimentary epithets of Sakyasinha, the Lion, and Buddha, the Sage.

By a comparison of the various epochs assigned to his birth, it is inferred that he lived about one thousand years before Christ.

He was the son of a king; and when in conformity to the usage of the country he was, a few days after his birth, presented before the altar of a deity, the image is said to have inclined its head, as a presage of the future greatness of the new-born prophet. The child soon developed faculties of the first order, and became equally distinguished by the uncommon beauty of his person. No sooner had he grown to years of maturity than he began to reflect deeply on the depravity and misery of mankind, and he conceived the idea of retiring from society and devoting himself to meditation. His father in vain opposed this design. Buddha escaped the vigilance of his guards, and having found a secure retreat, lived for six years undisturbed in his devout contemplations. At the expiration of that period he came forward at Benares as a religious teacher. At first some who heard him doubted of the soundness of his mind; but his doctrines soon gained credit, and were propagated so rapidly that Buddha himself lived to see them spread all over India.

The young prince distinguished himself by his personal and intellectual qualities, but still more by his early piety. It appears from the laws of Manu that it was not unusual, in the earliest periods of Brahmanism, for those seeking a superior piety to turn hermits, and to live alone in the forest, engaged in acts of prayer, meditation, abstinence, and the study of the Vedas. This practice, however, seems to have been confined to the Brahmans. It was, therefore, a grief to the king, when his son, in the flower of his youth and highly accomplished in every kingly faculty of body and mind, began to turn his thoughts toward the life of an anchorite.

* * * * * * * * * * * *

He first visited the Brahmans, and listened to their doctrines, but found no satisfaction therein. The wisest among them could not teach him true peace, that profound inward rest, which was already called Nirvana. He was twenty-nine years old. Although disapproving of the Brahmanic austerities as an end, he practised them during six years, in order to subdue the senses. He then became satisfied that the path to perfection did not lie that way. He therefore resumed his former diet and a more comfortable mode of life, and so lost many disciples who had been attracted by his amazing austerity. Alone in his hermitage, he came at last to that solid conviction, that KNOWLEDGE never to be shaken, of the laws of things, which had seemed to him the only foundation of a truly free life. The spot where, after a week of constant meditation, he at last arrived at this beatific vision, became one of the most sacred places in India. He was seated under a tree, his face to the east, not having moved for a day and night, when he attained the triple science, which was to rescue mankind from its woes. Twelve hundred years after the death of the Buddha, a Chinese pilgrim was shown what then passed for the sacred tree.

* * * * * * * * * * * *

Having attained this inward certainty of vision, he decided to teach the world his truth. He knew well what it would bring him, what opposition, insult, neglect, scorn. But he thought of three classes of men: those who were already on the way to the truth and did not need him; those who were fixed in error and whom he could not help; and the poor doubters, uncertain of their way. It was to help these last, the doubters, that the Buddha went forth to preach. On his way to the holy city of India, Benares, a serious difficulty arrested him at the Ganges, namely, his having no money to pay the boatman for his passage. At Benares he made his first converts, "turning the wheel of the law" for the first time. His discourses are contained in the sacred books of the Buddhists. He converted great numbers, his father among the rest, but met with fierce opposition from the Hindu Scribes and Pharisees, the leading Brahmans. So he lived and taught, and died at the age of eighty years.

The Buddhists reject entirely the authority of the Vedas, and the religious observances prescribed in them and kept by the Hindus. They also reject the distinction of castes, and prohibit all bloody sacrifices, and allow animal food. Their priests are chosen from all classes; they are expected to procure their maintenance by perambulation and begging, and, among other things, it is their duty to endeavor to turn to some use things thrown aside as useless by others, and to discover the medicinal power of plants. But in Ceylon three orders of priests are recognized; those of the highest order are usually men of high birth and learning, and are supported at the principal temples, most of which have been richly endowed by the former monarchs of the country.

For several centuries after the appearance of Buddha, his sect seems to have been tolerated by the Brahmans, and Buddhism appears to have penetrated the peninsula of Hindustan in every direction, and to have been carried to Ceylon, and to the eastern peninsula. But afterwards it had to endure in India a long continued persecution, which ultimately had the effect of entirely abolishing it in the country where it had originated, but to scatter it widely over adjacent countries. Buddhism appears to have been introduced into China about the year 65 of our era. From China it was subsequently extended to Korea, Japan, and Java.

The charming poem called the Light of Asia, by Mr. Edwin Arnold, has lately called general attention to Buddhism. The following is an extract from it:

"Fondly Siddatha drew the proud head down
Patted the shining neck, and said 'Be still,
White Kantaka! Be still, and bear me now
The farthest journey ever rider rode;
For this night take I horse to find the truth,
And where my quest will end yet know I not.
Save that it shall not end until I find.
Therefore to-night, good steed, be fierce and bold!
Let nothing stay thee, though a thousand blades
Deny the road! Let neither wall nor moat
Forbid our flight! Look! If I touch thy flank
And cry, "On, Kantaka!" let whirlwinds lag
Behind thy course! Be fire and air, my horse!
To stead thy lord, so shalt thou share with him
The greatness of this deed which helps the world;
For therefore ride I, not for men alone,
But for all things which, speechless, share our pain,
And have no hope, nor wit to ask for hope.
Now, therefore, hear thy master valorously!'"

THE GRAND LAMA, OR DALAI LAMA

It is a doctrine alike of the Brahminical Hindus and of the Buddhist sect that the confinement of the human soul, an emanation of the divine spirit, in a human body, is a state of misery, and the consequence of frailties and sins committed during former existences. But they hold that some few individuals have appeared on this earth from time to time, not under the necessity of terrestrial existence, but who voluntarily descend to the earth to promote the welfare of mankind. These individuals have gradually assumed the character of reappearances of Buddha himself, in which capacity the line is continued till the present day in the several Lamas of Tibet, China, and other countries where Buddhism prevails. In consequence of the victories of Gengis Khan and his successors, the Lama residing in Tibet was raised to the dignity of chief pontiff of the sect. A separate province was assigned to him as his own territory, and besides his spiritual dignity, he became to a limited extent a temporal monarch. He is styled the Dalai Lama.

The first Christian missionaries who proceeded to Tibet were surprised to find there in the heart of Asia a pontifical court and several other ecclesiastical institutions resembling those of the Roman Catholic church. They found convents for priests and nuns; also, processions and forms of religious worship, attended with much pomp and splendor; and many were induced by these similarities to consider Lamaism as a sort of degenerated Christianity. It is not improbable that the Lamas derived some of these practices from the Nestorial Christians, who were settled in Tartary when Buddhism was introduced into Tibet.

PRESTER JOHN

An early account, communicated probably by travelling merchants, of a Lama or spiritual chief among the Tartars, seems to have occasioned in Europe the report of a Presbyter or Prester John, a Christian pontiff, resident in Upper Asia. The Pope sent a mission in search of him, as did also Louis IX of France, some years later, but both missions were unsuccessful, though the small communities of Nestorial Christians, which they did find, served to keep up the belief in Europe that such a personage did exist somewhere in the East. At last in the fifteenth century, a Portuguese traveler, Pedro Covilham, happening to hear that there was a Christian prince in the country of the Abessines (Abyssinia), not far from the Red Sea, concluded that this must be the true Prester John. He accordingly went thither, and penetrated to the court of the king, whom he calls Negus. Milton alludes to him in Paradise Lost, Book XI, where, describing Adam's vision of his descendants in their various nations and cities, scattered over the face of the earth, he says,

"—— Nor did his eyes not ken
The empire of Negus, to his utmost port
Ercoco, and the less maritime kings,
Mombaza and Quiloa and Melind."

Figure 44: "Gran Lama" by Alain Manesson Mallet

Chapter 31

NORTHERN MYTHOLOGY VALHALLA THE VALKYRIE

The stories which have engaged our attention thus far relate to the mythology of southern regions. But there is another branch of ancient superstitions which ought not to be entirely overlooked, especially as it belongs to the nations from which we, through our English ancestors, derive our origin. It is that of the northern nations called Scandinavians, who inhabited the countries now known as Sweden, Denmark, Norway, and Iceland. These mythological records are contained in two collections called the Eddas, of which the oldest is in poetry and dates back to the year 1056, the more modern, or prose Edda, being of the date of 1640.

According to the Eddas there was once no heaven above nor earth beneath, but only a bottomless deep, and a world of mist in which flowed a fountain. Twelve rivers issued from this fountain, and when they had flowed far from their source, they froze into ice, and one layer accumulating above another, the great deep was filled up.

Southward from the world of mist was the world of light. From this flowed a warm wind upon the ice and melted it. The vapors rose in the air and formed clouds, from which sprang Ymir, the Frost giant and his progeny, and the cow Audhumbla, whose milk afforded nourishment and food to the giant. The cow got nourishment by licking the hoar frost and salt from the ice. While she was one day licking the salt stones there appeared at first the hair of a man, on the second day the whole head, and on the third the entire form endowed with beauty, agility, and power. This new being was a god, from whom and his wife, a daughter of the giant race, sprang the three brothers Odin, Vili, and Ve. They slew the giant Ymir, and out of his body formed the earth, of his blood the seas, of his bones the mountains, of his hair the trees, of his skull the heavens, and of his brain clouds, charged with hail and snow. Of Ymir's eyebrows the gods formed Midgard (mid earth), destined to become the abode of man.

Odin then regulated the periods of day and night and the seasons by placing in the heavens the sun and moon, and appointing to them their respective courses. As soon as the sun began to shed its rays upon the earth, it caused the vegetable world to bud and sprout. Shortly after the gods had created the world they walked by the side of the sea, pleased with their new work, but found that it was still incomplete, for it was without human beings. They therefore took an ash-tree and made a man out of it, and they made a woman out of an alder, and called the man Aske and the woman Embla. Odin then gave them life and soul, Vili reason and motion, and Ve bestowed upon them the senses, expressive features, and speech. Midgard was then given them as their residence, and they became the progenitors of the human race.

The mighty ash-tree Ygdrasil was supposed to support the whole universe. It sprang from the body of Ymir, and had three immense roots, extending one into Asgard (the dwelling of the gods), the other into Jotunheim (the abode of the giants), and the third to Niffleheim (the regions of darkness and cold). By the side of each of these roots is a spring, from which it is watered. The root that extends into Asgard is carefully tended by the three Norns, goddesses who are regarded as the dispensers of fate. They are Urdur (the past), Verdandi (the present), Skuld (the future). The spring at the Jotunheim side is Ymir's well, in which wisdom and wit lie hidden, but that of Niffleheim feeds the adder, Nidhogge (darkness), which perpetually gnaws at the root. Four harts run across the branches of the tree and bite the buds; they represent the four winds. Under the tree lies Ymir, and when he tries to shake off its weight the earth quakes.

Asgard is the name of the abode of the gods, access to which is only gained by crossing the bridge, Bifrost (the rainbow). Asgard consists of golden and silver palaces, the dwellings of the gods, but the most beautiful of these is Valhalla, the residence of Odin. When seated on his throne he overlooks all heaven and earth. Upon his shoulders are the ravens Hugin and Munin, who fly every day over the whole world, and on their return report to him all they have seen and heard. At his feet lie his two wolves, Geri, and Freki, to whom Odin gives all the meat that is set before him, for he himself stands in no need of food. Mead is for him both food and drink. He invented the Runic characters, and it is the business of the Norns to engrave the runes of fate upon a metal shield. From Odin's name, spelt Wodin, as it sometimes is, came Wednesday, the name of the fourth day of the week.

Odin is frequently called Alfadur (All-father), but this name is sometimes used in a way that shows that the Scandinavians had an idea of a deity superior to Odin, uncreated and eternal.

OF THE JOYS OF VALHALLA

Valhalla is the great hall of Odin, wherein he feasts with his chosen heroes, all those who have fallen bravely in battle, for all who die a peaceful death are excluded. The flesh of the boar Schrimnir is served up to them, and is abundant for all. For although this boar is cooked every morning, he becomes whole again every night. For drink the heroes are supplied abundantly with mead from the she-goat Heidrun. When the heroes are not feasting they amuse themselves with fighting. Every day they ride out into the court or field and fight until they cut each other in pieces. This is their pastime; but when meal-time comes, they recover from their wounds and return to feast in Valhalla.

Figure 45: "The Valkyrie" by Arthur Rackham

THE VALKYRIES

The Valkyrie are warlike virgins, mounted upon horses and armed with helmets, shields, and spears. Odin, who is desirous to collect a great many heroes in Valhalla, to be able to meet the giants in a day when the final contest must come, sends down to every battle-field to make choice of those who shall be slain. The Valkyrie are his messengers, and their name means "Choosers of the slain." When they ride forth on their errand their armor shed a strange flickering light, which flashes up over the northern skies, making what men call the "Aurora Borealis," or "Northern Lights." (Gray's ode, The Fatal Sisters, is founded on this superstition.)

The following is by Matthew Arnold:

"——He crew at dawn a cheerful note,
To wake the gods and heroes to their tasks
And all the gods and all the heroes woke.
And from their beds the heroes rose and donned
Their arms, and led their horses from the stall,
And mounted them, and in Valhalla's court
Were ranged; and then the daily fray began,
And all day long they there are hacked and hewn
'Mid dust and groans, and limbs lopped off, and blood;
But all at night return to Odin's hall
Woundless and fresh; such lot is theirs in heaven.
And the Valkyries on their steeds went forth
Toward earth and fights of men; and at their side
Skulda, the youngest of the Nornies, rode;
And over Bifrost, where is Heimdall's watch,
Past Midgard Fortress, down to Earth they came;
There through some battle-field, where men fall fast,
Their horses fetlock-deep in blood, they ride,
And pick the bravest warriors out for death,
Whom they bring back with them at night to heaven,
To glad the gods, and feast in Odin's hall."
BALDER DEAD

This description of The Funeral of Balder is by William Morris:

"——Guest
Gazed through the cool dusk, till his eyes did rest
Upon the noble stories, painted fair

On the high panelling and roof-boards there;
For over the high sea, in his ship, there lay
The gold-haired Balder, god of the dead day,
The spring-flowers round his high pile, waiting there
Until the gods there to the torch should bear;
And they were wrought on this side and on that,
Drawing on towards him. There was Frey, and sat
On the gold-bristled boar, who first they say
Ploughed the brown earth, and made it green for Frey;
Then came dark-bearded Niod; and after him
Freyia, thin-robed, about her ankles slim
The grey cats playing. In another place
Thor's hammer gleamed o'er Thor's red-bearded face;
And Heimdal, with the old horn slung behind,
That in the god's dusk he shall surely wind,
Sickening all hearts with fear; and last of all,
Was Odin's sorrow wrought upon the wall.
As slow-paced, weary faced, he went along,
Anxious with all the tales of woe and wrong
His ravens, Thought and Memory, bring to him."
THE EARTHLY PARADISE: THE LOVERS OF GODRUN THOR

THOR

OF THOR AND THE OTHER GODS

Thor, the thunderer, Odin's eldest son, is the strongest of gods and men, and possesses three very precious things. The first is his hammer, Miolnir, which both the Frost and the Mountain giants know to their cost, when they see it hurled against them in the air, for it has split many a skull of their fathers and kindred. When thrown, it returns to his hand of its own accord. The second rare thing he possesses is called the belt of strength. When he girds it about him his divine might is doubled. The third, also very precious, is his iron gloves, which he puts on whenever he would use his mallet efficiently. From Thor's name is derived our word Thursday.

This description of Thor is by Longfellow:

"I am the God Thor,
I am the War God,
I am the Thunderer!
Here in my Northland,
My fastness and fortress,
Reign I forever!

"Here amid icebergs
Rule I the nations;
This is my hammer,
Miolner the mighty;
Giants and sorcerers
Cannot withstand it!

"These are the gauntlets
Wherewith I wield it,
And hurl it afar off;
This is my girdle;
Whenever I brace it
Strength is redoubled!

"The light thou beholdest
Stream through the heavens,
In flashes of crimson,
Is but my red beard
Blown by the night wind,
Affrighting the nations!

"Jove is my brother;
Mine eyes are the lightning;
The wheels of my chariot
Roll in the thunder,
The blows of my hammer
Ring in the thunder."
TALES OF A WAYSIDE INN

Frey is one of the most celebrated of the gods. He presides over rain and sunshine and all the fruits of the earth. His sister Freya is the most propitious of the goddesses. She loves music, spring, and flowers, and is particularly fond of the Elves (fairies). She is very fond of love-ditties, and all lovers would do well to invoke her.

Bragi is the god of poetry, and his song records the deeds of warriors. His wife, Iduna, keeps in a box the apples which the gods, when they feel old age approaching, have only to taste of to become young again.

Heimdall is the watchman of the gods, and is therefore placed on the borders of heaven to prevent the giants from forcing their way over the bridge Bifrost (the rainbow.) He requires less sleep than a bird, and sees by night as well as by day a hundred miles all around him. So acute is his ear that no sound escapes him, for he can even hear the grass grow and the wool on a sheep's back.

OF LOKI AND HIS PROGENY

There is another deity who is described as the calumniator of the gods and the contriver of all fraud and mischief. His name is Loki. He is handsome and well made, but of a very fickle mood and most evil disposition. He is of the giant race, but forced himself into the company of the gods, and seems to take pleasure in bringing them into difficulties, and in extricating them out of the danger by his cunning, wit, and skill. Loki has three children. The first is the wolf Fenris, the second the Midgard serpent, the third Hela (Death). The gods were not ignorant that these monsters were growing up, and that they would one day bring much evil upon gods and men. So Odin deemed it advisable to send one to bring them to him. When they came he threw the serpent into that deep ocean by which the earth is surrounded. But the monster has grown to such an enormous size that holding his tail in his mouth he encircles the whole earth. Hela he cast into Niffleheim, and gave her power over nine worlds or regions, into which she distributes those who are sent to her; that is, all who die of sickness or old age. Her hall is called Elvidnia. Hunger is her table, Starvation her knife, Delay her man, Slowness her maid, Precipice her threshold, Care her bed, and Burning-anguish forms the hangings of her apartments. She may easily be recognized for her body is half flesh-color and half blue, and she has a dreadfully stern and forbidding countenance.

The wolf Fenris gave the gods a great deal of trouble before they succeeded in chaining him. He broke the strongest fetters as if they were made of cobwebs. Finally the gods sent a messenger to the mountain spirits, who made for them the chain called Gleipnir. It is fashioned of six things, viz., th noise made by the footfall of a cat, the beards of women, the roots of stones, the breath of fishes, the nerves (sensibilities) of bears, and the spittle of birds. When finished it was as smooth and soft as a silken string. But when the gods asked the wolf to suffer himself to be bound with this apparently slight ribbon, he suspected their design, fearing that it was made by enchantment. But Tyr (the sword god), to quiet his suspicions, placed his hand in Fenris' mouth. Then the other gods bound the wolf with Gleipnir. But when the wolf found that he could not break his fetters, and that the gods would not release him, he bit off Tyr's hand, and he has ever since remained one-handed.

HOW THOR PAID THE MOUNTAIN GIANT HIS WAGES

Once on a time, when the gods were constructing their abodes and had already finished Midgard and Valhalla, a certain artificer came and offered to build them a residence so well fortified that they should be perfectly safe from the incursions of the Frost giants and the giants of the mountains. But he demanded for his reward the goddess Freya, together with the sun and moon. The gods yielded to his terms provided he would finish the whole work himself without any one's assistance, and all within the space of one winter. But if anything remained unfinished on the first day of summer he should forfeit the recompense agreed on. On being told these terms the artificer stipulated that he should be allowed the use of his horse Svadilfari, and this by the advice of Loki was granted to him. He accordingly set to work on the first day of winter, and during the night let his horse draw stone for the building. The enormous size of the stones struck the gods with astonishment, and they saw clearly that the horse did one half more of the toilsome work than his mater. Their bargain, however, had been concluded, and confirmed by solemn oaths, for without these precautions a giant would not have thought himself safe among the gods, especially when Thor should return from an expedition he had then undertaken against the evil demons.

As the winter drew to a close, the building was far advanced, and the bulwarks were sufficiently high and massive to render the place impregnable. In short, when it wanted but three days to summer the only part that remained to be finished was the gateway. Then sat the gods on their seats of justice and entered into consultation, inquiring of one another who among them could have advised to give Freya away, or to plunge the heavens in darkness by permitting the giant to carry away the sun and the moon.

They all agreed that no one but Loki, the author of so many evil deeds, could have given such bad counsel, and that he should be put to a cruel death if he did not contrive some way to prevent the artificer from completing his task and obtaining the stipulated recompense. They proceeded to lay hands on Loki, who in his fright promised upon oath that, let it cost what it would, he would so manage matters that the man should lose his reward. That very night when the man went with Svadilfari for building- stone, a mare suddenly ran out of a forest and began to neigh. The horse thereat broke loose and ran after the mare into the forest, which obliged the man also to run after his horse, and thus between one and another the whole night was lost, so that at dawn the work had not made the usual progress. The man, seeing that he must fail of completing his task, resumed his own gigantic stature, and the gods now clearly perceived that it was in reality a mountain giant who had come amongst them. Feeling no longer bound by their oaths, they called on Thor, who immediately ran to their assistance, and lifting up his mallet, paid the workman his wages, not with the sun and moon, and not even by sending him back to Jotunheim, for with the first blow he shattered the giant's skull to pieces and hurled him headlong into Niffleheim.

THE RECOVERY OF THE HAMMER

Once upon a time it happened that Thor's hammer fell into the possession of the giant Thrym, who buried it eight fathoms deep under the rocks of Jotunheim. Thor sent Loki to negotiate with Thrym, but he could only prevail so far as to get the giant's promise to restore the weapon if Freya would consent to be his bride. Loki returned and reported the result of his mission, but the goddess of love was quite horrified at the idea of bestowing her charms on the king of the Frost giants. In this emergency Loki persuaded Thor to dress himself in Freya's clothes and accompany him to Jotunheim. Thrym received his veiled bride with due courtesy, but was greatly surprised at seeing her eat for her supper eight salmon and a full-grown ox, besides other delicacies, washing the whole down with three tuns of mead. Loki, however, assured him that she had not tasted anything for eight long nights, so great was her desire to see her lover, the renowned ruler or Jotunheim. Thrym had at length the curiosity to peep under his bride's veil, but started back in affright, and demanded why Freya's eyeballs glistened with fire. Loki repeated the same excuse and the giant was satisfied. He ordered the hammer to be brought in and laid on the maiden's lap. Thereupon Thor threw off his disguise, grasped his redoubted weapon and slaughtered Thrum and all his followers.

Frey also possessed a wonderful weapon, a sword which would of itself spread a field with carnage whenever the owner desired it. Frey parted with this sword, but was less fortunate than Thor and never recovered it. It happened in this way: Frey once mounted Odin's throne, from whence one can see over the whole universe, and looking round saw far off in the giant's kingdom a beautiful maid, at the sight of whom he was struck with sudden sadness, insomuch that from that moment he could neither sleep, nor drink, nor speak. At last Skirnir, his messenger, drew his secret from him, and undertook to get him the maiden for his bride, if he would give him his sword as a reward. Frey consented and gave him the sword, and Skirnir set off on his journey and obtained the maiden's promise that within nine nights she would come to a certain place and there wed Frey. Skirnir having reported the success of his errand, Frey exclaimed,

"Long is one night,
Long are two nights,
But how shall I hold out three?
Shorter hath seemed
A month to me oft
Than of this longing time the half."

So Frey obtained Gerda, the most beautiful of all women, for his wife, but he lost his sword.

This story, entitled Skirnir For, and the one immediately preceding it, Thrym's Quida, will be found poetically told in Longfellow's Poets and Poetry of Europe.

Chapter 32

THOR'S VISIT TO JOTUNHEIM

One day the god Thor, accompanied by his servant Thialfi, and also by Loki, set out on a journey to the giant's country. Thialfi was of all men the swiftest of foot. He bore Thor's wallet, containing their provisions. When night came on they found themselves in an immense forest, and searched on all sides for a place where they might pass the night, and at last came to a very large hall, with an entrance that took the whole breadth of one end of the building. Here they lay down to sleep, but towards midnight were alarmed by an earthquake which shook the whole edifice. Thor rising up called on his companion to seek with him a place of safety. On the right they found an adjoining chamber, into which the others entered, but Thor remained at the doorway with his mallet in his hand, prepared to defend himself, whatever might happen. A terrible groaning was heard during the night, and at dawn of day Thor went out and found lying near him a huge giant, who slept and snored in the way that had alarmed them so. It is said that for once Thor was afraid to use his mallet, and as the giant soon waked up, Thor contented himself with simply asking his name.

"My name is Skrymir," said the giant, "but I need not ask thy name, for I know that thou art the god Tor. But what has become of my glove?" Thor then perceived that what they had taken overnight for a hall was the giant's glove and the chamber where his two companions had sought refuge was the thumb. Skrymir then proposed that they should travel in company, and Thor consenting, they sat down to eat their breakfast, and when they had done, Skrymir packed all the provisions into one wallet, threw it over his shoulder, and strode on before them, taking such tremendous strides that they were hard put to it to keep up with him. So they travelled the whole day, and at dusk, Skrymir close a place for them to pass the night in under a large oak-tree. Skrymir then told them he would lie down to sleep. "But take ye the wallet," he added, "and prepare your supper."Skrymir soon fell asleep and began to snore strongly, but when Thor tried to open the wallet, he found the giant had tied it up so tight he could not untie a single knot. At last Thor became wroth, and grasping his mallet with both hands he struck a furious blow on the giant's head. Skrymir awakening merely asked whether a leaf had not fallen on his head, and whether they had supped and were ready to go to sleep. Thor answered that they were just going to sleep, and so saying went and laid himself down under another tree. But sleep came not that night to Thor, and when Skrymir snored again so loud that the forest re-echoed with the noise, he arose, and grasping his mallet launched it with such force at the giant's skull that it made a deep dint in it. Skrymir awakening cried out, "What's the matter? Are there any birds perched on this tree? I felt some moss from the branches fall on my head. How fares it with thee, Thor?" But Thor went away hastily, saying that he had just then awoke, and that as it was only midnight, there was still time for sleep. He however resolved that if he had an opportunity of striking

Figure 46: "I Am the Giant Skrymir" by Elmer Boyd Smith

a third blow, it should settle all matters between them. A little before daybreak he perceived that Skrymir was again fast asleep, and again grasping his mallet, he dashed it with such violence that it forced its way into the giant's skull up to the handle. But Skrymir sat up, and stroking his cheek, said, "An acorn fell on my head. What! Art thou awake, Thor? Methinks it is time for us to get up and dress ourselves; but you have not now a long way before you to the city called Utgard. I have heard you whispering to one another that I am not a man of small dimensions; but if you come to Utgard you will see there many men much taller than I. Wherefore I advise you, when you come there, not to make too much of yourselves, for the followers of Utgard-Loki will not brook the boasting of such little fellows as you are. You must take the road that leads eastward, mine lies northward, so we must part here."

Hereupon he threw his wallet over his shoulders, and turned away from them into the forest, and Thor had no wish to stop him or to ask for any more of his company.

Figure 47: "Thor's Fight with the Giants" by Marten Eskil Winge

Thor and his companions proceeded on their way, and towards noon descried a city standing in the middle of a plain. It was so lofty that they were obliged to bend their necks quite back on their shoulders in order to see to the top of it. On arriving they entered the city, and seeing a large palace before them with the door wide open, they went in, and found a number of men of prodigious stature, sitting on benches in the hall. Going further, they came before the king Utgard-Loki, whom they saluted with great respect. The king, regarding them with a scornful smile, said, "If I do not mistake me, that stripling yonder must be the god Thor." Then addressing himself to Thor, he said, "Perhaps thou mayst be more than thou appearest to be. What are the feats that thou and thy fellows deem yourselves skilled in, for no one is permitted to remain here who does not, in some feat or other, excel all other men?"

"The feat that I know," said Loki, "is to eat quicker than anyone else, and in this I am ready to give a proof against anyone here who may choose to compete with me."

"That will indeed be a feat," said Utgard-Loki, "if thou performest what thou promisest, and it shall be tried forthwith."

He then ordered one of his men who was sitting at the farther end of the bench, and whose name was Logi, to come forward and try his skill with Loki. A trough filled with meat having been set on the hall floor, Loki placed himself at one end, and Logi at the other, and each of them began to eat as fast as he could, until they met in the middle of the trough. But it was found that Loki had only eaten the flesh, while his adversary had devoured both flesh and bone, and the trough to boot. All the company therefore adjudged that Loki was vanquished.

Utgard-Loki then asked what feat the young man who accompanied Thor could perform. Thialfi answered that he would run a race with any one who might be matched against him. The king observed that skill in running was something to boast of, but if the youth would win the match he must display great agility. He then arose and went with all who were present to a plain where there was good ground for running on, and calling a young man named Hugi, bade him run a match with Thialfi. In the first course Hugi so much outstripped his competitor that he turned back and met him not far from the starting-place.

Then they ran a second and a third time, but Thialfi met with no better success. Utgard-Loki then asked Thor in what feats he would choose to give proofs of that prowess for which he was so famous. Thor answered that he would try a drinking-match with any one. Utgard-Loki bade his cupbearer bring the large horn which his followers were obliged to empty when they had trespassed in any way against the law of the feast. The cupbearer having presented it to Thor, Utgard- Loki said, "Whoever is a good drinker will empty that horn at a single draught, though most men make two of it, but the most puny drinker can do it in three."

Thor looked at the horn, which seemed of no extraordinary size though somewhat long; however, as he was very thirsty, he set it to his lips, and without drawing breath, pulled as long and as deeply as he could, that he might not be obliged to make a second draught of it; but when he set the horn down and looked in, he could scarcely perceive that the liquor was diminished.

After taking breath, Thor went to it again with all his might, but when he took the horn from his mouth, it seemed to him that he had drunk rather less than before, although the horn could now be carried without spilling.

"How now, Thor," said Utgard-Loki, "thou must not spare thyself; if thou meanest to drain the horn at the third draught thou must pull deeply; and I must needs say that thou wilt not be called so mighty a man here as thou art at home if thou showest no greater prowess in other feats than methinks will be shown in this."

Thor, full of wrath, again set the horn to his lips, and did his best to empty it; but on looking in found the liquor was only a little lower, so he resolved to make no further attempt, but gave back the horn to the cupbearer.

"I now see plainly," said Utgard-Loki, "that thou art not quite so stout as we thought thee; but wilt thou try any other feat, though methinks thou art not likely to bear any prize away with thee hence."

"What new trial hast thou to propose?" said Thor.

"We have a very trifling game here," answered Utgard-Loki, "in which we exercise none but children. It consists in merely lifting my cat from the ground; nor should I have dared to mention such a feat to the great Thor if I had not already observed that thou art by no means what we took thee for."

As he finished speaking, a large gray cat sprang on the hall floor. Thor put his hand under the cat's belly and did his utmost to raise him from the floor, but the cat, bending his back, had, notwithstanding all Thor's efforts, only one of his feet lifted up, seeing which Thor made no further attempt.

"This trial has turned out," said Utgard-Loki, "just as I imagined it would. The cat is large, but Thor is little in comparison to our men."

"Little as ye call me," answered Thor, "let me see who among you will come hither now I am in wrath and wrestle with me."

"I see no one here," said Utgard-Loki, looking at the men sitting on the benches, "who would not think it beneath him to wrestle with thee; let somebody, however, call hither that old crone, my nurse Elli, and let Thor wrestle with her if he will. She has thrown to the ground many a man not less strong than this Thor is."

A toothless old woman then entered the hall, and was told by Utgard-Loki to take hold of Thor. The tale is shortly told. The more Thor tightened his hold on the crone the firmer she stood. At length, after a very violent struggle, Thor began to lose his footing, and was finally brought down upon one knee. Utgard-Loki then told them to desist, adding that Thor had now no occasion to ask any one else in the hall to wrestle with him, and it was also getting late; so he showed Thor and his companions to their seats, and they passed the night there in good cheer.

The next morning at break of day, Thor and his companions dressed themselves and prepared for their departure. Utgard-Loki ordered a table to be set for them, on which there was no lack of victuals or drink. After the repast Utgard-Loki led them to the gate of the city, and on parting asked Thor how he thought his journey had turned out, and whether he had met with any men stronger than himself. Thor told him that he could not deny but that he had brought great shame on himself. "And what grieves me most," he added, is that ye will call me a person of little worth."

"Nay," said Utgard-Loki, "it behooves me to tell thee the truth, now thou art out of the city, which so long as I live and have my way thou shalt never enter again. And, by my troth, had I known beforehand that thou hadst so much strength in thee, and wouldst have brought me so near to a great mishap, I would not have suffered thee to enter this time. Know then that I have all along deceived thee by my illusions; first in the forest where I tied up the wallet with iron wire so that thou couldst not untie it. After this thou gavest me three blows with the mallet; the first, though the least, would have ended my days had it fallen on me, but I slipped aside and thy blows fell on the mountain where thou wilt find three glens, one of them remarkably deep. These are the dints made by thy mallet. I have made use of similar illusions in the contests you have had with my followers. In the first, Loki, like hunger itself, devoured all that was set before him, but Logi was in reality nothing else than Fire, and therefore consumed not only the meat, but the trough which held it. Hugi, with whom Thialfi contended in running, was Thought, and it was impossible for Thialfi to keep pace with that. When thou in thy turn didst attempt to empty the horn, thou didst perform, by my troth, a deed so marvellous, that had I not seen it myself, I should never have believed it. For one end of that horn reached the sea, which thou was not aware of, but when thou comest to the shore thou wilt perceive how much the sea has sunk by thy draughts. Thou didst perform a feat no less wonderful by lifting up the cat, and to tell thee the truth, when we saw that one of his paws was off the floor, we were all of us terror- stricken, for what thou tookest for a cat was in reality the Midgard serpent that encompasseth the earth, and he was so stretched by thee, that he was barely long enough to enclose it between his head and tail. Thy wrestling with Elli was also a most astonishing feat, for there was never yet a man, nor ever will be, whom Old Age, for such in fact was Elli, will not sooner or later lay low. But now, as we are going to part, let me tell thee that it will be better for both of us if thou never come near me again, for shouldst thou do so, I shall again defend myself by other illusions, so that thou wilt only lose thy labor and get no fame from the contest with me."

On hearing these words Thor in a rage laid hold of his mallet and would have launched it at him, but Utgard-Loki had disappeared, and when Thor would have returned to the city to destroy it, he found nothing around him but a verdant plain.

On another occasion Thor was more successful in an encounter with the giants. It happened that Thor met with a giant, Hrungnir by name, who was disputing with Odin as to the merits of their respective horses, Gullfaxi and Sleipnir, the eight-legged. Thor and the giant made an agreement to fight together on a certain day. But as the day approached, the giant, becoming frightened at the thought of encountering Thor alone, manufactured, with the assistance of his fellow-giants, a great giant of clay. He was nine miles high and three miles about the chest, and in his heart he had the heart of a mare. Accompanied by the clay giant, Hrungnir awaited Thor on the appointed day. Thor approached preceded by Thialfi, his servant, who, running ahead, shouted out to Hrungnir that it was useless to hold his shield before him, for the god Thor would attack him out of the ground. Hrungnir at this flung his shield on the ground, and, standing upon it, made ready. As Thor approached Hrungnir flung at him an immense club of stone. Thor flung his hammer. Miolnir met the club half way, broke it in pieces, and burying itself in the stone skull of Hrungnir, felled him to the ground. Meanwhile Thialfi had despatched the clay giant with a spade. Thor himself received but a slight wound from a fragment of the giant's hammer.

Figure 48: "My Hammer's Swing" by Arhtur Rackham

Chapter 33

THE DEATH OF BALDUR, OR BALDER, OR BALDR. THE ELVES. RUNIC LETTERS. SKALDS. ICELAND

Baldur, the Good, having been tormented with terrible dreams indicating that his life was in peril, told them to the assembled gods, who resolved to conjure all things to avert from him the threatened danger. Then Frigga, the wife of Odin, exacted an oath from fire and water, from iron and all other metals, from stones, trees, diseases, beasts, birds, poisons, and creeping things, that none of them would do any harm to Baldur. Odin, not satisfied with all this, and feeling alarmed for the fate of his son, determined to consult the prophetess Angerbode, a giantess, mother of Fenris, Hela, and the Midgard serpent. She was dead, and Odin was forced to seek her in Hela's dominions. This descent of Odin forms the subject of Gray's fine ode beginning,

---

"Up rose the king of men with speed
And saddled straight his coal-black steed."

But the other gods, feeling that what Frigga had done was quite sufficient, amused themselves with using Baldur as a mark, some hurling darts at him, some stones, while others hewed at him with their swords and battle-axes, for do what they would none of them could harm him. And this became a favorite pastime with them and was regarded as an honor shown to Baldur. But when Loki beheld the scene he was sorely vexed that Baldur was not hurt. Assuming, therefore, the shape of a woman, he went to Fensalir, the mansion of Frigga. That goddess, when she saw the pretended woman, inquired of her if she knew what the gods were doing at their meetings. She replied that they were throwing darts and stones at Baldur, without being able to hurt him. "Ay," said Frigga, "neither stones, nor sticks, nor anything else can hurt Baldur, for I have exacted an oath from all of them. " "What," exclaimed the woman, "have all things sworn to spare Baldur?" "All things," replied Frigga, "except one little shrub that grows on the eastern side of Valhalla, and is called Mistletoe, and which I thought too young and feeble to crave an oath from."

As soon as Loki heard this he went away, and resuming his natural shape, cut off the mistletoe, and repaired to the place where the gods were assembled. There he found Hodur standing apart, without partaking of the sports, on account of his blindness, and going up to him, said, "Why dost thou not also throw something at Baldur?"

"Because I am blind," answered Hodur, "and see not where Baldur is, and have moreover nothing to throw."

"Come, then," said Loki, "do like the rest and show honor to Baldur by throwing this twig at him, and I will direct thy arm towards the place where he stands."

Hodur then took the mistletoe, and under the guidance of Loki, darted it at Baldur, who, pierced through and through, fell down lifeless. Surely never was there witnessed, either among gods or men, a more atrocious deed than this. When Baldur fell, the gods were struck speechless with horror, and then they looked at each other, and all were of one mind to lay hands on him who had done the deed, but they were obliged to delay their vengeance out of respect for the sacred place where they were assembled. They gave vent to their grief by loud lamentations. When the gods came to themselves, Frigga asked who among them wished to gain all her love and good will. "For this," said she, "shall he have who will ride to Hel and offer Hela a ransom if she will let Baldur return to Asgard." Whereupon Hermod, surnamed the Nimble, the son of Odin, offered to undertake the journey. Odin's horse, Sleipnir, which has eight legs, and can outrun the wind, was then led forth, on which Hermod mounted and galloped away on his mission. For the space of nine days and as many nights he rode through deep glens so dark that he could not discern anything until he arrived at the river Gyoll, which he passed over on a bridge covered with glittering gold. The maiden who kept the bridge asked him his name and lineage, telling him that the day before five bands of dead persons had ridden over the bridge, and did not shake it as much as he alone. "But," she added, "thou hast not death's hue on thee; why then ridest thou here on the way to Hel?"

"I ride to Hel," answered Hermod, "to seek Baldur. Hast thou perchance seen him pass this way?"

She replied, "Baldur hath ridden over Gyoll's bridge, and yonder lieth the way he took to the abodes of death."

Hermod pursued his journey until he came to the barred gates of Hel. Here he alighted, girthed his saddle tighter, and remounting clapped both spurs to his horse, who cleared the gate by a tremendous leap without touching it. Hermod then rode on to the palace where he found his brother Baldur occupying the most distinguished seat in the hall, and passed the night in his company. The next morning he besought Hela to let Baldur ride home with him, assuring her that nothing but lamentations were to be heard among the gods. Hela answered that it should now be tried whether Baldur was so beloved as he was said to be. "If, therefore," she added, "all things in the world, both living and lifeless, weep for him, then shall he return to life; but if any one thing speak against him or refuse to weep, he shall be kept in Hel."

Hermod then rode back to Asgard and gave an account of all he had heard and witnessed.

The gods upon this despatched messengers throughout the world to beg every thing to weep in order that Baldur might be delivered from Hel. All things very willingly complied with this request, both men and every other living being, as well as earths, and stones, and trees, and metals, just as we have all seen these things weep when they are brought from a cold place into a hot one. As the messengers were returning, they found an old hag named Thaukt sitting in a cavern, and begged her to weep Baldur out of Hel. But she answered,

"Thaukt will wail
With dry tears
Baldur's bale-fire.
Let Hela keep her own."

It was strongly suspected that this hag was no other than Loki himself, who never ceased to work evil among gods and men. So Baldur was prevented from coming back to Asgard. (In Longfellow's Poems, vol. 1, page 379, will be found a poem entitled Tegner's Drapa, upon the subject of Baldur's death.)

Among Matthew Arnold's Poems is one called "Balder Death" beginning thus:

"So on the floor lay Balder dead; and round
Lay thickly strewn swords, axes, darts and spears,
Which all the Gods in sport had idly thrown
At Balder, whom no weapon pierced or clave;
But in his breast stood fixt the fatal bough
Of mistletoe, which Lok the Accuser gave
To Hoder, and unwitting Hoder threw;
"Gainst that alone had Balder's life no charm.
And all the Gods and all the heroes came
And stood round Balder on the bloody floor
Weeping and wailing; and Valhalla rang
Up to its golden roof with sobs and cries;
And on the table stood the untasted meats,
And in the horns and gold-rimmed skulls the wine;
And now would night have fallen and found them yet
Wailing; but otherwise was Odin's will."

THE FUNERAL OF BALDUR

The gods took up the dead body and bore it to the sea-shore where stood Baldur's ship Hringham, which passed for the largest in the world. Baldur's dead body was put on the funeral pile, on board the ship, and his wife Nanna was so struck with grief at the sight that she broke her heart, and her body was burned on the same pile with her husband's. There was a vast concourse of various kinds of people at Baldur's obsequies. First came Odin accompanied by Frigga, the Valkyrie, and his ravens; then Frey in his car drawn by Gullinbursti, the boar; Heimdall rode his horse Gulltopp, and Freya drove in her chariot drawn by cats. There were also a great many Frost giants and giants of the mountain present. Baldur's horse was led to the pile fully caparisoned and consumed in the same flames with his master.

But Loki did not escape his deserved punishment. When he saw how angry the gods were, he fled to the mountain, and there built himself a hut with four doors, so that he could see every approaching danger. He invented a net to catch the fishes, such as fishermen have used since his time. But Odin found out his hiding place and the gods assembled to take him. He, seeing this, changed himself into a salmon, and lay hid among the stones of the brook. But the gods took his net and dragged the brook, and Loki finding he must be caught, tried to leap over the net; but Thor caught him by the tail and compressed it so, that salmons ever since have had that part remarkably fine and

Figure 49: "Last Words to Baldr" by W. G. Collingwood

thin. They bound him with chains and suspended a serpent over his head, whose venom falls upon his face drop by drop. His wife Siguna sits by his side and catches the drops as they fall, in a cup; but when she carries it away to empty it, the venom falls upon Loki, which makes him howl with horror, and twist his body about so violently that the whole earth shakes, and this produces what men call earthquakes.

THE ELVES

The Edda mentions another class of beings, inferior to the gods, but still possessed of great power; these were called Elves. The white spirits, or Elves of Light, were exceedingly fair, more brilliant than the sun, and clad in garments of delicate and transparent texture. They loved the light, were kindly disposed to mankind, and generally appeared as fair and lovely children. Their country was called Alfheim, and was the domain of Freyr, the god of the sun, in whose light they were always sporting.

The black of Night Elves were a different kind of creatures. Ugly, long-nosed dwarfs, of a dirty brown color, they appeared only at night, for they avoided the sun as their most deadly enemy, because whenever his beams fell upon any of them they changed them immediately into stones. Their language was the echo of solitudes, and their dwelling-places subterranean caves and clefts. They were supposed to have come into existence as maggots, produced by the decaying flesh of Ymir's body, and were afterwards endowed by the gods with a human form and great understanding. They were particularly distinguished for a knowledge of the mysterious powers of nature, and for the runes which they carved and explained. They were the most skilful artificers of all created beings, and worked in metals and in wood. Among their most noted works were Thor's hammer, and the ship Skidbladnir, which they gave to Freyr, and which was so large that it could contain all the deities with their war and household implements, but so skilfully was it wrought that when folded together it could be put into a side pocket.

RAGNAROK, THE TWILIGHT OF THE GODS

It was a firm belief of the northern nations that a time would come when all the visible creation, the gods of Valhalla and Niffleheim, the inhabitants of Jotunheim, Alfheim, and Midgard, together with their habitations, would be destroyed. The fearful day of destruction will not, however, be without its forerunners. First will come a triple winter, during which snow will fall from the four corners of the heavens, the frost be very severe, the wind piercing, the weather tempestuous, and the sun impart no gladness. Three such winters will pass away without being tempered by a single summer. Three other similar winters will then follow, during which war and discord will spread over the universe. The earth itself will be frightened and begin to tremble, the sea leave its basin, the heavens tear asunder, and men perish in great numbers, and the eagles of the air feast upon their still quivering bodies. The wolf Fenris will now break his bands, the Midgard serpent rise out of her bed in the sea, and Loki, released from his bonds, will join the enemies of the gods. Amidst the general devastation the sons of Muspelheim will rush forth under their leader Surtur, before and behind whom are flames and burning fire. Onward they ride over Bifrost, the rainbow bridge, which breaks under the horses' hoofs. But they, disregarding its fall, direct their course to the battle-field called Vigrid. Thither also repair the wolf Fenris, the Midgard serpent, Loki with all the followers of Hela, and the Frost giants.

Heimdall now stands up and sounds the Giallar horn to assemble the gods and heroes for the contest. The gods advance, led on by Odin, who engages the wolf Fenris, but falls a victim to the monster, who is, however, slain by Vidar, Odin's son. Thor gains great renown by killing the Midgard serpent, but recoils and falls dead, suffocated with the venom which the dying monster vomits over him. Loki and Heimdall meet and fight till they are both slain.

The Gods and their enemies having fallen in battle, Surtur, who has killed Dreyr, darts fire and flames over the world, and the whole universe is burned up. The sun becomes dim, the earth sinks into the ocean, the stars fall from heaven, and time is no more.

After this Alfadur (the almighty) will cause a new heaven and a new earth to arise out of the sea. The new earth, filled with abundant supplies, will spontaneously produce its fruits without labor or care. Wickedness and misery will no more be known, but the gods and men will live happily together.

RUNIC LETTERS

One cannot travel far in Denmark, Norway, or Sweden, without meeting with great stones, of different forms, engraven with characters called Runic, which appear at first sight very different from all we know. The letters consist almost invariably of straight lines, in the shape of little sticks either singly or put together. Such sticks were in early times used by the northern nations for the purpose of ascertaining future events. The sticks were shaken up, and from the figures that they formed a kind of divination was derived.

The Runic characters were of various kinds. They were chiefly used for magical purposes. The noxious, or, as they called them, the BITTER runes, were employed to bring various evils on their enemies; the favorable averted misfortune. Some were medicinal, others employed to win love, etc. In later times they were frequently used for inscriptions, of which more than a thousand have been found. The language is a dialect of the Gothic, called Norse, still in use in Iceland. The inscriptions may therefore be read with certainty, but hitherto very few have been found which throw the least light on history. They are mostly epitaphs on tombstones.

Gray's ode on the Descent of Odin contains an allusion to the use of Runic letters for incantation:

"Facing to the northern clime,
Thrice he traced the Runic rhyme;
Thrice pronounced, in accents dread,
The thrilling verse that wakes the dead,
Till from out the hollow ground
Slowly breathed a sullen sound."

THE SKALDS

The Skalds were the bards and poets of the nation, a very important class of men in all communities in an early stage of civilization. They are the depositaries of whatever historic lore there is, and it is their office to mingle something of intellectual gratification with the rude feasts of the warriors, by rehearsing, with such accompaniments of poetry and music as their skill can afford, the exploits of their heroes living or dead. The compositions of the Skalds were called Sagas, many of which have come down to us, and contain valuable materials of history, and a faithful picture of the state of society at the time to which they relate.

ICELAND

The Eddas and Sagas have come to us from Iceland. The following extract from Carlyle's Lectures on Heroes and Hero worship gives an animated account of the region where the strange stories we have been reading had their origin. Let the reader contrast it for a moment with Greece, the parent of classical mythology.

"In that strange island, Iceland, burst up, the geologists say, by fire from the bottom of the sea, a wild land of barrenness and lava, swallowed many months of every year in black tempests, yet with a wild, gleaming beauty in summer time, towering up there stern and grim in the North Ocean, with its snow yokuls (mountains), roaring geysers (boiling springs), sulphur pools, and horrid volcanic chasms, like the vast, chaotic battle-field of Frost and Fire, where, of all places, we least looked for literature or written memorials, the record of these things was written down. On the seaboard of this wild land is a rim of grassy country, where cattle can subsist, and men by means of them and of what the sea yields; and it seems they were poetic men these, men who had deep thoughts in them and uttered musically their thoughts. Much would be lost had Iceland not been burst up from the sea, not been discovered by the Northmen!"

Chapter 34

THE DRUIDS IONA

The Druids were the priests or ministers of religion among the ancient Celtic nations in Gaul, Britain, and Germany. Our information respecting them is borrowed from notices in the Greek and Roman writers, compared with the remains of Welsh and Gaelic poetry still extant.

The Druids combined the functions of the priest, the magistrate, the scholar, and the physician. They stood to the people of the Celtic tribes in a relation closely analogous to that in which the Brahmans of India, the Magi of Persia, and the priests of the Egyptians stood to the people respectively by whom they were revered.

The Druids taught the existence of one God, to whom they gave a name "Be'al," which Celtic antiquaries tell us means "the life of everything," or "the source of all beings,:" and which seems to have affinity with the Phoenician Baal. What renders this affinity more striking is that the Druids as well as the Phoenicians identified this, their supreme deity, with the Sun. Fire was regarded as a symbol of the divinity. The Latin writers assert that the Druids also worshipped numerous inferior Gods. They used no images to represent the object of their worship, nor did they meet in temples or buildings of any kind for the performance of their sacred rites. A circle of stones (each stone generally of vast size) enclosing an area of from twenty feet to thirty yards in diameter, constituted their sacred place. The most celebrated of these now remaining is Stonehenge, on Salisbury Plain, England.

These sacred circles were generally situated near some stream, or under the shadow of a grove or widespreading oak. In the centre of the circle stood the Cromlech or altar, which was a large stone, placed in the manner of a table upon other stones set up on end. The Druids had also their high places, which were large stones or piles of stones on the summits of hills. These were called Cairns, and were used in the worship of the deity under the symbol of the sun.

That the Druids offered sacrifices to their deity there can be no doubt. But there is some uncertainty as to what they offered, and of the ceremonies connected with their religious services we know almost nothing. The classical (Roman) writers affirm that they offered on great occasions human sacrifices; as for success in war or for relief from dangerous diseases. Caesar has given a detailed account of the manner in which this was done. "They have images of immense size, the limbs of which are framed with twisted twigs and filled with living persons. These being set on fire, those within are encompassed by the flames." Many attempts have been made by Celtic writers to shake the testimony of the Roman historians to this fact, but without success.

The Druids observed two festivals in each year. The former took place in the beginning of May, and was called Beltane or "fire of God." On this occasion a large fire was kindled on some elevated spot, in honor of the sun, whose returning beneficence they thus welcomed after the gloom and desolation of winter. Of this custom a trace remains in the name given to Whitsunday in parts of Scotland to this day. Sir Walter Scott uses the word in the Boat Song in the Lady of the Lake:

"Ours is no sapling, chance-sown by the fountain,
Blooming at Beltane in winter to fade."

The other great festival of the Druids was called "Samh'in," or "fire of peace," and was held on Hallow-eve (first of November), which still retains this designation in the Highlands of Scotland. On this occasion the Druids assembled in solemn conclave, in the most central part of the district, to discharge the judicial functions of their order. All questions, whether public or private, all crimes against person or property, were at this time brought before them for adjudication. With these judicial acts were combined certain superstitious usages, especially the kindling of the sacred fire, from which all the fires in the district which had been beforehand scrupulously extinguished, might be relighted. This usage of kindling fires on Hallow-eve lingered in the British Islands long after the establishment of Christianity.

Besides these two great annual festivals, the Druids were in the habit of observing the full moon, and especially the sixth day of the moon. On the latter they sought the mistletoe, which grew on their favorite oaks, and to which, as well as to the oak itself, they ascribed a peculiar virtue and sacredness. The discovery of it was an occasion of rejoicing and solemn worship. "They call it," says Pliny, "by a word in their language which means 'heal- all,' and having made solemn preparation for feasting and sacrifice under the tree, they drive thither two milk-white bulls, whose horns are then for the first time bound. The priest then, robed in white, ascends the tree, and cuts off the mistletoe with a golden sickle. It is caught in a white mantle, after which they proceed to slay the victims, at the same time praying that god would render his gift prosperous to those to whom he had given it. They drink the water in which it has been infused, and think it a remedy for all diseases. The mistletoe is a parasitic plant, and is not always nor often found on the oak, so that when it is found it is the more precious."

The Druids were the teachers of morality as well as of religion. Of their ethical teaching a valuable specimen is preserved in the Triads of the Welsh Bards, and from this we may gather that their views of moral rectitude were on the whole just, and that they held and inculcated many very noble and valuable principles of conduct. They were also the men of science and learning of their age and people. Whether they were acquainted with letters or not has been disputed, though the probability is strong that they were, to some extent. But it is certain that they committed nothing of their doctrine, their history, or their poetry to writing. Their teaching was oral, and their literature (if such a word may be used in such a case) was preserved solely by tradition. But the Roman writers admit that "they paid much attention to the order and laws of nature, and investigated and taught to the youth under their charge many things concerning the stars and their motions, the size of the world and the lands, and concerning the might and power of the immortal gods."

Their history consisted in traditional tales, in which the heroic deeds of their forefathers were celebrated. These were apparently in verse, and thus constituted part of the poetry as well as the history of the Druids. In the poems of Ossian we have, if not the actual productions of Druidical times, what may be considered faithful representations of the songs of the Bards.

The Bards were an essential part of the Druidical hierarchy. One author, Pennant, says, "The bards were supposed to be endowed with powers equal to inspiration. They were the oral historians of all past transactions, public and private. They were also accomplished genealogists."

Pennant gives a minute account of the Eisteddfods or sessions of the bards and minstrels, which were held in Wales for many centuries, long after the Druidical priesthood in its other departments became extinct. At these meetings none but bards of merit were suffered to rehearse their pieces, and minstrels of skill to perform. Judges were appointed to decide on their respective abilities, and suitable degrees were conferred. In the earlier period the judges were appointed by the Welsh princes, and after the conquest of Wales, by commission from the kings of England. Yet the tradition is that Edward I., in revenge for the influence of the bards, in animating the resistance of the people to his sway, persecuted them with great cruelty. This tradition has furnished the poet Gray with the subject of his celebrated ode, the Bard.

There are still occasional meetings of the lovers of Welsh poetry and music, held under the ancient name. Among Mrs. Heman's poems is one written for an Eisteddfod, or meeting of Welsh Bards, held in London May 22, 1822. It begins with a description of the ancient meeting, of which the following lines are a part:

"—— midst the eternal cliffs, whose strength defied
The crested Roman in his hour of pride;
And where the Druid's ancient cromlech frowned,
And the oaks breathed mysterious murmurs round,
There thronged the inspired of yore! On plain or height,
In the sun's face, beneath the eye of light,
And baring unto heaven each noble head,
Stood in the circle, where none else might tread."

The Druidical system was at its height at the time of the Roman invasion under Julius Caesar. Against the Druids, as their chief enemies, these conquerors of the world directed their unsparing fury. The Druids, harassed at all points on the main-land, retreated to Anglesey and Iona, where for a season they found shelter, and continued their now-dishonored rites.

The Druids retained their predominance in Iona and over the adjacent islands and main-land until they were supplanted and their superstitions overturned by the arrival of St. Columba, the apostle of the Highlands, by whom the inhabitants of that district were first led to profess Christianity.

IONA

One of the smallest of the British Isles, situated near a ragged and barren coast, surrounded by dangerous seas, and possessing no sources of internal wealth, Iona has obtained an imperishable place in history as the seat of civilization and religion at a time when the darkness of heathenism hung over almost the whole of Northern Europe. Iona or Icolmkill is situated at the extremity of the island of Mull, from which it is separated by a strait of half a mile in breadth, its distance from the main-land of Scotland being thirty-six miles.

Columba was a native of Ireland, and connected by birth with the princes of the land. Ireland was at that time a land of gospel light, while the western and northern parts of Scotland were still immersed in the darkness of heathenism. Columba, with twelve friends landed on the island of Iona in the year of our Lord 563, having made the passage in a wicker boat covered with hides. The Druids who occupied the island endeavored to prevent his settling there, and the savage nations on the adjoining shores incommoded him with their hostility, and on several occasions endangered his life by their attacks. Yet by his perseverance and zeal he surmounted all opposition, procured from the king a gift of the island, and established there a monastery of which he was the abbot. He was unwearied in his labors to disseminate a knowledge of the Scriptures throughout the Highlands and Islands of Scotland, and such was the reverence paid him that though not a bishop, but merely a presbyter and monk, the entire province with its bishops was subject to him and his successors. The Pictish monarch was so impressed with a sense of his wisdom and worth that he held him in the highest honor, and the neighboring chiefs and princes sought his counsel and availed themselves of his judgment in settling their disputes.

When Columba landed on Iona he was attended by twelve followers whom he had formed into a religious body, of which he was the head. To these, as occasion required, others were from time to time added, so that the original number was always kept up. Their institution was called a monastery, and the superior an abbot, but the system had little in common with the monastic institutions of later times. The name by which those who submitted to the rule were known was that of Culdees, probably from the Latin "cultores Dei" worshippers of God. They were a body of religious persons associated together for the purpose of aiding each other in the common work of preaching the gospel and teaching youth, as well as maintaining in themselves the fervor of devotion by united exercises of worship. On entering the order certain vows were taken by the members, but they were not those which were usually imposed by monastic orders, for of these, which are three, celibacy, poverty, and obedience, the Culdees were bound to none except the third. To poverty they did not bind themselves; on the contrary, they seem to have labored diligently to procure for themselves and those dependent on them the comforts of life. Marriage also was allowed them, and most of them seem to have entered into that state. True, their wives were not permitted to reside with them at the institution, but they had a residence assigned to them in an adjacent locality. Near Iona there is an island which still bears the name of "Eilen nam ban," women's island, where their husbands seem to have resided with them, except when duty required their presence in the school or the sanctuary.

Campbell, in his poem of Reullura, alludes to the married monks of Iona:

"——The pure Culdees
Were Albyn's earliest priests of God,
Ere yet an island of her seas
By foot of Saxon monk was trod,
Long ere her churchmen by bigotry
Were barred from holy wedlock's tie.
'Twas then that Aodh, famed afar,
In Iona preached the word with power.
And Reullura, beauty's star,
Was the partner of his bower."

In one of his Irish Melodies, Moore gives the legend of St. Senanus and the lady who sought shelter on the island, but was repulsed:

"Oh, haste and leave this sacred isle,
Unholy bark, ere morning smile;
For on thy deck, though dark it be,
A female form I see;
And I have sworn this sainted sod
Shall ne'er by woman's foot be trod.

In these respects and in others the Culdees departed from the established rules of the Romish Church, and consequently were deemed heretical. The consequence was that as the power of the latter advanced, that of the Culdees was enfeebled. It was not, however, till the thirteenth century that the communities of the Culdees were suppressed and the members dispersed. They still continued to labor as individuals, and resisted the inroads of Papa usurpation as they best might till the light of the Reformation dawned on the world.

Ionia, from its position in the western seas, was exposed to the assaults of the Norwegian and Danish rovers by whom those seas were infested, and by them it was repeatedly pillaged, its dwellings burned, and its peaceful inhabitants put to the sword. These unfavorable circumstances led to its gradual decline, which was expedited by the supervision of the Culdees throughout Scotland. Under the reign of Popery the island became the seat of a nunnery, the ruins of which are still seen. At the Reformation, the nuns were allowed to remain, living in community, when the abbey was dismantled.

Ionia is now chiefly resorted to by travelers on account of the numerous ecclesiastical and sepulchral remains which are found upon it. The principal of these are the Cathedral or Abbey Church, and the Chapel of the Nunnery. Besides these remains of ecclesiastical antiquity, there are some of an earlier date, and pointing to the existence on the island of forms of worship and belief different from those of Christianity. These are the circular Cairns which are found in various parts, and which seem to have been of Druidical origin. It is in reference to all these remains of ancient religion that Johnson exclaims, "That man is little to be envied whose patriotism would not gain force upon the plains of Marathon, or whose piety would not grow warmer amid the ruins of Iona."

In the Lord of the Isles, Scott beautifully contrasts the church on Iona with the Cave of Staffa, opposite:

"Nature herself, it seemed, would raise
A minister to her Maker's praise!
Not for a meaner use ascend
Her columns or her arches bend;
Nor of a theme less solemn tells
The mighty surge that ebbs and swells,
And still between each awful pause,
From the high vault an answer draws,
In varied tone, prolonged and high,
That mocks the organ's melody;
Nor doth its entrance front in vain
To old Iona's holy fane,
That Nature's voice might seem to say,
Well hast thou done, frail child of clay,
Thy humble powers that stately shrine
Tasked high and hard but witness mine."

SKETCH OF THE HISTORY OF GREEK SCULPTURE

We have seen throughout the course of this book how the Greek and Norse myths have furnished material for the poets, not only of Greece and Scandinavia, but also of modern times. In the same way these stories have been found capable of artistic treatment by painters, sculptors, and even by musicians. The story of Cupid and Psyche has not only been retold by poets from Apuleius to William Morris, but also drawn out in a series of frescoes by Raphael, and sculptured in marble by Canova. Even to enumerate the works of art of the modern and ancient world which depend for their subject-matter upon mythology would be a task for a book by itself. As we have been able to give only a few illustrations of the poetic treatment of some of the principal myths, so we shall have to content ourselves with a similarly limited view of the part played by them in other fields of art.

Of the statues made by the ancients themselves to represent their greater deities, a few have been already commented on. But it must not be thought that these splendid examples of plastic art, the Olympian Jupiter and the Athene of the Parthenon, represent the earliest attempts of the Greeks to give form to their myths in sculpture. Our most primitive sources of knowledge of much of Greek mythology are the Homeric poems, where the stories of Achilles and Ulysses have already taken on a poetic form, almost the highest conceivable. But in the other arts, Greek genius lagged behind. At the time when the Homeric poems were written, we find no traces of columned temples or magnificent statues. Scarcely were the domestic arts sufficiently advanced to allow the poet to describe dwellings glorious enough for his heroes to live in, or articles of common utility fit for their use. Of the two most famous works of art mentioned in the Iliad we must think of the statue of Athene at Troy (the Palladium) as a rude carving perhaps of wood, the arms of the goddess separated from the body only enough to allow her to hold the lance and spindle, which were the signs of her divinity. The splendor of the shield of Achilles must be attributed largely to the rich imagination of the poet.

Other works of art of this primitive age we know from descriptions in later classical writers. They attributed the rude statues which had come down to them to Daedalus and his pupils, and beheld them with wonder at their uncouth ugliness. It was long thought that these beginnings of Greek sculpture were to be traced to Egypt, but now-a-days scholars are inclined to take a different view. Egyptian sculpture was closely allied to architecture; the statues were frequently used for the columns of temples. Thus sculpture was subordinated to purely mechanical principles, and human figures were represented altogether in accordance with established conventions. Greek sculpture, on the contrary, even in its primitive forms was eminently natural, capable of developing a high degree of realism. From the first it was decorative in character, and this left the artist free to execute in his own way, provided only that the result should be in accordance with the highest type of beauty which he could conceive. An example of this early decorative art was the chest of Kypselos, on which stories from Homer were depicted in successive bands, the reliefs being partly inlaid with gold and ivory.

From the sixth century before Christ date three processes of great importance in the development of sculpture; the art of casting in bronze, the chiselling of marble, and the inlaying of gold and ivory on wood (chryselephantine work). As early Greek literature developed first among the island Greeks, so the invention of these three methods of art must br attributed to the colonists away from the original Hellas. To the Samians is probably due the invention of bronze casting, to the Chians the beginning of sculpture in marble. This latter development opened to Greek sculpture its great future. Marble work was carried on by a race of artists beginning with Melas in the seventh century and coming down to Boupalos and Athenis, the sons of Achermos, whose works survived to the time of Augustus. Chryselephantine sculpture began in Crete.

Among the earliest of the Greek sculptors whose names have come down to us was Canachos, the Sicyonian. His masterpiece was the Apollo Philesios, in bronze, made for the temple of Didymas. The statue no longer exists, but there are a number of ancient monuments which may be taken as fairly close copies of it, or at least as strongly suggestive of the style of Canachos, among which are the Payne-Knight Apollo at the British Museum, and the Piombino Apollo at the Louvre. In this latter statue the god stands erect with the left foot slightly advanced, and the hands outstretched. The socket of the eye is hollow and was probably filled with some bright substance. Canachos was undoubtedly an innovator, and in the stronger modelling of the head and neck, the more vigorous posture of the body of his statue, he shows an advance on the more conventional and limited art of his generation.

As Greek sculpture progressed, schools of artists arose in various cities, dependent usually for their fame on the ability of some individual sculptor. "Among these schools, those of Aegina and Athens are the most important. Of the former school the works of Onatus are by far the most notable.

Onatus was a contemporary of Canachos, and reached the height of his fame in the middle of the fifth century before Christ. His most famous work was the scene where the Greek heroes draw lots for an opponent to Hector. It is not certain whether Onatus sculptured the groups which adorned the pediments of the temple of Athena at Aegina, groups now in the Glyptothek at Munich, but certainly these famous statues are decidedly in his style. Both pediments represent the battle over the body of Patroclus. The east pediment shows the struggle between Heracles and Laomedon. In each group a fallen warrior lies at the feet of the goddess, over whom she extends her protection. The Aeginetan marbles show the traces of dying archaism. The figures of the warriors are strongly moulded, muscular, but without grace. The same type is reproduced again and again among them. Even the wounded scarcely depart from it. The statues of the eastern pediment are probably later in date than those of the western, and in the former the dying warrior exhibits actual weakness and pain. In the western pediment the statue of the goddess is thoroughly archaic, stiff, uncompromisingly harsh, the features frozen into a conventional smile. In the eastern group the goddess, though still ungraceful, is more distinctly in action, and seems about to take part in the struggle. The Heracles of the eastern pediment, a warrior supported on one knee and drawing his bow, is, for the time, wonderfully vivid and strong. All of these statues are evidence of the rapid progress which Greek sculpture was making in the fifth century against the demands of hieratic conventionality.

The contemporary Athenian school boasted the names of Hegias, Critios, and Nesiotes. Their works have all perished, but a copy of one of the most famous works of Critios and Nesiotes, the statue of the Tyrannicides, is to be found in the Museum of Naples. Harmodius and Aristogeiton killed, in 514 B.C., the tyrant-ruler of Athens, Hipparchus. In consequence of this Athens soon became a republic, and the names of the first rebels were held in great honor. Their statues were set up on the Acropolis, first a group by Antenor, then the group in question by Critios and Nesiotes after the first had been carried away by Xerxes. The heroes, as we learn from the copies in Naples, were represented as rushing forward, one with a naked sword flashing above his head, the other with a mantle for defence thrown over his left arm. They differ in every detail of action and pose, yet they exemplify the same emotion, a common impulse to perform the same deed.

At Argus, contemporary with these early schools of Athens and Aegina, was a school of artists depending on the fame of the great sculptor Ageladas. He was distinguished for his statues in bronze of Zeus and Heracles, but his great distinction is not through works of his own, but is due to the fact that he was the teacher of Myron, Polycleitos, and Pheidias. These names with those of Pythagoras and Calamis bring us to the glorious flowering time of Greek sculpture.

Calamis, somewhat older than the others, was an Athenian, at least by residence. He carried on the measure of perfection which Athenian sculpture had already attained, and added grace and charm to the already powerful model which earlier workers had left him. None of his works survive, but from notices of critics we know that he excelled especially in modelling horses and other animals. His two race-horses in memory of the victory of Hiero of Syracuse at Olympia in 468 were considered unsurpassable. However, it is related that Praxiteles removed the charioteer from one of the groups of Calamis and replaced it by one of his own statues "that the men of Calamis might not be inferior to his horses." Thus it would appear that Calamis was less successful in dealing with the human body, though a statue of Aphrodite from his hand was proverbial, under the name Sosandra, for its grace and grave beauty.

Pythagoras of Rhegium carried on the realism, truth to nature, which was beginning to appear as an ideal of artistic representation. He is said to have been the first sculptor to mark the veins and sinews on the body.

In this vivid naturalness Pythagoras was himself far surpassed by Myron. Pythagoras had seen the importance of showing the effect of action in every portion of the body. Myron carried the minuteness of representation so far that his Statue of Ladas, the runner, was spoken of not as a runner, but as a BREATHER. This statue represented the victor of the foot-race falling, overstrained and dying, at the goal, the last breath from the tired lungs yet hovering upon the lips. More famous than the Ladas is the Discobolos , or disc-thrower, of which copies exist at Rome, one being at the Vatican, the other at the Palazzo Massimi alle Colonne. These, though doubtless far behind the original, serve to show the marvellous power of portraying intense action which the sculptor possessed. The athlete is represented at the precise instant when he has brought the greatest possible bodily strength into play in order to give to the disc its highest force. The body is bent forward, the toes of one foot cling to the ground, the muscles of the torso are strained, the whole body is in an attitude of violent tension which can endure only for an instant. Yet the face is free from contortion, free from any trace of effort, calm and beautiful. This shows that Myron, intent as he was upon reproducing nature, could yet depart from his realistic formulae when the requirements of beautiful art demanded it.

The same delight in rapid momentary action which characterized the two statues of Myron already mentioned appears in a third, the statue of Marsyas astonished at the flute which Athene had thrown away, and which was to lead its finder into his fatal contest with Apollo. A copy of this work at the Lateran Museum represents the satyr starting back in a rapid mingling of desire and fear, which is stamped on his heavy face, as well as indicated in the movement of his body.

Myron's realism again found expression in the bronze cow, celebrated by the epigrams of contemporary poets for its striking naturalness. "Shepherd, pasture thy flock at a little distance, lest thinking thou seest the cow of Myron breathe, thou shouldst wish to lead it away with thine oxen," was one of them.

The value and originality of Myron's contributions to the progress of Greek sculpture were so great that he left behind him a considerable number of artists devoted to his methods. His son Lykios followed his father closely. In statues on the Acropolis representing two boys, one bearing a basin, one blowing the coals in a censer into a flame, he reminds one of the Ladas, especially in the second, where the action of breathing is exemplified in every movement of the body. Another famous work by a follower of Myron was the boy plucking a thorn from his foot, a copy of which is in the Rothschild collection.

The frieze of the Temple of Apollo at Phigales has also been attributed to the school of Myron. The remnants of this frieze, now in the British Museum, show the battle of the Centaurs and Amazons. The figures have not the calm stateliness of bearing which characterizes those of the Parthenon frieze, but instead exhibit a wild vehemence of action which is, perhaps, directly due to the influence of Myron.

Another pupil of Ageladas, a somewhat younger contemporary of Pheidias, was Polycleitos. He excelled in representations of human, bodily beauty. Perfection of form was his aim, and so nearly did he seem to the ancients to have attained this object that his Doryphoros was taken by them as a model of the human figure. A copy of this statue exists in the Museum of Naples and represents a youth in the attitude of bearing a lance, quiet and reserved. The figure is rather heavily built, firm, powerful, and yet graceful, though hardly light enough to justify the praise of perfection which has been lavished upon it.

A companion statue to the Doryphorus of Polycleitos was his statue of the Diadumenos, or boy binding his head with a fillet. A supposed copy of this exists in the British Museum. It presents the same general characteristics as the Doryphorus, a well-modelled but thick-set figure standing in an attitude of repose.

What Polycleitos did for the male form in these two statues he did for the female form in his Amazon, which, according to a doubtful story, was adjudged in competition superior to a work by Pheidias. A statue supposed to be a copy of this masterpiece of Polycleitos is now in the Berlin Museum. It represents a woman standing in a graceful attitude beside a pillar, her left arm thrown above her head to free her wounded breast. The sculptor has succeeded admirably in catching the muscular force and firm hard flesh beneath the graceful curves of the woman warrior.

Polycleitos won his chief successes in portraying human figures. His statues of divinities are not numerous: a Zeus at Argos, an Aphrodite at Amyclae, and, more famous than either, the chryselephantine Hera for a temple between Argos and Mycenae. The goddess was represented as seated on a throne of gold, with bare head and arms. In her right hand was the sceptre crowned with the cuckoo, symbol of conjugal fidelity; in her left, the pomegranate. There exists no certain copy of the Hera of Polycleitos. The head of Hera in Naples may, perhaps, give us some idea of the type of divine beauty preferred by the sculptor who was preeminent for his devotion to human beauty.

Polycleitos was much praised by the Romans Quintilian and Cicero, who nevertheless, held that though he surpassed the beauty of man in nature, yet he did not approach the beauty of the gods. It was reserved for Pheidias to portray the highest conceptions of divinity of which the Greek mind was capable in his statues of Athene in the Parthenon at Athens, and the Zeus of Olympus.

Pheidias lived in the golden age of Athenian art. The victory of Greece against Persia had been due in large measure to Athens, and the results of the political success fell largely to her. It is true the Persians had held the ground of Athens for weeks, and when, after the victory of Salamis, the people returned to their city, they found it in ruins. But the spirit of the Athenians had been stirred, and in spite of the hostility of Persia, the jealousy of neighboring states, and the ruin of the city, the people felt new confidence in themselves and their divinity, and were more than ever ready to strive for the leadership of Greece. Religious feeling, gratitude to the gods who had preserved them, and civic pride in the glory of their own victorious city, all inspired the Athenians. After the winter in which the Persians were finally beaten at Plataea, the Athenians began to rebuild. For a while their efforts were confined to rendering the city habitable and defensible, since the activity of the little state was largely political. But when th leadership of Athens in Greece had become firmly established under Theistocles and Cimon, the third president of the democracy, Pericles, found leisure to turn to the artistic development of the city. The time was ripe, for the artistic progress of the people had been no less marked than their political. The same long training in valor and temperance which gave Athens her statesmen, Aristides and Pericles, gave her her artists and poets also. Pericles became president of the city in 444 B.C., just at the time when the decorative arts were approaching perfection under Pheidias.

Pheidias was an Athenian by birth, the son of Charmides. He studied first under Hegias, then under Ageladas the Argive. He became the most famous sculptor of his time, and when Pericles wanted a director for his great monumental works at Athens, he summoned Pheidias. Artists from all over Hellas put themselves at his disposal, and under his direction the Parthenon was built and adorned with the most splendid statuary the world has ever known.

The Parthenon was fashioned in honor of Athene or Minerva, the guardian deity of Athens, the preserver of Hellas, whom the Athenians in their gratitude sought to make the sovereign goddess of the land which she had saved. The eastern gable of the temple was adorned with a group representing the appearance of Minerva before the gods of Olympus. In the left angle of the gable appeared Helios, the dawn, rising from the sea. In the right angle Selene, evening, sank from sight. Next to Helios was a figure representing either Dionysus or Olympus, and beside were seated two figures, perhaps Persephone and Demeter, perhaps two Horae. Approaching these as a messenger was Iris. Balancing these figures on the side next Selene were two figures, representing Aphrodite in the arms of Peitho, or perhaps Thalassa, goddess of the sea, leaning against Gaia, the earth. Nearer the centre on this side was Hestia, to whom Hermes brought the tidings. The central group is totally lost, but must have been made up of Zeus, Athene, and Vulcan, with, perhaps, others of the greater divinities.

The group of the western pediment represented Athene and Poseidon, contesting for the supremacy of Athens. Athene's chariot is driven by Victory, Poseidon's by Amphitrite. Although the greater part of the attendant deities have disappeared, we know the gods of the rivers of Athens, Eridanas and Ilissos, in reclining postures filled the corners of the pediment. One of these has survived, and remains in its perfection of grace and immortal beauty to attest the wonderful skill that directed the chiselling of the whole group.

Although the gable groups have suffered terribly in the historic vicissitudes of the Parthenon, still enough remains of them to show the dignity of their conception, the rhythm of composition, and the splendid freedom of their workmanship. The fragments were purchased by Lord Elgin early in this century and are now in the British Museum.

The frieze of the Parthenon, executed under the supervision of Pheidias, represented one of the most glorious religious ceremonies of the Greek, the Pan-Athenaic procession. The deities surround Zeus as spectators of the scene, and toward them winds the long line of virgins bearing incense, herds of animals for sacrifice, players upon the lute and lyre, chariots and riders. On the western front the movement has not yet begun, and the youths and men stand in disorder, some binding their mantles, some mounting their horses. The frieze is noteworthy for its expression of physical and intellectual beauty which marked the highest conceptions of Greek art, and for the studied mingling of forcible action and gracious repose. The larger part of this frieze has been preserved and is to be seen at the British Museum.

The third group of Parthenon sculptures, the ornaments of the metope, represents the contest between centaurs and the Lapithae with some scenes interspersed of which the subjects cannot now be determined. The frieze is in low relief, the figures scarcely starting from the background. The sculptures of the metope, on the contrary, are in high relief, frequently giving the impression of marbles detached from the background altogether. They were, moreover, colored. Or course, Pheidias himself cannot have had more than the share of general director in the sculptures of the metope; many of them are manifestly executed by inferior hands. Nevertheless, the mind of a great designer is evident in the wonderful variety of posture and action which the figures show. Indeed, when we consider the immense number of figures employed, it becomes evident that not even all the sculptures of the pediments can have been executed entirely by Pheidias, who was already probably well advanced in life when he began the Parthenon decorations; yet all the sculptures were the work of Pheidias or of pupils working under him, and although traces may be found of the influence of other artists, of Myron, for example, in the freedom and naturalness of the action in the figures of the frieze, yet all the decorations of the Parthenon may fairly be said to belong to the Pheidian school of sculpture.

The fame of Pheidias himself, however, rested very largely on three great pieces of art work: The Athene Promachos, the Athene Parthenos, and the Olympian Zeus. The first of these was a work of Pheidias's youth. It represented the goddess standing gazing toward Athens lovingly and protectingly. She held a spear in one hand, the other supported a buckler. The statue was nine feet high. It was dignified and noble, but at the time of its conception Pheidias had not freed himself from the convention and traditions of the earlier school, and the stiff folds of the tunic, the cold demeanor of the goddess, recall the masters whom Pheidias was destined to supersede. No copy of this statue survives, and hence a description of it must be largely conjectural, made up from hints gleaned from Athenian coins.

Pheidias sculptured other statues of Athene, but none so wonderful as the Athene Parthenos, which, with the Olympian Zeus, was the wonder and admiration of the Greek world. The Athene Parthenos was designed to stand as an outward symbol of the divinity in whose protecting might the city had conquered and grown strong, in whose honor the temple had been built in which this statue was to shine as queen. The Olympian Zeus was the representative of that greater divinity which all Hellas united in honoring. We may gain from the words of Pausanias some idea of the magnificence of this statue, but of its unutterable majesty we can only form faint images in the mind, remembering the strength and grace of the figures of the pediments of the temple at Athens. "Zeus," says Pausanias, "is seated on a throne of ivory and gold; upon his head is laced a garland made in imitation of olive leaves. He bears a Victory in his right hand, also crowned and made in gold and ivory, and holding in her right hand a little fillet. In his left hand the god holds a sceptre, made of all kinds of metals; the bird perched on the tip of the sceptre is an eagle. The shoes of Zeus are also of gold, and of gold his mantle, and underneath this mantle are figures and lilies inlaid."

Both the Olympian Zeus and the Athene were of chryselephantine work offering enormous technical difficulties, but in spite of this both showed almost absolute perfection of form united with beauty of intellectual character to represent the godhead incarnate in human substance. These two statues may be taken as the noblest creations of the Greek imagination when directed to the highest objects of its contemplation. The beauty of the Olympian Zeus, according to Quintilian, "added a new element to religion."

In the works of art just mentioned the creative force of the Greeks attained its highest success. After the death of Pheidias his methods were carried on in a way by the sculptors who had worked under him and become subject to his influence; but as years went on, with less and less to remind us of the supreme perfection of the master. Among these pupils of Pheidias were Agoracritos and Colotes in Athens, Paionios, and Alcamenes. Of Paionios fortunately one statue survives in regard to which there can be no doubt. The Victory erected to the Olympian Zeus shows a tall goddess, strongly yet gracefully carved, posed forward with her drapery flattened closely against her body in front as if by the wind, and streaming freely behind. The masterpiece of Alcamenes, an Aphrodite, is known only by descriptions. The pediments of the temple at Olympia have been assigned, by tradition, one to Alcamenes, one to Paionios. They are, however, so thoroughly archaic in style that it seems impossible to reconcile them with what we know of the work of the men to whom they are attributed. The group of the eastern front represented the chariot races of Oinomaos and Pelops; that of the western, the struggle of the Centaurs and Lapithae. In the latter the action is extremely violent, only the Apollo in the midst is calm and commanding. In both pediments there are decided approaches to realism.

In Athens, after Pheidias, the greatest sculptures were those used to adorn the Erechtheion. The group of Caryatids, maidens who stand erect and firm, bearing upon their heads the weight of the porch, is justly celebrated as an architectural device. At the same time, the maidens, though thus performing the work of columns, do not lose the grace and charm which naturally belongs to them.

Another post-Pheidian work at Athens was the temple of Nike Apteros, the wingless Victory. The bas-reliefs from this temple, now in the Acropolis Museum at Athens, one representing the Victory stooping to tie her sandal, another, the Victory crowning a trophy, recall the consummate grace of the art of Pheidias, the greatest Greek art.

Agoracritos left behind him works at Athens which in their perfection could scarcely be distinguished from the works of Pheidias himself, none of which have come down to us. But from the time of the Peloponnesian war, the seeds of decay were in the art of Hellas, and they ripened fast. In one direction Callimachus carried refined delicacy and formal perfection to excess; and in the other Demetrios, the portrait sculptor, put by ideal beauty for the striking characteristics of realism. Thus the strict reserve, the earnest simplicity of Pheidias and his contemporaries, were sacrificed sacrificed partly, it is true, to the requirements of a fuller spiritual life, partly to the demands of a wider knowledge and deeper passion. The legitimate effects of sculpture are strictly limited. Sculpture is fitted to express not temporary, accidental feeling, but permanent character; not violent action, but repose. In the great work of the golden age the thought of the artist was happily limited so that the form was adequate to its expression. One single motive was all that he tried to express a motive uncomplicated by details of specific situation, a type of general beauty unmixed with the peculiar suggestions of special and individual emotion. When the onward impulse led the artist to pass over the severe limits which bounded the thought of the earlier school, he found his medium becoming less adequate to the demands of his more detailed and circumstantial mental conception. The later sculpture, therefore, lacks in some measure the repose and entire assurance of the earlier. The earlier sculpture confines itself to broad, central lines of heroic and divine character, as in the two masterpieces of Pheidias. The latter dealt in great elaboration with the details and elements of the stories and characters that formed its subjects, as in the Niobe group, or the Laocoon, to be mentioned later.

These modern tendencies produced as the greatest artists of the later Greek type Scopas and Praxiteles.

Between these, however, and the earlier school which they superseded came the Athenian Kephisodotos, the father, it may be supposed of Praxiteles. His fame rests upon a single work, a copy of which has been discovered, the Eirene and Ploutos. In this, while the simplicity and strictness of the Pheidian ideal have been largely preserved, it has been used as the vehicle of deeper feeling and more spiritual life.

Scopas was born at Paros, and lived during the fist half of the fourth century. He did much decorative work including the pediments of the temple of Athena at Tegea. He participated also in the decoration of the Mausoleum erected by Artemisia to the memory of her husband. In this latter, the battle of the Amazons, though probably not the work of Scopas himself, shows in the violence of its attitudes and the pathos of its action the new elements of interest in Greek art with the introduction of which Scopas is connected. The fame of Scopas rests principally on the Niobe group which is attributed to him. The sculpture represents the wife of Amphion at the moment when the curse of Apollo and Diana falls upon her, and her children are slain before her eyes. The children, already feeling the arrows of the gods, are flying to her for protection. She tries in vain to shield her youngest born beneath her mantle, and turns as if to hide her face with its motherly pride just giving place to despair and agony. The whole group is free from contortion and grandly tragic. The original exists no longer, but copies of parts of the group are found in the Uffizi Gallery at Florence.

The Niobe group shows the distinction between Scopas and Praxiteles and the earlier artists in choice of subject and mode of treatment. The same distinction is shown by the Raging Bacchante of Scopas. The head is thrown back, the hair loosened, the garments floating in the wind, an ecstacy of wild, torrent- like action.

Of the work of Praxiteles we know more directly than of the work of any other Greek sculptor of the same remoteness, for one statue has come down to us actually from the master's own hand, and we possess good copies of several others. His statues of Aphrodite, of which there were at least five, are known to us by the figures on coins and by two works in the same style, the Aphrodite in the Glyptothek, and that of the Vatican. The most famous of all was the Aphrodite of Cnidos, which was ranked with the Olympian Zeus and was called one of the wonders of te world. King Nicomedes of Bithynia offered vainly to the people of Cnidos the entire amount of their state debt for its possession. Lucian described the goddess as having a smile somewhat proud and disdainful; yet the eyes, moist and kindly, glowed with tenderness and passion, and the graceful lines of the shoulders, the voluptuous curves of the thighs, are full of sensuous feeling. The goddess, as represented in coins, stood beside a vase, over which her drapery is falling, while with her right hand she shields herself modestly. The head of Aphrodite in the British Museum, with its pure brows, its delicate, voluptuous lips, and sweet, soft skin, is, perhaps, the nearest approach which we possess to the glorious beauty of the original.

Other Aphrodites, the draped statue of Cos among them, and several statues of Eros, representing tender, effeminate youths, illustrate further the departure which Praxiteles marks from the restraint of Pheidias. Another of his masculine figures is the graceful Apollo with the Lizard. The god, strong in his youthful suppleness, is leaning against a tree threatening with his darts a small lizard which is seeking to climb up. Still another type of masculine grace left us by Praxiteles is his statue of the Satyr, of which a copy exists in the Capitoline Museum. The Satyr, in the hands of Praxiteles, lost all his ancient uncouthness, and became a strong, graceful youth, with soft, full form. In the Capitoline representation the boy is leaning easily against a tree, throwing his body into the most indolent posture, which brings out the soft, feminine curves of hips and legs. In fact, so thoroughly is the feminine principle worked into the statues of the Apollo, the Eros, and the Satyr, that this characteristic became considered typical of Praxiteles, and when, in 1877, was discovered the one authentic work which we possess of this artist, the great Hermes of Olympia, critics were at a loss to reconcile this figure with what was already known of the sculptor's work, some holding that it must be a work of his youth, when, through his father, Kephisodotos, he felt the force of the Pheidian tradition, others that there must have been two sculptors bearing the great name of Praxiteles.

The Hermes was found lacking the right arm and both legs below the knees, but the marvellous head and torso are perfectly preserved. The god is without the traditional symbols of his divinity. He is merely a beautiful man. He stands leaning easily against a tree, supporting on one arm the child Dionysus, to whom he turns his gracious head with the devotion and love of a protector. The face, in its expression of sweet majesty, is distinctly a personal conception. The low forehead, the eyes far apart, the small, playful mouth, the round, dimpled chin, all bear evidence to the individual quality which Praxiteles infused into the ideal thought of the god. The body, though at rest, is instinct with life and activity, in spite of its grace. In short, the form of the god has the superb perfection, as the face has the dignity, which was attributed to Pheidias. Nevertheless, the Hermes illustrates sensual loveliness of the later school. The freedom with which the god is conceived belongs to an age when the chains of religious belief sat lightly upon the artist. The gods of Praxiteles are the gods of human experience, and in his treatment of them he does not always escape the tendency of the age of decline to put pathos and passion in the place of eternal majesty.

The influence of Scopas and Praxiteles continued to be felt through a number of artists who worked in sufficient harmony with them to be properly called of their school. To one of these followers of Praxiteles, some say as a copy of a work of the master himself, we must attribute the Demeter now in the British Museum. This is a pathetic illustration of suffering motherhood. There is no exaggeration in the grief, only the calm dignity of a sorrow which in spite of hope refuses to be comforted.

Another work of an unknown artist, probably a follower of Scopas, is the splendid Victory of Samothrace, now in the Louvre. The goddess, with her great wings outspread behind her, is being carried forward, her firm rounded limbs striking through the draperies which flutter behind her, and fall about her in soft folds. Vigorous and stately, the goddess poises herself on the prow of the ship, swaying with the impulse of conquering daring and strength.

Another statue which belongs, so far as artistic reasoning may carry us, to the period and school of Praxiteles, is the so- called Venus of Milo. The proper title to be given to this statue is doubtful, for the drapery corresponds to that of the Roman type of Victory, and if we could be sure that the goddess once held the shield of conquest in her now broken arms we should be forced to call the figure a Victory and place its date no earlier than the second century B.C. However this may be, the statue is justly one of the most famous in the world. It represents an ideal of purity and sweetness. There is not a trace of coarseness or immodesty in the half-naked woman who stands perfect in the maidenly dignity of her own conquering fairness. Her serious yet smiling face, her graceful form, the delicacy of feeling in attitude and gaze, the tender moulding of breast and limbs, make it a worthy companion of the Hermes or Praxiteles. It seems scarcely possible that it should not have sprung from the inspiration of his example.

The last of the great sculptors of Greece was Lysippos of Sikyou. He differed from Pheidias on the one hand and from Polycleitos on the other. Pheidias strove to make his gods all god-like; Lysippos was content to represent them merely as exaggerated human beings; but therein he differed also from Polycleitos, who aimed to model the human body with the beauty only which actually existed in it. Lysippos felt that he must set the standard of human perfection higher than it appears in the average of human examples. Hence we have from him the statues of Heracles, in which the ideal of manly strength was carried far beyond the range of human possibility. A reminiscence of this conception of Lysippos may be found in the Farnese Heracles of Glycon, now in the Museum of Naples. Lysippos also sculptured four statues of Zeus, which depended for their interest largely on their heroic size.

Lysippos won much fame by his statues of Alexander the Great, but he is chiefly known to us by his statue of the athlete scraping himself with a strigil, of which an authentic copy is in the Vatican. The figure differs decidedly from the thick-set, rather heavy figures of Polycleitos, being tall, and slender in spite of its robustness. The head is small, the torso is small at the waist, but strong, and the whole body is splendidly active.

The changes in the models of earlier sculptors made by Lysippos were of sufficient importance to give rise to a school which was carried on by his sons and others, producing among many famous works the Barberini Faun, now at the Glyptothek, Munich. The enormous Colossus of Rhodes was also the work of a disciple of Lysippos.

But from this time the downward tendency in Greek art is only too apparent, and very rapid. The spread of Greek influence over Asia, and later, in consequence of the conquest of Greece by Rome, over Europe, had the effect of widening the market for Greek production, but of drying up the sources of what was vital in that production. Athens and Sikyou became mere provincial cities, and were shorn thenceforth of all artistic significance; and Greek art, thus deprived of the roots of its life, continued to grow for a while with a rank luxuriance of production, but soon became normal and conventional. The artists who followed Lysippos contented themselves chiefly with seeking a merely technical perfection in reproducing the creations of the earlier and more original age.

At Pergamon under Attalus, in the last years of the third century, there was something of an artistic revival. This Attalus successfully defended his country against an overwhelming attack of the Gauls from the north. To celebrate this victory, an altar was erected to Zeus on the Acropolis of Pergamon, of which the frieze represented the contest between Zeus and the giants. These sculptures are now to be found in Berlin. They are carved in high relief; the giants with muscles strained and distended, their bodies writhing in the contortions of effort and suffering; the gods, no longer calm and restrained, but themselves overcome with the ardor of battle. Zeus stretches his arms over the battle-field hurling destruction everywhere. Athene turns from the field, dragging at her heels a young giant whom she has conquered, and reaches forward to the crown of victory. The wild, passionate action of the whole work remove it far from the firm, orderly work of Pheidias, and carry it almost to the extreme of pathetic representation in sculpture shown by the Laocoon.

The contests with the Gauls, the fear inspired by the huge forms of the barbarians, seem to have influenced powerfully the imaginative conceptions of the sculptors of the school of Pergamon. One of the most famous works which they have left is the figure long known as the Dying Gladiator, of which a copy exists in the Capitoline Museum. This represents a Gaul sinking wounded to the ground, supporting himself on his right arm. It is remarkable for its stern realism. The pain and sense of defeat comes out in every feature. Moreover, the nationality of the fallen warrior is clearly expressed in the deep indentation between the heavy brow and the prominent nose, in the face, shaven, except the upper lip, in the uncouth, fleshy body, in the rough hands and feet. Usually the artist preferred to hint at the race by some peculiarities of costume. Here nothing but uncompromising realism of feature will satisfy the sculptor. A companion piece to the Wounded Gaul, though less famous, is the group of the Villa Ludovisi, which represents a Gaul, who has slain his wife, in the act of stabbing himself in the neck.

In addition to inspiring the sculptures at Pergamon, Attalus dedicated to the gods of Athens a votive offering in return for the help which they had given him. This was placed on the Acropolis at Athens. It consisted of four groups, representing the gigantomachia or giant combat, the battle of the Amazons, the battle of Marathon, and the victory of Attalus. Figures from these survive, a dead Amazon at Naples and a kneeling Persian at the Vatican being the best known.

Another state which became famous in the declining days of Greek art was the republic of Rhodes. The Rhodian sculptors learned their anatomy from Lysippos, and caught their dramatic instinct from the artists of Pergamon. Two of the most famous sculpture groups in the world were produced at Rhodes, the Laocoon, now at the Vatican, and the Farnese Bull, now at Naples. The former was the work of three artists, given by Pliny as Agesandros, Athanodorus, and Polydorus. It has been accepted as one of the masterpieces of the world, but as we shall see, it is manifestly a work of a time of decadence.

The Laocoon illustrates excellently the extreme results of the pathetic tendency. The priest Laocoon is represented at the moment when the serpents of Apollo surround him and his two sons, born through their father's sin, and bear them all three down to destruction. The younger son, fatally bitten, falls back in death agony. The father yields slowly, his desperation giving way before the merciless strength of the serpents. The elder son shrinks away in horror though bound fast by the inevitable coils.

The Laocoon shows the pathetic tendency at its utmost. The technical difficulties have been overcome with astonishing success, and though the combination of figures is impossible in life, it is marvellously effective in art. But the group depends for its interest purely on the accidental horror of the situation. There is no hint in the sculpture of the motive of the tragedy, no suggestion of ethical significance in the suffering portrayed. It does not connect itself with any principle of life. In this way the work became a superb piece of display, a TOUR DE FORCE of surprising composition but with little serious meaning.

The same judgment may be extended to the Farnese Bull, the work of Apollonius and Tauriscos, artists from Tralles who lived at Rhodes. This group represents the punishment of the cruel Dirke at the hands of the sons of Antiope. The beautiful queen clasps the knee of one of the sons praying for grace, while the other boy is about to throw over her the noose which is to bind her to the bull. Antiope stands in the background, a mere lay figure,and scattered about are numerous small symbolical figures. Like the Laocoon the Farnese Bull exhibits surprising mastery of technical obstacles, but, like the Laocoon, it falls short of true tragic grandeur. In a greater degree than the Laocoon it trenches upon the province of painting. It is more complicated in its subject-matter; and the appearance in the group of many small subsidiary figures, which in a painting might have been given their proper value, being in the marble of the same relief and distinction as the major characters, give a somewhat absurd effect. The little goddess who sits in the foreground, for instance, is smaller than the dog. Again, there is less of the motive shown than in the Laocoon. The group is seized at the moment preceding the frightful catastrophe, but that moment is as full of agony as the succeeding ones, and in addition there is the feeling of suspense and oppression that comes from the unfinished tragedy. Altogether, the group, in spite of the marvellous technical skill shown in details, is a failure when judged on general lines. Its interest lies in momentary and apparently ummotived suffering, not in any truly serious conception of life.

With the conquest of Greece by Rome, the final stage of Greek art begins. But the vigor and originality had departed. The sculptors aimed at and attained technical correctness, academic beauty of form, sensuous feeling, perfection of details, but they lost all imaginative power. A good example of the work of this period is found in the Apollo Belvidere now in the Vatican. This famous statue is an early Roman copy of a Greek original. It represents the god advancing easily, full of vigor and grace. It is marvellously correct in drawing, but quite without feeling of any kind.

Another work of this period is the sleeping Ariadne of the Vatican. This represents a woman reclining in a studied sentimental attitude, her arms thrown about her head, her body swathed in its protecting drapery. To the same period also belongs almost the last notable work of Greek art, the degenerate and sensuous conception of the Venus de Medici. In this statue the goddess stands as if rising from the sea, her attitude reserved, yet coquettish and self-conscious. The form is technically perfect, graceful, and soft in its refinement, but compared with the earlier Aphrodites it is an unworthy successor.

Still another famous statue is the Borghese Gladiator, of Agasius of Ephesus, now in the Louvre. The statue is merely a bit of display, an effort to parade technical skill and anatomical knowledge. The gladiator throws his weight strongly on his right leg, and holds one arm high above his head, giving to his whole body an effect of straining. The figure is strong and wiry. Agasius was distinctly an imitator, as were most of the artists of this age, among whom must be reckoned the skilful sculptor of the crouching Venus, also in the Louvre. The goddess is shown as bending down in graceful curves until her body is supported on the right leg, which is bent double. The form is strong and healthy, graceful and easy in its somewhat constrained posture.

During all of this final period Greek art was very largely influenced by the relations which existed between Greece and Rome. About the year 200 B.C. the Roman conquest of Greece led to an important traffic in works of art between Rome and the Greek cities. For a time, indeed, statues formed a recognized part of the booty which graced every Roman triumph. M. Fulvius Nobilior carried away not less than five hundred and fifteen. After the period of conquest the importation of Greek statues continued at Rome, and in time Greek artists also began to remove thither, so that Rome became not only the centre for the collection of Greek works of art, but the chief seat of their production. At this time the Roman religious conceptions were identified with those of Greece, and the Greek gods received the Latin names by which we now know them. The influence of the Greeks upon Rome was very marked, but the reflex influence of the material civilization of Italy upon Greek art was altogether bad, and thus the splendor of classical art went out in dilletantism and weakness.

The destruction of the Roman Empire by the barbarians makes a break in the artistic history of the world. Not for many centuries was there a vestige of artistic production. Even when in Italy and France the monks began to make crude attempts to reach out for and represent in painting and sculpture imaginative conceptions of things beautiful, they took their material exclusively from Christian sources. The tradition of classical stories had nearly vanished from the mind of Europe. Not until the Renaissance restored the knowledge of classical culture to Europe do we find artists making any use of the wealth of imaginative material stored up in the myths of Greece. Then, indeed, by the discovery and circulation of the poets of mythology, the Greek stories and conceptions of characters, divine and human, became known once more and were used freely, remaining until the present day one chief source of material and subject-matter for the use of the painter and sculptor.

Figure 50: "Struth Winkelreid" by Adolf Ehrhardt

King Arthur and His Knights

Chapter 1

INTRODUCTION

On the decline of the Roman power, about five centuries after Christ, the countries of Northern Europe were left almost destitute of a national government. Numerous chiefs, more or less powerful, held local sway, as far as each could enforce his dominion, and occasionally those chiefs would unite for a common object; but, in ordinary times, they were much more likely to be found in hostility to one another. In such a state of things the rights of the humbler classes of society were at the mercy of every assailant; and it is plain that, without some check upon the lawless power of the chiefs, society must have relapsed into barbarism. Such checks were found, first, in the rivalry of the chiefs themselves, whose mutual jealousy made them restraints upon one another; secondly, in the influence of the Church, which, by every motive, pure or selfish, was pledged to interpose for the protection of the weak; and lastly, in the generosity and sense of right which, however crushed under the weight of passion and selfishness, dwell naturally in the heart of man. From this last source sprang Chivalry, which framed an ideal of the heroic character, combining invincible strength and valor, justice, modesty, loyalty to superiors, courtesy to equals, compassion to weakness, and devotedness to the Church; an ideal which, if never met with in real life, was acknowledged by all as the highest model for emulation.

The word "Chivalry" is derived from the French "cheval," a horse. The word "knight," which originally meant boy or servant, was particularly applied to a young man after he was admitted to the privilege of bearing arms. This privilege was conferred on youths of family and fortune only, for the mass of the people were not furnished with arms. The knight then was a mounted warrior, a man of rank, or in the service and maintenance of some man of rank, generally possessing some independent means of support, but often relying mainly on the gratitude of those whom he served for the supply of his wants, and often, no doubt, resorting to the means which power confers on its possessor.

In time of war the knight was, with his followers, in the camp of his sovereign, or commanding in the field, or holding some castle for him. In time of peace he was often in attendance at his sovereign's court, gracing with his presence the banquets and tournaments with which princes cheered their leisure. Or he was traversing the country in quest of adventure, professedly bent on redressing wrongs and enforcing rights, sometimes in fulfilment of some vow of religion or of love. These wandering knights were called knights-errant; they were welcome guests in the castles of the nobility, for their presence enlivened the dulness of those secluded abodes, and they were received with honor at the abbeys, which often owed the best part of their revenues to the patronage of the knights; but if no castle or abbey or hermitage were at hand their hardy habits made it not intolerable to them to lie down, supperless, at the foot of some wayside cross, and pass the night.

It is evident that the justice administered by such an instrumentality must have been of the rudest description. The force whose legitimate purpose was to redress wrongs might easily be perverted to inflict them Accordingly, we find in the romances, which, however fabulous in facts, are true as pictures of manners, that a knightly castle was often a terror to the surrounding country; that is, dungeons were full of oppressed knights and ladies, waiting for some champion to appear to set them free, or to be ransomed with money; that hosts of idle retainers were ever at hand to enforce their lord's behests, regardless of law and justice; and that the rights of the unarmed multitude were of no account. This contrariety of fact and theory in regard to chivalry will account for the opposite impressions which exist in men's minds respecting it. While it has been the theme of the most fervid eulogium on the one part, it has been as eagerly denounced on the other. On a cool estimate, we cannot but see reason to congratulate ourselves that it has given way in modern times to the reign of law, and that the civil magistrate, if less picturesque, has taken the place of the mailed champion.

THE TRAINING OF A KNIGHT

The preparatory education of candidates for knighthood was long and arduous. At seven years of age the noble children were usually removed from their father's house to the court or castle of their future patron, and placed under the care of a governor, who taught them the first articles of religion, and respect and reverence for their lords and superiors, and initiated them in the ceremonies of a court. They were called pages, valets, or varlets, and their office was to carve, to wait at table, and to perform other menial services, which were not then considered humiliating. In their leisure hours they learned to dance and play on the harp, were instructed in the mysteries of woods and rivers, that is, in hunting, falconry, and fishing, and in wrestling, tilting with spears, and performing other military exercises on horseback. At fourteen the page became an esquire, and began a course of severer and more laborious exercises. To vault on a horse in heavy armor; to run, to scale walls, and spring over ditches, under the same encumbrance; to wrestle, to wield the battle-axe for a length of time, without raising the visor or taking breath; to perform with grace all the evolutions of horsemanship,—were necessary preliminaries to the reception of knighthood, which was usually conferred at twenty-one years of age, when the young man's education was supposed to be completed. In the meantime, the esquires were no less assiduously engaged in acquiring all those refinements of civility which formed what was in that age called courtesy. The same castle in which they received their education was usually thronged with young persons of the other sex, and the page was encouraged, at a very early age, to select some lady of the court as the mistress of his heart, to whom he was taught to refer all his sentiments, words, and actions. The service of his mistress was the glory and occupation of a knight, and her smiles, bestowed at once by affection and gratitude, were held out as the recompense of his well-directed valor. Religion united its influence with those of loyalty and love, and the order of knighthood, endowed with all the sanctity and religious awe that attended the priesthood, became an object of ambition to the greatest sovereigns.

The ceremonies of initiation were peculiarly solemn. After undergoing a severe fast, and spending whole nights in prayer, the candidate confessed, and received the sacrament. He then clothed himself in snow-white garments, and repaired to the church, or the hall, where the ceremony was to take place, bearing a knightly sword suspended from his neck, which the officiating priest took and blessed, and then returned to him. The candidate then, with folded arms, knelt before the presiding knight, who, after some questions about his motives and purposes in requesting admission, administered to him the oaths, and granted his request. Some of the knights present, sometimes even ladies and damsels, handed to him in succession the spurs, the coat of mail, the hauberk, the armlet and gauntlet, and lastly he girded on the sword. He then knelt again before the president, who, rising from his seat, gave him the "accolade," which consisted of three strokes, with the flat of a sword, on the shoulder or neck of the candidate, accompanied by the words: "In the name of God, of St. Michael, and St. George, I make thee a knight; be valiant, courteous, and loyal!" Then he received his helmet, his shield, and spear; and thus the investiture ended.

FREEMAN, VILLAINS, SERFS, AND CLERKS

The other classes of which society was composed were, first, FREEMEN, owners of small portions of land independent, though they sometimes voluntarily became the vassals of their more opulent neighbors, whose power was necessary for their protection. The other two classes, which were much the most numerous, were either serfs or villains, both of which were slaves.

The SERFS were in the lowest state of slavery. All the fruits of their labor belonged to the master whose land they tilled, and by whom they were fed and clothed.

The VILLIANS were less degraded. Their situation seems to have resembled that of the Russian peasants at this day. Like the serfs, they were attached to the soil, and were transferred with it by purchase; but they paid only a fixed rent to the landlord, and had a right to dispose of any surplus that might arise from their industry.

The term "clerk" was of very extensive import. It comprehended, originally, such persons only as belonged to the clergy, or clerical order, among whom, however, might be found a multitude of married persons, artisans or others. But in process of time a much wider rule was established; every one that could read being accounted a clerk or clericus, and allowed the "benefit of clergy," that is, exemption from capital and some other forms of punishment, in case of crime.

TOURNAMENTS

The splendid pageant of a tournament between knights, its gaudy accessories and trappings, and its chivalrous regulations, originated in France. Tournaments were repeatedly condemned by the Church, probably on account of the quarrels they led to, and the often fatal results. The "joust," or "just," was different from the tournament. In these, knights fought with their lances, and their object was to unhorse their antagonists; while the tournaments were intended for a display of skill and address in evolutions, and with various weapons, and greater courtesy was observed in the regulations. By these it was forbidden to wound the horse, or to use the point of the sword, or to strike a knight after he had raised his vizor, or unlaced his helmet. The ladies encouraged their knights in these exercises; they bestowed prizes, and the conqueror's feats were the theme of romance and song. The stands overlooking the ground, of course, were varied

Figure 51: "Knight Wood" by Charles S. Ricketts

in the shapes of towers, terraces, galleries, and pensile gardens, magnificently decorated with tapestry, pavilions, and banners. Every combatant proclaimed the name of the lady whose servant d'amour he was. He was wont to look up to the stand, and strengthen his courage by the sight of the bright eyes that were raining their influence on him from above. The knights also carried FAVORS, consisting of scarfs, veils, sleeves, bracelets, clasps,—in short, some piece of female habiliment,—attached to their helmets, shields, or armor. If, during the combat, any of these appendages were dropped or lost the fair donor would at times send her knight new ones, especially if pleased with his exertions.

MAIL ARMOR

Mail armor, of which the hauberk is a species, and which derived its name from maille, a French word for MESH, was of two kinds, PLATE or SCALE mail, and CHAIN mail. It was originally used for the protection of the body only, reaching no lower than the knees. It was shaped like a carter's frock, and bound round the waist by a girdle. Gloves and hose of mail were afterwards added, and a hood, which, when necessary, was drawn over the head, leaving the face alone uncovered. To protect the skin from the impression of the iron network of the chain mail, a quilted lining was employed, which, however, was insufficient, and the bath was used to efface the marks of the armor.

The hauberk was a complete covering of double chain mail. Some hauberks opened before, like a modern coat; others were closed like a shirt.

The chain mail of which they were composed was formed by a number of iron links, each link having others inserted into it, the whole exhibiting a kind of network, of which (in some instances at least) the meshes were circular, with each link separately riveted.

The hauberk was proof against the most violent blow of a sword; but the point of a lance might pass through the meshes, or drive the iron into the flesh. To guard against this, a thick and well- stuffed doublet was worn underneath, under which was commonly added an iron breastplate. Hence the expression "to pierce both plate and mail," so common in the earlier poets.

Mail armor continued in general use till about the year 1300, when it was gradually supplanted by plate armor, or suits consisting of pieces or plates of solid iron, adapted to the different parts of the body.

Shields were generally made of wood, covered with leather, or some similar substance. To secure them, in some sort, from being cut through by the sword, they were surrounded with a hoop of metal.

HELMETS

The helmet was composed of two parts: the HEADPIECE, which was strengthened within by several circles of iron, and the VISOR, which, as the name implies, was a sort of grating to see through, so contrived as, by sliding in a groove, or turning on a pivot, to be raised or lowered at pleasure. Some helmets had a further improvement called a BEVER, from the Italian bevere, to drink. The VENTAYLE, or "air-passage," is another name for this.

To secure the helmet from the possibility of falling, or of being struck off, it was tied by several laces to the meshes of the hauberk; consequently, when a knight was overthrown it was necessary to undo these laces before he could be put to death; though this was sometimes effected by lifting up the skirt of the hauberk, and stabbing him in the belly. The instrument of death was a small dagger, worn on the right side.

ROMANCES

In ages when there were no books, when noblemen and princes themselves could not read, history or tradition was monopolized by the story-tellers. They inherited, generation after generation, the wondrous tales of their predecessors, which they retailed to the public with such additions of their own as their acquired information supplied them with. Anachronisms became of course very common, and errors of geography, of locality, of manners, equally so. Spurious genealogies were invented, in which Arthur and his knights, and Charlemagne and his paladins, were made to derive their descent from Aeneas, Hector, or some other of the Trojan heroes.

With regard to the derivation of the word "Romance," we trace it to the fact that the dialects which were formed in Western Europe, from the admixture of Latin with the native languages, took the name of Langue Romaine. The French language was divided into two dialects. The river Loire was their common boundary. In the provinces to the south of that river the affirmative, YES, was expressed by the word oc; in the north it was called oil (oui); and hence Dante has named the southern language langue d'oc, and the northern langue d'oil. The latter, which was carried into England by the Normans, and is the origin of the present French, may be called the French Romane; and the former the Provencal, or Provencial Romane, because it was spoken by the people of Provence and Languedoc, southern provinces of France.

These dialects were soon distinguished by very opposite characters. A soft and enervating climate, a spirit of commerce encouraged by an easy communication with other maritime nations, the influx of wealth, and a more settled government, may have tended to polish and soften the diction of the Provencials, whose poets, under the name of Troubadours, were the masters of the Italians, and particularly of Petrarch. Their favorite pieces were Sirventes (satirical pieces), love-songs, and Tensons, which last were a sort of dialogue in verse between two poets, who questioned each other on some refined points of loves' casuistry. It seems the Provencials were so completely absorbed in these delicate questions as to neglect and despise the composition of fabulous histories of adventure and knighthood, which they left in a great measure to the poets of the northern part of the kingdom, called Trouveurs.

At a time when chivalry excited universal admiration, and when all the efforts of that chivalry were directed against the enemies of religion, it was natural that literature should receive the same impulse, and that history and fable should be ransacked to furnish examples of courage and piety that might excite increased emulation. Arthur and Charlemagne were the two heroes selected for this purpose. Arthur's pretensions were that he was a brave, though not always a successful warrior; he had withstood with great resolution the arms of the infidels, that is to say of the Saxons, and his memory was held in the highest estimation by his countrymen, the Britons, who carried with them into Wales, and into the kindred country of Armorica, or Brittany, the memory of his exploits, which their national vanity insensibly exaggerated, till the little prince of the Silures (South Wales) was magnified into the conqueror of England, of Gaul, and of the greater part of Europe. His genealogy was gradually carried up to an imaginary Brutus, and to the period of the Trojan war, and a sort of chronicle was composed in the Welsh, or Armorican language, which, under the pompous title of the "History of the Kings of Britain," was translated into Latin by Geoffrey of Monmouth, about the year 1150. The Welsh critics consider the material of the work to have been an older history, written by St. Talian, Bishop of St. Asaph, in the seventh century.

As to Charlemagne, though his real merits were sufficient to secure his immortality, it was impossible that his HOLY WARS against the Saracens should not become a favorite topic for fiction. Accordingly, the fabulous history of these wars was written, probably towards the close of the eleventh century, by a monk, who, thinking it would add dignity to his work to embellish it with a contemporary name, boldly ascribed it to Turpin, who was Archbishop of Rheims about the year 773.

These fabulous chronicles were for a while imprisoned in languages of local only or of professional access. Both Turpin and Geoffrey might indeed be read by ecclesiastics, the sole Latin scholars of those times, and Geoffrey's British original would contribute to the gratification of Welshmen; but neither could become extensively popular till translated into some language of general and familiar use. The Anglo-Saxon was at that time used only by a conquered and enslaved nation; the Spanish and Italian languages were not yet formed; the Norman French alone was spoken and understood by the nobility in the greater part of Europe, and therefore was a proper vehicle for the new mode of composition.

That language was fashionable in England before the Conquest, and became, after that event, the only language used at the court of London. As the various conquests of the Normans, and the enthusiastic valor of that extraordinary people, had familiarized the minds of men with the most marvellous events, their poets eagerly seized the fabulous legends of Arthur and Charlemagne, translated them into the language of the day, and soon produced a variety of imitations. The adventures attributed to these monarchs, and to their distinguished warriors, together with those of many other traditionary or imaginary heroes, composed by degrees that formidable body of marvellous histories which, from the dialect in which the most ancient of them were written, were called "Romances."

METRICAL ROMANCES

The earliest form in which romances appear is that of a rude kind of verse. In this form it is supposed they were sung or recited at the feasts of princes and knights in their baronial halls. The following specimen of the language and style of Robert de Beauvais, who flourished in 1257, is from Sir Walter Scott's "Introduction to the Romance of Sir Tristrem":

"Ne voil pas emmi dire,
Ici diverse la matyere,
Entre ceus qui solent cunter,
E de le cunte Tristran parler."
"I will not say too much about it,
So diverse is the matter,
Among those who are in the habit of telling
And relating the story of Tristran."

This is a specimen of the language which was in use among the nobility of England, in the ages immediately after the Norman conquest. The following is a specimen of the English that existed at the same time, among the common people. Robert de Brunne, speaking of his Latin and French authorities, says:

"Als thai haf wryten and sayd
Haf I alle in myn Inglis layd,
In symple speche as I couthe,
That is lightest in manne's mouthe.
Alle for the luf of symple men,
That strange Inglis cannot ken."

The "strange Inglis" being the language of the previous specimen.

It was not till toward the end of the thirteenth century that the PROSE romances began to appear. These works generally began with disowning and discrediting the sources from which in reality they drew their sole information. As every romance was supposed to be a real history, the compilers of those in prose would have forfeited all credit if they had announced themselves as mere copyists of the minstrels. On the contrary, they usually state that, as the popular poems upon the matter in question contain many "lesings," they had been induced to translate the real and true history of such or such a knight from the original Latin or Greek, or from the ancient British or Armorican authorities, which authorities existed only in their own assertion.

A specimen of the style of the prose romances may be found in the following extract from one of the most celebrated and latest of them, the "Morte d'Arthur" of Sir Thomas Mallory, of the date of 1485. From this work much of the contents of this volume has been drawn, with as close an adherence to the original style as was thought consistent with our plan of adapting our narrative to the taste of modern readers.

"It is notoyrly knowen thorugh the vnyuersal world that there been ix worthy and the best that ever were. That is to wete thre paynyms, three Jewes, and three crysten men. As for the paynyms, they were tofore the Incarnacyon of Cryst whiche were named, the fyrst Hector of Troye; the second Alysaunder the grete, and the thyrd Julyus Cezar, Emperour of Rome, of whome thystoryes ben wel kno and had. And as for the thre Jewes whyche also were tofore thyncarnacyon of our Lord, of whome the fyrst was Duc Josue, whyche brought the chyldren of Israhel into the londe of beheste; the second Dauyd, kyng of Jherusalem, and the thyrd Judas Machabeus; of these thre the byble reherceth al theyr noble hystoryes and actes. And sythe the sayd Incarnacyon haue ben the noble crysten men stalled and admytted thorugh the vnyuersal world to the nombre of the ix beste and worthy, of whome was fyrst the noble Arthur, whose noble actes I purpose to wryte in this person book here folowyng. The second was Charlemayn, or Charles the grete, of whome thystorye is had in many places both in frensshe and englysshe, and the thyrd and last was Godefray of boloyn."

Chapter 2

THE MYTHICAL HISTORY OF ENGLAND

The illustrious poet, Milton, in his "History of England," is the author whom we chiefly follow in this chapter.

According to the earliest accounts, Albion, a giant, and son of Neptune, a contemporary of Hercules, ruled over the island, to which he gave his name. Presuming to oppose the progress of Hercules in his western march, he was slain by him.

Another story is that Histion, the son of Japhet, the son of Noah, had four sons, Francus, Romanus, Alemannus, and Britto, from whom descended the French, Roman, German, and British people.

Rejecting these and other like stories, Milton gives more regard to the story of Brutus, the Trojan, which, he says, is supported by "descents of ancestry long continued, laws and exploits not plainly seeming to be borrowed or devised, which on the common belief have wrought no small impression; defended by many, denied utterly by few." The principal authority is Geoffrey of Monmouth, whose history, written in the twelfth century, purports to be a translation of a history of Britain brought over from the opposite shore of France, which, under the name of Brittany, was chiefly peopled by natives of Britain who, from time to time, emigrated thither, driven from their own country by the inroads of the Picts and Scots. According to this authority, Brutus was the son of Silvius, and he of Ascanius, the son of Aeneas, whose flight from Troy and settlement in Italy are narrated in "Stories of Gods and Heroes."

Brutus, at the age of fifteen, attending his father to the chase, unfortunately killed him with an arrow. Banished therefor by his kindred, he sought refuge in that part of Greece where Helenus, with a band of Trojan exiles, had become established. But Helenus was now dead and the descendants of the Trojans were oppressed by Pandrasus, the king of the country. Brutus, being kindly received among them, so throve in virtue and in arms as to win the regard of all the eminent of the land above all others of his age. In consequence of this the Trojans not only began to hope, but secretly to persuade him to lead them the way to liberty. To encourage them, they had the promise of help from Assaracus, a noble Greek youth, whose mother was a Trojan. He had suffered wrong at the hands of the king, and for that reason the more willingly cast in his lost with the Trojan exiles.

Choosing a fit opportunity, Brutus with his countrymen withdrew to the woods and hills, as the safest place from which to expostulate, and sent this message to Pandrasus: "That the Trojans, holding it unworthy of their ancestors to serve in a foreign land, had retreated to the woods, choosing rather a savage life than a slavish one. If that displeased him, then, with his leave, they would depart to some other country." Pandrasus, not expecting so bold a message from the sons of captives, went in pursuit of them, with such forces as he could gather, and met them on the banks of the Achelous, where Brutus got the advantage, and took the king captive. The result was, that the terms demanded by the Trojans were granted; the king gave his daughter Imogen in marriage to Brutus, and furnished shipping, money, and fit provision for them all to depart from the land.

The marriage being solemnized, and shipping from all parts got together, the Trojans, in a fleet of no less than three hundred and twenty sail, betook themselves to the sea. On the third day they arrived at a certain island, which they found destitute of inhabitants, though there were appearances of former habitation, and among the ruins a temple of Diana. Brutus, here performing sacrifice at the shrine of the goddess, invoked an oracle for his guidance, in these lines:

"Goddess of shades, and huntress, who at will
Walk'st on the rolling sphere, and through the deep;
On thy third realm, the earth, look now, and tell
What land, what seat of rest, thou bidd'st me seek;
What certain seat where I may worship thee
For aye, with temples vowed and virgin choirs."
To whom, sleeping before the altar, Diana in a vision thus answered:
"Brutus! far to the west, in the ocean wide,
Beyond the realm of Gaul, a land there lies,
Seagirt it lies, where giants dwelt of old;

Now, void, it fits thy people: thither bend
Thy course; there shalt thou find a lasting seat;
There to thy sons another Troy shall rise,
And kings be born of thee, whose dreaded might
Shall awe the world, and conquer nations bold"

Brutus, guided now, as he thought, by divine direction, sped his course towards the west, and, arriving at a place on the Tyrrhene sea, found there the descendants of certain Trojans who, with Antenor, came into Italy, of whom Corineus was the chief. These joined company, and the ships pursued their way till they arrived at the mouth of the river Loire, in France, where the expedition landed, with a view to a settlement, but were so rudely assaulted by the inhabitants that they put to sea again, and arrived at a part of the coast of Britain, now called Devonshire, where Brutus felt convinced that he had found the promised end of his voyage, landed his colony, and took possession.

The island, not yet Britain, but Albion, was in a manner desert and inhospitable, occupied only by a remnant of the giant race whose excessive force and tyranny had destroyed the others. The Trojans encountered these and extirpated them, Corineus, in particular, signalizing himself by his exploits against them; from whom Cornwall takes its name, for that region fell to his lot, and there the hugest giants dwelt, lurking in rocks and caves, till Corineus rid the land of them.

Brutus built his capital city, and called it Trojanova (New Troy), changed in time to Trinovantus, now London;

[Footnote:
"For noble Britons sprong from Trojans bold,
And Troynovant was built of old Troy's ashes cold"
SPENSER,
Book III, Canto IX., 38.]

---

and, having governed the isle twenty-four years, died, leaving three sons, Locrine, Albanact and Camber. Locrine had the middle part, Camber the west, called Cambria from him, and Albanact Albania, now Scotland. Locrine was married to Guendolen, the daughter of Corineus, but having seen a fair maid named Estrildis, who had been brought captive from Germany, he became enamoured of her, and had by her a daughter, whose name was Sabra. This matter was kept secret while Corineus lived, but after his death Locrine divorced Guendolen, and made Estrildis his queen. Guendolen, all in rage, departed to Cornwall, where Madan, her son, lived, who had been brought up by Corineus, his grandfather. Gathering an army of her father's friends and subjects, she gave battle to her husband's forces and Locrine was slain. Guendolen caused her rival, Estrildis, with her daughter Sabra, to be thrown into the river, from which cause the river thenceforth bore the maiden's name, which by length of time is now changed into Sabrina or Severn. Milton alludes to this in his address to the rivers,—

"Severn swift, guilty of maiden's death";—

---

and in his "Comus" tells the story with a slight variation, thus:

"There is a gentle nymph not far from hence,
That with moist curb sways the smooth Severn stream;
Sabrina is her name, a virgin pure:
Whilom she was the daughter of Locrine,
That had the sceptre from his father, Brute,
She, guiltless damsel, flying the mad pursuit
Of her enraged step-dame, Guendolen,
Commended her fair innocence to the flood,
That stayed her night with his cross-flowing course
The water-nymphs that in the bottom played,
Held up their pearled wrists and took her in,
Bearing her straight to aged Nereus' hall,
Who, piteous of her woes, reared her lank head,
And gave her to his daughters to imbathe
In nectared lavers strewed with asphodel,
And through the porch and inlet of each sense
Dropped in ambrosial oils till she revived,
And underwent a quick, immortal change,
Made goddess of the river," etc.

If our readers ask when all this took place, we must answer, in the first place, that mythology is not careful of dates; and next, that, as Brutus was the great-grandson of Aeneas, it must have been not far from a century subsequent to the Trojan war, or about eleven hundred years before the invasion of the island by Julius Caesar. This long interval is filled with the names of princes whose chief occupation was in warring with one another.

Figure 52: "King Lear: Cordelia's Farewell" by Edwin Austin Abbey

Some few, whose names remain connected with places, or embalmed in literature, we will mention.

BLADUD

Bladud built the city of Bath, and dedicated the medicinal waters to Minerva. He was a man of great invention, and practised the arts of magic, till, having made him wings to fly, he fell down upon the temple of Apollo, in Trinovant, and so died, after twenty years' reign.

LEIR, OR LEAR

Leir, who next reigned, built Leicester, and called it after his name. He had no male issue, but only three daughters. When grown old he determined to divide his kingdom among his daughters, and bestow them in marriage. But first, to try which of them loved him best, he determined to ask them solemnly in order, and judge of the warmth of their affection by their answers. Goneril, the eldest, knowing well her father's weakness, made answer that she loved him "above her soul." "Since thou so honorest my declining age," said the old man, "to thee and to thy husband I give the third part of my realm." Such good success for a few words soon uttered was ample instruction to Regan, the second daughter, what to say. She therefore to the same question replied that "she loved him more than all the world beside;" and so received an equal reward with her sister. But Cordelia, the youngest, and hitherto the best beloved, though having before her eyes the reward of a little easy soothing, and the loss likely to attend plain- dealing, yet was not moved from the solid purpose of a sincere and virtuous answer, and replied: "Father, my love towards you is as my duty bids. They who pretend beyond this flatter." When the old man, sorry to hear this, and wishing her to recall these words, persisted in asking, she still restrained her expressions so as to say rather less than more than the truth. Then Leir, all in a passion, burst forth: "Since thou hast not reverenced thy aged father like thy sisters, think not to have any part in my kingdom or what else I have;"—and without delay, giving in marriage his other daughters, Goneril to the Duke of Albany, and Regan to the Duke of Cornwall, he divides his kingdom between them, and goes to reside with his eldest daughter, attended only by a hundred knights. But in a short time his attendants, being complained of as too numerous and disorderly, are reduced to thirty. Resenting that affront, the old king betakes him to his second daughter; but she, instead of soothing his wounded pride, takes part with her sister, and refuses to admit a retinue of more than five. Then back he returns to the other, who now will not receive him with more than one attendant. Then the remembrance of Cordeilla comes to his thoughts, and he takes his journey into France to seek her, with little hope of kind consideration from one whom he had so injured, but to pay her the last recompense he can render,— confession of his injustice. When Cordeilla is informed of his approach, and of his sad condition, she pours forth true filial tears. And, not willing that her own or others' eyes should see him in that forlorn condition, she sends one of her trusted servants to meet him, and convey him privately to some comfortable abode, and to furnish him with such state as befitted his dignity. After which Cordeilla, with the king her husband, went in state to meet him, and, after an honorable reception, the king permitted his wife, Cordeilla, to go with an army and set her father again upon his throne. They prospered, subdued the wicked sisters and their consorts, and Leir obtained the crown and held it three years. Cordeilla succeeded him and reigned five years; but the sons of her sisters, after that, rebelled against her, and she lost both her crown and life.

Shakspeare has chosen this story as the subject of his tragedy of "King Lear," varying its details in some respects. The madness of Leir, and the ill success of Cordeilla's attempt to reinstate her father, are the principal variations, and those in the names will also be noticed. Our narrative is drawn from Milton's "History;" and thus the reader will perceive that the story of Leir has had the distinguished honor of being told by the two acknowledged chiefs of British literature.

FERREX AND PORREX

Ferrex and Porrex were brothers, who held the kingdom after Leir. They quarrelled about the supremacy, and Porrex expelled his brother, who, obtaining aid from Suard, king of the Franks, returned and made war upon Porrex. Ferrex was slain in battle and his forces dispersed. When their mother came to hear of her son's death, who was her favorite, she fell into a great rage, and conceived a mortal hatred against the survivor. She took, therefore, her opportunity when he was asleep, fell upon him, and, with the assistance of her women, tore him in pieces. This horrid story would not be worth relating, were it not for the fact that it has furnished the plot for the first tragedy which was written in the English language. It was entitled "Gorboduc," but in the second edition "Ferrex and Porrex," and was the production of Thomas Sackville, afterwards Earl of Dorset, and Thomas Norton, a barrister. Its date was 1561.

DUNWALLO MOLMUTIUS

This is the next name of note. Molmutius established the Molmutine laws, which bestowed the privilege of sanctuary on temples, cities, and the roads leading to them, and gave the same protection to ploughs, extending a religious sanction to the labors of the field. Shakspeare alludes to him in "Cymbeline," Act III., Scene 1:

"... Molmutius made our laws;
Who was the first of Britain which did put
His brows within a golden crown, and called
Himself a king."

BRENNUS AND BELINUS

The sons of Molmutius, succeeded him. They quarrelled, and Brennus was driven out of the island, and took refuge in Gaul, where he met with such favor from the king of the Allobroges that he gave him his daughter in marriage, and made him his partner on the throne. Brennus is the name which the Roman historians give to the famous leader of the Gauls who took Rome in the time of Camillus. Geoffrey of Monmouth claims the glory of the conquest for the British prince, after he had become king of the Allobroges.

ELIDURE

After Belinus and Brennus there reigned several kings of little note, and then came Elidure. Arthgallo, his brother, being king, gave great offence to his powerful nobles, who rose against him, deposed him, and advanced Elidure to the throne. Arthgallo fled, and endeavored to find assistance in the neighboring kingdoms to reinstate him, but found none. Elidure reigned prosperously and wisely. After five years' possession of the kingdom, one day, when hunting, he met in the forest his brother,

Arthgallo, who had been deposed. After long wandering, unable longer to bear the poverty to which he was reduced, he had returned to Britain, with only ten followers, designing to repair to those who had formerly been his friends. Elidure, at the sight of his brother in distress, forgetting all animosities, ran to him, and embraced him. He took Arthgallo home with him, and concealed him in the palace. After this he feigned himself sick, and, calling his nobles about him, induced them, partly by persuasion, partly by force, to consent to his abdicating the kingdom, and reinstating his brother on the throne. The agreement being ratified, Elidure took the crown from his own head, and put it on his brother's head. Arthgallo after this reigned ten years, well and wisely, exercisng strict justice towards all men.

He died, and left the kingdom to his sons, who reigned with various fortunes, but were not long-lived, and left no offspring, so that Elidure was again advanced to the throne, and finished the course of his life in just and virtuous actions, receiving the name of THE PIOUS, from the love and admiration of his subjects.

Wordsworth has taken the story of Artegal and Elidure for the subject of a poem, which is No. 2 of "Poems founded on the Affections."

LUD

After Elidure, the Chronicle names many kings, but none of special note, till we come to Lud, who greatly enlarged Trinovant, his capital, and surrounded it with a wall. He changed its name, bestowing upon it his own, so that henceforth it was called Lud's town, afterwards London. Lud was buried by the gate of the city called after him Ludgate. He had two sons, but they were not old enough at the time of their father's death to sustain the cares of government, and therefore their uncle, Caswallaun, or Cassibellaunus, succeeded to the kingdom. He was a brave and magnificent prince, so that his fame reached to distant countries.

CASSIBELLAUNUS

About this time it happened (as is found in the Roman histories) that Julius Caesar, having subdued Gaul, came to the shore opposite Britain. And having resolved to add this island also to his conquests, he prepared ships and transported his army across the sea, to the mouth of the River Thames. Here he was met by Cassibellaun with all his forces, and a battle ensued, in which Nennius, the brother of Cassibellaun, engaged in single combat with Csesar. After several furious blows given and received, the sword of Caesar stuck so fast in the shield of Nennius that it could not be pulled out, and the combatants being separated by the intervention of the troops Nennius remained possessed of this trophy. At last, after the greater part of the day was spent, the Britons poured in so fast that Caesar was forced to retire to his camp and fleet. And finding it useless to continue the war any longer at that time, he returned to Gaul.

Shakspeare alludes to Cassibellaunus, in "Cymbeline":

"The famed Cassibelan, who was once at point
(O giglot fortune!) to master Caesar's sword,
Made Lud's town with rejoicing fires bright,
And Britons strut with courage."

KYMBELINUS, OR CYMBELINE

Caesar, on a second invasion of the island, was more fortunate, and compelled the Britons to pay tribute. Cymbeline, the nephew of the king, was delivered to the Romans as a hostage for the faithful fulfilment of the treaty, and, being carried to Rome by Caesar, he was there brought up in the Roman arts and accomplishments. Being afterwards restored to his country, and placed on the throne, he was attached to the Romans, and continued through all his reign at peace with them. His sons, Guiderius and Arviragus, who made their appearance in Shakspeare's play of "Cymbeline," succeeded their father, and, refusing to pay tributc to thc Romans, brought on another invasion. Guiderius was slain, but Arviragus afterward made terms with the Romans, and reigned prosperously many years.

ARMORICA

The next event of note is the conquest and colonization of Armorica, by Maximus, a Roman general, and Conan, lord of Miniadoc or Denbigh-land, in Wales. The name of the country was changed to Brittany, or Lesser Britain; and so completely was it possessed by the British colonists, that the language became assimilated to that spoken in Wales, and it is said that to this day the peasantry of the two countries can understand each other when speaking their native language.

The Romans eventually succeeded in establishing themselves in the island, and after the lapse of several generations they became blended with the natives so that no distinction existed between the two races. When at length the Roman armies were withdrawn from Britain, their departure was a matter of regret to the inhabitants, as it left them without protection against the barbarous tribes, Scots, Picts, and Norwegians, who harassed the country incessantly. This was the state of things when the era of King Arthur began.

The adventure of Albion, the giant, with Hercules is alluded to by Spenser, "Faery Queene," Book IV., Canto xi:

"For Albion the son of Neptune was;
Who for the proof of his great puissance,
Out of his Albion did on dry foot pass
Into old Gaul that now is cleped France,
To fight with Hercules, that did advance
To vanquish all the world with matchless might:
And there his mortal part by great mischance
Was slain."

Figure 53: "Vercingetorix Surrenders to Caesar" by Lionel Royer

Chapter 3

MERLIN

Merlin was the son of no mortal father, but of an Incubus, one of a class of beings not absolutely wicked, but far from good, who inhabit the regions of the air. Merlin's mother was a virtuous young woman, who, on the birth of her son, intrusted him to a priest, who hurried him to the baptismal fount, and so saved him from sharing the lot of his father, though he retained many marks of his unearthly origin.

At this time Vortigern reigned in Britain. He was a usurper, who had caused the death of his sovereign, Moines, and driven the two brothers of the late king, whose names were Uther and Pendragon, into banishment. Vortigern, who lived in constant fear of the return of the rightful heirs of the kingdom, began to erect a strong tower for defence. The edifice, when brought by the workmen to a certain height, three times fell to the ground, without any apparent cause. The king consulted his astrologers on this wonderful event, and learned from them that it would be necessary to bathe the corner-stone of the foundation with the blood of a child born without a mortal father.

In search of such an infant, Vortigern sent his messengers all over the kingdom, and they by accident discovered Merlin, whose lineage seemed to point him out as the individual wanted. They took him to the king; but Merlin, young as he was, explained to the king the absurdity of attempting to rescue the fabric by such means, for he told him the true cause of the instability of the tower was its being placed over the den of two immense dragons, whose combats shook the earth above them. The king ordered his workmen to dig beneath the tower, and when they had done so they discovered two enormous serpents, the one white as milk the other red as fire. The multitude looked on with amazement, till the serpents, slowly rising from their den, and expanding their enormous folds, began the combat, when everyone fled in terror, except Merlin, who stood by clapping his hands and cheering on the conflict. The red dragon was slain, and the white one, gliding through a cleft in the rock, disappeared.

These animals typified, as Merlin afterwards explained, the invasion of Uther and Pendragon, the rightful princes, who soon after landed with a great army. Vortigern was defeated, and afterwards burned alive in the castle he had taken such pains to construct. On the death of Vortigern, Pendragon ascended the throne. Merlin became his chief adviser, and often assisted the king by his magical arts.

"Merlin, who knew the range of all their arts,
Had built the King his havens, ships and halls."
—Vivian.

Among other endowments, he had the power of transforming himself into any shape he pleased. At one time he appeared as a dwarf, at others as a damsel, a page, or even a greyhound or a stag. This faculty he often employed for the service of the king, and sometimes also for the diversion of the court and the sovereign.

Merlin continued to be a favorite counsellor through the reigns of Pendragon, Uther, and Arthur, and at last disappeared from view, and was no more found among

Figure 54: "Vivien Pa II" by Paul Gustave Dore

Figure 55: "O Master, Do You Love My Tender Rhyme" by Eleanor Fortescue-Brickdale

men, through the treachery of his mistress, Viviane, the Fairy, which happened in this wise.

Merlin, having become enamoured of the fair Viviane, the Lady of the Lake, was weak enough to impart to her various important secrets of his art, being impelled by fatal destiny, of which he was at the same time fully aware. The lady, however, was not content with his devotion, unbounded as it seems to have been, but "cast about," the Romance tells us, how she might "detain him for evermore," and one day addressed him in these terms: "Sir, I would that we should make a fair place and a suitable, so contrived by art and by cunning that it might never be undone, and that you and I should be there in joy and solace." "My lady," said Merlin, "I will do all this." "Sir," said she, "I would not have you do it, but you shall teach me, and I will do it, and then it will be more to my mind." "I grant you this," said Merlin. Then he began to devise, and the damsel put it all in writing. And when he had devised the whole, then had the damsel full great joy, and showed him greater semblance of love than she had ever before made, and they sojourned together a long while. At length it fell out that, as they were going one day hand in hand through the forest of Breceliande, they found a bush of white-thorn, which was laden with flowers; and they seated themselves under the shade of this white-thorn, upon the green grass, and Merlin laid his head upon the damsel's lap, and fell asleep. Then the damsel rose, and made a ring with her wimple round the bush, and round Merlin, and began her enchantments, such as he himself had taught her; and nine times she made the ring, and nine times she made the enchantment, and then she went and sat down by him, and placed his head again upon her lap.

"And a sleep
Fell upon Merlin more like death, so deep
Her finger on her lips; then Vivian rose,
And from her brown-locked head the wimple throws,
And takes it in her hand and waves it over
The blossomed thorn tree and her sleeping lover.
Nine times she waved the fluttering wimple round,
And made a little plot of magic ground."
—Matthew Arnold.

And when he awoke, and looked round him, it seemed to him that he was enclosed in the strongest tower in the world, and laid upon a fair bed. Then said he to the dame: "My lady, you have deceived me, unless you abide with me, for no one hath power to unmake this tower but you alone." She then promised she would be often there, and in this she held her covenant with him. And Merlin never went out of that tower where his Mistress Viviane had enclosed him; but she entered and went out again when she listed.

After this event Merlin was never more known to hold converse with any mortal but Viviane, except on one occasion. Arthur, having for some time missed him from his court, sent several of his knights in search of him, and, among the number, Sir Gawain, who met with a very unpleasant adventure while engaged in this quest. Happening to pass a damsel on his road, and neglecting to salute her, she revenged herself for his incivility by transforming him into a hideous dwarf. He was bewailing aloud his evil fortune as he went through the forest of Breceliande, when suddenly he heard the voice of one groaning on his right hand; and, looking that way, he could see nothing save a kind of smoke, which seemed like air, and through which he could not pass. Merlin then addressed him from out the smoke, and told him by what misadventure he was imprisoned there. "Ah, sir!" he added, "you will never see me more, and that grieves me, but I cannot remedy it; I shall never more speak to you, nor to any other person, save only my mistress. But do thou hasten to King Arthur, and charge him from me to undertake, without delay, the quest of the Sacred Graal. The knight is already born, and has received knighthood at his hands, who is destined to accomplish this quest." And after this he comforted Gawain under his transformation, assuring him that he should speedily be disenchanted; and he predicted to him that he should find the king at Carduel, in Wales, on his return, and that all the other knights who had been on like quest would arrive there the same day as himself. And all this came to pass as Merlin had said.

Merlin is frequently introduced in the tales of chivalry, but it is chiefly on great occasions, and at a period subsequent to his death, or magical disappearance. In the romantic poems of Italy, and in Spenser, Merlin is chiefly represented as a magical artist. Spenser represents him as the artificer of the impenetrable shield and other armor of Prince Arthur ("Faery Queene," Book I., Canto vii.), and of a mirror, in which a damsel viewed her lover's shade. The Fountain of Love, in the "Orlando Innamorata," is described as his work; and in the poem of "Ariosto" we are told of a hall adorned with prophetic paintings, which demons had executed in a single night, under the direction of Merlin.

The following legend is from Spenser's "Faery Queene," Book III.,Canto iii.:

CAER-MERDIN, OR CAERMARTHEN (IN WALES), MERLIN'S TOWER, AND THE IMPRISONED FIENDS.

"Forthwith themselves disguising both, in straunge
And base attire, that none might them bewray,
To Maridunum, that is now by chaunge
Of name Caer-Merdin called, they took their way:
There the wise Merlin whylome wont (they say)
To make his wonne, low underneath the ground
In a deep delve, far from the view of day,
That of no living wight he mote be found,
Whenso he counselled with his sprights encompassed round.
"And if thou ever happen that same way
To travel, go to see that dreadful place;
It is a hideous hollow cave (they say)
Under a rock that lies a little space
From the swift Barry, tombling down apace
Amongst the woody hills of Dynevor;
But dare not thou, I charge, in any case,
To enter into that same baleful bower,
For fear the cruel fiends should thee unwares devour.
"But standing high aloft, low lay thine ear,
And there such ghastly noise of iron chains
And brazen cauldrons thou shalt rumbling hear,
Which thousand sprites with long enduring pains
Do toss, that it will stun thy feeble brains;
And oftentimes great groans, and grievous stounds,
When too huge toil and labor them constrains;
And oftentimes loud strokes and ringing sounds
From under that deep rock most horribly rebounds.
"The cause some say is this. A little while
Before that Merlin died, he did intend
A brazen wall in compas to compile
About Caermerdin, and did it commend
Unto these sprites to bring to perfect end;
During which work the Lady of the Lake,
Whom long he loved, for him in haste did send;
Who, thereby forced his workmen to forsake,
Them bound till his return their labor not to slack.
"In the mean time, through that false lady's train,
He was surprised, and buried under beare,
He ever to his work returned again;
Nathless those fiends may not their work forbear,
So greatly his commandement they fear;
But there do toil and travail day and night,
Until that brazen wall they up do rear.
For Merlin had in magic more insight
Than ever him before or after living wight."

[Footnote: Buried under beare. Buried under something which enclosed him like a coffin or bier.]

Chapter 4

ARTHUR

We shall begin our history of King Arthur by giving those particulars of his life which appear to rest on historical evidence; and then proceed to record those legends concerning him which form the earliest portion of British literature.

Arthur was a prince of the tribe of Britons called Silures, whose country was South Wales, the son of Uther, named Pendragon, a title given to an elective sovereign, paramount over the many kings of Britain. He appears to have commenced his martial career about the year 500, and was raised to the Pendragonship about ten years later. He is said to have gained twelve victories over the Saxons. The most important of them was that of Badon, by some supposed to be Bath, by others Berkshire. This was the last of his battles with the Saxons, and checked their progress so effectually, that Arthur experienced no more annoyance from them, and reigned in peace, until the revolt of his nephew Modred, twenty years later, which led to the fatal battle of Camlan, in Cornwall, in 542. Modred was slain, and Arthur, mortally wounded, was conveyed by sea to Glastonbury, where he died, and was buried. Tradition preserved the memory of the place of his interment within the abbey, as we are told by Giraldus Cambrensis, who was present when the grave was opened by command of Henry II. about 1150, and saw the bones and sword of the monarch, and a leaden cross let into his tombstone, with the inscription in rude Roman letters, "Here lies buried the famous King Arthur, in the island Avalonia." This story has been elegantly versified by Warton. A popular traditional belief was long entertained among the Britons, that Arthur was not dead, but had been carried off to be healed of his wounds in Fairy-land, and that he would reappear to avenge his countrymen and reinstate them in the sovereignty of Britain. In Warton's "Ode" a bard relates to King Henry the traditional story of Arthur's death, and closes with these lines.

"Yet in vain a paynim foe
Armed with fate the mighty blow:
For when he fell, the Elfin queen,
All in secret and unseen,
O'er the fainting hero threw
Her mantle of ambrosial blue,
And bade her spirits bear him far,
In Merlin's agate-axled car,
To her green isle's enamelled steep,
Far in the navel of the deep.
O'er his wounds she sprinkled dew
From flowers that in Arabia grew.
There he reigns a mighty king,
Thence to Britain shall return,
If right prophetic rolls I learn,
Borne on victory's spreading plume,
His ancient sceptre to resume,
His knightly table to restore,
And brave the tournaments of yore."

After this narration another bard came forward who recited a different story:

"When Arthur bowed his haughty crest,
No princess veiled in azure vest
Snatched him, by Merlin's powerful spell,
In groves of golden bliss to dwell;
But when he fell, with winged speed,
His champions, on a milk-white steed,
From the battle's hurricane,
Bore him to Joseph's towered fane,
In the fair vale of Avalon;
There, with chanted orison
And the long blaze of tapers clear,
The stoled fathers met the bier;
Through the dim aisles, in order dread
Of martial woe, the chief they led,
And deep entombed in holy ground,
Before the altar's solemn bound."

[Footnote: Glastonbury Abbey, said to be founded by Joseph of Arimathea, in a spot anciently called the island or valley of Avalonia.

Tennyson, in his "Palace of Art," alludes to the legend of Arthur's rescue by the Faery queen, thus:

"Or mythic Uther's deeply wounded son,
In some fair space of sloping greens,
Lay dozing in the vale of Avalon,
And watched by weeping queens."]

It must not be concealed that the very existence of Arthur has been denied by some. Milton says of him: "As to Arthur, more renowned in songs and romances than in true stories, who he was, and whether ever any such reigned in Britain, hath been doubted heretofore, and may again, with good reason." Modern critics, however, admit that there was a prince of this name, and find proof of it in the frequent mention of him in the writings of the Welsh bards. But the Arthur of romance, according to Mr. Owen, a Welsh scholar and antiquarian, is a mythological person. "Arthur," he says, "is the Great Bear, as the name literally implies (Arctos, Arcturus), and perhaps this constellation, being so near the pole, and visibly describing a circle in a small space, is the origin of the famous Round Table."

KING ARTHUR

Constans, king of Britain, had three sons, Moines, Ambrosius, otherwise called Uther, and Pendragon. Moines, soon after his accession to the crown, was vanquished by the Saxons, in consequence of the treachery of his seneschal, Vortigern, and growing unpopular, through misfortune, he was killed by his subjects, and the traitor Vortigern chosen in his place.

Vortigern was soon after defeated in a great battle by Uther and Pendragon, the surviving brothers of Moines, and Pendragon ascended the throne.

This prince had great confidence in the wisdom of Merlin, and made him his chief adviser. About this time a dreadful war arose between the Saxons and Britons. Merlin obliged the royal brothers to swear fidelity to each other, but predicted that one of them must fall in the first battle. The Saxons were routed, and Pendragon, being slain, was succeeded by Uther, who now assumed in addition to his own name the appellation of Pendragon.

Merlin still continued a favorite counsellor. At the request of Uther he transported by magic art enormous stones from Ireland, to form the sepulchre of Pendragon. These stones constitute the monument now called Stonehenge, on Salisbury plain.

Merlin next proceeded to Carlisle to prepare the Round Table, at which he seated an assemblage of the great nobles of the country. The companions admitted to this high order were bound by oath to assist each other at the hazard of their own lives, to attempt singly the most perilous adventures, to lead, when necessary, a life of monastic solitude, to fly to arms at the first summons, and never to retire from battle till they had defeated the enemy, unless night intervened and separated the combatants.

Soon after this institution, the king invited all his barons to the celebration of a great festival, which he proposed holding annually at Carlisle.

As the knights had obtained the sovereign's permission to bring their ladies along with them, the beautiful Igerne accompanied her husband, Gorlois, Duke of Tintadel, to one of these anniversaries. The king became deeply enamoured of the duchess, and disclosed his passion; but Igerne repelled his advances, and revealed his solicitations to her husband. On hearing this, the duke instantly removed from court with Igerne, and without taking leave of Uther. The king complained to his council of this want of duty, and they decided that the duke should be summoned to court, and, if refractory, should be treated as a rebel. As he refused to obey the citation, the king carried war into the estates of his vassal and besieged him in the strong castle of Tintadel. Merlin transformed the king into the likeness of Gorlois, and enabled him to have many stolen interviews with Igerne. At length the duke was killed in battle and the king espoused Igerne.

From this union sprang Arthur, who succeeded his father, Uther, upon the throne.

ARTHUR CHOSEN KING

Arthur, though only fifteen years old at his father's death, was elected king, at a general meeting of the nobles. It was not done without opposition, for there were many ambitious competitors.

"For while he linger'd there
A doubt that ever smoulder'd in the hearts

Of those great Lords and Barons of his realm
Flash'd forth and into war: for most of these
Made head against him, crying, 'Who is he
That he should rule us? who hath proven him
King Uther's son? for lo! we look at him,
And find nor face nor bearing, limbs nor voice,
Are like to those of Uther whom we knew."
—Coming of Arthur.

But Bishop Brice, a person of great sanctity, on Christmas eve addressed the assembly, and represented that it would well become them, at that solemn season, to put up their prayers for some token which should manifest the intentions of Providence respecting their future sovereign. This was done, and with such success, that the service was scarcely ended when a miraculous stone was discovered before the church door, and in the stone was firmly fixed a sword, with the following words engraven on its hilt:

"I am hight Escalibore,
Unto a king fair tresore."

Bishop Brice, after exhorting the assembly to offer up their thanksgiving for this signal miracle, proposed a law, that whoever should be able to draw out the sword from the stone, should be acknowledged as sovereign of the Britons; and his proposal was decreed by general acclamation. The tributary kings of Uther, and the most famous knights, successively put their strength to the proof, but the miraculous sword resisted all their efforts. It stood till Candlemas; it stood till Easter, and till Pentecost, when the best knights in the kingdom usually assembled for the annual tournament. Arthur, who was at that time serving in the capacity of squire to his foster-brother, Sir Kay, attended his master to the lists. Sir Kay fought with great valor and success, but had the misfortune to break his sword, and sent Arthur to his mother for a new one. Arthur hastened home, but did not find the lady; but having observed near the church a sword, sticking in a stone, he galloped to the place, drew out the sword with great ease, and delivered it to his master. Sir Kay would willingly have assumed to himself the distinction conferred by the possession of the sword, but when, to confirm the doubters, the sword was replaced in the stone he was utterly unable to withdraw it, and it would yield a second time to no hand but Arthur's. Thus decisively pointed out by Heaven as their king, Arthur was by general consent proclaimed as such, and an early day appointed for his solemn coronation.

Immediately after his election to the crown, Arthur found himself opposed by eleven kings and one duke, who with a vast army were actually encamped in the forest of Rockingham. By Merlin's advice Arthur sent an embassy to Brittany, to solicit the aid of King Ban and King Bohort, two of the best knights in the world. They accepted the call, and with a powerful army crossed the sea, landing at Portsmouth, where they were received with great rejoicing. The rebel kings were still superior in numbers; but Merlin, by a powerful enchantment, caused all their tents to fall down at once, and in the confusion Arthur with his allies fell upon them and totally routed them.

After defeating the rebels, Arthur took the field against the Saxons. As they were too strong for him unaided, he sent an embassy to Armorica, beseeching the assistance of Hoel, who soon after brought over an army to his aid. The two kings joined their forces, and sought the enemy, whom they met, and both sides prepared for a decisive engagement. "Arthur himself," as Geoffrey of Monmouth relates, "dressed in a breastplate worthy of so great a king, places on his head a golden helmet engraved with the semblance of a dragon. Over his shoulders he throws his shield called Priwen, on which a picture of the Holy Virgin constantly recalled her to his memory. Girt with Caliburn, a most excellent sword, and fabricated in the isle of Avalon, he graces his right hand with the lance named Ron. This was a long and broad spear, well contrived for slaughter." After a severe conflict, Arthur, calling on the name of the Virgin, rushes into the midst of his enemies, and destroys multitudes of them with the formidable Caliburn, and puts the rest to flight. Hoel, being detained by sickness, took no part in this battle.

This is called the victory of Mount Badon, and, however disguised by fable, it is regarded by historians as a real event.

The feats performed by Arthur at the battle of Badon Mount are thus celebrated in Drayton's verse:

"They sung how he himself at Badon bore, that day,
When at the glorious goal his British sceptre lay;
Two daies together how the battel stronglie stood;

Pendragon's worthie son, who waded there in blood,
Three hundred Saxons slew with his owne valiant hand."
—Song IV.

GUENEVER, OR GUINEVERE, OR GENEURA

Merlin had planned for Arthur a marriage with the daughter of King Laodegan of Carmalide. By his advice Arthur paid a visit to the court of that sovereign, attended only by Merlin and by thirty- nine knights whom the magician had selected for that service. On their arrival they found Laodegan and his peers sitting in council, endeavoring, but with small prospect of success, to devise means of resisting the impending attack of Ryence, king of Ireland, who, with fifteen tributary kings and an almost innumerable army, had nearly surrounded the city. Merlin, who acted as leader of the band of British knights, announced them as strangers, who came to offer the king their services in his wars; but under the express condition that they should be at liberty to conceal their names and quality until they should think proper to divulge them. These terms were thought very strange, but were thankfully accepted, and the strangers, after taking the usual oath to the king, retired to the lodging which Merlin had prepared for them.

A few days after this, the enemy, regardless of a truce into which they had entered with King Laodegan, suddenly issued from their camp and made an attempt to surprise the city. Cleodalis, the king's general, assembled the royal forces with all possible despatch. Arthur and his companions also flew to arms, and Merlin appeared at their head, bearing a standard on which was emblazoned a terrific dragon. Merlin advanced to the gate, and commanded the porter to open it, which the porter refused to do, without the king's order. Merlin thereupon took up the gate, with all its appurtenances of locks, bars, bolts, etc., and directed his troops to pass through, after which he replaced it in perfect order. He then set spurs to his horse and dashed, at the head of his little troop, into a body of two thousand pagans. The disparity of numbers being so enormous, Merlin cast a spell upon the enemy, so as to prevent their seeing the small number of their assailants; notwithstanding which the British knights were hard pressed. But the people of the city, who saw from the walls this unequal contest, were ashamed of leaving the small body of strangers to their fate, so they opened the gate and sallied forth. The numbers were now more nearly equal, and Merlin revoked his spell, so that the two armies encountered on fair terms. Where Arthur, Ban, Bohort, and the rest fought the king's army had the advantage; but in another part of the field the king himself was surrounded and carried off by the enemy. The sad sight was seen by Guenever, the fair daughter of the king, who stood on the city wall and looked at the battle. She was in dreadful distress, tore her hair, and swooned away.

But Merlin, aware of what passed in every part of the field, suddenly collected his knights, led them out of the battle, intercepted the passage of the party who were carrying away the king, charged them with irresistible impetuosity, cut in pieces or dispersed the whole escort, and rescued the king. In the fight Arthur encountered Caulang, a giant fifteen feet high, and the fair Guenever, who had already began to feel a strong interest in the handsome young stranger, trembled for the issue of the contest. But Arthur, dealing a dreadful blow on the shoulder of the monster, cut through his neck so that his head hung over on one side, and in this condition his horse carried him about the field, to the great horror and dismay of the Pagans. Guenever could not refrain from expressing aloud her wish that the gentle knight, who dealt with giants so dexterously, were destined to become her husband, and the wish was echoed by her attendants. The enemy soon turned their backs and fled with precipitation, closely pursued by Laodegan and his allies.

After the battle Arthur was disarmed and conducted to the bath by the princess Guenever, while his friends were attended by the other ladies of the court. After the bath the knights were conducted to a magnificent entertainment, at which they were diligently served by the same fair attendants. Laodegan, more and more anxious to know the name and quality of his generous deliverers, and occasionally forming a secret wish that the chief of his guests might be captivated by the charms of his daughter, appeared silent and pensive, and was scarcely roused from his reverie by the banters of his courtiers. Arthur, having had an opportunity of explaining to Guenever his great esteem for her merit, was in the joy of his heart, and was still further delighted by hearing from Merlin the late exploits of Gawain at London, by means of which his

Figure 56: "Queen Guinevere Bidding Farewell to Sir Lancelot" by Emil Teschendorff

immediate return to his dominions was rendered unnecessary, and he was left at liberty to protract his stay at the court of Laodegan. Every day contributed to increase the admiration of the whole court for the gallant strangers, and the passion of Guenever for their chief; and when at last Merlin announced to the king that the object of the visit of the party was to procure a bride for their leader, Laodegan at once presented Guenever to Arthur, telling him that, whatever might be his rank, his merit was sufficient to entitle him to the possession of the heiress of Carmalide.

"And could he find a woman in her womanhood
As great as he was in his manhood—
The twain together might change the world."
—Guinevere.

Arthur accepted the lady with the utmost gratitude, and Merlin then proceeded to satisfy the king of the rank of his son-in-law; upon which Laodegan, with all his barons, hastened to do homage to their lawful sovereign, the successor of Uther Pendragon. The fair Guenever was then solemnly betrothed to Arthur, and a magnificent festival was proclaimed, which lasted seven days. At the end of that time, the enemy appearing again with renewed force, it became necessary to resume military operations. [Footnote: Guenever, the name of Arthur's queen, also written Genievre and Geneura, is familiar to all who are conversant with chivalric lore. It is to her adventures, and those of her true knight, Sir Launcelot, that Dante alludes in the beautiful episode of Francesca di Rimini.]

We must now relate what took place at and near London, while Arthur was absent from his capital. At this very time a band of young heroes were on their way to Arthur's court, for the purpose of receiving knighthood from him. They were Gawain and his three brothers, nephews of Arthur, sons of King Lot, and Galachin, another nephew, son of King Nanters. King Lot had been one of the rebel chiefs whom Arthur had defeated, but he now hoped by means of the young men to be reconciled to his brother-in-law. He equipped his sons and his nephew with the utmost magnificence, giving them a splendid retinue of young men, sons of earls and barons, all mounted on the best horses, with complete suits of choice armor. They numbered in all seven hundred, but only nine had yet received the order of knighthood; the rest were candidates for that honor, and anxious to earn it by an early encounter with the enemy. Gawain, the leader, was a knight of wonderful strength; but what was most remarkable about him was that his strength was greater at certain hours of the day than at others. From nine o'clock till noon his strength was doubled, and so it was from three to evensong; for the rest of the time it was less remarkable, though at all times surpassing that of ordinary men.

After a march of three days they arrived in the vicinity of London, where they expected to find Arthur and his court, and very unexpectedly fell in with a large convoy belonging to the enemy, consisting of numerous carts and wagons, all loaded with provisions, and escorted by three thousand men, who had been collecting spoil from all the country round. A single charge from Gawain's impetuous cavalry was sufficient to disperse the escort and recover the convoy, which was instantly despatched to London. But before long a body of seven thousand fresh soldiers advanced to the attack of the five princes and their little army. Gawain, singling out a chief named Choas, of gigantic size, began the battle by splitting him from the crown of the head to the breast. Galachin encountered King Sanagran, who was also very huge, and cut off his head. Agrivain and Gahariet also performed prodigies of valor. Thus they kept the great army of assailants at bay, though hard pressed, till of a sudden they perceived a strong body of the citizens advancing from London, where the convoy which had been recovered by Gawain had arrived, and informed the mayor and citizens of the danger of their deliverer. The arrival of the Londoners soon decided the contest. The enemy fled in all directions, and Gawain and his friends, escorted by the grateful citizens, entered London, and were received with acclamations.

Chapter 5

ARTHUR (CONTINUED)

After the great victory of Mount Badon, by which the Saxons were for the time effectually put down, Arthur turned his arms against the Scots and Picts, whom he routed at Lake Lomond, and compelled to sue for mercy. He then went to York to keep his Christmas, and employed himself in restoring the Christian churches which the Pagans had rifled and overthrown. The following summer he conquered Ireland, and then made a voyage with his fleet to Iceland, which he also subdued. The kings of Gothland and of the Orkneys came voluntarily and made their submission, promising to pay tribute. Then he returned to Britain, where, having established the kingdom, he dwelt twelve years in peace.

Figure 57: "Guinever" by Henry Justice Ford

During this time he invited over to him all persons whatsoever that were famous for valor in foreign nations, and augmented the number of his domestics, and introduced such politeness into his court as people of the remotest countries thought worthy of their imitation. So that there was not a nobleman who thought himself of any consideration unless his clothes and arms were made in the same fashion as those of Arthur's knights.

Finding himself so powerful at home, Arthur began to form designs for extending his power abroad. So, having prepared his fleet, he first attempted Norway, that he might procure the crown of it for Lot, his sister's husband. Arthur landed in Norway, fought a great battle with the king of that country, defeated him, and pursued the victory till he had reduced the whole country under his dominion, and established Lot upon the throne. Then Arthur made a voyage to Gaul and laid siege to the city of Paris. Gaul was at that time a Roman province, and governed by Flollo, the Tribune. When the siege of Paris had continued a month, and the people began to suffer from famine, Flollo challenged Arthur to single combat, proposing to decide the conquest of the province in that way. Arthur gladly accepted the challenge, and slew his adversary in the contest, upon which the citizens surrendered the city to him. After the victory Arthur divided his army into two parts, one of which he committed to the conduct of Hoel, whom he ordered to march into Aquitaine, while he with the other part should endeavor to subdue the other provinces. At the end of nine years, in which time all the parts of Gaul were entirely reduced, Arthur returned to Paris, where he kept his court, and, calling an assembly of the clergy and people, established peace and the just administration of the laws in that kingdom. Then he bestowed Normandy upon Bedver, his butler, and the province of Andegavia upon Kay, his steward, [Footnote: This name, in the French romances, is spelled Queux, which means head cook. This would seem to imply that it was a title, and not a name; yet the personage who bore it is never mentioned by any other. He is the chief, if not the only, comic character among the heroes of Arthur's court. He is the Seneschal or Steward, his duties also embracing those of chief of the cooks. In the romances, his general character is a compound of valor and buffoonery, always ready to fight, and generally getting the worst of the battle. He is also sarcastic and abusive in his remarks, by which he often gets into trouble. Yet Arthur seems to have an attachment to him, and often takes his advice, which is generally wrong.] and several other provinces upon his great men that attended him. And, having settled the peace of the cities and countries, he returned back in the beginning of spring to Britain.

Upon the approach of the feast of Pentecost, Arthur, the better to demonstrate his joy after such triumphant successes, and for the more solemn observation of that festival, and reconciling the minds of the princes that were now subject to him, resolved during that season to hold a magnificent court, to place the crown upon his head, and to invite all the kings and dukes under his subjection to the solemnity. And he pitched upon Caerleon, the City of Legions, as the proper place for his purpose. For, besides its great wealth above the other cities, its situation upon the river Usk, near the Severn sea, was most pleasant and fit for so great a solemnity. For on one side it was washed by that noble river, so that the kings and princes from the countries beyond the seas might have the convenience of sailing up to it. On the other side the beauty of the meadows and groves, and magnificence of the royal palaces, with lofty gilded roofs that adorned it, made it even rival the grandeur of Rome. It was also famous for two churches, whereof one was adorned with a choir of virgins, who devoted themselves wholly to the service of God, and the other maintained a convent of priests. Besides, there was a college of two hundred philosophers, who, being learned in astronomy and the other arts, were diligent in observing the courses of the stars, and gave Arthur true predictions of the events that would happen. In this place, therefore, which afforded such delights, were preparations made for the ensuing festival.

[Footnote: Several cities are allotted to King Arthur by the romance-writers. The principal are Caerleon, Camelot, and Carlisle.

Caerleon derives its name from its having been the station of one of the legions, during the dominion of the Romans. It is called by Latin writers Urbs Legionum, the City of Legions. The former word being rendered into Welsh by Caer, meaning city, and the latter contracted into lleon. The river Usk retains its name in modern geography, and there is a town or city of Caerleon upon it, though the city of Cardiff is thought to be the scene of Arthur's court. Chester also bears in Welsh the name of Caerleon; for Chester, derived from castra, Latin for camp, is the designation of military headquarters.

Camelot is thought to be Winchester.

Shalott is Guilford.

Hamo's Port is Southampton.

Carlisle is the city still retaining that name, near the Scottish border. But this name is also sometimes applied to other places, which were, like itself, military stations.]

Ambassadors were then sent into several kingdoms, to invite to court the princes both of Gaul and of the adjacent islands. Accordingly, there came Augusel, king of Albania, now Scotland, Cadwallo, king of Venedotia, now North Wales, Sater, king of Demetia, now South Wales; also the archbishops of the metropolitan sees, London and York, and Dubricius, bishop of Caerleon, the City of Legions. This prelate, who was primate of Britain, was so eminent for his piety that he could cure any sick person by his prayers. There were also the counts of the principal cities, and many other worthies of no less dignity.

From the adjacent islands came Guillamurius, king of Ireland, Gunfasius, king of the Orkneys, Malvasius, king of Iceland, Lot, king of Norway, Bedver, the butler, Duke of Normandy, Kay, the sewer, Duke of Andegavia; also the twelve peers of Gaul, and Hoel, Duke of the Armorican Britons, with his nobility, who came with such a train of mules, horses, and rich furniture as it is difficult to describe. Besides these there remained no prince of any consideration on this side of Spain who came not upon this invitation. And no wonder, when Arthur's munificence, which was celebrated over the whole world, made him beloved by all people.

When all were assembled upon the day of the solemnity the archbishops were conducted to the palace, in order to place the crown upon the king's head. Then Dubricius, inasmuch as the court was held in his diocese, made himself ready to celebrate the office. As soon as the king was invested with his royal habiliments he was conducted in great pomp to the metropolitan church, having four kings, viz., of Albania, Cornwall, Demetia,

Figure 58: Merlin Presenting the Future King Arthur" by Emil Johann Lauffer

and Venedotia, bearing four golden swords before him. On another part was the queen, dressed out in her richest ornaments, conducted by the archbishops and bishops to the Church of Virgins; the four queens, also, of the kings last mentioned, bearing before her four white doves, according to ancient custom. When the whole procession was ended so transporting was the harmony of the musical instruments and voices, whereof there was a vast variety in both churches, that the knights who attended were in doubt which to prefer, and therefore crowded from the one to the other by turns, and were far from being tired of the solemnity, though the whole day had been spent in it. At last, when divine service was over at both churches, the king and queen put off their crowns, and, putting on their lighter ornaments, went to the banquet. When they had all taken their seats according to precedence, Kay, the sewer, in rich robes of ermine, with a thousand young noblemen all in like manner clothed in rich attire, served up the dishes. From another part Bedver, the butler, was followed by the same number of attendants, who waited with all kinds of cups and drinking-vessels. And there was food and drink in abundance, and everything was of the best kind, and served in the best manner. For at that time Britain had arrived at such a pitch of grandeur that in riches, luxury, and politeness it far surpassed all other kingdoms.

As soon as the banquets were over they went into the fields without the city to divert themselves with various sports, such as shooting with bows and arrows, tossing the pike, casting of heavy stones and rocks, playing at dice, and the like, and all these inoffensively, and without quarrelling. In this manner were three days spent, and after that they separated, and the kings and noblemen departed to their several homes.

After this Arthur reigned five years in peace. Then came ambassadors from Lucius Tiberius, Procurator under Leo, Emperor of Rome, demanding tribute. But

Arthur refused to pay tribute, and prepared for war. As soon as the necessary dispositions were made he committed the government of his kingdom to his nephew Modred and to Queen Guenever, and marched with his army to Hamo's Port, where the wind stood fair for him. The army crossed over in safety, and landed at the mouth of the river Barba. And there they pitched their tents to wait the arrival of the kings of the islands.

As soon as all the forces were arrived Arthur marched forward to Augustodunum, and encamped on the banks of the river Alba. Here repeated battles were fought, in all which the Britons, under their valiant leaders, Hoel, Duke of Armorica, and Gawain, nephew to Arthur, had the advantage. At length Lucius Tiberius determined to retreat, and wait for the Emperor Leo to join him with fresh troops. But Arthur, anticipating this event, took possession of a certain valley, and closed up the way of retreat to Lucius, compelling him to fight a decisive battle, in which Arthur lost some of the bravest of his knights and most faithful followers. But on the other hand Lucius Tiberius was slain, and his army totally defeated. The fugitives dispersed over the country, some to the by-ways and woods, some to cities and towns, and all other places where they could hope for safety.

Arthur stayed in those parts till the next winter was over, and employed his time in restoring order and settling the government. He then returned into England, and celebrated his victories with great splendor.

Then the king stablished all his knights, and to them that were not rich he gave lands, and charged them all never to do outrage nor murder, and always to flee treason; also, by no means to be cruel, but to give mercy unto him that asked mercy, upon pain of forfeiture of their worship and lordship; and always to do ladies, damosels, and gentlewomen service, upon pain of death. Also that no man take battle in a wrongful quarrel, for no law, nor for any world's goods. Unto this were all the knights sworn of the Table Round, both old and young. And at every year were they sworn at the high feast of Pentecost.

KING ARTHUR SLAYS THE GIANT OF ST. MICHAEL'S MOUNT

While the army was encamped in Brittany, awaiting the arrival of the kings, there came a countryman to Arthur, and told him that a giant, whose cave was on a neighboring mountain, called St. Michael's Mount, had for a long time been accustomed to carry off the children of the peasants to devour them. "And now he hath taken the Duchess of Brittany, as she rode with her attendants, and hath carried her away in spite of all they could do." "Now, fellow," said King Arthur, "canst thou bring me there where this giant haunteth?" "Yea, sure," said the good man; "lo, yonder where thou seest two great fires, there shalt thou find him, and more treasure than I suppose is in all France beside." Then the king called to him Sir Bedver and Sir Kay, and commanded them to make ready horse and harness for himself and them; for after evening he would ride on pilgrimage to St. Michael's Mount.

So they three departed, and rode forth till they came to the foot of the mount. And there the king commanded them to tarry, for he would himself go up into that mount. So he ascended the hill till he came to a great fire, and there he found an aged woman sitting by a new-made grave, making great sorrow. Then King Arthur saluted her, and demanded of her wherefore she made such lamentation; to whom she answered: "Sir knight, speak low, for yonder is a devil, and if he hear thee speak, he will come and destroy thee. For ye cannot make resistance to him, he is so fierce and so strong. He hath murdered the Duchess, which here lieth, who was the fairest of all the world, wife to Sir Hoel, Duke of Brittany." "Dame," said the king, "I come from the noble conqueror, King Arthur, to treat with that tyrant." "Fie on such treaties," said she; "he setteth not by the king, nor by no man else." "Well," said Arthur, "I will accomplish my message for all your fearful words." So he went forth by the crest of the hill, and saw where the giant sat at supper, gnawing on the limb of a man, and baking his broad limbs at the fire, and three fair damsels lying bound, whose lot it was to be devoured in their turn. When King Arthur beheld that, he had great compassion on them, so that his heart bled for sorrow. Then he hailed the giant, saying, "He that all the world ruleth give thee short life and shameful death. Why hast thou murdered this Duchess? Therefore come forth, for this day thou shalt die by my hand." Then the giant started up, and took a great club, and smote at the king, and smote off his coronal; and then the king struck him in the belly with his sword, and made a fearful wound. Then the giant threw away his club, and caught the king in his arms, so that he crushed his ribs. Then the three maidens kneeled down and prayed for help and comfort for Arthur. And Arthur weltered and wrenched, so that he was one while under, and another time above. And so weltering and wallowing they rolled down the hill, and ever as they weltered Arthur smote him with his dagger; and it fortuned they came to the place where the two knights were. And when they saw the king fast in the giant's arms they came and loosed him. Then the king commanded Sir Kay to smite off the giant's head, and to set it on the truncheon of a spear, and fix it on the barbican, that all the people might see and behold it. This was done, and anon it was known through all the country, wherefore the people came and thanked the king. And he said, "Give your thanks to God; and take ye the giant's spoil and divide it among you." And King Arthur caused a church to be builded on that hill, in honor of St. Michael.

KING ARTHUR GETS A SWORD FROM THE LADY OF THE LAKE

One day King Arthur rode forth, and on a sudden he was ware of three churls chasing Merlin, to have slain him. And the king rode unto them and bade them, "Flee, churls!" Then were they afraid when they saw a knight, and fled. "O Merlin," said Arthur, "here hadst thou been slain, for all thy crafts, had I not been by." "Nay," said Merlin, "not so, for I could save myself if I would; but thou art more near thy death than I am." So, as they went thus talking, King Arthur perceived where sat a knight on horseback, as if to guard the pass. "Sir knight," said Arthur, "for what cause abidest thou here?" Then the knight said, "There may no knight ride this way unless he just with me, for such is the custom of the pass." "I will amend that custom," said the king. Then they ran together, and they met so hard that their spears were shivered. Then they drew their swords and fought a strong battle, with many great strokes. But at length the sword of the knight smote King Arthur's sword in two pieces. Then said the knight unto Arthur, "Thou art in my power, whether to save thee or slay thee, and unless thou yield thee as overcome and recreant, thou shalt die." "As for death," said King Arthur, "welcome be it when it cometh; but to yield me unto thee as recreant, I will not." Then he leapt upon the knight, and took him by the middle and threw him down; but the knight was a passing strong man, and anon he brought Arthur under him, and would have razed off his helm to slay him. Then said Merlin, "Knight, hold thy hand, for this knight is a man of more worship than thou art aware of." "Why, who is he?" said the knight. "It is King Arthur." Then would he have slain him for dread of his wrath, and lifted up his sword to slay him; and therewith Merlin cast an enchantment on the knight, so that he fell to the earth in a great sleep. Then Merlin took up King Arthur, and set him on his horse. "Alas!" said Arthur, "what hast thou done, Merlin? hast thou slain this good knight by thy crafts?" "Care ye not," said Merlin; "he is wholer than ye be. He is only asleep, and will wake in three hours."

Then the king and he departed, and went till they came to a hermit, that was a good man and a great leech. So the hermit searched all his wounds, and applied good salves; and the king was there three days, and then were his wounds well amended, that he might ride and go. So they departed, and as they rode Arthur said, "I have no sword." "No matter," said Merlin; "hereby is a sword that shall be yours." So they rode till they came to a lake, which was a fair water and broad. And in the midst of the lake Arthur was aware of an arm clothed in white samite, [Footnote: Samite, a sort of silk stuff.] that held a fair sword in the hand. "Lo!" said Merlin, "yonder is that sword that I spake of. It belongeth to the Lady of the Lake, and, if she will, thou mayest take it; but if she will not, it will not be in thy power to take it."

So Sir Arthur and Merlin alighted from their horses, and went into a boat. And when they came to the sword that the hand held Sir Arthur took it by the handle and took it to him, and the arm and the hand went under the water.

Then they returned unto the land and rode forth. And Sir Arthur looked on the sword and liked it right well.

So they rode unto Caerleon, whereof his knights were passing glad. And when they heard of his adventures they marvelled that he would jeopard his person so alone. But all men of worship said it was a fine thing to be under such a chieftain as would put his person in adventure as other poor knights did.

Chapter 6

SIR GAWAIN

Sir Gawain was nephew to King Arthur, by his sister Morgana, married to Lot, king of Orkney, who was by Arthur made king of Norway. Sir Gawain was one of the most famous knights of the Round Table, and is characterized by the romancers as the SAGE and COURTEOUS Gawain. To this Chaucer alludes in his "Squiere's Tale," where the strange knight "salueth" all the court

"With so high reverence and observance,
As well in speeche as in countenance,
That Gawain, with his olde curtesie,
Though he were come agen out of faerie,
Ne coude him not amenden with a word."

Gawain's brothers were Agrivain, Gahariet, and Gareth.

SIR GAWAIN'S MARRIAGE

Once upon a time King Arthur held his court in merry Carlisle, when a damsel came before him and craved a boon. It was for vengeance upon a caitiff knight, who had made her lover captive and despoiled her of her lands. King Arthur commanded to bring him his sword, Excalibar, and to saddle his steed, and rode forth without delay to right the lady's wrong. Ere long he reached the castle of the grim baron, and challenged him to the conflict. But the castle stood on magic ground, and the spell was such that no knight could tread thereon but straight his courage fell and his strength decayed. King Arthur felt the charm, and before a blow was struck, his sturdy limbs lost their strength, and his head grew faint. He was fain to yield himself prisoner to the churlish knight, who refused to release him except upon condition that he should return at the end of a year, and bring a true answer to the question, "What thing is it which women most desire?" or in default thereof surrender himself and his lands. King Arthur accepted the terms, and gave his oath to return at the time appointed. During the year the king rode east, and he rode west, and inquired of all whom he met what thing it is which all women most desire. Some told him riches; some, pomp and state; some, mirth; some, flattery; and some, a gallant knight. But in the diversity of answers he could find no sure dependence. The year was well-nigh spent, when one day, as he rode thoughtfully through a forest, he saw sitting beneath a tree a lady of such hideous aspect that he turned away his eyes, and when she greeted him in seemly sort, made no answer. "What wight art thou," the lady said, "that will not speak to me? It may chance that I may resolve thy doubts, though I be not fair of aspect." "If thou wilt do so," said King Arthur, "choose what reward thou wilt, thou grim lady, and it shall be given thee." "Swear me this upon thy faith," she said, and Arthur swore it. Then the lady told him the secret, and demanded her reward, which was that the king should find some fair and courtly knight to be her husband.

King Arthur hastened to the grim baron's castle and told him one by one all the answers which he had received from his various advisers, except the last, and not one was admitted as the true one. "Now yield thee, Arthur," the giant said, "for thou hast not paid thy ransom, and thou and thy lands are forfeited to me." Then King Arthur said:

"Yet hold thy hand, thou proud baron,
I pray thee hold thy hand,
And give me leave to speak once more,
In rescue of my land.
This morn as I came over a moor,
I saw a lady set,
Between an oak and a green holly,
All clad in red scarlett.
She says ALL WOMEN WOULD HAVE THEIR WILL,
This is their chief desire;
Now yield, as thou art a baron true,
That I have paid my hire."

"It was my sister that told thee this," the churlish baron exclaimed. "Vengeance light on her! I will some time or other do her as ill a turn."

King Arthur rode homeward, but not light of heart, for he remembered the promise he was under to the loathly lady to—give her one of his young and gallant knights for

Figure 59: "Sir Gawain & the Lady Lys" by Morris M. Williams

a husband. He told his grief to Sir Gawain, his nephew, and he replied, "Be not sad, my lord, for I will marry the loathly lady." King Arthur replied:

"Now nay, now nay, good Sir Gawaine,
My sister's son ye be;
The loathly lady's all too grim,
And all too foule for thee."

But Gawain persisted, and the king at last, with sorrow of heart, consented that Gawain should be his ransom. So one day the king and his knights rode to the forest, met the loathly lady, and brought her to the court. Sir Gawain stood the scoffs and jeers of his companions as he best might, and the marriage was solemnized, but not with the usual festivities. Chaucer tells us:

"... There was no joye ne feste at alle;
There n' as but hevinesse and mochel sorwe,
For prively he wed her on the morwe,
And all day after hid him as an owle,
So wo was him his wife loked so foule!"

[Footnote: N'AS is NOT WAS, contracted; in modern phrase, THERE WAS NOT. MOCHEL SORWE is much sorrow; MORWE is MORROW.]

When night came, and they were alone together, Sir Gawain could not conceal his aversion; and the lady asked him why he sighed so heavily, and turned away his face. He candidly confessed it was on account of three things, her age, her ugliness, and her low degree. The lady, not at all offended, replied with excellent arguments to all his objections. She showed him that with age is discretion, with ugliness security from rivals, and that all true gentility depends, not upon the accident of birth, but upon the character of the individual.

Sir Gawain made no reply; but, turning his eyes on his bride, what was his amazement to perceive that she wore no longer the unseemly aspect that had so distressed him. She then told him that the form she had worn was not her true form, but a disguise imposed upon her by a wicked enchanter, and that she was condemned to wear it until two things should happen: one, that she should obtain some young and gallant knight to be her husband. This having been done, one-half of the charm was removed. She was now at liberty to wear her true form for half the time, and she bade him choose whether he would have her fair by day, and ugly by night, or the reverse. Sir Gawain would fain have had her look her best by night, when he alone would see her, and show her repulsive visage, if at all, to others. But she reminded him how much more pleasant it would be to her to wear her best looks in the throng of knights and ladies by day. Sir Gawain yielded, and gave up his will to hers. This alone was wanting to dissolve the charm. The lovely lady now with joy assured him that she should change no more, but as she now was, so would she remain by night as well as by day.

"Sweet blushes stayned her rud-red cheek,
Her eyen were black as sloe,
The ripening cherrye swelled her lippe,
And all her neck was snow.
Sir Gawain kist that ladye faire
Lying upon the sheete,
And swore, as he was a true knight,
The spice was never so swete."

The dissolution of the charm which had held the lady also released her brother, the "grim baron," for he too had been implicated in it. He ceased to be a churlish oppressor, and became a gallant and generous knight as any at Arthur's court.

Chapter 7

CARADOC BRIEFBRAS, OR CARADOC WITH THE SHRUNKEN ARM

Caradoc was the son of Ysenne, the beautiful niece of Arthur. He was ignorant who his father was, till it was discovered in the following manner: When the youth was of proper years to receive the honors of knighthood, King Arthur held a grand court for the purpose of knighting him. On this occasion a strange knight presented himself, and challenged the knights of Arthur's court to exchange blow for blow with him. His proposal was this—to lay his neck on a block for any knight to strike, on condition that, if he survived the blow, the knight should submit in turn to the same experiment. Sir Kay, who was usually ready to accept all challenges, pronounced this wholly unreasonable, and declared that he would not accept it for all the wealth in the world. And when the knight offered his sword, with which the operation was to be performed, no person ventured to accept it, till Caradoc, growing angry at the disgrace which was thus incurred by the Round Table, threw aside his mantle and took it. "Do you do this as one of the best knights?" said the stranger. "No," he replied, "but as one of the most foolish." The stranger lays his head upon the block, receives a blow which sends it rolling from his shoulders, walks after it, picks it up, replaces it with great success, and says he will return when the court shall be assembled next year, and claim his turn. When the anniversary arrived, both parties were punctual to their engagement. Great entreaties were used by the king and queen, and the whole court, in behalf of Caradoc, but the stranger was inflexible. The young knight laid his head upon the block, and more than once desired him to make an end of the business, and not keep him longer in so disagreeable a state of expectation. At last the stranger strikes him gently with the side of the sword, bids him rise, and reveals to him the fact that he is his father, the enchanter Eliaures, and that he gladly owns him for a son, having proved his courage and fidelity to his word.

But the favor of enchanters is short-lived and uncertain. Eliaures fell under the influence of a wicked woman, who, to satisfy her pique against Caradoc, persuaded the enchanter to fasten on his arm a serpent, which remained there sucking at his flesh and blood, no human skill sufficing either to remove the reptile or alleviate the torments which Caradoc endured.

Caradoc was betrothed to Guimier, sister to his bosom friend, Cador, and daughter to the king of Cornwall. As soon as they were informed of his deplorable condition, they set out for Nantes, where Caradoc's castle was, that Guimier might attend upon him. When Caradoc heard of their coming, his first emotion was that of joy and love. But soon he began to fear that the sight of his emaciated form, and of his sufferings, would disgust Guimier; and this apprehension became so strong, that he departed secretly from Nantes, and hid himself in a hermitage. He was sought far and near by the knights of Arthur's court, and Cador made a vow never to desist from the quest till he should have found him. After long wandering, Cador discovered his friend in the hermitage, reduced almost to a skeleton, and apparently near his death. All other means of relief having already been tried in vain, Cador at last prevailed on the enchanter Eliaures to disclose the only method which could avail for his rescue. A maiden must be found, his equal in birth and beauty, and loving him better than herself, so that she would expose herself to the same torment to deliver him. Two vessels were then to be provided, the one filled with sour wine, and the other with milk. Caradoc must enter the first, so that the wine should

Figure 60: "Sir Kay Nreakth His Sword" by Howard Pyle

reach his neck, and the maiden must get into the other, and, exposing her bosom upon the edge of the vessel, invite the serpent to forsake the withered flesh of his victim for this fresh and inviting food. The vessels were to be placed three feet apart, and as the serpent crossed from one to the other. a knight was to cut him in two. If he failed in his blow, Caradoc would indeed be delivered, but it would be only to see his fair champion suffering the same cruel and hopeless torment. The sequel may be easily foreseen. Guimier willingly exposed herself to the perilous adventure, and Cador, with a lucky blow, killed the serpent. The arm in which Caradoc had suffered so long recovered its strength, but not its shape, in consequence of which he was called Caradoc Briefbras, Caradoc of the Shrunken Arm.

Caradoc and Guimier are the hero and heroine of the ballad Of the "Boy and the Mantle," which follows:

"THE BOY AND THE MANTLE
"In Carlisle dwelt King Arthur,
A prince of passing might,
And there maintained his Table Round,
Beset with many a knight.
"And there he kept his Christmas,
With mirth and princely cheer,
When lo! a strange and cunning boy
Before him did appear.
"A kirtle and a mantle
This boy had him upon,
With brooches, rings, and ouches,
Full daintily bedone.
"He had a sash of silk
About his middle meet;
And thus with seemly curtesie
He did King Arthur greet:
"'God speed thee, brave King Arthur.
Thus feasting in thy bower,
And Guenever, thy goodly queen,
That fair and peerless flower.
"'Ye gallant lords and lordlings,
I wish you all take heed,
Lest what ye deem a blooming rose
Should prove a cankered weed.'
"Then straightway from his bosom
A little wand he drew;
And with it eke a mantle,
Of wondrous shape and hue.
"'Now have thou here, King Arthur,
Have this here of me,
And give unto thy comely queen,
All shapen as you see.
"'No wife it shall become,
That once hath been to blame.'
Then every knight in Arthur's court
Sly glanced at his dame.
"And first came Lady Guenever,
The mantle she must try.
This dame she was new-fangled, [1]
And of a roving eye.
"When she had taken the mantle,
And all with it was clad,
From top to toe it shivered down,
As though with shears beshred.
"One while it was too long,
Another while too short,
And wrinkled on her shoulders,
In most unseemly sort.
"Now green, now red it seemed,
Then all of sable hue;
'Beshrew me,' quoth King Arthur,
'I think thou be'st not true!'
"Down she threw the mantle,
No longer would she stay;
But, storming like a fury,
To her chamber flung away.
"She cursed the rascal weaver,
That had the mantle wrought;
And doubly cursed the froward imp
Who thither had it brought.
I had rather live in deserts,
Beneath the greenwood tree,
Than here, base king, among thy grooms
The sport of them and thee.'
"Sir Kay called forth his lady,
And bade her to come near:
'Yet dame, if thou be guilty,
I pray thee now forbear.'

"This lady, pertly giggling,
With forward step came on,
And boldly to the little boy
With fearless face is gone.
"When she had taken the mantle,
With purpose for to wear,
It shrunk up to her shoulder,
And left her back all bare.
"Then every merry knight,
That was in Arthur's court,
Gibed and laughed and flouted,
To see that pleasant sport.
"Down she threw the mantle,
No longer bold or gay,
But, with a face all pale and wan
To her chamber slunk away.
"Then forth came an old knight
A pattering o'er his creed,
And proffered to the little boy
Five nobles to his meed:
"'And all the time of Christmas
Plum-porridge shall be thine,
If thou wilt let my lady fair
Within the mantle shine.'
"A saint his lady seemed,
With step demure and slow,
And gravely to the mantle
With mincing face doth go.
"When she the same had taken
That was so fine and thin,
It shrivelled all about her,
And showed her dainty skin.
"Ah! little did her mincing,
Or his long prayers bestead;
She had no more hung on her
Than a tassel and a thread.
"Down she threw the mantle,
With terror and dismay,
And with a face of scarlet
To her chamber hied away.
"Sir Cradock called his lady,
And bade her to come near:
'Come win this mantle, lady,
And do me credit here:
"'Come win this mantle, lady,
For now it shall be thine,
If thou hast never done amiss,
Since first I made thee mine.'
"The lady, gently blushing,
With modest grace came on;
And now to try the wondrous charm
Courageously is gone.
"When she had ta'en the mantle,
And put it on her back,
About the hem it seemed
To wrinkle and to crack.
"'Lie still,' she cried, 'O mantle!
And shame me not for naught;
I'll freely own whate'er amiss
Or blameful I have wrought.
"'Once I kissed Sir Cradock
Beneath the greenwood tree;
Once I kissed Sir Cradock's mouth,
Before he married me.'
"When she had thus her shriven,
And her worst fault had told,
The mantle soon became her,
Right comely as it should.
"Most rich and fair of color,
Like gold it glittering shone,
And much the knights in Arthur's court
Admired her every one."

[Footnote 1: New-fangled—fond of novelty.]

The ballad goes on to tell of two more trials of a similar kind, made by means of a boar's head and a drinking horn, in both of which the result was equally favorable with the first to Sir Cradock and his lady. It then concludes as follows:

"Thus boar's head, horn, and mantle
Were this fair couple's meed;
And all such constant lovers,
God send them well to speed"
—Percy's Reliques.

Chapter 8

LAUNCELOT OF THE LAKE

King Ban, of Brittany, the faithful ally of Arthur was attacked by his enemy Claudas, and after a long war saw himself reduced to the possession of a single fortress, where he was besieged by his enemy. In this extremity he determined to solicit the assistance of Arthur, and escaped in a dark night, with his wife Helen and his infant son Launcelot, leaving his castle in the hands of his seneschal, who immediately surrendered the place to Claudas. The flames of his burning citadel reached the eyes of the unfortunate monarch during his flight and he expired with grief. The wretched Helen, leaving her child on the brink of a lake, flew to receive the last sighs of her husband, and on returning perceived the little Launcelot in the arms of a nymph, who, on the approach of the queen, threw herself into the lake with the child. This nymph was Viviane, mistress of the enchanter Merlin, better known by the name of the Lady of the Lake. Launcelot received his appellation from having been educated at the court of this enchantress, whose palace was situated in the midst, not of a real, but, like the appearance which deceives the African traveller, of an imaginary lake, whose deluding resemblance served as a barrier to her residence. Here she dwelt not alone, but in the midst of a numerous retinue, and a splendid court of knights and damsels.

The queen, after her double loss, retired to a convent, where she was joined by the widow of Bohort, for this good king had died of grief on hearing of the death of his brother Ban. His two sons, Lionel and Bohort, were rescued by a faithful knight, and arrived in the shape of greyhounds at the palace of the lake, where, having resumed their natural form, they were educated along with their cousin Launcelot.

The fairy, when her pupil had attained the age of eighteen, conveyed him to the court of Arthur for the purpose of demanding his admission to the honor of knighthood; and at the first appearance of the youthful candidate the graces of his person, which were not inferior to his courage and skill in arms, made an instantaneous and indelible impression on the heart of Guenever, while her charms inspired him with an equally ardent and constant passion. The mutual attachment of these lovers exerted, from that time forth, an influence over the whole history of Arthur. For the sake of Guenever, Launcelot achieved the conquest of Northumberland, defeated Gallehaut, King of the Marches, who afterwards became his most faithful friend and ally, exposed himself in numberless encounters, and brought hosts of prisoners to the feet of his sovereign.

SIR LAUNCELOT, OR LANCELOT

After King Arthur was come from Rome into England all the knights of the Table Round resorted unto him and made him many justs and tournaments. And in especial Sir Launcelot of the Lake in all tournaments and justs and deeds of arms, both for life and death, passed all other knights, and was never overcome, except it were by treason or enchantment; and he increased marvellously in worship, wherefore Queen Guenever had him in great favor, above all other knights. And for certain he loved the queen again above all other ladies; and for her he did many deeds of arms, and saved her from peril, through his noble chivalry. Thus Sir Launcelot rested him long with play and game, and then he thought to prove himself in strange adventures; so he bade his nephew, Sir Lionel, to make him ready,— "for we two will seek adventures." So they mounted on their horses, armed at all sights, and rode into a forest, and so into a deep plain. And the weather was hot about noon, and Sir Launcelot had great desire to sleep. Then Sir Lionel espied a great apple-tree that stood by a hedge, and he said: "Brother, yonder is a fair shadow— there may we rest us and our horses." "It is well said," replied Sir Launcelot. So they there alighted, and Sir Launcelot laid him down, and his helm under his head, and soon was asleep passing fast. And Sir Lionel waked while he slept. And presently there came three knights riding as fast as ever they might ride, and there followed them but one knight. And Sir Lionel thought he never saw so great a knight before. So within a while this great knight overtook one of those knights, and smote him so that he fell to the earth. Then he rode to the second knight and smote him, and so he did to the third knight. Then he alighted down and bound all the three knights fast with their own bridles. When Sir Lionel saw him do thus, he

Figure 61: "Lancelot & Hellawes" by Aubrey Beardsley

thought to assay him, and made him ready silently, not to awake Sir Launcelot, and rode after the strong knight, and bade him turn. And the other smote Sir Lionel so hard that horse and man fell to the earth; and then he alighted down and bound Sir Lionel, and threw him across his own horse; and so he served them all four, and rode with them away to his own castle. And when he came there he put them in a deep prison, in which were many more knights in great distress.

Now while Sir Launcelot lay under the apple-tree sleeping, there came by him four queens of great estate. And that the heat should not grieve them, there rode four knights about them, and bare a cloth of green silk on four spears, betwixt them and the sun. And the queens rode on four white mules.

Thus, as they rode they heard by them a great horse grimly neigh. Then they were aware of a sleeping knight, that lay all armed under an apple-tree; and as the queens looked on his face, they knew it was Sir Launcelot. Then they began to strive for that knight, and each one said she would have him for her love. "We will not strive," said Morgane le Fay, that was King Arthur's sister, "for I will put an enchantment upon him, that he shall not wake for six hours, and we will take him away to my castle; and then when he is surely within my hold, I will take the enchantment from him, and then let him choose which of us he will have for his love." So the enchantment was cast upon Sir Launcelot. And then they laid him upon his shield, and bare him so on horseback between two knights, and brought him unto the castle and laid him in a chamber, and at night they sent him his supper. And on the morning came early those four queens, richly dight, and bade him good morning, and he them again. "Sir knight," they said, "thou must understand thou art our prisoner; and we know thee well, that thou art Sir Launcelot of the Lake, King Ban's son, and that thou art the noblest knight living. And we know well that there can no lady have thy love but one, and that is Queen Guenever; and now thou shalt lose her for ever, and she thee; and therefore it behooveth thee now to choose one of us. I am the Queen Morgane le Fay, and here is the Queen of North Wales, and the Queen of Eastland, and the Queen of the Isles. Now choose one of us which thou wilt have, for if thou choose not, in this prison thou shalt die." "This is a hard case," said Sir Launcelot, "that either I must die, or else choose one of you; yet had I liever to die in this prison with worship, than to have one of you for my paramour, for ye be false enchantresses." "Well," said the queens, "is this your answer, that ye will refuse us." "Yea, on my life it is," said Sir Launcelot. Then they departed, making great sorrow.

Then at noon came a damsel unto him with his dinner, and asked him, "What cheer?" "Truly, fair damsel," said Sir Launcelot, "never so ill." "Sir," said she, "if you will be ruled by me, I will help you out of this distress. If ye will promise me to help my father on Tuesday next, who hath made a tournament betwixt him and the king of North Wales; for last Tuesday my father lost the field." "Fair maiden," said Sir Launcelot, "tell me what is your father's name, and then will I give you an answer." "Sir knight," she said, "my father is King Bagdemagus." "I know him well," said Sir Launcelot, "for a noble king and a good knight; and, by the faith of my body, I will be ready to do your father and you service at that day."

So she departed, and came on the next morning early and found him ready, and brought him out of twelve locks, and brought him to his own horse, and lightly he saddled him, and so rode forth.

And on the Tuesday next he came to a little wood where the tournament should be. And there were scaffolds and holds, that lords and ladies might look on, and give the prize. Then came into the field the king of North

Wales, with eightscore helms, and King Badgemagus came with fourscore helms. And then they couched their spears, and came together with a great dash, and there were overthrown at the first encounter twelve of King Bagdemagus's party and six of the king of North Wales's party, and King Bagdemagus's party had the worse.

With that came Sir Launcelot of the Lake, and thrust in with his spear in the thickest of the press; and he smote down five knights ere he held his hand; and he smote down the king of North Wales, and he brake his thigh in that fall. And then the knights of the king of North Wales would just no more; and so the gree was given to King Bagdemagus.

And Sir Launcelot rode forth with King Bagdemagus unto his castle; and there he had passing good cheer, both with the king and with his daughter. And on the morn he took his leave, and told the king he would go and seek his brother, Sir Lionel, that went from him when he slept. So he departed, and by adventure he came to the same forest where he was taken sleeping. And in the highway he met a damsel riding on a white palfrey, and they saluted each other. "Fair damsel," said Sir Launcelot, "know ye in this country any adventures?" "Sir knight," said the damsel, "here are adventures near at hand, if thou durst pursue them." "Why should I not prove adventures?" said Sir Launcelot, "since for that cause came I hither." "Sir," said she, "hereby dwelleth a knight that will not be overmatched for any man I know, except thou overmatch him. His name is Sir Turquine, and, as I understand, he is a deadly enemy of King Arthur, and he has in his prison good knights of Arthur's court, threescore and more, that he hath won with his own hands." "Damsel," said Launcelot, "I pray you bring me unto this knight." So she told him, "Hereby, within this mile, is his castle, and by it on the left hand is a ford for horses to drink of, and over that ford there groweth a fair tree, and on that tree hang many shields that good knights wielded aforetime, that are now prisoners; and on the tree hangeth a basin of copper and latten, and if thou strike upon that basin thou shalt hear tidings." And Sir Launcelot departed, and rode as the damsel had shown him, and shortly he came to the ford, and the tree where hung the shields and the basin. And among the shields he saw Sir Lionel's and Sir Hector's shields, besides many others of knights that he knew.

Then Sir Launcelot struck on the basin with the butt of his spear; and long he did so, but he saw no man. And at length he was ware of a great knight that drove a horse before him, and across the horse there lay an armed knight bounden. And as they came near, Sir Launcelot thought he should know the captive knight. Then Sir Launcelot saw that it was Sir Gaheris, Sir Gawain's brother, a knight of the Table Round. "Now, fair knight," said Sir Launcelot, "put that wounded knight off the horse, and let him rest awhile, and let us two prove our strength. For, as it is told me, thou hast done great despite and shame unto knights of the Round Table, therefore now defend thee." "If thou be of the Table Round," said Sir Turquine, "I defy thee and all thy fellowship." "That is overmuch said," said Sir Launcelot.

Then they put their spears in the rests, and came together with their horses as fast as they might run. And each smote the other in the middle of their shields, so that their horses fell under them, and the knights were both staggered; and as soon as they could clear their horses they drew out their swords and came together eagerly, and each gave the other many strong strokes, for neither shield nor harness might withstand their strokes. So within a while both had grimly wounds, and bled grievously. Then at the last they were breathless both, and stood leaning upon their swords. "Now, fellow," said Sir Turquine, "thou art the stoutest man that ever I met with, and best breathed; and so be it thou be not the knight that I hate above all other knights, the knight that slew my brother, Sir Carados, I will gladly accord with thee; and for thy love I will deliver all the prisoners that I have."

"What knight is he that thou hatest so above others?" "Truly," said Sir Turquine, "his name is Sir Launcelot of the Lake." "I am Sir Launcelot of the Lake, King Ban's son of Benwick, and very knight of the Table Round; and now I defy thee do thy best." "Ah!" said Sir Turquine, "Launcelot, thou art to me the most welcome that ever was knight; for we shall never part till the one of us be dead." And then they hurtled together like two wild bulls, rashing and lashing with their swords and shields, so that sometimes they fell, as it were, headlong. Thus they fought two hours and more, till the ground where they fought was all bepurpled with blood.

Then at the last Sir Turquine waxed sore faint, and gave somewhat aback, and bare his shield full low for weariness. That spied Sir Launcelot, and leapt then upon him fiercely as a lion, and took him by the beaver of his helmet, and drew him down on his knees. And he raised off his helm, and smote his neck in sunder.

And Sir Gaheris, when he saw Sir Turquine slain, said, "Fair lord, I pray you tell me your name, for this day I say ye are the best knight in the world, for ye have slain this day in my sight the mightiest man and the best knight except you that ever I saw." "Sir, my name is Sir Launcelot du Lac, that ought to help you of right for King Arthur's sake, and in especial for Sir Gawain's sake, your own dear brother. Now I pray you, that ye go into yonder castle, and set free all the prisoners ye find there, for I am sure ye shall find there many knights of the Table Round, and especially my brother Sir Lionel. I pray you greet them all from me, and tell them I bid them take there such stuff as they find; and tell my brother to go unto the court and abide me there, for by the feast of Pentecost I think to be there; but at this time I may not stop, for I have adventures on hand." So he departed, and Sir Gaheris rode into the castle, and took the keys from the porter, and hastily opened the prison door and let out all the prisoners. There was Sir Kay, Sir Brandeles, and Sir Galynde, Sir Bryan, and Sir Alyduke, Sir Hector de Marys, and Sir Lionel, and many more. And when they saw Sir Gaheris they all thanked him, for they thought, because he was wounded, that he had slain Sir Turquine. "Not so," said Sir Gaheris; "it was Sir Launcelot that slew him, right worshipfully; I saw it with mine eyes."

Sir Launcelot rode till at nightfall he came to a fair castle, and therein he found an old gentlewoman, who lodged him with good- will, and there he had good cheer for him and his horse. And when time was, his host brought him to a fair chamber over the gate to his bed. Then Sir Launcelot unarmed him, and set his harness by him, and went to bed, and anon he fell asleep. And soon after, there came one on horseback and knocked at the gate in great haste; and when Sir Launcelot heard this, he arose and looked out of the window, and saw by the moonlight three knights riding after that one man, and all three lashed on him with their swords, and that one knight turned on them knightly again and defended himself. "Truly," said Sir Launcelot, "yonder one knight will I help, for it is shame to see three knights on one." Then he took his harness and went out at the window by a sheet down to the four knights; and he said aloud, "Turn you knights unto me, and leave your fighting with that knight." Then the knights left Sir Kay, for it was he they were upon, and turned unto Sir Launcelot, and struck many great strokes at Sir Launcelot, and assailed him on every side. Then Sir Kay addressed him to help Sir Launcelot, but he said, "Nay, sir, I will none of your help; let me alone with them." So Sir Kay suffered him to do his will, and stood one side. And within six strokes Sir Launcelot had stricken them down.

Then they all cried, "Sir knight, we yield us unto you." "As to that," said Sir Launcelot, "I will not take your yielding unto me. If so be ye will yield you unto Sir Kay the Seneschal, I will save your lives, but else not." "Fair knight," then they said, "we will do as thou commandest us." "Then shall ye," said Sir Launcelot, "on Whitsunday next, go unto the court of King Arthur, and there shall ye yield you unto Queen Guenever, and say that Sir Kay sent you thither to be her prisoners." "Sir," they said, "it shall be done, by the faith of our bodies;" and then they swore, every knight upon his sword. And so Sir Launcelot suffered them to depart.

On the morn Sir Launcelot rose early and left Sir Kay sleeping; and Sir Launcelot took Sir Kay's armor, and his shield, and armed him, and went to the stable and took his horse, and so he departed. Then soon after arose Sir Kay, and missed Sir Launcelot. And then he espied that he had taken his armor and his horse. "Now, by my faith, I know well," said Sir Kay, "that he will grieve some of King Arthur's knights, for they will deem that it is I, and will be bold to meet him. But by cause of his armor I am sure I shall ride in peace." Then Sir Kay thanked his host and departed.

Sir Launcelot rode in a deep forest, and there he saw four knights, under an oak, and they were of Arthur's court. There was Sir Sagramour le Desirus, and Hector de Marys, and Sir Gawain, and Sir Uwaine. As they spied Sir Launcelot they judged by his arms it had been Sir Kay. "Now, by my faith," said Sir Sagramour, "I will prove Sir Kay's might;" and got his spear in his hand, and came towards Sir Launcelot. Therewith Sir Launcelot couched his spear against him, and smote Sir Sagramour so sore that horse and man fell both to the earth. Then said Sir Hector, "Now shall ye see what I may do with him." But he fared worse than Sir Sagramour, for Sir Launcelot's spear went through his shoulder and bare him from his horse to the ground. "By my faith," said Sir Uwaine, "yonder is a strong knight, and I fear he hath slain Sir Kay, and taken his armor." And therewith Sir Uwaine took his spear in hand, and rode toward Sir Launcelot; and Sir Launcelot met him on the plain and gave him such a buffet that he was staggered, and wist not where he was. "Now see I well," said Sir Gawain, "that I must encounter with that knight." Then he adjusted his shield, and took a good spear in his hand, and Sir Launcelot knew him well. Then they let run their horses with all their mights, and each knight smote the other in the middle of his shield. But Sir Gawain's spear broke, and Sir Launcelot charged so sore upon him that his horse fell over backward. Then Sir Launcelot passed by smiling with himself, and he said, "Good luck be with him that made this spear, for never came a better into my hand." Then the four knights went each to the other and comforted one another. "What say ye to this adventure," said Sir Gawain, "that one spear hath felled us all four?" "I dare lay my head it is Sir Launcelot," said Sir Hector; "I know it by his riding."

And Sir Launcelot rode through many strange countries, till by fortune he came to a fair castle; and as he passed beyond the castle he thought he heard two bells ring. And then he perceived how a falcon came flying over his head, toward a high elm; and she had long lunys [Footnote: LUNYS, the string with which the falcon is held.] about her feet, and she flew unto the elm to take her perch, and the lunys got entangled in the bough; and when she would have taken her flight, she hung by the legs fast, and Sir Launcelot saw how she hung, and beheld the fair falcon entangled, and he was sorry for her. Then came a lady out of the castle and cried aloud, "O Launcelot, Launcelot, as thou art the flower of all knights, help me to get my hawk; for if my hawk be lost, my lord will slay me, he is so hasty." "What is your lord's name?" said Sir Launcelot. "His name is Sir Phelot, a knight that belongeth to the king of North Wales." "Well, fair lady, since ye know my name, and require me of knighthood to help you, I will do what I may to get your hawk; and yet in truth I am an ill climber, and the tree is passing high, and few boughs to help me." And therewith Sir Launcelot alighted and tied his horse to the tree, and prayed the lady to unarm him. And when he was unarmed, he put off his jerkin, and with might and force he clomb up to the falcon, and tied the lunys to a rotten bough, and threw the hawk down with it; and the lady got the hawk in her hand. Then suddenly there came out of the castle her husband, all armed, and with his naked sword in his hand, and said, "O Knight Launcelot, now have I got thee as I would," and stood at the boll of the tree to slay him. "Ah, lady!" said Sir Launcelot, "why have ye betrayed me?" "She hath done," said Sir Phelot, "but as I commanded her; and therefore there is none other way but thine hour is come, and thou must die." "That were shame unto thee," said Sir Launcelot; "thou an armed knight to slay a naked man by treason." "Thou gettest none other grace," said Sir Phelot, "and therefore help thyself if thou canst." "Alas!" said Sir Launcelot, "that ever a knight should die weaponless!" And therewith he turned his eyes upward and downward; and over his head he saw a big bough leafless, and he brake it off from the trunk. And then he came lower, and watched how his own horse stood; and suddenly he leapt on the further side of his horse from the knight. Then Sir Phelot lashed at him eagerly, meaning to have slain him. But Sir Launcelot put away the stroke, with the big bough, and smote Sir Phelot therewith on the side of the head, so that he fell down in a swoon to the ground. Then Sir Launcelot took his sword out of his hand and struck his head from the body. Then said the lady, "Alas! why hast thou slain my husband?" "I am not the cause," said Sir Launcelot, "for with falsehood ye would have slain me, and now it is fallen on yourselves." Thereupon Sir Launcelot got all his armor, and put it upon him hastily, for fear of more resort, for the knight's castle was so nigh. And as soon as he might, he took his horse and departed, and thanked God he had escaped that adventure.

And two days before the feast of Pentecost, Sir Launcelot came home; and the king and all the court were passing glad of his coming. And when Sir Gawain, Sir Uwaine, Sir Sagramour, and Sir Hector de Marys saw Sir Launcelot in Sir Kay's armor then they wist well it was he that smote them down, all with one spear. Then there was laughing and merriment among them; and from time to time came all the knights that Sir Turquine had prisoners, and they all honored and worshipped Sir Launcelot. Then Sir Gaheris said, "I saw all the battle from the beginning to the end," and he told King Arthur all how it was. Then Sir Kay told the king how Sir Launcelot had rescued him, and how he "made the knights yield to me, and not to him." And there they were, all three, and confirmed it all "And, by my faith," said Sir Kay, "because Sir Launcelot took my harness and left me his, I rode in peace, and no man would have to do with me."

And so at that time Sir Launcelot had the greatest name of any knight of the world, and most was he honored of high and low.

Chapter 9

THE ADVENTURE OF THE CART

It befell in the month of May, Queen Guenever called to her knights of the Table Round, and gave them warning that early upon the morrow she would ride a-maying into the woods and fields beside Westminster; "and I warn you that there be none of you but he be well horsed, and that ye all be clothed in green, either silk or cloth; and I shall bring with me ten ladies, and every knight shall have a lady behind him, and every knight shall have a squire and two yeoman, and all well horsed."

"For thus it chanced one morn when all the court,
Green-suited, but with plumes that mock'd the May,
Had been, their wont, a-maying"
—Guinevere.

So they made them ready; and these were the names of the knights: Sir Kay the Seneschal, Sir Agrivaine, Sir Brandiles, Sir Sagramour le Desirus, Sir Dodynas le Sauvage, Sir Ozanna, Sir Ladynas, Sir Persant of Inde, Sir Ironside, and Sir Pelleas; and these ten knights made them ready, in the freshest manner, to ride with the queen. So upon the morn they took their horses with the queen, and rode a-maying in woods and meadows, as it pleased them, in great joy and delight. Now there was a knight named Maleagans, son to King Brademagus, who loved Queen Guenever passing well, and so had he done long and many years. Now this knight, Sir Maleagans, learned the queen's purpose, and that she had no men of arms with her but the ten noble knights all arrayed in green for maying; so he prepared him twenty men of arms, and a hundred archers, to take captive the queen and her knights.

"In the merry month of May,
In a morn at break of day,
With a troop of damsels playing,
The Queen, forsooth, went forth a-maying."
—Old Song.

So when the queen had mayed, and all were bedecked with herbs, mosses, and flowers in the best manner and freshest, right then came out of a wood Sir Maleagans with eightscore men well harnessed, and bade the queen and her knights yield them prisoners. "Traitor knight," said Queen Guenever, "what wilt thou do? Wilt thou shame thyself? Bethink thee how thou art a king's son, and a knight of the Table Round, and how thou art about to dishonor all knighthood and thyself?" "Be it as it may," said Sir Maleagans, "know you well, madam, I have loved you many a year and never till now could I get you to such advantage as I do now; and therefore I will take you as I find you." Then the ten knights of the Round Table drew their swords, and the other party run at them with their spears, and the ten knights manfully abode them, and smote away their spears. Then they lashed together with swords till several were smitten to the earth. So when the queen saw her knights thus dolefully oppressed, and needs must be slain at the last, then for pity and sorrow she cried, "Sir Maleagans, slay not my noble knights and I will go with you, upon this covenant, that they be led with me wheresoever thou leadest me." "Madame," said Maleagans, "for your sake they shall be led with you into my own castle, if that ye will be ruled, and ride with me." Then Sir Maleagans charged them all that none should depart from the queen, for he dreaded lest Sir Launcelot should have knowledge of what had been done.

Then the queen privily called unto her a page of her chamber that was swiftly horsed, to whom she said, "Go thou when thou seest thy time, and bear this ring unto Sir Launcelot, and pray him as he loveth me, that he will see me and rescue me. And spare not thy horse," said the queen, "neither for water nor for land." So the child espied his time, and lightly he took his horse with the spurs and departed as fast as he might. And when Sir Maleagans saw him so flee, he understood that it was by the queen's commandment for to warn Sir Launcelot. Then they that were best horsed chased him, and shot at him, but the child went from them all. Then Sir Maleagans said to the queen, "Madam, ye are about to betray me, but I shall arrange for Sir Launcelot that he shall not come lightly at you." Then he rode with her and them all to his castle, in all the haste that they might. And by the way Sir Maleagans laid in ambush the best archers that he had to wait for Sir Launcelot. And the child came to Westminster and found Sir Launcelot and told his message and delivered him the queen's ring. "Alas!" said Sir Launcelot, "now am I shamed for ever, unless I may rescue that noble lady."

Chapter 9: The Adventure of the Cart

Figure 62: "Guinevre's Maying" by John Collier

Then eagerly he asked his armor and put it on him, and mounted his horse and rode as fast as he might; and men say he took the water at Westminster Bridge, and made his horse swim over Thames unto Lambeth. Then within a while he came to a wood where was a narrow way; and there the archers were laid in ambush. And they shot at him and smote his horse so that he fell. Then Sir Launcelot left his horse and went on foot, but there lay so many ditches and hedges betwixt the archers and him that he might not meddle with them. "Alas! for shame," said Sir Launcelot, "that ever one knight should betray another! but it is an old saw, a good man is never in danger, but when he is in danger of a coward." Then Sir Launcelot went awhile and he was exceedingly cumbered by his armor, his shield, and his spear, and all that belonged to him. Then by chance there came by him a cart that came thither to fetch wood.

Now at this time carts were little used except for carrying offal and for conveying criminals to execution. But Sir Launcelot took no thought of anything but the necessity of haste for the purpose of rescuing the queen; so he demanded of the carter that he should take him in and convey him as speedily as possible for a liberal reward. The carter consented, and Sir Launcelot placed himself in the cart and only lamented that with much jolting he made but little progress. Then it happened Sir Gawain passed by and seeing an armed knight travelling in that unusual way he drew near to see who it might be. Then Sir Launcelot told him how the queen had been carried off, and how, in hastening to her rescue, his horse had been disabled and he had been compelled to avail himself of the cart rather than give up his enterprise. Then Sir Gawain said, "Surely it is unworthy of a knight to travel in such sort;" but Sir Launcelot heeded him not.

At nightfall they arrived at a castle and the lady thereof came out at the head of her damsels to welcome Sir Gawain. But to admit his companion, whom she supposed to be a criminal, or at least a prisoner, it pleased her not; however, to oblige Sir Gawain, she consented. At supper Sir Launcelot came near being consigned to the kitchen and was only admitted to the lady's table at the earnest solicitation of Sir Gawain. Neither would the damsels prepare a bed for him. He seized the first he found unoccupied and was left undisturbed.

Next morning he saw from the turrets of the castle a train accompanying a lady, whom he imagined to be the queen. Sir Gawain thought it might be so, and became equally eager to depart. The lady of the castle supplied Sir Launcelot with a horse and they traversed the plain at full speed. They learned from some travellers whom they met, that there were two roads which led to the castle of Sir Maleagans. Here therefore the friends separated. Sir Launcelot found his way beset with obstacles, which he encountered successfully, but not without much loss of time. As evening approached he was met by a young and sportive damsel, who gayly proposed to him a supper at her castle. The knight, who was hungry and weary, accepted the offer, though with no very good grace. He followed the lady to her castle and ate voraciously of her supper, but was quite impenetrable to all her amorous advances. Suddenly the scene changed and he was assailed by six furious ruffians, whom he dealt with so vigorously that most of them were speedily disabled, when again there was a change and he found himself alone with his fair hostess, who informed him that she was none other than his guardian fairy, who had but subjected him to tests of his courage and fidelity. The next day the fairy brought him on his road, and before parting gave him a ring, which she told him would by its changes of color disclose to him all enchantments, and enable him to subdue them.

Sir Launcelot pursued his journey, without being much incommoded except by the taunts of travellers, who all seemed to have learned, by some means, his disgraceful drive in the cart. One, more insolent than the rest, had the audacity to interrupt him during dinner, and even to risk a battle in support of his pleasantry. Launcelot, after an easy victory, only doomed him to be carted in his turn.

At night he was received at another castle, with great apparent hospitality, but found himself in the morning in a dungeon, and loaded with chains. Consulting his ring, and finding that this was an enchantment, he burst his chains, seized his armor in spite of the visionary monsters who attempted to defend it, broke open the gates of the tower, and continued his journey. At length his progress was checked by a wide and rapid torrent, which could only be passed on a narrow bridge, on which a false step would prove his destruction. Launcelot, leading his horse by the bridle, and making him swim by his side, passed over the bridge, and was attacked as soon as he reached the bank by a lion and a leopard, both of which he slew, and then, exhausted and bleeding, seated himself on the grass, and endeavored to bind up his wounds, when he was accosted by Brademagus, the father of Maleagans, whose castle was then in sight, and at no great distance. This king, no less courteous than his son was haughty and insolent, after complimenting Sir Launcelot on the valor and skill he had displayed in the perils of the bridge and the wild beasts, offered him his assistance, and informed him that the queen was safe in his castle, but could only be rescued by encountering Maleagans. Launcelot demanded the battle for the next day, and accordingly it took place, at the foot of the tower, and under the eyes of the fair captive. Launcelot was enfeebled by his wounds, and fought not with his usual spirit, and the contest for a time was doubtful; till Guenever exclaimed, "Ah, Launcelot! my knight, truly have I been told that thou art no longer worthy of me!" These words instantly revived the drooping knight; he resumed at once his usual superiority, and soon laid at his feet his haughty adversary.

He was on the point of sacrificing him to his resentment, when Guenever, moved by the entreaties of Brademagus, ordered him to withhold the blow, and he obeyed. The castle and its prisoners were now at his disposal. Launcelot hastened to the apartment of the queen, threw himself at her feet, and was about to kiss her hand, when she exclaimed, "Ah, Launcelot! why do I see thee again, yet feel thee to be no longer worthy of me, after having been disgracefully drawn about the country in a— " She had not time to finish the phrase, for her lover suddenly started from her, and, bitterly lamenting that he had incurred the displeasure of his sovereign lady, rushed out of the castle, threw his sword and his shield to the right and left, ran furiously into the woods, and disappeared.

It seems that the story of the abominable cart, which haunted Launcelot at every step, had reached the ears of Sir Kay, who had told it to the queen, as a proof that her knight must have been dishonored. But Guenever had full leisure to repent the haste with which she had given credit to the tale. Three days elapsed, during which Launcelot wandered without knowing where he went, till at last he began to reflect that his mistress had doubtless been deceived by misrepresentation, and that it was his duty to set her right. He therefore returned, compelled Maleagans to release his prisoners, and, taking the road by which they expected the arrival of Sir Gawain, had the satisfaction of meeting him the next day; after which the whole company proceeded gayly towards Camelot.

Figure 63: "Idylls of the King: Camelot" by Paul Gustave Dore

Chapter 10

THE LADY OF THE SHALOTT

King Arthur proclaimed a solemn tournament to be held at Winchester. The king, not less impatient than his knights for this festival, set off some days before to superintend the preparations, leaving the queen with her court at Camelot. Sir Launcelot, under pretence of indisposition, remained behind also. His intention was to attend the tournament—in disguise; and having communicated his project to Guenever, he mounted his horse, set off without any attendant, and, counterfeiting the feebleness of age, took the most unfrequented road to Winchester, and passed unnoticed as an old knight who was going to be a spectator of the sports. Even Arthur and Gawain, who happened to behold him from the windows of a castle under which he passed, were the dupes of his disguise. But an accident betrayed him. His horse happened to stumble, and the hero, forgetting for a moment his assumed character, recovered the animal with a strength and agility so peculiar to himself, that they instantly recognized the inimitable Launcelot. They suffered him, however, to proceed on his journey without interruption, convinced that his extraordinary feats of arms must discover him at the approaching festival.

In the evening Launcelot was magnificently entertained as a stranger knight at the neighboring castle of Shalott. The lord of this castle had a daughter of exquisite beauty, and two sons lately received into the order of knighthood, one of whom was at that time ill in bed, and thereby prevented from attending the tournament, for which both brothers had long made preparation. Launcelot offered to attend the other, if he were permitted to borrow the armor of the invalid, and the lord of Shalott, without knowing the name of his guest, being satisfied from his appearance that his son could not have a better assistant in arms, most thankfully accepted the offer. In the meantime the young lady, who had been much struck by the first appearance of the stranger knight, continued to survey him with increased attention, and, before the conclusion of supper, became so deeply enamoured of him, that after frequent changes of color, and other symptoms which Sir Launcelot could not possibly mistake, she was obliged to retire to her chamber, and seek relief in tears. Sir Launcelot hastened to convey to her, by means of her brother, the information that his heart was already disposed of, but that it would be his pride and pleasure to act as her knight at the approaching tournament. The lady, obliged to be satisfied with that courtesy, presented him her scarf to be worn at the tournament.

Launcelot set off in the morning with the young knight, who, on their approaching Winchester, carried him to the castle of a lady, sister to the lord of Shalott, by whom they were hospitably entertained. The next day they put on their armor, which was perfectly plain and without any device, as was usual to youths during the first year of knighthood, their shields being only painted red, as some color was necessary to enable them to be recognized by their attendants. Launcelot wore on his crest the scarf of the maid of Shalott, and, thus equipped, proceeded to the tournament, where the knights were divided into two companies, the one commanded by Sir Galehaut, the other by King Arthur. Having surveyed the combat for a short time from without the lists, and observed that Sir Galehaut's party began to give way, they joined the press and attacked the royal knights, the young man choosing such adversaries as were suited to his strength, while his companion selected the principal champions of the Round Table, and successively overthrew Gawain, Bohort, and Lionel. The astonishment of the spectators was extreme, for it was thought that no one but Launcelot could possess such invincible force; yet the favor on his crest seemed to preclude the possibility of his being thus disguised, for Launcelot had never been known to wear the badge of any but his sovereign lady. At length Sir Hector, Launcelot's brother, engaged him, and, after a dreadful combat, wounded him dangerously in the head, but was himself completely stunned by a blow on the helmet, and felled to the ground; after which the conqueror rode off at full speed, attended by his companion.

They returned to the castle of Shalott, where Launcelot was attended with the greatest care by the good earl, by his two sons, and, above all, by his fair daughter, whose medical skill probably much hastened the period of his recovery. His health was almost completely restored, when Sir Hector, Sir Bohort, and Sir Lionel, who, after the return of the court to Camelot, had undertaken the quest of their relation, discovered him walking on the walls of

Figure 64: "The Lady of the Sahlott" by John Everett Millais

the castle. Their meeting was very joyful; they passed three days in the castle amidst constant festivities, and bantered each other on the events of the tournament. Launcelot, though he began by vowing vengeance against the author of his wound, yet ended by declaring that he felt rewarded for the pain by the pride he took in witnessing his brother's extraordinary prowess. He then dismissed them with a message to the queen, promising to follow immediately, it being necessary that he should first take a formal leave of his kind hosts, as well as of the fair maid of Shalott.

The young lady, after vainly attempting to detain him by her tears and solicitations, saw him depart without leaving her any ground for hope.

It was early summer when the tournament took place; but some months had passed since Launcelot's departure, and winter was now near at hand. The health and strength of the Lady of Shalott had gradually sunk, and she felt that she could not live apart from the object of her affections. She left the castle, and descending to the river's brink placed herself in a boat, which she loosed from its moorings, and suffered to bear her down the current toward Camelot.

One morning, as Arthur and Sir Lionel looked from the window of the tower, the walls of which were washed by a river, they descried a boat richly ornamented, and covered with an awning of cloth of gold, which appeared to be floating down the stream without any human guidance. It struck the shore while they watched it, and they hastened down to examine it. Beneath the awning they discovered the dead body of a beautiful woman, in whose features Sir Lionel easily recognized the lovely maid of Shalott. Pursuing their search, they discovered a purse richly embroidered with gold and jewels, and within the purse a letter, which Arthur opened, and found addressed to himself and all the knights of the Round Table, stating that Launcelot of the Lake, the most accomplished of knights and most beautiful of men, but at the same time the most cruel and inflexible, had by his rigor produced the death of the wretched maiden, whose love was no less invincible than his cruelty. The king immediately gave orders for the interment of the lady with all the honors suited to her rank, at the same time explaining to the knights the history of her affection for Launcelot, which moved the compassion and regret of all.

Tennyson has chosen the story of the "Lady of Shalott" for the subject of a poem. The catastrophe is told thus:

"Under tower and balcony,
By garden-wall and gallery,
A gleaming shape she floated by,
A corse between the houses high,
Silent into Camelot.
Out upon the wharfs they came,
Knight and burgher, lord and dame,
And round the prow they read her name,
'The Lady of Shalott'
"Who is this? and what is here?
And in the lighted palace near
Died the sound of royal cheer;
And they crossed themselves for fear,
All the knights at Camelot.
But Launcelot mused a little space;
He said, 'She has a lovely face;
God in his mercy lend her grace,
The Lady of Shalott.'"

Chapter 11

QUEEN GUENEVER'S PERIL

It happened at this time that Queen Guenever was thrown into great peril of her life. A certain squire who was in her immediate service, having some cause of animosity to Sir Gawain, determined to destroy him by poison, at a public entertainment. For this purpose, he concealed the poison in an apple of fine appearance, which he placed on the top of several others, and put the dish before the queen, hoping that, as Sir Gawain was the knight of greatest dignity, she would present the apple to him. But it happened that a Scottish knight of high distinction, who arrived on that day, was seated next to the queen, and to him as a stranger she presented the apple, which he had no sooner eaten than he was seized with dreadful pain, and fell senseless. The whole court was, of course, thrown into confusion; the knights rose from table, darting looks of indignation at the wretched queen, whose tears and protestations were unable to remove their suspicions. In spite of all that could be done the knight died, and nothing remained but to order a magnificent funeral and monument for him, which was done.

Some time after Sir Mador, brother of the murdered knight, arrived at Arthur's court in quest of him. While hunting in the forest he by chance came to the spot where the monument was erected, read the inscription, and returned to court determined on immediate and signal vengeance. He rode into the hall, loudly accused the queen of treason, and insisted on her being given up for punishment, unless she should find by a certain day a knight hardy enough to risk his life in support of her innocence. Arthur, powerful as he was, did not dare to deny the appeal, but was compelled with a heavy heart to accept it, and Mador sternly took his departure, leaving the royal couple plunged in terror and anxiety.

During all this time Launcelot was absent, and no one knew where he was. He fled in anger from his fair mistress, upon being reproached by her with his passion for the Lady of Shalott, which she had hastily inferred from his wearing her scarf at the tournament. He took up his abode with a hermit in the forest, and resolved to think no more of the cruel beauty, whose conduct he thought must flow from a wish to get rid of him. Yet calm reflection had somewhat cooled his indignation, and he had begun to wish, though hardly able to hope, for a reconciliation when the news of Sir Mador's challenge fortunately reached his ears. The intelligence revived his spirits, and he began to prepare with the utmost cheerfulness for a contest which, if successful, would insure him at once the affection of his mistress and the gratitude of his sovereign.

The sad fate of the Lady of Shalott had ere this completely acquitted Launcelot in the queen's mind of all suspicion of his fidelity, and she lamented most grievously her foolish quarrel with him, which now, at her time of need, deprived her of her most efficient champion.

As the day appointed by Sir Mador was fast approaching, it became necessary that she should procure a champion for her defence; and she successively adjured Sir Hector, Sir Lionel, Sir Bohort, and Sir Gawain to undertake the battle. She fell on her knees before them, called heaven to witness her innocence of the crime alleged against her, but was sternly answered by all that they could not fight to maintain the innocence of one whose act, and the fatal consequence of it, they had seen with their own eyes. She retired, therefore, dejected and disconsolate; but the sight of the fatal pile on which, if guilty, she was doomed to be burned, exciting her to fresh effort, she again repaired to Sir Bohort, threw herself at his feet, and piteously calling on him for mercy, fell into a swoon. The brave knight was not proof against this. He raised her up, and hastily promised that he would undertake her cause, if no other or better champion should present himself. He then summoned his friends, and told them his resolution; and as a mortal combat with Sir Mador was a most fearful enterprise, they agreed to accompany him in the morning to the hermitage in the forest, where he proposed to receive absolution from the hermit, and to make his peace with Heaven before he entered the lists. As they approached the hermitage, they espied a knight riding in the forest, whom they at once recognized as Sir Launcelot. Overjoyed at the meeting, they quickly, in answer to his questions, confirmed the news of the queen's imminent danger, and received his instructions to return to court, to comfort her as well as they could, but to say nothing of his intention of

Figure 65: "Sir Mador's Spear Brake All to Pieces, But the Other's Spear Held" by Newell Convers Wyeth

undertaking her defence, which he meant to do in tne character of an unknown adventurer.

On their return to the castle they found that mass was finished, and had scarcely time to speak to the queen before they were summoned into the hall to dinner. A general gloom was spread over the countenances of all the guests. Arthur himself was unable to conceal his dejection, and the wretched Guenever, motionless and bathed in tears, sat in trembling expectation of Sir Mador's appearance. Nor was it long ere he stalked into the hall, and with a voice of thunder, rendered more impressive by the general silence, demanded instant justice on the guilty party. Arthur replied with dignity, that little of the day was yet spent, and that perhaps a champion might yet be found capable of satisfying his thirst for battle. Sir Bohort now rose from table, and shortly returning in complete armor, resumed his place, after receiving the embraces and thanks of the king, who now began to resume some degree of confidence. Sir Mador, growing impatient, again repeated his denunciations of vengeance, and insisted that the combat should no longer be postponed.

In the height of the debate there came riding into the hall a knight mounted on a black steed, and clad in black armor, with his visor down, and lance in hand. "Sir," said the king, "is it your will to alight and partake of our cheer?" "Nay, sir," he replied; "I come to save a lady's life. The queen hath ill bestowed her favors, and honored many a knight, that in her hour of need she should have none to take her part. Thou that darest accuse her of treachery, stand forth, for to-day shalt thou need all thy might."

Sir Mador, though surprised, was not appalled by the stern challenge and formidable appearance of his antagonist, but prepared for the encounter. At the first shock both were unhorsed. They then drew their swords, and commenced a combat which lasted from noon till evening, when Sir Mador, whose strength began to fail, was felled to the ground by Launcelot, and compelled to sue for mercy. The victor, whose arm was already raised to terminate the life of his opponent, instantly dropped his sword, courteously lifted up the fainting Sir Mador, frankly confessing that he had never before encountered so formidable an enemy. The other, with similar courtesy, solemnly renounced all further projects of vengeance for his brother's death; and the two knights, now become fast friends, embraced each other with the greatest cordiality. In the meantime, Arthur, having recognized Sir Launcelot, whose helmet was now unlaced, rushed down into the lists, followed by all his knights, to welcome and thank his deliverer. Guenever swooned with joy, and the place of combat suddenly exhibited a scene of the most tumultuous delight.

The general satisfaction was still further increased by the discovery of the real culprit. Having accidentally incurred some suspicion, he confessed his crime, and was publicly punished in the presence of Sir Mador.

The court now returned to the castle, which, with the title of "La Joyeuse Garde" bestowed upon it in memory of the happy event, was conferred on Sir Launcelot by Arthur, as a memorial of his gratitude.

Chapter 12

TRISTRAM AND ISOUDE, OR TRISTAN AND ISEULT, OR ISOLDE

Meliadus was king of Leonois, or Lionesse, a country famous in the annals of romance, which adjoined the kingdom of Cornwall, but has now disappeared from the map, having been, it is said, overwhelmed by the ocean. Meliadus was married to Isabella, sister of Mark, king of Cornwall. A fairy fell in love with him, and drew him away by enchantment while he was engaged in hunting. His queen set out in quest of him, but was taken ill on her journey, and died, leaving an infant son, whom, from the melancholy circumstances of his birth, she called Tristram.

Gouvernail, the queen's squire, who had accompanied her, took charge of the child, and restored him to his father, who had at length burst the enchantments of the fairy, and returned home.

Meliadus after seven years married again, and the new queen, being jealous of the influence of Tristram with his father, laid plots for his life, which were discovered by Gouvernail, who in consequence fled with the boy to the court of the king of France, where Tristram was kindly received, and grew up improving in every gallant and knightly accomplishment, adding to his skill in arms the arts of music and of chess. In particular, he devoted himself to the chase and to all woodland sports, so that he became distinguished above all other chevaliers of the court for his knowledge of all that relates to hunting. No wonder that Belinda, the king's daughter, fell in love with him; but as he did not return her passion, she, in a sudden impulse of anger, excited her father against him, and he was banished the kingdom. The princess soon repented of her act, and in despair destroyed herself, having first written a most tender letter to Tristram, sending him at the same time a beautiful and sagacious dog, of which she was very fond, desiring him to keep it as a memorial of her. Meliadus was now dead, and as his queen, Tristram's stepmother, held the throne, Gouvernail was afraid to carry his pupil to his native country, and took him to Cornwall, to his uncle Mark, who gave him a kind reception.

King Mark resided at the castle of Tintadel, already mentioned in the history of Uther and Igerne. In this court Tristram became distinguished in all the exercises incumbent on a knight; nor was it long before he had an opportunity of practically employing his valor and skill. Moraunt, a celebrated champion, brother to the queen of Ireland, arrived at the court, to demand tribute of King Mark. The knights of Cornwall are in ill repute in romance for their cowardice, and they exhibited it on this occasion. King Mark could find no champion who dared to encounter the Irish knight, till his nephew Tristram, who had not yet received the honors of knighthood, craved to be admitted to the order, offering at the same time to fight the battle of Cornwall against the Irish champion. King Mark assented with reluctance; Tristram received the accolade, which conferred knighthood upon him, and the place and time were assigned for the encounter.

Without attempting to give the details of this famous combat, the first and one of the most glorious of Tristram's exploits, we shall only say that the young knight, though severely wounded, cleft the head of Moraunt, leaving a portion of his sword in the wound. Moraunt, half dead with his wound and the disgrace of his defeat, hastened to hide himself in his ship, sailed away with all speed for Ireland, and died soon after arriving in his own country.

The kingdom of Cornwall was thus delivered from its tribute. Tristram, weakened by loss of blood, fell senseless. His friends flew to his assistance. They dressed his wounds, which in general healed readily; but the lance of Moraunt was poisoned, and one wound which it made yielded to no remedies, but grew worse day by day. The surgeons could do no more. Tristram asked permission of his uncle to depart, and seek for aid in the kingdom of Loegria (England). With his consent he embarked, and after tossing for many days on the sea, was driven by the winds to the coast of Ireland. He landed, full of joy and gratitude that he had escaped the peril of the sea; took his rote,[Footnote: A musical instrument.] and began to play. It was a summer evening, and the king of Ireland and his daughter, the beautiful Isoude, were at a window which overlooked the sea. The strange harper was sent for, and conveyed to the palace, where, finding that he was in Ireland, whose champion he had lately slain, he concealed his name, and called himself Tramtris. The queen undertook his cure, and by a medicated bath gradually restored him to health. His skill in music and in games occasioned his being frequently called to court, and he became the instructor of the princess Isoude in minstrelsy and poetry, who profited so well under his care, that she soon had no equal in the kingdom, except her instructor.

At this time a tournament was held, at which many knights of the Round Table, and others, were present. On the first day a Saracen prince, named Palamedes, obtained the advantage over all. They brought him to the court, and gave him a feast, at which Tristram, just recovering from his wound, was present. The fair Isoude appeared on this occasion in all her charms. Palamedes could not behold them without emotion, and made no effort to conceal his love. Tristram perceived it, and the pain he felt from jealousy taught him how dear the fair Isoude had already become to him.

Next day the tournament was renewed. Tristram, still feeble from his wound, rose during the night, took his arms, and concealed them in a forest near the place of the contest, and, after it had begun, mingled with the combatants. He overthrew all that encountered him, in particular Palamedes, whom he brought to the ground with a stroke of his lance, and then fought him hand to hand, bearing off the prize of the tourney. But his exertions caused his wound to reopen; he bled fast, and in this sad state, yet in triumph, they bore him to the palace. The fair Isoude devoted herself to his relief with an interest which grew more vivid day by day; and her skilful care soon restored him to health.

It happened one day that a damsel of the court, entering the closet where Tristram's arms were deposited, perceived that a part of the sword had been broken off. It occurred to her that the missing portion was like that which was left in the skull of Moraunt, the Irish champion. She imparted her thought to the queen, who compared the fragment taken from her brother's wound with the sword of Tristram, and was satisfied that it was part of the same, and that the weapon of Tristram was that which reft her brother's life. She laid her griefs and resentment before the king, who satisfied himself with his own eyes of the truth of her suspicions. Tristram was cited before the whole court, and reproached with having dared to present himself before them after having slain their kinsman. He acknowledged that he had fought with Moraunt to settle the claim for tribute, and said that it was by force of winds and waves alone that he was thrown on their coast. The queen demanded vengeance for the death of her brother; the fair Isoude trembled and grew pale, but a murmur rose from all the assembly that the life of one so handsome and so brave should not be taken for such a cause, and

Figure 66: "Tristan and Iseult" by Herbert James Draper

generosity finally triumphed over resentment in the mind of the king. Tristram was dismissed in safety, but commanded to leave the kingdom without delay, and never to return thither under pain of death Tristram went back, with restored health, to Cornwall.

King Mark made his nephew give him a minute recital of his adventures. Tristram told him all minutely; but when he came to speak of the fair Isoude he described her charms with a warmth and energy such as none but a lover could display. King Mark was fascinated with the description, and, choosing a favorable time, demanded a boon of his nephew, who readily granted it. The king made him swear upon the holy reliques that he would fulfil his commands. Then Mark directed him to go to Ireland, and obtain for him the fair Isoude to be queen of Cornwall.

[Footnote: "Good faith was the very corner-stone of chivalry. Whenever a knight's word was pledged (it mattered not how rashly) it was to be redeemed at any price. Hence the sacred obligation of the boon granted by a knight to his suppliant. Instances without number occur in romance, in which a knight, by rashly granting an indefinite boon, was obliged to do or suffer something extremely to his prejudice. But it is not in romance alone that we find such singular instances of adherence to an indefinite promise. The history of the times presents authentic transactions equally embarrassing and absurd"—SCOTT, note to Sir Tristram.]

Tristram believed it was certain death for him to return to Ireland; and how could he act as ambassador for his uncle in such a cause? Yet, bound by his oath, he hesitated not for an instant. He only took the precaution to change his armor. He embarked for Ireland; but a tempest drove him to the coast of England, near Camelot, where King Arthur was holding his court, attended by the knights of the Round Table, and many others, the most illustrious in the world.

Tristram kept himself unknown. He took part in many justs; he fought many combats, in which he covered himself with glory. One day he saw among those recently arrived the king of Ireland, father of the fair Isoude. This prince, accused of treason against his liege sovereign, Arthur, came to Camelot to free himself from the charge. Blaanor, one of the most redoubtable warriors of the Round Table, was his accuser, and Argius, the king, had neither youthful vigor nor strength to encounter him. He must therefore seek a champion to sustain his innocence. But the knights of the Round Table were not at liberty to fight against one another, unless in a quarrel of their own. Argius heard of the great renown of the unknown knight; he also was witness of his exploits. He sought him, and conjured him to adopt his defence, and on his oath declared that he was innocent of the crime of which he was accused. Tristram readily consented, and made himself known to the king, who on his part promised to reward his exertions, if successful, with whatever gift he might ask.

Tristram fought with Blaanor, and overthrew him, and held his life in his power. The fallen warrior called on him to use his right of conquest, and strike the fatal blow. "God forbid," said Tristram, "that I should take the life of so brave a knight!" He raised him up and restored him to his friends. The judges of the field decided that the king of Ireland was acquitted of the charge against him, and they led Tristram in triumph to his tent. King Argius, full of gratitude, conjured Tristram to accompany him to his kingdom. They departed together, and arrived in Ireland; and the queen, forgetting her resentment for her brother's death, exhibited to the preserver of her husband's life nothing but gratitude and good-will.

How happy a moment for Isoude, who knew that her father had promised his deliverer whatever boon he might ask! But the unhappy Tristram gazed on her with despair, at the thought of the cruel oath which bound him. His magnanimous soul subdued the force of his love. He revealed the oath which he had taken, and with trembling voice demanded the fair Isoude for his uncle.

Argius consented, and soon all was prepared for the departure of Isoude. Brengwain, her favorite maid of honor, was to accompany her. On the day of departure the queen took aside this devoted attendant, and told her that she had observed that her daughter and Tristram were attached to one another, and that to avert the bad effects of this inclination she had procured from a powerful fairy a potent philter (love-draught), which she directed Brengwain to administer to Isoude and to King Mark on the evening of their marriage.

Isoude and Tristram embarked together. A favorable wind filled the sails, and promised them a fortunate voyage. The lovers gazed upon one another, and could not repress their sighs. Love seemed to light up all his fires on their lips, as in their hearts. The day was warm; they suffered from thirst. Isoude first complained. Tristram descried the bottle containing the love-draught, which Brengwain had been so imprudent as to leave in sight. He took it, gave some of it to the charming Isoude, and drank the remainder himself. The dog Houdain licked the cup. The ship arrived in Cornwall, and Isoude was married to King Mark, The old monarch was delighted with his bride, and his gratitude to Tristram was unbounded. He loaded him with honors, and made him chamberlain of his palace, thus giving him access to the queen at all times.

In the midst of the festivities of the court which followed the royal marriage, an unknown minstrel one day presented himself, bearing a harp of peculiar construction. He excited the curiosity of King Mark by refusing to play upon it till he should grant him a boon. The king having promised to grant his request, the minstrel, who was none other than the Saracen knight, Sir Palamedes, the lover of the fair Isoude, sung to the harp a lay, in which he demanded Isoude as the promised gift. King Mark could not by the laws of knighthood withhold the boon. The lady was mounted on her horse, and led away by her triumphant lover. Tristram, it is needless to say, was absent at the time, and did not return until their departure. When he heard what had taken place he seized his rote, and hastened to the shore, where Isoude and her new master had already embarked. Tristram played upon his rote, and the sound reached the ears of Isoude, who became so deeply affected, that Sir Palamedes was induced to return with her to land, that they might see the unknown musician. Tristram watched his opportunity, seized the lady's horse by the bridle, and plunged with her into the forest, tauntingly informing his rival that "what he had got by the harp he had lost by the rote." Palamedes pursued, and a combat was about to commence, the result of which must have been fatal to one or other of these gallant knights; but Isoude stepped between them, and, addressing Palamedes, said, "You tell me that you love me; you will not then deny me the request I am about to make?" "Lady," he replied, "I will perform your bidding." "Leave, then," said she, "this contest, and repair to King Arthur's court, and salute Queen Guenever from me; tell her that there are in the world but two ladies, herself and I, and two lovers, hers and mine; and come thou not in future in any place where I am." Palamedes burst into tears. "Ah, lady," said he, "I will obey you; but I beseech you that you will not for ever steel your heart against me." "Palamedes," she replied, "may I never taste of joy again if I ever quit my first love." Palamedes then went his way. The lovers remained a week in concealment, after which Tristram restored Isoude to her husband, advising him in future to reward minstrels in some other way.

The king showed much gratitude to Tristram, but in the bottom of his heart he cherished bitter jealousy of him. One day Tristram and Isoude were alone together in her private chamber. A base and cowardly knight of the court, named Andret, spied them through a keyhole. They sat at a table of chess, but were not attending to the game. Andret brought the king, having first raised his suspicions, and placed him so as to watch their motions. The king saw enough to confirm his suspicions, and he burst into the apartment with his sword drawn, and had nearly slain Tristram before he was put on his guard. But Tristram avoided the blow, drew his sword, and drove before him the cowardly monarch, chasing him through all the apartments of the palace, giving him frequent blows with the flat of his sword, while he cried in vain to his knights to save him. They were not inclined, or did not dare, to interpose in his behalf.

A proof of the great popularity of the tale of Sir Tristram is the fact that the Italian poets, Boiardo and Ariosto, have founded upon it the idea of the two enchanted fountains, which produced the opposite effects of love and hatred. Boiardo thus describes the fountain of hatred:

"Fair was that fountain, sculptured all of gold,
With alabaster sculptured, rich and rare;
And in its basin clear thou might'st behold
The flowery marge reflected fresh and fair.
Sage Merlin framed the font,—so legends bear,—
When on fair Isoude doated Tristram brave,
That the good errant knight, arriving there,
Might quaff oblivion in the enchanted wave,
And leave his luckless love, and 'scape his timeless grave.
'But ne'er the warrior's evil fate allowed
His steps that fountain's charmed verge to gain.
Though restless, roving on adventure proud,
He traversed oft the land and oft the main."

Chapter 13

TRISTRAM AND ISOUDE (CONTINUED)

After this affair Tristram was banished from the kingdom, and Isoude shut up in a tower, which stood on the bank of a river. Tristram could not resolve to depart without some further communication with his beloved; so he concealed himself in the forest, till at last he contrived to attract her attention, by means of twigs which he curiously peeled, and sent down the stream under her window. By this means many secret interviews were obtained. Tristram dwelt in the forest, sustaining himself by game, which the dog Houdain ran down for him; for this faithful animal was unequalled in the chase, and knew so well his master's wish for concealment, that, in the pursuit of his game, he never barked. At length Tristram departed, but left Houdain with Isoude, as a remembrancer of him.

Sir Tristram wandered through various countries, achieving the most perilous enterprises, and covering himself with glory, yet unhappy at the separation from his beloved Isoude. At length King Mark's territory was invaded by a neighboring chieftain, and he was forced to summon his nephew to his aid. Tristram obeyed the call, put himself at the head of his uncle's vassals, and drove the enemy out of the country. Mark was full of gratitude, and Tristram, restored to favor and to the society of his beloved Isoude, seemed at the summit of happiness. But a sad reverse was at hand.

Tristram had brought with him a friend named Pheredin, son of the king of Brittany. This young knight saw Queen Isoude, and could not resist her charms. Knowing the love of his friend for the queen, and that that love was returned, Pheredin concealed his own, until his health failed, and he feared he was drawing near his end. He then wrote to the beautiful queen that he was dying for love of her.

The gentle Isoude, in a moment of pity for the friend of Tristram, returned him an answer so kind and compassionate that it restored him to life. A few days afterwards Tristram found this letter. The most terrible jealousy took possession of his soul; he would have slain Pheredin, who with difficulty made his escape. Then Tristram mounted his horse, and rode to the forest, where for ten days he took no rest nor food. At length he was found by a damsel lying almost dead by the brink of a fountain. She recognized him, and tried in vain to rouse his attention. At last recollecting his love for music she went and got her harp, and played thereon. Tristram was roused from his reverie; tears flowed; he breathed more freely; he took the harp from the maiden, and sung this lay, with a voice broken with sobs:

"Sweet I sang in former days,
Kind love perfected my lays:
Now my art alone displays
The woe that on my being preys.
"Charming love, delicious power,
Worshipped from my earliest hour,
Thou who life on all dost shower,
Love! my life thou dost devour.
"In death's hour I beg of thee,
Isoude, dearest enemy,
Thou who erst couldst kinder be,
When I'm gone, forget not me.
"On my gravestone passers-by
Oft will read, as low I lie,
'Never wight in love could vie
With Tristram, yet she let him die.'"

Tristram, having finished his lay, wrote it off and gave it to the damsel, conjuring her to present it to the queen.

Meanwhile Queen Isoude was inconsolable at the absence of Tristram. She discovered that it was caused by the fatal letter which she had written to Pheredin. Innocent, but in despair at the sad effects of her letter, she wrote another to Pheredin, charging him never to see her again. The unhappy lover obeyed this cruel decree. He plunged into the forest, and died of grief and love in a hermit's cell.

Isoude passed her days in lamenting the absence and unknown fate of Tristram. One day her jealous husband, having entered her chamber unperceived, overheard her singing the following lay:

Figure 67: "Tristan and Isolde" by Edmund Leighton

"My voice to piteous wail is bent,
My harp to notes of languishment;
Ah, love! delightsome days be meant
For happier wights, with hearts content.
"Ah, Tristram' far away from me,
Art thou from restless anguish free?
Ah! couldst thou so one moment be,
From her who so much loveth thee?"

The king hearing these words burst forth in a rage; but Isoude was too wretched to fear his violence. "You have heard me," she said; "I confess it all. I love Tristram, and always shall love him. Without doubt he is dead, and died for me. I no longer wish to live. The blow that shall finish my misery will be most welcome."

The king was moved at the distress of the fair Isoude, and perhaps the idea of Tristram's death tended to allay his wrath. He left the queen in charge of her women, commanding them to take especial care lest her despair should lead her to do harm to herself.

Tristram meanwhile, distracted as he was, rendered a most important service to the shepherds by slaying a gigantic robber named Taullas, who was in the habit of plundering their flocks and rifling their cottages. The shepherds, in their gratitude to Tristram, bore him in triumph to King Mark to have him bestow on him a suitable reward. No wonder Mark failed to recognize in the half-clad, wild man, before him his nephew Tristram; but grateful for the service the unknown had rendered he ordered him to be well taken care of, and gave him in charge to the queen and her women. Under such care Tristram rapidly recovered his serenity and his health, so that the romancer tells us he became handsomer than ever.

King Mark's jealousy revived with Tristram's health and good looks, and, in spite of his debt of gratitude so lately increased, he again banished him from the court.

Sir Tristram left Cornwall, and proceeded into the land of Loegria (England) in quest of adventures. One day he entered a wide forest. The sound of a little bell showed him that some inhabitant was near. He followed the sound, and found a hermit, who informed him that he was in the forest of Arnantes, belonging to the fairy Viviane, the Lady of the Lake, who, smitten with love for King Arthur, had found means to entice him to this forest, where by enchantments she held him a prisoner, having deprived him of all memory of who and what he was. The hermit informed him that all the knights of the Round Table were out in search of the king, and that he (Tristram) was now in the scene of the most grand and important adventures.

This was enough to animate Tristram in the search. He had not wandered far before he encountered a knight of Arthur's court, who proved to be Sir Kay the Seneschal, who demanded of him whence he came. Tristram answering, "From Cornwall," Sir Kay did not let slip the opportunity of a joke at the expense of the Cornish knight. Tristram chose to leave him in his error, and even confirmed him in it; for meeting some other knights Tristram declined to just with them. They spent the night together at an abbey, where Tristram submitted patiently to all their jokes. The Seneschal gave the word to his companions that they should set out early next day, and intercept the Cornish knight on his way, and enjoy the amusement of seeing his fright when they should insist on running a tilt with him. Tristram next morning found himself alone; he put on his armor, and set out to continue his quest. He soon saw before him the Seneschal and the three knights, who barred the way, and insisted on a just. Tristram excused himself a long time; at last he reluctantly took his stand. He encountered them, one after the other, and overthrew them all four, man and horse, and then rode off, bidding them not to forget their friend the knight of Cornwall.

Tristram had not ridden far when he met a damsel, who cried out, "Ah, my lord! hasten forward, and prevent a horrid treason!" Tristram flew to her assistance, and soon reached a spot where he beheld a knight, whom three others had borne to the ground, and were unlacing his helmet in order to cut off his head.

Tristram flew to the rescue, and slew with one stroke of his lance one of the assailants. The knight, recovering his feet, sacrificed another to his vengeance, and the third made his escape. The rescued knight then raised the visor of his helmet, and a long white beard fell down upon his breast. The majesty and venerable air of this knight made Tristram suspect that it was none other than Arthur himself, and the prince confirmed his conjecture. Tristram would have knelt before him, but Arthur received him in his arms, and inquired his name and country; but Tristram declined to disclose them, on the plea that he was now on a quest requiring secrecy. At this moment the damsel who had brought Tristram to the rescue darted forward, and, seizing the king's hand, drew from his finger a ring, the gift of the fairy, and by that act dissolved the enchantment. Arthur, having recovered his reason and his memory, offered to Tristram to attach him to his court, and to confer honors and dignities upon him; but Tristram declined all, and only consented to accompany him till he should see him safe in the hands of his knights. Soon after, Hector de Marys rode up, and saluted the king, who on his part introduced him to Tristram as one of the bravest of his knights. Tristram took leave of the king and his faithful follower, and continued his quest.

We cannot follow Tristram through all the adventures which filled this epoch of his history. Suffice it to say, he fulfilled on all occasions the duty of a true knight, rescuing the oppressed, redressing wrongs, abolishing evil customs, and suppressing injustice, thus by constant action endeavoring to lighten the pains of absence from her he loved. In the meantime, Isoude, separated from her dear Tristram, passed her days in languor and regret. At length she could no longer resist the desire to hear some news of her lover. She wrote a letter, and sent it by one of her damsels, niece of her faithful Brengwain. One day Tristram, weary with his exertions, had dismounted and laid himself down by the side of a fountain and fallen asleep. The damsel of Queen Isoude arrived at the same fountain, and recognized Passebreul, the horse of Tristram, and presently perceived his master asleep. He was thin and pale, showing evident marks of the pain he suffered in separation from his beloved. She awakened him, and gave him the letter which she bore, and Tristram enjoyed the pleasure, so sweet to a lover, of hearing from and talking about the object of his affections. He prayed the damsel to postpone her return till after the magnificent tournament which Arthur had proclaimed should have taken place, and conducted her to the castle of Persides, a brave and loyal knight, who received her with great consideration.

Tristram conducted the damsel of Queen Isoude to the tournament, and had her placed in the balcony among the ladies of the queen.

"He glanced and saw the stately galleries,
Dame, damsel, each through worship of their Queen
White-robed in honor of the stainless child,
And some with scatter'd jewels, like a bank
Of maiden snow mingled with sparks of fire.
He looked but once, and veiled his eyes again."
—The Last Tournament.

He then joined the tourney. Nothing could exceed his strength and valor. Launcelot admired him, and by a secret presentiment declined to dispute the honor of the day with a knight so gallant and so skilful. Arthur descended from the balcony to greet the conqueror; but the modest and devoted Tristram, content with having borne off the prize in the sight of the messenger of Isoude, made his escape with her, and disappeared.

The next day the tourney recommenced. Tristram assumed different armor, that he might not be known; but he was soon detected by the terrible blows that he gave, Arthur and Guenever had no doubt that it was the same knight who had borne off the prize of the day before. Arthur's gallant spirit was roused. After Launcelot of the Lake and Sir Gawain he was accounted the best knight of the Round Table. He went privately and armed himself, and came into the tourney in undistinguished armor. He ran a just with Tristram, whom he shook in his seat; but Tristram, who did not know him, threw him out of the saddle. Arthur recovered himself, and content with having made proof of the stranger knight bade Launcelot finish the adventure, and vindicate the honor of the Round Table. Sir Launcelot, at the bidding of the monarch, assailed Tristram, whose lance was already broken in former encounters. But the law of this sort of combat was that the knight after having broken his lance must fight with his sword, and must not refuse to meet with his shield the lance of his antagonist. Tristram met Launcelot's charge upon his shield, which that terrible lance could not fail to pierce. It inflicted a wound upon Tristram's side, and, breaking, left the iron in the wound. But Tristram also with his sword smote so vigorously on Launcelot's casque that he cleft it, and wounded his head. The wound was not deep, but the blood flowed into his eyes, and blinded him for a moment, and Tristram, who thought himself mortally wounded, retired from the field. Launcelot declared to the king that he had never received such a blow in his life before.

Tristram hastened to Gouvernail, his squire, who drew forth the iron, bound up the wound, and gave him immediate ease. Tristram after the tournament kept retired in his tent, but Arthur, with the consent of all the knights of the Round Table, decreed him the honors of the second day. But it was no longer a secret that the victor of the two days was the same individual, and Gouvernail, being questioned, confirmed the suspicions of Launcelot and Arthur that it was no other than Sir Tristram of Leonais, the nephew of the king of Cornwall.

King Arthur, who desired to reward his distinguished valor, and knew that his Uncle Mark had ungratefully banished him, would have eagerly availed himself of the opportunity to attach Tristram to his court,—all the knights of the Round Table declaring with acclamation that it would be impossible to find a more worthy companion. But Tristram had already departed in search of adventures, and the damsel of Queen Isoude returned to her mistress.

Figure 68: "King Mark Slew the Noble Knight Sir Tristram" by Newell Convers Wyeth

Chapter 14

SIR TRISTRAM'S BATTLE WITH SIR LAUNCELOT

Sir Tristram rode through a forest and saw ten men fighting, and one man did battle against nine. So he rode to the knights and cried to them, bidding them cease their battle, for they did themselves great shame, so many knights to fight against one. Then answered the master of the knights (his name was Sir Breuse sans Pitie, who was at that time the most villanous knight living): "Sir knight, what have ye to do to meddle with us? If ye be wise depart on your way as you came, for this knight shall not escape us." "That were pity," said Sir Tristram, "that so good a knight should be slain so cowardly; therefore I warn you I will succor him with all my puissance."

Then Sir Tristram alighted off his horse, because they were on foot, that they should not slay his horse. And he smote on the right hand and on the left so vigorously that well-nigh at every stroke he struck down a knight. At last they fled, with Breuse sans Pitie, into the tower, and shut Sir Tristram without the gate. Then Sir Tristram returned back to the rescued knight, and found him sitting under a tree, sore wounded. "Fair knight," said he, "how is it with you?" "Sir knight," said Sir Palamedes, for he it was, "I thank you of your great goodness, for ye have rescued me from death." "What is your name?" said Sir Tristram. He said, "My name is Sir Palamedes." "Say ye so?" said Sir Tristram; "now know that thou art the man in the world that I most hate; therefore make thee ready, for I will do battle with thee." "What is your name?" said Sir Palamedes. "My name is Sir Tristram, your mortal enemy." "It may be so," said Sir Palamedes; "but you have done overmuch for me this day, that I should fight with you. Moreover, it will be no honor for you to have to do with me, for you are fresh and I am wounded. Therefore, if you will needs have to do with me, assign me a day, and I shall meet you without fail." "You say well, "said Sir Tristram; "now I assign you to meet me in the meadow by the river of Camelot, where Merlin set the monument." So they were agreed. Then they departed and took their ways diverse. Sir Tristram passed through a great forest into a plain, till he came to a priory, and there he reposed him with a good man six days.

Figure 69: "Lancelot Killing Fire-breathing Dragon" by Arthur Rackham

Then departed Sir Tristram, and rode straight into Camelot to the monument of Merlin, and there he looked about him for Sir Palamedes. And he perceived a seemly knight, who came riding against him all in white, with a covered shield. When he came nigh Sir Tristram said aloud, "Welcome, sir knight, and well and truly have you kept your promise." Then they made ready their shields and spears, and came together with all the might of their horses, so fiercely, that both the horses and the knights fell to the earth. And as soon as they might they quitted their horses, and struck together with bright swords as men of might, and each wounded the other wonderfully sore, so that the blood ran out upon the grass. Thus they fought for the space of four hours and never one would speak to the other one word. Then at last spake the white knight, and said, "Sir, thou fightest wonderful well, as ever I saw knight; therefore, if it please you, tell me your name." "Why dost thou ask my name?" said Sir Tristram; "art thou not Sir Palamedes?" "No, fair knight," said he, "I am Sir

Launcelot of the Lake." "Alas!" said Sir Tristram, "what have I done? for you are the man of the world that I love best." "Fair knight," said Sir Launcelot, "tell me your name." "Truly," said he, "my name is Sir Tristram de Lionesse." "Alas! alas!" said Sir Launcelot, "what adventure has befallen me!" And therewith Sir Launcelot kneeled down and yielded him up his sword; and Sir Tristram kneeled down and yielded him up his sword; and so either gave other the degree. And then they both went to the stone, and sat them down upon it and took off their helms and each kissed the other a hundred times. And then anon they rode toward Camelot, and on the way they met with Sir Gawain and Sir Gaheris, that had made promise to Arthur never to come again to the court till they had brought Sir Tristram with them.

"Return again," said Sir Launcelot, "for your quest is done; for I have met with Sir Tristram. Lo, here he is in his own person." Then was Sir Gawain glad, and said to Sir Tristram, "Ye are welcome." With this came King Arthur, and when he wist there was Sir Tristram, he ran unto him, and took him by the hand, and said, "Sir Tristram, ye are as welcome as any knight that ever came to this court." Then Sir Tristram told the king how he came thither for to have had to do with Sir Palamedes, and how he had rescued him from Sir Breuse sans Pitie and the nine knights. Then King Arthur took Sir Tristram by the hand, and went to the Table Round, and Queen Guenever came, and many ladies with her, and all the ladies said with one voice, "Welcome, Sir Tristram." "Welcome," said the knights. "Welcome," said Arthur, "for one of the best of knights, and the gentlest of the world, and the man of most worship; for of all manner of hunting thou bearest the prize, and of all measures of blowing thou art the beginning, and of all the terms of hunting and hawking ye are the inventor, and of all instruments of music ye are the best skilled; therefore, gentle knight," said Arthur, "ye are welcome to this court." And then King Arthur made Sir Tristram knight of the Table Round with great nobley and feasting as can be thought.

SIR TRISTRAM AS A SPORTSMAN

Tristram is often alluded to by the Romancers as the great authority and model in all matters relating to the chase. In the "Faery Queene," Tristram, in answer to the inquiries of Sir Calidore, informs him of his name and parentage, and concludes:

Figure 70: "Questing Beast" by Arthur Rackham

"All which my days I have not lewdly spent,
Nor spilt the blossom of my tender years
In idlesse; but, as was convenient,
Have trained been with many noble feres
In gentle thewes, and such like seemly leers;
'Mongst which my most delight hath always been
To hunt the salvage chace, amongst my peers,
Of all that rangeth in the forest green,
Of which none is to me unknown that yet was seen.
"Ne is there hawk which mantleth on her perch,
Whether high towering or accosting low,
But I the measure of her flight do search,
And all her prey, and all her diet know.
Such be our joys, which in these forests grow."

[Footnote: Feres, companions; thewes, labors; leers, learning.]

Chapter 15

THE ROUND TABLE

The famous enchanter, Merlin, had exerted all his skill in fabricating the Round Table. Of the seats which surrounded it he had constructed thirteen, in memory of the thirteen Apostles. Twelve of these seats only could be occupied, and they only by knights of the highest fame; the thirteenth represented the seat of the traitor Judas. It remained always empty. It was called the PERILOUS SEAT, ever since a rash and haughty Saracen knight had dared to place himself in it, when the earth opened and swallowed him up.

"In our great hall there stood a vacant chair,
Fashion'd by Merlin ere he past away,
And carven with strange figures; and in and out
The figures, like a serpent, ran a scroll
Of letters in a tongue no man could read
And Merlin call'd it 'The Siege perilous,'
Perilous for good and ill; 'for there,' he said,
'No man could sit but he should lose himself.'"
—The Holy Grail.

A magic power wrote upon each seat the name of the knight who was entitled to sit in it. No one could succeed to a vacant seat unless he surpassed in valor and glorious deeds the knight who had occupied it before him; without this qualification he would be violently repelled by a hidden force. Thus proof was made of all those who presented themselves to replace any companions of the order who had fallen.

One of the principal seats, that of Moraunt of Ireland, had been vacant ten years, and his name still remained over it ever since the time when that distinguished champion fell beneath the sword of Sir Tristram. Arthur now took Tristram by the hand and led him to that seat. Immediately the most melodious sounds were heard, and exquisite perfumes filled the place; the name of Moraunt disappeared, and that of Tristram blazed forth in light. The rare modesty of Tristram had now to be subjected to a severe task; for the clerks charged with the duty of preserving the annals of the Round Table attended, and he was required by the law of his order to declare what feats of arms he had accomplished to entitle him to take that seat. This ceremony being ended, Tristram received the congratulations of all his companions. Sir Launcelot and Guenever took the occasion to speak to him of the fair Isoude, and to express their wish that some happy chance might bring her to the kingdom of Loegria.

While Tristram was thus honored and caressed at the court of King Arthur, the most gloomy and malignant jealousy harassed the soul of Mark. He could not look upon Isoude without remembering that she loved Tristram, and the good fortune of his nephew goaded him to thoughts of vengeance. He at last resolved to go disguised into the kingdom of Loegria, attack Tristram by stealth, and put him to death. He took with him two knights, brought up in his court, who he thought were devoted to him; and, not willing to leave Isoude behind, named two of her maidens to attend her, together with her faithful Brengwain, and made them accompany him.

Having arrived in the neighborhood of Camelot, Mark imparted his plan to his two knights, but they rejected it with horror; nay, more, they declared that they would no longer remain in his service; and left him, giving him reason to suppose that they should repair to the court to accuse him before Arthur. It was necessary for Mark to meet and rebut their accusation; so, leaving Isoude in an abbey, he pursued his way alone to Camelot.

Mark had not ridden far when he encountered a party of knights of Arthur's court, and would have avoided them, for he knew their habit of challenging to a just every stranger knight whom they met. But it was too late. They had seen his armor, and recognized him as a Cornish knight, and at once resolved to have some sport with him. It happened they had with them Daguenet, King Arthur's fool, who, though deformed and weak of body, was not wanting in courage. The knights as Mark approached laid their plan that Daguenet should personate Sir Launcelot of the Lake, and challenge the Cornish knight. They equipped him in armor belonging to one of their number who was ill, and sent him forward to the cross-road to defy the strange knight. Mark, who saw that his antagonist was by no means formidable in appearance, was not disinclined to the combat; but when the dwarf rode towards him, calling out that he was Sir Launcelot of the

Figure 71: "Holy Grail and the Knights of the Round Table" by Edvrard d'Espinques

Lake, his fears prevailed, he put spurs to his horse, and rode away at full speed, pursued by the shouts and laughter of the party.

Meanwhile Isoude, remaining at the abbey with her faithful Brengwain, found her only amusement in walking occasionally in a forest adjoining the abbey. There, on the brink of a fountain girdled with trees, she thought of her love, and sometimes joined her voice and her harp in lays reviving the memory of its pains or pleasures. One day the caitiff knight, Breuse the Pitiless, heard her voice, concealed himself, and drew near. She sang:

"Sweet silence, shadowy bower, and verdant lair,
Ye court my troubled spirit to repose,
Whilst I, such dear remembrance rises there,
Awaken every echo with my woes
"Within these woods, by nature's hand arrayed,
A fountain springs, and feeds a thousand flowers;

Ah! how my groans do all its murmurs aid!
How my sad eyes do swell it with their showers!
"What doth my knight the while? to him is given
A double meed; in love and arms' emprise,
Him the Round Table elevates to heaven!
Tristram! ah me! he hears not Isoude's cries."

Breuse the Pitiless, who like most other caitiffs had felt the weight of Tristram's arm, and hated him accordingly, at hearing his name breathed forth by the beautiful songstress, impelled by a double impulse, rushed forth from his concealment and laid hands on his victim. Isoude fainted, and Brengwain filled the air with her shrieks. Breuse carried Isoude to the place where he had left his horse; but the animal had got away from his bridle, and was at some distance. He was obliged to lay down his fair burden, and go in pursuit of his horse. Just then a knight came up, drawn by the cries of Brengwain, and demanded the cause of her distress. She could not speak, but pointed to her mistress lying insensible on the ground.

Breuse had by this time returned, and the cries of Brengwain, renewed at seeing him, sufficiently showed the stranger the cause of the distress. Tristram spurred his horse towards Breuse, who, not unprepared, ran to the encounter. Breuse was unhorsed, and lay motionless, pretending to be dead; but when the stranger knight left him to attend to the distressed damsels, he mounted his horse, and made his escape.

The knight now approached Isoude, gently raised her head, drew aside the golden hair which covered her countenance, gazed thereon for an instant, uttered a cry, and fell back insensible. Brengwain came; her cares soon restored her mistress to life, and they then turned their attention to the fallen warrior. They raised his visor, and discovered the countenance of Sir Tristram. Isoude threw herself on the body of her lover, and bedewed his face with her tears. Their warmth revived the knight, and Tristram on awaking found himself in the arms of his dear Isoude.

It was the law of the Round Table that each knight after his admission should pass the next ten days in quest of adventures, during which time his companions might meet him in disguised armor and try their strength with him. Tristram had now been out seven days, and in that time had encountered many of the best knights of the Round Table, and acquitted himself with honor. During the remaining three days, Isoude remained at the abbey, under his protection, and then set out with her maidens, escorted by Sir Tristram, to rejoin King Mark at the court of Camelot.

This happy journey was one of the brightest epochs in the lives of Tristram and Isoude. He celebrated it by a lay upon the harp in a peculiar measure, to which the French give the name of Triolet.

"With fair Isoude, and with love,
Ah! how sweet the life I lead!
How blest for ever thus to rove,
With fair Isoude, and with love!
As she wills, I live and move,
And cloudless days to days succeed:
With fair Isoude, and with love,
Ah! how sweet the life I lead!
"Journeying on from break of day,
Feel you not fatigued, my fair?
Yon green turf invites to play;
Journeying on from day to day,
Ah! let us to that shade away,
Were it but to slumber there!
Journeying on from break of day,
Feel you not fatigued, my fair?"

They arrived at Camelot, where Sir Launcelot received them most cordially. Isoude was introduced to King Arthur and Queen Guenever, who welcomed her as a sister. As King Mark was held in arrest under the accusation of the two Cornish knights, Queen Isoude could not rejoin her husband, and Sir Launcelot placed his castle of La Joyeuse Garde at the disposal of his friends, who there took up their abode.

King Mark, who found himself obliged to confess the truth of the charge against him, or to clear himself by combat with his accusers, preferred the former, and King Arthur, as his crime had not been perpetrated, remitted the penalty, only enjoining upon him, under pain of his signal displeasure, to lay aside all thoughts of vengeance against his nephew. In the presence of the king and his court all parties were formally reconciled; Mark and his queen departed for their home, and Tristram remained at Arthur's court.

Chapter 16

SIR PALAMEDES, OR PALOMIDES, OR PELLINORE

While Sir Tristram and the fair Isoude abode yet at La Joyeuse Garde, Sir Tristram rode forth one day, without armor, having no weapon but his spear and his sword. And as he rode he came to a place where he saw two knights in battle, and one of them had gotten the better and the other lay overthrown. The knight who had the better was Sir Palamedes. When Sir Palamedes knew Sir Tristram, he cried out, "Sir Tristram, now we be met, and ere we depart we will redress our old wrongs." "As for that," said Sir Tristram, "there never yet was Christian man that might make his boast that I ever fled from him, and thou that art a Saracen shalt never say that of me." And therewith Sir Tristram made his horse to run, and with all his might came straight upon Sir Palamedes, and broke his spear upon him. Then he drew his sword and struck at Sir Palamedes six great strokes, upon his helm. Sir Palamedes saw that Sir Tristram had not his armor on, and he marvelled at his rashness and his great folly; and said to himself, "If I meet and slay him, I am shamed wheresoever I go." Then Sir Tristram cried out and said, "Thou coward knight, why wilt thou not do battle with me? for have thou no doubt I shall endure all thy malice." "Ah, Sir Tristram!" said Sir Palamedes, "thou knowest I may not fight with thee for shame; for thou art here naked, and I am armed; now I require that thou answer me a question that I shall ask you." "Tell me what it is," said Sir Tristram. "I put the case," said Palamedes, "that you were well armed, and I naked as ye be; what would you do to me now, by your true knighthood?" "Ah!" said Sir Tristram, "now I understand thee well, Sir Palamedes; and, as God bless me, what I shall say shall not be said for fear that I have of thee. But if it were so, thou shouldest depart from me, for I would not have to do with thee." "No more will I with thee," said Sir Palamedes, "and therefore ride forth on thy way." "As for that, I may choose," said Sir Tristram, "either to ride or to abide. But, Sir Palamedes, I marvel at one thing,—that thou art so good a knight, yet that thou wilt not be christened." "As for that," said Sir Palamedes, "I may not yet be christened, for a vow which I made many years ago; yet in my heart I believe in our Saviour and his mild mother, Mary; but I have yet one battle to do, and when that is done I will be christened, with a good will." "By my head," said Sir Tristram, "as for that one battle, thou shalt seek it no longer; for yonder is a knight, whom

Figure 72: "Idylls of the King, Lord Tennyson" by Paul Gustave Dore

you have smitten down. Now help me to be clothed in his armor, and I will soon fulfil thy vow." "As ye will," said Sir Palamedes, "so shall it be." So they rode both unto that knight that sat on a bank; and Sir Tristram saluted him, and he full weary saluted him again. "Sir," said Sir Tristram, "I pray you to lend me your whole armor; for I am unarmed, and I must do battle with this knight." "Sir," said the hurt knight, "you shall have it, with a right good will," Then Sir Tristram unarmed Sir Galleron, for that was the name of the hurt knight, and he as well as he could helped to arm Sir Tristram. Then Sir Tristram mounted upon his own horse, and in his hand he took Sir Galleron's spear. Thereupon Sir Palamedes was ready, and so they came hurling together, and each smote the other in the midst of their shields. Sir Palamedes' spear broke, and Sir Tristram smote down the horse. Then Sir Palamedes leapt from his horse, and drew out his sword. That saw Sir Tristram, and therewith he alighted and tied his horse to a tree. Then they came together as two wild beasts, lashing the one on the other, and so fought more than two hours; and often Sir Tristram smote such strokes at Sir Palamedes that he made him to kneel, and Sir Palamedes broke away Sir Tristram's shield, and wounded him. Then Sir Tristram was wroth out of measure, and he rushed to Sir Palamedes and wounded him passing sore through the shoulder, and by fortune smote Sir Palamedes' sword out of his hand And if Sir Palamedes had stooped for his sword Sir Tristram had slain him. Then Sir Palamedes stood and beheld his sword with a full sorrowful heart. "Now," said Sir Tristram, "I have thee at a vantage, as thou hadst me to-day; but it shall never be said, in court, or among good knights, that Sir Tristram did slay any knight that was weaponless; therefore take thou thy sword, and let us fight this battle to the end." Then spoke Sir Palamedes to Sir Tristram: "I have no wish to fight this battle any more. The offence that I have done unto you is not so great but that, if it please you, we may be friends. All that I have offended is for the love of the queen, La Belle Isoude, and I dare maintain that she is peerless among ladies; and for that offence ye have given me many grievous and sad strokes, and some I have given you again. Wherefore I require you, my lord Sir Tristram, forgive me all that I have offended you, and this day have me unto the next church; and first I will be clean confessed, and after that see you that I be truly baptized, and then we will ride together unto the court of my lord, King Arthur, so that we may be there at the feast of Pentecost." "Now take your horse," said Sir Tristram, "and as you have said, so shall it be done." So they took their horses, and Sir Galleron rode with them. When they came to the church of Carlisle, the bishop commanded to fill a great vessel with water; and when he had hallowed it, he then confessed Sir Palamedes clean, and christened him, and Sir Tristram and Sir Galleron were his godfathers. Then soon after they departed, and rode towards Camelot, where the noble King Arthur and Queen Guenever were keeping a court royal. And the king and all the court were glad that Sir Palamedes was christened. Then Sir Tristram returned again to La Joyeuse Garde, and Sir Palamedes went his way.

Not long after these events Sir Gawain returned from Brittany, and related to King Arthur the adventure which befell him in the forest of Breciliande, how Merlin had there spoken to him, and enjoined him to charge the king to go without delay upon the quest of the Holy Greal. While King Arthur deliberated Tristram determined to enter upon the quest, and the more readily, as it was well known to him that this holy adventure would, if achieved, procure him the pardon of all his sins. He immediately departed for the kingdom of Brittany, hoping there to obtain from Merlin counsel as to the proper course to pursue to insure success.

Figure 73: "King Pellinore and the Damsel at the Well" by Francis Arthur Fraser

Chapter 17

SIR TRISTRAM

On arriving in Brittany Tristram found King Hoel engaged in a war with a rebellious vassal, and hard pressed by his enemy. His best knights had fallen in a late battle, and he knew not where to turn for assistance. Tristram volunteered his aid. It was accepted; and the army of Hoel, led by Tristram, and inspired by his example, gained a complete victory. The king, penetrated by the most lively sentiments of gratitude, and having informed himself of Tristram's birth, offered him his daughter in marriage. The princess was beautiful and accomplished, and bore the same name with the Queen of Cornwall; but this one is designated by the Romancers as Isoude of the White Hands, to distinguish her from Isoude the Fair.

How can we describe the conflict that agitated the heart of Tristram? He adored the first Isoude, but his love for her was hopeless, and not unaccompanied by remorse. Moreover, the sacred quest on which he had now entered demanded of him perfect purity of life. It seemed as if a happy destiny had provided for him in the charming princess Isoude of the White Hands the best security for all his good resolutions. This last reflection determined him. They were married, and passed some months in tranquil happiness at the court of King Hoel. The pleasure which Tristram felt in his wife's society increased day by day. An inward grace seemed to stir within him from the moment when he took the oath to go on the quest of the Holy Greal; it seemed even to triumph over the power of the magic love-potion.

The war, which had been quelled for a time, now burst out anew. Tristram as usual was foremost in every danger. The enemy was worsted in successive conflicts, and at last shut himself up in his principal city. Tristram led on the attack of the city. As he mounted a ladder to scale the walls he was struck on the head by a fragment of rock, which the besieged threw down upon him. It bore him to the ground, where he lay insensible.

As soon as he recovered consciousness he demanded to be carried to his wife. The princess, skilled in the art of surgery, would not suffer any one but herself to touch her beloved husband. Her fair hands bound up his wounds; Tristram kissed them with gratitude, which began to grow into love. At first the devoted cares of Isoude seemed to meet with great success; but after a while these flattering appearances vanished, and, in spite of all her care, the malady grew more serious day by day.

In this perplexity, an old squire of Tristram's reminded his master that the princess of Ireland, afterwards queen of Cornwall, had once cured him under circumstances quite as discouraging. He called Isoude of the White Hands to him, told her of his former cure, added that he believed that the Queen Isoude could heal him, and that he felt sure that she would come to his relief, if sent for.

Isoude of the White Hands consented that Gesnes, a trusty man and skilful navigator, should be sent to Cornwall. Tristram called him, and, giving him a ring, "Take this," he said, "to the Queen of Cornwall. Tell her that Tristram, near to death, demands her aid. If you succeed in bringing her with you, place white sails to your vessel on your return, that we may know of your success

Figure 74: "Trsitan e Iseo (La vida)" by Rogelio de Egusquiza

when the vessel first heaves in sight. But if Queen Isoude refuses, put on black sails; they will be the presage of my impending death."

Gesnes performed his mission successfully. King Mark happened to be absent from his capital, and the queen readily consented to return with the bark to Brittany. Gesnes clothed his vessel in the whitest of sails, and sped his way back to Brittany.

Meantime the wound of Tristram grew more desperate day by day. His strength, quite prostrated, no longer permitted him to be carried to the seaside daily, as had been his custom from the first moment when it was possible for the bark to be on the way homeward. He called a young damsel, and gave her in charge to keep watch in the direction of Cornwall, and to come and tell him the color of the sails of the first vessel she should see approaching.

When Isoude of the White Hands consented that the queen of Cornwall should be sent for, she had not known all the reasons which she had for fearing the influence which renewed intercourse with that princess might have on her own happiness. She had now learned more, and felt the danger more keenly. She thought, if she could only keep the knowledge of the queen's arrival from her husband, she might employ in his service any resources which her skill could supply, and still avert the dangers which she apprehended. When the vessel was seen approaching, with its white sails sparkling in the sun, the damsel, by command of her mistress, carried word to Tristram that the sails were black.

Tristram, penetrated with inexpressible grief, breathed a profound sigh, turned away his face, and said, "Alas, my beloved! we shall never see one another again!" Then he commended himself to God, and breathed his last.

The death of Tristram was the first intelligence which the queen of Cornwall heard on landing. She was conducted almost senseless into the chamber of Tristram, and expired holding him in her arms.

Tristram, before his death, had requested that his body should be sent to Cornwall, and that his sword, with a letter he had written, should be delivered to King Mark. The remains of Tristram and Isoude were embarked in a vessel, along with the sword, which was presented to the king of Cornwall. He was melted with tenderness when he saw the weapon which slew Moraunt of Ireland,— which had so often saved his life, and redeemed the honor of his kingdom. In the letter Tristram begged pardon of his uncle, and related the story of the amorous draught.

Mark ordered the lovers to be buried in his own chapel. From the tomb of Tristram there sprung a vine, which went along the walls, and descended into the grave of the queen. It was cut down three times, but each time sprung up again more vigorous than before, and this wonderful plant has ever since shaded the tombs of Tristram and Isoude.

Spenser introduces Sir Tristram in his "Faery Queene." In Book VI., Canto ii., Sir Calidore encounters in the forest a young hunter, whom he thus describes:

"Him steadfastly he marked, and saw to be
A goodly youth of amiable grace,
Yet but a slender slip, that scarce did see
Yet seventeen yeares; but tall and faire of face,
That sure he deemed him borne of noble race.
All in a woodman's jacket he was clad
Of Lincoln greene, belayed with silver lace;
And on his head an hood with aglets sprad,
And by his side his hunter's horne he hanging had.

[Footnote: Aglets, points or tags]

"Buskins he wore of costliest cordawayne,
Pinckt upon gold, and paled part per part,
As then the guize was for each gentle swayne.
In his right hand he held a trembling dart,
Whose fellow he before had sent apart;
And in his left he held a sharp bore-speare,
With which he wont to launch the salvage heart
Of many a lyon, and of many a beare,
That first unto his hand in chase did happen neare."

[Footnote: PINCKT UPON GOLD, ETC., adorned with golden points, or eyelets, and regularly intersected with stripes. PALED (in heraldry), striped]

Chapter 18

PERCEVAL

The father and two elder brothers of Perceval had fallen in battle or tournaments, and hence, as the last hope of his family, his mother retired with him into a solitary region, where he was brought up in total ignorance of arms and chivalry. He was allowed no weapon but "a lyttel Scots spere," which was the only thing of all "her lordes faire gere" that his mother carried to the wood with her. In the use of this he became so skilful, that he could kill with it not only the animals of the chase for the table, but even birds on the wing. At length, however, Perceval was roused to a desire of military renown by seeing in the forest five knights who were in complete armor. He said to his mother, "Mother, what are those yonder?" "They are angels, my son," said she. "By my faith, I will go and become an angel with them." And Perceval went to the road and met them. "Tell me, good lad," said one of them, "sawest thou a knight pass this way either today or yesterday?" "I know not," said he, "what a knight is." "Such an one as I am," said the knight. "If thou wilt tell me what I ask thee, I will tell thee what thou askest me." "Gladly will I do so," said Sir Owain, for that was the knight's name. "What is this?" demanded Perceval, touching the saddle. "It is a saddle," said Owain. Then he asked about all the accoutrements which he saw upon the men and the horses, and about the arms, and what they were for, and how they were used. And Sir Owain showed him all those things fully. And Perceval in return gave him such information as he had

Then Perceval returned to his mother, and said to her, "Mother, those were not angels, but honorable knights." Then his mother swooned away. And Perceval went to the place where they kept the horses that carried firewood and provisions for the castle, and he took a bony, piebald horse, which seemed to him the strongest of them. And he pressed a pack into the form of a saddle, and with twisted twigs he imitated the trappings which he had seen upon the horses. When he came again to his mother, the countess had recovered from her swoon. "My son," said she, "desirest thou to ride forth?" "Yes, with thy leave," said he. "Go forward, then," she said, "to the court of Arthur, where there are the best and the noblest and the most bountiful of men, and tell him thou art Perceval, the son of Pelenore, and ask of him to bestow knighthood on thee. And whenever thou seest a church, repeat there thy pater- noster; and if thou see meat and drink, and hast need of them, thou mayest take them. If thou hear an outcry of one in distress, proceed toward it, especially if it be the cry of a woman, and render her what service thou canst. If thou see a fair jewel, win it, for thus shalt thou acquire fame; yet freely give it to another, for thus thou shalt obtain praise. If thou see a fair woman, pay court to her, for thus thou wilt obtain love."

After this discourse Perceval mounted the horse and taking a number of sharp-pointed sticks in his hand he rode forth. And he rode far in the woody wilderness without food or drink. At last he came to an opening in the wood where he saw a tent, and as he thought it might be a church he said his pater-noster to it. And he went towards it; and the door of the tent was open. And Perceval dismounted and entered the tent. In the tent he found a maiden sitting, with a golden frontlet on her forehead and a gold ring on her hand. And Perceval said, "Maiden, I salute you, for my mother told me whenever I met a lady I must respectfully salute her." Perceiving in one corner of the tent some food, two flasks full of wine, and some boar's flesh roasted, he said, "My mother told me, whenever I saw meat and drink to take it." And he ate greedily, for he was very hungry. The maiden said, "Sir, thou hadst best go quickly from here, for fear that my friends should come, and evil should befall you." But Perceval said, "My mother told me wheresoever I saw a fair jewel to take it," and he took the gold ring from her finger, and put it on his own; and he gave the maiden his own ring in exchange for hers; then he mounted his horse and rode away.

Perceval journeyed on till he arrived at Arthur's court. And it so happened that just at that time an uncourteous knight had offered Queen Guenever a gross insult. For when her page was serving the queen with a golden goblet, this knight struck the arm of the page and dashed the wine in the queen's face and over her stomacher. Then he said, "If any have boldness to avenge this insult to Guenever, let him follow me to the meadow." So the knight took his horse and rode to the meadow, carrying away the golden goblet. And all the household hung down their heads and no one offered to follow the knight to take vengeance upon him. For it seemed to them that no one would have ventured on so daring an outrage unless he possessed such powers, through magic or charms, that none could be able to punish him. Just then, behold, Perceval entered the hall upon the bony, piebald horse, with his uncouth trappings. In the centre of the hall stood Kay the Seneschal. "Tell me, tall man," said Perceval, "is that Arthur yonder?" "What wouldst thou with Arthur?" asked Kay. "My mother told me to go to Arthur and receive knighthood from him." "By my faith," said he, "thou art all too meanly equipped with horse and with arms." Then all the household began to jeer and laugh at him. But there was a certain damsel who had been a whole year at Arthur's court, and had never been known to smile. And the king's fool [Footnote: A fool was a common appendage of the courts of those days when this romance was written. A fool was the ornament held in next estimation to a dwarf. He wore a white dress with a yellow bonnet, and carried a bell or bawble in his hand. Though called a fool, his words were often weighed and remembered as if there were a sort of oracular meaning in them.] had said that this damsel would not smile till she had seen him who would be the flower of chivalry. Now this damsel came up to Perceval and told him, smiling, that if he lived he would be one of the bravest and best of knights. "Truly," said Kay, "thou art ill taught to remain a year at Arthur's court, with choice of society, and smile on no one, and now before the face of Arthur and all his knights to call such a man as this the flower of knighthood;" and he gave her a box on the ear, that she fell senseless to the ground. Then said Kay to Perceval, "Go after the knight who went hence to the meadow, overthrow him and recover the golden goblet, and possess thyself of his horse and arms, and thou shalt have knighthood." "I will do so, tall man," said Perceval. So he turned his horse's head toward the meadow. And when he came there, the knight was riding up and down, proud of his strength and valor and noble mien. "Tell me," said the knight, "didst thou see any one coming after me from the court?" "The tall man that was there," said Perceval, "told me to come and overthrow thee, and to take from thee the goblet and thy horse and armor for myself." "Silence!" said the knight; "go back to the court, and tell Arthur either to come himself, or to send some other to fight with me; and unless he do so quickly, I will not wait for him." "By my faith," said Perceval, "choose thou whether it shall be willingly or unwillingly, for I will have the horse and the arms and the goblet." Upon this the knight ran at him furiously, and struck him a violent blow with the shaft of his spear, between the neck and the shoulder. "Ha, ha, lad!" said Perceval, "my mother's servants were not used to play with me in this wise; so thus will I play with thee." And he threw at him one of his sharp-pointed sticks, and it struck him in the eye, and came out at the back of his head, so that he fell down lifeless.

"Verily," said Sir Owain, the son of Urien, to Kay the Seneschal, "thou wast ill-advised to send that madman after the knight, for he must either be overthrown or flee, and either way it will be a disgrace to Arthur and his warriors; therefore will I go to see what has befallen him." So Sir Owain went to the meadow, and he found Perceval trying in vain to get the dead knight's armor off, in order to clothe himself with it. Sir Owain unfastened the armor, and helped Perceval to put it on, and taught him how to put his foot in the stirrup, and use the spur; for Perceval had never used stirrup nor spur, but rode without saddle, and urged on his horse with a stick. Then Owain would have had him return to the court to receive the praise that was his due; but Perceval said, "I will not come to the court till I have encountered the tall man that is there, to revenge the injury he did to the maiden. But take thou the goblet to Queen Guenever, and tell King Arthur that, wherever I am, I will be his vassal, and will do him what profit and service I can." And Sir Owain went back to the court, and related all these things to Arthur and Guenever, and to all the household.

And Perceval rode forward. And he came to a lake on the side of which was a fair castle, and on the border of the lake he saw a hoary-headed man sitting upon a velvet cushion, and his attendants were fishing in the lake. When the hoary-headed man beheld Perceval approaching, he arose and went into the castle. Perceval rode to the castle, and the door was open, and he entered the hall. And the hoary-headed man received Perceval courteously, and asked him to sit by him on the cushion. When it was time the tables were set, and they went to meat. And when they had finished their meat the hoary-headed man asked Perceval if he knew how to fight with the sword "I know not," said Perceval, "but were I to be taught, doubtless I should." And the hoary-headed man said to him, "I am thy uncle, thy mother's brother; I am called King Pecheur.[Footnote: The word means both FISHER and SINNER.] Thou shalt remain with me a space, in order to learn the manners and customs of different countries, and courtesy and noble bearing. And this do thou remember, if thou seest aught to cause thy wonder, ask not the meaning of it; if no one has the courtesy to inform thee, the reproach will not fall upon thee, but upon me that am thy teacher." While Perceval and his uncle discoursed together, Perceval beheld two youths enter the hall bearing a golden cup and a spear of mighty size, with blood dropping from its point to the ground. And when all the company saw this they began to weep and lament. But for all that, the man did not break off his discourse with Perceval. And as he did not tell him the meaning of what he saw, he forebore to ask him concerning it. Now the cup that Perceval saw was the Sangreal, and the spear the sacred spear; and afterwards King Pecheur removed with those sacred relics into a far country.

One evening Perceval entered a valley, and came to a hermit's cell; and the hermit welcomed him gladly, and there he spent the night. And in the morning he arose, and when he went forth, behold! a shower of snow had fallen in the night, and a hawk had killed a wild-fowl in front of the cell. And the noise of the horse had scared the hawk away, and a raven alighted on the bird. And Perceval stood and compared the blackness of the raven and the whiteness of the snow and the redness of the blood to the hair of the lady that best he loved, which was blacker than jet, and to her skin, which was whiter than the snow, and to the two red spots upon her cheeks, which were redder than the blood upon the snow.

Now Arthur and his household were in search of Perceval, and by chance they came that way. "Know ye," said Arthur, "who is the knight with the long spear that stands by the brook up yonder?" "Lord," said one of them, "I will go and learn who he is." So the youth came to the place where Perceval was, and asked him what he did thus, and who he was. But Perceval was so intent upon his thought that he gave him no answer. Then the youth thrust at Perceval with his lance; and Perceval turned upon him, and struck him to the ground. And when the youth returned to the king, and told how rudely he had been treated, Sir Kay said, "I will go myself." And when he greeted Perceval, and got no answer, he spoke to him rudely and angrily. And Perceval thrust at him with his lance, and cast him down so that he broke his arm and his shoulder-blade. And while he lay thus stunned his horse returned back at a wild and prancing pace.

Then said Sir Gawain, surnamed the Golden-Tongued, because he was the most courteous knight in Arthur's court: "It is not fitting that any should disturb an honorable knight from his thought unadvisedly; for either he is pondering some damage that he has sustained, or he is thinking of the lady whom best he loves. If it seem well to thee, lord, I will go and see if this knight has changed from his thought, and if he has, I will ask him courteously to come and visit thee."

And Perceval was resting on the shaft of his spear, pondering the same thought, and Sir Gawain came to him, and said: "If I thought it would be as agreeable to thee as it would be to me, I would converse with thee. I have also a message from Arthur unto thee, to pray thee to come and visit him. And two men have been before on this errand." "That is true," said Perceval; "and uncourteously they came. They attacked me, and I was annoyed thereat" Then he told him the thought that occupied his mind, and Gawain said, "This was not an ungentle thought, and I should marvel if it were pleasant for thee to be drawn from it." Then said Perceval, "Tell me, is Sir Kay in Arthur's court?" "He is," said Gawain; "and truly he is the knight who fought with thee last." "Verily," said Perceval, "I am not sorry to have thus avenged the insult to the smiling maiden. "Then Perceval told him his name, and said, "Who art thou?" And he replied, "I am Gawain." "I am right glad to meet thee," said Perceval, "for I have everywhere heard of thy prowess and uprightness; and I solicit thy fellowship." "Thou shalt have it, by my faith; and grant me thine," said he. "Gladly will I do so," answered Perceval.

So they went together to Arthur, and saluted him.

"Behold, lord," said Gawain, "him whom thou hast sought so long." "Welcome unto thee, chieftain," said Arthur. And hereupon there came the queen and her handmaidens, and Perceval saluted them. And they were rejoiced to see him, and bade him welcome. And Arthur did him great honor and respect and they returned towards Caerleon.

Chapter 19

THE SANGREAL, OR HOLY GRAIL

The Sangreal was the cup from which our Saviour drank at his last supper. He was supposed to have given it to Joseph of Arimathea, who carried it to Europe, together with the spear with which the soldier pierced the Saviour's side. From generation to generation, one of the descendants of Joseph of Arimathea had been devoted to the guardianship of these precious relics; but on the sole condition of leading a life of purity in thought, word, and deed. For a long time the Sangreal was visible to all pilgrims, and its presence conferred blessings upon the land in which it was preserved. But at length one of those holy men to whom its guardianship had descended so far forgot the obligation of his sacred office as to look with unhallowed eye upon a young female pilgrim whose robe was accidentally loosened as she knelt before him. The sacred lance instantly punished his frailty, spontaneously falling upon him, and inflicting a deep wound. The marvellous wound could by no means be healed, and the guardian of the Sangreal was ever after called "Le Roi Pescheur,"—The Sinner King. The Sangreal withdrew its visible presence from the crowds who came to worship, and an iron age succeeded to the happiness which its presence had diffused among the tribes of Britain.

"But then the times
Grew to such evil that the Holy cup
Was caught away to heaven and disappear'd."
—The Holy Grail.

We have told in the history of Merlin how that great prophet and enchanter sent a message to King Arthur by Sir Gawain, directing him to undertake the recovery of the Sangreal, informing him at the same time that the knight who should accomplish that sacred quest was already born, and of a suitable age to enter upon it. Sir Gawain delivered his message, and the king was anxiously revolving in his mind how best to achieve the enterprise, when, at the vigil of Pentecost, all the fellowship of the Round Table being met together at Camelot, as they sat at meat, suddenly there was heard a clap of thunder, and then a bright light burst forth, and every knight, as he looked on his fellow, saw him, in seeming, fairer than ever before. All the hall was filled with sweet odors, and every knight had such meat and drink as he best loved. Then there entered into the hall the Holy Graal, covered with white samite, so that none could see it, and it passed through the hall suddenly, and disappeared. During this time no one spoke a word, but when they had recovered breath to speak King Arthur said, "Certainly we ought greatly to thank the Lord for what he hath showed us this day." Then Sir Gawain rose up, and made a vow that for twelve months and a day he would seek the Sangreal, and not return till he had seen it, if so he might speed. When they of the Round Table heard Sir Gawain say so, they arose, the most part of them, and vowed the same. When King Arthur heard this, he was greatly displeased, for he knew well that they might not gainsay their vows. "Alas!" said he to Sir Gawain, "you have nigh slain me with the vow and promise that ye have made, for ye have bereft me of the fairest fellowship that ever were seen together in any realm of the world; for when they shall depart hence, I am sure that all shall never meet more in this world."

SIR GALAHAD

At that time there entered the hall a good old man, and with him he brought a young knight, and these words he said: "Peace be with you, fair lords." Then the old man said unto King Arthur, "Sir, I bring you here a young knight that is of kings' lineage, and of the kindred of Joseph of Arimathea, being the son of Dame Elaine, the daughter of King Pelles, king of the foreign country." Now the name of the young knight was Sir Galahad, and he was the son of Sir Launcelot du Lac; but he had dwelt with his mother, at the court of King Pelles, his grandfather, till now he was old enough to bear arms, and his mother had sent him in the charge of a holy hermit to King Arthur's court. Then Sir Launcelot beheld his son, and had great joy of him. And Sir Bohort told his fellows, "Upon my life, this young knight shall come to great worship." The noise was great in all the court, so that it came to the queen. And she said, "I would fain see him, for he must needs be a noble knight, for so is his father." And the queen and her ladies all said that he resembled much unto his father; and he was seemly and demure as a dove, with

Figure 75: "Sir Galahad" by George Frederic Watts

all manner of good features, that in the whole world men might not find his match. And King Arthur said, "God make him a good man, for beauty faileth him not, as any that liveth."

Then the hermit led the young knight to the Siege Perilous; and he lifted up the cloth, and found there letters that said, "This is the seat of Sir Galahad, the good knight;" and he made him sit in that seat. And all the knights of the Round Table marvelled greatly at Sir Galahad, seeing him sit securely in that seat, and said, "This is he by whom the Sangreal shall be achieved, for there never sat one before in that seat without being mischieved."

On the next day the king said, "Now, at this quest of the Sangreal shall all ye of the Round Table depart, and never shall I see you again altogether; therefore I will that ye all repair to the meadow of Camelot, for to just and tourney yet once more before ye depart." But all the meaning of the king was to see Sir Galahad proved. So then were they all assembled in the meadow. Then Sir Galahad, by request of the king and queen, put on his harness and his helm, but shield would he take none for any prayer of the king. And the queen was in a tower, with all her ladies, to behold that tournament. Then Sir Galahad rode into the midst of the meadow; and there he began to break spears marvellously, so that all men had wonder of him, for he surmounted all knights that encountered with him, except two, Sir Launcelot and Sir Perceval.

"So many knights, that all the people cried,
And almost burst the barriers in their heat,
Shouting 'Sir Galahad and Sir Perceval!'"
—Sir Galahad

Then the king, at the queen's request, made him to alight, and presented him to the queen; and she said, "Never two men resembled one another more than he and Sir Launcelot, and therefore it is no marvel that he is like him in prowess."

Then the king and the queen went to the minster, and the knights followed them. And after the service was done they put on their helms and departed, and there was great sorrow. They rode through the streets of Camelot, and there was weeping of the rich and poor; and the king turned away, and might not speak for weeping. And so they departed, and every knight took the way that him best liked.

Sir Galahad rode forth without shield, and rode four days, and found no adventure. And on the fourth day he came to a white abbey; and there he was received with great reverence, and led to a chamber. He met there two knights, King Bagdemagus and Sir Uwaine, and they made of him great solace. "Sirs," said Sir Galahad, "what adventure brought you hither?" "Sir," said they, "it is told us that within this place is a shield, which no man may bear unless he be worthy; and if one unworthy should attempt to bear it, it shall surely do him a mischief." Then King Bagdemagus said, "I fear not to bear it, and that shall ye see to- morrow."

So on the morrow they arose, and heard mass; then King Bagdemagus asked where the adventurous shield was. Anon a monk led him behind an altar, where the shield hung, as white as snow; but in the midst there was a red cross. Then King Bagdemagus took the shield, and bare it out of the minster; and he said to Sir Galahad, "If it please you, abide here till ye know how I shall speed."

Then King Bagdemagus and his squire rode forth: and when they had ridden a mile or two, they saw a goodly knight come towards them, in white armor, horse and all; and he came as fast as his horse might run, with his spear in the rest; and King Bagdemagus directed his spear against him, and broke it upon the white knight, but the other struck him so hard that he broke the mails, and thrust him through the right shoulder, for the shield covered him not, and so he bare him from his horse. Then the white knight turned his horse and rode away.

Then the squire went to King Bagdemagus, and asked him whether he were sore wounded or not. "I am sore wounded," said he, "and full hardly shall I escape death." Then the squire set him on his horse, and brought him to an abbey; and there he was taken down softly, and unarmed, and laid in a bed, and his wound was looked to, for he lay there long, and hardly escaped with his life. And the squire brought the shield back to the abbey.

The next day Sir Galahad took the shield, and within a while he came to the hermitage, where he met the white knight, and each saluted the other courteously. "Sir," said Sir Galahad, "can you tell me the marvel of the shield?" "Sir," said the white knight, "that shield belonged of old to the gentle knight, Joseph of Arimathea; and when he came to die he said, 'Never shall man bear this shield about his neck but he shall repent it, unto the time that Sir Galahad the good knight bear it, the last of my lineage, the which shall do many marvellous deeds.'" And then the white knight vanished away.

SIR GAWAIN

After Sir Gawain departed, he rode many days, both toward and forward, and at last he came to the abbey where Sir Galahad took the white shield. And they told Sir Gawain of the marvellous adventure that Sir Galahad had done. "Truly," said Sir Gawain, "I am not happy that I took not the way that he went, for, if I may meet with him, I will not part from him lightly, that I may partake with him all the marvellous adventures which he shall achieve." "Sir," said one of the monks, "he will not be of your fellowship." "Why?" said Sir Gawain. "Sir," said he, "because ye be sinful, and he is blissful." Then said the monk, "Sir Gawain, thou must do penance for thy sins." "Sir, what penance shall I do?" "Such as I will show," said the good man. "Nay," said Sir Gawain, "I will do no penance, for we knights adventurous often suffer great woe and pain." "Well," said the good man; and he held his peace. And Sir Gawain departed.

Now it happened, not long after this, that Sir Gawain and Sir Hector rode together, and they came to a castle where was a great tournament. And Sir Gawain and Sir Hector joined themselves to the party that seemed the weaker, and they drove before them the other party. Then suddenly came into the lists a knight, bearing a white shield with a red cross, and by adventure he came by Sir Gawain, and he smote him so hard that he clave his helm and wounded his head, so that Sir Gawain fell to the earth. When Sir Hector saw that, he knew that the knight with the white shield was Sir Galahad, and he thought it no wisdom to abide him, and also for natural love, that he was his uncle. Then Sir Galahad retired privily, so that none knew where he had gone. And Sir Hector raised up Sir Gawain, and said, "Sir, me seemeth your quest is done." "It is done," said Sir Gawain; "I shall seek no further." Then Gawain was borne into the castle, and unarmed, and laid in a rich bed, and a leech found to search his wound. And Sir Gawain and Sir Hector abode together, for Sir Hector would not away till Sir Gawain were whole.

Figure 76: "The Holy Grail" by Dante Gabriel Rossetti

Chapter 20

THE SANGREAL (CONTINUED)

SIR LAUNCELOT

Sir Launcelot rode overthwart and endlong in a wide forest, and held no path but as wild adventure lee him.

"My golden spurs now bring to me,
And bring to me my richest mail,
For to-morrow I go over land and sea
In search of the Holy, Holy Grail
Shall never a bed for me be spread,
Nor shall a pillow be under my head,
Till I begin my vow to keep.
Here on the rushes will I sleep,
And perchance there may come a vision true
Ere day create the world anew"
—Lowell's Holy Grail.

And at last he came to a stone cross. Then Sir Launcelot looked round him, and saw an old chapel. So he tied his horse to a tree, and put off his shield, and hung it upon a tree; and then he went into the chapel, and looked through a place where the wall was broken. And within he saw a fair altar, full richly arrayed with cloth of silk; and there stood a fair candlestick, which bare six great candles, and the candlestick was of silver. When Sir Launcelot saw this sight, he had a great wish to enter the chapel, but he could find no place where he might enter. Then was he passing heavy and dismayed. And he returned and came again to his horse, and took off his saddle and his bridle, and let him pasture; and unlaced his helm, and ungirded his sword, and laid him down to sleep upon his shield before the cross.

And as he lay, half waking and half sleeping, he saw come by him two palfreys, both fair and white, which bare a litter, on which lay a sick knight. And when he was nigh the cross, he there abode still. And Sir Launcelot heard him say, "O sweet Lord, when shall this sorrow leave me, and when shall the holy vessel come by me whereby I shall be healed?" And thus a great while complained the knight, and Sir Launcelot heard it. Then Sir Launcelot saw the candlestick, with the lighted tapers, come before the cross, but he could see nobody that brought it. Also there came a salver of silver and the holy vessel of the Sangreal; and therewithal the sick knight sat him upright, and held up both his hands, and said, "Fair, sweet Lord, which is here within the holy vessel, take heed to me, that I may be whole of this great malady." And therewith, upon his hands and upon his knees, he went so nigh that he touched the holy vessel and kissed it. And anon he was whole. Then the holy vessel went into the chapel again, with the candlestick and the light, so that Sir Launcelot wist not what became of it.

Then the sick knight rose up and kissed the cross; and anon his squire brought him his arms and asked his lord how he did. "I thank God right heartily," said he, "for, through the holy vessel, I am healed. But I have great marvel of this sleeping knight, who hath had neither grace nor power to awake during the time that the holy vessel hath been here present." "I dare it right well say," said the squire, "that this same knight is stained with some manner of deadly sin, whereof he was never confessed." So they departed.

Then anon Sir Launcelot waked, and set himself upright, and bethought him of what he had seen and whether it were dreams or not. And he was passing heavy, and wist not what to do. And he said: "My sin and my wretchedness hath brought me into great dishonor. For when I sought worldly adventures and worldly desires, I ever achieved them, and had the better in every place, and never was I discomfited in any quarrel, were it right or wrong. And now I take upon me the adventure of holy things, I see and understand that mine old sin hindereth me, so that I had no power to stir nor to speak when the holy blood appeared before me." So thus he sorrowed till it was day, and heard the fowls of the air sing. Then was he somewhat comforted.

Then he departed from the cross into the forest. And there he found a hermitage, and a hermit therein, who was going to mass. So when mass was done Sir Launcelot called the hermit to him, and prayed him for charity to hear his confession. "With a good will," said the good man. And then he told that good man all his life, and how he had loved a queen unmeasurably many years. "And all my great deeds of arms that I have done I did the most part for

Figure 77: "Sir Galahad Discovers the Fabled Holy Grail" by Edwin Austin Abbey

the queen's sake, and for her sake would I do battle, were it right or wrong, and never did I battle all only for God's sake, but for to win worship, and to cause me to be better beloved; and little or naught I thanked God for it. I pray you counsel me."

"I will counsel you," said the hermit, "if ye will insure me that ye will never come in that queen's fellowship as much as ye may forbear." And then Sir Launcelot promised the hermit, by his faith, that he would no more come in her company. "Look that your heart and your mouth accord," said the good man, "and I shall insure you that ye shall have more worship than ever ye had."

Then the good man enjoined Sir Launcelot such penance as he might do, and he assailed Sir Launcelot and made him abide with him all that day. And Sir Launcelot repented him greatly.

SIR PERCEVAL

Sir Perceval departed and rode till the hour of noon; and he met in a valley about twenty men of arms. And when they saw Sir Perceval, they asked him whence he was; and he answered: "Of the court of King Arthur." Then they cried all at once, "Slay him." But Sir Perceval smote the first to the earth, and his horse upon him. Then seven of the knights smote upon his shield all at once, and the remnant slew his horse, so that he fell to the earth. So had they slain him or taken him, had not the good knight Sir Galahad, with the red cross, come there by adventure. And when he saw all the knights upon one, he cried out, "Save me that knight's life." Then he rode toward the twenty men of arms as fast as his horse might drive, with his spear in the rest, and smote the foremost horse and man to the earth. And when his spear was broken, he set his hand to his sword, and smote on the right hand and on the left, that it was marvel to see; and at every stroke he smote down one, or put him to rebuke, so that they would fight no more, but fled to a thick forest, and Sir Galahad followed them. And when Sir Perceval saw him chase them so, he made great sorrow that his horse was slain. And he wist well it was Sir Galahad. Then he cried aloud, "Ah, fair knight, abide, and suffer me to do thanks unto thee; for right well have ye done for me." But Sir Galahad rode so fast that at last he passed out of his sight. When Sir Perceval saw that he would not turn, he said, "Now am I a very wretch, and most unhappy above all other knights." So in his sorrow he abode all that day till it was night; and then he was faint, and laid him down and slept till midnight; and then he awaked and saw before him a woman, who said unto him, "Sir Perceval, what dost thou here?" He answered, "I do neither good, nor great ill." "If thou wilt promise me," said she, "that thou wilt fulfil my will when I summon thee, I will lend thee my own horse, which shall bear thee whither thou wilt." Sir Perceval was glad of her proffer, and insured her to fulfil all her desire. "Then abide me here, and I will go fetch you a horse." And so she soon came again, and brought a horse with her that was inky black. When Perceval beheld that horse he marvelled, it was so great and so well apparelled. And he leapt upon him and took no heed of himself. And he thrust him with his spurs, and within an hour and less he bare him four days' journey thence, until he came to a rough water, which roared, and his horse would have borne him into it. And when Sir Perceval came nigh the brim and saw the water so boisterous he doubted to overpass it. And then he made the sign of the cross on his forehead. When the fiend felt him so charged, he shook off Sir Perceval, and went into the water crying and roaring; and it seemed unto him that the water burned. Then Sir Perceval perceived it was a fiend that would have brought him unto his perdition. Then he commended himself unto God, and prayed our Lord to keep him from all such temptations; and so he prayed all that night till it was day. Then he saw that he was in a wild place, that was closed with the sea nigh all about. And Sir Perceval looked forth over the sea, and saw a ship come sailing towards him; and it came and stood still under the rock. And when Sir Perceval saw this, he hied him thither, and found the ship covered with silk; and therein was a lady of great beauty, and clothed so richly that none might be better.

And when she saw Sir Perceval, she saluted him, and Sir Perceval returned her salutation. Then he asked her of her country and her lineage. And she said, "I am a gentlewoman that am disinherited, and was once the richest woman of the world." "Damsel," said Sir Perceval, "who hath disinherited you? for I have great pity of you." "Sir," said she, "my enemy is a great and powerful lord, and aforetime he made much of me, so that of his favor and of my beauty I had a little pride more than I ought to have had. Also I said a word that pleased him not. So he drove me from his company and from mine heritage. Therefore I know no good knight nor good man, but I get him on my side if I may. And for that I know that thou art a good knight, I beseech thee to help me."

Then Sir Perceval promised her all the help that he might, and she thanked him.

And at that time the weather was hot, and she called to her a gentlewoman, and bade her bring forth a pavilion. And she did so, and pitched it upon the gravel. "Sir," said she, "now may ye rest you in this heat of the day." Then he thanked her, and she put off his helm and his shield, and there he slept a great while. Then he awoke, and asked her if she had any meat, and she said yea, and so there was set upon the table all manner of meats that he could think on. Also he drank there the strongest wine that ever he drank, and therewith he was a little chafed more than he ought to be. With that he beheld the lady, and he thought she was the fairest creature that ever he saw. And then Sir Perceval proffered her love, and prayed her that she would be his. Then she refused him in a manner, for the cause he should be the more ardent on her, and ever he ceased not to pray her of love. And when she saw him well enchafed, then she said, "Sir Perceval, wit you well I shall not give ye my love, unless you swear from henceforth you will be my true servant, and do no thing but that I shall command you. Will you insure me this, as ye be a true knight?" "Yea," said he, "fair lady, by the faith of my body." And as he said this, by adventure and grace, he saw his sword lie on the ground naked, in whose pommel was a red cross, and the sign of the crucifix thereon. Then he made the sign of the cross on his forehead, and therewith the pavilion shrivelled up, and changed into a smoke and a black cloud. And the damsel cried aloud, and hasted into the ship, and so she went with the wind roaring and yelling that it seemed all the water burned after her. Then Sir Perceval made great sorrow, and called himself a wretch, saying, "How nigh was I lost!" Then he took his arms, and departed thence.

Chapter 21

THE SANGREAL (CONTINUED)

SIR BOHORT, OR BORS

When Sir Boliort departed from Camelot he met with a religious man, riding upon an ass; and Sir Bohort saluted him. "What are ye?" said the good man. "Sir," said Sir Bohort, "I am a knight that fain would be counselled in the quest of the Sangreal." So rode they both together till they came to a hermitage; and there he prayed Sir Bohort to dwell that night with him. So he alighted, and put away his armor, and prayed him that he might be confessed. And they went both into the chapel, and there he was clean confessed. And they ate bread and drank water together. "Now," said the good man, "I pray thee that thou eat none other till thou sit at the table where the Sangreal shall be." "Sir," said Sir Bohort, "but how know ye that I shall sit there?" "Yea," said the good man, "that I know well; but there shall be few of your fellows with you." Then said Sir Bohort, "I agree me thereto" And the good man when he had heard his confession found him in so pure a life and so stable that he marvelled thereof.

On the morrow, as soon as the day appeared, Sir Bohort departed thence, and rode into a forest unto the hour of midday. And there befell him a marvellous adventure. For he met, at the parting of two ways, two knights that led Sir Lionel, his brother, all naked, bound upon a strong hackney, and his hands bound before his breast; and each of them held in his hand thorns wherewith they went beating him, so that he was all bloody before and behind; but he said never a word, but, as he was great of heart, he suffered all that they did to him as though he had felt none anguish. Sir Bohort prepared to rescue his brother. But he looked on the other side of him, and saw a knight dragging along a fair gentlewoman, who cried out, "Saint Mary! succor your maid!" And when she saw Sir Bohort, she called to him, and said, "By the faith that ye owe to knighthood, help me!" When Sir Bohort heard her say thus he had such sorrow that he wist not what to do. "For if I let my brother be he must be slain, and that would I not for all the earth; and if I help not the maid I am shamed for ever." Then lift he up his eyes and said, weeping, "Fair Lord, whose liegeman I am, keep Sir Lionel, my brother, that none of these knights slay him, and for pity of you, and our Lady's sake, I shall succor this maid."

Then he cried out to the knight, "Sir knight, lay your hand off that maid, or else ye be but dead." Then the knight set down the maid, and took his shield, and drew out his sword. And Sir Bohort smote him so hard that it went through his shield and habergeon, on the left shoulder, and he fell down to the earth. Then came Sir Bohort to the maid, "Ye be delivered of this knight this time." "Now," said she, "I pray you lead me there where this knight took me." "I shall gladly do it," said Sir Bohort. So he took the horse of the wounded knight, and set the gentlewoman upon it, and brought her there where she desired to be. And there he found twelve knights seeking after her; and when she told them how Sir Bohort had delivered her, they made great joy, and besought him to come to her father, a great lord, and he should be right welcomed. "Truly," said Sir Bohort, "that may not be; for I have a great adventure to do." So he commended them to God and departed.

Then Sir Bohort rode after Sir Lionel, his brother, by the trace of their horses. Thus he rode seeking, a great while. Then he overtook a man clothed in a religious clothing, who said, "Sir Knight, what seek ye?" "Sir," said Sir Bohort, "I seek my brother, that I saw within a little space beaten of two knights." "Ah, Sir Bohort, tiouble not thyself to seek for him, for truly he is dead." Then he showed him a new-slain body, lying in a thick bush; and it seemed him that it was the body of Sir Lionel. And then he made such sorrow that he fell to the ground in a swoon, and lay there long. And when he came to himself again, he said, "Fair brother, since the fellowship of you and me is sundered, shall I never have joy again; and now He that I have taken for my Master, He be my help!" And when he had said thus he took up the body in his arms, and put it upon the horse. And then he said to the man, "Canst thou tell me the way to some chapel, where I may bury this body?" "Come on," said the man, "here is one fast by." And so they rode till they saw a fair tower, and beside it a chapel. Then they alighted both, and put the body into a tomb of marble.

Then Sir Bohort commended the good man unto God, and departed. And he rode all that day, and harbored with an old lady. And on the morrow he rode unto the castle in a valley, and there he met with a yeoman. "Tell me," said Sir Bohort, "knowest thou of any adventure?" "Sir," said he, "here shall be, under this castle, a great and marvellous tournament." Then Sir Bohort thought to be there, if he might meet with any of the fellowship that were in quest of the Sangreal; so he turned to a hermitage that was on the border of the forest. And when he was come hither, he found there Sir Lionel his brother, who sat all armed at the entry of the chapel door. And when Sir Bohort saw him, he had great joy, and he alighted off his horse, and said. "Fair brother, when came ye hither?" As soon as Sir Lionel saw him he said, "Ah, Sir Bohort, make ye no false show, for, as for you, I might have been slain, for ye left me in peril of death to go succor a gentlewoman; and for that misdeed I now assure you but death, for ye have right well deserved it." When Sir Bohort perceived his brother's wrath he kneeled down to the earth and cried him mercy, holding up both his hands, and prayed him to forgive him. "Nay," said Sir Lionel, "thou shalt have but death for it, if I have the upper hand; therefore leap upon thy horse and keep thyself, and if thou do not I will run upon thee there as thou standest on foot, and so the shame shall be mine, and the harm thine, but of that I reck not." When Sir Bohort saw that he must fight with his brother or else die, he wist not what to do. Then his heart counselled him not so to do, inasmuch as Sir Lionel was his elder brother, wherefore he ought to bear him reverence. Yet kneeled he down before Sir Lionel's horse's feet, and said, "Fair brother, have mercy upon me and slay me not." But Sir Lionel cared not, for the fiend had brought him in such a will that he should slay him. When he saw that Sir Bohort would not rise to give him battle, he rushed over him, so that he smote him with his horse's feet to the earth, and hurt him sore, that he swooned of distress. When Sir Lionel saw this he alighted from his horse for to have smitten off his head; and so he took him by the helm, and would have rent it from his head. But it happened that Sir Colgrevance, a knight of the Round Table, came at that time thither, as it was our Lord's will; and then he beheld how Sir Lionel would have slain his brother, and he knew Sir Bohort, whom he loved right well.

Then leapt he down from his horse and took Sir Lionel by the shoulders, and drew him strongly back from Sir Bohort, and said, "Sir Lionel, will ye slay your brother?" "Why," said Sir Lionel, "will ye stay me? If ye interfere in this I will slay you, and him after." Then he ran upon Sir Bohort, and would have smitten him; but Sir Colgrevance ran between them, and said, "If ye persist to do so any more, we two shall meddle together." Then Sir Lionel defied him, and gave him a great stroke through the helm. Then he drew his sword, for he was a passing good knight, and defended himself right manfully. So long endured the battle, that Sir Bohort rose up all anguishly, and beheld Sir Colgrevance, the good knight, fight with his brother for his quarrel. Then was he full sorry and heavy, and thought that if Sir Colgrevance slew him that was his brother he should never have joy, and if his brother slew Sir Colgrevance the shame should ever be his.

Then would he have risen for to have parted them, but he had not so much strength to stand on his feet; so he staid so long that Sir Colgrevance had the worse; for Sir Lionel was of great chivalry and right hardy. Then cried Sir Colgrevance, "Ah, Sir Bohort, why come ye not to bring me out of peril of death, wherein I have put me to succor you?" With that, Sir Lionel smote off his helm and bore him to the earth. And when he had slain Sir Colgrevance he ran upon his brother as a fiendly man, and gave him such a stroke that he made him stoop. And he that was full

Figure 78: "Lancelot and Guinever" by Andrew Lang

of humility prayed him, "for God's sake leave this battle, for if it befell, fair brother, that I slew you, or ye me, we should be dead of that sin." "Pray ye not me for mercy," said Sir Lionel. Then Sir Bohort, all weeping, drew his sword, and said, "Now God have mercy upon me, though I defend my life against my brother." With that Sir Bohort lifted up his sword, and would have smitten his brother. Then he heard a voice that said, "Flee, Sir Bohort, and touch him not." Right so alighted a cloud between them, in the likeness of a fire and a marvellous flame, so that they both fell to the earth, and lay there a great while in a swoon. And when they came to themselves, Sir Bohort saw that his brother had no harm; and he was right glad, for he dread sore that God had taken vengeance upon him. Then Sir Lionel said to his brother, "Brother, forgive me, for God's sake, all that I have trespassed against you." And Sir Bohort answered, "God forgive it thee, and I do."

With that Sir Bohort heard a voice say, "Sir Bohort, take thy way anon, right to the sea, for Sir Perceval abideth thee there." So Sir Bohort departed, and rode the nearest way to the sea. And at last he came to an abbey that was nigh the sea. That night he rested him there, and in his sleep there came a voice unto him and bade him go to the sea-shore. He started up, and made a sign of the cross on his forehead, and armed himself, and made ready his horse and mounted him, and at a broken wall he rode out, and came to the sea-shore. And there he found a ship, covered all with white samite. And he entered into the ship; but it was anon so dark that he might see no man, and he laid him down and slept till it was day. Then he awaked, and saw in the middle of the ship a knight all armed, save his helm. And then he knew it was Sir Perceval de Galis, and each made of other right great joy. Then said Sir Perceval, "We lack nothing now but the good knight Sir Galahad."

SIR LAUNCELOT (RESUMED)

It befell upon a night Sir Launcelot arrived before a castle, which was rich and fair. And there was a postern that was opened toward the sea, and was open without any keeping, save two lions kept the entry; and the moon shined clear. Anon Sir Launcelot heard a voice that said, "Launcelot, enter into the castle, where thou shalt see a great part of thy desire." So he went unto the gate, and saw the two lions; then he set hands to his sword, and drew it. Then there came suddenly as it were a stroke upon the arm, so sore that the sword fell out of his hand, and he heard a voice that said, "O man of evil faith, wherefore believest thou more in thy armor than in thy Maker?" Then said Sir Launcelot, "Fair Lord, I thank thee of thy great mercy, that thou reprovest me of my misdeed; now see I well that thou holdest me for thy servant." Then he made a cross on his forehead, and came to the lions; and they made semblance to do him harm, but he passed them without hurt, and entered into the castle, and he found no gate nor door but it was open. But at the last he found a chamber whereof the door was shut; and he set his hand thereto, to have opened it, but he might not. Then he listened, and heard a voice which sung so sweetly that it seemed none earthly thing; and the voice said, "Joy and honor be to the Father of heaven." Then Sir Launcelot kneeled down before the chamber, for well he wist that there was the Sangreal in that chamber. Then said he, "Fair, sweet Lord, if ever I did anything that pleased thee, for thy pity show me something of that which I seek." And with that he saw the chamber door open, and there came out a great clearness, that the house was as bright as though all the torches of the world had been there. So he came to the chamber door, and would have entered; and anon a voice said unto him, "Stay, Sir Launcelot, and enter not." And he withdrew him back, and was right heavy in his mind. Then looked he in the midst of the chamber, and saw a table of silver, and the holy vessel, covered with red samite, and many angels about it; whereof one held a candle of wax burning, and another held a cross, and the ornaments of the altar.

"O, yet methought I saw the Holy Grail,
All pall'd in crimson samite, and around
Great angels, awful shapes, and wings and eyes"
—The Holy Grail.

Then for very wonder and thankfulness Sir Launcelot forgot himself and he stepped forward and entered the chamber. And suddenly a breath that seemed intermixed with fire smote him so sore in the visage that therewith he fell to the ground, and had no power to rise. Then felt he many hands about him, which took him up and bare him out of the chamber, without any amending of his swoon, and left him there, seeming dead to all the people. So on the morrow, when it was fair daylight, and they within were arisen, they found Sir Launcelot lying before the

Figure 79: "How Sir Galahad, Sir Bors, and Sir Pervival Were Fed with the Sanct Grael; but Sir Percival's Sister Died by the Way" by Dante Gabriel Rosetti

chamber door. And they looked upon him and felt his pulse, to know if there were any life in him. And they found life in him, but he might neither stand nor stir any member that he had. So they took him and bare him into a chamber, and laid him upon a bed, far from all folk, and there he lay many days. Then the one said he was alive, and the others said nay. But said an old man, "He is as full of life as the mightiest of you all, and therefore I counsel you that he be well kept till God bring him back again." And after twenty-four days he opened his eyes; and when he saw folk he made great sorrow, and said, "Why have ye wakened me? for I was better at ease than I am now." "What have ye seen?" said they about him. "I have seen," said he, "great marvels that no tongue can tell, and more than any heart can think." Then they said, "Sir, the quest of the Sangreal is achieved right now in you, and never shall ye see more of it than ye have seen." "I thank God," said Sir Launcelot, "of his great mercy, for that I have seen, for it sufficeth me." Then he rose up and clothed himself; and when he was so arrayed they marvelled all, for they knew it was Sir Launcelot the good knight. And after four days he took his leave of the lord of the castle, and of all the fellowship that were there, and thanked them for their great labor and care of him. Then he departed, and turned to Camelot, where he found King Arthur and Queen Guenever; but many of the knights of the Round Table were slain and destroyed, more than half. Then all the court was passing glad of Sir Launcelot; and he told the king all his adventures that had befallen him since he departed.

SIR GALAHAD

Now, when Sir Galahad had rescued Perceval from the twenty knights, he rode into a vast forest, wherein he abode many days. Then he took his way to the sea, and it befell him that he was benighted in a hermitage. And the good man was glad when he saw he was a knight-errant. And when they were at rest, there came a gentlewoman knocking at the door; and the good man came to the door to wit what she would. Then she said, "I would speak with the knight which is with you." Then Galahad went to her, and asked her what she would. "Sir Galahad," said she, "I will that ye arm you, and mount upon your horse, and follow me; for I will show you the highest adventure that ever knight saw." Then Galahad armed himself and commended himself to God, and bade the damsel go before, and he would follow where she led.

So she rode as fast as her palfrey might bear her, till she came to the sea; and there they found the ship where Sir Bohort and Sir Perceval were, who cried from the ship, "Sir Galahad, you are welcome; we have waited you long." And when he heard them, he asked the damsel who they were. "Sir," said she, "leave your horse here, and I shall leave mine, and we will join ourselves to their company." So they entered into the ship, and the two knights received them both with great joy. For they knew the damsel, that she was Sir Perceval's sister. Then the wind arose and drove them through the sea all that day and the next, till the ship arrived between two rocks, passing great and marvellous; but there they might not land, for there was a whirlpool; but there was another ship, and upon it they might go without danger. "Go we thither," said the gentlewoman, "and there we shall see adventures, for such is our Lord's will." Then Sir Galahad blessed him, and entered therein, and then next the gentlewoman, and then Sir Bohort and Sir Perceval. And when they came on board they found there the table of silver, and the Sangreal, which was covered with red samite. And they made great reverence thereto, and Sir Galahad prayed a long time to our Lord, that at what time he should ask to pass out of this world he should do so; and a voice said to him, "Galahad, thou shalt have thy request; and when thou askest the death of thy body, thou shalt have it, and then shalt thou find the life of thy soul."

And anon the wind drove them across the sea, till they came to the city of Sarras. Then took they out of the ship the table of silver, and Sir Perceval and Sir Bohort took it before, and Sir Galahad came behind, and right so they went to the city. And at the gate of the city they saw an old man, a cripple.

"And Sir Launfal said, 'I behold in thee
An image of Him who died on the tree
Thou also hast had thy crown of thorns,
Thou also hast had the world's buffets and scorns;
And to thy life were not denied
The wounds in thy hands and feet and side
Mild Mary's son, acknowledge me;
Behold, through Him I give to thee!'"
—Lowell's Holy Grail.

Then Galahad called him, and bade him help to bear this heavy thing. "Truly," said the old man, "it is ten years since I could not go but with crutches." "Care thou not," said Sir Galahad, "but arise up, and show thy good will." Then the old man rose up, and assayed, and found himself as whole as ever he was; and he ran to the table, and took one part with Sir Galahad.

When they came to the city it chanced that the king was just dead, and all the city was dismayed, and wist not who might be their king. Right so, as they were in counsel, there came a voice among them, and bade them choose the youngest knight of those three to be their king. So they made Sir Galahad king, by all the assent of the city. And when he was made king, he commanded to make a chest of gold and of precious stones to hold the holy vessel. And every day the three companions would come before it and make their prayers.

Now at the year's end, and the same day of the year that Sir Galahad received the crown, he got up early, and, with his fellows, came to where the holy vessel was; and they saw one kneeling before it that had about him a great fellowship of angels; and he called Sir Galahad, and said, "Come, thou servant of the Lord, and thou shalt see what thou hast much desired to see." And Sir Galahad's mortal flesh trembled right hard when he began to behold the spiritual things. Then said the good man, "Now wottest thou who I am?" "Nay," said Sir Galahad. "I am Joseph of Arimathea, whom our Lord hath sent here to thee, to bear thee fellowship." Then Sir Galahad held up his hands toward heaven, and said, "Now, blessed Lord, would I not longer live, if it might please thee." And when he had said these words, Sir Galahad went to Sir Perceval and to Sir Bohort and kissed them, and commended them to God. And then he kneeled down before the table, and made his prayers, and suddenly his soul departed, and a great multitude of angels bare his soul up to heaven, so as the two fellows could well behold it. Also they saw come from heaven a hand, but they saw not the body; and the hand came right to the vessel and bare it up to heaven. Since then was there never one so hardy as to say that he had seen the Sangreal on earth any more.

Chapter 22

SIR AGRIVAIN'S TREASON

"Modred's narrow foxy face,
Heart-hiding smile, and gray persistent eye:
Henceforward, too, the Powers that tend the soul
To help it from the death that cannot die,
And save it even in extremes, began
To vex and plague."
—Guinevere.

When Sir Perceval and Sir Bohort saw Sir Galahad dead they made as much sorrow as ever did two men. And if they had not been good men they might have fallen into despair. As soon as Sir Galahad was buried Sir Perceval retired to a hermitage out of the city, and took a religious clothing; and Sir Bohort was always with him, but did not change his secular clothing, because he purposed to return to the realm of Loegria. Thus a year and two months lived Sir Perceval in the hermitage a full holy life, and then passed out of this world, and Sir Bohort buried him by his sister and Sir Galahad. Then Sir Bohort armed himself and departed from Sarras, and entered into a ship, and sailed to the kingdom of Loegria, and in due time arrived safe at Camelot, where the king was. Then was there great joy made of him in the whole court, for they feared he had been dead. Then the king made great clerks to come before him, that they should chronicle of the high adventures of the good knights. And Sir Bohort told him of the adventures that had befallen him, and his two fellows, Sir Perceval and Sir Galahad. And Sir Launcelot told the adventures of the Sangreal that he had seen. All this was made in great books, and put up in the church at Salisbury.

So King Arthur and Queen Guenever made great joy of the remnant that were come home, and chiefly of Sir Launcelot and Sir Bohort. Then Sir Launcelot began to resort unto Queen Guenever again, and forgot the promise that he made in the quest: so that many in the court spoke of it, and in especial Sir Agrivain, Sir Gawain's brother, for he was ever open-mouthed. So it happened Sir Gawain and all his brothers were in King Arthur's chamber, and then Sir Agrivain said thus openly, "I marvel that we all are not ashamed to see and to know so noble a knight as King Arthur so to be shamed by the conduct of Sir Launcelot and the queen. "Then spoke Sir Gawain, and said, "Brother, Sir Agrivain, I pray you and charge you move not such matters any more before me, for be ye assured I will not be of your counsel." "Neither will we," said Sir Gaheris and Sir Gareth. "Then will I," said Sir Modred. "I doubt you not," said Sir Gawain, "for to all mischief ever were ye prone; yet I would that ye left all this, for I know what will come of it."

"Fall of it what fall may," said Sir Agrivain, "I will disclose it to the king." With that came to them King Arthur. "Now, brothers, hold your peace," said Sir Gawain. "We will not," said Sir Agrivain. Then said Sir Gawain, "I will not hear your tales nor be of your counsel." "No more will I," said Sir Gareth and Sir Gaheris, and therewith they departed, making great sorrow.

Then Sir Agrivain told the king all that was said in the court of the conduct of Sir Launcelot and the queen, and it grieved the king very much. But he would not believe it to be true without proof. So Sir Agrivain laid a plot to entrap Sir Launcelot and the queen, intending to take them together unawares. Sir Agrivain and Sir Modred led a party for this purpose, but Sir Launcelot escaped from them, having slain Sir Agrivain and wounded Sir Modred. Then Sir Launcelot hastened to his friends, and told them what had happened, and withdrew with them to the forest; but he left spies to bring him tidings of whatever might be done.

So Sir Launcelot escaped, but the queen remained in the king's power, and Arthur could no longer doubt of her guilt. And the law was such in those days that they who committed such crimes, of what estate or condition soever they were, must be burned to death, and so it was ordained for Queen Guenever. Then said King Arthur to Sir Gawain, "I pray you make you ready, in your best armor, with your brethren, Sir Gaheris and Sir Gareth, to bring my queen to the fire, there to receive her death." "Nay, my most noble lord," said Sir Gawain, "that will I never do; for know thou well, my heart will never serve me to see her die, and it shall never be said that I was of your counsel in her death." Then the king commanded Sir Gaheris and Sir Gareth to be there, and they said, "We will be there, as ye command us, sire, but in peaceable wise, and bear no armor upon us."

So the queen was led forth, and her ghostly father was brought to her to shrive her, and there was weeping and wailing of many lords and ladies. And one went and told Sir Launcelot that the queen was led forth to her death. Then Sir Launcelot and the knights that were with him fell upon the troop that guarded the queen, and dispersed them, and slew all who withstood them. And in the confusion Sir Gareth and Sir Gaheris were slain, for they were unarmed and defenceless. And Sir Launcelot carried away the queen to his castle of La Joyeuse Garde.

Then there came one to Sir Gawain and told him how that Sir Launcelot had slain the knights and carried away the queen. "O Lord, defend my brethren!" said Sir Gawain. "Truly," said the man, "Sir Gareth and Sir Gaheris are slain." "Alas!" said Sir Gawain, "now is my joy gone." And then he fell down and swooned, and long he lay there as he had been dead.

When he arose out of his swoon Sir Gawain ran to the king, crying, "O King Arthur, mine uncle, my brothers are slain." Then the king wept and he both. "My king, my lord, and mine uncle," said Sir Gawain, "bear witness now that I make you a promise that I shall hold by my knighthood, and from this day I will never fail Sir Launcelot until the one of us have slain the other. I will seek Sir Launcelot throughout seven kings' realms, but I shall slay him or he shall slay me." "Ye shall not need to seek him," said the king, "for as I hear, Sir Launcelot will abide me and you in the Joyeuse Garde; and much people draweth unto him, as I hear say." "That may I believe," said Sir Gawain; "but, my lord, summon your friends, and I will summon mine." "It shall be done," said the king. So then the king sent letters and writs throughout all England, both in the length and breadth, to summon all his knights. And unto Arthur drew many knights, dukes, and earls, so that he had a great host. Thereof heard Sir Launcelot, and collected all whom he could; and many good knights held with him, both for his sake and for the queen's sake. But King Arthur's host was too great for Sir Launcelot to abide him in the field; and he was full loath to do battle against the king. So Sir Launcelot drew him to his strong castle, with all manner of provisions. Then came King Arthur with Sir Gawain, and laid siege all about La Joyeuse Garde, both the town and the castle; but in no wise would Sir Launcelot ride out of his castle, neither suffer any of his knights to issue out, until many weeks were past.

Then it befell upon a day in harvest-time, Sir Launcelot looked over the wall, and spoke aloud to King Arthur and Sir Gawain, "My lords both, all is in vain that ye do at this siege, for here ye shall win no worship, but only dishonor; for if I list to come out, and my good knights, I shall soon make an end of this war." "Come forth," said Arthur, "if thou darest, and I promise thee I shall meet thee in the midst of the field." "God forbid me," said Sir Launcelot, "that I should encounter with the most noble king that made me knight." "Fie upon thy fair language," said the king, "for know thou well I am thy mortal foe, and ever will be to my dying day." And Sir Gawain said, "What cause hadst thou to slay my brother, Sir Gaheris, who bore no arms against thee, and Sir Gareth, whom thou madest knight, and who loved thee more than all my kin? Therefore know thou well I shall make war to thee all the while that I may live."

When Sir Bohort, and Sir Hector de Marys, and Sir Lionel heard this outcry, they called to them Sir Palamedes, and Sir Saffire his brother, and Sir Lawayn, with many more, and all went to Sir Launcelot. And they said, "My lord, Sir Launcelot, we pray you, if you will have our service keep us no longer within these walls, for know well all your fair speech and forbearance will not avail you." "Alas!" said Sir Launcelot, "to ride forth and to do battle I am full loath." Then he spake again unto the king and Sir Gawain, and willed them to keep out of the battle; but they despised his words. So then Sir Launcelot's fellowship came out of the castle in full good array. And always Sir Launcelot charged all his knights, in any wise, to save King Arthur and Sir Gawain.

Then came forth Sir Gawain from the king's host and offered combat, and Sir Lionel encountered with him, and there Sir Gawain smote Sir Lionel through the body, that he fell to the earth as if dead. Then there began a great conflict, and much people were slain; but ever Sir Launcelot did what he might to save the people on King Arthur's party, and ever King Arthur followed Sir Launcelot to slay him; but Sir Launcelot suffered him, and would not strike again. Then Sir Bohort encountered with King Arthur, and smote him down; and he alighted and drew his sword, and said to Sir Launcelot, "Shall I make an end of this war?" for he meant to have slain King Arthur. "Not so," said Sir Launcelot, "touch him no more, for I will never see that most noble king that made me knight either slain or shamed;" and therewith Sir Launcelot alighted off his horse, and took up the king, and horsed him again, and said thus: "My lord Arthur, for God's love, cease this strife." And King Arthur looked upon Sir Launcelot, and the tears burst from his eyes, thinking on the great courtesy that was in Sir Launcelot more than in any other man; and therewith the king rode his way. Then anon both parties withdrew to repose them, and buried the dead.

But the war continued, and it was noised abroad through all Christendom, and at last it was told afore the pope; and he, considering the great goodness of King Arthur, and of Sir Launcelot, called unto him a noble clerk, which was the Bishop of Rochester, who was then in his dominions, and sent him to King Arthur, charging him that he take his queen, dame Guenever, unto him again, and make peace with Sir Launcelot.

So, by means of this bishop, peace was made for the space of one year; and King Arthur received back the queen, and Sir Launcelot departed from the kingdom with all his knights, and went to his own country. So they shipped at Cardiff, and sailed unto Benwick, which some men call Bayonne. And all the people of those lands came to Sir Launcelot, and received him home right joyfully. And Sir Launcelot stablished and garnished all his towns and castles, and he greatly advanced all his noble knights, Sir Lionel and Sir Bohort, and Sir Hector de Marys, Sir Blamor, Sir Lawayne, and many others, and made them lords of lands and castles; till he left himself no more than any one of them.

"Then Arthur made vast banquets, and strange knights
From the four winds came in: and each one sat,
Tho' served with choice from air, land, stream and sea,
Oft in mid-banquet measuring with his eyes
His neighbor's make and might."
—Pelleas and Ettarre.

But when the year was passed, King Arthur and Sir Gawain came with a great host, and landed upon Sir Launcelot's lands, and burned and wasted all that they might overrun. Then spake Sir Bohort and said, "My lord, Sir Launcelot, give us leave to meet them in the field, and we shall make them rue the time that ever they came to this country." Then said Sir Launcelot, "I am full loath to ride out with my knights for shedding of Christian blood;

Figure 80: "How Sir Launcelot was espied in the Queen's Chamber, and how Sir Agravaine and Sir Mordred came with twelve knights to slay him" by Dante Gabriel Rossetti:

so we will yet a while keep our walls, and I will send a messenger unto my lord Arthur, to propose a treaty; for better is peace than always war." So Sir Launcelot sent forth a damsel, and a dwarf with her, requiring King Arthur to leave his warring upon his lands; and so she started on a palfrey, and the dwarf ran by her side. And when she came to the pavilion of King Arthur, she alighted, and there met her a gentle knight, Sir Lucan, the butler, and said, "Fair damsel, come ye from Sir Launcelot du Lac?" "Yea, sir," she said, "I come hither to speak with the king." "Alas!" said Sir Lucan, "my lord Arthur would be reconciled to Sir Launcelot, but Sir Gawain will not suffer him." And with this Sir Lucan led the damsel to the king, where he sat with Sir Gawain, to hear what she would say. So when she had told her tale, the tears ran out of the king's eyes; and all the lords were forward to advise the king to be accorded with Sir Launcelot, save only Sir Gawain; and he said, "My lord, mine uncle, what will ye do? Will you now turn back, now you are so far advanced upon your journey? If ye do all the world will speak shame of you." "Nay," said King Arthur, "I will do as ye advise me; but do thou give the damsel her answer, for I may not speak to her for pity."

Then said Sir Gawain, "Damsel, say ye to Sir Launcelot, that it is waste labor to sue to mine uncle for peace, and say that I, Sir Gawain, send him word that I promise him, by the faith I owe unto God and to knighthood, I shall never leave him till he have slain me or I him." So the damsel returned; and when Sir Launcelot had heard this answer the tears ran down his cheeks.

Then it befell on a day Sir Gawain came before the gates, armed at all points, and cried with a loud voice, "Where art thou now, thou false traitor, Sir Launcelot? Why hidest thou thyself within holes and walls like a coward? Look out now, thou traitor knight, and I will avenge upon thy body the death of my three brethren." All this language heard Sir Launcelot, and the knights which were about him; and they said to him, "Sir Launcelot, now must ye defend you like a knight, or else be shamed for ever, for you have slept overlong and suffered overmuch." Then Sir Launcelot spake on high unto King Arthur, and said, "My lord Arthur, now I have forborne long, and suffered you and Sir Gawain to do what ye would, and now must I needs defend myself, inasmuch as Sir Gawain hath appealed me of treason." Then Sir Launcelot armed him and mounted upon his horse, and the noble knights came out of the city, and the host without stood all apart; and so the covenant was made that no man should come near the two knights, nor deal with them, till one were dead or yielded.

Then Sir Launcelot and Sir Gawain departed a great way asunder, and then they came together with all their horses' might, and each smote the other in the middle of their shields, but neither of them was unhorsed, but their horses fell to the earth. And then they leapt from their horses, and drew their swords, and gave many sad strokes, so that the blood burst out in many places. Now Sir Gawain had this gift from a holy man, that every day in the year, from morning to noon, his strength was increased threefold, and then it fell again to its natural measure. Sir Launcelot was aware of this, and therefore, during the three hours that Sir Gawain's strength was at the height, Sir Launcelot covered himself with his shield, and kept his might in reserve. And during that time Sir Gawain gave him many sad brunts, that all the knights that looked on marvelled how Sir Launcelot might endure them. Then, when it was past noon, Sir Gawain had only his own might; and when Sir Launcelot felt him so brought down he stretched himself up, and doubled his strokes, and gave Sir Gawain such a buffet that he fell down on his side; and Sir Launcelot drew back and would strike no more. "Why withdrawest thou, false traitor?" then said Sir Gawain; "now turn again and slay me, for if thou leave me thus when I am whole again, I shall do battle with thee again." "I shall endure you, sir, by God's grace," said Sir Launcelot, "but know thou well Sir Gawain, I will never smite a felled knight." And so Sir Launcelot went into the city, and Sir Gawain was borne into King Arthur's pavilion, and his wounds were looked to.

Thus, the siege endured, and Sir Gawain lay helpless near a month; and when he was near recovered came tidings unto King Arthur that made him return with all his host to England.

Chapter 23

MORTE D'ARTHUR

Sir Modred was left ruler of all England, and he caused letters to be written, as if from beyond sea, that King Arthur was slain in battle. So he called a Parliament, and made himself be crowned king; and he took the queen Guenever, and said plainly that he would wed her, but she escaped from him and took refuge in the Tower of London. And Sir Modred went and laid siege about the Tower of London, and made great assaults thereat, but all might not avail him. Then came word to Sir Modred that King Arthur had raised the siege of Sir Launcelot, and was coming home. Then Sir Modred summoned all the barony of the land; and much people drew unto Sir Modred, and said they would abide with him for better and for worse; and he drew a great host to Dover, for there he heard say that King Arthur would arrive.

"I hear the steps of Modred in the west,
And with him many of thy people, and knights
Once thine, whom thou hast loved, but grosser grown
Than heathen, spitting at their vows and thee"
—The Passing of Arthur.

And as Sir Modred was at Dover with his host, came King Arthur, with a great number of ships and galleys, and there was Sir Modred awaiting upon the landing. Then was there launching of great boats and small, full of noble men of arms, and there was much slaughter of gentle knights on both parts. But King Arthur was so courageous, there might no manner of knights prevent him to land, and his knights fiercely followed him; and so they landed, and put Sir Modred aback so that he fled, and all his people. And when the battle was done, King Arthur commanded to bury his people that were dead. And then was noble Sir Gawain found, in a great boat, lying more than half dead. And King Arthur went to him, and made sorrow out of measure. "Mine uncle," said Sir Gawain, "know thou well my death-day is come, and all is through mine own hastiness and wilfulness, for I am smitten upon the old wound which Sir Launcelot gave me, of which I feel I must die. And had Sir Launcelot been with you as of old, this war had never begun, and of all this I am the cause." Then Sir Gawain prayed the king to send for Sir Launcelot, and to cherish him above all other knights. And so at the hour of noon Sir Gawain yielded up his spirit, and then the king bade inter him in a chapel within Dover Castle; and there all men may see the skull of him, and the same wound is seen that Sir Launcelot gave him in battle.

Then was it told the king that Sir Modred had pitched his camp upon Barrendown; and the king rode thither, and there was a great battle betwixt them, and King Arthur's party stood best, and Sir Modred and his party fled unto Canterbury.

And there was a day assigned betwixt King Arthur and Sir Modred that they should meet upon a down beside Salisbury, and not far from the sea-side, to do battle yet again. And at night, as the king slept, he dreamed a wonderful dream. It seemed him verily that there came Sir Gawain unto him, with a number of fair ladies with him. And when King Arthur saw him, he said, "Welcome, my sister's son; I weened thou hadst been dead; and now I see thee alive great is my joy. But, O fair nephew, what be

Figure 81: "Sir Mordred" by Andrew Lang

these ladies that hither be come with you?" "Sir," said Sir Gawain, "all these be ladies for whom I have fought when I was a living man; and because I did battle for them in righteous quarrel they have given me grace to bring me hither unto you to warn you of your death, if ye fight to-morrow with Sir Modred. Therefore, take ye treaty, and proffer you largely for a month's delay; for within a month shall come Sir Launcelot and all his noble knights, and rescue you worshipfully, and slay Sir Modred and all that hold with him." And then Sir Gawain and all the ladies vanished. And anon the king called to fetch his noble lords and wise bishops unto him. And when they were come, the king told them his vision, and what Sir Gawain had told him. Then the king sent Sir Lucan, the butler, and Sir Bedivere, with two bishops, and charged them in any wise to take a treaty for a month and a day with Sir Modred. So they departed, and came to Sir Modred; and so, at the last, Sir Modred was agreed to have Cornwall and Kent during Arthur's life, and all England after his death.

"Sir Modred; he the nearest to the king,
His nephew, ever like a subtle beast
Lay couchant with his eyes upon the throne,
Ready to spring, waiting a chance."
—Guinevere

Then was it agreed that King Arthur and Sir Modred should meet betwixt both their hosts, and each of them should bring fourteen persons, and then and there they should sign the treaty. And when King Arthur and his knights were prepared to go forth, he warned all his host, "If so be ye see any sword drawn, look ye come on fiercely, and slay whomsoever withstandeth, for I in no wise trust that traitor, Sir Modred." In like wise Sir Modred warned his host. So they met, and were agreed and accorded thoroughly. And wine was brought, and they drank. Right then came an adder out of a little heath-bush, and stung a knight on the foot. And when the knight felt him sting, he looked down and saw the adder, and then he drew his sword to slay the adder, and thought of no other harm. And when the host on both sides saw that sword drawn, they blew trumpets and horns, and shouted greatly. And King Arthur took his horse, and rode to his party, saying, "Alas, this unhappy day!" And Sir Modred did in like wise. And never was there a more doleful battle in Christian land. And ever King Arthur rode throughout the battle, and did full nobly, as a worthy king should, and Sir Modred that day did his devoir, and put himself in great peril. And thus they fought all the long day, till the most of all the noble knights lay dead upon the ground. Then the king looked about him, and saw of all his host were left alive but two knights, Sir Lucan, the butler, and Sir Bedivere, his brother, and they were full sore wounded. Then King Arthur saw where Sir Modred leaned upon his sword among a great heap of dead men. "Now give me my spear," said Arthur unto Sir Lucan; "for yonder I espy the traitor that hast wrought all this woe." "Sir, let him be," said Sir Lucan; "for if ye pass this unhappy day, ye shall be right well revenged upon him. Remember what the sprite of Sir Gawain told you, and leave off now, for ye have won the field; and if ye leave off now this evil day of destiny is past." "Betide me life, betide me death," said King Arthur, "he shall not now escape my hands." Then the king took his spear in both hands, and ran toward Sir Modred, crying, "Traitor, now is thy death-day come." And there King Arthur smote Sir Modred under the shield, with a thrust of his spear through the body. And when Sir Modred felt that he had his death-wound, with the might that he had he smote King Arthur, with his sword holden in both his hands, on the side of the head, that the sword pierced the helmet and the brain-pan; and then Sir Modred fell stark dead upon the earth. And the noble Arthur fell in a swoon to the earth. And Sir Lucan, the butler, and Sir Bedivere raised him up, and gently led him betwixt them both to a little chapel not far from the sea-side. And when the king was there he thought him well eased. Then heard they people cry in the field. And Sir Lucan went to see what that cry betokened; and he saw by the moonlight that pillers and robbers were come to rob the dead. And he returned, and said to the king, "By my rede, it is best that we bring you to some town." "I would it were so," said the king. And when the king tried to go he fainted. Then Sir Lucan took up the king on the one part, and Sir Bedivere on the other part; and in the lifting, Sir Lucan fell in a swoon to the earth, for he was grievously wounded. And then the noble knight's heart burst. And when the king awoke he beheld Sir Lucan how he lay foaming at the mouth, and speechless. "Alas!" said the king, "this is to me a full heavy sight, to see this noble duke so die for my sake; for he would have holpen me that had more need of help than I, and he would not complain, his heart was so set to help me." Then Sir Bedivere wept for his brother. "Leave this mourning and weeping," said the king, "for wilt thou well, if I might live myself, the death of Sir

Lucan would grieve me evermore; but my time hieth fast. Therefore," said Arthur unto Sir Bedivere, "take thou Excalibar, my good sword, and go with it to yonder water-side; and when thou comest there I charge thee throw my sword in that water, and come again and tell me what thou there seest." "My lord," said Sir Bedivere, "your commandment shall be done." So Sir Bedivere departed, and by the way he beheld that noble sword, that the pommel and the haft were all of precious stones; and then he said to himself, "If I throw this rich sword into the water no good shall come thereof, but only harm and loss." And then Sir Bedivere hid Excalibar under a tree. And so, as soon as he might, he came again to the king. "What sawest thou there?" said the king. "Sir," he said, "I saw nothing." "Alas! thou hast deceived me," said the king. "Go thou lightly again, and as thou love me, spare not to throw it in." Then Sir Bedivere went again, and took the sword in his hand to throw it; but again it beseemed him but sin and shame to throw away that noble sword, and he hid it away again, and returned, and told the king he had done his commandment. "What sawest thou there?" said the king. "Sir," he said, "I saw nothing but waters deep and waves wan." "Ah, traitor untrue!" said King Arthur, "now hast thou betrayed me twice. And yet thou art named a noble knight, and hast been lief and dear to me. But now go again, and do as I bid thee, for thy long tarrying putteth me in jeopardy of my life." Then Sir Bedivere went to the sword, and lightly took it up, and went to the water-side, and he bound the girdle about the hilt, and then he threw the sword as far into the water as he might. And there came an arm and a hand out of the water, and met it, and caught it, and shook it thrice and brandished it, and then vanished away the hand with the sword in the water.

Then Sir Bedivere came again to the king, and told him what he saw. "Help me hence," said the king, "for I fear I have tarried too long." Then Sir Bedivere took the king on his back, and so went with him to that water-side; and when they came there, even fast by the bank there rode a little barge with many fair ladies in it, and among them was a queen; and all had black hoods, and they wept and shrieked when they saw King Arthur.

"Now put me in the barge," said the king. And there received him three queens with great mourning, and in one of their laps King Arthur laid his head. And the queen said, "Ah, dear brother, why have ye tarried so long? Alas! this wound on your head hath caught over-much cold." And then they rowed from the land, and Sir Bedivere beheld them go from him. Then he cried: "Ah, my lord Arthur, will ye leave me here alone among mine enemies?" "Comfort thyself," said the king, "for in me is no further help; for I will to the Isle of Avalon, to heal me of my grievous wound." And as soon as Sir Bedivere had lost sight of the barge, he wept and wailed; then he took the forest, and went all that night, and in the morning he was ware of a chapel and a hermitage.

Then went Sir Bedivere thither; and when he came into the chapel, he saw where lay an hermit on the ground, near a tomb that was newly graven. "Sir," said Sir Bedivere, "what man is there buried that ye pray so near unto?" "Fair son," said the hermit, "I know not verily. But this night there came a number of ladies, and brought hither one dead, and prayed me to bury him." "Alas!" said Sir Bedivere, "that was my lord, King Arthur." Then Sir Bedivere swooned; and when he awoke he prayed the hermit he might abide with him, to live with fasting and prayers. "Ye are welcome," said the hermit. So there bode Sir Bedivere with the hermit; and he put on poor clothes, and served the hermit full lowly in fasting and in prayers.

Thus of Arthur I find never more written in books that be authorized, nor more of the very certainty of his death; but thus was he led away in a ship, wherein were three queens; the one was King Arthur's sister, Queen Morgane le Fay; the other was Viviane, the Lady of the Lake; and the third was the queen of North Galis. And this tale Sir Bedivere, knight of the Table Round, made to be written.

Yet some men say that King Arthur is not dead, but hid away into another place, and men say that he shall come again and reign over England. But many say that there is written on his tomb this verse:

"Hie facet Arthurus, Rex quondam, Rexque futurus."
Here Arthur lies, King once and King to be.

And when Queen Guenever understood that King Arthur was slain, and all the noble knights with him, she stole away, and five ladies with her; and so she went to Almesbury, and made herself a nun, and ware white clothes and black, and took great penance as ever did sinful lady, and lived in fasting, prayers, and alms-deeds. And there she was abbess and ruler of the nuns.

Chapter 23: Morte D'Arthur

"And when she came to Almesbury she spake
There to the nuns, and said, 'Mine enemies
Pursue me, but, O peaceful Sisterhood,
Receive, and yield me sanctuary, nor ask
Her name to whom ye yield it, till her time
To tell you;' and her beauty, grace and power
Wrought as a charm upon them, and they spared
To ask it."
—Guinevere.

Now turn we from her, and speak of Sir Launcelot of the Lake.

When Sir Launcelot heard in his country that Sir Modred was crowned king of England, and made war against his own uncle, King Arthur, then was Sir Launcelot wroth out of measure, and said to his kinsmen: "Alas, that double traitor, Sir Modred! now it repenteth me that ever he escaped out of my hands." Then Sir Launcelot and his fellows made ready in all haste, with ships and galleys, to pass into England; and so he passed over till he came to Dover, and there he landed with a great army. Then Sir Launcelot was told that King Arthur was slain. "Alas!" said Sir Launcelot, "this is the heaviest tidings that ever came to me." Then he called the kings, dukes, barons, and knights, and said thus: "My fair lords, I thank you all for coming into this country with me, but we came too late, and that shall repent me while I live. But since it is so," said Sir Launcelot, "I will myself ride and seek my lady, Queen Guenever, for I have heard say she hath fled into the west; therefore ye shall abide me here fifteen days, and if I come not within that time, then take your ships and your host, and depart into your country."

So Sir Launcelot departed and rode westerly, and there he sought many days; and at last he came to a nunnery, and was seen of Queen Guenever as he walked in the cloister; and when she saw him she swooned away. And when she might speak she bade him to be called to her. And when Sir Launcelot was brought to her she said: "Sir Launcelot, I require thee and beseech thee, for all the love that ever was betwixt us, that thou never see me more, but return to thy kingdom and take thee a wife, and live with her with joy and bliss; and pray for me to my Lord, that I may get my soul's health." "Nay, madam," said Sir Launcelot, "wit you well that I shall never do; but the same destiny that ye have taken you to will I take me unto, for to please and serve God." And so they parted, with tears and much lamentation; and the ladies bare the queen to her chamber, and Sir Launcelot took his horse and rode away, weeping.

And at last Sir Launcelot was ware of a hermitage and a chapel, and then he heard a little bell ring to mass; and thither he rode and alighted, and tied his horse to the gate, and heard mass. And he that sang the mass was the hermit with whom Sir Bedivere had taken up his abode; and Sir Bedivere knew Sir Launcelot, and they spake together after mass. But when Sir Bedivere had told his tale, Sir Launcelot's heart almost burst for sorrow. Then he kneeled down, and prayed the hermit to shrive him, and besought that he might be his brother. Then the hermit said, "I will gladly;" and then he put a habit upon Sir Launcelot, and there he served God day and night, with prayers and fastings.

And the great host abode at Dover till the end of the fifteen days set by Sir Launcelot, and then Sir Bohort made them to go home again to their own country; and Sir Bohort, Sir Hector de Marys, Sir Blamor, and many others, took on them to ride through all England to seek Sir Launcelot. So Sir Bohort by fortune rode until he came to the same chapel where Sir Launcelot was; and when he saw Sir Launcelot in that manner of clothing he, prayed the hermit that he might be in that same. And so there was an habit put upon him, and there he lived in prayers and fasting. And within half a year came others of the knights, their fellows, and took such a habit as Sir Launcelot and Sir Bohort had. Thus they endured in great penance six years.

And upon a night there came a vision to Sir Launcelot, and charged him to haste toward Almesbury, and "by the time thou come there, thou shalt find Queen Guenever dead." Then Sir Launcelot rose up early and told the hermit thereof. Then said the hermit, "It were well that ye disobey not this vision." And Sir Launcelot took his seven companions with him, and on foot they went from Glastonbury to Almesbury, which is more than thirty miles. And when they were come to Almesbury, they found that Queen Guenever died but half an hour before. Then Sir Launcelot saw her visage, but he wept not greatly, but sighed. And so he did all the observance of the service himself, both the "dirige" at night, and at morn he sang mass. And there was prepared an horse-bier, and Sir Launcelot and his fellows followed the bier on foot from

Almesbury until they came to Glastonbury; and she was wrapped in cered clothes, and laid in a coffin of marble. And when she was put in the earth Sir Launcelot swooned, and lay long as one dead.

And Sir Launcelot never after ate but little meat, nor drank; but continually mourned. And within six weeks Sir Launcelot fell sick; and he sent for the hermit and all his true fellows, and said, "Sir hermit, I pray you give me all my rights that a Christian man ought to have." "It shall not need," said the hermit and all his fellows; "it is but heaviness of your blood, and to-morrow morn you shall be well" "My fair lords," said Sir Launcelot, "my careful body will into the earth; I have warning more than now I will say; therefore give me my rights." So when he was houseled and aneled, and had all that a Christian man ought to have, he prayed the hermit that his fellows might bear his body to Joyous Garde. (Some men say it was Alnwick, and some say it was Bamborough.) "It repenteth me sore," said Sir Launcelot, "but I made a vow aforetime that in Joyous Garde I would be buried." Then there was weeping and wringing of hands among his fellows. And that night Sir Launcelot died; and when Sir Bohort and his fellows came to his bedside the next morning they found him stark dead; and he lay as if he had smiled, and the sweetest savor all about him that ever they knew.

And they put Sir Launcelot into the same horse-bier that Queen Guenever was laid in, and the hermit and they altogether went with the body till they came to Joyous Garde. And there they laid his corpse in the body of the quire, and sang and read many psalms and prayers over him. And ever his visage was laid open and naked, that all folks might behold him. And right thus, as they were at their service, there came Sir Hector de Maris, that had seven years sought Sir Launcelot, his brother, through all England, Scotland and Wales. And when Sir Hector heard such sounds in the chapel of Joyous Garde he alighted and came into the quire. And all they knew Sir Hector. Then went Sir Bohort, and told him how there lay Sir Launcelot, his brother, dead. Then Sir Hector threw his shield, his sword, and helm from him. And when he beheld Sir Launcelot's visage it were hard for any tongue to tell the doleful complaints he made for his brother. "Ah, Sir Launcelot!" he said, "there thou liest. And now I dare to say thou wert never matched of none earthly knight's hand. And thou wert the courteousest knight that ever bare shield; and thou wert the truest friend to thy lover that ever bestrode horse; and thou wert the truest lover, of a sinful man, that ever loved woman; and thou wert the kindest man that ever struck with sword. And thou wert the goodliest person that ever came among press of knights. And thou wert the meekest man, and the gentlest, that ever ate in hall among ladies. And thou wert the sternest knight to thy mortal foe that ever put spear in the rest." Then there was weeping and dolor out of measure. Thus they kept Sir Launcelot's corpse fifteen days, and then they buried it with great devotion.

Then they went back with the hermit to his hermitage. And Sir Bedivere was there ever still hermit to his life's end. And Sir Bohort, Sir Hector, Sir Blamor, and Sir Bleoberis went into the Holy Land. And these four knights did many battles upon the miscreants, the Turks; and there they died upon a Good Friday, as it pleased God.

Thus endeth this noble and joyous book, entitled "La Morte d'Arthur;" notwithstanding it treateth of the birth, life, and acts of the said King Arthur, and of his noble Knights of the Round Table, their marvellous enquests and adventures, the achieving of the Sangreal, and, in the end, le Morte d'Arthur, with the dolorous death and departing out of this world of them all. Which book was reduced into English by Sir Thomas Mallory, Knight, and divided into twenty-one books, chaptered and imprinted and finished in the Abbey Westmestre, the last day of July, the year of our Lord MCCCCLXXXV.

Caxton me fieri fecit.

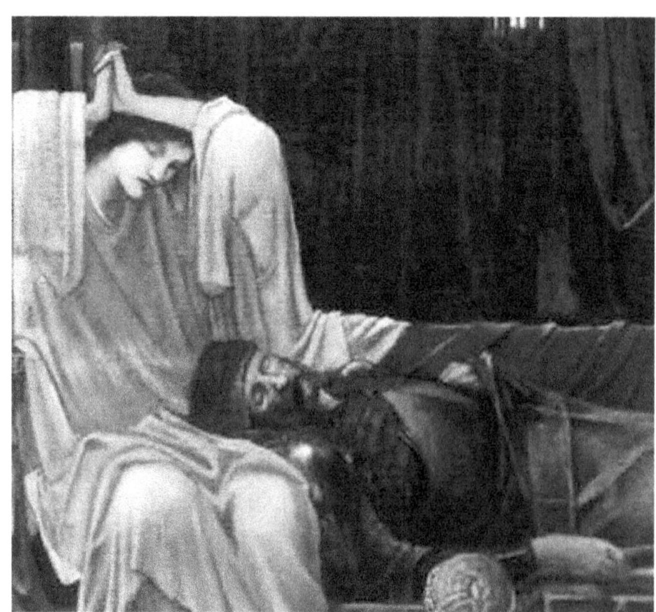

Figure 82: Detail from "The Last Sleep of Arthur" by Edward Burne-Jones

The Mabinogion

Introductory Note

It has been well known to the literati and antiquarians of Europe that there exist in the great public libraries voluminous manuscripts of romances and tales once popular, but which on the invention of printing had already become antiquated, and fallen into neglect. They were therefore never printed, and seldom perused even by the learned, until about half a century ago, when attention was again directed to them, and they were found very curious monuments of ancient manners, habits, and modes of thinking. Several have since been edited, some by individuals, as Sir Walter Scott and the poet Southey, others by antiquarian societies. The class of readers which could be counted on for such publications was so small that no inducement of profit could be found to tempt editors and publishers to give them to the world. It was therefore only a few, and those the most accessible, which were put in print. There was a class of manuscripts of this kind which were known, or rather suspected, to be both curious and valuable, but which it seemed almost hopeless to expect ever to see in fair printed English. These were the Welsh popular tales called Mabinogeon, a plural word, the singular being Mabinogi, a tale. Manuscripts of these were contained in the Bodleian Library at Oxford and elsewhere, but the difficulty was to find translators and editors. The Welsh is a spoken language among the peasantry of Wales, but is entirely neglected by the learned, unless they are natives of the principality. Of the few Welsh scholars none were found who took sufficient interest in this branch of learning to give these productions to the English public. Southey and Scott, and others, who like them, loved the old romantic legends of their country, often urged upon the Welsh literati the duty of reproducing the Mabinogeon. Southey, in the preface of his edition of "Moted'Arthur," says: "The specimens which I have seen are exceedingly curious; nor is there a greater desideratum in British literature than an edition of these tales, with a literal version, and such comments as Mr. Davies of all men is best qualified to give. Certain it is that many of the round table fictions originated in Wales, or in Bretagne, and probably might still be traced there."

Again, in a letter to Sir Charles W. W. Wynn, dated 1819, he says:

"I begin almost to despair of ever seeing more of the Mabinogeon; and yet if some competent Welshman could be found to edit it carefully, with as literal a version as possible, I am sure it might be made worth his while by a subscription, printing a small edition at a high price, perhaps two hundred at five guineas. I myself would gladly subscribe at that price per volume for such an edition of the whole of your genuine remains in prose and verse. Till some such collection is made, the 'gentlemen of Wales' ought to be prohibited from wearing a leek; ay, and interdicted from toasted cheese also. Your bards would have met with better usage if they had been Scotchmen."

Sharon Turner and Sir Walter Scott also expressed a similar wish for the publication of the Welsh manuscripts. The former took part in an attempt to effect it, through the instrumentality of a Mr. Owen, a Welshman, but, we judge, by what Southey says of him, imperfectly

Figure 83: "Cuchulain Desires the Arms of a King" by Stephen Reid

acquainted with English. Southey's language is "William Owen lent me three parts of the Mabinogeon, delightfully translated into so Welsh an idiom and syntax that such a translation is as instructive as an original." In another letter he adds, "Let Sharon make his language grammatical, but not alter their idiom in the slightest point."

It is probable Mr. Owen did not proceed far in an undertaking which, so executed, could expect but little popular patronage. It was not till an individual should appear possessed of the requisite knowledge of the two languages, of enthusiasm sufficient for the task, and of pecuniary resources sufficient to be independent of the booksellers and of the reading public, that such a work could be confidently expected. Such an individual has, since Southey's day and Scott's, appeared in the person of Lady Charlotte Guest, an English lady united to a gentleman of property in Wales, who, having acquired the language of the principality, and become enthusiastically fond of its literary treasures, has given them to the English reader, in a dress which the printer's and the engraver's arts have done their best to adorn. In four royal octavo volumes containing the Welsh originals, the translation, and ample illustrations from French, German, and other contemporary and affiliated literature, the Mabinogeon is spread before us. To the antiquarian and the student of language and ethnology an invaluable treasure, it yet can hardly in such a form win its way to popular acquaintance. We claim no other merit than that of bringing it to the knowledge of our readers, of abridging its details, of selecting its most attractive portions, and of faithfully preserving throughout the style in which Lady Guest has clothed her legends. For this service we hope that our readers will confess we have laid them under no light obligation.

Figure 84: From J.M. Edwards "Y Mabingion" 1901, artist unknown

Chapter 1

THE BRITONS

The earliest inhabitants of Britain are supposed to have been a branch of that great family known in history by the designation of Celts. Cambria, which is a frequent name for Wales, is thought to be derived from Cymri, the name which the Welsh traditions apply to an immigrant people who entered the island from the adjacent continent. This name is thought to be identical with those of Cimmerians and Cimbri, under which the Greek and Roman historians describe a barbarous people, who spread themselves from the north of the Euxine over the whole of Northwestern Europe.

The origin of the names Wales and Welsh has been much canvassed. Some writers make them a derivation from Gael or Gaul, which names are said to signify "woodlanders;" others observe that Walsh, in the northern languages, signifies a stranger, and that the aboriginal Britons were so called by those who at a later era invaded the island and possessed the greater part of it, the Saxons and Angles.

The Romans held Britain from the invasion of Julius Caesar till their voluntary withdrawal from the island, A.D. 420,—that is, about five hundred years. In that time there must have been a wide diffusion of their arts and institutions among the natives. The remains of roads, cities, and fortifications show that they did much to develop and improve the country, while those of their villas and castles prove that many of the settlers possessed wealth and taste for the ornamental arts. Yet the Roman sway was sustained chiefly by force, and never extended over the entire island. The northern portion, now Scotland, remained independent, and the western portion, constituting Wales and Cornwall, was only nominally subjected.

Neither did the later invading hordes succeed in subduing the remoter sections of the island. For ages after the arrival of the Saxons under Hengist and Horsa, A.D. 449, the whole western coast of Britain was possessed by the aboriginal inhabitants, engaged in constant warfare with the invaders.

It has, therefore, been a favorite boast of the people of Wales and Cornwall that the original British stock flourishes in its unmixed purity only among them. We see this notion flashing out in poetry occasionally, as when Gray, in "The Bard," prophetically describing Queen Elizabeth, who was of the Tudor, a Welsh race, says:

"Her eye proclaims her of the Briton line;"

and, contrasting the princes of the Tudor with those of the Norman race, he exclaims:

"All hail, ye genuine kings, Britannia's issue, hail!"

THE WELSH LANGUAGE AND LITERATURE

The Welsh language is one of the oldest in Europe. It possesses poems the origin of which is referred with probability to the sixth century. The language of some of these is so antiquated that the best scholars differ about the interpretation of many passages; but, generally speaking, the body of poetry which the Welsh possess, from the year 1000 downwards, is intelligible to those who are acquainted with the modern language.

Till within the last half-century these compositions remained buried in the libraries of colleges or of individuals, and so difficult of access that no successful attempt was made to give them to the world. This reproach was removed after ineffectual appeals to the patriotism of the gentry of Wales, by Owen Jones, a furrier of London, who at his own expense collected and published the chief productions of Welsh literature, under the title of the Myvyrian Archaeology of Wales. In this task he was assisted by Dr. Owen and other Welsh scholars.

After the cessation of Jones' exertions the old apathy returned, and continued till within a few years. Dr. Owen exerted himself to obtain support for the publication of the Mabinogeon or Prose Tales of the Welsh, but died without accomplishing his purpose, which has since been carried into execution by Lady Charlotte Guest. The legends which fill the remainder of this volume are taken from this

Figure 85: "The Bard" by Thomas Jones

work, of which we have already spoken more fully in the introductory chapter to the First Part.

THE WELSH BARDS

The authors to whom the oldest Welsh poems are attributed are Aneurin, who is supposed to have lived A.D. 500 to 550, and Taliesin, Llywarch Hen (Llywarch the Aged), and Myrddin or Merlin, who were a few years later. The authenticity of the poems which bear their names has been assailed, and it is still an open question how many and which of them are authentic, though it is hardly to be doubted that some are so. The poem of Aneurin entitled the "Gododin" bears very strong marks of authenticity. Aneurin was one of the Northern Britons of Strath-Clyde, who have left to that part of the district they inhabited the name of Cumberland, or Land of the Cymri. In this poem he laments the defeat of his countrymen by the Saxons at the battle of Cattraeth, in consequence of having partaken too freely of the mead before joining in combat. The bard himself and two of his fellow-warriors were all who escaped from the field. A portion of this poem has been translated by Gray, of which the following is an extract:

"To Cattraeth's vale, in glittering row,
Twice two hundred warriors go;
Every warrior's manly neck
Chains of regal honor deck,
Wreathed in many a golden link;
From the golden cup they drink
Nectar that the bees produce,
Or the grape's exalted juice.
Flushed with mirth and hope they burn,
But none to Cattraeth's vale return,
Save Aeron brave, and Conan strong,
Bursting through the bloody throng,

And I, the meanest of them all,
That live to weep, and sing their fall."

The works of Taliesin are of much more questionable authenticity. There is a story of the adventures of Taliesin so strongly marked with mythical traits as to cast suspicion on the writings attributed to him. This story will be found in the subsequent pages.

THE TRIADS

The Triads are a peculiar species of poetical composition, of which the Welsh bards have left numerous examples. They are enumerations of a triad of persons, or events, or observations, strung together in one short sentence. This form of composition, originally invented, in all likelihood, to assist the memory, has been raised by the Welsh to a degree of elegance of which it hardly at first sight appears susceptible. The Triads are of all ages, some of them probably as old as anything in the language. Short as they are individually, the collection in the Myvyrian Archaeology occupies more than one hundred and seventy pages of double columns. We will give some specimens, beginning with personal triads, and giving the first place to one of King Arthur's own composition:

"I have three heroes in battle:
Mael the tall, and Llyr, with his army,
And Caradoc, the pillar of Wales."
"The three principal bards of the island of Britain:—
Merlin Ambrose
Merlin the son of Mprfyn, called also Merlin the Wild,
And Taliesin, the chief of the bards."
"The three golden-tongued knights of the court of
Arthur:—
Gawain, son of Gwyar,
Drydvas, son of Tryphin,
And Ehwlod, son of Madag, ap Uther."
"The three honorable feasts of the island of Britain:—
The feast of Caswallaun, after repelling Julius Caesar
from this
isle;
The feast of Aurelius Ambrosius, after he had conquered
the
Saxons;
And the feast of King Arthur, at Carleon upon Usk."
"Guenever, the daughter of Laodegan the giant,
Bad when little, worse when great."
Next follow some moral triads:
"Hast thou heard what Dremhidydd sung,
An ancient watchman on the castle walls?
A refusal is better than a promise unperformed."
"Hast thou heard what Llenleawg sung,
The noble chief wearing the golden torques?
The grave is better than a life of want."
"Hast thou heard what Garselit sung,
The Irishman whom it is safe to follow?
Sin is bad, if long pursued."
"Hast thou heard what Avaon sung,
The son of Taliesin, of the recording verse?
The cheek will not conceal the anguish of the heart."
"Didst thou hear what Llywarch sung,
The intrepid and brave old man?
Greet kindly, though there be no acquaintance."

Figure 86: "The Bard" by Phillippe Jacques de Loutherbourg

THE LADY OF THE FOUNTAIN

KYNON'S ADVENTURE

King Arthur was at Caerleon upon Usk; and one day he sat in his chamber, and with him were Owain, the son of Urien, and Kynon, the son of Clydno, and Kay, the son of Kyner, and Guenever and her handmaidens at needlework by the window. In the centre of the chamher King Arthur sat, upon a seat of green rushes, [Footnote: The use of green rushes in apartments was by no means peculiar to the court of Carleon upon Usk. Our ancestors had a great predilection for them, and they seem to have constituted an essential article, not only of comfort, but of luxury. The custom of strewing the floor with rushes is well known to have existed in England during the Middle Ages, and also in France.] over which was spread a covering of flame-covered satin, and a cushion of red satin was under his elbow.

Then Arthur spoke. "If I thought you would not disparage me," said he, "I would sleep while I wait for my repast; and you can entertain one another with relating tales, and can obtain a flagon of mead and some meat from Kay." And the king went to sleep. And Kynon the son of Clydno asked Kay for that which Arthur had promised them. "I too will have the good tale which he promised me," said Kay. "Nay," answered Kynon; "fairer will it be for thee to fulfil Arthur's behest in the first place, and then we will tell thee the best tale that we know." So Kay went to the kitchen and to the mead-cellar, and returned, bearing a flagon of mead, and a golden goblet, and a handful of skewers, upon which were broiled collops of meat. Then they ate the collops, and began to drink the mead. "Now," said Kay, "it is time for you to give me my story." "Kynon," said Owain, "do thou pay to Kay the tale that is his due." "I will do so," answered Kynon.

"I was the only son of my mother and father, and I was exceedingly aspiring, and my daring was very great. I thought there was no enterprise in the world too mighty for me: and after I had achieved all the adventures that were in my own country, I equipped myself, and set forth to journey through deserts and distant regions. And at length it chanced that I came to the fairest valley in the world, wherein were trees all of equal growth; and a river ran through the valley, and a path was by the side of the river. And I followed the path until midday, and continued my journey along the remainder of the valley until the evening; and at the extremity of the plain I came to a large and lustrous castle, at the foot of which was a torrent. And I approached the castle, and there I beheld two youths with yellow curling hair, each with a frontlet of gold upon his head, and clad in a garment of yellow satin; and they had gold clasps upon their insteps. In the hand of each of them was an ivory bow, strung with the sinews of the stag, and their arrows and their shafts were of the bone of the whale, and were winged with peacock's feathers. The shafts also had golden heads. And they had daggers with blades of gold, and with hilts of the bone of the whale. And they were shooting at a mark.

"And a little away from them I saw a man in the prime of life, with his beard newly shorn, clad in a robe and mantle of yellow satin, and round the top of his mantle was a band of gold lace. On his feet were shoes of variegated leather, [Footnote: Cordwal is the word in the original, and from the manner in which it is used it is evidently intended for the French Cordouan or Cordovan leather, which derived its name from Cordova, where it was manufactured. From this comes also our English word cordwainer.] fastened by two bosses of gold. When I saw him I went towards him and saluted him; and such was his courtesy, that he no sooner received my greeting than he returned it. And he went with me towards the castle. Now there were no dwellers in the castle, except those who were in one hall. And there I saw four and twenty damsels, embroidering satin at a window. And this I tell thee, Kay, that the least fair of them was fairer than the fairest maid thou didst ever behold in the island of Britain; and the least lovely of them was more lovely than Guenever, the wife of Arthur, when she appeared loveliest, at the feast of Easter. They rose up at my coming, and six of them took my horse, and divested me of my armor, and six others took my arms and washed them in a vessel till they were perfectly bright. And the third six spread cloths upon the tables and prepared meat. And the fourth six took off my soiled garments and placed others upon me, namely, an under vest and a doublet of fine linen, and a robe and a surcoat, and a mantle of yellow satin, with a broad gold

Figure 87: "Spirit of the Fountain" by Herbert James Draper

band upon the mantle. And they placed cushions both beneath and around me, with coverings of red linen, and I sat down. Now the six maidens who had taken my horse unharnessed him as well as if they had been the best squires in the island of Britain.

"Then behold they brought bowls of silver, wherein was water to wash and towels of linen, some green and some white; and I washed. And in a little while the man sat down at the table. And I sat next to him, and below me sat all the maidens, except those who waited on us. And the table was of silver, and the cloths upon the table were of linen. And no vessel was served upon the table that was not either of gold or of silver or of buffalo horn. And our meat was brought to us. And verily, Kay, I saw there every sort of meat, and every sort of liquor that I ever saw elsewhere; but the meat and the liquor were better served there than I ever saw them in any other place.

"Until the repast was half over, neither the man nor any one of the damsels spoke a single word to me; but when the man perceived that it would be more agreeable for me to converse than to eat any more, he began to inquire of me who I was. Then I told the man who I was and what was the cause of my journey, and said that I was seeking whether any one was superior to me, or whether I could gain mastery over all. The man looked upon me, and he smiled and said, 'If I did not fear to do thee a mischief, I would show thee that which thou seekest.' Then I desired him to speak freely. And he said: 'Sleep here to-night, and in the morning arise early, and take the road upwards through the valley, until thou readiest the wood. A little way within the wood thou wilt come to a large sheltered glade, with a mound in the centre. And thou wilt see a black man of great stature on the top of the mound. He has but one foot, and one eye in the middle of his forehead. He is the wood- ward of that wood. And thou wilt see a thousand wild animals grazing around him. Inquire of him the way out of the glade, and he will reply to thee briefly, and will point out the road by which thou shalt find that which thou art in quest of.'

"And long seemed that night to me. And the next morning I arose and equipped myself, and mounted my horse, and proceeded straight through the valley to the wood, and at length I arrived at the glade. And the black man was there, sitting upon the top of the mound; and I was three times more astonished at the number of wild animals that I beheld than the man had said I should be. Then I inquired of him the way and he asked me roughly whither I would go. And when I had told him who I was and what I sought, 'Take,' said he, 'that path that leads toward the head of the glade, and there thou wilt find an open space like to a large valley, and in the midst of it a

Figure 88: "The Rainbow Woman" by Arthur Rackham

tall tree. Under this tree is a fountain, and by the side of the fountain a marble slab, and on the marble slab a silver bowl, attached by a chain of silver, that it may not be carried away. Take, the bowl and throw a bowlful of water on the slab. And if thou dost not find trouble in that adventure, thou needest not seek it during the rest of thy life.'

"So I journeyed on until I reached the summit of the steep. And there I found everything as the black man had described it to me. And I went up to the tree, and beneath it I saw the fountain, and by its side the marble slab, and the silver bowl fastened by the chain. Then I took the bowl, and cast a bowlful of water upon the slab, and immediately I heard a mighty peal of thunder, so that heaven and earth seemed to tremble with its fury. And after the thunder came a, shower; and of a truth I tell thee, Kay, that it was such a shower as neither man nor beast could endure and live. I turned my horse's flank toward the shower, and placed the beak of my shield over his head and neck, while I held the upper part of it over my own neck. And thus I withstood the shower. And presently the sky became clear, and with that, behold, the birds lighted upon the tree, and sang. And truly, Kay, I never heard any melody equal to that, either before or since. And when I was most charmed with listening to the birds, lo! a chiding voice was heard of one approaching me and saying: 'O knight, what has brought thee hither? What evil have I done to thee that thou shouldst act towards me and my possessions as thou hast this day? Dost thou not know that the shower to-day has left in my dominions neither man nor beast alive that was exposed to it?' And thereupon, behold, a knight on a black horse appeared, clothed in jet-black velvet, and with a tabard of black linen about him. And we charged each other, and, as the onset was furious, it was not long before I was overthrown. Then the knight passed the shaft of his lance through the bridle-rein of my horse, and rode off with the two horses, leaving me where I was. And he did not even bestow so much notice upon me as to imprison me, nor did he despoil me of my arms. So I returned along the road by which I had come. And when I reached the glade where the black man was, I confess to thee, Kay, it is a marvel that I did not melt down into a liquid pool, through the shame that I felt at the black man's derision. And that night I came to the same castle where I had spent the night preceding. And I was more agreeably entertained that night than I had been the night before. And I conversed freely with the inmates of the castle; and none of them alluded to my expedition to the fountain, neither did I mention it to any. And I remained there that night. When I arose on the morrow I found ready saddled a dark bay palfrey, with nostrils as red as scarlet. And after putting on my armor, and leaving there my blessing, I returned to my own court. And that horse I still possess, and he is in the stable yonder. And I declare that I would not part with him for the best palfrey in the island of Britain.

"Now, of a truth, Kay, no man ever before confessed to an adventure so much to his own discredit; and verily it seems strange to me that neither before nor since have I heard of any person who knew of this adventure, and that the subject of it should exist within King Arthur's dominions without any other person lighting upon it."

Chapter 3

THE LADY OF THE FOUNTAIN (CONTINUED)

OWAIN'S ADVENTURE

[Footnote: Amongst all the characters of early British history none is the more interesting, or occupies more conspicuous place, than the hero of this tale. Urien, his father, was prince of Rheged, a district comprising the present Cumberland and part of the adjacent country. His valor, and the consideration in which he was held, are a frequent theme of Bardic song, and form the subject of several very spirited odes by Taliesin. Among the Triads there is one relating to him; it is thus translated:

"Three Knights of Battle were in court of Arthur Cadwr, the Earl of Cornwall, Launcelot du Lac, and Owain, the son of Urien. And this was their characteristic—that they would not retreat from battle, neither for spear, nor for arrow, nor for sword. And Arthur never had shame in battle the day he saw their faces there. And they were called the Knights of Battle."]

"Now," quoth Owain, "would it not be well to go and endeavor to discover that place?"

"By the hand of my friend," said Kay, "often dost thou utter that with thy tongue which thou wouldest not make good with thy deeds."

"In very truth," said Guenever, "it were better thou wert hanged, Kay, than to use such uncourteous speech towards a man like Owain."

"By the hand of my friend, good lady," said Kay, "thy praise of Owain is not greater than mine."

With that Arthur awoke, and asked if he had not been sleeping a little.

"Yes, lord," answered Owain, "thou hast slept awhile."

"Is it time for us to go to meat?"

"It is, lord," said Owain.

Then the horn for washing was sounded, and the king and all his household sat down to eat. And when the meal was ended Owain withdrew to his lodging, and made ready his horse and his arms.

On the morrow with the dawn of day he put on his armor, and mounted his charger, and travelled through distant lands, and over desert mountains. And at length he arrived at the valley which Kynon had described to him, and he was certain that it was the same that he sought. And journeying along the valley, by the side of the river, he followed its course till he came to the plain, and within sight of the castle. When he approached the castle he saw the youths shooting with their bows, in the place where Kynon had seen them, and the yellow man, to whom the castle belonged, standing hard by. And no sooner had Owain saluted the yellow man, than he was saluted by him in return.

And he went forward towards the castle, and there he saw the chamber; and when he had entered the chamber, he beheld the maidens working at satin embroidery, in chains of gold. And their beauty and their comeliness seemed to Owain far greater than Kynon had represented to him. And they arose to wait upon Owain, as they had done to Kynon. And the meal which they set before him gave even more satisfaction to Owain than it had done to Kynon.

About the middle of the repast the yellow man asked Owain the object of his journey. And Owain made it known to him, and said, "I am in quest of the knight who guards the fountain." Upon this the yellow man smiled, and said that he was as loth to point out that adventure to him as he had been to Kynon. However, he described the whole to Owain, and they retired to rest.

The next morning Owain found his horse made ready for him by the damsels, and he set forward and came to the glade where the black man was. And the stature of the black man seemed more wonderful to Owain than it had done to Kynon; and Owain asked of him his road, and he showed it to him. And Owain followed the road till he came to the green tree; and he beheld the fountain, and the slab beside the fountain, with the bowl upon it. And Owain took the bowl and threw a bowlful of water upon the slab. And, lo! the thunder was heard, and after the thunder came the shower, more violent than Kynon had described, and after the shower the sky became bright. And immediately the birds came and settled upon the tree and sang. And when their song was most pleasing to Owain he beheld a knight coming towards him through the valley; and he prepared to receive him, and encountered him violently. Having broken both their lances, they drew their swords and fought blade to blade. Then Owain struck the knight a blow through his helmet, head-piece, and visor, and through the skin, and the flesh, and the bone, until it wounded the very brain. Then the black knight felt that he had received a mortal wound, upon which he turned his horse's head and fled. And Owain pursued him and followed close upon him, although he was not near enough to strike him with his sword. Then Owain descried a vast and resplendent castle; and they came to the castle gate. And the black knight was allowed to enter, and the portcullis was let fall upon Owain; and it struck his horse behind the saddle, and cut him in two, and carried away the rowels of the spurs that were upon Owains' heels. And the portcullis descended to the floor. And the rowels of the spurs and part of the horse were without, and Owain with the other part of the horse remained between the two gates, and the inner gate was closed, so that Owain could not go thence; and Owain was in a perplexing situation. And while he was in this state, he could see through an aperture in the gate a street facing him, with a row of houses on each side. And he beheld a maiden, with yellow, curling hair, and a frontlet of gold upon her head; and she was clad in a dress of yellow satin, and on her feet were shoes of variegated leather. And she approached the gate, and desired that it should be opened. "Heaven knows, lady," said Owain, "it is no more possible for me to open to thee from hence, than it is for thee to set me free." And he told her his name, and who he was. "Truly," said the damsel, "it is very sad that thou canst not be released; and every woman ought to succor thee, for I know there is no one more faithful in the service of ladies than thou. Therefore," quoth she, "whatever is in my power to do for thy release, I will do it. Take this ring and put it on thy finger, with the stone inside thy hand, and close thy hand upon the stone. And as long as thou concealest it, it will conceal thee. When they come forth to fetch thee, they will be much grieved that they cannot find thee. And I will await thee on the horseblock yonder, and thou wilt be able to see me, though I cannot see thee. Therefore come and place thy hand upon my shoulder, that I may know that thou art near me. And by the way that I go hence do thou accompany me."

Figure 89: "The Accolade" by Edmund Leighton

Then the maiden went away from Owain, and he did all that she had told him. And the people of the castle came to seek Owain to put him to death; and when they found nothing but the half of his horse, they were sorely grieved.

And Owain vanished from among them, and went to the maiden, and placed his hand upon her shoulder; whereupon she set off, and Owain followed her, until they came to the door of a large and beautiful chamber, and the maiden opened it, and they went in. And Owain looked around the chamber, and behold there was not a single nail in it that was not painted with gorgeous colors, and there was not a single panel that had not sundry images in gold portrayed upon it.

The maiden kindled a fire, and took water in a silver bowl, and gave Owain water to wash. Then she placed before him a silver table, inlaid with gold; upon which was a cloth of yellow linen, and she brought him food. And, of a truth, Owain never saw any kind of meat that was not there in abundance, but it was better cooked there than he had ever found it in any other place. And there was not one vessel from which he was served that was not of gold or of silver. And Owain eat and drank until late in the afternoon, when lo! they heard a mighty clamor in the castle, and Owain asked the maiden what it was. "They are administering extreme unction," said she, "to the nobleman who owns the castle." And she prepared a couch for Owain which was meet for Arthur himself, and Owain went to sleep.

And a little after daybreak he heard an exceeding loud clamor and wailing, and he asked the maiden what was the cause of it. "They are bearing to the church the body of the nobleman who owned the castle."

And Owain rose up, and clothed himself, and opened a window of the chamber, and looked towards the castle; and he could see neither the bounds nor the extent of the hosts that filled the streets. And they were fully armed; and a vast number of women were with them, both on horseback and on foot, and all the ecclesiastics in the city singing. In the midst of the throng he beheld the bier, over which was a veil of white linen; and wax tapers were burning beside and around it; and none that supported the bier was lower in rank than a powerful baron.

Never did Owain see an assemblage so gorgeous with silk [Footnote: Before the sixth century all the silk used by Europeans had been brought to them by the Seres, the ancestors of the present Boukharians, whence it derived its Latin name of Serica. In 551 the silkworm was brought by two monks to Constantinople, but the manufacture of silk was confined to the Greek empire till the year 1130, when Roger, king of Sicily, returning from a crusade, collected some manufacturers from Athens and Corinth, and established them at Palermo, whence the trade was gradually disseminated over Italy. The varieties of silk stuffs known at this time were velvet, satin (which was called samite), and taffety (called cendal or sendall), all of which were occasionally stitched with gold and silver.] and satin. And, following the train, he beheld a lady with yellow hair falling over her shoulders, and stained with blood; and about her a dress of yellow satin, which was torn. Upon her feet were shoes of variegated leather. And it was a marvel that the ends of her fingers were not bruised from the violence with which she smote her hands together. Truly she would have been the fairest lady Owain ever saw, had she been in her usual guise. And her cry was louder than the shout of the men or the clamor of the trumpets. No sooner had he beheld the lady than he became inflamed with her love, so that it took entire possession of him.

Then he inquired of the maiden who the lady was. "Heaven knows," replied the maiden, "she is the fairest and the most chaste, and the most liberal, and the most noble of women. She is my mistress, and she is called the Countess of the Fountain, the wife of him whom thou didst slay yesterday." "Verily," said Owain, "she is the woman that I love best." "Verily," said the maiden, "she shall also love thee, not a little."

Then the maiden prepared a repast for Owain, and truly he thought he had never before so good a meal, nor was he ever so well served. Then she left him, and went towards the castle. When she came there, she found nothing but mourning and sorrow; and the Countess in her chamber could not bear the sight of any one through grief. Luned, for that was the name of the maiden, saluted her, but the Countess answered her not. And the maiden bent down towards her, and said, "What aileth thee, that thou answereth no one to-day?" "Luned," said the Countess, "what change hath befallen thee, that thou hast not come to visit me in my grief. It was wrong in thee, and I so sorely afflicted." "Truly," said Luned, "I thought thy good sense was greater than I find it to be. Is it well for thee to mourn after that good man, or for anything else that thou canst not have?" "I declare to Heaven," said the Countess, "that in the whole world there is not a man equal to him." "Not so," said Luned, "for an ugly man would be as good as or better than he." "I declare to Heaven," said the Countess, "that were it not repugnant to me to put to death one whom I have brought up, I would have thee executed for making such a comparison to me. As it is, I will banish thee." "I am glad," said Luned, "that thou hast no other cause to do so than that I would have been of service to thee, where thou didst not know what was to thine advantage. Henceforth, evil betide whichever of us shall make the first advance towards reconciliation to the other, whether I should seek an invitation from thee, or thou of thine own accord should send to invite."

With that Luned went forth; and the Countess arose and followed her to the door of the chamber, and began coughing loudly. And when Luned looked back, the Countess beckoned to her, and she returned to the Countess. "In truth," said the Countess, "evil is thy disposition; but if thou knowest what is to my advantage, declare it to me." "I will do so," said she.

"Thou knowest that, except by warfare and arms, it is impossible for thee to preserve thy possessions; delay not, therefore, to seek some one who can defend them." "And how can I do that?" said the Countess. "I will tell thee," said Luned; "unless thou canst defend the fountain, thou canst not maintain thy dominions; and no one can defend the fountain except it be a knight of Arthur's household. I will go to Arthur's court, and ill betide me if I return not thence with a warrior who can guard the fountain as well as, or even better than, he who defended it formerly." "That will be hard to perform," said the Countess. "Go, however, and make proof of that which thou hast promised,"

Luned set out under the pretence of going to Arthur's court; but she went back to the mansion where she had left Owain, and she tarried there as long as it might have taken her to travel to the court of King Arthur and back. And at the end of that time she apparelled herself, and went to visit the Countess. And the Countess was much rejoiced when she saw her, and inquired what news she brought from the court. "I bring thee the best of news," said Luned, "for I have compassed the object of my mission. When wilt thou that I should present to thee the chieftain who has come with me hither?" "Bring him here to visit me to-morrow," said the Countess, "and I will cause the town to be assembled by that time."

And Luned returned home. And the next day at noon, Owain arrayed himself in a coat and a surcoat, and a mantle of yellow satin, upon which was a broad band of gold lace; and on his feet were high shoes of variegated leather, which were fastened by golden clasps, in the form of lions. And they proceeded to the chamber of the Countess.

Right glad was the Countess of their coming. And she gazed steadfastly upon Owain, and said, "Luned, this knight has not the look of a traveller." "What harm is there in that, lady?" said Luned. "I am certain," said the Countess, "that no other man than this chased the soul from the body of my lord." "So much the better for thee, lady," said Luned, "for had he not been stronger than thy lord, he could not have deprived him of life. There is no remedy for that which is past, be it as it may." "Go back to thine abode," said the Countess, "and I will take counsel."

The next day the Countess caused all her subjects to assemble, and showed them that her earldom was left defenceless, and that it could not be protected but with horse and arms, and military skill. "Therefore," said she, "this is what I offer for your choice: either let one of you take me, or give your consent for me to take a husband from elsewhere, to defend my dominions."

So they came to the determination that it was better that she should have permission to marry some one from elsewhere; and thereupon she sent for the bishops and archbishops, to celebrate her nuptials with Owain. And the men of the earldom did Owain homage.

And Owain defended the fountain with lance and sword. And this is the manner in which he defended it. Whensoever a knight came there, he overthrew him, and sold him for his full worth. And what he thus gained he divided among his barons and his knights, and no man in the whole world could be more beloved than he was by his subjects. And it was thus for the space of three years.

[Footnote: There exists an ancient poem, printed among those of Taliesin, called the "Elegy of Owain ap Urien," and containing several very beautiful and spirited passages It commences:

"The soul of Owain ap Urien,
May its Lord consider its exigencies'
Reged's chief the green turf covers."

In the course of this Elegy the bard, alluding to the incessant warfare with which this chieftain harassed his Saxon foes, exclaims,

"Could England sleep with the light upon her eyes'"

Chapter 4

THE LADY OF THE FOUNTAIN (CONTINUED)

GAWAIN'S ADVENTURE

It befell that, as Gawain went forth one day with King Arthur, he perceived him to be very sad and sorrowful. And Gawain was much grieved to see Arthur in his state, and he questioned him, saying, "O my lord, what has befallen thee?" "In sooth, Gawain," said Arthur, "I am grieved concerning Owain, whom I have lost these three years; and I shall certainly die if the fourth year pass without my seeing him. Now I am sure that it is through the tale which Kynon, the son of Clydno, related, that I have lost Owain." "There is no need for thee," said Gawain, "to summon to arms thy whole dominions on this account, for thou thyself, and the men of thy household, will be able to avenge Owain if he be slain or to set him free if he be in prison; and, if alive, to bring him back with thee." And it was settled according to what Gawain had said.

Then Arthur and the men of his household prepared to go and seek Owain. And Kynon, the son of Clydno, acted as their guide. And Arthur came to the castle where Kynon had been before. And when he came there, the youths were shooting in the same place, and the yellow man was standing hard by. When the yellow man saw Arthur, he greeted him, and invited him to the castle. And Arthur accepted his invitation, and they entered the castle together. And great as was the number of his retinue, their presence was scarcely observed in the castle, so vast was its extent. And the maidens rose up to wait on them. And the service of the maidens appeared to them all to excel any attendance they had ever met with; and even the pages, who had charge of the horses, were no worse served that night than Arthur himself would have been in his own palace.

The next morning Arthur set out thence, with Kynon for his guide, and came to the place where the black man was. And the stature of the black man was more surprising to Arthur than it had been represented to him. And they came to the top of the wooded steep, and traversed the valley, till they reached the green tree, where they saw the fountain and the bowl and the slab. And upon that Kay came to Arthur, and spoke to him. "My lord," said he, "I know the meaning of all this, and my request is that thou wilt permit me to throw the water on the slab, and to receive the first adventure that may befall." And Arthur gave him leave.

Then Kay threw a bowlful of water upon the slab, and immediately there came the thunder, and after the thunder the shower. And such a thunder-storm they had never known before. After the shower had ceased, the sky became clear, and on looking at the tree, they beheld it completely leafless. Then the birds descended upon the tree. And the song of the birds was far sweeter than any strain they had ever heard before. Then they beheld a knight, on a coal- black horse, clothed in black satin, coming rapidly towards them. And Kay met him and encountered him, and it was not long before Kay was overthrown. And the knight withdrew. And Arthur and his host encamped for the night.

And when they arose in the morning, they perceived the signal of combat upon the lance of the knight. Then, one by one, all the household of Arthur went forth to combat the knight, until there was not one that was not overthrown by him, except Arthur and Gawain. And Arthur armed himself to encounter the knight. "O my

Figure 90: "Owain, or Cynon Shelter from a Hailstorm" by S. Williams

Figure 91: "Sir Gawain" by Howrd Pyle

lord," said Gawain, "permit me to fight with him first." And Arthur permitted him. And he went forth to meet the knight, having over himself and his horse a satin robe of honor, which had been sent him by the daughter of the Earl of Rhangyr, and in this dress he was not known by any of the host. And they charged each other, and fought all that day until the evening. And neither of them was able to unhorse the other. And so it was the next day; they broke their lances in the shock, but neither of them could obtain the mastery.

And the third day they fought with exceeding strong lances. And they were incensed with rage, and fought furiously, even until noon. And they gave each other such a shock that the girths of their horses were broken, so that they fell over their horses' cruppers to the ground. And they rose up speedily and drew their swords, and resumed the combat. And all they that witnessed their encounter felt assured that they had never before seen two men so valiant or so powerful. And had it been midnight, it would have been light, from the fire that flashed from their weapons. And the knight gave Gawain a blow that turned his helmet from off his face, so that the knight saw that it was Gawain. Then Owain said, "My lord Gawain, I did not know thee for my cousin, owing to the robe of honor that enveloped thee; take my sword and my arms." Said Gawain, "Thou, Owain, art the victor; take thou my sword." And with that Arthur saw that they were conversing, and advanced toward them. "My lord Arthur," said Gawam, "here is Owain who has vanquished me, and will not take my arms." "My lord," said Owain, "it is he that has vanquished me, and he will not take my sword." "Give me your swords," said Arthur, "and then neither of you has vanquished the other." Then Owain put his arms around Arthur's neck, and they embraced. And all the host hurried forward to see Owain, and to embrace him. And there was nigh being a loss of life, so great was the press.

And they retired that night, and the next day Arthur prepared to depart. "My lord," said Owain, "this is not well of thee. For I have been absent from thee these three years, and during all that time, up to this very day, I have been preparing a banquet for thee, knowing that thou wouldst come to seek me. Tarry with me, therefore, until thou and thy attendants have recovered the fatigues of the journey, and have been anointed."

And they all proceeded to the castle of the Countess of the Fountain, and the banquet which had been three years preparing was consumed in three months. Never had they a more delicious or agreeable banquet. And Arthur prepared to depart. Then he sent an embassy to the Countess to beseech her to permit Owain to go with him, for the space of three months, that he might show him to the nobles and the fair dames of the island of Britain. And the Countess gave her consent, although it was very painful to her. So Owain came with Arthur to the island of Britain. And when he was once more amongst his kindred and friends, he remained three years, instead of three months, with them.

THE ADVENTURE OF THE LION

And as Owain one day sat at meat, in the city of Caerleon upon Usk, behold a damsel entered the hall, upon a bay horse, with a curling mane, and covered with foam; and the bridle, and as much as was seen of the saddle, were of gold. And the damsel was arrayed in a dress of yellow satin. And she came up to Owain, and took the ring from off his hand. "Thus," said she, "shall be treated the deceiver, the traitor, the faithless, the disgraced, and the beardless." And she turned her horse's head and departed.

[Footnote: The custom of riding into a hall while the lord and his guests sat at meat might be illustrated by numerous passages of ancient romance and history. But a quotation from Chaucer's beautiful and half-told tale of "Cambuscan" is sufficient:

"And so befell that after the thridde cours,
While that this king sat thus in his nobley,
Herking his minstralles thir thinges play,
Beforne him at his bord deliciously,
In at the halle door all sodenly
Ther came a knight upon a stede of bras,
And in his hond a brod mirrour of glas;
Upon his thombe he had of gold a ring,
And by his side a naked sword hanging;
And up he rideth to the highe bord.
In all the halle ne was ther spoke a word,
For meryaille of this knight; him to behold
Full besily they waiten, young and old."]

Then his adventure came to Owain's remembrance, and he was sorrowful. And having finished eating, he went to his own abode, and made preparations that night. And the next day he arose, but did not go to the court, nor did he return to the Countess of the Fountain, but wandered to the distant parts of the earth and to uncultivated mountains. And he remained there until all his apparel was worn out, and his body was wasted away, and his hair was grown long. And he went about with the wild beasts, and fed with them, until they became familiar with him. But at length he became so weak that he could no longer bear them company. Then he descended from the mountains to the valley, and came to a park, that was the fairest in the world, and belonged to a charitable lady.

One day the lady and her attendants went forth to walk by a lake that was in the middle of the park. And they saw the form of a man, lying as if dead. And they were terrified. Nevertheless they went near him, and touched him, and they saw that there was life in him. And the lady returned to the castle, and took a flask full of precious ointment and gave it to one of her maidens. "Go with this," said she, "and take with thee yonder horse, and clothing, and place them near the man we saw just now; and anoint him with this balsam near his heart; and if there is life in him, he will revive, through the efficiency of this balsam. Then watch what he will do."

And the maiden departed from her, and went and poured of the balsam upon Owain, and left the horse and the garments hard by, and went a little way off and hid herself to watch him. In a short time, she saw him begin to move; and he rose up, and looked at his person, and became ashamed of the unseemliness of his appearance. Then he perceived the horse and the garments that were near him. And he clothed himself, and with difficulty mounted the horse. Then the damsel discovered herself to him, and saluted him. And he and the maiden proceeded to the castle, and the maiden conducted him to a pleasant chamber, and kindled a fire, and left him.

And he stayed at the castle three months, till he was restored to his former guise, and became even more comely than he had ever been before. And Owain rendered signal service to the lady, in a controversy with a powerful neighbor, so that he made ample requital to her for her hospitality; and he took his departure.

And as he journeyed he heard a loud yelling in a wood. And it was repeated a second and a third time. And Owain went towards the spot, and beheld a huge craggy mound, in the middle of the wood, on the side of which was a gray rock. And there was a cleft in the rock, and a serpent was within the cleft. And near the rock stood a black lion, and every time the lion sought to go thence the serpent darted towards him to attack him. And Owain unsheathed his sword, and drew near to the rock; and as the serpent sprung out he struck him with his sword and cut him in two. And he dried his sword, and went on his way as before. But behold the lion followed him, and played about him, as though it had been a greyhound that he had reared.

They proceeded thus throughout the day, until the evening. And when it was time for Owain to take his rest he dismounted, and turned his horse loose in a flat and wooded meadow. And he struck fire, and when the fire was kindled, the lion brought him fuel enough to last for three nights. And the lion disappeared. And presently the lion returned, bearing a fine large roebuck. And he threw it down before Owain, who went towards the fire with it.

And Owain took the roebuck, and skinned it, and placed collops of its flesh upon skewers round the fire. The rest of the buck he gave to the lion to devour. While he was so employed, he heard a deep groan near him, and a second, and a third. And the place whence the groans proceeded was a cave in the rock; and Owain went near, and called out to know who it was that groaned so piteously. And a voice answered, "I am Luned, the hand-maiden of the Countess of the Fountain." "And what dost thou here?" said he. "I am imprisoned," said she, "on account of the knight who came from Arthur's court, and married the Countess. And he staid a short time with her, but he afterwards departed for the court of Arthur, and has not returned since. And two of the Countess's pages traduced him, and called him a deceiver. And because I said I would vouch for it he would come before long and maintain his cause against both of them, they imprisoned me in this cave, and said that I should be put to death, unless he came to deliver me, by a certain day; and that is no further off than to-morrow, and I have no one to send to seek him for me. His name is Owain, the son of Urien." "And art thou certain that if that knight knew all this, he would come to thy rescue?" "I am most certain of it," said she.

When the collops were cooked, Owain divided them into two parts, between himself and the maiden, and then Owain laid himself down to sleep; and never did sentinel keep stricter watch over his lord than the lion that night over Owain.

And the next day there came the two pages with a great troop of attendants to take Luned from her cell, and put her to death. And Owain asked them what charge they had against her. And they told him of the compact that was between them; as the maiden had done the night before. "And," said they, "Owain has failed her, therefore we are taking her to be burnt." "Truly," said Owain, "he is a good knight; and if he knew that the maiden was in such peril, I marvel that he came not to her rescue. But if you will accept me in his stead, I will do battle with you." "We will," said the youth.

And they attacked Owain, and he was hard beset by them. And with that, the lion came to Owain's assistance, and they two got the better of the young men And they said to him, "Chieftain, it was not agreed that we should fight save with thyself alone, and it is harder for us to contend with yonder animal than with thee." And Owain put the lion in the place where Luned had been imprisoned, and blocked up the door with stones. And he went to fight with the young men as before. But Owain had not his usual strength, and the two youths pressed hard upon him. And the lion roared incessantly at seeing Owain in trouble. And he brust through the wall, until he found a way out, and rushed upon the young men and instantly slew them. So Luned was saved from being burned.

Then Owain returned with Luned to the castle of the Lady of the Fountain. And when he went thence, he took the Countess with him to Arthur's court, and she was his wife as long as she lived.

Figure 92: "Androcles and the Lion" by John Dickson Batten

Chapter 5

GERAINT, THE SON OF ERBIN

Arthur was accustomed to hold his court at Caerleon upon Usk. And there he held it seven Easters and five Christmases. And once upon a time he held his court there at Whitsuntide. For Caerleon was the place most easy of access in his dominions, both by sea and by land. And there were assembled nine crowned kings, who were his tributaries, and likewise earls and barons. For they were his invited guests at all the high festivals, unless they were prevented by any great hinderatice. And when he was at Caerleon holding his court, thirteen churches were set apart for mass. And thus they were appointed: one church for Arthur and his kings, and his guests; and the second for Guenever and her ladies; and the third for the steward of the household and the suitors; and the fourth for the Franks and the other officers; and the other nine churches were for the nine masters of the household, and chiefly for Gawain, for he, from the eminence of his warlike fame, and from the nobleness of his birth, was the most exalted of the nine. And there was no other arrangement respecting the churches than that which we have here mentioned.

And on Whit-Tuesday, as the king sat at the banquet, lo, there entered a tall, fair-headed youth, clad in a coat and surcoat of satin, and a golden-hilted sword about his neck, and low shoes of leather upon his feet. And he came and stood before Arthur. "Hail to thee, lord," said he. "Heaven prosper thee," he answered, "and be thou welcome. Dost thou bring any new tidings?" "I do, lord," he said. "I am one of thy foresters, lord, in the forest of Dean, and my name is Madoc, son of Turgadarn. In the forest I saw a stag, the like of which beheld I never yet." "What is there about him," asked Arthur, "that thou never yet didst see his like?" "He is of pure white, lord, and he does not herd with any other animal, through stateliness and pride, so royal is his bearing. And I come to seek thy counsel, lord, and to know thy will concerning him." "It seems best to me," said Arthur, "to go and hunt him to-morrow at break of day, and to cause general notice thereof to be given to-night, in all quarters of the court."

"For Arthur on the Whitsuntide before
Held court at old Caerleon upon Usk.
There on a day, he sitting high in hall,
Before him came a forester of Dean,
Wet from the woods, with notice of a hart
Taller than all his fellows, milky-white,
First seen that day: these things he told the king.
Then the good king gave order to let blow
His horns for hunting on the morrow morn."
—Enid.

And Arryfuerys was Arthur's chief huntsman, and Arelivri his chief page. And all received notice; and thus it was arranged.

Then Guenever said to Arthur, "Wilt thou permit me, lord, to go to-morrow to see and hear the hunt of the stag of which the young man spoke?" "I will gladly," said Arthur. And Gawain said to Arthur, "Lord, if it seem well to thee, permit that into whose hunt soever the stag shall come, that one, be he a knight or one on foot, may cut off his head, and give it to whom he pleases, whether to his

Figure 93: "Went Along" by Arthur Rackham

own lady-love, or to the lady of his friend." "I grant it gladly," said Arthur, "and let the steward of the household be chastised, if all things are not ready to-morrow for the chase."

And they passed the night with songs, and diversions, and discourse, and ample entertainment. And when it was time for them all to go to sleep, they went. And when the next day came, they arose. And Arthur called the attendants who guarded his couch. And there were four pages whose names were Cadyrnerth, the son of Gandwy, and Ambreu, the son of Bedwor and Amhar, the son of Arthur and Goreu, the son of Custennin. And these men came to Arthur and saluted him, and arrayed him in his garments. And Arthur wondered that Guenever did not awake, and the attendants wished to awaken her. "Disturb her not," said Arthur, "for she had rather sleep than go to see the hunting."

Then Arthur went forth, and he heard two horns sounding, one from near the lodging of the chief huntsman, and the other from near that of the chief page. And the whole assembly of the multitudes came to Arthur, and they took the road to the forest.

And after Arthur had gone forth from the palace, Guenever awoke, and called to her maidens, and apparalled herself. "Maidens," said she, "I had leave last night to go and see the hunt. Go one of you to the stable, and order hither a horse such as a woman may ride." And one of them went, and she found but two horses in the stable; and Guenever and one of her maidens mounted them, and went through the Usk, and followed the track of the men and the horses. And as they rode thus, they heard a loud and rushing sound; and they looked behind them, and beheld a knight upon a hunter foal of mighty size. And the rider was a fairhaired youth, bare-legged, and of princely mien; and a golden-hilted sword was at his side, and a robe and a surcoat of satin were upon him, and two low shoes of leather upon his feet; and around him was a scarf of blue purple, at each corner of which was a golden apple.

"For Prince Geraint,
Late also, wearing neither hunting-dress
Nor weapon, save a golden-hilted brand,
Came quickly flashing through the shallow ford."
—Enid.

And his horse stepped stately, and swift, and proud; and he overtook Guenever, and saluted her. "Heaven prosper thee, Geraint," said she; "and why didst thou not go with thy lord to hunt?" "Because I knew not when he went," said he. "I marvel too," said she, "how he could go, unknown to me. But thou, O young man, art the most agreeable companion I could have in the whole kingdom; and it may be I shall be more amused with the hunting than they; for we shall hear the horns when they sound and we shall hear the dogs when they are let loose and begin to cry."

So they went to the edge of the forest, and there they stood. "From this place," said she, "we shall hear when the dogs are let loose." And thereupon they heard a loud noise; and they looked towards the spot whence it came, and they beheld a dwarf riding upon a horse, stately and foaming and prancing and strong and spirited. And in the hand of the dwarf was a whip. And near the dwarf they saw a lady upon a beautiful white horse, of steady and stately pace; and she was clothed in a garment of gold brocade. And near her was a knight upon a war-horse of large size, with heavy and bright armor both upon himself and upon his horse. And truly they never before saw a knight, or a horse, or armor, of such remarkable size.

"Geraint," said Guenever, "knowest thou the name of that tall knight yonder?" "I know him not," said he, "and the strange armor that he wears prevents my either seeing his face or his features." "Go, maiden," said Guenever, "and ask the dwarf who that knight is." Then the maiden went up to the dwarf; and she inquired of the dwarf who the knight was. "I will not tell thee," he answered. "Since thou art so churlish," said she, "I will ask him, himself." "Thou shalt not ask him, by my faith," said he. "Wherefore not?" said she. "Because thou art not of honor sufficient to befit thee to speak to my lord." Then the maiden turned her horse's head towards the knight, upon which the dwarf struck her with the whip that was in his hand across the face and the eyes, so that the blood flowed forth. And the maiden returned to Guenever, complaining of the hurt she had received. "Very rudely has the dwarf treated thee," said Geraint, and he put his hand upon the hilt of his sword. But he took counsel with himself, and considered that it would be no vengeance for him to slay the dwarf, and to be attacked unarmed by the armed knight; so he refrained.

"Lady," said he, "I will follow him, with thy permission, and at last he will come to some inhabited place, where I may have arms, either as a loan or for a pledge, so that I may encounter the knight." "Go," said she, "and do not attack him until thou hast good arms; and I shall be very anxious concerning thee, until I hear tidings of thee." "If I am alive," said he, "thou shalt hear tidings of me by to-morrow afternoon;" and with that he departed.

And the road they took was below the palace of Caerleon, and across the ford of the Usk; and they went along a fair and even and lofty ridge of ground, until they came to a town, and at the extremity of the town they saw a fortress and a castle. And as the knight passed through the town all the people arose and saluted him, and bade him welcome. And when Geraint came into the town, he looked at every house to see if he knew any of those whom he saw. But he knew none, and none knew him, to do him the kindness to let him have arms, either as a loan or for a pledge. And every house he saw was full of men, and arms, and horses. And they were polishing shields, and burnishing swords, and washing armor, and shoeing horses. And the knight and the lady and the dwarf rode up to the castle, that was in the town, and every one was glad in the castle. And from the battlements and the gates they risked their necks, through their eagerness to greet them, and to show their joy.

Geraint stood there to see whether the knight would remain in the castle; and when he was certain that he would do so, he looked around him. And at a little distance from the town he saw an old palace in ruins, wherein was a hall that was falling to decay.

"And high above a piece of turret-stair,
Worn by the feet that now were silent, wound
Bare to the sun"
—Enid.

And as he knew not any one in the town, he went towards the old palace. And when he came near to the palace, he saw a hoary-headed man, standing by it, in tattered garments. And Geraint gazed steadfastly upon him. Then the hoary-headed man said to him, "Young man, wherefore art thou thoughtful?" "I am thoughtful," said he, "because I know not where to pass the night." "Wilt thou come forward this way, chieftain," said he, "and thou shalt have of the best that can be procured for thee." So Geraint went forward. And the hoary-headed man led the way into the hall. And in the hall he dismounted, and he left there his horse. Then he went on to the upper chamber with the hoary-headed man. And in the chamber he beheld an old woman, sitting on a cushion, with old, worn-out garments upon her; yet it seemed to him that she must have been comely when in the bloom of youth. And beside her was a maiden, upon whom were a vest and a veil that were old and beginning to be worn out. And truly he never saw a maiden more full of comeliness and grace and beauty than she. And the hoary- headed man said to the maiden, "There is no attendant for the horse of this youth but thyself." "I will render the best service I am able," said she, "both to him and to his horse." And the maiden disarrayed the youth, and then she furnished his horse with straw and corn; and then she returned to the chamber. And the hoary-headed man said to the maiden, "Go to the town and bring hither the best that thou canst find, both of food and of liquor." "I will gladly, lord," said she. And to the town went the maiden. And they conversed together while the maiden was at the town. And, behold, the maiden came back, and a youth with her, bearing on his back a costrel full of good purchased mead, and a quarter of a young bullock. And in the hands of the maiden was a quantity of white bread, and she had some manchet bread in her veil, and she came into the chamber. "I would not obtain better than this," said she, "nor with better should I have been trusted." "It is good enough," said Geraint. And they caused the meat to be boiled; and when their food was ready, they sat down. And it was in this wise. Geraint sat between the hoary-headed man and his wife, and the maiden served them. And they ate and drank.

And when they had finished eating, Geraint talked with the hoary- headed man, and he asked him in the first place to whom belonged the palace that he was in. "Truly," said he, "it was I that built it, and to me also belonged the city and the castle which thou sawest." "Alas!" said Geraint, "how is it that thou hast lost them now?" "I lost a great earldom as well as these," said he, "and this is how I lost them. I had a nephew, the son of my brother, and I took care of his possessions; but he was impatient to enter upon them, so he made war upon me, and wrested from me not only his own, but also my estates, except this castle." "Good sir," said Geraint, "wilt thou tell me wherefore came the knight and the lady and the dwarf just now into the town, and what is the preparation which I saw, and the putting of arms in order?" "I will do so," said he. "The preparations are for the game that is to be held to-morrow by the young earl, which will be on this wise. In the midst of a meadow which is here, two forks will be set up, and upon the two forks a silver rod, and upon the silver rod a sparrow-hawk, and for the sparrow-hawk there will be a tournament. And to the tournament will go all the array thou didst see in the city, of men and of horses and of arms. And with each man will go the lady he loves best; and no man can joust for the sparrow-hawk, except the lady he loves best be with him. And the knight that thou sawest has gained the sparrow-hawk these two years; and if he gains it the third year, he will be called the Knight of the Sparrow-hawk from that time forth." "Sir," said Geraint, "what is thy counsel to me concerning this knight, on account of the insult which the maiden of Guenever received from the dwarf?" And Geraint told the hoary-headed man what the insult was that the maiden had received. "It is not easy to counsel thee, inasmuch as thou hast neither dame nor maiden belonging to thee, for whom thou canst joust. Yet I have arms here, which thou couldst have, and there is my horse also, if he seem to thee better than thine own." "Ah, sir," said he, "Heaven reward thee! But my own horse to which I am accustomed, together with thine arms, will suffice me. And if, when the appointed time shall come to-morrow thou wilt permit me, sir, to challenge for yonder maiden that is thy daughter, I will engage, if I escape from the tournament, to love the maiden as long as I live." "Gladly will I permit thee," said the hoary-headed man; "and since thou dost thus resolve, it is necessary that thy horse and arms should be ready to-morrow at break of day. For then the Knight of the Sparrow-hawk will make proclamation, and ask the lady he loves best to take the sparrow-hawk; and if any deny it to her, by force will he defend her claim. And therefore," said the hoary-headed man, "it is needful for thee to be there at daybreak, and we three will be with thee." And thus was it settled.

And at night they went to sleep. And before the dawn they arose and arrayed themselves; and by the time that it was day, they were all four in the meadow. And there was the Knight of the Sparrow- hawk making the proclamation, and asking his lady-love to take the sparrow-hawk. "Take it not," said Geraint, "for here is a maiden who is fairer, and more noble, and more comely, and who has a better claim to it than thou." Then said the knight, "If thou maintainest the sparrow-hawk to be due to her, come forward and do battle with me." And Geraint went forward to the top of the meadow, having upon himself and upon his horse armor which was heavy and rusty, and of uncouth shape. Then they encountered each other, and they broke a set of lances; and they broke a second set, and a third. And when the earl and his company saw the Knight of the Sparrow-hawk gaining the mastery, there was shouting and joy and mirth amongst them; and the hoary-headed man and his wife and his daughter were sorrowful. And the hoary-headed man served Geraint with lances as often as he broke them, and the dwarf served the Knight of the Sparrow-hawk. Then the hoary-headed man said to Geraint, "O chieftain, since no other will hold with thee, behold, here is the lance which was in my hand on the day when I received the honor of knighthood, and from that time to this I never broke it, and it has an excellent point." Then Geraint took the lance, thanking the hoary-headed man. And thereupon the dwarf also brought a lance to his lord. "Behold, here is a lance for thee, not less good than his," said the dwarf. "And bethink thee that no knight ever withstood thee so long as this one has done." "I declare to Heaven," said Geraint, "that unless death takes me quickly hence, he shall fare never the better for thy service." And Geraint pricked his horse towards him from afar, and, warning him, he rushed upon him, and gave him a blow so severe, and furious, and fierce, upon the face of his shield, that he cleft it in two, and broke his armor, and burst his girths, so that both he and his saddle were borne to the ground over the horse's crupper. And Geraint dismounted quickly. And he was wroth, and he drew his sword, and rushed fiercely upon him. Then the knight also arose, and drew his sword against Geraint. And they fought on foot with their swords until their arms struck sparks of fire like stars from one another; and thus they continued fighting until the blood and sweat obscured the light from their eyes. At length Geraint called to him all his strength, and struck the knight upon the crown of his head, so that he broke all his head-armor, and cut through all the flesh and the skin, even to the skull, until he wounded the bone.

Then the knight fell upon his knees, and cast his sword from his hand, and besought mercy from Geraint. "Of a truth," said he, "I relinquish my overdaring and my pride, and crave thy mercy; and unless I have time to commit myself to Heaven for my sins, and to talk with a priest, thy mercy will avail me little." "I will grant thee grace upon this condition," said Geraint, "that thou go to Guenever, the wife of Arthur, to do her satisfaction for the insult which her maiden received from thy dwarf. Dismount not from the time thou goest hence until thou comest into the presence of Guenever, to make her what atonement shall be adjudged at the court of Arthur." "This will I do gladly; and who art thou?" "I am Geraint, the son of Erbin; and declare thou also who thou art." "I am Edeym, the son of Nudd." Then he threw himself upon his horse, and went forward to Arthur's court; and the lady he loved best went before him, and the dwarf, with much lamentation.

Then came the young earl and his hosts to Geraint, and saluted him, and bade him to his castle. "I may not go," said Geraint; "but where I was last night, there will I be to-night also." "Since thou wilt none of my inviting, thou shalt have abundance of all that I can command for thee; and I will order ointment for thee, to recover thee from thy fatigues, and from the weariness that is upon thee." "Heaven reward thee," said Geraint, "and I will go to my lodging." And thus went Geraint and Earl Ynywl, and his wife and his daughter. And when they reached the old mansion, the household servants and attendants of the young earl had arrived, and had arranged all the apartments, dressing them with straw and with fire; and in a short time the ointment was ready, and Geraint came there, and they washed his head. Then came the young earl, with forty honorable knights from among his attendants, and those who were bidden to the tournament. And Geraint came from the anointing. And the earl asked him to go to the hall to eat. "Where is the Earl Ynywl," said Geraint, "and his wife and his daughter?" "They are in the chamber yonder," said the earl's chamberlain, "arraying themselves in garments which the earl has caused to be brought for them." "Let not the damsel array herself," said he, "except in her vest and her veil, until she come to the court of Arthur, to be clad by Guenever in such garments as she may choose." So the maiden did not array herself.

Figure 94: "Queen Guinevere" by William Morris

Then they all entered the hall, and they washed, and sat down to meat. And thus were they seated. On one side of Geraint sat the young earl, and Earl Ynywl beyond him, and on the other side of Geraint was the maiden and her mother. And after these all sat according to their precedence in honor. And they ate. And they were served abundantly, and they received a profusion of divers kinds of gifts. Then they conversed together. And the young earl invited Geraint to visit him next day. "I will not, by Heaven," said Geraint. "To the court of Arthur will I go with this maiden to-morrow. And it is enough for me, as long as Earl Ynywl is in poverty and trouble; and I go chiefly to seek to add to his maintenance." "Ah, chieftain," said the young earl, "it is not by my fault that Earl Ynywl is without his possessions." "By my faith," said Geraint, "he shall not remain without them, unless death quickly takes me hence." "O chieftain," said he, "with regard to the disagreement between me and Ynywl, I will gladly abide by thy counsel, and agree to what thou mayest judge right between us." "I but ask thee," said Geraint, "to restore to him what is his, and what he should have received from the time he lost his possessions even until this day." "That will I do, gladly, for thee," answered he. "Then," said Geraint, "whosoever is here who owes homage to Ynywl, let him come forward, and perform it on the spot." And all the men did so; and by that treaty they abided. And his castle and his town, and all his possessions, were restored to Ynywl. And he received back all that he had lost, even to the smallest jewel.

Then spoke Earl Ynywl to Geraint. "Chieftain," said he, "behold the maiden for whom thou didst challenge at the tournament; I bestow her upon thee." "She shall go with me," said Geraint, "to the court of Arthur, and Arthur and Guenever, they shall dispose of her as they will." And the next day they proceeded to Arthur's court. So far concerning Geraint.

Chapter 6

GERAINT, THE SON OF ERBIN (CONTINUED)

Now this is how Arthur hunted the stag. The men and the dogs were divided into hunting-parties, and the dogs were let loose upon the stag. And the last dog that was let loose was the favorite dog of Arthur; Cavall was his name. And he left all the other dogs behind him and turned the stag. And at the second turn the stag came toward the hunting-party of Arthur. And Arthur set upon him; and before he could be slain by any other, Arthur cut off his head. Then they sounded the death-horn for slaying and they all gathered round.

They came Kadyriath to Arthur and spoke to him. "Lord," said he, "behold, yonder is Guenever, and none with her save only one maiden." "Command Gildas, the son of Caw, and all the scholars of the court," said Arthur, "to attend Guenever to the palace." And they did so.

Then they all set forth, holding converse together concerning the head of the stag, to whom it should be given. One wished that it should be given to the lady best beloved by him, and another to the lady whom he loved best. And so they came to the palace. And when Arthur and Guenever heard them disputing about the head of the stag, Guenever said to Arthur: "My lord, this is my counsel concerning the stag's head; let it not be given away until Geraint, the son of Erbin, shall return from the errand he is upon." And Guenever told Arthur what that errand was. "Right gladly shall it be so," said Arthur. And Guenever caused a watch to be set upon the ramparts for Geraint's coming. And after midday they beheld an unshapely little man upon a horse, and after him a dame or a damsel, also on horseback, and after her a knight of large stature, bowed down, and hanging his head low and sorrowfully, and clad in broken and worthless armor.

And before they came near to the gate one of the watch went to Guenever, and told her what kind of people they saw, and what aspect they bore. "I know not who they are," said he, "But I know," said Guenever; "this is the knight whom Geraint pursued, and methinks that he comes not here by his own free will. But Geraint has overtaken him, and avenged the insult to the maiden to the uttermost." And thereupon, behold, a porter came to the spot where Guenever was. "Lady," said he, "at the gate there is a knight, and I saw never a man of so pitiful an aspect to look upon as he. Miserable and broken is the armor that he wears, and the hue of blood is more conspicuous upon it than its own color." "Knowest thou his name?" said she. "I do," said he; "he tells me that he is Edeyrn, the son of Nudd." Then she replied, "I know him not."

So Guenever went to the gate to meet him and he entered. And Guenever was sorry when she saw the condition he was in, even though he was accompanied by the churlish dwarf. Then Edeyrn saluted Guenever. "Heaven protect thee," said she. "Lady," said he, "Geraint, the son of Erbin, thy best and most valiant servant, greets thee." "Did he meet with thee?" she asked. "Yes," said he, "and it was not to my advantage; and that was not his fault, but mine, lady. And Geraint greets thee well; and in greeting thee he compelled me to come hither to do thy pleasure for the insult which thy maiden received from the dwarf." "Now where did he overtake thee?" "At the place where we were jousting and contending for the sparrow-hawk, in the town which is now called Cardiff. And it was for the avouchment of the love of the maiden, the daughter of Earl Ynywl, that Geraint jousted at the tournament. And thereupon we encountered each other, and he left me, lady, as thou seest." "Sir," said she, "when thinkest thou that Geraint will be here?" "To-morrow, lady, I think he will be here with the maiden."

Then Arthur came to them. And he saluted Arthur, and Arthur gazed a long time upon him and was amazed to see him thus. And thinking that he knew him, he inquired of him, "Art thou Edeyrn, the son of Nudd?" "I am, lord," said he, "and I have met with much trouble and received wounds unsupportable." Then he told Arthur all his adventure. "Well," said Arthur, "from what I hear it behooves Guenever to be merciful towards thee." "The mercy which thou desirest, lord," said she. "will I grant to him, since it is as insulting to thee that an insult should be offered to me as to thyself." "Thus will it be best to do," said Arthur; "let this man have medical care until it be known whether he may live. And if he live, he shall do such satisfaction as shall be judged best by the men of the court. And if he die, too much will be the death of such a youth as Edeyrn for an insult to a maiden." "This pleases me," said Guenever. And Arthur caused Morgan Tud to be called to him. He was the chief physician. "Take with thee Edeyrn, the son of Nudd, and cause a chamber to be prepared for him, and let him have the aid of medicine as thou wouldst do unto myself, if I were wounded, and let none into his chamber to molest him, but thyself and thy disciples, to administer to him remedies." "I will do so, gladly, lord," said Morgan Tud. Then said the steward of the household, "Whither is it right, lord, to order the maiden?" "To Guenever and her handmaidens," said he. And the steward of the household so ordered her.

"And rising up, he rode to Arthur's court,
And there the queen forgave him easily.
And being young, he changed himself, and grew
To hate the sin that seem'd so like his own
Of Modred, Arthur's nephew, and fell at last
In the great battle fighting for the king."
—Enid.

The next day came Geraint towards the court; and there was a watch set on the ramparts by Guenever, lest he should arrive unawares. And one of the watch came to Guenever. "Lady," said he, "methinks that I see Geraint, and a maiden with him. He is on horseback, but he has his walking gear upon him, and the maiden appears to be in white, seeming to be clad in a garment of linen." "Assemble all the women," said Guenever, "and come to meet Geraint, to welcome him, and wish him joy." And Guenever went to meet Geraint and the maiden. And when Geraint came to the place where Guenever was, he saluted her. "Heaven prosper thee," said she, "and welcome to thee." "Lady," said he, "I earnestly desired to obtain thee satisfaction, according to thy will; and, behold, here is the maiden through whom thou hadst thy revenge." "Verily," said Guenever, "the welcome of Heaven be unto her; and it is fitting that we should receive her joyfully." Then they went in and dismounted. And Geraint came to where Arthur was, and saluted him. "Heaven protect thee," said Arthur, "and the welcome of Heaven be unto thee. And inasmuch as thou hast vanquished Edeyrn, the son of Nudd, thou hast had a prosperous career." "Not upon me be the blame," said Geraint; "it was through the arrogance of Edeyrn, the son of Nudd, himself, that we were not friends." "Now," said Arthur, "where is the maiden for whom I heard thou didst give challenge?" "She is gone with Guenever to her chamber." Then went Arthur to see the maiden. And Arthur, and all his companions, and his whole court, were glad concerning the maiden. And certain were they all, that, had her array been suitable to her beauty, they had never seen a maid fairer than she. And Arthur gave away the maiden to Geraint. And the usual bond made between two persons was made between Geraint and the maiden, and the choicest of all Guenever's apparel was given to the maiden; and thus arrayed, she appeared comely and graceful to all who beheld her. And that day and the night were spent in abundance of minstrelsy, and ample gifts of liquor, and a multiude of games. And when it was time for them to go to sleep they went. And in the chamber where the couch of Arthur and Guenever was, the couch of Geraint and Enid was prepared. And from that time she became his wife. And the next day Arthur satisfied all the claimants upon Geraint with bountiful gifts. And the maiden took up her abode in the palace, and she had many companions, both men and women, and there was no maiden more esteemed than she in the island of Britain.

Then spake Guenever. "Rightly did I judge," said she, "concerning the head of the stag, that it should not be

Figure 95: "Sir Geraint and Lady Enid in the deserted Roman town" by Walter Crane

given to any until Geraint's return; and behold, here is a fit occasion for bestowing it. Let it be given to Enid, the daughter of Ynywl, the most illustrious maiden. And I do not believe that any will begrudge it her, for between her and every one here there exists nothing but love and friendship." Much applauded was this by them all, and by Arthur also. And the head of the stag was given to Enid. And thereupon her fame increased, and her friends became more in number than before. And Geraint from that time forth loved the hunt, and the tournament, and hard encounters; and he came victorious from them all. And a year, and a second, and a third, he proceeded thus, until his fame had flown over the face of the kingdom.

And, once upon a time, Arthur was holding his court at Caerleon upon Usk; and behold, there came to him ambassadors, wise and prudent, full of knowledge and eloquent of speech, and they saluted Arthur. "Heaven prosper you!" said Arthur; "and whence do you come?" "We come, lord," said they, "from Cornwall; and we are ambassadors from Erbin, the son of Custennin, thy uncle, and our mission is unto thee. And he greets thee well, as an uncle should greet his nephew, and as a vassal should greet his lord. And he represents unto thee that he waxes heavy and feeble, and is advancing in years. And the neighboring chiefs, knowing this, grow insolent towards him, and covet his land and possessions. And he earnestly beseeches thee, lord, to permit Geraint, his son, to return to him, to protect his possessions, and to become acquainted with his boundaries. And unto him he represents that it were better for him to spend the flower of his youth and the prime of his age in preserving his own boundaries, than in tournaments which are productive of no profit, although he obtains glory in them."

Figure 96: "King Arthur" by Arthur Rackham

"Well," said Arthur, "go and divest yourselves of your accoutrements, and take food, and refresh yourselves after your fatigues; and before you go from hence you shall have an answer." And they went to eat. And Arthur considered that it would go hard with him to let Geraint depart from him, and from his court; neither did he think it fair that his cousin should be restrained from going to protect his dominions and his boundaries, seeing that his father was unable to do so. No less was the grief and regret of Guenever, and all her women, and all her damsels, through fear that the maiden would leave them. And that day and that night were spent in abundance of feasting. And Arthur told Geraint the cause of the mission, and of the coming of the ambassadors to him out of Cornwall. "Truly," said Geraint, "be it to my advantage or disadvantage, lord, I will do according to thy will concerning this embassy." "Behold," said Arthur, "though it grieves me to part with thee, it is my counsel that thou go to dwell in thine own dominions, and to defend thy boundaries, and take with thee to accompany thee as many as thou wilt of those thou lovest best among my faithful ones, and among thy friends, and among thy companions in arms." "Heaven reward thee! and this will I do," said Geraint. "What discourse," said Guenever, "do I hear between you? Is it of those who are to conduct Geraint to his country?" "It is," said Arthur. "Then is it needful for me to consider," said she, "concerning companions and a provision for the lady that is with me." "Thou wilt do well," said Arthur.

And that night they went to sleep. And the next day the ambassadors were permitted to depart, and they were told that Geraint should follow them. And on the third day Geraint set forth, and many went with him—Gawain, the son of Gwyar, and Riogoned, the son of the king of

Figure 97: "Geriant and Enid" by Louis Rhead

Ireland, and Ondyaw, the son of the Duke of Burgundy, Gwilim, the son of the ruler of the Franks, Howel, the son of the Earl of Brittany, Perceval, the son of Evrawk, Gwyr, a judge in the court of Arthur, Bedwyr, the son of Bedrawd, Kai, the son of Kyner, Odyar, the Frank, and Ederyn, the son of Nudd. Said Geraint, "I think I shall have enough of knighthood with me." And they set forth. And never was there seen a fairer host journeying towards the Severn. And on the other side of the Severn were the nobles of Erbin, the son of Custennin, and his foster-father at their head, to welcome Geraint with gladness; and many of the women of the court, with his mother, came to receive Enid, the daughter of Ynywl, his wife. And there was great rejoicing and gladness throughout the whole court, and through all the country, concerning Geraint, because of the greatness of their love to him, and of the greatness of the fame which he had gained since he went from amongst them, and because he was come to take possession of his dominions, and to preserve his boundaries. And they came to the court. And in the court they had ample entertainment, and a multitude of gifts, and abundance of liquor, and a sufficiency of service, and a variety of games. And to do honor to Geraint, all the chief men of the country were invited that night to visit him. And they passed that day and that night in the utmost enjoyment. And at dawn next day Erbin arose and summoned to him Geraint, and the noble persons who had borne him company. And he said to Geraint: "I am a feeble and an aged man, and whilst I was able to maintain the dominion for thee and for myself, I did so. But thou art young, and in the flower of thy vigor and of thy youth. Henceforth do thou preserve thy possessions." "Truly," said Geraint, "with my consent thou shalt not give the power over thy dominions at this time into my hands, and thou shalt not take me from Arthur's court." "Into thy hands will I give them," said Erbin, "and this day also shalt thou receive the homage of thy subjects."

Then said Gawain, "It were better for thee to satisfy those who have boons to ask, to-day, and to-morrow thou canst receive the homage of thy dominions." So all that had boons to ask were summoned into one place. And Kadyriath came to them to know what were their requests. And every one asked that which he desired. And the followers of Arthur began to make gifts, and immediately the men of Cornwall came, and gave also. And they were not long in giving, so eager was every one to bestow gifts, and of those who came to ask gifts, none departed unsatisfied. And that day and that night were spent in the utmost enjoyment.

And the next day at dawn, Erbin desired Geraint to send messengers to the men to ask them whether it was displeasing to them that he should come to receive their homage, and whether they had anything to object to him. Then Geraint sent ambassadors to the men of Cornwall to ask them this. And they all said that it would be the fulness of joy and honor to them for Geraint to come and receive their homage. So he received the homage of such as were there. And the day after the followers of Arthur intended to go away. "It is too soon for you to go away yet," said he; "stay with me until I have finished receiving the homage of my chief men, who have agreed to come to me." And they remained with him until he had done so. Then they set forth towards the court of Arthur. And Geraint went to bear them company, and Enid also, as far as Diganwy; there they parted. And Ondyaw, the son of the Duke of Burgundy, said to Geraint, "Go, now, and visit the uttermost parts of thy dominions, and see well to the boundaries of thy territories; and if thou hast any trouble respecting them, send unto thy companions." "Heaven reward thee!" said Geraint; "and this will I do." And Geraint journeyed to the uttermost parts of his dominions. And experienced guides, and the chief men of his country, went with him. And the furthermost point that they showed him he kept possession of.

Chapter 7

GERAINT, THE SON OF ERBIN (CONTINUED)

Geraint, as he had been used to do when he was at Arthur's court, frequented tournaments. And he became acquainted with valiant and mighty men, until he had gained as much fame there as he had formerly done elsewhere. And he enriched his court, and his companions, and his nobles, with the best horses and the best arms, and with the best and most valuable jewels, and he ceased not until his fame had flown over the face of the whole kingdom.

"Before Geraint, the scourge of the enemy,
I saw steeds white with foam,
And after the shout of battle a fearful torrent."
—Hen.

When he knew that it was thus, he began to love ease and pleasure, for there was no one who was worth his opposing. And he loved his wife, and liked to continue in the palace with minstrelsy and diversions. So he began to shut himself up in the chamber of his wife, and he took no delight in anything besides, insomuch that he gave up the friendship of his nobles, together with his hunting and his amusements, and lost the hearts of all the host in his court. And there was murmuring and scoffing concerning him among the inhabitants of the palace, on account of his relinquishing so completely their companionship for the love of his wife.

"They
Began to scoff and jeer and babble of him
As of a prince whose manhood was all gone,
And molten down in mere uxoriousness."

These tidings came to Erbin. And when Erbin had heard these things, he spoke unto Enid, and inquired of her whether it was she that had caused Geraint to act thus, and to forsake his people and his hosts. "Not I, by my confession unto Heaven," said she; "there is nothing more hateful unto me than this." And she knew not what she should do, for, although it was hard for her to own this to Geraint, yet was it not more easy for her to listen to what she heard, without warning Geraint concerning it. And she was very sorrowful.

One morning in the summer-time they were upon their couch, and Geraint lay upon the edge of it. And Enid was without sleep in the apartment, which had windows of glass; [Footnote: The terms of admiration in which the older writers invariably speak of GLASS WINDOWS would be sufficient proof, if other evidence were wanting, how rare an article of luxury they were in the houses of our ancestors. They were first introduced in ecclesiastical architecture, to which they were for a long time confined. Glass is said not to have been employed in domestic architecture before the fourteenth century.] and the sun shone upon the couch. And the clothes had slipped from off his arms and his breast, and he was asleep. Then she gazed upon the marvellous beauty of his appearance, and she said, "Alas! and am I the cause that these arms and this breast have lost their glory, and the warlike fame which they once so richly enjoyed!" As she said this the tears dropped from her eyes, and they fell upon his breast. And the tears she shed and the words she had spoken, awoke him. And another thing contributed to awaken him, and that was the idea that it was not in thinking of him that she spoke thus, but that it was because she loved some other man more than him, and that she wished for other society. Thereupon Geraint was troubled in his mind, and he called his squire; and when he came to him, "Go quickly," said he, "and prepare my horse and my arms, and make them ready. And do thou rise," said he to Enid, "and apparel thyself; and cause thy horse to be accoutred, and clothe thee in the worst riding-dress that thou hast in thy possession. And evil betide me," said he, "if thou returnest here until thou knowest whether I have lost my strength so completely as thou didst say. And if it be so, it will then be easy for thee to seek the society thou didst wish for of him of whom thou wast thinking." So she arose, and clothed herself in her meanest garments. "I know nothing, lord," said she, "of thy meaning." "Neither wilt thou know at this time," said he.

Then Geraint went to see Erbin. "Sir," said he, "I am going upon a quest, and I am not certain when I may come back. Take heed, therefore, unto thy possessions until my return." "I will do so," said he; "but it is strange to me that thou shouldst go so suddenly. And who will proceed with thee, since thou art not strong enough to traverse the land of Loegyr alone?" "But one person only will go with me." "Heaven counsel thee, my son," said Erbin, "and may many attach themselves to thee in Loegyr." Then went Geraint to the place where his horse was, and it was equipped with foreign armor, heavy and shining. And he desired Enid to mount her horse, and to ride forward, and to keep a long way before him. "And whatever thou mayst see, and whatever thou mayst hear concerning me," said he, "do thou not turn back. And unless I speak unto thee, say not thou one word, either." So they set forward. And he did not choose the pleasantest and most frequented road, but that which was the wildest and most beset by thieves and robbers and venomous animals.

And they came to a high road, which they followed till they saw a vast forest; and they saw four armed horsemen come forth from the forest. When the armed men saw them, they said one to another. "Here is a good occasion for us to capture two horses and armor, and a lady likewise; for this we shall have no difficulty in doing against yonder single knight who hangs his head so pensively and heavily." Enid heard this discourse, and she knew not what she should do through fear of Geraint, who had told her to be silent. "The vengeance of Heaven be upon me," said she, "if I would not rather receive my death from his hand than from the hand of any other; and though he should slay me, yet will I speak to him, lest I should have the misery to witness his death." So she waited for Geraint until he came near to her. "Lord," said she, "didst thou hear the words of those men concerning thee?" Then he lifted up his eyes, and looked at her angrily. "Thou hadst only," said he, "to hold thy peace as I bade thee. I wish but for silence, and not for warning. And though thou shouldst desire to see my defeat and my death by the hands of those men, yet do I feel no dread." Then the foremost of them couched his lance, and rushed upon Geraint. And he received him, and that not feebly. But he let the thrust go by him, while he struck the horseman upon the centre of his shield, in such a manner that his shield was split, and his armor broken, so that a cubit's length of the shaft of Geraint's lance passed through his body, and sent him to the earth, the length of the lance over his horse's crupper. Then the second horseman attacked him furiously, being wroth at the death of his companion. But with one thrust Geraint overthrew him also, and killed him as he had done the other. Then the third set upon him, and he killed him in like manner. And thus also he slew the

Figure 98: "Geriant and Enid Ride Away" by Gustave Dore

fourth. Sad and sorrowful was the maiden as she saw all this. Geraint dismounted his horse, and took the arms of the men he had slain, and placed them upon their saddles, and tied together the reins of their horses; and he mounted his horse again. "Behold what thou must do," said he; "take the four horses and drive them before thee, and proceed forward as I bade thee just now. And say not one word unto me, unless I speak first unto thee. And I declare unto Heaven," said he, "if thou doest not thus, it will be to thy cost." "I will do as far as I can, lord," said she, "according to thy desire."

So the maiden went forward, keeping in advance of Geraint, as he had desired her; and it grieved him as much as his wrath would permit, to see a maiden so illustrious as she having so much trouble with the care of the horses. Then they reached a wood, and it was both deep and vast, and in the wood night overtook them. "Ah, maiden," said he, "it is vain to attempt proceeding forward." "Well, lord," said she, "whatever thou wishest, we will do." "It will be best for us," he answered, "to rest and wait for the day, in order to pursue our journey." "That we will, gladly," said she. And they did so. Having dismounted himself, he took her down from her horse. "I cannot by any means refrain from sleep, through weariness," said he;

"do thou therefore watch the horses, and sleep not." "I will, lord," said she. Then he went to sleep in his armor, and thus passed the night, which was not long at that season. And when she saw the dawn of day appear, she looked around her to see if he were waking, and thereupon he woke. Then he arose, and said unto her, "Take the horses and ride on, and keep straight on as thou didst yesterday." And they left the wood, and they came to an open country, with meadows on one hand, and mowers mowing the meadows. And there was a river before them, and the horses bent down and drank of the water. And they went up out of the river by a lofty steep; and there they met a slender stripling with a satchel about his neck, and they saw that there was something in the satchel, but they knew not what it was. And he had a small blue pitcher in his hand, and a bowl on the mouth of the pitcher. And the youth saluted Geraint. "Heaven prosper thee!" said Geraint; "and whence dost thou come?" "I come," said he, "from the city that lies before thee. My lord," he added, "will it be displeasing to thee if I ask whence thou comest also?" "By no means; through yonder wood did I come." "Thou camest not through the wood to-day." "No," he replied, "we were in the wood last night." "I warrant," said the youth, "that thy condition there last night was not the most pleasant, and that thou hadst neither meat nor drink." "No, by my faith," said he. "Wilt thou follow my counsel," said the youth, "and take thy meal from me?" "What sort of meal?" he inquired. "The breakfast which is sent for yonder mowers, nothing less than bread and meat and wine, and if thou wilt, sir, they shall have none of it." "I will," said he, "and Heaven reward thee for it."

"as thou sayest." Thereupon the man of the house came to Geraint and welcomed him. And after they had eaten and drank, Geraint went to sleep, and so did Enid also.

In the evening, behold, the earl came to visit Geraint, and his twelve honorable knights with him. And Geraint rose up and welcomed him. Then they all sat down according to their precedence in honor. And the earl conversed with Geraint, and inquired of him the object of his journey. "I have none," he replied, "but to seek adventures and to follow mine own inclination." Then the earl cast his eye upon Enid, and he looked at her steadfastly. And he thought he had never seen a maiden fairer or more comely than she. And he set all his thoughts

So Geraint alighted, and the youth took the maiden from off her horse. Then they washed, and took their repast. And the youth cut the bread in slices, and gave them drink, and served them withal. And when they had finished, the youth arose and said to Geraint, "My lord, with thy permission, I will now go and fetch some food for the mowers." "Go first to the town," said Geraint, "and take a lodging for me in the best place that thou knowest, and the most commodious one for the horses; and take thou whichever horse and arms thou choosest, in payment for thy service and thy gift." "Heaven reward thee, lord!" said the youth; "and this would be ample to repay services much greater than those I have rendered unto thee." And to the town went the youth, and he took the best and the most pleasant lodgings that he knew; and after that he went to the palace, having the horse and armor with him, and proceeded to the place where the earl was, and told him all his adventure. "I go now, lord," said he, "to meet the knight, and to conduct him to his lodging." "Go, gladly," said the earl; "and right joyfully shall he be received here, if he so come." And the youth went to meet Geraint, and told him that he would be received gladly by the earl in his own palace; but he would go only to his lodgings. And he had a goodly chamber, in which was plenty of straw and drapery, and a spacious and commodious place he had for the horses; and the youth prepared for them plenty of provender. After they had disarrayed themselves, Geraint spoke thus to Enid: "Go," said he, "to the other side of the chamber, and come not to this side of the house; and thou mayst call to thee the woman of the house, if thou wilt." "I will do, lord," said she,

and his affections upon her. Then he asked of Geraint, "Have I thy permission to go and converse with yonder maiden, for I see that she is apart from thee?" "Thou hast it gladly," said he. So the earl went to the place where the maiden was, and spake with her. "Ah! maiden," said he, "it cannot be pleasant to thee to journey with yonder man." "It is not unpleasant to me," said she. "Thou hast neither youths nor maidens to serve thee," said he. "Truly," she replied, "it is more pleasant for me to follow yonder man, than to be served by youths and maidens." "I will give thee good counsel," said he: "all my earldom will I place in thy possession, if thou wilt dwell with me."

"Enid, the pilot star of my lone life,
Enid, my early and my only love."

—Enid.

"That will I not, by Heaven," she said; "yonder man was the first to whom my faith was ever pledged; and shall I prove inconstant to him?" "Thou art in the wrong," said the earl; "if I slay the man yonder, I can keep thee with me as long as I choose; and when thou no longer pleasest me, I can turn thee away. But if thou goest with me by thy own good-will, I protest that our union shall continue as long as I remain alive." Then she pondered those words of his, and she considered that it was advisable to encourage him in his request. "Behold then, chieftain, this is most expedient for thee to do to save me from all reproach; come here to-morrow and take me away as though I knew nothing thereof." "I will do so," said he. So he arose and took his leave, and went forth with his attendants. And she told not then to Geraint any of the conversation which she had had with the earl, lest it should rouse his anger, and cause him uneasiness and care.

And at the usual hour they went to sleep. And at the beginning of the night Enid slept a little; and at midnight she arose, and placed all Geraint's armor together so that it might be ready to put on. And although fearful of her errand, she came to the side of Geraint's bed; and she spoke to him softly and gently, saying, "My lord, arise, and clothe thyself, for these were the words of the earl to me and his intention concerning me." So she told Geraint all that had passed. And although he was wroth with her, he took warning, and clothed himself. And she lighted a candle, that he might have light to do so. "Leave there the candle," said he, "and desire the man of the house to come here." Then she went, and the man of the house came to him. "Dost thou know how much I owe thee?" asked Geraint. "I think thou owest but little." "Take the three horses and the three suits of armor." "Heaven reward thee, lord," said he, "but I spent not the value of one suit of armor upon thee." "For that reason," said he, "thou wilt be the richer. And now, wilt thou come to guide me out of the town?" "I will gladly," said he; "and in which direction dost thou intend to go?" "I wish to leave the town by a different way from that by which I entered it." So the man of the lodgings accompanied him as far as he desired. Then he bade the maiden to go on before him, and she did so, and went straight forward, and his host returned home.

And Geraint and the maiden went forward along the high-road. And as they journeyed thus, they heard an exceeding loud wailing near to them. "Stay thou here," said he, "and I will go and see what is the cause of this wailing." "I will," said she. Then he went forward into an open glade that was near the road. And in the glade he saw two horses, one having a man's saddle, and the other a woman's saddle upon it. And behold there was a knight lying dead in his armor, and a young damsel in a riding-dress standing over him lamenting. "Ah, lady," said Geraint, "what hath befallen thee?" "Behold," she answered, "I journeyed here with my beloved husband, when lo! three giants came upon us, and without any cause in the world, they slew him." "Which way went they hence?" said Geraint. "Yonder by the high-road," she replied. So he returned to Enid. "Go," said he, "to the lady that is below yonder, and await me there till I come." She was sad when he ordered her to do thus, but nevertheless she went to the damsel, whom it was ruth to hear, and she felt certain that Geraint would never return.

Meanwhile Geraint followed the giants, and overtook them. And each of them was greater in stature than three other men, and a huge club was on the shoulder of each. Then he rushed upon one of them, and thrust his lance through his body. And having drawn it forth again, he pierced another of them through likewise. But the third turned upon him and struck him with his club so that he split his shield and crushed his shoulder. But Geraint drew his sword and gave the giant a blow on the crown of his head, so severe, and fierce, and violent, that his head and his neck were split down to his shoulders, and he fell dead. So Geraint left him thus and returned to Enid. And when he reached the place where she was he fell down lifeless from his horse. Piercing and loud and thrilling was the cry that Enid uttered. And she came and stood over him where he had fallen. And at the sound of her cries came the Earl of Limours, and they who journeyed with him, whom her lamentations brought out of their road. And the earl said to Enid, "Alas, lady, what hath befallen thee?" "Ah, good sir," said she, "the only man I have loved, or ever shall love, is slain." Then he said to the other, "And what is the cause of thy grief?" "They have slain my beloved husband also," said she. "And who was it that slew them?" "Some giants," she answered, "slew my best-beloved, and the other knight went in pursuit of them, and came back in the state thou seest." The earl caused the knight that was dead to be buried, but he thought that there still remained some life in Geraint; and to see if he yet would live, he had him carried with him in the hollow of his shield, and upon a bier. And the two damsels went to the court; and when they arrived there, Geraint was placed upon a little couch in front of the table that was in the hall. Then they all took off their traveling-gear, and the earl besought Enid to do the same, and to clothe herself in other garments. "I will not, by Heaven," said she. "Ah, lady," said he, "be not so sorrowful for this matter." "It were hard to persuade me to be otherwise," said she. "I will act towards thee in such wise that thou needest not be sorrowful, whether yonder knight live or die. Behold, a good earldom, together with myself, will I bestow upon thee; be therefore happy and joyful." "I declare to Heaven," said she, "that henceforth I shall never be joyful while I live." "Come," said he, "and eat." "No, by Heaven, I will not." "But, by Heaven, thou shalt," said he. So he took her with him to the table against her will, and many times desired her to eat. "I call Heaven to witness," said she, "that I will not until the man that is upon yonder bier shall eat likewise." "Thou canst not fulfil that," said the earl, "yonder man is dead already." "I will prove that I can," said she. Then he offered her a goblet of liquor. "Drink this goblet," he said, "and it will cause thee to change thy mind." "Evil betide me," she answered, "if I drink aught until he drink also." "Truly," said the earl, "it is of no more avail for me to be gentle with thee than ungentle." And he gave her a box in the ear. Thereupon she raised a loud and piercing shriek, and her lamentations were much greater than they had been before; for she considered in her mind, that, had Geraint been alive, he durst not have struck her thus. But, behold, at the sound of her cry, Geraint revived from his swoon, and he sat upon the bier; and finding his sword in the hollow of his shield, he rushed to the place where the earl was, and struck him a fiercely-wounding, severely-venomous, and sternly-smiting blow upon the crown of his head, so that he clove him in twain, until his sword was staid by the table. Then all left the board and fled away. And this was not so much through fear of the living, as through the dread they felt at seeing the dead man rise up to slay them. And Geraint looked upon Enid, and he was grieved for two causes; one was to see that Enid had lost her color and her wonted aspect; and the other, to know that she was in the right. "Lady," said he, "knowest thou where our horses are?" "I know, lord, where thy horse is," she replied, "but I know not where is the other. Thy horse is in the house yonder." So he went to the house, and brought forth his horse, and mounted him, and took up Enid, and placed her upon the horse with him. And he rode forward. And their road lay between two hedges; and the night was gaining on the day. And lo! they saw behind them the shafts of spears betwixt them and the sky, and they heard the tramping of horses, and the noise of a host approaching. "I hear something following us," said he, "and I will put thee on the other side of the hedge." And thus he did. And thereupon, behold a knight pricked towards him, and couched his lance. When Enid saw this, she cried out, saying, "O chieftain, whoever thou art, what renown wilt thou gain by slaying a dead man?" "O Heaven!" said he, "is it Geraint?" "Yes, in truth," said she; "and who art thou?" "I am Gwiffert Petit," said he, "thy husband's ally, coming to thy assistance, for I heard that thou wast in trouble. Come with me to the court of a son-in-law of my sister, which is near here, and thou shalt have the best medical assistance in the kingdom." "I will do so gladly," said Geraint. And Enid was placed upon the horse of one of Gwiffert's squires, and they went forward to the baron's palace. And they were received there with gladness, and they met with hospitality and attention. The next morning they went to seek physicians; and it was not long before they came, and they attended Geraint until he was perfectly well. And while Geraint was under medical care Gwiffert caused his armor to be repaired, until it was as good as it had ever been. And they remained there a month and a fortnight. Then they separated, and Geraint went towards his own dominions, and thenceforth he reigned prosperously, and his warlike fame and splendor lasted with renown and honor, both to him and to Enid, from that time forward.

[Footnote: Throughout the broad and varied region of romance it would be difficult to find a character of greater simplicity and truth than that of Enid, the daughter of Earl Ynywl. Conspicuous for her beauty and noble bearing, we are at a loss whether more to admire the patience with which she bore all the hardships she was destined to undergo or the constancy and affection which finally achieved the truimph she so richly deserved.

The character of Enid is admirably sustained through the whole tale; and as it is more natural, because less overstrained, so perhaps it is even more touching than that of Griselda, over which, however, Chaucer has thrown a charm that leads us to forget the improbability of her story.]

Chapter 8

PWYLL, PRINCE OF DYVED

Once upon a time Pwyll was at Narberth, his chief palace, where a feast had been prepared for him, and with him was a great host of men. And after the first meal Pwyll arose to walk; and he went to the top of a mound that was above the palace, and was called Gorsedd Arberth. "Lord," said one of the court, "it is peculiar to the mound that whosoever sits upon it cannot go thence without either receiving wounds or blows, or else seeing a wonder." "I fear not to receive wounds or blows," said Pwyll; "but as to the wonder, gladly would I see it. I will therefore go and sit upon the mound."

And upon the mound he sat. And while he sat there, they saw a lady, on a pure white horse of large size, with a garment of shining gold around her, coming along the highway that led from the mound. "My men," said Pwyll, "is there any among you who knows yonder lady?" "There is not, lord," said they. "Go one of you and meet her, that we may know who she is." And one of them arose, and as he came upon the road to meet her, she passed by; and he followed as fast as he could, being on foot, and the greater was his speed, the further was she from him. And when he saw that it profited him nothing to follow her, he returned to Pwyll, and said unto him, "Lord, it is idle for any one in the world to follow her on foot." "Verily," said Pwyll, "go unto the palace, and take the fleetest horse that thou seest, and go after her."

And he took a horse and went forward. And he came to an open, level plain, and put spurs to his horse; and the more he urged his horse, the further was she from him. And he returned to the place where Pwyll was, and said, "Lord, it will avail nothing for any one to follow yonder lady. I know of no horse in these realms swifter than this, and it availed me not to pursue her." "Of a truth," said Pwyll, "there must be some illusion here; let us go towards the palace." So to the palace they went, and spent the day.

And the next day they amused themselves until it was time to go to meat. And when meat was ended, Pwyll said, "Where are the hosts that went yesterday to the top of the mound?" "Behold, lord, we are here," said they. "Let us go," said he, "to the mound, and sit there. And do thou," said he to the page who tended his horse, "saddle my horse well, and hasten with him to the road, and bring also my spurs with thee." And the youth did thus. And they went and sat upon the mound; and ere they had been there but a short time, they beheld the lady coming by the same road, and in the same manner, and at the same pace. "Young man," said Pwyll, "I see the lady coming; give me my horse." And before he had mounted his horse she passed him. And he turned after her and followed her. And he let his horse go bounding playfully, and thought that he should soon come up with her. But he came no nearer to her than at first. Then he urged his horse to his utmost speed, yet he found that it availed not. Then said Pwyll, "O maiden, for the sake of him whom thou best lovest, stay for me." "I will stay gladly," said she; "and it were better for thy horse hadst thou asked it long since." So the maiden stopped; and she threw back that part of her head-dress which covered her face. Then he thought that the beauty of all the maidens and all the ladies that he had ever seen was as nothing compared to her beauty. "Lady," he said, "wilt thou tell me aught concerning thy purpose?" "I will tell thee," said she; "my chief quest was to see thee." "Truly," said Pwyll, "this is to me the most pleasing quest on which thou couldst have come; and wilt thou tell me who thou art?" "I will tell thee, lord," said she. "I am Rhiannon, the daughter of Heveydd, and they sought to give me a husband against my will. But no husband would I have, and that because of my love for thee; neither will I yet have one, unless thou reject me; and hither have I come to hear thy answer." "By Heaven," said Pwyll, "behold this is my answer. If I might choose among all the ladies and damsels in the world, thee would I choose." "Verily," said she, "if thou art thus minded, make a pledge to meet me ere I am given to another." "The sooner I may do so, the more pleasing will it be to me," said Pwyll; "and wheresoever thou wilt, there will I meet with thee." "I will that thou meet me this day twelvemonth at the palace of Heveydd." "Gladly," said he, "will I keep this tryst." So they parted, and he went back to his hosts, and to them of his household. And whatsoever questions they asked him respecting the damsel, he always turned the discourse upon other matters.

And when a year from that time was gone, he caused a hundred knights to equip themselves, and to go with him to the palace of Heveydd. And he came to the palace, and

Figure 99: "Guest Rhiannon" by W.Williams

there was great joy concerning him, with much concourse of people, and great rejoicing, and vast preparations for his coming. And the whole court was placed under his orders.

And the hall was garnished, and they went to meat, and thus did they sit: Heveydd was on one side of Pwyll, and Rhiannon on the other; and all the rest according to their rank. And they ate and feasted, and talked one with another. And at the beginning of the carousal after the meat, there entered a tall, auburn-haired youth, of royal bearing, clothed in a garment of satin. And when he came into the hall, he saluted Pwyll and his companions. "The greeting of Heaven be unto thee," said Pwyll; "come thou and sit down." "Nay," said he, "a suitor am I, and I will do my errand." "Do so willingly," said Pwyll. "Lord," said he, "my errand is unto thee, and it is to crave a boon of thee that I come." "What boon soever thou mayest ask of me, so far as I am able, thou shalt have." "Ah!" said Rhiannon, "wherefore didst thou give that answer?" "Has he not given it before the presence of these nobles?" asked the youth. "My soul," said Pwyll, "what is the boon thou askest?" "The lady whom best I love is to be thy bride this night; I come to ask her of thee, with the feast and the banquet that are in this place." And Pwyll was silent, because of the promise which he had given. "Be silent as long as thou wilt," said Rhiannon, "never did man make worse use of his wits than thou hast done." "Lady," said he, "I knew not who he was." "Behold, this is the man to whom they would have given me against my will," said she; "and he is Gawl, the son of Clud, a man of great power and wealth, and because of the word thou hast spoken, bestow me upon him, lest shame befall thee." "Lady," said he, "I understand not thy answer; never can I do as thou sayest." "Bestow me upon him," said she, "and I will cause that I shall never be his." "By what means will that be?" asked Pwyll. Then she told him the thought that was in her mind. And they talked long together. Then Gawl said, "Lord, it is meet that I have an answer to my request." "As much of that thou hast asked as it is in my power to give, thou shalt have," replied Pwyll. "My soul," said Rhiannon unto Gawl, "as for the feast and the banquet that are here, I have bestowed them upon the men of Dyved, and the household and the warriors that are with us. These can I not suffer to be given to any. In a year from to-night, a banquet shall be prepared for thee in this palace, that I may become thy bride."

So Gawl went forth to his possessions, and Pwyll went also back to Dyved. And they both spent that year until it was the time for the feast at the palace of Heveydd. Then Gawl, the son of Clud, set out to the feast that was prepared for him; and he came to the palace, and was received there with rejoicing. Pwyll, also, the chief of Dyved, came to the orchard with a hundred knights, as Rhiannon had commanded him. And Pwyll was clad in coarse and ragged garments, and wore large, clumsy old shoes upon his feet. And when he knew that the carousal after the meat had begun, he went toward the hall; and when he came into the hall he saluted Gawl, the son of Clud, and his company, both men and women. "Heaven prosper thee," said Gawl, "and friendly greeting be unto thee!" "Lord," said he, "may Heaven reward thee! I have an errand unto thee." "Welcome be thine errand, and if thou ask of me that which is right, thou shalt have it gladly." "It is fitting," answered he; "I crave but from want, and the boon I ask is to have this small bag that thou seest filled with meat." "A request within reason is this," said he, "and gladly shalt thou have it. Bring him food." A great number of attendants arose and began to fill the bag; but for all they put into it, it was no fuller than at first. "My

Figure 100: "The Hands of Pryderi and Rhiannon were Held Fast by the Enchanted Bowl" by Albert Herter

soul," said Gawl, "will thy bag ever be full?" "It will not, I declare to Heaven," said he, "for all that may be put into it, unless one possessed of lands, and domains, and treasure, shall arise and tread down with both his feet the food that is within the bag, and shall say, 'Enough has been put therein.'" Then said Rhiannon unto Gawl, the son of Clud, "Rise up quickly." "I will willingly arise," said he. So he rose up, and put his two feet into the bag. And Pwyll turned up the sides of the bag, so that Gawl was over his head in it. And he shut it up quickly, and slipped a knot upon the thongs, and blew his horn. And thereupon, behold, his knights came down upon the palace. And they seized all the host that had come with Gawl, and cast them into his own prison. And Pwyll threw off his rags, and his old shoes, and his tattered array. And as they came in, every one of Pwyll's knights struck a blow upon the bag, and asked, "What is here?" "A badger," said they. And in this manner they played, each of them striking the bag, either with his foot or with a staff. And thus played they with the bag. And then was the game of Badger in the Bag first played.

"Lord," said the man in the bag, "if thou wouldst but hear me, I merit not to be slain in a bag." Said Heveydd, "Lord, he speaks truth; it were fitting that thou listen to him, for he deserves not this." "Verily," said Pwyll, "I will do thy counsel concerning him." "Behold, this is my counsel then," said Rhiannon. "Thou art now in a position in which it behooves thee to satisfy suitors and minstrels. Let him give unto them in thy stead, and take a pledge from him that he will never seek to revenge that which has been done to him. And this will be punishment enough." "I will do this gladly," said the man in the bag. "And gladly will I accept it," said Pwyll, "since it is the counsel of Heveydd and Rhiannon. Seek thyself sureties." "We will be for him," said Heveydd, "until his men be free to answer for him." And upon this he was let out of the bag, and his liegemen were liberated. "Verily, lord," said Gawl, "I am greatly hurt, and I have many bruises. With thy leave, I will go forth. I will leave nobles in my stead to answer for me in all that thou shalt require." "Willingly," said Pwyll, "mayest thou do this." So Gawl went to his own possessions.

And the hall was set in order for Pwyll and the men of his host, and for them also of the palace, and they went to the tables and sat down. And as they had sat that time twelvemonth, so sat they that night. And they ate and feasted, and spent the night in mirth and tranquility. And the time came that they should sleep, and Pwyll and Rhiannon went to their chamber.

And next morning at break of day, "My lord," said Rhiannon, "arise and begin to give thy gifts unto the minstrels. Refuse no one to- day that may claim thy bounty." "Thus shall it be gladly," said Pwyll, "both to-day and every day while the feast shall last." So Pwyll arose, and he caused silence to be proclaimed, and desired all the suitors and minstrels to show and to point out what gifts they desired. And this being done, the feast went on, and he denied no one while it lasted. And when the feast was ended, Pwyll said unto Heveydd, "My lord, with thy permission, I will set out for Dyved to-morrow." "Certainly," said Heveydd; "may Heaven prosper thee! Fix also a time when Rhiannon shall follow thee." "By Heaven," said Pwyll, "we will go hence together." "Willest thou this, lord?" said Heveydd. "Yes, lord," answered Pwyll.

And the next, day they set forward towards Dyved, and journeyed to the palace of Narberth, where a feast was made ready for them. And there came to them great numbers of the chief men and the most noble ladies of the land, and of these there were none to whom Rhiannon did not give some rich gift, either a bracelet, or a ring, or a precious stone. And they ruled the land prosperously that year and the next.

Chapter 9

BRANWEN, THE DAUGHTER OF LLYR

Bendigeid Vran, the son of Llyr, was the crowned king of this island, and he was exalted from the crown of London. And one afternoon he was at Harlech, in Ardudwy, at his court; and he sat upon the rock of Harlech, looking over the sea. And with him were his brother, Manawyddan, the son of Llyr, and his brothers by the mother's side, Nissyen and Evnissyen, and many nobles likewise, as was fitting to see around a king. His two brothers by the mother's side were the sons of Euroswydd, and one of these youths was a good youth, and of gentle nature, and would make peace between his kindred, and cause his family to be friends when their wrath was at the highest, and this one was Nissyen; but the other would cause strife between his two brothers when they were most at peace. And as they sat thus they beheld thirteen ships coming from the south of Ireland, and making towards them; and they came with a swift motion, the wind being behind them; and they neared them rapidly. "I see ships afar," said the king, "coming swiftly towards the land. Command the men of the court that they equip themselves, and go and learn their intent." So the men equipped themselves, and went down towards them. And when they saw the ships near, certain were they that they had never seen ships better furnished. Beautiful flags of satin were upon them. And, behold, one of the ships outstripped the others, and they saw a shield lifted up above the side of the ship, and the point of the shield was upwards, in token of peace. And the men drew near, that they might hold converse. Then they put out boats, and came toward the land. And they saluted the king. Now the king could hear them from the place where he was upon the rock above their heads. "Heaven prosper you." said he, "and be ye welcome! To whom do these ships belong, and who is the chief amongst you?" "Lord," said they, "Matholch, king of Ireland, is here, and these ships belong to him." "Wherefore comes he?" asked the king, "and will he come to the land?" "He is a suitor unto thee, lord," said they, "and he will not land unless he have his boon." "And what may that be?" inquired the king. "He desires to ally himself, lord, with thee," said they, "and he comes to ask Branwen, the daughter of Llyr, that, if it seem well to thee, the Island of the Mighty [Footnote: The Island of the Mighty is one of the many names bestowed upon Britain by the Welsh.] may be leagued with Ireland, and both become more powerful." "Verily," said he, "let him come to land, and we will take counsel thereupon." And this answer was brought to Matholch. "I will go willingly," said he. So he landed, and they received him joyfully; and great was the throng in the palace that night, between his hosts and those of the court; and next day they took counsel, and they resolved to bestow Branwen upon Matholch. Now she was one of the three chief ladies of this island, and she was the fairest damsel in the world.

And they fixed upon Aberfraw as the place where she should become his bride. And they went thence, and towards Aberfraw the hosts proceeded, Matholch and his host in their ships, Bendigeid Vran and his host by land, until they came to Aberfraw. And at Aberfraw they began the feast, and sat down. And thus sat they: the king of the Island of the Mighty and Manawyddan, the son of Llyr, on one side, and Matholch on the other side, and Branwen, the daughter of Llyr, beside him. And they were not within a house, but under tents. No house could ever contain Bendigeid Vran. And they began the banquet, and caroused and discoursed. And when it was more pleasing to them to sleep than to carouse, they went to rest, and Branwen became Matholch's bride.

And next day they arose, and all they of the court, and the officers began to equip, and to range the horses and the attendants, and they ranged them in order as far as the sea.

And, behold, one day Evnissyen, the quarrelsome man, of whom it is spoken above, came by chance into the place where the horses of Matholch were, and asked whose horses they might be. "They are the horses of Matholch, king of Ireland, who is married to Branwen, thy sister; his horses are they." "And is it thus they have done with a maiden such as she, and moreover my sister, bestowing her without my consent? They could have offered no greater insult to me than this," said he. And thereupon he rushed under the horses, and cut off their lips at the teeth, and their ears close to their heads, and their tails close to their backs; and he disfigured the horses, and rendered them useless.

Figure 101: "Branwen and her Drudwy" by W. Williams

And they came with these tidings unto Matholch, saying that the horses were disfigured and injured, so that not one of them could ever be of any use again. "Verily, lord," said one, "it was an insult unto thee, and as such was it meant." "Of a truth, it is a marvel to me that, if they desire to insult me, they should have given me a maiden of such high rank, and so much beloved of her kindred, as they have done." "Lord," said another, "thou seest that thus it is, and there is nothing for thee to do but to go to thy ships." And thereupon towards his ships he set out.

And tidings came to Bendigeid Vran that Matholch was quitting the court without asking leave, and messengers were sent to inquire of him wherefore he did so. And the messengers that went were Iddic, the son of Anarawd, and Heveyd Hir. And these overtook him, and asked of him what he designed to do, and wherefore he went forth. "Of a truth," said he, "if I had known, I had not come hither. I have been altogether insulted; no one had ever worse treatment than I have had here." "Truly, lord, it was not the will of any that are of the court," said they, "nor of any that are of the council, that thou shouldst have received this insult; and as thou hast been insulted, the dishonor is greater unto Bendigeid Vran than unto thee." "Verily," said he, "I think so. Nevertheless, he cannot recall the insult." These men returned with that answer to the place where Bendigeid Vran was, and they told him what reply Matholch had given them. "Truly," said he, "there are no means by which we may prevent his going away at enmity with us that we will not take." "Well, lord," said they, "send after him another embassy." "I will do so," said he. "Arise, Manawyddan, son of Llyr, and Heveyd Hir, and go after him, and tell him that he shall have a sound horse for every one that has been injured. And beside that, as an atonement for the insult, he shall have a staff of silver as large and as tall as himself, and a plate of gold of the breadth of his face. And show unto him who it was that did this, and that it was done against my will; but that he who did it is my brother, and therefore it would be hard for me to put him to death. And let him come and meet me," said he, "and we will make peace in any way he may desire."

The embassy went after Matholch, and told him all these sayings in a friendly manner; and he listened thereunto. "Men," said he, "I will take counsel." So to the council he went. And in the council they considered that, if they should refuse this, they were likely to have more shame rather than to obtain so great an atonement. They resolved, therefore, to accept it, and they returned to the court in peace.

Then the pavilions and the tents were set in order, after the fashion of a hall; and they went to meat, and as they had sat at the beginning of the feast so sat they there. And Matholch and Bendigeid Vran began to discourse; and, behold, it seemed to Bendigeid Vran, while they talked, that Matholch was not so cheerful as he had been before. And he thought that the chieftain might be sad because of the smallness of the atonement which he had for the wrong that had been done him. "O man," said Bendigeid Vran, "thou dost not discourse to-night so cheerfully as thou wast wont. And if it be because of the smallness of the atonement, thou shalt add thereunto whatsoever thou mayest choose, and to-morrow I will pay thee for the horses." "Lord," said he, "Heaven reward thee!" "And I will enhance the atonement," said Bendigeid Vran, "for I will give unto thee a caldron, the property of which is, that if one of thy men be slain to-day, and be cast therein, to-morrow he will be as well as ever he was at the best, except that he will not regain his speech." And thereupon he gave him great thanks, and very joyful was he for that cause.

That night they continued to discourse as much as they would, and had minstrelsy and carousing; and when it was more pleasant to them to sleep than to sit longer, they went to rest. And thus was the banquet carried on with joyousness; and when it was finished, Matholch journeyed towards Ireland, and Branwen with him; and they went from Aber Menei with thirteen ships, and came to Ireland. And in Ireland was there great joy because of their coming. And not one great man nor noble lady visited Branwen unto whom she gave not either a clasp or a ring, or a royal jewel to keep, such as it was honorable to be seen departing with. And in these things she spent that year in much renown, and she passed her time pleasantly, enjoying honor and friendship. And in due time a son was born unto her, and the name that they gave him was Gwern, the son of Matholch, and they put the boy out to be nursed in a place where were the best men of Ireland.

And, behold, in the second year a tumult arose in Ireland, on account of the insult which Matholch had received in Wales, and the payment made him for his horses. And his foster-brothers, and such as were nearest to him, blamed him openly for that matter. And he might have no peace by reason of the tumult, until they should revenge upon him this disgrace. And the vengeance which they took was to drive away Branwen from the same chamber with him, and to make her cook for the court; and they caused the butcher, after he had cut up the meat, to come to her and give her every day a blow on the ear; and such they made her punishment.

"Verily, lord," said his men to Matholch, "forbid now the ships and the ferry-boats, and the coracles, that they go not into Wales, and such as come over from Wales hither, imprison them, that they go not back for this thing to be known there." And he did so; and it was thus for no less than three years.

And Branwen reared a starling in the cover of the kneading-trough, and she taught it to speak, and she taught the bird what manner of man her brother was. And she wrote a letter of her woes, and the despite with which she was treated, and she bound the letter to the root of the bird's wing, and sent it toward Wales. And the bird came to that island; and one day it found Bendigeid Vran at Caer Seiont in Arvon, conferring there, and it alighted upon his shoulder, and ruffled its feathers, so that the letter was seen, and they knew that the bird had been reared in a domestic manner.

Then Bendigeid Vran took the letter and looked upon it. And when he had read the letter, he grieved exceedingly at the tidings of Branwen's woes. And immediately he began sending messengers to summon the island together. And he caused seven-score and four of his chief men to come unto him, and he complained to them of the grief that his sister endured. So they took counsel. And in the counsel they resolved to go to Ireland, and to leave seven men as princes at home, and Caradoc, [Footnote: Caractacus.] the son of Bran, as the chief of them.

Bendigeid Vran, with the host of which we spoke, sailed towards Ireland; and it was not far across the sea, and he came to shoal water. Now the swine-herds of Matholch were upon the sea-shore, and they came to Matholch. "Lord," said they, "greeting be unto thee." "Heaven protect you!" said he; "have you any news?" "Lord," said they, "we have marvellous news. A wood have we seen upon the sea, in a place where we never yet saw a single tree." "This is indeed a marvel," said he; "saw you aught else?" "We saw, lord," said they, "a vast mountain beside the wood, which moved, and there was a lofty ridge on the top of the mountain, and a lake on each side of the ridge. And the wood and the mountain, and all these things, moved." "Verily," said he, "there is none who can know aught concerning this unless it be Branwen."

Messengers then went unto Branwen. "Lady," said they, "what thinkest thou that this is?" "The men of the Island of the Mighty, who have come hither on hearing of my ill-treatment and of my woes." "What is the forest that is seen upon the sea?" asked they. "The yards and the masts of ships," she answered. "Alas!" said they; "what is the mountain that is seen by the side of the ships?" "Bendigeid Vran, my brother," she replied, "coming to shoal water, and he is wading to the land." "What is the lofty ridge, with the lake on each side thereof?" "On looking towards this island he is wroth, and his two eyes on each side of his nose are the two lakes on each side of the ridge."

The warriors and chief men of Ireland were brought together in haste, and they took counsel. "Lord," said the neighbors unto Matholch, "there is no other counsel than this alone. Thou shalt give the kingdom to Gwern, the son of Branwen his sister, as a compensation for the wrong and despite that have been done unto Branwen. And he will make peace with thee." And in the council it was resolved that this message should be sent to Bendigeid Vran, lest the country should be destroyed. And this peace was made. And Matholch caused a great house to be built for Bendigeid Vran, and his host. Thereupon came the hosts into the house. The men of the island of Ireland entered the house on the one side, and the men of the Island of the Mighty on the other. And as soon as they had sat down, there was concord between them; and the sovereignty was conferred upon the boy. When the peace was concluded, Bendigeid Vran called the boy unto him, and from Bendigeid Vran the boy went unto Manawyddan; and he was beloved by all that beheld him. And from Manawyddan the boy was called by Nissyen, the son of Euroswydd, and the boy went unto him lovingly. "Wherefore," said Evnissyen, "comes not my nephew, the son of my sister, unto me? Though he were not king of Ireland, yet willingly would I fondle the boy." "Cheerfully let him go to thee," said Bendigeid Vran; and the boy went unto him cheerfully. "By my confession to Heaven," said Evnissyen in his heart, "unthought of is the slaughter that I will this instant commit."

Then he arose and took up the boy, and before any one in the house could seize hold of him he thrust the boy headlong into the blazing fire. And when Branwen saw her son burning in the fire, she strove to leap into the fire also, from the place where she sat between her two brothers. But Bendigeid Vran grasped her with one hand, and his shield with the other. Then they all hurried about the house, and never was there made so great a tumult by any host in one house as was made by them, as each man armed himself. And while they all sought their arms Bendigeid Vran supported Branwen between his shield and his shoulder. And they fought.

Then the Irish kindled a fire under the caldron of renovation, and they cast the dead bodies into the caldron until it was full; and the next day they came forth fighting men, as good as before, except that they were not able to speak. Then when Evnissyen saw the dead bodies of the men of the Island of the Mighty nowhere resuscitated, he said in his heart, "Alas! woe is me, that I should have been the cause of bringing the men of the Island of the Mighty into so great a strait. Evil betide me if I find not a deliverance therefrom." And he cast himself among the dead bodies of the Irish; and two unshod Irishmen came to him, and, taking him to be one of the Irish, flung him into the caldron. And he stretched himself out in the caldron, so that he rent the caldron into four pieces, and burst his own heart also.

In consequence of this, the men of the Island of the Mighty obtained such success as they had; but they were not victorious, for only seven men of them all escaped, and Bendigeid Vran himself was wounded in the foot with a poisoned dart. Now the men that escaped were Pryderi, Manawyddan, Taliesin, and four others.

And Bendigeid Vran commanded them that they should cut off his head. "And take you my head," said he, "and bear it even unto the White Mount in London, and bury it there with the face towards France. And so long as it lies there, no enemy shall ever land on the island." So they cut off his head, and these seven went forward therewith. And Branwen was the eighth with them. And they came to land on Aber Alaw, and they sat down to rest. And Branwen looked towards Ireland, and towards the Island of the Mighty, to see if she could descry them. "Alas!" said she, "woe is me that I was ever born; two islands have been destroyed because of me." Then she uttered a groan, and there broke her heart. And they made her a four-sided grave, and buried her upon the banks of the Alaw.

Then the seven men journeyed forward, bearing the head with them; and as they went, behold there met them a multitude of men and women. "Have you any tidings?" said Manawyddan. "We have none," said they, "save that Caswallawn, [Footnote: Cassivellaunus.] the son of Beli, has conquered the Island of the Mighty, and is crowned king in London." "What has become," said they, "of Caradoc, the son of Bran, and the seven men who were left with him in this island?" "Caswallawn came upon them, and slew six of the men, and Caradoc's heart broke for grief thereof." And the seven men journeyed on towards London, and they buried the head in the White Mount, as Bendigeid Vran had directed them. [Footnote: There is a Triad upon the story of the head buried under the White Tower of London, as a charm against invasion. Arthur, it seems, proudly disinterred the head, preferring to hold the island by his own strength alone.]

Chapter 10

MANAWYDDAN

Pwyll and Rhiannon had a son, whom they named Pryderi. And when he was grown up, Pwyll, his father, died. And Pryderi married Kicva, the daughter of Gwynn Gloy.

Now Manawyddan returned from the war in Ireland, and he found that his cousin had seized all his possessions, and much grief and heaviness came upon him. "Alas! woe is me!" he exclaimed; "there is none save myself without a home and a resting-place." "Lord," said Pryderi, "be not so sorrowful. Thy cousin is king of the Island of the Mighty, and though he has done thee wrong, thou hast never been a claimant of land or possessions." "Yea," answered he, "but although this man is my cousin, it grieveth me to see any one in the place of my brother, Bendigeid Vran; neither can I be happy in the same dwelling with him." "Wilt thou follow the counsel of another?" said Pryderi. "I stand in need of counsel," he answered, "and what may that counsel be?" "Seven cantrevs belong unto me," said Pryderi, "wherein Rhiannon, my mother, dwells. I will bestow her upon thee, and the seven cantrevs with her; and though thou hadst no possessions but those cantrevs only, thou couldst not have any fairer than they. Do thou and Rhiannon enjoy them, and if thou desire any possessions thou wilt not despise these." "I do not, chieftain," said he. "Heaven reward thee for the friendship! I will go with thee to seek Rhiannon, and to look at thy possessions." "Thou wilt do well," he answered; "and I believe that thou didst never hear a lady discourse better than she, and when she was in her prime, none was ever fairer. Even now her aspect is not uncomely."

They set forth, and, however long the journey, they came at last to Dyved; and a feast was prepared for them by Rhiannon and Kicva. Then began Manawyddan and Rhiannon to sit and to talk together; and his mind and his thoughts became warmed towards her, and he thought in his heart he had never beheld any lady more fulfilled of grace and beauty than she. "Pryderi," said he, "I will that it be as thou didst say." "What saying was that?" asked Rhiannon. "Lady," said Pryderi, "I did offer thee as a wife to Manawyddan, the son of Llyr." "By that will I gladly abide," said Rhiannon. "Right glad am I also," said Manawyddan, "may Heaven reward him who hath shown unto me friendship so perfect as this!"

And before the feast was over she became his bride. Said Pryderi, "Tarry ye here the rest of the feast, and I will go into England to tender my homage unto Caswallawn, the son of Beli." "Lord," said Rhiannon, "Caswallawn is in Kent; thou mayest therefore tarry at the feast, and wait until he shall be nearer." "We will wait," he answered. So they finished the feast. And they began to make the circuit of Dyved, and to hunt, and to take their pleasure. And as they went through the country, they had never seen lands more pleasant to live in, nor better hunting grounds, nor greater plenty of honey and fish. And such was the friendship between these four, that they would not be parted from each other by night nor by day.

And in the midst of all this he went to Caswallawn at Oxford, and tendered his homage; and honorable was his reception there, and highly was he praised for offering his homage.

And after his return Pryderi and Manawyddan feasted and took their ease and pleasure. And they began a feast at Narberth, for it was the chief palace. And when they had ended the first meal, while those who served them ate, they arose and went forth, and proceeded to the Gorsedd, that is, the Mount of Narberth, and their retinue with them. And as they sat thus, behold a peal of thunder, and with the violence of the thunder-storm, lo! there came a fall of mist, so thick that not one of them could see the other. And after the mist it became light all around. And when they looked towards the place where they were wont to see the cattle and herds and dwellings, they saw nothing now, neither house, nor beast, nor smoke, nor fire, nor man, nor dwelling, but the buildings of the court empty, and desert, and uninhabited, without either man or beast within them. And truly all their companions were lost to them, without their knowing aught of what had befallen them, save those four only.

"In the name of Heaven," said Manawyddan, "where are they of the court, and all my host beside? Let us go and see."

Figure 102: "Manawyddan" by Stephen Reid

So they came to the castle, and saw no man, and into the hall, and to the sleeping-place, and there was none; and in the mead-cellar and in the kitchen there was naught but desolation. Then they began to go through the land, and all the possessions that they had; and they visited the houses and dwellings, and found nothing but wild beasts. And when they had consumed their feast and all their provisions, they fed upon the prey they killed in hunting, and the honey of the wild swans.

And one morning Pryderi and Manawyddan rose up to hunt, and they ranged their dogs and went forth. And some of the dogs ran before them, and came to a bush which was near at hand; but as soon as they were come to the bush, they hastily drew back, and returned to the men, their hair bristling up greatly. "Let us go near to the bush," said Pryderi, "and see what is in it." And as they came near, behold, a wild boar of a pure white color rose up from the bush. Then the dogs, being set on by the men, rushed towards him; but he left the bush, and fell back a little way from the men, and made a stand against the dogs, without retreating from them, until the men had come near. And when the men came up, he fell back a second time, and betook him to flight. Then they pursued the boar until they beheld a vast and lofty castle, all newly built, in a place where they had never before seen either stone or building. And the boar ran swiftly into the castle, and the dogs after him. Now when the boar and the dogs had gone into the castle, the men began to wonder at finding a castle in a place where they had never before seen any building whatsoever. And from the top of the Gorsedd they looked and listened for the dogs. But so long as they were there, they heard not one of the dogs, nor aught concerning them.

"Lord," said Pryderi, "I will go into the castle to get tidings of the dogs." "Truly," he replied, "thou wouldst be unwise to go into this castle, which thou hast never seen till now. If thou wouldst follow my counsel, thou wouldst not enter therein. Whosoever has cast a spell over this land, has caused this castle to be here." "Of a truth," answered Pryderi, "I cannot thus give up my dogs." And for all the counsel that Manawyddan gave him, yet to the castle he went.

When he came within the castle, neither man nor beast, nor boar, nor dogs, nor house, nor dwelling, saw he within it. But in the centre of the castle-floor he beheld a fountain with marble-work around it, and on the margin of the fountain a golden bowl upon a marble slab, and chains hanging from the air, to which he saw no end.

And he was greatly pleased with the beauty of the gold, and with the rich workmanship of the bowl; and he went up to the bowl, and laid hold of it. And when he had taken hold of its his hands stuck to the bowl, and his feet to the slab on which the bowl was placed; and all his joyousness forsook him, so that he could not utter a word. And thus he stood.

And Manawyddan waited for him till near the close of the day. And late in the evening, being certain that he should have no tidings of Pryderi or the dogs, he went back to the palace. And as he entered, Rhiannon looked at him. "Where," said she, "are thy companion and thy dogs?" "Behold," he answered, "the adventure that has befallen me." And he related it all unto her. "An evil companion hast thou been," said Rhiannon, "and a good companion hast thou lost." And with that word she went out, and proceeded towards the castle, according to the direction which he gave her. The gate of the castle she found open. She was nothing daunted, and she went in. And as she went in, she perceived Pryderi laying hold of the bowl, and she went towards him. "O my lord," said she, "what dost thou here?" And she took hold of the bowl with him; and as she did so, her hands also became fast to the bowl, and her feet to the slab, and she was not able to utter a word. And with that, as it became night, lo! there came thunder upon them, and a fall of mist; and thereupon the castle vanished, and they with it.

When Kicva, the daughter of Gwynn Gloy, saw that there was no one in the palace but herself and Manawyddan, she sorrowed so that she cared not whether she lived or died. And Manawyddan saw this. "Thou art in the wrong," said he, "if through fear of me thou grievest thus. I call Heaven to witness that thou hast never seen friendship more pure than that which I will bear thee as long as Heaven will that thou shouldst be thus. I declare to thee, that, were I in the dawn of youth, I would keep my faith unto Pryderi, and unto thee also will I keep it. Be there no fear upon thee, therefore." "Heaven reward thee!" she said; "and that is what I deemed of thee." And the damsel thereupon took courage, and was glad.

"Truly, lady," said Manawyddan, "it is not fitting for us to stay here; we have lost our dogs, and cannot get food. Let us go into England; it is easiest for us to find support there." "Gladly, lord," said she, "we will do so." And they set forth together to England.

"Lord," said she, "what craft wilt thou follow? Take up one that is seemly." "None other will I take," answered he, "but that of making shoes." "Lord," said she, "such a craft becomes not a man so nobly born as thou." "By that however will I abide," said he. "I know nothing thereof," said Kicva. "But I know," answered Manawyddan, "and I will teach thee to stitch. We will not attempt to dress the leather, but we will buy it ready dressed, and will make the shoes from it."

Figure 103: "Manawydan" by W.William

So they went into England, and went as far as Hereford; and they betook themselves to making shoes. And he began by buying the best cordwain that could be had in the town, and none other would buy. And he associated himself with the best goldsmith in the town, and caused him to make clasps for the shoes, and to gild the clasps; and he marked how it was done until he learned the method. And therefore is he called one of the three makers of gold shoes. And when they could be had from him, not a shoe nor hose was bought of any of the cordwainers in the town. But when the cordwainers perceived that their gains were failing (for as Manawyddan shaped the work, so Kicva stitched it), they came together and took counsel, and agreed that they would slay them. And he had warning thereof, and it was told him how the cordwainers had agreed together to slay him.

"Lord," said Kicva, "wherefore should this be borne from these boors?" "Nay," said he, "we will go back unto Dyved." So towards Dyved they set forth.

Now Manawyddan, when he set out to return to Dyved, took with him a burden of wheat. And he proceeded towards Narberth, and there he dwelt. And never was he better pleased than when he saw Narberth again, and the lands where he had been wont to hunt with Pryderi and with Rhiannon. And he accustomed himself to fish, and to hunt the deer in their covert. And then he began to prepare some ground, and he sowed a croft, and a second, and a third. And no wheat in the world ever sprung up better. And the three crofts prospered with perfect growth, and no man ever saw fairer wheat than it.

And thus passed the seasons of the year until the harvest came. And he went to look at one of his crofts, and, behold, it was ripe. "I will reap this to-morrow," said he. And that night he went back to Narberth, and on the morrow, in the gray dawn, he went to reap the croft; and when he came there, he found nothing but the bare straw. Every one of the ears of the wheat was cut off from the stalk, and all the ears carried entirely away, and nothing but the straw left. And at this he marvelled greatly.

Then he went to look at another croft, and, behold, that also was ripe. "Verily," said he, "this will I reap to-morrow." And on the morrow he came with the intent to reap it; and when he came there, he found nothing but the bare straw. "O gracious Heaven!" he exclaimed. "I know that whosoever has begun my ruin is completing it, and has also destroyed the country with me."

Then he went to look at the third croft; and when he came there, finer wheat had there never been seen, and this also was ripe. "Evil betide me," said he, "if I watch not here to-night. Whoever carried off the other corn will come in like manner to take this, and I will know who it is." And he told Kicva all that had befallen. "Verily," said she, "what thinkest thou to do?" "I will watch the croft to-night," said he. And he went to watch the croft.

And at midnight he heard something stirring among the wheat; and he looked, and behold, the mightiest host of mice in the world, which could neither be numbered nor measured. And he knew not what it was until the mice had made their way into the croft, and each of them, climbing up the straw, and bending it down with its weight, had cut off one of the ears of wheat, and had carried it away, leaving there the stalk; and he saw not a single straw there that had not a mouse to it. And they all took their way, carrying the ears with them.

In wrath and anger did he rush upon the mice; but he could no more come up with them than if they had been gnats or birds of the air, except one only, which, though it was but sluggish, went so fast that a man on foot could scarce overtake it. And after this one he went, and he caught it, and put it in his glove, and tied up the opening of the glove with a string, and kept it with him, and returned to the palace. Then he came to the hall where Kicva was, and he lighted a fire, and hung the glove by the string upon a peg. "What hast thou there, lord?" said Kicva. "A thief," said he, "that I found robbing me." "What kind of a thief may it be, lord, that thou couldst put into thy glove?" said she. Then he told her how the mice came to the last of the fields in his sight. "And one of them was less nimble than the rest, and is now in my glove; to-morrow I will hang it." "My lord," said she, "this is marvellous; but yet it would be unseemly for a man of dignity like thee to be hanging such a reptile as this." "Woe betide me," said he, "if I would not hang them all, could I catch them, and such as I have I will hang." "Verily, lord," said she, "there is no reason that I should succor this reptile, except to prevent discredit unto thee. Do therefore, lord, as thou wilt."

Then he went to the Mound of Narberth, taking the mouse with him. And he set up two forks on the highest part of the mound. And while he was doing this, behold, he saw a scholar coming towards him, in old and poor and tattered garments. And it was now seven years since he had seen in that place either man or beast, except those four persons who had remained together until two of them were lost.

"My lord," said the scholar, "good-day to thee." "Heaven prosper thee, and my greeting be unto thee! And whence dost thou come, scholar?" asked he. "I come, lord, from singing in England; and wherefore dost thou inquire?" "Because for the last seven years," answered he, "I have seen no man here save four secluded persons, and thyself this moment." "Truly, lord," said he, "I go through this land unto mine own. And what work art thou upon, lord?" "I am hanging a thief that I caught robbing me," said he. "What manner of thief is that?" asked the scholar. "I see a creature in thy hand like unto a mouse, and ill does it become a man of rank equal to thine to touch a reptile such as this. Let it go forth free." "I will not let it go free, by Heaven," said he; "I caught it robbing me, and the doom of a thief will I inflict upon it, and I will hang it." "Lord," said he, "rather than see a man of rank equal to thine at such a work as this, I would give thee a pound, which I have received as alms, to let the reptile go forth free." "I will not let it go free," said he, "neither will I sell it." "As thou wilt, lord," he answered; "I care naught." And the scholar went his way.

And as he was placing the cross-beam upon the two forks, behold, a priest came towards him, upon a horse covered with trappings. "Good day to thee, lord," said he. "Heaven prosper thee!" said Manawyddan; "thy blessing." "The blessing of Heaven be upon thee! And what, lord, art thou doing?" "I am hanging a thief that I caught robbing me," said he. "What manner of thief, lord?" asked he. "A creature," he answered, "in form of a mouse. It has been robbing me, and I am inflicting upon it the doom of a thief." "Lord," said he, "rather than see thee touch this reptile, I would purchase its freedom." "By my confession to Heaven, neither will I sell it nor set it free." "It is true, lord, that it is worth nothing to buy; but rather than see thee defile thyself by touching such a reptile as this, I will give thee three pounds to let it go." "I will not, by Heaven," said he, "take any price for it. As it ought, so shall it be hanged." And the priest went his way.

Then he noosed the string around the mouse's neck, and as he was about to draw it up, behold, he saw a bishop's retinue, with his sumpter-horses and his attendants. And the bishop himself came towards him. And he stayed his work. "Lord Bishop," said he, "thy blessing." "Heaven's blessing be unto thee!" said he. "What work art thou upon?" "Hanging a thief that I caught robbing me," said he. "Is not that a mouse that I see in thy hand?" "Yes," answered he, "and she has robbed me." "Ay," said he, "since I have come at the doom of this reptile I will ransom it of thee. I will give thee seven pounds for it, and that rather than see a man of rank equal to thine destroying so vile a reptile as this. Let it loose, and thou shalt have the money." "I declare to Heaven that I will not let it loose." "If thou wilt not loose it for this, I will give thee four and twenty pounds of ready money to set it free." "I will not set it free, by Heaven, for as much again," said he. "If thou wilt not set it free for this, I will give thee all the horses that thou seest in this plain, and the seven loads of baggage, and the seven horses that they are upon." "By Heaven, I will not," he replied. "Since for this thou wilt not set it free, do so at what price soever thou wilt." "I will that Rhiannon and Pryderi be free," said he. "That thou shalt have," he answered. "Not yet will I loose the mouse, by Heaven." "What then wouldst thou?" "That the charm and the illusion be removed from the seven cantrevs of Dyved." "This shalt thou have also; set therefore the mouse free." "I will not set it free, by Heaven," said he, "till I know who the mouse may be." "She is my wife." "Wherefore came she to me?" "To despoil thee," he answered. "I am Lloyd, the son of Kilwed, and I cast the charm over the seven cantrevs of Dyved. And it was to avenge Gawl, the son of Clud, from the friendship I had towards him, that I cast the charm. And upon Pryderi did I avenge Gawl, the son of Clud, for the game of Badger in the Bag, that Pwyll, the son of Auwyn, played upon him. And when it was known that thou wast come to dwell in the land, my household came and besought me to transform them into mice, that they might destroy thy corn. And they went the first and the second night, and destroyed thy two crops. And the third night came unto me my wife and the ladies of the court, and besought me to transform them. And I transformed them. Now she is not in her usual health. And had she been in her usual health, thou wouldst not have been able to overtake her; but since this has taken place, and she has been caught, I will restore to thee Pryderi and Rhiannon, and I will take the charm and illusion from off Dyved. Set her therefore free." "I will not set her free yet." "What wilt thou more?" he asked. "I will that there be no more charm upon the seven cantrevs of Dyved, and that none shall be put upon it henceforth; moreover, that vengeance be never taken for this, either upon Pryderi or Rhiannon, or upon me." "All this shalt thou have. And truly thou hast done wisely in asking this. Upon thy head would have lit all this trouble." "Yea," said he, "for fear thereof was it that I required this." "Set now my wife at liberty." "I will not," said he, "until I see Pryderi and Rhiannon with me free." "Behold, here they come," he answered.

And thereupon behold Pryderi and Rhiannon. And he rose up to meet them, and greeted them, and sat down beside them. "Ah, chieftain, set now my wife at liberty," said the bishop. "Hast thou not received all thou didst ask?" "I will release her, gladly," said he. And thereupon he set her free.

Then he struck her with a magic wand, and she was changed back into a young woman, the fairest ever seen. "Look round upon thy land," said he, "and thou wilt see it all tilled and peopled as it was in its best estate." And he rose up and looked forth. And when he looked he saw all the lands tilled, and full of herds and dwellings.

And thus ends this portion of the Mabinogion.

The following allusions to the preceding story are found in a letter of the poet Southey to John Rickman, Esq., dated June 6th, 1802:

"You will read the Mabinogeon, concerning which I ought to have talked to you. In the last, that most odd and Arabian-like story of the mouse, mention is made of a begging scholar, that helps to the date; but where did the Cymri get the imagination that could produce such a tale? That enchantment of the basin hanging by the chain from heaven is in the wildest spirit of the Arabian Nights. I am perfectly astonished that such fictions should exist in Welsh. They throw no light on the origin of romance, everything being utterly dissimilar to what we mean by that term, but they do open a new world of fiction; and if the date of their language be fixed about the twelfth or thirteenth century, I cannot but think the mythological substance is of far earlier date; very probably brought from the East by some of the first settlers or conquerors."

Chapter 11

KILWICH AND OLWEN, OR CULHWCH

Kilydd, a son of Prince Kelyddon, desired a wife as a helpmate, and the wife that he chose was Goleudid, the daughter of Prince Anlawd. And after their union the people put up prayers that they might have an heir. And they had a son through the prayers of the people; and called his name Kilwich.

After this the boy's mother, Goleudid, the daughter of Prince Anlawd, fell sick. Then she called her husband to her, and said to him, "Of this sickness I shall die, and thou wilt take another wife. Now wives are the gift of the Lord, but it would be wrong for thee to harm thy son. Therefore I charge thee that thou take not a wife until thou see a briar with two blossoms upon my grave." And this he promised her. Then she besought him to dress her grave every year, that no weeds might grow thereon. So the queen died. Now the king sent an attendant every morning to see if anything were growing upon the grave. And at the end of the seventh year they neglected that which they had promised to the queen.

One day the king went to hunt; and he rode to the place of burial, to see the grave, and to know if it were time that he should take a wife: and the King saw the briar. And when he saw it, the king took counsel where he should find a wife. Said one of his counsellors, "I know a wife that will suit thee well; and she is the wife of King Doged." And they resolved to go to seek her; and they slew the king, and brought away his wife. And they conquered the kings' lands. And he married the widow of King Doged, the sister of Yspadaden Penkawr.

And one day his stepmother said to Kilwich, "It were well for thee to have a wife." "I am not yet of an age to wed," answered the youth. Then said she unto him, "I declare to thee that it is thy destiny not to be suited with a wife until thou obtain Olwen, the daughter of Yspadaden Penkawr." And the youth blushed, and the love of the maiden diffused itself through all his frame, although he had never seen her. And his father inquired of him, "What has come over thee, my son, and what aileth thee?" "My stepmother has declared to me that I shall never have a wife until I obtain Olwen, the daughter of Yspadaden Penkawr." "That will be easy for thee," answered his father. "Arthur is thy cousin. Go, therefore, unto Arthur, to cut thy hair, and ask this of him as a boon."

And the youth pricked forth upon a steed with head dappled gray, four winters old, firm of limb, with shell-formed hoofs, having a bridle of linked gold on his head, and upon him a saddle of costly gold. And in the youth's hand were two spears of silver, sharp, well-tempered, headed with steel, three ells in length, of an edge to wound the wind, and cause blood to flow, and swifter than the fall of the dew-drop from the blade of reed-grass, when the dew of June is at the heaviest. A gold-hilted sword was upon his thigh, the blade of which was gilded, bearing a cross of inlaid gold of the hue of the lightning of heaven. His war-horn was of ivory. Before him were two brindled, white-breasted greyhounds, having strong collars of rubies about their necks, reaching from the shoulder to the ear. And the one that was upon the left side bounded across to the right side, and the one on the right to the left, and, like two sea-swallows, sported around him. And his courser cast up four sods, with his four hoofs, like four swallows in the air, about his head, now above, now below. About him was a four-cornered cloth of purple, and an apple of gold was at each corner, and every one of the apples was of the value of an hundred kine. And there was precious gold of the value of three hundred kine upon his shoes, and upon his stirrups, from his knee to the tip of his toe. And the blade of grass bent not beneath him, so light was his courser's tread, as he journeyed toward the gate of Arthur's palace.

Spoke the youth: "Is there a porter?" "There is; and if thou holdest not thy peace, small will be thy welcome. I am Arthur's porter every first day of January." "Open the portal." "I will not open it." "Wherefore not?" "The knife is in the meat, and the drink is in the horn, and there is revelry in Arthur's hall; and none may enter therein but the son of a king of a privileged country, or a craftsman bringing his craft. But there will be refreshment for thy dogs and for thy horse; and for thee there will be collops cooked and peppered, and luscious wine, and mirthful songs; and food for fifty men shall be brought unto thee in the guest-chamber, where the stranger and the sons of other countries eat, who come not into the precincts of the palace of Arthur. Thou wilt fare no worse there than thou wouldst with Arthur in the court. A lady shall smooth thy couch, and shall lull thee with songs; and early to-morrow morning, when the gate is open for the multitude that came hither to-day, for thee shall it be opened first, and thou mayest sit in the place that thou shalt choose in Arthur's hall, from the upper end to the lower." Said the youth: "That will I not do. If thou openest the gate, it is well. If thou dost not open it, I will bring disgrace upon thy lord, and evil report upon thee. And I will set up three shouts at this very gate, than which none were ever heard more deadly." "What clamor soever thou mayest make," said Glewlwyd, the porter, "against the laws of Arthur's palace, shalt thou not enter therein, until I first go and speak with Arthur."

Then Glewlwyd went into the hall. And Arthur said to him, "Hast thou news from the gate?" "Half of my life is passed," said Glewlwyd, "and half of thine. I was heretofore in Kaer Se and Asse, in Sach and Salach, in Lotor and Fotor, and I have been in India the Great and India the Lesser, and I have also been in Europe and Africa, and in the islands of Corsica, and I was present when thou didst conquer Greece in the East. Nine supreme sovereigns, handsome men, saw we there, but never did I behold a man of equal dignity with him who is now at the door of the portal." Then said Arthur: "If walking thou didst enter here, return thou running. It is unbecoming to keep such a man as thou sayest he is in the wind and the rain." Said Kay: "By the hand of my friend, if thou wouldst follow my counsel, thou wouldst not break through the laws of the court because of him." "Not so, blessed Kay," said Arthur; "it is an honor to us to be resorted to, and the greater our courtesy, the greater will be our renown and our fame and our glory."

And Glewlwyd came to the gate, and opened the gate before Kilwich: and although all dismounted upon the horse-block at the gate, yet did he not dismount, but he rode in upon his charger. Then said he, "Greeting be unto thee, sovereign ruler of this island, and be this greeting no less unto the lowest than unto the highest, and be it equally unto thy guests, and thy warriors, and thy chieftains; let all partake of it as completely as thyself. And complete be thy favor, and thy fame, and thy glory, throughout all this

Figure 104: "Culwch" by W. Williams

island." "Greeting unto thee also," said Arthur; "sit thou between two of my warriors, and thou shalt have minstrels before thee, and thou shalt enjoy the privileges of a king born to a throne, as long as thou remainest here. And when I disperse my presents to the visitors and strangers in this court, they shall be in thy hand at my commencing." Said the youth, "I came not here to consume meat and drink; but if I obtain the boon that I seek, I will requite it thee, and extol thee; but if I have it not, I will bear forth thy dispraise to the four quarters of the world, as far as thy renown has extended." Then said Arthur, "Since thou wilt not remain here, chieftain, thou shalt receive the boon, whatsoever thy tongue may name, as far as the wind dries, and the rain moistens, and the sun revolves, and the sea encircles, and the earth extends; save only my ship Prydwen, and my mantle, and Caliburn, my sword, and Rhongomyant, my lance, and Guenever, my wife. By the truth of Heaven, thou shalt have it cheerfuly, name what thou wilt." "I would that thou bless my hair," said he. "That shall be granted thee."

And Arthur took a golden comb, and scissors whereof the loops were of silver, and he combed his hair. And Arthur inquired of him who he was; "for my heart warms unto thee, and I know that thou art come of my blood. Tell me, therefore, who thou art." "I will tell thee," said the youth. "I am Kilwich, the son of Kilydd, the son of Prince Kelyddon, by Goleudyd, my mother, the daughter of Prince Anlawd." "That is true," said Arthur; "thou art my cousin. Whatsoever boon thou mayest ask, thou shalt receive, be it what it may that thy tongue shall name." "Pledge the truth of Heaven and the faith of thy kingdom thereof." "I pledge it thee gladly." "I crave of thee, then, that thou obtain for me Olwen, the daughter of Yspadaden Penkawr, to wife; and this boon I likewise seek at the hands of thy warriors. I seek it from Kay and from Bedwyr; and from Gwynn, the son of Nudd, and Gadwy, the son of Geraint, and Prince Flewddur Flam and Iona, king of France, and Sel, the son of Selgi, and Taliesin, the chief of the bards, and Geraint, the son of Erbin, Garanwyn, the son of Kay, and Amren, the son of Bedwyr, Ol, the son of Olwyd, Bedwin, the bishop, Guenever, the chief lady, and Guenhywach, her sister, Morved, the daughter of Urien, and Gwenlian Deg, the majestic maiden, Creiddylad, [Footnote: Creiddylad is no other than Shakspeare's Cordelia, whose father, King Lear, is by the Welsh authorities called indiscriminately Llyr or Lludd. All the old chronicles give the story of her devotion to her aged parent, but none of them seem to have been aware that she is destined to remain with him till the day of doom, whilst Gwyn ap Nudd, the king of the fairies, and Gwythyr op Greidiol, fight for her every first of May, and whichever of them may be fortunate enough to be the conqueror at that time will obtain her as a bride.] the daughter of Lludd, the constant maiden, and Ewaedah, the daughter of Kynvelyn, [Footnote: The Welsh have a fable on the subject of the half man, taken to be illustrative of the force of habit. In this allegory Arthur is supposed to be met by a sprite, who appears at first in a small and indistinct form, but who, on approaching nearer, increases in size, and, assuming the semblance of half a man, endeavors to provoke the king to wrestle. Despising his weakness, and considering that he should gain no credit by the encounter, Arthur refuses to do so, and delays the contest until at length the half man (Habit) becomes so strong that it requires his utmost efforts to overcome him.] the half-man." All these did Kilwich, the son of Kilydd, adjure to obtain his boon.

Then said Arthur, "O chieftain, I have never heard of the maiden of whom thou speakest, nor of her kindred, but I will gladly send messengers in search of her. Give me time to seek her." And the youth said, "I will willingly grant from this night to that at the end of the year to do so." Then Arthur sent messengers to every land within his dominions to seek for the maiden, and at the end of the year Arthur's messengers returned without having gained any knowledge or intelligence concerning Olwen, more than on the first day. Then said Kilwich, "Every one has received his boon, and I yet lack mine. I will depart, and bear away thy honor with me." Then said Kay, "Rash chieftain! dost thou reproach Arthur? Go with us, and we will not part until thou dost either confess that the maiden exists not in the world, or until we obtain her." Thereupon Kay rose up. And Arthur called Bedwyr, who never shrank from any enterprise upon which Kay was bound. None were equal to him in swiftness throughout this island except Arthur alone; and although he was one handed; three warriors could not shed blood faster than he on the field of battle.

And Arthur called to Kyndelig, the guide, "Go thou upon this expedition with the chieftain." For as good a guide was he in a land which he had never seen as he was in his own.

He called Gurhyr Gwalstat, because he knew all tongues.

He called Gawain, the son of Gwyar, because he never returned home without achieving the adventure of which he went in quest.

And Arthur called Meneu, the son of Teirgwed, in order that, if they went into a savage country, he might cast a charm and an illusion over them, so that none might see them, whilst they could see every one.

They journeyed until they came to a vast open plain, wherein they saw a great castle, which was the fairest of the castles of the world. And when they came before the castle, they beheld a vast flock of sheep. And upon the top of a mound there was a herdsman keeping the sheep. And a rug made of skins was upon him, and by his side was a shaggy mastiff, larger than a steed nine winters old.

Then said Kay, "Gurhyr Gwalstat, go thou and salute yonder man." "Kay," said he, "I engaged not to go further than thou thyself." "Let us go then together." answered Kay. Said Meneu, "Fear not to go thither, for I will cast a spell upon the dog, so that he shall injure no one." And they went up to the mound whereon the herdsman was, and they said to him, "How dost thou fare, herdsman?" "Not less fair be it to you than to me." "Whose are the sheep that thou dost keep, and to whom does yonder castle belong?" "Stupid are ye, truly! not to know that this is the castle of Yspadaden Penkawr. And ye also, who are ye?" "We are an embassy from Arthur, come to seek Olwen, the daughter of Yspadaden Penkawr." "O men! the mercy of Heaven be upon you; do not that for all the world. None who ever came hither on this quest has returned alive." And the herdsman rose up. And as he rose Kilwich gave unto him a ring of gold. And he went home and gave the ring to his spouse to keep. And she took the ring when it was given her, and she said, "Whence came this ring, for thou art not wont to have good fortune." "O wife, him to whom this ring belonged thou shalt see here this evening." "And who is he?" asked the woman. "Kilwich, the son of Kilydd, by Goleudid, the daughter of Prince Anlawd, who is come to seek Olwen as his wife." And when she heard that, she had joy that her nephew, the son of her sister, was coming to her, and sorrow, because she had never known any one depart alive who had come on that quest.

And the men went forward to the gate of the herdsman's dwelling. And when she heard their footsteps approaching, she ran out with joy to meet them. And Kay snatched a billet out of the pile. And when she met them, she sought to throw her arms about their necks. And Kay placed the log between her two hands, and she squeezed it so that it became a twisted coil. "O woman," said Kay, "if thou hadst squeezed me thus, none could ever again have set their affections on me. Evil love were this." They entered into the house and were served; and soon after, they all went forth to amuse themselves. Then the woman opened a stone chest that was before the chimney-corner, and out of it arose a youth with yellow, curling hair. Said Gurhyr, "It is a pity to hide this youth. I know that it is not his own crime that is thus visited upon him." "This is but a remnant," said the woman. "Three and twenty of my sons has Yspadaden Penkawr slain, and I have no more hope of this one than of the others." Then said Kay, "Let him come and be a companion with me, and he shall not be slain unless I also am slain with him." And they ate. And the woman asked them, "Upon what errand come you here?" "We come to seek Olwen for this youth." Then said the woman, "In the name of Heaven, since no one from the castle hath yet seen you, return again whence you came." "Heaven is our witness, that we will not return until we have seen the maiden. Does she ever come hither, so that she may be seen?" "She comes here every Saturday to wash her head, and in the vessel where she washes she leaves all her rings, and she never either comes herself or sends any messengers to fetch them." "Will she come here if she is sent to?" "Heaven knows that I will not destroy my soul, nor will I betray those that trust me; unless you will pledge me your faith that you will not harm her, I will not send to her." "We pledge it," said they. So a message was sent, and she came.

The maiden was clothed in a robe of flame-colored silk, and about her neck was a collar of ruddy gold, on which were precious emeralds and rubies. More yellow was her head than the flower of the broom, [Footnote: The romancers dwell with great complacency on the fair hair and delicate complexion of their heroines. This taste continued for a long time, and to render the hair light was an object of education. Even when wigs came into fashion they were all flaxen. Such was the color of the hair of the Gauls and of their German conquerors. It required some centuries to reconcile their eyes to the swarthy beauties of their Spanish and Italian neighbors.] and her skin was whiter than the foam of the wave, and fairer were her hands and her fingers than the blossoms of the wood-

Figure 105: "Culhwch at Ysbadadden's Court" by E. Wallcousins

anemone amidst the spray of the meadow fountain. The eye of the trained hawk was not brighter than hers. Her bosom was more snowy than the breast of the white swan, her cheek was redder than the reddest roses. Whoso beheld her was filled with her love. Four white trefoils sprung up wherever she trod. And therefore was she called Olwen.

She entered the house and sat beside Kilwich upon the foremost bench; and as soon as he saw her, he knew her. And Kilwich said unto her, "Ah! maiden, thou art she whom I have loved; come away with me, lest they speak evil of thee and of me. Many a day have I loved thee." "I cannot do this, for I have pledged my faith to my father not to go without his counsel, for his life will last only until the time of my espousals. Whatever is to be, must be. But I will give thee advice, if thou wilt take it. Go, ask me of my father, and that which he shall require of thee, grant it, and thou wilt obtain me; but if thou deny him anything, thou wilt not obtain me, and it will be well for thee if thou escape with thy life." "I promise all this, if occasion offer," said he.

She returned to her chamber, and they all rose up, and followed her to the castle. And they slew the nine porters, that were at the nine gates, in silence. And they slew the nine watch-dogs without one of them barking. And they went forward to the hall.

"The greeting of Heaven and of man be unto thee, Yspadaden Penkawr," said they. "And you, wherefore come you?" "We come to ask thy daughter Olwen for Kilwich, the son of Kilydd, the son of Prince Kelyddon." "Where are my pages and my servants? Raise up the forks beneath my two eyebrows, which have fallen over my eyes, that I may see the fashion of my son-in-law." And they did so. "Come hither to-morrow, and you shall have an answer."

They rose to go forth, and Yspadaden Penkawr seized one of the three poisoned darts that lay beside him, and threw it after them. And Bedwyr caught it, and flung it, and pierced Yspadaden Penkawr grievously with it through the knee. Then he said, "A cursed ungentle son-in-law, truly! I shall ever walk the worse for his rudeness, and shall ever be without a cure. This poisoned iron pains me like the bite of a gad-fly. Cursed be the smith who forged it, and the anvil on which it was wrought! So sharp is it!"

That night also they took up their abode in the house of the herdsman. The next day, with the dawn, they arrayed themselves and proceeded to the castle, and entered the hall; and they said, "Yspadaden Penkawr, give us thy daughter in consideration of her dower and her maiden fee, which we will pay to thee, and to her two kinswomen likewise." Then he said, "Her four great-grandmothers and her four great-grandsires are yet alive; it is needful that I take counsel of them." "Be it so," they answered, "we will go to meat." As they rose up he took the second dart that was beside him, and cast it after them. And Meneu, the son of Gawedd, caught it, and flung it back at him, and wounded him in the centre of the breast. "A cursed ungentle son-in-law, truly!" said he; "the hard iron pains me like the bite of a horse-leech. Cursed be the hearth whereon it was heated, and the smith who formed it! So sharp is it! Henceforth, whenever I go up hill, I shall have a scant in my breath, and a pain in my chest, and I shall often loathe my food." And they went to meat.

And the third day they returned to the palace. And Yspadaden Penkawr said to them, "Shoot not at me again unless you desire death. Where are my attendants? Lift up the forks of my eyebrows, which have fallen over my eyeballs, that I may see the fashion of my son-in-law." Then they arose, and, as they did so, Yspadaden Penkawr took the third poisoned dart and cast it at them. And Kilwich caught it, and threw it vigorously, and wounded him through the eyeball. "A cursed ungentle son-in-law, truly! As long as I remain alive, my eyesight will be the worse. Whenever I go against the wind, my eyes will water; and peradventure my head will burn, and I shall have a giddiness every new moon. Like the bite of a mad dog is the stroke of this poisoned iron. Cursed be the fire in which it was forged!" And they went to meat.

And the next day they came again to the palace, and they said, "Shoot not at us any more, unless thou desirest such hurt and harm and torture as thou now hast, and even more." Said Kilwich, "Give me thy daughter; and if thou wilt not give her, thou shalt receive thy death because of her." "Where is he that seeks my daughter? Come hither where I may see thee." And they placed him a chair face to face with him.

Said Yspadaden Penkawr, "Is it thou that seekest my daughter?"

"It is I," answered Kilwich.

"I must have thy pledge that thou wilt not do toward me otherwise than is just; and when I have gotten that which I shall name, my daughter thou shalt have."

"I promise thee that willingly," said Kilwich; "name what thou wilt."

"I will do so," said he. "Seest thou yonder red tilled ground?"

"I see it."

"When first I met the mother of this maiden, nine bushels of flax were sown therein, and none has yet sprung up, white nor black. I require to have the flax to sow in the new land yonder, that when it grows up it may make a white wimple for my daughter's head on the day of thy wedding."

"It will be easy for me to compass this, although thou mayest think it will not be easy."

"Though thou get this, there is yet that which thou wilt not get— the harp of Teirtu, to play to us that night. When a man desires that it should play, it does so of itself; and when he desires that it should cease, it ceases. And this he will not give of his own free will, and thou wilt not be able to compel him."

"It will be easy for me to compass this, although thou mayest think it will not be easy."

"Though thou get this, there is yet that which thou wilt not get. I require thee to get me for my huntsman Mabon, the son of Modron. He was taken from his mother when three nights old, and it is not known where he now is, nor whether he is living or dead."

"It will be easy for me to compass this, although thou mayest think it will not be easy."

"Though thou get this, there is yet that which thou wilt not get— the two cubs of the wolf Gast Rhymhi; no leash in the world will hold them, but a leash made from the beard of Dillus Varwawc, the robber. And the leash will be of no avail unless it be plucked from his beard while he is alive. While he lives he will not suffer this to be done to him, and the leash will be of no use should he be dead, because it will be brittle."

"It will be easy for me to compass this, although thou mayest think it will not be easy."

"Though thou get this, there is yet that which thou wilt not get— the sword of Gwernach the Giant; of his own free will he will not give it, and thou wilt never be able to compel him."

"It will be easy for me to compass this, although thou mayest think it will not be easy."

"Though thou get this, there is yet that which thou wilt not get. Difficulties shalt thou meet with, and nights without sleep, in seeking this, and if thou obtain it not, neither shalt thou obtain my daughter."

"Horses shall I have, and chivalry; and my lord and kinsman, Arthur, will obtain for me all these things. And I shall gain thy daughter, and thou shalt lose thy life."

"Go forward. And thou shalt not be chargeable for food or raiment for my daughter while thou art seeking these things; and when thou hast compassed all these marvels, thou shalt have my daughter for thy wife."

Chapter 12

KILWICH AND OLWEN (CONTINUED)

All that day they journeyed until the evening, and then they beheld a vast castle, which was the largest in the world. And lo! a black man, larger than three of the men of this world, came out from the castle. And they spoke unto him, and said, "O man, whose castle is that?" "Stupid are ye, truly, O men! There is no one in the world that does not know that this is the castle of Gwernach the Giant." "What treatment is there for guests and strangers that alight in that castle?" "O chieftain, Heaven protect thee! No guests ever returned thence alive, and no one may enter therein unless he brings with him his craft."

Then they proceeded towards the gate. Said Gurhyr Gwalstat, "Is there a porter?" "There is; wherefore dost thou call?" "Open the gate." "I will not open it." "Wherefore wilt thou not?" "The knife is in the meat, and the drink is in the horn, and there is revelry in the hall of Gwernach the Giant; and except for a craftsman who brings his craft, the gate will not be opened to-night." "Verily, porter," then said Kay, "my craft bring I with me." "What is thy craft?" "The best burnisher of swords am I in the world." "I will go and tell this unto Gwernach the Giant, and I will bring thee an answer."

So the porter went in, and Gwernach said to him, "Hast thou news from the gate?" "I have. There is a party at the door of the gate who desire to come in." "Didst thou inquire of them if they possessed any art?" "I did inquire," said he, "and one told me that he was well skilled in the burnishing of swords." "We have need of him then. For some time have I sought for some one to polish my sword, and could find no one. Let this man enter, since he brings with him his craft."

The porter thereupon returned and opened the gate. And Kay went in by himself, and he saluted Gwernach the Giant. And a chair was placed for him opposite to Gwernach. And Gwernach said to him, "O man, is it true that is reported of thee, that thou knowest how to burnish swords?" "I know full well how to do so," answered Kay. Then was the sword of Gwernach brought to him. And Kay took a blue whetstone from under his arm, and asked whether he would have it burnished white or blue. "Do with it as it seems good to thee, or as thou wouldst if it were thine own." Then Kay polished one half of the blade, and put it in his hand. "Will this please thee?" asked he. "I would rather than all that is in my dominions that the whole of it were like this. It is a marvel to me that such a man as thou should be without a companion." "O noble sir, I have a companion, albeit he is not skilled in this art." "Who may he be?" "Let the porter go forth, and I will tell him whereby he may know him. The head of his lance will leave its shaft, and draw blood from the wind, and will descend upon its shaft again." Then the gate was opened, and Bedwyr entered. And Kay said, "Bedwyr is very skilful, though he knows not this art."

And there was much discourse among those who were without, because that Kay and Bedwyr had gone in. And a young man who was with them, the only son of the herdsman, got in also; and he contrived to admit all the rest, but they kept themselves concealed.

The sword was now polished, and Kay gave it unto the hand of Gwernach the Giant, to see if he were pleased with his work. And the giant said, "The work is good; I am content therewith." Said Kay, "It is thy scabbard that hath rusted thy sword; give it to me, that I may take out the wooden sides of it, and put in new ones." And he took the scabbard from him, and the sword in the other hand. And he came and stood over against the giant, as if he would have put the sword into the scabbard; and with it he struck at the head of the giant, and cut off his head at one blow. Then they despoiled the castle, and took from it what goods and jewels they would. And they returned to Arthur's court, bearing with them the sword of Gwernach the Giant.

And when they told Arthur how they had sped, Arthur said, "It is a good beginning." Then they took counsel, and said, "Which of these marvels will it be best for us to seek next?" "It will be best," said one, "to seek Mabon, the son of Modron; and he will not be found unless we first find Eidoel, the son of Aer, his kinsman." Then Arthur rose up, and the warriors of the island of Britain with him, to seek for Eidoel; and they proceeded until they came to the castle of Glivi, where Eidoel was imprisoned. Glivi stood on the summit of his castle, and he said, "Arthur, what requirest thou of me, since nothing remains to me in this fortress, and I have neither joy nor pleasure in it, neither wheat nor oats? Seek not, therefore, to do me harm." Said Arthur, "Not to injure thee came I hither, but to seek for the prisoner that is with thee." "I will give thee my prisoner, though I had not thought to give him up to any one, and therewith shalt thou have my support and my aid."

His followers said unto Arthur, "Lord, go thou home, thou canst not proceed with thy host in quest of such small adventures as these." Then said Arthur, "It were well for thee, Gurhyr Gwalstat, to go upon this quest, for thou knowest all languages, and art familiar with those of the birds and the beasts. Thou, Eidoel, oughtest likewise to go with thy men in search of thy cousin. And as for you, Kay and Bedwyr, I have hope of whatever adventure ye are in quest of, that ye will achieve it. Achieve ye this adventure for me."

They went forward until they came to the Ousel of Cilgwri. And Gurhyr adjured her, saying, "Tell me if thou knowest aught of Mabon, the son of Modron, who was taken when three nights old from between his mother and the wall?" And the Ousel answered, "When I first came here, there was a smith's anvil in this place, and I was then a young bird; and from that time no work has been done upon it, save the pecking of my beak every evening; and now there is not so much as the size of a nut remaining thereof; yet during all that time I have never heard of the man for whom you inquire. Nevertheless, I will do that which it is fitting that I should for an embassy from Arthur. There is a race of animals who were formed before me, and I will be your guide to them."

So they proceeded to the place where was the Stag of Redynvre. "Stag of Redynvre, behold, we are come to thee, an embassy from Arthur, for we have not heard of any animal older than thou. Say, knowest thou aught of Mabon, the son of Modron, who was taken from his mother when three nights old?" The Stag said, "When first I came hither there was a plain all around me, without any trees save one oak sapling, which grew up to be an oak with an hundred branches; and that oak has since perished, so that now nothing remains of it but the withered stump; and from that day to this I have been here, yet have I never heard of the man for whom you inquire. Nevertheless, being an embassy from Arthur, I will be your guide to the place where there is an animal which was formed before I was, and the oldest animal in the world, and the one that has travelled most, the Eagle of Gwern Abwy."

Gurhyr said, "Eagle of Gwern Abwy, we have come to thee, an embassy from Arthur, to ask thee if thou knowest aught of Mabon, the son of Modron, who was taken from his mother when he was three nights old?" The Eagle said, "I have been here for a great space of time, and when I first came hither, there was a rock here from the top of which I pecked at the stars every evening; and it has crumbled away, and now it is not so much as a span high. All that time I have been here, and I have never heard of the man for whom you inquire, except once when I went in search of food as far as Llyn Llyw. And when I came there, I struck my talons into a salmon, thinking he would serve me as food for a long time. But he drew me into the water, and I was scarcely able to escape from him. After that I made peace with him. And I drew fifty fish- spears out of his back, and relieved him. Unless he know something of him whom you seek, I cannot tell who may. However, I will guide you to the place where he is."

So they went thither; and the Eagle said, "Salmon of Llyn Llyw, I have come to thee with an embassy from Arthur, to ask thee if thou knowest aught of Mabon, the son of Modron, who was taken away at three nights old from his mother." "As much as I know I will tell thee. With

Figure 106: "The Wooing of Olwen" by John D. Batten

every tide I go along the river upward, until I come near to the walls of Gloucester, and there have I found such wrong as I never found elsewhere; and to the end that ye may give credence thereto, let one of you go thither upon each of my two shoulders." So Kay and Gurhyr Gwalstat went upon the two shoulders of the Salmon, and they proceeded until they came unto the wall of the prison; and they heard a great wailing and lamenting from the dungeon. Said Gurhyr, "Who is it that laments in this house of stone?" "Alas! it is Mabon, the son of Modron, who is here imprisoned; and no imprisonment was ever so grievous as mine." "Hast thou hope of being released for gold or for silver, or for any gifts of wealth, or through battle and fighting?" "By fighting will what ever I may gain be obtained."

Then they went thence, and returned to Arthur, and they told him where Mabon, the son of Modron, was imprisoned. And Arthur summoned the warriors of the island, and they journeyed as far as Gloucester, to the place where Mabon was in prison. Kay and Bedwyr went upon the shoulders of the fish, whilst the warriors of Arthur attacked the castle. And Kay broke through the wall into the dungeon, and brought away the prisoner upon his back, whilst the fight was going on between the warriors. And Arthur returned home, and Mabon with him at liberty.

On a certain day as Gurhyr Gwalstat was walking over a mountain, he heard a wailing and a grievous cry. And when he heard it, he sprang forward and went towards it. And when he came there, he saw a fire burning among the turf, and an ant-hill nearly surrounded with the fire. And he drew his sword, and smote off the ant-hill close to the earth, so that it escaped being burned in the fire. And the ants said to him, "Receive from us the blessing of Heaven, and that which no man can give, we give thee." Then they fetched the nine bushels of flax-seed which Yspadaden Penkawr had required of Kilwich, and they brought the full measure, without lacking any, except one flax-seed, and that the lame pismire brought in before night.

Then said Arthur, "Which of the marvels will it be best for us to seek next?" "It will be best to seek for the two cubs of the wolf Gast Rhymhi."

"Is it known," said Arthur, "where she is?" "She is in Aber Cleddyf," said one. Then Arthur went to the house of Tringad, in Aber Cleddyf, and he inquired of him whether he had heard of her there. "She has often slain my herds, and she is there below in a cave in Aber Cleddyf."

Ther Arthur went in his ship Prydwen by sea, and the others went by land to hunt her. And they surrounded her and her two cubs, and took them and carried them away.

As Kay and Bedwyr sat on a beacon-cairn on the summit of Plinlimmon, in the highest wind that ever was, they looked around them and saw a great smoke, afar off. Then said Kay, "By the hand of my friend, yonder is the fire of a robber." Then they hastened towards the smoke, and they came so near to it that they could see Dillus Varwawc scorching a wild boar. "Behold, yonder is the greatest robber that ever fled from Arthur," said Bedwyr to Kay. "Dost thou know him?" "I do know him," answered Kay; "he is Dillus Varwarc, and no leash in the world will be able to hold the cubs of Gast Rhymi, save a leash made from the beard of him thou seest yonder. And even that will be useless unless his beard be plucked out alive, with wooden tweezers; for if dead it will be brittle." "What thinkest thou that we should do concerning this?" said Bedwyr. "Let us suffer him." said Kay, "to eat as much as he will of the meat, and after that he will fall asleep." And during that time they employed themselves in making the wooden tweezers. And when Kay knew certainly that he was asleep, he made a pit under his feet, and he struck him a violent blow, and squeezed him into the pit. And there they twitched out his beard completely with the wooden tweezers, and after that they slew him altogether. And from thence they went, and took the leash made of Dillus Varwawc's beard, and they gave it into Arthur's hand.

Thus they got all the marvels that Yspadaden Penkawr had required of Kilwich; and they set forward, and took the marvels to his court. And Kilwich said to Yspadaden Penkawr, "Is thy daughter mine now?" "She is thine," said he, "but therefore needest thou not thank me, but Arthur, who hath accomplished this for thee." Then Goreu, the son of Custennin, the herdsman, whose brothers Yspadaden Penkawr had slain, seized him by the hair of his head, and dragged him after him to the keep, and cut off his head, and placed it on a stake on the citadel. Then they took possession of his castle, and of his treasures. And that night Olwen became Kilwich's bride, and she continued to be his wife as long as she lived.

Chapter 13

TALIESIN

Gwyddno Garanhir was sovereign of Gwaelod, a territory bordering on the sea. And he possessed a weir upon the strand between Dyvi and Aberystwyth, near to his own castle, and the value of an hundred pounds was taken in that weir every May eve. And Gwyddno had an only son named Elphin, the most hapless of youths, and the most needy. And it grieved his father sore, for he thought that he was born in an evil hour. By the advice of his council, his father had granted him the drawing of the weir that year, to see if good luck would ever befall him, and to give him something wherewith to begin the world. And this was on the twenty-ninth of April.

The next day, when Elphin went to look, there was nothing in the weir but a leathern bag upon a pole of the weir. Then said the weir-ward unto Elphin, "All thy ill-luck aforetime was nothing to this; and now thou hast destroyed the virtues of the weir, which always yielded the value of an hundred pounds every May eve; and to-night there is nothing but this leathern skin within it." "How now," said Elphin, "there may be therein the value of a hundred pounds." Well! they took up the leathern bag, and he who opened it saw the forehead of an infant, the fairest that ever was seen; and he said, "Behold a radiant brow?" (In the Welsh language, taliesin.) "Taliesin be he called," said Elphin. And he lifted the bag in his arms, and, lamenting his bad luck, placed the boy sorrowfully behind him. And he made his horse amble gently, that before had been trotting, and he carried him as softly as if he had been sitting in the easiest chair in the world. And presently the boy made a Consolation, and praise to Elphin; and the Consolation was as you may here see:

"Fair Elphin, cease to lament!
Never in Gwyddno's weir
Was there such good luck as this night.
Being sad will not avail;
Better to trust in God than to forbode ill;
Weak and small as I am,
On the foaming beach of the ocean,
In the day of trouble I shall be
Of more service to thee than three hundred salmon."

This was the first poem that Taliesin ever sung, being to console Elphin in his grief for that the produce of the weir was lost, and what was worse, that all the world would consider that it was through his fault and ill-luck. Then Elphin asked him what he was, whether man or spirit. And he sung thus:

"I have been formed a comely person;
Although I am but little, I am highly gifted;
Into a dark leathern bag I was thrown,
And on a boundless sea I was sent adrift.
From seas and from mountains
God brings wealth to the fortunate man."

Then came Elphin to the house of Gwyddno, his father, and Taliesin with him. Gwyddno asked him if he had had a good haul at the weir, and he told him that he had got that which was better than fish. "What was that?" said Gwyddno. "A bard," said Elphin. Then said Gwyddno, "Alas! what will he profit thee?" And Taliesin himself replied and said, "He will profit him more than the weir ever profited thee." Asked Gwyddno, "Art thou able to speak, and thou so little?" And Taliesin answered him, "I am better able to speak than thou to question me." "Let me hear what thou canst say," quoth Gwyddno. Then Taliesin sang:

"Three times have I been born, I know by meditation;
All the sciences of the world are collected in my breast,
For I know what has been, and what hereafter will
occur."

Elphin gave his haul to his wife, and she nursed him tenderly and lovingly. Thenceforward Elphin increased in riches more and more, day after day, and in love and favor with the king; and there abode Taliesin until he was thirteen years old, when Elphin, son of Gwyddno, went by a Christmas invitation to his uncle, Maelgan Gwynedd, who held open court at Christmas-tide in the castle of Dyganwy, for all the number of his lords of both degrees, both spiritual and temporal, with a vast and thronged host of knights and squires. And one arose and said, "Is there in the whole world a king so great as Maelgan, or one on whom Heaven has bestowed so many gifts as upon him;—

form, and beauty, and meekness, and strength, besides all the powers of the soul?" And together with these they said that Heaven had given one gift that exceeded all the others, which was the beauty, and grace, and wisdom, and modesty of his queen, whose virtues surpassed those of all the ladies and noble maidens throughout the whole kingdom. And with this they put questions one to another, Who had braver men? Who had fairer or swifter horses or greyhounds? Who had more skilful or wiser bards than Maelgan?

When they had all made an end of their praising the king and his gifts, it befell that Elphin spoke on this wise. "Of a truth, none but a king may vie with a king; but were he not a king, I would say that my wife was as virtuous as any lady in the kingdom, and also that I have a bard who is more skilful than all the king's bards." In a short space some of his fellows told the king all the boastings of Elphin; and the king ordered him to be thrown into a strong prison, until he might show the truth as to the virtues of his wife, and the wisdom of his bard.

Now when Elphin had been put in a tower of the castle, with a thick chain about his feet (it is said that it was a silver chain, because he was of royal blood), the king, as the story relates, sent his son Rhun to inquire into the demeanor of Elphin's wife. Now Rhun was the most graceless man in the world, and there was neither wife nor maiden with whom he held converse but was evil spoken of. While Rhun went in haste towards Elphin's dwelling, being fully minded to bring disgrace upon his wife, Taliesin told his mistress how that the king had placed his master in durance in prison, and how that Rhun was coming in haste to strive to bring disgrace upon her. Wherefore he caused his mistress to array one of the maids of her kitchen in her apparel; which the noble lady gladly did, and she loaded her hands with the best rings that she and her husband possessed.

In this guise Taliesin caused his mistress to put the maiden to sit at the board in her room at supper; and he made her to seem as her mistress, and the mistress to seem as the maid. And when they were in due time seated at their supper, in the manner that has been said, Rhun suddenly arrived at Elphin's dwelling, and was received with joy, for the servants knew him; and they brought him to the room of their mistress, in the semblance of whom the maid rose up from supper and welcomed him gladly. And afterwards she sat down to supper again, and Rhun with her. Then Rhun began jesting with the maid, who still kept the semblance of her mistress. And verily this story shows that the maiden became so intoxicated that she fell asleep; and the story relates that it was a powder that Rhun put into the drink, that made her sleep so soundly that she never felt it when he cut off from her hand her little finger, whereon was the signet ring of Elphin, which he had sent to his wife as a token a short time before. And Rhun returned to the king with the finger and the ring as a proof, to show that he had cut it off from her hand without her awaking from her sleep of intemperance.

The king rejoiced greatly at these tidings, and he sent for his councillors, to whom he told the whole story from the beginning. And he caused Elphin to be brought out of prison, and he chided him because of his boast. And he spake on this wise: "Elphin, be it known to thee beyond a doubt, that it is but folly for a man to trust in the virtues of his wife further than he can see her; and that thou mayest be certain of thy wife's vileness, behold her finger, with thy signet ring upon it, which was cut from her hand last night, while she slept the sleep of intoxication." Then thus spake Elphin: "With thy leave, mighty king, I cannot deny my ring, for it is known of many; but verily I assert that the finger around which it is was never attached to the hand of my wife; for in truth and certainty there are three notable things pertaining to it, none of which ever belonged to any of my wife's fingers. The first of the three is, that it is certainly known to me that this ring would never remain upon her thumb, whereas you can plainly see that it is hard to draw it over the joint of the little finger of the hand whence this was cut. The second thing is, that my wife has never let pass one Saturday since I have known her, without paring her nails before going to bed, and you can see fully that the nail of this little finger has not been pared for a month. The third is, truly, that the hand whence this finger came was kneading rye dough within three days before the finger was cut therefrom, and I can assure your highness that my wife has never kneaded rye dough since my wife she has been."

The king was mightily wroth with Elphin for so stoutly withstanding him, respecting the goodness of his wife; wherefore he ordered him to his prison a second time, saying that he should not be loosed thence until he had proved the truth of his boast, as well concerning the wisdom of his bard as the virtues of his wife.

Chapter 13: Taliesin

In the meantime, his wife and Taliesin remained joyful at Elphin's dwelling. And Taliesin showed his mistress how that Elphin was in prison because of them; but he bade her be glad, for that he would go to Maelgan's court to free his master. So he took leave of his mistress, and came to the court of Maelgan, who was going to sit in his hall, and dine in his royal state, as it was the custom in those days for kings and princes to do at every chief feast. As soon as Taliesin entered the hall he placed himself in a quiet corner, near the place where the bards and the minstrels were wont to come, in doing their service and duty to the king, as is the custom at the high festivals, when the bounty is proclaimed. So, when the bards and the heralds came to cry largess, and to proclaim the power of the king, and his strength, at the moment when they passed by the corner wherein he was crouching, Taliesin pouted out his lips after them, and played "Blerwm, blerwm!" with his finger upon his lips. Neither took they much notice of him as they went by but proceeded forward till they came before the king, unto whom they made their obeisance with their bodies, as they were wont, without speaking a single word, but pouting out their lips, and making mouths at the king, playing, "Blerwm, blerwm!" upon their lips with their fingers, as they had seen the boy do. This sight caused the king to wonder, and to deem within himself that they were drunk with many liquors. Wherefore he commanded one of his lords, who served at the board, to go to them and desire them to collect their wits, and to consider where they stood, and what it was fitting for them to do. And this lord did so gladly. But they ceased not from their folly any more than before. Whereupon he sent to them a second time, and a third, desiring them to go forth from the hall. At the last the king ordered one of his squires to give a blow to the chief of them, named Heinin Vardd; and the squire took a broom and struck him on the head, so that he fell back in his seat. Then he arose, and went on his knees, and besought leave of the king's grace to show that this their fault was not through want of knowledge, neither through drunkenness, but by the influence of some spirit that was in the hall. And he spoke on this wise: "O honorable king, be it known to your grace that not from the strength of drink, or of too much liquor, arc wc dumb, but through the influence of a spirit that sits in the corner yonder, in the form of a child." Forthwith the king commanded the squire to fetch him; and he went to the nook where Taliesin sat, and brought him before the king, who asked him what he was, and whence he came. And he answered the king in verse:

"Primary chief bard am I to Elphin,
And my native country is the region of the summer stars;
I have been in Asia with Noah in the ark,
I have seen the destruction of Sodom and Gomorrah,
I was in India when Rome was built,
I have now come here to the remnant of Troia."

When the king and his nobles had heard the song, they wondered much, for they had never heard the like from a boy so young as he. And when the king knew that he was the bard of Elphin he bade Heinin, his first and wisest bard, to answer Taliesin, and to strive with him. But when he came he could do no other than play "Blerwm!" on his lips; and when he sent for the others of the four and twenty bards, they all did likewise, and could do no other. And Maelgan asked the boy Taliesin what was his errand, and he answered him in song:

"Elphin, the son of Gwyddno,
Is in the land of Artro,
Secured by thirteen locks,
For praising his instructor.
Therefore I, Taliesin,
Chief of the bards of the west,
Will loosen Elphin
Out of a golden fetter."
Then he sang to them a riddle:
"Discover thou what is
The strong creature from before the flood,
Without flesh, without bone,
Without vein, without blood,
Without head, without feet;
It will neither be older nor younger
Than at the beginning.
Behold how the sea whitens
When first it comes,
When it comes from the south,
When it strikes on coasts
It is in the field, it is in the wood,
But the eye cannot perceive it.
One Being has prepared it,
By a tremendous blast,

To wreak vengeance
On Maelgan Gwynedd."

While he was thus singing his verse, there arose a mighty storm of wind, so that the king and all his nobles thought that the castle would fall upon their heads. And the king caused them to fetch Elphin in haste from his dungeon, and placed him before Taliesin. And it is said that immediately he sung a verse, so that the chains opened from about his feet.

After that Taliesin brought Elphin's wife before them, and showed that she had not one finger wanting. And in this manner did he set his master free from prison, and protect the innocence of his mistress, and silence the bards so that not one of them dared to say a word. Right glad was Elphin, right glad was Taliesin.

HERO MYTHS OF THE BRITISH RACE

BEOWULF

Notable among the names of heroes of the British race is that of Beowulf, which appeals to all English-speaking people in a very special way, since he is the one hero in whose story we may see the ideals of our English forefathers before they left their Continental home to cross to the islands of Britain.

Although this hero had distinguished himself by numerous feats of strength during his boyhood and early youth, it was as the deliverer of Hrothgar, king of Denmark, from the monster Grendel that he first gained wide renown. Grendel was half monster and half man, and had his abode in the fen-fastnesses in the vicinity of Hrothgar's residence. Night after night he would steal into the king's great palace called Heorot and slay sometimes as many as thirty at one time of the knights sleeping there.

Beowulf put himself at the head of a selected band of warriors, went against the monster, and after a terrible fight slew it. The following night Grendel's mother, a fiend scarcely less terrible than her son, carried off one of Hrothgar's boldest thanes. Once more Beowulf went to the help of the Danish king, followed the she-monster to her lair at the bottom of a muddy lake in the midst of the swamp, and with his good sword Hrunting and his own muscular arms broke the sea-woman's neck.

Upon his return to his own country of the Geats, loaded with honors bestowed upon him by Hrothgar, Beowulf served the king of Geatland as the latter's most trusted counsellor and champion. When, after many years, the king fell before an enemy, the Geats unanimously chose Beowulf for their new king. His fame as a warrior kept his country free from invasion, and his wisdom as a statesman increased its prosperity and happiness.

In the fiftieth year of Beowulf's reign, however, a great terror fell upon the land in the way of a monstrous fire-dragon, which flew forth by night from its den in the rocks, lighting up the blackness with its blazing breath, and burning houses and homesteads, men and cattle, with the flames from its mouth. When the news came to Beowulf that his people were suffering and dying, and that no warrior dared to risk his life in an effort to deliver the country from this deadly devastation, the aged king took up his shield and sword and went forth to his last fight. At the entrance of the dragon's cave Beowulf raised his voice and shouted a furious defiance to the awesome guardian of the den. Roaring hideously and napping his glowing wings together, the dragon rushed forth and half flew, half sprang, on Beowulf. Then began a fearful combat, which ended in Beowulf's piercing the dragon's scaly armor and inflicting a mortal wound, but alas! in himself being given a gash in the neck by his opponent's poisoned fangs which resulted in his death. As he lay stretched on the ground, his head supported by Wiglaf, an honored warrior who had helped in the fight with the dragon, Beowulf roused himself to say, as he grasped Wiglaf's hand:

"Thou must now look to the needs of the nation;
Here dwell I no longer, for Destiny calleth me!
Bid thou my warriors after my funeral pyre
Build me a burial-cairn high on the sea-cliff's head;
So that the seafarers Beowulf's Barrow
Henceforth shall name it, they who drive far and wide
Over the mighty flood their foamy keels.
Thou art the last of all the kindred of Wagmund!
Wyrd has swept all my kin, all the brave chiefs away!
Now must I follow them!"

These last words spoken, the king of the Geats, brave to seek danger and brave to look on death and Fate

Figure 107: "Cuchulain in Battle" by Joseph Christian Leyendecker

undaunted, fell back dead. According to his last desires, his followers gathered wood and piled it on the cliff-head. Upon this funeral pyre was laid Beowulf's body and consumed to ashes. Then, upon the same cliff of Hronesness, was erected a huge burial cairn, wide-spread and lofty, to be known thereafter as Beowulf's Barrow.

CUCHULAIN, CHAMPION OF IRELAND

Among all the early literatures of Europe, there are two which, at exactly opposite corners of the continent, display most strikingly similar characteristics. These are the Greek and the Irish, and the legend of the Irish champion Cuchulain, which well illustrates the similarity of the literatures, bears so close a resemblance to the story of Achilles as to win for this hero the title of "the Irish Achilles." Certainly in reckless courage, power of inspiring dread, sense of personal merit, and frankness of speech the Irish hero is fully equal to the mighty Greek.

Cuchulain was the nephew of King Conor of Ulster, son of his sister Dechtire, and it is said that his father was no mortal man, but the great god Lugh of the Long Hand. Cuchulain was brought up by King Conor himself, and even while he was still a boy his fame spread all over Ireland. His warlike deeds were those of a proved warrior, not of a child of nursery age; and by the time Cuchulain was seventeen he was without peer among the champions of Ulster.

Upon Cuchulain's marriage to Emer, daughter of Forgall the Wily, a Druid of great power, the couple took up their residence at Armagh, the capital of Ulster, under the protection of King Conor. Here there was one chief, Bricriu of the Bitter Tongue, who, like Thersites among the Grecian leaders, delighted in making mischief. Soon he had on foot plans for stirring up strife among the heroes of Ulster, leaders among whom were the mighty Laegaire, Conall Cearnach, cousin of Cuchulain, and Cuchulain himself. Inviting the members of King Conor's court to dinner, Bricriu arranged that a contest should arise over who should have the "champion's portion," and so successful was he that, to avoid a bloody fight, the three heroes mentioned decided to submit their claims to the championship of Ireland to King Ailill of Connaught.

Ailill put the heroes to an unexpected test. Their dinner was served them in a separate room, into which three magic beasts, in the shape of monstrous cats, were sent by the king. When they saw them Laegire and Conall rose from their meal, climbed among the rafters, and stayed there all night. Cuchulain waited until one cat attacked him, and then, drawing his sword, struck the monster. It showed no further sign of fight, and at daybreak the magic beasts disappeared.

As Laegire and Conall claimed that this test was an unfair one, Ailill sent the three rivals to Curoi of Kerry, a just and wise man, who set out to discover by wizardry and enchantments the best among the heroes. In turn they stood watch outside Curoi's castle, where Laegire and Conall were overcome by a huge giant, who hurled spears of mighty oak trees, and ended by throwing them over the wall into the courtyard. Cuchulain alone withstood the giant, whereupon he was attacked by other magic foes. Among these was a dragon, which flew on horrible wings from a neighboring lake, and seemed ready to devour everything in its way. Cuchulain sprang up, giving his wonderful hero-leap, thrust his arm into the dragon's mouth and down its throat, and tore out its heart. After the monster fell dead, he cut off its scaly head.

As even yet Cuchulain's opponents would not admit his championship, they were all three directed to return to Armagh, to await Curoi's judgment. Here it happened that all the Ulster heroes were in the great hall one night, except Cuchulain and his cousin Conall. As they sat in order of rank, a terrible stranger, gigantic in stature, hideous of aspect, with ravening yellow eyes, entered. In his hand he bore an enormous axe, with keen and shining edge. Upon King Conor's inquiring his business there, the stranger replied:

"Behold my axe! The man who will grasp it to-day may cut my head off with it, provided that I may, in like manner, cut off his head to-morrow. If you have no champion who dare face me, I will say that Ulster has lost her courage and is dishonored."

At once Laegire accepted the challenge. The giant laid his head on a block, and at a blow the hero severed it from the body. Thereupon the giant arose, took the head and the axe, and thus, headless, strode from the hall. But the following night, when he returned, sound as ever, to claim the fulfilment of Laegire's promise, the latter's heart failed him and he did not come forward. The stranger then jeered at the men of Ulster because their great champion durst not keep his agreement, nor face the blow he should receive in return for the one he gave.

The men of Ulster were utterly ashamed, but Conall Cearnach, who was present that night, made a new agreement with the stranger. He gave a blow which beheaded the giant, but again, when the latter returned whole and sound on the following evening, the champion was not to be found.

Now it was the turn of Cuchulain, who, as the others had done, cut off the giant's head at one stroke. The next day the members of Conor's court watched Cuchulain to see what he would do. They would not have been surprised if he had failed like the others, who now were present. The champion, however, showed no signs of failing or retreat. He sat sorrowfully in his place, and with a sigh said to King Conor as they waited: "Do not leave this place till all is over. Death is coming to me very surely, but I must fulfil my agreement, for I would rather die than break my word."

Towards the close of day the stranger strode into the hall exultant.

"Where is Cuchulain?" he cried.

"Here I am," was the reply.

"Ah, poor boy! your speech is sad to-night, and the fear of death lies heavy on you; but at least you have redeemed your word and have not failed me."

The youth rose from his seat and went towards him, as he stood with the great axe ready, and knelt to receive the blow.

The hero of Ulster laid his head on the block; but the giant was not satisfied. "Stretch out your neck better," said he.

"You are playing with me, to torment me," said Cuchulain. "Slay me now speedily, for I did not keep you waiting last night."

However, he stretched out his neck as ordered, and the stranger raised his axe till it crashed upwards through the rafters of the hall, like the crash of trees falling in a storm. When the axe came down with a terrific sound all men looked fearfully at Cuchulain. The descending axe had not even touched him; it had come down with the blunt side on the ground, and the youth knelt there unharmed. Smiling at him, and leaning on his axe, stood no terrible and hideous stranger, but Curoi of Kerry, come to give his decision at last.

"Rise up, Cuchulain," said Curoi. "There is none among all the heroes of Ulster to equal you in courage and loyalty and truth. The Championship of the Heroes of Ireland is yours from this day forth, and the Champion's Portion at all feasts; and to your wife I adjudge the first place among all the women of Ulster. Woe to him who dares to dispute this decision!" Thereupon Curoi vanished, and the warriors gathered around Cuchulain, and all with one voice acclaimed him the Champion of the Heroes of all Ireland—a title which has clung to him until this day.

This is one of many stories told of the Irish champion, whose deeds of bravery would fill many pages. Cuchulain finally came to his end on the field of battle, after a fight in which he displayed all his usual gallantry but in which unfair means were used to overcome him.

For Wales and for England during centuries Arthur has been the representative "very gentle perfect knight." In a similar way, in England's sister isle, Cuchulain stands ever for the highest ideals of the Irish Gaels.

HEREWARD THE WAKE

In Hereward the Wake (or "Watchful") is found one of those heroes whose date can be ascertained with a fair amount of exactness and yet in whose story occur mythological elements which seem to belong to all ages. The folklore of primitive races is a great storehouse whence a people can choose tales and heroic deeds to glorify its own national hero, careless that the same tales and deeds have done duty for other peoples and other heroes. Hence it happens that Hereward the Saxon, a patriot hero as real and actual as Nelson or George Washington, whose deeds were recorded in prose and verse within forty years of his death, was even then surrounded by a cloud of romance and mystery, which hid in vagueness his family, his marriage, and even his death.

Briefly it may be stated that Hereward was a native of Lincolnshire, and was in his prime about 1070. In that year he joined a party of Danes who appeared in England, attacked Peterborough and sacked the abbey there, and afterward took refuge in the Isle of Ely. Here he was besieged by William the Conqueror, and was finally forced to yield to the Norman. He thus came to stand for the defeated Saxon race, and his name has been passed down as that of the darling hero of the Saxons. For his splendid defence of Ely they forgave his final surrender to Duke William; they attributed to him all the virtues supposed to be inherent in the free-born, and all the glorious valor on which the English prided themselves; and, lastly, they surrounded his death with a halo of desperate fighting, and made his last conflict as wonderful as that of Roland at Roncesvalles. If Roland is the ideal of Norman feudal chivalry, Hereward is equally the ideal of Anglo-Saxon sturdy manliness and knighthood.

An account of one of Hereward's adventures as a youth will serve as illustration of the stories told of his prowess. On an enforced visit to Cornwall, he found that King Alef, a petty British chief, had betrothed his fair daughter to a terrible Pictish giant, breaking off, in order to do it, her troth-plight with Prince Sigtryg of Waterford, son of a Danish king in Ireland. Hereward, ever chivalrous, picked a quarrel with the giant and killed him in fair fight, whereupon the king threw him into prison. In the following night, however, the released princess arranged that the gallant Saxon should be freed and sent hot-foot for her lover, Prince Sigtryg. After many adventures Hereward reached the prince, who hastened to return to Cornwall with the young hero. But to the grief of both, they learned upon their arrival that the princess had just been betrothed to a wild Cornish hero, Haco, and the wedding feast was to be held that very day. Sigtryg at once sent a troop of forty Danes to King Alef demanding the fulfilment of the troth-plight between himself and his daughter, and threatening vengeance if it were broken. To this threat the king returned no answer, and no Dane came back to tell of their reception.

Sigtryg would have waited till morning, trusting in the honor of the king, but Hereward disguised himself as a minstrel and obtained admission to the bridal feast, where he soon won applause by his beautiful singing. The bridegroom, Haco, in a rapture offered him any boon he liked to ask, but he demanded only a cup of wine from the hands of the bride. When she brought it to him he flung into the empty cup the betrothal ring, the token she had sent to Sigtryg, and said: "I thank thee, lady, and would reward thee for thy gentleness to a wandering minstrel; I give back the cup, richer than before by the kind thoughts of which it bears the token." The princess looked at him, gazed into the goblet, and saw her ring; then, looking again, she recognized her deliverer and knew that rescue was at hand.

While men feasted Hereward listened and talked, and found out that the forty Danes were prisoners, to be released on the morrow when Haco was sure of his bride, but released useless and miserable, since they would be turned adrift blinded. Haco was taking his lovely bride back to his own land, and Hereward saw that any rescue, to be successful, must be attempted on the march.

Returning to Sigtryg, the young Saxon told all that he had learned, and the Danes planned an ambush in the ravine where Haco had decided to blind and set free his captives. The whole was carried out exactly as Hereward arranged it. The Cornishmen, with the Danish captives, passed first without attack; next came Haco, riding grim and ferocious beside his silent bride, he exulting in his success, she looking eagerly for any signs of rescue. As they passed Hereward sprang from his shelter, crying, "Upon them, Danes, and set your brethren free!" and himself struck down Haco and smote off his head. There was a short struggle, but soon the rescued Danes were able to aid their deliverers, and the Cornish guards were all slain; the men of King Alef, never very zealous for the cause of Haco, fled, and the Danes were left masters of the field.

Sigtryg had in the meantime seen to the safety of the princess, and now, placing her between himself and Hereward, he escorted her to the ship, which soon brought them to Waterford and a happy bridal. The Prince and Princess of Waterford always recognized in Hereward their deliverer and best friend, and in their gratitude wished him to dwell with them always; but the hero's roving and daring temper forbade his settling down, but rather urged him on to deeds of arms in other lands, where he quickly won a renown second to none.

ROBIN HOOD

Among the earliest heirlooms of the Anglo-Saxon tongue are the songs and legends of Robin Hood and his merry outlaws, which have charmed readers young and old for more than six hundred years. These entertaining stories date back to the time when Chaucer wrote his "Canterbury Tales," when the minstrel and scribe stood in the place of the more prim and precise modern printed book.

The question of whether or not Robin Hood was a real person has been asked for many years, just as a similar question has been asked about William Tell and others whom everyone would much rather accept on faith. It cannot be answered by a brief "yes" or "no," even though learned men have pored over ancient records and have written books on the subject. According to the general belief Robin was an outlaw in the reign of Richard I, when in the depths of Sherwood Forest he entertained one hundred tall men, all good archers, with the spoil he took; but "he suffered no woman to be oppressed or otherwise molested; poore men's goods he spared, abundantlie relieving them with that which by theft he got from abbeys and houses of rich carles." Consequently Robin was an immense favorite with the common people.

This popularity extended from the leader to all the members of his hardy band. "God save Robin Hood and all his good yeomanry" is the ending of many old ballads. The clever archer who could outshoot his fellows, the brave yeoman inured to blows, and the man who could be true to his friends through thick and thin were favorites for all time; and they have been idealized in the persons of Robin Hood and his merry outlaws.

One of the best-known stories of this picturesque figure of early English times is that given by Sir Walter Scott in "Ivanhoe," concerning the archery contest during the rule or misrule of Prince John, in the absence of Richard from the kingdom. Robin Hood, under the assumed name of Locksley, boldly presents himself at a royal tournament at Ashby, as competitor for the prize in shooting with the long-bow. From the eight or ten archers who enter the contest, the number finally narrows down to two,— Hubert, a forester in the service of one of the king's nobles, and Locksley or Robin Hood. Hubert takes the first shot in the final trial of skill, and lands his arrow within the inner ring of the target, but not exactly in the centre.

"'You have not allowed for the wind, Hubert,' said Locksley, 'or that had been a better shot.'

"So saying, and without showing the least anxiety to pause upon his aim, Locksley stepped to the appointed station, and shot his arrow as carelessly in appearance as if he had not even looked at the mark. He was speaking almost at the instant that the shaft left the bow-string, yet it alighted in the target two inches nearer to the white spot which marked the centre than that of Hubert.

"'By the light of Heaven!' said Prince John to Hubert, 'an thou suffer that runagate knave to overcome thee, thou art worthy of the gallows!'

"Hubert had but one set speech for all occasions. 'An your highness were to hang me,' he said, 'a man can but do his best. Nevertheless, my grandsire drew a good bow—'

"'The foul fiend on thy grandsire and all his generation!' interrupted John; 'shoot, knave, and shoot thy best, or it shall be worse for thee!'

Figure 108: "Robin Hood and Little John Search for Adventure" by Howard Pyle

"Thus exhorted, Hubert resumed his place, and not neglecting the caution which he had received from his adversary, he made the necessary allowance for a very light air of wind, which had just risen, and shot so successfully that his arrow alighted in the very centre of the target.

"'A Hubert! a Hubert!' shouted the populace, more interested in a known person than in a stranger. 'In the clout!—in the clout!—a Hubert forever!'

"'Thou canst not mend that shot, Locksley,' said the Prince, with an insulting smile.

"'I will notch his shaft for him, however,' replied Locksley.

"And letting fly his arrow with a little more precaution than before, it lighted right upon that of his competitor, which it split to shivers. The people who stood around were so astonished at his wonderful dexterity, that they could not even give vent to their surprise in their usual clamor. 'This must be the devil, and no man of flesh and blood,' whispered the yeomen to each other; 'such archery was never seen since a bow was first bent in Britain.'

"'And now,' said Locksley, 'I will crave your Grace's permission to plant such a mark as is used in the North Country; and welcome every brave yeoman who shall try a shot at it to win a smile from the bonny lass he loves best.'"

Locksley thereupon sets up a willow wand, six feet long and as thick as a man's thumb. Hubert is forced to decline the honor of taking part in such a trial of archery skill, but his rival easily splits the wand at a distance of three hundred feet and carries off the prize.

"Even Prince John, in admiration of Locksley's skill, lost for an instant his dislike to his person. 'These twenty nobles,' he said, 'which, with the bugle, thou hast fairly won, are thine own; we will make them fifty, if thou wilt take livery and service with us as a yeoman of our bodyguard, and be near to our person. For never did so strong a hand bend a bow, or so true an eye direct a shaft.'" [Footnote: Ivanhoe, Vol. 1, chap. XIII.]

Locksley, however, declares that it is impossible for him to enter the Prince's service, generously shares his prize with the worthy Hubert, and retires once more to his beloved haunts among the lights and shadows of the good greenwood.

Legends of Charlemagne

INTRODUCTION

Those who have investigated the origin of the romantic fables relating to Charlemagne and his peers are of opinion that the deeds of Charles Martel, and perhaps of other Charleses, have been blended in popular tradition with those properly belonging to Charlemagne. It was indeed a most momentous era; and if our readers will have patience, before entering on the perusal of the fabulous annals which we are about to lay before them, to take a rapid survey of the real history of the times, they will find it hardly less romantic than the tales of the poets.

In the century beginning from the year 600, the countries bordering upon the native land of our Saviour, to the east and south, had not yet received his religion. Arabia was the seat of an idolatrous religion resembling that of the ancient Persians, who worshipped the sun, moon, and stars. In Mecca, in the year 571, Mahomet was born, and here, at the age of forty, he proclaimed himself the prophet of God, in dignity as superior to Christ as Christ had been to Moses. Having obtained by slow degrees a considerable number of disciples, he resorted to arms to diffuse his religion. The energy and zeal of his followers, aided by the weakness of the neighboring nations, enabled him and his successors to spread the sway of Arabia and the religion of Mahomet over the countries to the east as far as the Indus, northward over Persia and Asia Minor, westward over Egypt and the southern shores of the Mediterranean, and thence over the principal portion of Spain. All this was done within one hundred years from the Hegira, or flight of Mahomet from Mecca to Medina, which happened in the year 622, and is the era from which Mahometans reckon time, as we do from the birth of Christ.

From Spain the way was open for the Saracens (so the followers of Mahomet were called) into France, the conquest of which, if achieved, would have been followed very probably by that of all the rest of Europe, and would have resulted in the banishment of Christianity from the earth. For Christianity was not at that day universally professed, even by those nations which we now regard as foremost in civilization. Great part of Germany, Britain, Denmark, and Russia were still pagan or barbarous.

At that time there ruled in France, though without the title of king, the first of those illustrious Charleses of whom we have spoken, Charles Martel, the grandfather of Charlemagne. The Saracens of Spain had made incursions into France in 712 and 718, and had retired, carrying with them a vast booty. In 725, Anbessa, who was then the Saracen governor of Spain, crossed the Pyrenees with a numerous army, and took by storm the strong town of Carcassone. So great was the terror excited by this invasion, that the country for a wide extent submitted to the conqueror, and a Mahometan governor for the province was appointed and installed at Narbonne. Anbessa, however, received a fatal wound in one of his engagements, and the Saracens, being thus checked from further advance, retired to Narbonne.

In 732 the Saracens again invaded France under Abdalrahman, advanced rapidly to the banks of the Garonne, and laid siege to Bordeaux. The city was taken by assault and delivered up to the soldiery. The invaders still pressed forward, and spread over the territories of Orleans, Auxerre and Sens. Their advanced parties were suddenly called in by their chief, who had received information of the rich abbey of St. Martin of Tours, and resolved to plunder and destroy it.

Charles during all this time had done nothing to oppose the Saracens, for the reason that the portion of France over which their incursions had been made was not at that time under his dominion, but constituted an independent kingdom, under the name of Aquitaine, of which Eude was king. But now Charles became convinced of the danger, and prepared to encounter it. Abdalrahman was advancing toward Tours, when intelligence of the approach of Charles, at the head of an army of Franks, compelled him to fall back upon Poitiers, in order to seize an advantageous field of battle.

Charles Martel had called together his warriors from every part of his dominions, and, at the head of such an army as had hardly ever been seen in France, crossed the Loire, probably at Orleans, and, being joined by the remains of the army of Aquitaine, came in sight of the Arabs in the month of October, 732. The Saracens seem to have been aware of the terrible enemy they were now to encounter, and for the first time these formidable conquerors hesitated. The two armies remained in presence during seven days before either ventured to begin the attack; but at length the signal for battle was given by Abdalrahman, and the immense mass of the Saracen army rushed with fury on the Franks. But the heavy line of the

Northern warriors remained like a rock, and the Saracens, during nearly the whole day, expended their strength in vain attempts to make any impression upon them. At length, about four o'clock in the afternoon, when Abdalrahman was preparing for a new and desperate attempt to break the line of the Franks, a terrible clamor was heard in the rear of the Saracens. It was King Eude, who, with his Aquitanians, had attacked their camp, and a great part of the Saracen army rushed tumultuously from the field to protect their plunder. In this moment of confusion the line of the Franks advanced, and, sweeping the field before it, carried fearful slaughter amongst the enemy. Abdalrahman made desperate efforts to rally his troops, but when he himself, with the bravest of his officers, fell beneath the swords of the Christians, all order disappeared, and the remains of his army sought refuge in their immense camp, from which Eude and his Aquitanians had been repulsed. It was now late, and Charles, unwilling to risk an attack on the camp in the dark, withdrew his army, and passed the night in the plain, expecting to renew the battle in the morning.

Accordingly, when daylight came, the Franks drew up in order of battle, but no enemy appeared; and when at last they ventured to approach the Saracen camp they found it empty. The invaders had taken advantage of the night to begin their retreat, and were already on their way back to Spain, leaving their immense plunder behind to fall into the hands of the Franks.

This was the celebrated battle of Tours, in which vast numbers of the Saracens were slain, and only fifteen hundred of the Franks. Charles received the surname of Martel (the Hammer) in consequence of this victory.

The Saracens, notwithstanding this severe blow, continued to hold their ground in the south of France; but Pepin, the son of Charles Martel, who succeeded to his father's power, and assumed the title of king, successively took from them the strong places they held; and in 759, by the capture of Narbonne, their capital, extinguished the remains of their power in France.

Charlemagne, or Charles the Great, succeeded his father, Pepin, on the throne in the year 768. This prince, though the hero of numerous romantic legends, appears greater in history than in fiction. Whether we regard him as a warrior or as a legislator, as a patron of learning or as the civilizer of a barbarous nation, he is entitled to our warmest admiration. Such he is in history; but the romancers represent him as often weak and passionate, the victim of treacherous counsellors, and at the mercy of turbulent barons, on whose prowess he depends for the maintenance of his throne. The historical representation is doubtless the true one, for it is handed down in trustworthy records, and is confirmed by the events of the age. At the height of his power, the French empire extended over what we now call France, Germany, Switzerland, Holland, Belgium, and great part of Italy.

In the year 800 Charlemagne, being in Rome, whither he had gone with a numerous army to protect the Pope, was crowned by the Pontiff Emperor of the West. On Christmas day Charles entered the Church of St. Peter, as if merely to take his part in the celebration of the mass with the rest of the congregation. When he approached the altar and stooped in the act of prayer the Pope stepped forward and placed a crown of gold upon his head; and immediately the Roman people shouted, "Life and victory to Charles the August, crowned by God the great and pacific Emperor of the Romans." The Pope then prostrated himself before him, and paid him reverence, according to the custom established in the times of the ancient Emperors, and concluded the ceremony by anointing him with consecrated oil.

Charlemagne's wars were chiefly against the pagan and barbarous people, who, under the name of Saxons, inhabited the countries now called Hanover and Holland. He also led expeditions against the Saracens of Spain; but his wars with the Saracens were not carried on, as the romances assert, in France, but on the soil of Spain. He entered Spain by the Eastern Pyrenees, and made an easy conquest of Barcelona and Pampeluna. But Saragossa refused to open her gates to him, and Charles ended by negotiating and accepting a vast sum of gold as the price of his return over the Pyrenees.

On his way back, he marched with his whole army through the gorges of the mountains by way of the valleys of Engui, Eno, and Roncesvalles. The chief of this region had waited upon Charlemagne, on his advance, as a faithful vassal of the monarchy; but now, on the return of the Franks, he had called together all the wild mountaineers who acknowledged him as their chief, and they occupied the heights of the mountains under which the army had to pass. The main body of the troops met with no obstruction, and received no intimation of danger;

Figure 109: "Three Worthy Christians: Charlemenge, King Arthur, and Geoffrey of Bouillon" by Daniel Hopfer

but the rear-guard, which was considerably behind, and encumbered with its plunder, was overwhelmed by the mountaineers in the pass of Roncesvalles, and slain to a man. Some of the bravest of the Prankish chiefs perished on this occasion, among whom is mentioned Roland or Orlando, governor of the marches or frontier of Brittany. His name became famous in after times, and the disaster of Roncesvalles and death of Roland became eventually the most celebrated episode in the vast cycle of romance.

Though after this there were hostile encounters between the armies of Charlemagne and the Saracens, they were of small account, and generally on the soil of Spain. Thus the historical foundation for the stories of the romancers is but scanty, unless we suppose the events of an earlier and of a later age to be incorporated with those of Charlemagne's own time.

There is, however, a pretended history, which for a long time was admitted as authentic, and attributed to Turpin, Archbishop of Rheims, a real personage of the time of Charlemagne. Its title is "History of Charles the Great and Orlando." It is now unhesitatingly considered as a collection of popular traditions, produced by some credulous and unscrupulous monk, who thought to give dignity to his romance by ascribing its authorship to a well- known and eminent individual. It introduces its pretended author, Bishop Turpin, in this manner:

"Turpin, Archbishop of Rheims, the friend and secretary of Charles the Great, excellently skilled in sacred and profane literature, of a genius equally adapted to prose and verse, the advocate of the poor, beloved of God in his life and conversation, who often fought the Saracens, hand to hand, by the Emperor's side, he relates the acts of Charles the Great in one book, and flourished under Charles and his son Louis, to the year of our Lord eight hundred and thirty."

The titles of some of Archbishop Turpin's chapters will show the nature of his history. They are these: "Of the Walls of Pampeluna, that fell of themselves." "Of the War of the holy Facundus, where the Spears grew." (Certain of the Christians fixed their spears in the evening, erect in the ground, before the castle; and found them, in the morning, covered with bark and branches.) "How the Sun stood still for Three Days, and of the Slaughter of Four Thousand Saracens."

Turpin's history has perhaps been the source of the marvellous adventures which succeeding poets and romancers have accumulated around the names of Charlemagne and his Paladins, or Peers. But Ariosto and the other Italian poets have drawn from different sources, and doubtless often from their own invention, numberless other stories which they attribute to the same heroes, not hesitating to quote as their authority "the good Turpin," though his history contains no trace of them; and the more outrageous the improbability, or rather the impossibility, of their narrations, the more attentive are they to cite "the Archbishop," generally adding their testimonial to his unquestionable veracity.

The principal Italian poets who have sung the adventures of the peers of Charlemagne are Pulci, Boiardo, and Ariosto. The characters of Orlando, Rinaldo, Astolpho, Gano, and others, are the same in all, though the adventures attributed to them are different. Boiardo tells us of the loves of Orlando, Ariosto of his disappointment and consequent madness, Pulci of his death.

Ogier, the Dane, is a real personage. History agrees with romance in representing him as a powerful lord who, originally from Denmark and a Pagan, embraced Christianity, and took service under Charlemagne. He revolted from the Emperor, and was driven into exile. He afterwards led one of those bands of piratical Northmen which ravaged France under the reigns of Charlemagne's degenerate successors. The description which an ancient chronicler gives of Charlemagne, as described by Ogier, is so picturesque, that we are tempted to transcribe it. Charlemagne was advancing to the siege of Pavia. Didier, King of the Lombards, was in the city with Ogier, to whom he had given refuge. When they learned that the king was approaching they mounted a high tower, whence they could see far and wide over the country. "They first saw advancing the engines of war, fit for the armies of Darius or Julius Caesar. 'There is Charlemagne,' said Didier. 'No,' said Ogier. The Lombard next saw a vast body of soldiers, who filled all the plain. 'Certainly Charles advanced with that host,' said the king. 'Not yet,' replied Ogier. 'What hope for us,' resumed the king, 'if he brings with him a greater host than that?' At last Charles appeared, his head covered with an iron helmet, his hands with iron gloves, his breast and shoulders with a cuirass of iron, his left hand holding an iron lance, while his right hand grasped his sword. Those who went before the monarch, those who marched at his side, and those who followed him, all had similar arms. Iron covered the fields and the roads; iron points reflected the rays of the sun. This iron, so hard, was borne by a people whose hearts were harder still. The blaze of the weapons flashed terror into the streets of the city."

This picture of Charlemagne in his military aspect would be incomplete without a corresponding one of his "mood of peace." One of the greatest of modern historians, M. Guizot, has compared the glory of Charlemagne to a brilliant meteor, rising suddenly out of the darkness of barbarism to disappear no less suddenly in the darkness of feudalism. But the light of this meteor was not extinguished, and reviving civilization owed much that was permanently beneficial to the great Emperor of the Franks. His ruling hand is seen in the legislation of his time, as well as in the administration of the laws. He encouraged learning; he upheld the clergy, who were the only peaceful and intellectual class, against the encroaching and turbulent barons; he was an affectionate father, and watched carefully over the education of his children, both sons and daughters. Of his encouragement of learning we will give some particulars.

He caused learned men to be brought from Italy and from other foreign countries to revive the public schools of France, which had been prostrated by the disorders of preceding times. He recompensed these learned men liberally, and kept some of them near himself, honoring them with his friendship. Of these the most celebrated is Alcuin, an Englishman, whose writings still remain, and prove him to have been both a learned and a wise man. With the assistance of Alcuin, and others like him, he founded an academy or royal school, which should have the direction of the studies of all the schools of the kingdom. Charlemagne himself was a member of this academy on equal terms with the rest. He attended its meetings, and fulfilled all the duties of an academician. Each member took the name of some famous man of antiquity. Alcuin called himself Horace, another took the name of Augustin, a third of Pindar. Charlemagne, who knew the Psalms by heart, and who had an ambition to be, according to his conception, A KING AFTER GOD'S OWN HEART, received from his brother academicians the name of David.

Of the respect entertained for him by foreign nations an interesting proof is afforded in the embassy sent to him by the Caliph of the Arabians, the celebrated Haroun al Raschid, a prince in character and conduct not unlike to Charlemagne. The ambassadors brought with them, besides other rich presents, a clock, the first that was seen in Europe, which excited universal admiration. It had the form of a twelve-sided edifice with twelve doors. These doors formed niches, in each of which was a little statue representing one of the hours. At the striking of the hour the doors, one for each stroke, was seen to open, and from the doors to issue as many of the little statues, which, following one another, marched gravely round the tower. The motion of the clock was caused by water, and the striking was effected by balls of brass equal to the number of the hours, which fell upon a cymbal of the same metal, the number falling being determined by the discharge of the water, which, as it sunk in the vessel, allowed their escape.

Charlemagne was succeeded by his son Louis, a well-intentioned but feeble prince, in whose reign the fabric reared by Charles began rapidly to crumble. Louis was followed successively by two Charleses, incapable princes, whose weak and often tyrannical conduct is no doubt the source of incidents of that character ascribed in the romances to Charlemagne.

The lawless and disobedient deportment of Charles's paladins, instances of which are so frequent in the romantic legends, was also a trait of the declining empire, but not of that of Charlemagne.

THE PEERS, OR PALADINS

The twelve most illustrious knights of Charlemagne were called Peers, for the equality that reigned among them; while the name of Paladins, also conferred on them, implies that they were inmates of the palace and companions of the king. Their names are always given alike by the romancers, yet we may enumerate the most distinguished of them as follows: Orlando or Roland (the former the Italian, the latter the French form of the name), favorite nephew of Charlemagne; Rinaldo of Montalban, cousin of Orlando; Namo, Duke of Bavaria; Salomon, king of Brittany; Turpin, the Archbishop; Astolpho, of England; Ogier, the Dane; Malagigi, the Enchanter; and Florismart, the friend of Orlando. There were others who are sometimes named as paladins, and the number cannot be strictly limited to twelve. Charlemagne himself must be counted one, and Ganelon, or Gano, of Mayence, the treacherous enemy of all the rest, was rated high on the list by his deluded sovereign, who was completely the victim of his arts.

We shall introduce more particularly to our readers a few of the principal peers, leaving the others to make their own introduction as they appear in the course of our narrative. We begin with Orlando.

ORLANDO

Milon, or Milone, a knight of great family, and distantly related to Charlemagne, having secretly married Bertha, the Emperor's sister, was banished from France, and excommunicated by the Pope. After a long and miserable wandering on foot as mendicants Milon and his wife arrived at Sutri, in Italy, where they took refuge in a cave, and in that cave Orlando was born. There his mother continued, deriving a scanty support from the compassion of the neighboring peasants; while Milon, in quest of honor and fortune, went into foreign lands. Orlando grew up among the children of the peasantry, surpassing them all in strength and manly graces. Among his companions in age, though in station far more elevated, was Oliver, son of the governor of the town. Between the two boys a feud arose that led to a fight, in which Orlando thrashed his rival; but this did not prevent a friendship springing up between the two, which lasted through life.

Orlando was so poor that he was sometimes half naked. As he was a favorite of the boys, one day four of them brought some cloth to make him clothes. Two brought white and two red; and from this circumstance Orlando took his coat-of-arms, or quarterings.

When Charlemagne was on his way to Rome to receive the imperial crown he dined in public in Sutri. Orlando and his mother that day had nothing to eat, and Orlando coming suddenly upon the royal party, and seeing abundance of provisions, seized from the attendants as much as he could carry off, and made good his retreat in spite of their resistance. The Emperor, being told of this incident, was reminded of an intimation he had received in a dream, and ordered the boy to be followed. This was done by three of the knights, whom Orlando would have encountered with a cudgel on their entering the grotto, had not his mother restrained him. When they heard from her who she was they threw themselves at her feet, and promised to obtain her pardon from the Emperor. This was easily effected. Orlando was received into favor by the Emperor, returned with him to France, and so distinguished himself that he became the most powerful support of the throne and of Christianity. [Footnote: It is plain that Shakspeare borrowed from this source the similar incident in his "As you Like it." The names of characters in the play, Orlando, Oliver, Rowland indicate the same thing.]

ROLAND AND FERRAGUS

Orlando, or Roland, particularly distinguished himself by his combat with Ferragus. Ferragus was a giant, and moreover his skin was of such impenetrable stuff that no sword could make any impression upon it. The giant's mode of fighting was to seize his adversary in his arms and carry him off, in spite of all the struggles he could make. Roland's utmost skill only availed to keep him out of the giant's clutches, but all his efforts to wound him with the sword were useless. After long fighting Ferragus was so weary that he proposed a truce, and when it was agreed upon he lay down and immediately fell asleep. He slept in perfect security, for it was against all the laws of chivalry to take advantage of an adversary under such circumstances. But Ferragus lay so uncomfortably for the want of a pillow that Orlando took pity upon him, and brought a smooth stone and placed it under his head. When the giant woke up, after a refreshing nap, and perceived what Orlando had done, he seemed quite grateful, became sociable, and talked freely in the usual boastful style of such characters. Among other things he told Orlando that he need not attempt to kill him with a sword, for that every part of his body was invulnerable, except this; and as he spoke, he put his hand to the vital part, just in the middle of his breast. Aided by this information Orlando succeeded, when the fight was renewed, in piercing the giant in the very spot he had pointed out, and giving him a death-wound. Great was the rejoicing in the Christian camp, and many the praises showered upon the victorious paladin by the Emperor and all his host.

On another occasion Orlando encountered a puissant Saracen warrior, and took from him, as the prize of victory, the sword Durindana. This famous weapon had once belonged to the illustrious prince Hector of Troy. It was of the finest workmanship, and of such strength and temper that no armor in the world could stand against it.

A ROLAND FOR AN OLIVER

Guerin de Montglave held the lordship of Vienne, subject to Charlemagne. He had quarrelled with his sovereign, and Charles laid siege to his city, having ravaged the neighboring country. Guerin was an aged warrior, but relied for his defence upon his four sons and two grandsons, who were among the bravest knights of the age. After the siege had continued two months Charlemagne received tidings that Marsilius, king of Spain, had invaded France, and, finding himself unopposed, was advancing rapidly in the Southern provinces. At this intelligence Charles listened to the counsel of his peers, and consented to put the quarrel with Guerin to the decision of Heaven, by single combat between two knights, one of each party, selected by lot. The proposal was acceptable to Guerin and his sons. The names of the four, together with Guerin's own, who would not be excused, and of the two grandsons, who claimed their lot, being put into a helmet, Oliver's was drawn forth, and to him, the youngest of the grandsons, was assigned the honor and the peril of the combat. He accepted the award with delight, exulting in being thought worthy to maintain the cause of his family. On Charlemagne's side Roland was the designated champion, and neither he nor Oliver knew who his antagonist was to be.

Chapter 13: A Roland for an Oliver

Figure 110: "Rinaldo and Armida" by Anthony van Dyck

They met on an island in the Rhone, and the warriors of both camps were ranged on either shore, spectators of the battle. At the first encounter both lances were shivered, but both riders kept their seats, immovable. They dismounted, and drew their swords. Then ensued a combat which seemed so equal, that the spectators could not form an opinion as to the probable issue. Two hours and more the knights continued to strike and parry, to thrust and ward, neither showing any sign of weariness, nor ever being taken at unawares. At length Orlando struck furiously upon Oliver's shield, burying Durindana in its edge so deeply that he could not draw it back, and Oliver, almost at the same moment, thrust so vigorously upon Orlando's breastplate that his sword snapped off at the handle. Thus were the two warriors left weaponless. Scarcely pausing a moment, they rushed upon one another, each striving to throw his adversary to the ground, and failing in that, each snatched at the other's helmet to tear it away. Both succeeded, and at the same moment they stood bare-headed face to face, and Roland recognized Oliver, and Oliver Roland. For a moment they stood still; and the next, with open arms, rushed into one another's embrace. "I am conquered," said Orlando. "I yield me." said Oliver.

The people on the shore knew not what to make of all this. Presently they saw the two late antagonists standing hand in hand, and it was evident the battle was at an end. The knights crowded round them, and with one voice hailed them as equals in glory. If there were any who felt disposed to murmur that the battle was left undecided they were silenced by the voice of Ogier the Dane, who proclaimed aloud that all had been done that honor required, and declared that he would maintain that award against all gainsayers.

The quarrel with Guerin and his sons being left undecided, a truce was made for four days, and in that time, by the efforts of Duke Namo on the one side, and of Oliver on the other, a reconciliation was effected. Charlemagne, accompanied by Guerin and his valiant family, marched to meet Marsilius, who hastened to retreat across the frontier.

RINALDO

Rinaldo was one of the four sons of Aymon, who married Aya, the sister of Charlemagne. Thus Rinaldo was nephew to Charlemagne and cousin of Orlando.

When Rinaldo had grown old enough to assume arms Orlando had won for himself an illustrious name by his exploits against the Saracens, whom Charlemagne and his brave knights had driven out of France. Orlando's fame excited a noble emulation in Rinaldo. Eager to go in pursuit of glory, he wandered in the country near Paris, and one day saw at the foot of a tree a superb horse, fully equipped and loaded with a complete suit of armor. Rinaldo clothed himself in the armor and mounted the horse, but took not the sword. On the day when, with his brothers, he had received the honor of knighthood from the Emperor he had sworn never to bind a sword to his side till he had wrested one from some famous knight.

Rinaldo took his way to the forest of Arden, celebrated for so many adventures. Hardly had he entered it when he met an old man, bending under the weight of years, and learned from him that the forest was infested with a wild horse, untamable, that broke and overturned everything that opposed his career. To attack him, he said, or even to meet him, was certain death. Rinaldo, far from being alarmed, showed the most eager desire to combat the animal. This was the horse Bayard, afterward so famous. He had formerly belonged to Amadis of Gaul. After the death of that hero he had been held under enchantment by the power of a magician, who predicted that, when the time came to break the spell, he should be subdued by a knight of the lineage of Amadis, and not less brave than he.

To win this wonderful horse it was necessary to conquer him by force or skill; for from the moment when he should be thrown down he would become docile and manageable. His habitual resort was a cave on the borders of the forest; but woe be to any one who should approach him, unless gifted with strength and courage more than mortal. Having told this, the old man departed. He was not, in fact, an old man, but Malagigi, the enchanter, cousin of Rinaldo, who, to favor the enterprises of the young knight, had procured for him the horse and armor which he so opportunely found, and now put him in the way to acquire a horse unequalled in the world.

Rinaldo plunged into the forest, and spent many days in seeking Bayard, but found no traces of him. One day he encountered a Saracen knight, with whom he made acquaintance, as often happened to knights, by first meeting him in combat. This knight, whose name was Isolier, was also in quest of Bayard. Rinaldo succeeded in the encounter, and so severe was the shock that Isolier was a long time insensible. When he revived, and was about to resume the contest, a peasant who passed by (it was Malagigi) interrupted them with the news that the terrible horse was near at hand, advising them to unite their powers to subdue him, for it would require all their ability.

Rinaldo and Isolier, now become friends, proceeded together to the attack of the horse. They found Bayard, and stood a long time, concealed by the wood, admiring his strength and beauty.

A bright bay in color (whence he was called Bayard), with a silver star in his forehead, and his hind feet white, his body slender, his head delicate, his ample chest filled out with swelling muscles, his shoulders broad and full, his legs straight and sinewy, his thick mane falling over his arching neck,—he came rushing through the forest, regardless of rocks, bushes, or trees, rending everything that opposed his way, and neighing defiance.

He first descried Isolier, and rushed upon him. The knight received him with lance in rest, but the fierce animal broke the spear, and his course was not delayed by it for an instant. The Spaniard adroitly stepped aside, and gave way to the rushing tempest. Bayard checked his career, and turned again upon the knight, who had already drawn his sword. He drew his sword, for he had no hope of taming the horse; that, he was satisfied, was impossible.

Bayard rushed upon him; fiercely rearing, now on this side, now on that. The knight struck him with his sword, where the white star adorned his forehead, but struck in vain, and felt ashamed, thinking that he had struck feebly, for he did not know that the skin of that horse was so tough that the keenest sword could make no impression upon it.

Whistling fell the sword once more, and struck with greater force, and the fierce horse felt it, and drooped his head under the blow, but the next moment turned upon his foe with such a buffet that the Pagan fell stunned and lifeless to the earth.

Rinaldo, who saw Isolier fall, and thought that his life was reft, darted towards the horse, and, with his fist gave him such a blow on the jaws that the blood tinged his mouth with vermilion. Quicker than an arrow leaves the bow the horse turned upon him, and tried to seize his arm with his teeth.

The knight stepped back, and then, repeating his blow, struck him on the forehead. Bayard turned, and kicked with both his feet with a force that would have shattered a mountain. Rinaldo was on his guard, and evaded his attacks, whether made with head or heels. He kept at his side avoiding both; but, making a false step, he at last received a terrible blow from the horse's foot, and at the shock almost fainted away. A second such blow would have killed him, but the horse kicked at random, and a second blow did not reach Rinaldo, who in a moment recovered himself. Thus the contest continued until by chance Bayard's foot got caught between the branches of an oak. Rinaldo seized it and putting forth all his strength and address, threw him on the ground.

No sooner had Bayard touched the ground than all his rage subsided. No longer an object of terror, he became gentle and quiet, yet with dignity in his mildness.

The paladin patted his neck, stroked his breast, and smoothed his mane, while the animal neighed and showed delight to be caressed by his master. Rinaldo, seeing him now completely subdued, took the saddle and trappings from the other horse, and adorned Bayard with the spoils.

Rinaldo became one of the most illustrious knights of Charlemagne's court,—indeed, the most illustrious, if we except Orlando. Yet he was not always so obedient to the Emperor's commands as he should have been, and every fault he committed was sure to be aggravated by the malice of Gan, Duke of Maganza, the treacherous enemy of Rinaldo and all his house.

At one time Rinaldo had incurred the severe displeasure of Charlemagne, and been banished from court. Seeing no chance of being ever restored to favor, he went to Spain, and entered into the service of the Saracen king, Ivo. His brothers, Alardo, Ricardo, and Ricciardetto, accompanied him, and all four served the king so faithfully that they rose to high favor with him. The king gave them land in the mountains on the frontiers of France and Spain, and subjected all the country round to Rinaldo's authority. There was plenty of marble in the mountains, the king furnished workmen, and they built a castle for Rinaldo, surrounded with high walls, so as to be almost impregnable. Built of white stone, and placed on the brow of a marble promontory, the castle shone like a star, and Rinaldo gave it the name of Montalban. Here he assembled his friends, many of whom were banished men like himself, and the country people furnished them with provisions in return for the protection the castle afforded. Yet some of Rinaldo's men were lawless, and sometimes the supplies were not furnished in sufficient abundance, so that Rinaldo and his garrison got a bad name for taking by force what they could not obtain by gift; and we sometimes find Montalban spoken of as a nest of freebooters, and its defenders called a beggarly garrison.

Charlemagne's displeasure did not last long, and, at the time our history commences, Rinaldo and his brothers were completely restored to the favor of the Emperor, and none of his cavaliers served him with greater zeal and fidelity than they, throughout all his wars with the Saracens and Pagans.

THE TOURNAMENT

It was the month of May, and the feast of Pentecost. Charlemagne had ordered magnificent festivities, and summoned to them, besides his paladins and vassals of the crown, all strangers, Christian or Saracen, then sojourning at Paris. Among the guests were King Grandonio, from Spain; and Ferrau, the Saracen, with eyes like an eagle; Orlando and Rinaldo, the Emperor's nephews; Duke Namo; Astolpho, of England, the handsomest man living; Malagigi, the Enchanter; and Gano, of Maganza, that wily traitor, who had the art to make the Emperor think he loved him, while he plotted against him.

High sat Charlemagne at the head of his vassals and his paladins, rejoicing in the thought of their number and their might, while all were sitting and hearing music, and feasting, when suddenly there came into the hall four enormous giants, having between them a lady of incomparable beauty, attended by a single knight. There were many ladies present who had seemed beautiful till she made her appearance, but after that they all seemed nothing. Every Christian knight turned his eyes to her, and every Pagan crowded round her, while she, with a sweetness that might have touched a heart of stone, thus addressed the Emperor:

"High-minded lord, the renown of your worthiness, and of the valor of these your knights, which echoes from sea to sea, encourages me to hope that two pilgrims, who have come from the ends of the world to behold you, will not have encountered their fatigue in vain. And, before I show the motive which has brought us hither, learn that this knight is my brother Uberto, and that I am his sister Angelica. Fame has told us of the jousting this day appointed, and so the prince my brother has come to prove his valor, and to say that, if any of the knights here assembled choose to meet him in the joust, he will encounter them, one by one, at the stair of Merlin, by the Fountain of the Pine. And his conditions are these: No knight who chances to be thrown shall be allowed to renew the combat, but shall remain prisoner to my brother; but if my brother be overthrown he shall depart out of the country, leaving me as the prize of the conqueror."

Now it must be stated that this Angelica and her brother, who called himself Uberto, but whose real name was Argalia, were the children of Galafron, king of Cathay, who had sent them to be the destruction of the Christian host; for Argalia was armed with an enchanted lance, which unfailingly overthrew everything it touched, and he was mounted on a horse, a creature of magic, whose swiftness outstripped the wind. Angelica possessed also a ring which was a defence against all enchantments, and when put into the mouth rendered the bearer invisible. Thus Argalia was expected to subdue and take prisoners whatever knights should dare to encounter him; and the charms of Angelica were relied on to entice the paladins to make the fatal venture, while her ring would afford her easy means of escape.

When Angelica ceased sneaking she knelt before the king and awaited his answer, and everybody gazed on her with admiration. Orlando especially felt irresistibly drawn towards her, so that he trembled and changed countenance. Every knight in the hall was infected with the same feeling, not excepting old white-headed Duke Namo and Charlemagne himself.

All stood for a while in silence, lost in the delight of looking at her. The fiery youth Ferrau could hardly restrain himself from seizing her from the giants and carrying her away; Rinaldo turned as red as fire, while Malagigi, who had discovered by his art that the stranger was not speaking truth, muttered softly, as he looked at her, "Exquisite false creature! I will play thee such a trick for this, as will leave thee no cause to boast of thy visit."

Charlemagne, to detain her as long as possible before him, delayed his assent till he had asked her a number of questions, all which she answered discreetly, and then the challenge was accepted.

As soon as she was gone Malagigi consulted his book, and found out the whole plot of the vile, infidel king, Galafron, as we have explained it, so he determined to seek the damsel and frustrate her designs. He hastened to the appointed spot, and there found the prince and his sister in a beautiful pavilion, where they lay asleep, while the four giants kept watch. Malagigi took his book and cast a spell out of it, and immediately the four giants fell into a deep sleep. Drawing his sword (for he was a belted knight), he softly approached the young lady, intending to despatch her at once; but, seeing her look so lovely, he paused for a moment, thinking there was no need of hurry, as he believed his spell was upon her, and she could not wake. But the ring which she wore secured her from the effect of the spell, and some slight noise, or whatever else it was, caused her at that moment to awake. She uttered a great cry, and flew to her brother, and waked him. By the help of her knowledge of enchantment, they took and bound fast the magician, and, seizing his book, turned his arts against himself. Then they summoned a crowd of demons, and bade them seize their prisoner and bear him to King Galafron, at his great city of Albracca, which they did, and, on his arrival, he was locked up in a rock under the sea.

While these things were going on all was uproar at Paris, since Orlando insisted upon being the first to try the adventure at the stair of Merlin. This was resented by the other pretenders to Angelica, and all contested his right to the precedence. The tumult was stilled by the usual expedient of drawing lots, and the first prize was drawn by Astolpho. Ferrau, the Saracen, had the second, and Grandonio the third. Next came Berlinghieri, and Otho; then Charles himself, and, as his ill-fortune would have it, after thirty more, the indignant Orlando.

Astolpho, who drew the first lot, was handsome, brave, and rich. But, whether from heedlessness or want of skill; he was an unlucky jouster, and very apt to be thrown, an accident which he bore with perfect good-humor, always ready to mount again and try to mend his fortune, generally with no better success.

Astolpho went forth upon his adventure with great gayety of dress and manner, encountered Argalia, and was immediately tilted out of the saddle. He railed at fortune, to whom he laid all the fault; but his painful feelings were somewhat relieved by the kindness of Angelica, who, touched by his youth and good looks, granted him the liberty of the pavilion, and caused him to be treated with all kindness and respect.

The violent Ferrau had the next chance in the encounter, and was thrown no less speedily than Astolpho; but he did not so easily put up with his mischance. Crying out, "What are the emperor's engagements to me?" he rushed with his sword against Argalia, who, being forced to defend himself, dismounted and drew his sword, but got so much the worse of the fight that he made a signal of surrender, and, after some words, listened to a proposal of marriage from Ferrau to his sister. The beauty, however, feeling no inclination to match with such a rough and savage-looking person, was so dismayed at the offer, that, hastily bidding her brother to meet her in the forest of Arden, she vanished from the sight of both by means of the enchanted ring. Argalia, seeing this, took to his horse of swiftness, and dashed away in the same direction. Ferrau pursued him, and Astolpho, thus left to himself, took possession of the enchanted lance in place of his own, which was broken, not knowing the treasure he possessed in it, and returned to the tournament. Charlemagne, finding the lady and her brother gone, ordered the jousting to proceed as at first intended, in which Astolpho, by aid of the enchanted lance, unhorsed all comers against him, equally to their astonishment and his own.

The paladin Rinaldo, on learning the issue of the combat of Ferrau and the stranger, galloped after the fair fugitive in an agony of love and impatience. Orlando, perceiving his disappearance, pushed forth in like manner; and, at length, all three are in the forest of Arden, hunting about for her who is invisible.

Now in this forest there were two fountains, the one constructed by the sage Merlin, who designed it for Tristram and the fair Isoude; [Footnote: See their story in "King Arthur and His Knights."] for such was the virtue of this fountain, that a draught of its waters produced on oblivion of the love which the drinker might feel, and even produced aversion for the object formerly beloved. The other fountain was endowed with exactly opposite qualities, and a draught of it inspired love for the first living object that was seen after tasting it. Rinaldo happened to come to the first mentioned fountain, and, being flushed with heat, dismounted, and quenched in one draught both his thirst and his passion. So far from loving Angelica as before he hated her from the bottom of his heart, became disgusted with the search he was upon, and, feeling fatigued with his ride, finding a sheltered and flowery nook, laid himself down and fell asleep.

Shortly after came Angelica, but, approaching in a different direction, she espied the other fountain, and there quenched her thirst. Then resuming her way, she came upon the sleeping Rinaldo. Love instantly seized her, and she stood rooted to the spot.

The meadow round was all full of lilies of the valley and wild roses. Angelica, not knowing what to do, at length plucked a handful of these, and dropped them, one by one, on the face of the sleeper. He woke up, and, seeing who it was, received her salutations with averted countenance, remounted his horse, and galloped away. In vain the beautiful creature followed and called after him, in vain asked him what she had done to be so despised. Rinaldo disappeared, leaving her in despair, and she returned in tears to the spot where she had found him sleeping. There, in her turn, she herself lay down, pressing the spot of earth on which he had lain, and, out of fatigue and sorrow, fell asleep.

As Angelica thus lay, fortune conducted Orlando to the same place. The attitude in which she was sleeping was so lovely that it is not to be conceived, much less expressed. Orlando stood gazing like a man who had been transported to another sphere. "Am I on earth," he exclaimed, "or am I in Paradise? Surely it is I that sleep, and this is my dream."

But his dream was proved to be none in a manner which he little desired. Ferrau, who had slain Argalia, came up, raging with jealousy, and a combat ensued which awoke the sleeper.

Terrified at what she beheld, she rushed to her palfrey, and, while the fighters were occupied with one another, fled away through the forest. The champions continued their fight till they were interrupted by a messenger, who brought word to Ferrau that king Marsilius, his sovereign, was in pressing need of his assistance, and conjured him to return to Spain. Ferrau, upon this, proposed to suspend the combat, to which Orlando, eager to pursue Angelica, agreed. Ferrau, on the other hand, departed with the messenger to Spain.

Orlando's quest for the fair fugitive was all in vain. Aided by the powers of magic, she made a speedy return to her own country.

But the thought of Rinaldo could not be banished from her mind, and she determined to set Malagigi at liberty, and to employ him to win Rinaldo, if possible, to make her a return of affection. She accordingly freed him from his dungeon, unlocking his fetters with her own hands, and restored him his book, promising him ample honors and rewards on condition of his bringing Rinaldo to her feet.

Malagigi accordingly, with the aid of his book, called up a demon, mounted him, and departed. Arrived at his destination, he inveigled Rinaldo into an enchanted bark, which conveyed him, without any visible pilot, to an island where stood an edifice called Joyous Castle. The whole island was a garden. On the western side, close to the sea, was the palace, built of marble, so clear and polished that it reflected the landscape about it. Rinaldo leapt ashore, and soon met a lady, who invited him to

Figure 111: "The Courageous Gradasso and The Beautiful Marfisa" by Antonio Tempesta

enter. The house was as beautiful within as without, full of rooms adorned with azure and gold, and with noble paintings. The lady led the knight into an apartment painted with stories, and opening to the garden, through pillars of crystal, with golden capitals. Here he found a bevy of ladies, three of whom were singing in concert, while another played on an instrument of exquisite accord, and the rest danced round about them. When the ladies beheld him coming they turned the dance into a circuit round him, and then one of them, in the sweetest manner, said, "Sir knight, the tables are set, and the hour for the banquet is come;" and, with these words, still dancing, they drew him across the lawn in front of the apartment, to a table that was spread with cloth of gold and fine linen, under a bower of damask roses by the side of a fountain.

Four ladies were already seated there, who rose, and placed Rinaldo at their head, in a chair set with pearls. And truly indeed was he astonished. A repast ensued, consisting of viands the most delicate, and wines as fragrant as they were fine, drunk out of jewelled cups; and, when it drew towards its conclusion, harps and lutes were heard in the distance, and one of the ladies said in the knight's ear: "This house and all that you see in it are yours; for you alone was it built, and the builder is a queen. Happy indeed must you think yourself, for she loves you, and she is the greatest beauty in the world! Her name is Angelica."

The moment Rinaldo heard the name he so detested he started up, with a changed countenance, and, in spite of all that the lady could say, broke off across the garden, and never ceased hastening till he reached the place where he landed. The bark was still on the shore. He sprang into it, and pushed off, though he saw nobody in it but himself. It was in vain for him to try to control its movements, for it dashed on as if in fury, till it reached a distant shore covered with a gloomy forest. Here Rinaldo, surrounded by enchantments of a very different sort from those which he had lately resisted, was entrapped into a pit.

The pit belonged to a castle called Altaripa, which was hung with human heads, and painted red with blood. As the paladin was viewing the scene with amazement a hideous old woman made her appearance at the edge of the pit, and told him that he was destined to be thrown to a monster, who was only kept from devastating the whole country by being supplied with living human flesh. Rinaldo said, "Be it so; let me but remain armed as I am, and I fear nothing." The old woman laughed in derision. Rinaldo remained in the pit all night, and the next morning was taken to the place where the monster had his den. It was a court surrounded by a high wall. Rinaldo was shut in with the beast, and a terrible combat ensued. Rinaldo was unable to make any impression on the scales of the monster, while he, on the contrary, with his dreadful claws, tore away plate and mail from the paladin. Rinaldo began to think his last hour was come, and cast his eyes around and above to see if there was any means of escape. He perceived a beam projecting from the wall at the height of some ten feet, and, taking a leap almost miraculous, he succeeded in reaching it, and in flinging himself up across it. Here he sat for hours, the hideous brute continually trying to reach him. All at once he heard the sound of something coming through the air like a bird, and suddenly Angelica herself alighted on the end of the beam. She held something in her hand towards him, and spoke to him in a loving voice. But the moment Rinaldo saw her he commanded her to go away, refused all her offers of assistance, and at length declared that, if she did not leave him, he would cast himself down to the monster, and meet his fate.

Angelica, saying she would lose her life rather than displease him, departed; but first she threw to the monster a cake of wax she had prepared, and spread around him a rope knotted with nooses. The beast took the bait, and, finding his teeth glued together by the wax, vented his fury in bounds and leaps, and, soon getting entangled in the nooses, drew them tight by his struggles, so that he could scarcely move a limb.

Rinaldo, watching his chance, leapt down upon his back, seized him round the neck, and throttled him, not relaxing his gripe till the beast fell dead.

Another difficulty remained to be overcome. The walls were of immense height, and the only opening in them was a grated window of such strength that he could not break the bars. In his distress Rinaldo found a file, which Angelica had left on the ground, and, with the help of this, effected his deliverance.

What further adventures he met with will be told in another chapter.

THE SEIGE OF ALBRACCA

At the very time when Charlemagne was holding his plenary court and his great tournament his kingdom was invaded by a mighty monarch, who was moreover so valiant and strong in battle that no one could stand against him. He was named Gradasso, and his kingdom was called Sericane. Now, as it often happens to the greatest and the richest to long for what they cannot have, and thus to lose what they already possess, this king could not rest content without Durindana, the sword of Orlando, and Bayard, the horse of Rinaldo. To obtain these he determined to war upon France, and for this purpose put in array a mighty army.

He took his way through Spain, and, after defeating Marsilius, the king of that country, in several battles, was rapidly advancing on France. Charlemagne, though Marsilius was a Saracen, and had been his enemy, yet felt it needful to succor him in this extremity from a consideration of common danger, and, with the consent of his peers, despatched Rinaldo with a strong body of soldiers against Gradasso.

There was much fighting, with doubtful results, and Gradasso was steadily advancing into France. But, impatient to achieve his objects, he challenged Rinaldo to single combat, to be fought on foot, and upon these conditions: If Rinaldo conquered, Gradasso agreed to give up all his prisoners and return to his own country; but if Gradasso won the day, he was to have Bayard.

The challenge was accepted, and would have been fought had it not been for the arts of Malagigi, who just then returned from Angelica's kingdom with set purpose to win Rinaldo to look with favor upon the fair princess who was dying for love of him. Malagigi drew Rinaldo away from the army by putting on the semblance of Gradasso, and, after a short contest, pretending to fly before him, by which means Rinaldo was induced to follow him into a boat, in which he was borne away, and entangled in various adventures, as we have already related.

The army, left under the command of Ricciardetto, Rinaldo's brother, was soon joined by Charlemagne and all his peerage, but experienced a disastrous rout, and the Emperor and many of his paladins were taken prisoners. Gradasso, however, did not abuse his victory; he took Charles by the hand, seated him by his side, and told him he warred only for honor. He renounced all conquests, on condition that the Emperor should deliver to him Bayard and Durindana, both of them the property of his vassals, the former of which, as he maintained, was already forfeited to him by Rinaldo's failure to meet him as agreed. To these terms Charlemagne readily acceded.

Bayard, after the departure of his master, had been taken in charge by Ricciardetto, and sent back to Paris, where Astolpho was in command, in the absence of Charlemagne. Astolpho received with great indignation the message despatched for Bayard, and replied by a herald that "he would not surrender the horse of his kinsman Rinaldo without a contest. If Gradasso wanted the steed he might come and take him, and that he, Astolpho, was ready to meet him in the field."

Gradasso was only amused at this answer, for Astolpho's fame as a successful warrior was not high, and Gradasso willingly renewed with him the bargain which he had made with Rinaldo. On these conditions the battle was fought. The enchanted lance, in the hands of Astolpho, performed a new wonder; and Gradasso, the terrible Gradasso, was unhorsed.

He kept his word, set free his prisoners, and put his army on the march to return to his own country, renewing his oath, however, not to rest till he had taken from Rinaldo his horse, and from Orlando his sword, or lost his life in the attempt.

Charlemagne, full of gratitude to Astolpho, would have kept him near his person and loaded him with honors, but Astolpho preferred to seek Rinaldo, with the view of restoring to him his horse, and departed from Paris with that design.

Our story now returns to Orlando, whom we left fascinated with the sight of the sleeping beauty, who, however, escaped him while engaged in the combat with Ferrau. Having long sought her in vain through the recesses of the wood, he resolved to follow her to her father's court. Leaving, therefore, the camp of Charlemagne, he travelled long in the direction of the East, making inquiry everywhere, if, perchance, he might get tidings of the fugitive. After many adventures, he arrived one day at a place where many roads crossed, and meeting there a courier, he asked him for news. The courier replied that he had been despatched by Angelica to solicit the aid of Sacripant, king of Circassia, in favor of her father

Galafron, who was besieged in his city, Albracca, by Agrican, king of Tartary. This Agrican had been an unsuccessful suitor to the damsel, whom he now pursued with arms. Orlando thus learned that he was within a day's journey of Albracca; and, feeling now secure of Angelica, he proceeded with all speed to her city.

Thus journeying he arrived at a bridge, under which flowed a foaming river. Here a damsel met him with a goblet, and informed him that it was the usage of this bridge to present the traveller with a cup. Orlando accepted the offered cup and drank its contents. He had no sooner done so than his brain reeled, and he became unconscious of the object of his journey, and of everything else. Under the influence of this fascination he followed the damsel into a magnificent and marvellous palace. Here he found himself in company with many knights, unknown to him and to each other, though if it had not been for the Cup of Oblivion of which they all had partaken they would have found themselves brothers in arms.

Astolpho, proceeding on his way to seek Rinaldo, splendidly dressed and equipped, as was his wont, arrived in Circassia, and found there a great army encamped under the command of Sacripant, the king of that country, who was leading it to the defence of Galafron, the father of Angelica. Sacripant, much struck by the appearance of Astolpho and his horse, accosted him courteously, and tried to enlist him in his service; but Astolpho, proud of his late victories, scornfully declined his offers, and pursued his way. King Sacripant was too much attracted by his appearance to part with him so easily, and having laid aside his kingly ornaments, set out in pursuit of him.

Astolpho next day encountered on his way a stranger knight, named Sir Florismart, Lord of the Sylvan Tower, one of the bravest and best of knights, having as his guide a damsel, young, fair, and virtuous, to whom he was tenderly attached, whose name was Flordelis. Astolpho, as he approached, defied the knight, bidding him yield the lady, or prepare to maintain his right by arms. Florismart accepted the contest, and the knights encountered. Florismart was unhorsed and his steed fell dead, while Bayard sustained no injury by the shock.

Florismart was so overwhelmed with despair at his own disgrace and the sight of the damsel's distress, that he drew his sword, and was about to plunge it into his own bosom. But Astolpho held his hand, told him that he contended only for glory, and was contented to leave him the lady.

While Florismart and Flordelis were vowing eternal gratitude King Sacripant arrived, and coveting the damsel of the one champion as much as the horse and arms of the other, defied them to the joust. Astolpho met the challenger, whom he instantly overthrew, and presented his courser to Florismart, leaving the king to return to his army on foot.

The friends pursued their route, and ere long Flordelis discovered, by signs which were known to her, that they were approaching the waters of Oblivion, and advised them to turn back, or to change their course. This the knights would not hear of, and, continuing their march, they soon arrived at the bridge where Orlando had been taken prisoner.

The damsel of the bridge appeared as before with the enchanted cup, but Astolpho, forewarned, rejected it with scorn. She dashed it to the ground, and a fire blazed up which rendered the bridge unapproachable. At the same moment the two knights were assailed by sundry warriors, known and unknown, who, having no recollection of anything, joined blindly in defence of their prison-house. Among these was Orlando, at sight of whom Astolpho, with all his confidence not daring to encounter him, turned and fled, owing his escape to the strength and fleetness of Bayard.

Florismart, meanwhile, overlaid by fearful odds, was compelled to yield to necessity, and comply with the usage of the fairy. He drank of the cup and remained prisoner with the rest. Flordelis, deprived of her two friends, retired from the scene, and devoted herself to untiring efforts to effect her lover's deliverance. Astolpho pursued his way to Albracca, which Agrican was about to besiege. He was kindly welcomed by Angelica, and enrolled among her defenders. Impatient to distinguish himself, he one night sallied forth alone, arrived in Agrican's camp, and unhorsed his warriors right and left by means of the enchanted lance. But he was soon surrounded and overmatched, and made prisoner to Agrican.

Relief was, however, at hand; for as the citizens and soldiers were one day leaning over their walls they descried a cloud of dust, from which horsemen were seen to prick forth, as it rolled on towards the camp of the besiegers. This turned out to be the army of Sacripant, which immediately attacked that of Agrican, with the view of cutting a passage through his camp to the besieged city. But Agrican, mounted upon Bayard, taken from Astolpho, but not armed with the lance of gold, the virtues of which were unknown to him, performed wonders, and rallied his scattered troops, which had given way to the sudden and unexpected assault. Sacripant, on the other hand, encouraged his men by the most desperate acts of valor, having as an additional incentive to his courage the sight of Angelica, who showed herself upon the city walls.

There she witnessed a single combat between the two leaders, Agrican and Sacripant. In this, at length, her defender appeared to be overmatched, when the Circassians broke the ring, and separated the combatants, who were borne asunder in the rush. Sacripant, severely wounded, profited by the confusion, and escaped into Albracca, where he was kindly received and carefully tended by Angelica.

The battle continuing, the Circassians were at last put to flight, and, being intercepted between the enemy's lines and the town, sought for refuge under the walls. Angelica ordered the drawbridge to be let down, and the gates thrown open to the fugitives. With these Agrican, not distinguished in the crowd, entered the place, driving both Circassians and Cathayans before him, and the portcullis being dropped, he was shut in.

For a time the terror which he inspired put to flight all opposers, but when at last it came to be known that few or none of his followers had effected an entrance with him, the fugitives rallied and surrounded him on all sides. While he was thus apparently reduced to the last extremities, he was saved by the very circumstance which threatened him with destruction. The soldiers of Angelica, closing upon him from all sides, deserted their defences; and his own besieging army entered the city in a part where the wall was broken down.

In this way was Agrican rescued, the city taken, and the inhabitants put to the sword. Angelica, however, with some of the knights who were her defenders, among whom was Sacripant, saved herself in the citadel, which was planted upon a rock.

The fortress was impregnable, but it was scantily victualled, and ill provided with other necessaries. Under these circumstances Angelica announced to those blockaded with her in the citadel her intention to go in quest of assistance, and, having plighted her promise of a speedy return, she set out, with the enchanted ring upon her finger. Mounted upon her palfrey, the damsel passed through the enemy's lines, and by sunrise was many miles clear of their encampment.

It so happened that her road led her near the fatal bridge of Oblivion, and as she approached it she met a damsel weeping bitterly. It was Flordelis, whose lover, Florismart, as we have related, had met the fate of Orlando and many more, and fallen a victim to the enchantress of the cup. She related her adventures to Angelica, and conjured her to lend what aid she might to rescue her lord and his companions. Angelica, accordingly, watching her opportunity and aided by her ring, slipped into the castle unseen, when the door was opened to admit a new victim. Here she speedily disenchanted Orlando and the rest by a touch of her talisman. But Florismart was not there. He had been given up to Falerina, a more powerful enchantress, and was still in durance. Angelica conjured the rescued captives to assist her in the recovery of her kingdom, and all departed together for Albracca.

The arrival of Orlando, with his companions, nine in all, and among the bravest knights of France, changed at once the fortunes of the war. Wherever the great paladin came, pennon and standard fell before him. Agrican in vain attempted to rally his troops. Orlando kept constantly in his front, forcing him to attend to nobody else. The Tartar king at length bethought him of a stratagem. He turned his horse, and made a show of flying in despair. Orlando dashed after him as he desired, and Agrican fled till he reached a green place in a wood, where there was a fountain.

The place was beautiful, and the Tartar dismounted to refresh himself at the fountain, but without taking off his helmet, or laying aside any of his armor. Orlando was quickly at his back, crying out, "So bold, and yet a fugitive! How could you fly from a single arm and think to escape?"

The Tartar king had leaped on his saddle the moment he saw his enemy, and when the paladin had done speaking, he said in a mild voice, "Without doubt you are the best knight I ever encountered, and fain would I leave you untouched for your own sake, if you would cease to hinder me from rallying my people. I pretended to fly, in order to bring you out of the field. If you insist upon fighting I must needs fight and slay you, but I call the sun in the heavens to witness I would rather not. I should be very sorry for your death."

The Count Orlando felt pity for so much gallantry, and he said, "The nobler you show yourself the more it grieves me to think that in dying without a knowledge of the true faith you will be lost in the other world. Let me advise you to save body and soul at once. Receive baptism, and go your way in peace."

Agrican replied: "I suspect you to be the paladin Orlando. If you are I would not lose this opportunity of fighting with you to be king of Paradise. Talk to me no more about your things of another world, for you will preach in vain. Each of us for himself, and let the sword be umpire."

The Saracen drew his sword, boldly advancing upon Orlando, and a combat began, so obstinate and so long, each warrior being a miracle of prowess, that the story says it lasted from noon till night. Orlando then seeing the stars come out was the first to propose a respite.

"What are we to do," said he, "now that daylight has left us?"

Agrican answered readily enough, "Let us repose in this meadow, and renew the combat at dawn."

The repose was taken accordingly. Each tied up his horse, and reclined himself on the grass, not far from the other, just as if they had been friends, Orlando by the fountain, Agrican beneath a pine. It was a beautiful clear night, and, as they talked together before addressing themselves to sleep, the champion of Christendom, looking up at the firmament, said, "That is a fine piece of workmanship, that starry spectacle; God made it all, that moon of silver, and those stars of gold, and the light of day, and the sun,—all for the sake of human kind."

"You wish, I see, to talk of matters of faith," said the Tartar. "Now I may as well tell you at once that I have no sort of skill in such matters, nor learning of any kind. I never could learn anything when I was a boy. I hated it so that I broke the man's head who was commissioned to teach me; and it produced such an effect on others that nobody ever afterwards dared so much as show me a book. My boyhood was therefore passed, as it should be, in horsemanship and hunting, and learning to fight. What is the good of a gentleman's poring all day over a book? Prowess to the knight, and preaching to the clergyman, that is my motto."

"I acknowledge," returned Orlando, "that arms are the first consideration of a gentleman; but not at all that he does himself dishonor by knowledge. On the contrary, knowledge is as great an embellishment of the rest of his attainments, as the flowers are to the meadow before us; and as to the knowledge of his Maker, the man that is without it is no better than a stock or a stone or a brute beast. Neither without study can he reach anything of a due sense of the depth and divineness of the contemplation."

"Learned or not learned," said Agrican, "you might show yourself better bred than by endeavoring to make me talk on a subject on which you have me at a disadvantage. If you choose to sleep I wish you good night; but if you prefer talking I recommend you to talk of fighting or of fair ladies. And, by the way, pray tell me, are you not that Orlando who makes such a noise in the world? And what is it, pray, that brings you into these parts? Were you ever in love? I suppose you must have been; for to be a knight, and never to have been in love, would be like being a man without a heart in his breast."

The count replied: "Orlando I am, and in love I am. Love has made me abandon everything, and brought me into these distant regions, and, to tell you all in one word, my heart is in the hands of the daughter of King Galafron. You have come against him with fire and sword, to get possession of his castles and his dominions; and I have come to help him, for no object in the world but to please his daughter and win her beautiful hand. I care for nothing else in existence."

Now when the Tartar king, Agrican, heard his antagonist speak in this manner, and knew him to be indeed Orlando, and to be in love with Angelica, his face changed color for grief and jealousy, though it could not be seen for the darkness. His heart began beating with such violence that he felt as if he should have died. "Well," said he to Orlando, "we are to fight when it is daylight, and one or other is to be left here, dead on the ground. I have a proposal to make to you—nay, an entreaty. My love is so excessive for the same lady that I beg you to leave her to me. I will owe you my thanks, and give up the siege and put an end to the war. I cannot bear that any one should love her, and that I should live to see it. Why, therefore, should either of us perish? Give her up. Not a soul shall know it."

"I never yet," answered Orlando, "made a promise which I did not keep, and nevertheless I own to you that, were I to make a promise like that, and even swear to keep it, I should not. You might as well ask me to tear away the limbs from my body, and the eyes out of my head. I could as well live without breath itself as cease loving Angelica."

Agrican had hardly patience to let him finish speaking, ere he leapt furiously on horseback, though it was midnight. "Quit her," said he, "or die!"

Orlando seeing the infidel getting up, and not being sure that he would not add treachery to fierceness, had been hardly less quick in mounting for the combat. "Never," exclaimed he; "I never could have quitted her if I would, and now I would not if I could. You must seek her by other means than these."

Fiercely dashed their horses together, in the nighttime, on the green mead. Despiteful and terrible were the blows they gave and took by the moonlight. Agrican fought in a rage, Orlando was cooler. And now the struggle had lasted more than five hours, and day began to dawn, when the Tartar king, furious to find so much trouble given him, dealt his enemy a blow sharp and violent beyond conception. It cut the shield in two as if it had been made of wood, and, though blood could not be drawn from Orlando, because he was fated, it shook and bruised him as if it had started every joint in his body.

His body only, however, not a particle of his soul. So dreadful was the blow which the paladin gave in return, that not only shield, but every bit of mail on the body of Agrican was broken in pieces, and three of his ribs cut asunder.

The Tartar, roaring like a lion, raised his sword with still greater vehemence than before, and dealt a blow on the paladin's helmet, such as he had never yet received from mortal man. For a moment it took away his senses. His sight failed, his ears tingled, his frightened horse turned about to fly; and he was falling from the saddle, when the very action of falling threw his head upwards, and thus recalled his recollection.

"What a shame is this!" thought he; "how shall I ever again dare to face Angelica! I have been fighting hour after hour with this man, and he is but one, and I call myself Orlando! If the combat last any longer I will bury myself in a monastery, and never look on sword again."

Orlando muttered with his lips closed and his teeth ground together; and you might have thought that fire instead of breath came out of his nose and mouth. He raised his sword Durindana with both his hands, and sent it down so tremendously on Agrican's shoulder that it cut through breastplate down to the very haunch, nay, crushed the saddle-bow, though it was made of bone and iron, and felled man and horse to the earth. Agrican turned as white as ashes, and felt death upon him. He called Orlando to come close to him, with a gentle voice, and said, as well as he could: "I believe on Him who died on the cross. Baptize me, I pray thee, with the fountain, before my senses are gone. I have lived an evil life, but need not be rebellious to God in death also. May He who came to save all the rest of the world save me!" And he shed tears, that great king, though he had been so lofty and fierce.

Orlando dismounted quickly, with his own face in tears. He gathered the king tenderly in his arms, and took and laid him by the fountain, on a marble rim that it had, and then he wept in concert with him heartily, and asked his pardon, and so baptized him in the water of the fountain, and knelt and prayed to God for him with joined hands.

He then paused and looked at him; and when he perceived his countenance changed, and that his whole person was cold, he left him there on the marble rim of the fountain, all armed as he was, with the sword by his side, and the crown upon his head.

ADVENTURES OF RINALDO AND ORLANDO

We left Rinaldo when, having overcome the monster, he quitted the castle of Altaripa, and pursued his way on foot. He soon met with a weeping damsel, who, being questioned as to the cause of her sorrow, told him she was in search of one to do battle to rescue her lover, who had been made prisoner by a vile enchantress, together with

Orlando and many more. The damsel was Flordelis, the lady-love of Florismart, and Rinaldo promised his assistance, trusting to accomplish the adventure either by valor or skill. Flordelis insisted upon Rinaldo's taking her horse, which he consented to do, on condition of her mounting behind him.

As they rode on through a wood, they heard strange noises, and Rinaldo, reassuring the damsel, pressed forward towards the quarter from which they proceeded. He soon perceived a giant standing under a vaulted cavern, with a huge club in his hand, and of an appearance to strike the boldest spirit with dread. By the side of the cavern was chained a griffin, which, together with the giant, was stationed there to guard a wonderful horse, the same which was once Argalia's. This horse was a creature of enchantment, matchless in vigor, speed, and form, which disdained to share the diet of his fellow-steeds,—corn or grass,—and fed only on air. His name was Rabican.

This marvellous horse, after his master Argalia had been slain by Ferrau, finding himself at liberty, returned to his native cavern, and was here stabled under the protection of the giant and the griffin. As Rinaldo approached, the giant assailed him with his club. Rinaldo defended himself from the giant's blows, and gave him one in return, which, if his skin had not been of the toughest, would have finished the combat. But the giant, though wounded, escaped, and let loose the griffin. This monstrous bird towered in air, and thence pounced down upon Rinaldo, who, watching his opportunity, dealt her a desperate wound. She had, however, strength for another flight, and kept repeating her attacks, which Rinaldo parried as he could, while the damsel stood trembling by, witnessing the contest.

The battle continued, rendered more terrible by the approach of night, when Rinaldo determined upon a desperate expedient to bring it to a conclusion. He fell, as if fainting from his wounds, and, on the close approach of the griffin, dealt her a blow which sheared away one of her wings. The beast, though sinking, griped him fast with her talons, digging through plate and mail; but Rinaldo plied his sword in utter desperation, and at last accomplished her destruction.

Rinaldo then entered the cavern, and found there the wonderful horse, all caparisoned. He was coal-black, except for a star of white on his forehead, and one white foot behind. For speed he was unrivalled, though in strength he yielded to Bayard. Rinaldo mounted upon Rabican, and issued from the cavern.

As he pursued his way he met a fugitive from Agrican's army, who gave such an account of the prowess of a champion who fought on the side of Angelica, that Rinaldo was persuaded this must be Orlando, though at a loss to imagine how he could have been freed from captivity. He determined to repair to the scene of the contest to satisfy his curiosity, and Flordelis, hoping to find Florismart with Orlando, consented to accompany him.

While these things were doing, all was rout and dismay in the Tartarian army, from the death of Agrican. King Galafron, arriving at this juncture with an army for the relief of his capital, Albracca, assaulted the enemy's camp, and carried all before him. Rinaldo had now reached the scene of action, and was looking on as an unconcerned spectator, when he was espied by Galafron. The king instantly recognized the horse Rabican, which he had given to Argalia when he sent him forth on his ill-omened mission to Paris. Possessed with the idea that the rider of the horse was the murderer of Argalia, Galafron rode at Rinaldo, and smote him with all his force. Rinaldo was not slow to avenge the blow, and it would have gone hard with the king had not his followers instantly closed round him and separated the combatants.

Rinaldo thus found himself, almost without his own choice, enlisted on the side of the enemies of Angelica, which gave him no concern, so completely had his draught from the fountain of hate steeled his mind against her.

For several successive days the struggle continued, without any important results, Rinaldo meeting the bravest knights of Angelica's party, and defeating them one after the other. At length he encountered Orlando, and the two knights bitterly reproached one another for the cause they had each adopted, and engaged in a furious combat. Orlando was mounted upon Bayard, Rinaldo's horse, which Agrican had by chance become possessed of, and Orlando had taken from him as the prize of victory. Bayard would not fight against his master, and Orlando was getting the worse of the encounter, when suddenly Rinaldo, seeing Astolpho, who for love of him had arrayed himself on his side, hard beset by numbers, left Orlando to rush to the defence of his friend. Night prevented the combat from being renewed; but a challenge was given and accepted for their next meeting.

But Angelica, sighing in her heart for Rinaldo, was not willing that he should be again exposed to so terrible a venture. She begged a boon of Orlando, promising she would be his if he would do her bidding. On receiving his promise, she enjoined him to set out without delay to destroy the garden of the enchantress Falerina, in which many valiant knights had been entrapped, and were imprisoned.

Orlando departed on his horse Brigliadoro, leaving Bayard in disgrace for his bad deportment the day before. Angelica, to conciliate Rinaldo, sent Bayard to him; but Rinaldo remained unmoved by this as by all her former acts of kindness.

When Rinaldo learned Orlando's departure, he yielded to the entreaties of the lady of Florismart, and prepared to fulfil his promise, and rescue her lover from the power of the enchantress. Thus both Rinaldo and Orlando were bound upon the same adventure, but unknown to one another.

The castle of Falerina was protected by a river, which was crossed by a bridge, kept by a ruffian, who challenged all comers to the combat; and such was his strength that he had thus far prevailed in every encounter, as appeared by the arms of various knights which he had taken from them, and piled up as a trophy on the shore. Rinaldo attacked him, but with as bad success as the rest, for the bridge-ward struck him so violent a blow with an iron mace that he fell to the ground. But when the villain approached to strip him of his armor, Rinaldo seized him, and the bridge-ward, being unable to free himself, leapt with Rinaldo into the lake, where they both disappeared.

Orlando, meanwhile, in discharge of his promise to Angelica, pursued his way in quest of the same adventure. In passing through a wood he saw a cavalier armed at all points, and mounted, keeping guard over a lady who was bound to a tree, weeping bitterly. Orlando hastened to her relief, but was exhorted by the knight not to interfere, for she had deserved her fate by her wickedness. In proof of which he made certain charges against her. The lady denied them all, and Orlando believed her, defied the knight, overthrew him, and, releasing the lady, departed with her seated on his horse's croup.

While they rode another damsel approached on a white palfrey, who warned Orlando of impending danger, and informed him that he was near the garden of the enchantress. Orlando was delighted with the intelligence, and entreated her to inform him how he was to gain admittance. She replied that the garden could only be entered at sunrise and gave him such instructions as would enable him to gain admittance. She gave him also a book in which was painted the garden and all that it contained, together with the palace of the false enchantress, where she had secluded herself for the purpose of executing a magic work in which she was engaged. This was the manufacture of a sword capable of cutting even through enchanted substances The object of this labor, the damsel told him, was the destruction of a knight of the west, by name Orlando, who she had read in the book of Fate was coming to demolish her garden. Having thus instructed him, the damsel departed.

Orlando, finding he must delay his enterprise till the next morning, now lay down and was soon asleep. Seeing this, the base woman whom he had rescued, and who was intent on making her escape to rejoin her paramour, mounted Brigliadoro, and rode off, carrying away Durindana.

When Orlando awoke, his indignation, as may be supposed, was great on the discovery of the theft; but, like a good knight and true, he was not to be diverted from his enterprise. He tore off a huge branch of an elm to supply the place of his sword; and, as the sun rose, took his way towards the gate of the garden, where a dragon was on his watch. This he slew by repeated blows, and entered the garden, the gate of which closed behind him, barring retreat. Looking round him, he saw a fair fountain, which overflowed into a river, and in the centre of the fountain a figure, on whose forehead was written:

"The stream which waters violet and rose,
From hence to the enchanted palace goes."

Following the banks of this flowing stream, and rapt in the delights of the charming garden, Orlando arrived at the palace, and entering it, found the mistress, clad in white, with a crown of gold upon her head, in the act of viewing herself in the surface of the magic sword. Orlando surprised her before she could escape, deprived her of the weapon, and holding her fast by her long hair, which floated behind, threatened her with immediate death if she did not yield up her prisoners, and afford him the means of egress. She, however, was firm of purpose, making no reply, and Orlando, unable to move her either by threats or entreaties, was under the necessity of binding her to a beech, and pursuing his quest as he best might.

He then bethought him of his book, and, consulting it, found that there was an outlet to the south, but that to reach it a lake was to be passed, inhabited by a siren, whose song was so entrancing as to be quite irresistible to whoever heard it; but his book instructed him how to protect himself against this danger. According to its directions, while pursuing his path, he gathered abundance of flowers, which sprung all around, and filled his helmet and his ears with them; then listened if he heard the birds sing. Finding that, though he saw the gaping beak, the swelling throat, and ruffled plumes, he could not catch a note, he felt satisfied with his defence, and advanced toward the lake. It was small but deep, and so clear and tranquil that the eye could penetrate to the bottom.

He had no, sooner arrived upon the banks than the waters were seen to gurgle, and the siren, rising midway out of the pool, sung so sweetly that birds and beasts came trooping to the water-side to listen. Of this Orlando heard nothing, but, feigning to yield to the charm, sank down upon the bank. The siren issued from the water with the intent to accomplish his destruction. Orlando seized her by the hair, and while she sang yet louder (song being her only defence) cut off her head. Then, following the directions of the book, he stained himself all over with her blood.

Guarded by this talisman, he met successively all the monsters set for defence of the enchantress and her garden, and at length found himself again at the spot where he had made captive the enchantress, who still continued fastened to the beech. But the scene was changed. The garden had disappeared, and Falerina, before so haughty, now begged for mercy, assuring him that many lives depended upon the preservation of hers. Orlando promised her life upon her pledging herself for the deliverance of her captives.

This, however, was no easy task. They were not in her possession, but in that of a much more powerful enchantress, Morgana, the Lady of the Lake, the very idea of opposing whom made Falerina turn pale with fear. Representing to him the hazards of the enterprise, she led him towards the dwelling of Morgana. To approach it he had to encounter the same uncourteous bridge-ward who had already defeated and made captive so many knights, and last of all, Rinaldo. He was a churl of the most ferocious character, named Arridano. Morgana had provided him with impenetrable armor, and endowed him in such a manner that his strength always increased in proportion to that of the adversary with whom he was matched. No one had ever yet escaped from the contest, since, such was his power of endurance, he could breathe freely under water. Hence, having grappled with a knight, and sunk with him to the bottom of the lake, he returned, bearing his enemy's arms in triumph to the surface.

While Falerina was repeating her cautions and her counsels Orlando saw Rinaldo's arms erected in form of a trophy, among other spoils made by the villain, and, forgetting their late quarrel, determined upon revenging his friend. Arriving at the pass, the churl presuming to bar the way, a desperate contest ensued, during which Falerina escaped. The churl finding himself overmatched at a contest of arms, resorted to his peculiar art, grappled his antagonist, and plunged with him into the lake. When he reached the bottom Orlando found himself in another world, upon a dry meadow, with the lake overhead, through which shone the beams of our sun, while the water stood on all sides like a crystal wall. Here the battle was renewed, and Orlando had in his magic sword an advantage which none had hitherto possessed. It had been tempered by Falerina so that no spells could avail against it. Thus armed, and countervailing the strength of his adversary by his superior skill and activity, it was not long before he laid him dead upon the field.

Orlando then made all haste to return to the upper air, and, passing through the water, which opened a way before him (such was the power of the magic sword), he soon regained the shore, and found himself in a field as thickly covered with precious stones as the sky is with stars.

Orlando crossed the field, not tempted to delay his enterprise by gathering any of the brilliant gems spread all around him. He next passed into a flowery meadow planted with trees, covered with fruit and flowers, and full of all imaginable delights.

Figure 112: "Orlando Furioso" by Ludovico Ariosto

In the middle of this meadow was a fountain, and fast by it lay Morgana asleep; a lady of a lovely aspect, dressed in white and vermilion garments, her forehead well furnished with hair, while she had scarcely any behind.

While Orlando stood in silence contemplating her beauty he heard a voice exclaim: "Seize the fairy by the forelock, if thou hopest fair success." But his attention was arrested by another object, and he heeded not the warning. He saw on a sudden an array of towers, pinnacles and columns, palaces with balconies and windows, extended alleys with trees, in short a scene of architectural magnificence surpassing all he had ever beheld. While he stood gazing in silent astonishment the scene slowly melted away and disappeared. [Footnote: This is a poetical description of a phenomenon which is said to be really exhibited in the strait of Messina, between Sicily and Calabria. It is called Fata Morgana, or Mirage.]

When he had recovered from his amazement he looked again toward the fountain. The fairy had awaked and risen, and was dancing round its border with the lightness of a leaf, timing her footsteps to this song:

"Who in this world would wealth and treasure share,
Honor, delight, and state, and what is best,
Quick let him catch me by the lock of hair
Which flutters from my forehead; and be blest.
"But let him not the proffered good forbear,
Nor till he seize the fleeting blessing rest;
For present loss is sought in vain to-morrow,
And the deluded wretch is left in sorrow."

The fairy, having sung thus, bounded off, and fled from the flowery meadow over a high and inaccessible mountain. Orlando pursued her through thorns and rocks, while the sky gradually became overcast, and at last he was assailed by tempest, lightning, and hail.

While he thus pursued, a pale and meagre woman issued from a cave, armed with a whip, and, treading close upon his steps, scourged him with vigorous strokes. Her name was Repentance, and she told him it was her office to punish those who neglected to obey the voice of Prudence, and seize the fairy Fortune when he might.

Orlando, furious at this chastisement, turned upon his tormentor, but might as well have stricken the wind. Finding it useless to resist, he resumed his chase of the fairy, gained upon her, and made frequent snatches at her white and vermilion garments, which still eluded his grasp. At last, on her turning her head for an instant, he profited by the chance, and seized her by the forelock. In an instant the tempest ceased, the sky became serene, and Repentance retreated to her cave.

Orlando now demanded of Morgana the keys of her prison, and the fairy, feigning a complacent aspect, delivered up a key of silver, bidding him to be cautious in the use of it, since to break the lock would be to involve himself and all in inevitable destruction; a caution which gave the Count room for long meditation, and led him to consider:

How few amid the suitors who importune
The dame, know how to turn the keys of Fortune.

Keeping the fairy still fast by the forelock, Orlando proceeded toward the prison, turned the key, without occasioning the mischiefs apprehended, and delivered the prisoners.

Among these were Florismart, Rinaldo, and many others of the bravest knights of France. Morgana had disappeared, and the knights, under the guidance of Orlando, retraced the path by which he had come. They soon reached the field of treasure. Rinaldo, finding himself amidst this mass of wealth, remembered his needy garrison of Montalban, and could not resist the temptation of seizing part of the booty. In particular a golden chain, studded with diamonds, was too much for his self-denial, and he took it and was bearing it off, notwithstanding the remonstrances of Orlando, when a violent wind caught him and whirled him back, as he approached the gate. This happened a second and a third time, and Rinaldo at length yielded to necessity, rather than to the entreaties of his friends, and cast away his prize.

They soon reached the bridge and passed over without hindrance to the other side, where they found the trophy decorated with their arms. Here each knight resumed his own, and all, except the paladins and their friends, separated as their inclinations or duty prompted. Dudon, the Dane, one of the rescued knights, informed the cousins that he had been made prisoner by Morgana while in the discharge of an embassy to them from Charlemagne, who called upon them to return to the defence of Christendom. Orlando was too much fascinated by Angelica to obey this summons, and, followed by the faithful Florismart, who would not leave him, returned towards Albracca. Rinaldo, Dudon, Iroldo, Prasildo, and the others took their way toward the west.

THE INVASION OF FRANCE

Agramant, King of Africa, convoked the kings, his vassals, to deliberate in council. He reminded them of the injuries he had sustained from France, that his father had fallen in battle with Charlemagne, and that his early years had hitherto not allowed him to wipe out the stain of former defeats. He now proposed to them to carry war into France.

Sobrino, his wisest councillor, opposed the project, representing the rashness of it; but Rodomont, the young and fiery king of Algiers, denounced Sobrino's counsel as base and cowardly, declaring himself impatient for the enterprise. The king of the Garamantes, venerable for his

Figure 113: "Rinaldo Valoroso" by Antonio Tempesta

age and renowned for his prophetic lore, interposed, and assured the King that such an attempt would be sure to fail, unless he could first get on his side a youth marked out by destiny as the fitting compeer of the most puissant knights of France, the young Rogero, descended in direct line from Hector of Troy. This prince was now a dweller upon the mountain Carena, where Atlantes, his foster-father, a powerful magician, kept him in retirement, having discovered by his art that his pupil would be lost to him if allowed to mingle with the world. To break the spells of Atlantes, and draw Rogero from his retirement, one only means was to be found. It was a ring possessed by Angelica, Princess of Cathay, which was a talisman against all enchantments. If this ring could be procured all would go well; without it the enterprise was desperate.

Rodomont treated this declaration of the old prophet with scorn, and it would probably have been held of little weight by the council, had not the aged king, oppressed by the weight of years, expired in the very act of reaffirming his prediction. This made so deep an impression on the council that it was unanimously resolved to postpone the war until an effort should be made to win Rogero to the camp.

King Agramant thereupon proclaimed that the sovereignty of a kingdom should be the reward of whoever should succeed in obtaining the ring of Angelica. Brunello the dwarf, the subtlest thief in all Africa, undertook to procure it.

In prosecution of this design, he made the best of his way to Angelica's kingdom, and arrived beneath the walls of Albracca while the besieging army was encamped before the fortress. While the attention of the garrison was absorbed by the battle that raged below he scaled the walls, approached the Princess unnoticed, slipped the ring from her finger, and escaped unobserved. He hastened to the seaside, and, finding a vessel ready to sail, embarked, and arrived at Biserta, in Africa. Here he found Agramant impatient for the talisman which was to foil the enchantments of Atlantes and to put Rogero into his hands. The dwarf, kneeling before the king, presented him with the ring, and Agramant, delighted at the success of his mission, crowned him in recompense King of Tingitana.

All were now anxious to go in quest of Rogero. The cavalcade accordingly departed, and in due time arrived at the mountain of Carena.

At the bottom of this was a fruitful and well-wooded plain, watered by a large river, and from this plain was descried a beautiful garden on the mountain-top, which contained the mansion of Atlantes; but the ring, which discovered what was before invisible, could not, though it revealed this paradise, enable Agramant or his followers to enter it. So steep and smooth was the rock by nature, that even Brunello failed in every attempt to scale it. He did not, for this, despair of accomplishing the object; but, having obtained Agramant's consent, caused the assembled courtiers and knights to celebrate a tournament upon the plain below. This was done with the view of seducing Rogero from his fastness, and the stratagem was attended with success.

Rogero joined the tourney, and was presented by Agramant with a splendid horse, Frontino, and a magnificent sword. Having learned from Agramant his intended invasion of France, he gladly consented to join the expedition.

Rodomont, meanwhile, was too impatient to wait for Agramant's arrangements, and embarked with all the forces he could raise, made good his landing on the coast of France, and routed the Christians in several encounters. Previously to this, however, Gano, or Ganelon (as he is sometimes called), the traitor, enemy of Orlando and the other nephews of Charlemagne, had entered into a traitorous correspondence with Marsilius, the Saracen king of Spain, whom he invited into France. Marsilius, thus encouraged, led an army across the frontiers, and joined Rodomont. This was the situation of things when Rinaldo and the other knights who had obeyed the summons of Dudon set forward on their return to France.

When they arrived at Buda in Hungary they found the king of that country about despatching his son, Ottachiero, with an army to the succor of Charlemagne. Delighted with the arrival of Rinaldo, he placed his son and troops under his command. In due time the army arrived on the frontiers of France, and, united with the troops of Desiderius, king of Lombardy, poured down into Provence. The confederate armies had not marched many days through this gay tract before they heard a crash of drums and trumpets behind the hills, which spoke the conflict between the paynims, led by Rodomont, and the Christian forces. Rinaldo, witnessing from a mountain the prowess of Rodomont, left his troops in charge of his friends, and galloped towards him with his lance in rest. The impulse was irresistible, and Rodomont was unhorsed. But Rinaldo, unwilling to avail himself of his advantage, galloped back to the hill, and having secured Bayard among the baggage, returned to finish the combat on foot.

During this interval the battle had become general, the Hungarians were routed, and Rinaldo, on his return, had the mortification to find that Ottachiero was wounded, and Dudon taken prisoner. While he sought Rodomont in order to renew the combat a new sound of drums and trumpets was heard, and Charlemagne, with the main body of his army, was descried advancing in battle array.

Rodomont, seeing this, mounted the horse of Dudon, left Rinaldo, who was on foot, and galloped off to encounter this new enemy.

Agramant, accompanied by Rogero, had by this time made good his landing, and joined Rodomont with all his forces. Rogero eagerly embraced this first opportunity of distinguishing himself, and spread terror wherever he went, encountering in turn and overthrowing many of the bravest knights of France. At length he found himself opposite to Rinaldo, who, being interrupted, as we have said, in his combat with Rodomont, and unable to follow him, being on foot, was shouting to his late foe to return and finish their combat. Rogero also was on foot, and seeing the Christian knight so eager for a contest, proffered himself to supply the place of his late antagonist. Rinaldo saw at a glance that the Moorish prince was a champion worthy of his arm, and gladly accepted the defiance. The combat was stoutly maintained for a time; but now fortune declared decisively in favor of the infidel army, and Charlemagne's forces gave way at all points in irreparable confusion. The two combatants were separated by the crowd of fugitives and pursuers, and Rinaldo hastened to recover possession of his horse. But Bayard, in the confusion, had got loose, and Rinaldo followed him into a thick wood, thus becoming effectually separated from Rogero.

Rogero, also seeking his horse in the medley, came where two warriors were engaged in mortal combat. Though he knew not who they were, he could distinguish that one was a paynim and the other a Christian; and moved by the spirit of courtesy he approached them and exclaimed, "Let him of the two who worships Christ pause, and hear what I have to say. The army of Charles is routed and in flight, so that if he wishes to follow his leader he has no time for delay." The Christian knight, who was none other than Bradamante, a female warrior, in prowess equal to the best of knights, was thunderstruck with the tidings, and would gladly leave the contest undecided, and retire from the field; but Rodomont, her antagonist, would by no means consent. Rogero, indignant at his discourtesy, insisted upon her departure, while he took up her quarrel with Rodomont.

The combat, obstinately maintained on both sides, was interrupted by the return of Bradamante. Finding herself unable to overtake the fugitives, and reluctant to leave to another the burden and risk of a contest which belonged to herself, she had returned to reclaim the combat. She arrived, however, when her champion had dealt his enemy such a blow as obliged him to drop both his sword and bridle. Rogero, disdaining to profit by his adversary's defenceless situation, sat apart upon his horse, while that of Rodomont bore his rider, stunned and stupefied, about the field.

Bradamante approached Rogero, conceiving a yet higher opinion of his valor on beholding such an instance of forbearance. She addressed him, excusing herself for leaving him exposed to an enemy from his interference in her cause; pleading her duty to her sovereign as the motive. While she spoke Rodomont, recovered from his confusion, rode up to them. His bearing was, however, changed; and he disclaimed all thoughts of further contest with one who, he said, "had already conquered him by his courtesy." So saying, he quitted his antagonist, picked up his sword, and spurred out of sight.

Bradamante was now again desirous of retiring from the field, and Rogero insisted on accompanying her, though yet unaware of her sex.

As they pursued their way, she inquired the name and quality of her new associate; and Rogero informed her of his nation and family. He told her that Astyanax, the son of Hector of Troy, established the kingdom of Messina in Sicily. From him were derived two branches, which gave origin to two families of renown. From one sprang the royal race of Pepin and Charlemagne, and from the other, that of Reggio, in Italy. "From that of Reggio am I derived," he continued. "My mother, driven from her home by the chance of war, died in giving me life, and I was taken in charge by a sage enchanter, who trained me to feats of arms amidst the dangers of the desert and the chase."

Having thus ended his tale, Rogero entreated a similar return of courtesy from his companion, who replied, without disguise, that she was of the race of Clermont, and sister to Rinaldo, whose fame was perhaps known to him. Rogero, much moved by this intelligence, entreated her to take off her helmet, and at the discovery of her face remained transported with delight.

While absorbed in this contemplation, an unexpected danger assailed them. A party which was placed in a wood, in order to intercept the retreating Christians, broke from its ambush upon the pair, and Bradamante, who was uncasqued, was wounded in the head. Rogero was in a fury at this attack; and Bradamante, replacing her helmet, joined him in taking speedy vengeance on their enemies. They cleared the field of them, but became separated in the pursuit, and Rogero, quitting the chase, wandered by hill and vale in search of her whom he had no sooner found than lost.

While pursuing this quest he fell in with two knights, whom he joined, and engaged them to assist him in the search of his companion, describing her arms, but concealing, from a certain feeling of jealousy, her quality and sex.

It was evening when they joined company, and having ridden together through the night the morning was beginning to break, when one of the strangers, fixing his eyes upon Rogero's shield, demanded of him by what right he bore the Trojan arms. Rogero declared his origin and race, and then, in his turn, interrogated the inquirer as to his pretensions to the cognizance of Hector, which he bore. The stranger replied, "My name is Mandricardo, son of Agrican, the Tartar king, whom Orlando treacherously slew. I say treacherously, for in fair fight he could not have done it. It is in search of him that I have come to France, to take vengeance for my father, and to wrest from him Durindana, that famous sword, which belongs to me, and not to him." When the knights demanded to know by what right he claimed Durindana, Mandricardo thus related his history:

"I had been, before the death of my father, a wild and reckless youth. That event awakened my energies, and drove me forth to seek for vengeance. Determined to owe success to nothing but my own exertions, I departed without attendants or horse or arms. Travelling thus alone, and on foot, I espied one day a pavilion, pitched near a fountain, and entered it, intent on adventure. I found therein a damsel of gracious aspect, who replied to my inquiries that the fountain was the work of a fairy, whose castle stood beyond a neighboring hill, where she kept watch over a treasure which many knights had tried to win, but fruitlessly, having lost their life or liberty in the attempt. This treasure was the armor of Hector, prince of Troy, whom Achilles treacherously slew. Nothing was wanting but his sword, Durindana, and this had fallen into the possession of a queen named Penthesilea, from whom it passed through her descendants to Almontes, whom Orlando slew, and thus became possessed of the sword. The rest of Hector's arms were saved and carried off by Aeneas, from whom this fairy received them in recompense of service rendered. 'If you have the courage to attempt their acquisition,' said the damsel, 'I will be your guide.'"

Mandricardo went on to say that he eagerly embraced the proposal, and being provided with horse and armor by the damsel, set forth on his enterprise, the lady accompanying him.

As they rode she explained the dangers of the quest. The armor was defended by a champion, one of the numerous unsuccessful adventurers for the prize, all of whom had been made prisoners by the fairy, and compelled to take their turn, day by day, in defending the arms against all comers. Thus speaking they arrived at the castle, which was of alabaster, overlaid with gold. Before it, on a lawn, sat an armed knight on horseback, who was none other than Gradasso, king of Sericane, who, in his return home from his unsuccessful inroad into France, had fallen into the power of the fairy, and was held to do her bidding. Mandricardo, upon seeing him, dropt his visor, and laid his lance in rest. The champion of the castle was equally ready, and each spurred towards his opponent. They met one another with equal force, splintered their spears, and, returning to the charge, encountered with their swords. The contest was long and doubtful, when Mandricardo, determined to bring it to an end, threw his arms about Gradasso, grappled with him, and both fell to the ground. Mandricardo, however, fell uppermost, and, preserving his advantage, compelled Gradasso to yield himself conquered. The damsel now interfered, congratulating the victor, and consoling the vanquished as well as she might.

Mandricardo and the damsel proceeded to the gate of the castle, which they found undefended. As they entered they beheld a shield suspended from a pilaster of gold. The device was a white eagle on an azure field, in memory of the bird of Jove, which bore away Ganymede, the flower of the Phrygian race. Beneath was engraved the following couplet:

"Let none with hand profane my buckler wrong
Unless he be himself as Hector strong."

The damsel, alighting from her palfrey, made obeisance to the arms, bending herself to the ground. The Tartar king bowed his head with equal reverence; then advancing towards the shield, touched it with his sword. Thereupon an earthquake shook the ground, and the way by which he had entered closed. Another and an opposite gate opened, and displayed a field bristling with stalks and grain of gold. The damsel, upon this, told him that he had no means of retreat but by cutting down the harvest which was before him, and by uprooting a tree which grew in the middle of the field. Mandricardo, without replying, began to mow the harvest with his sword, but had scarce smitten thrice when he perceived that every stalk that fell was instantly transformed into some poisonous or ravenous animal, which prepared to assail him. Instructed by the damsel, he snatched up a stone and cast it among the pack. A strange wonder followed; for no sooner had the stone fallen among the beasts, than they turned their rage against one another, and rent each other to pieces. Mandricardo did not stop to marvel at the miracle, but proceeded to fulfil his task, and uproot the tree. He clasped it round the trunk, and made vigorous efforts to tear it up by the roots. At each effort fell a shower of leaves, that were instantly changed into birds of prey, which attacked the knight, flapping their wings in his face, with horrid screeching. But undismayed by this new annoyance, he continued to tug at the trunk till it yielded to his efforts. A burst of wind and thunder followed, and the hawks and vultures flew screaming away.

But these only gave place to a new foe; for from the hole made by tearing up the tree issued a furious serpent, and, darting at Mandricardo, wound herself about his limbs with a strain that almost crushed him. Fortune, however, again stood his friend, for, writhing under the folds of the monster, he fell backwards into the hole, and his enemy was crushed beneath his weight.

Mandricardo, when he was somewhat recovered, and assured himself of the destruction of the serpent, began to contemplate the place into which he had fallen, and saw that he was in a vault, incrusted with costly metals, and illuminated by a live coal. In the middle was a sort of ivory bier, and upon this was extended what appeared to be a knight in armor, but was in truth an empty trophy, composed of the rich and precious arms once Hector's, to which nothing was wanting but the sword. While Mandricardo stood contemplating the prize a door opened behind him, and a bevy of fair damsels entered, dancing, who, taking up the armor piece by piece, led him away to the place where the shield was suspended; where he found the fairy of the castle seated in state. By her he was invested with the arms he had won, first pledging his solemn oath to wear no other blade but Durindana, which he was to wrest from Orlando, and thus complete the conquest of Hector's arms.

THE INVASION OF FRANCE (CONTINUED)

Mandricardo, having completed his story, now turned to Rogero, and proposed that arms should decide which of the two was most worthy to bear the symbol of the Trojan knight.

Rogero felt no other objection to this proposal than the scruple which arose on observing that his antagonist was without a sword. Mandricardo insisted that this need be no impediment, since his oath prevented him from using a sword until he should have achieved the conquest of Durindana.

This was no sooner said than a new antagonist started up in Gradasso, who now accompanied Mandricardo. Gradasso vindicated his prior right to Durindana, to obtain which he had embarked (as was related in the beginning) in that bold inroad upon France. A quarrel was thus kindled between the kings of Tartary and Sericane. While the dispute was raging a knight arrived upon the ground, accompanied by a damsel, to whom Rogero related the cause of the strife. The knight was Florismart, and his companion Flordelis. Florismart succeeded in bringing the two champions to accord, by informing them that he could bring them to the presence of Orlando, the master of Durindana.

Gradasso and Mandricardo readily made truce, in order to accompanyFlorismart, nor would Rogero be left behind.

As they proceeded on their quest they were met by a dwarf, who entreated their assistance in behalf of his lady, who had been carried off by an enchanter, mounted on a winged horse. However unwilling to leave the question of the sword undecided, it was not possible for the knights to resist this appeal. Two of their number, Gradasso and Rogero, therefore accompanied the dwarf. Mandricardo persisted in his search for Orlando, and Florismart, with Flordelis, pursued their way to the camp of Charlemagne.

Figure 114: "Roger Delivering Angelica" by Jean Auguste Dominque Ingres

Atlantes, the enchanter, who had brought up Rogero, and cherished for him the warmest affection, knew by his art that his pupil was destined to be severed from him, and converted to the Christian faith through the influence of Bradamante, that royal maiden with whom chance had brought him acquainted. Thinking to thwart the will of Heaven in this respect, he now put forth all his arts to entrap Rogero into his power. By the aid of his subservient demons he reared a castle on an inaccessible height, in the Pyrenean mountains, and to make it a pleasant abode to his pupil, contrived to entrap and convey thither knights and damsels many a one, whom chance had brought into the vicinity of his castle. Here, in a sort of sensual paradise, they were but too willing to forget glory and duty, and to pass their time in indolent enjoyment

It was by the enchanter that the dwarf had now been sent to tempt the knights into his power.

But we must now return to Rinaldo, whom we left interrupted in his combat with Rodomont. In search of his late antagonist and intent on bringing their combat to a decision he entered the forest of Arden, whither he suspected Rodomont had gone. While engaged on this quest he was surprised by the vision of a beautiful child dancing naked, with three damsels as beautiful as himself. While he was lost in admiration at the sight the child approached him, and, throwing at him handfuls of roses and lilies, struck him from his horse. He was no sooner down than he was seized by the dancers, by whom he was dragged about and scourged with flowers till he fell into a swoon. When he began to revive one of the group approached him, and told him that his punishment was the consequence of his rebellion against that power before whom all things bend; that there was but one remedy to heal the wounds that had been inflicted, and that was to drink of the waters of Love. Then they left him.

Rinaldo, sore and faint, dragged himself toward a fountain which flowed near by, and, being parched with thirst, drank greedily and almost unconsciously of the water, which was sweet to the taste, but bitter to the heart. After repeated draughts he recovered his strength and recollection, and found himself in the same place where Angelica had formerly awakened him with a rain of flowers, and whence he had fled in contempt of her courtesy.

This remembrance of the scene was followed by the recognition of his crime; and, repenting bitterly his ingratitude, he leaped upon Bayard, with the intention of hastening to Angelica's country, and soliciting his pardon at her feet.

Let us now retrace our steps, and revert to the time when the paladins having learned from Dudon the summons of Charlemagne to return to France to repel the invaders, had all obeyed the command with the exception of Orlando, whose passion for Angelica still held him in attendance on her. Orlando, arriving before Albracca, found it closely beleaguered. He, however, made his way into the citadel, and related his adventures to Angelica, from the time of his departure up to his separation from Rinaldo and the rest, when they departed to the assistance of Charlemagne. Angelica, in return, described the distresses of the garrison, and the force of the besiegers; and in conclusion prayed Orlando to favor her escape from the pressing danger, and escort her into France. Orlando, who did not suspect that love for Rinaldo was her secret motive, joyfully agreed to the proposal, and the sally was resolved upon.

Leaving lights burning in the fortress, they departed at nightfall, and passed in safety through the enemy's camp. After encountering numerous adventures they reached the sea-side, and embarked on board a pinnace for France. The vessel arrived safely, and the travellers, disembarking in Provence, pursued their way by land. One day, heated and weary, they sought shelter from the sun in the forest of Arden, and chance directed Angelica to the fountain of Disdain, of whose waters she eagerly drank.

Issuing thence, the Count and damsel encountered a stranger- knight. It was no other than Rinaldo, who was just on the point of setting off on a pilgrimage in search of Angelica, to implore her pardon for his insensibility, and urge his new found passion. Surprise and delight at first deprived him of utterance, but soon recovering himself, he joyfully saluted her, claiming her as his, and exhorting her to put herself under his protection. His presumption was repelled by Angelica with disdain, and Orlando, enraged at the invasion of his rights, challenged him to decide their claims by arms.

Terrified at the combat which ensued, Angelica fled amain through the forest, and came out upon a plain covered with tents. This was the camp of Charlemagne, who led the army of reserve destined to support the troops which had advanced to oppose Marsilius. Charles having heard the damsel's tale, with difficulty separated the two cousins, and then consigned Angelica, as the cause of quarrel, to the care of Namo, Duke of Bavaria, promising that she should be his who should best deserve her in the impending battle.

But these plans and hopes were frustrated. The Christian army, beaten at all points, fled from the Saracens; and Angelica, indifferent to both her lovers, mounted a swift palfrey and plunged into the forest, rejoicing, in spite of her terror, at having regained her liberty. She stopped at last in a tufted grove, where a gentle zephyr blew, and whose young trees were watered by two clear runnels, which came and mingled their waters, making a pleasing murmur. Believing herself far from Rinaldo, and overcome by fatigue and the summer heat, she saw with delight a bank covered with flowers so thick that they almost hid the green turf, inviting her to alight and rest. She dismounted from her palfrey, and turned him loose to recruit his strength with the tender grass which bordered the streamlets. Then, in a sheltered nook tapestried with moss and fenced in with roses and hawthorn- flowers, she yielded herself to grateful repose.

She had not slept long when she was awakened by the noise made by the approach of a horse. Starting up, she saw an armed knight who had arrived at the bank of the stream. Not knowing whether he was to be feared or not, her heart beat with anxiety. She pressed aside the leaves to allow her to see who it was, but scarce dared to breathe for fear of betraying herself. Soon the knight threw himself on the flowery bank, and leaning his head on his hand fell into a profound reverie. Then arousing himself from his silence he began to pour forth complaints, mingled with deep sighs. Rivers of tears flowed down his cheeks, and his breast seemed to labor with a hidden flame. "Ah, vain regrets!" he exclaimed; "cruel fortune! others triumph, while I endure hopeless misery! Better a thousand times to lose life, than wear a chain so disgraceful and so oppressive!"

Angelica by this time had recognized the stranger, and perceived that it was Sacripant, king of Circassia, one of the worthiest of her suitors. This prince had followed Angelica from his country, at the very gates of the day, to France, where he heard with dismay that she was under the guardianship of the Paladin Orlando, and that the Emperor had announced his decree to award her as the prize of valor to that one of his nephews who should best deserve her.

As Sacripant continued to lament, Angelica, who had always opposed the hardness of marble to his sighs, thought with herself that nothing forbade her employing his good offices in this unhappy crisis. Though firmly resolved never to accept him as a spouse, she yet felt the necessity of giving him a gleam of hope in reward for the service she required of him. All at once, like Diana, she stepped forth from the arbor. "May the gods preserve thee," she said, "and put far from thee all hard thoughts of me!" Then she told him all that had befallen her since she parted with him at her father's court, and how she had availed herself of Orlando's protection to escape from the beleaguered city. At that moment the noise of horse and armor was heard as of one approaching; and Sacripant, furious at the interruption, resumed his helmet, mounted his horse, and placed his lance in rest. He saw a knight advancing, with scarf and plume of snowy whiteness. Sacripant regarded him with angry eyes, and, while he was yet some distance off, defied him to the combat. The other, not moved by his angry tone to make reply, put himself on his defence. Their horses, struck at the same moment with the spur, rushed upon one another with the impetuosity of a tempest. Their shields were pierced each with the other's lance, and only the temper of their breastplates saved their lives. Both the horses recoiled with the violence of the shock; but the unknown knight's recovered itself at the touch of the spur; the Saracen king's fell dead, and bore down his master with him. The white knight, seeing his enemy in this condition, cared not to renew the combat, but, thinking he had done enough for glory, pursued his way through the forest, and was a mile off before Sacripant had got free from his horse.

As a ploughman, stunned by a thunder-clap which has stricken dead the oxen at his plough, stands motionless, sadly contemplating his loss, so Sacripant stood confounded and overwhelmed with mortification at having Angelica a witness of his defeat. He groaned, he sighed, less from the pain of his bruises than for the shame of being reduced to such a state before her. The princess took pity on him, and consoled him as well as she could. "Banish your regrets, my lord," she said, "this accident has happened solely in consequence of the feebleness of your horse, which had more need of rest and food than of such an encounter as this. Nor can your adversary gain any credit by it, since he has hurried away, not venturing a second trial." While she thus consoled Sacripant they perceived a person approach, who seemed a courier, with bag and horn. As soon as he came up, he accosted Sacripant, and inquired if he had seen a knight pass that way, bearing a white shield and with a white plume to his helmet. "I have, indeed, seen too much of him," said Sacripant, "it is he who has brought me to the ground; but at least I hope to learn from you who that knight is." "That I can easily inform you," said the man; "know then that, if you have been overthrown, you owe your fate to the high prowess of a lady as beautiful as she is brave. It is the fair and illustrious Bradamante who has won from you the honors of victory."

At these words the courier rode on his way, leaving Sacripant more confounded and mortified than ever. In silence he mounted the horse of Angelica, taking the lady behind him on the croup, and rode away in search of a more secure asylum. Hardly had they ridden two miles when a new sound was heard in the forest, and they perceived a gallant and powerful horse, which, leaping the ravines and dashing aside the branches that opposed his passage, appeared before them, accoutred with a rich harness adorned with gold.

"If I may believe my eyes, which penetrate with difficulty the underwood," said Angelica, "that horse that dashes so stoutly through the bushes is Bayard, and I marvel how he seems to know the need we have of him, mounted as we are both on one feeble animal." Sacripant, dismounting from the palfrey, approached the fiery courser, and attempted to seize his bridle, but the disdainful animal, turning from him, launched at him a volley of kicks enough to have shattered a wall of marble. Bayard then approached Angelica with an air as gentle and loving as a faithful dog could his master after a long separation. For he remembered how she had caressed him, and even fed him, in Albracca. She took his bridle in her left hand, while with her right she patted his neck. The beautiful animal, gifted with wonderful intelligence, seemed to submit entirely. Sacripant, seizing the moment to vault upon him, controlled his curvetings, and Angelica, quitting the croup of the palfrey, regained her seat.

But, turning his eyes toward a place where was heard a noise of arms, Sacripant beheld Rinaldo. That hero now loves Angelica more than his life, and she flies him as the timid crane the falcon.

The fountain of which Angelica had drunk produced such an effect on the beautiful queen that, with distressed countenance and trembling voice, she conjured Sacripant not to wait the approach of Rinaldo, but to join her in flight.

"Am I, then," said Sacripant, "of so little esteem with you that you doubt my power to defend you? Do you forget the battle of Albracca, and how, in your defence, I fought single-handed against Agrican and all his knights?"

Angelica made no reply, uncertain what to do; but already Rinaldo was too near to be escaped. He advanced menacingly to the Circassian king, for he recognized his horse.

"Vile thief," he cried, "dismount from that horse, and prevent the punishment that is your due for daring to rob me of my property. Leave, also, the princess in my hands; for it would indeed be a sin to suffer so charming a lady and so gallant a charger to remain in such keeping."

The king of Circassia, furious at being thus insulted, cried out, "Thou liest, villain, in giving me the name of thief, which better belongs to thyself than to me. It is true, the beauty of this lady and the perfection of this horse are unequalled; come on, then, and let us try which of us is most worthy to possess them."

At these words the king of Circassia and Rinaldo attacked one another with all their force, one fighting on foot, the other on horseback. You need not, however, suppose that the Saracen king found any advantage in this; for a young page, unused to horsemanship, could not have failed more completely to manage Bayard than did this accomplished knight. The faithful animal loved his master too well to injure him, and refused his aid as well as his obedience to the hand of Sacripant, who could strike but ineffectual blows, the horse backing when he wished him to go forward, and dropping his head and arching his back, throwing out with his legs, so as almost to shake the knight out of the saddle. Sacripant, seeing that he could not manage him, watched his opportunity, rose on his saddle, and leapt lightly to the earth; then, relieved from the embarrassment of the horse, renewed the combat on more equal terms. Their skill to thrust and parry were equal; one rises, the other stoops; with one foot set firm they turn and wind, to lay on strokes or to dodge them. At last Rinaldo, throwing himself on the Circassian, dealt him a blow so terrible that Fusberta, his good sword, cut in two the buckler of Sacripant, although it was made of bone, and covered with a thick plate of steel well tempered. The arm of the Saracen was deprived of its defence, and almost palsied with the stroke. Angelica, perceiving how victory was likely to incline, and shuddering at the thought of becoming the prize of Rinaldo, hesitated no longer. Turning her horse's head, she fled with the utmost speed; and, in spite of the round pebbles which covered a steep descent, she plunged into a deep valley, trembling with the fear that Rinaldo was in pursuit. At the bottom of this valley she encountered an aged hermit, whose white beard flowed to his middle, and whose venerable appearance seemed to assure his piety.

This hermit, who appeared shrunk by age and fasting, travelled slowly, mounted upon a wretched ass. The princess, overcome with fear, conjured him to save her life; and to conduct her to some port of the sea, whence she might embark and quit France, never more to hear the odious name of Rinaldo.

The old hermit was something of a wizard. He comforted Angelica, and promised to protect her from all peril. Then he opened his scrip, and took from thence a book, and had read but a single page when a goblin, obedient to his incantations, appeared, under the form of a laboring man, and demanded his orders. He received them, transported himself to the place where the knights still maintained their conflict, and boldly stepped between the two.

"Tell me, I pray you," he said, "what benefit will accrue to him who shall get the better in this contest? The object you are contending for is already disposed of; for the Paladin Orlando, without effort and without opposition, is now carrying away the princess Angelica to

Paris. You had better pursue them promptly; for if they reach Paris you will never see her again."

At these words you might have seen those rival warriors confounded, stupefied, silently agreeing that they were affording their rival a fair opportunity to triumph over them. Rinaldo, approaching Bayard, breathes a sigh of shame and rage, and swears a terrible oath that, if he overtakes Orlando, he will tear his heart out. Then mounting Bayard and pressing his flanks with his spurs, he leaves the king of Circassia on foot in the forest.

Let it not appear strange that Rinaldo found Bayard obedient at last, after having so long prevented any one from even touching his bridle; for that fine animal had an intelligence almost human; he had fled from his master only to draw him on the track of Angelica, and enable him to recover her. He saw when the princess fled from the battle, and Rinaldo being then engaged in a fight on foot, Bayard found himself free to follow the traces of Angelica. Thus he had drawn his master after him, not permitting him to approach, and had brought him to the sight of the princess. But Bayard now, deceived like his master with the false intelligence of the goblin, submits to be mounted and to serve his master as usual, and Rinaldo, animated with rage, makes him fly toward Paris, more slowly than his wishes, though the speed of Bayard outstripped the winds. Full of impatience to encounter Orlando, he gave but a few hours that night to sleep. Early the next day he saw before him the great city, under the walls of which the Emperor Charles had collected the scattered remains of his army. Foreseeing that he would soon be attacked on all sides, the Emperor had caused the ancient fortifications to be repaired, and new ones to be built, surrounded by wide and deep ditches. The desire to hold the field against the enemy made him seize every means of procuring new allies. He hoped to receive from England aid sufficient to enable him to form a new camp, and as soon as Rinaldo rejoined him he selected him to go as his ambassador into England, to plead for auxiliaries. Rinaldo was far from pleased with his commission, but he obeyed the Emperor's commands, without giving himself time to devote a single day to the object nearest his heart. He hastened to Calais, and lost not a moment in embarking for England, ardently desiring a hasty despatch of his commission, and a speedy return to France.

BRADAMANTE AND ROGERO

Bradamante, the knight of the white plume and shield, whose sudden appearance and encounter with Sacripant we have already told, was in quest of Rogero, from whom chance had separated her, almost at the beginning of their acquaintance. After her encounter with Sacripant Bradamante pursued her way through the forest, in hopes of rejoining Rogero, and arrived at last on the brink of a fair fountain.

This fountain flowed through a broad meadow. Ancient trees overshadowed it, and travellers, attracted by the sweet murmur of its waters, stopped there to cool themselves. Bradamante, casting her eyes on all sides to enjoy the beauties of the spot, perceived, under the shade of a tree, a knight reclining, who seemed to be oppressed with the deepest grief

Figure 115: "Bradamante Valorola" by Antonio Tempesta

Bradamante accosted him, and asked to be informed of the cause of his distress. "Alas! my lord," said he, "I lament a young and charming friend, my affianced wife, who has been torn from me by a villain,—let me rather call him a demon,—who, on a winged horse, descended from the air, seized her, and bore her screaming to his den. I have pursued them over rocks and through ravines till my horse is no longer able to bear me, and I now wait only for death." He added that already a vain attempt on his behalf had been made by two knights, whom chance had brought to the spot. Their names were Gradasso, king of Sericane, and Rogero, the Moor. Both had been overcome by the wiles of the enchanter, and were added to the number of the captives, whom he held in an impregnable castle, situated on the height of the mountain. At the mention of Rogero's name Bradamante started with delight, which was soon changed to an opposite sentiment when she heard that her lover was a prisoner in the toils of the enchanter. "Sir Knight," she said, "do not surrender yourself to despair; this day may be more happy for you than you think, if you will only lead me to the castle which enfolds her whom you deplore."

The knight responded, "After having lost all that made life dear to me I have no motive to avoid the dangers of the enterprise, and I will do as you request; but I forewarn you of the perils you will have to encounter. If you fall impute it not to me."

Having thus spoken, they took their way to the castle, but were overtaken by a messenger from the camp, who had been sent in quest of Bradamante to summon her back to the army, where her presence was needed to reassure her disheartened forces, and withstand the advance of the Moors.

The mournful knight, whose name was Pinabel, thus became aware that Bradamante was a scion of the house of Clermont, between which and his own of Mayence there existed an ancient feud. From this moment the traitor sought only how he might be rid of the company of Bradamante, from whom he feared no good would come to him, but rather mortal injury, if his name and lineage became known to her. For he judged her by his own base model, and, knowing his ill deserts, he feared to receive his due.

Bradamante, in spite of the summons to return to the army, could not resolve to leave her lover in captivity, and determined first to finish the adventure on which she was engaged. Pinabel leading the way, they at length arrived at a wood, in the centre of which rose a steep, rocky mountain. Pinabel, who now thought of nothing else but how he might escape from Bradamante, proposed to ascend the mountain to extend his view, in order to discover a shelter for the night, if any there might be within sight. Under this pretence he left Bradamante, and advanced up the side of the mountain till he came to a cleft in the rock, down which he looked, and perceived that it widened below into a spacious cavern. Meanwhile Bradamante, fearful of losing her guide, had followed close on his footsteps, and rejoined him at the mouth of the cavern. Then the traitor, seeing the impossibility of escaping her, conceived another design. He told her that before her approach he had seen in the cavern a young and beautiful damsel, whose rich dress announced her high birth, who with tears and lamentations implored assistance; that before he could descend to relieve her a ruffian had seized her, and hurried her away into the recesses of the cavern.

Bradamante, full of truth and courage, readily believed this lie of the Mayencian traitor. Eager to succor the damsel, she looked round for the means of facilitating the descent, and seeing a large elm with spreading branches she lopped off with her sword one of the largest, and thrust it into the opening. She told Pinabel to hold fast to the larger end, while, grasping the branches with her hands, she let herself down into the cavern.

The traitor smiled at seeing her thus suspended, and, asking her in mockery, "Are you a good leaper?" he let go the branch with perfidious glee, and saw Bradamante precipitated to the bottom of the cave. "I wish your whole race were there with you," he muttered, "that you might all perish together."

But Pinabel's atrocious design was not accomplished. The twigs and foliage of the branch broke its descent, and Bradamante, not seriously injured, though stunned with her fall, was reserved for other adventures.

As soon as she recovered from the shock Bradamante cast her eyes around and perceived a door, through which she passed into a second cavern, larger and loftier than the first. It had the appearance of a subterranean temple. Columns of the purest alabaster adorned it, and supported the roof; a simple altar rose in the middle; a lamp, whose radiance was reflected by the alabaster walls, cast a mild light around.

Bradamante, inspired by a sense of religious awe, approached the altar, and, falling on her knees, poured forth her prayers and thanks to the Preserver of her life, invoking the protection of his power. At that moment a small door opened, and a female issued from it with naked feet, and flowing robe and hair, who called her by her name, and thus addressed her: "Brave and generous Bradamante, know that it is a power from above that has brought you hither. The spirit of Merlin, whose last earthly abode was in this place, has warned me of your arrival, and of the fate that awaits you. This famous grotto," she continued, "was the work of the enchanter Merlin; here his ashes repose. You have no doubt heard how this sage and virtuous enchanter ceased to be. Victim of the artful fairy of the lake, Merlin, by a fatal compliance with her request, laid himself down living in his tomb, without power to resist the spell laid upon him by that ingrate, who retained him there as long as he lived. His spirit hovers about this spot, and will not leave it, until the last trumpet shall summon the dead to judgment. He answers the questions of those who approach his tomb, where perhaps you may be privileged to hear his voice."

Bradamante, astonished at these words, and the objects which met her view, knew not whether she was awake or asleep. Confused, but modest, she cast down her eyes, and a blush overspread her face. "Ah, what am I," said she, "that so great a prophet should deign to speak to me!" Still, with a secret satisfaction, she followed the priestess, who led her to the tomb of Merlin. This tomb was constructed of a species of stone hard and resplendent like fire. The rays which beamed from the stone sufficed to light up that terrible place, where the sun's rays never penetrated; but I know not whether that light was the effect of a certain phosphorescence of the stone itself, or of the many talismans and charms with which it was wrought over.

Bradamante had hardly passed the threshold of this sacred place when the spirit of the enchanter saluted her with a voice firm and distinct: "May thy designs be prosperous, O chaste and noble maiden, the future mother of heroes, the glory of Italy, and destined to fill the whole world with their fame. Great captains, renowned knights, shall be numbered among your descendants, who shall defend the Church and restore their country to its ancient splendor. Princes, wise as Augustus and the sage Numa, shall bring back the age of gold. [Footnote: This prophecy is introduced by Ariosto in this place to compliment the noble house of Este, the princes of his native state, the dukedom of Ferrara.] To accomplish these grand destinies it is ordained that you shall wed the illustrious Rogero. Fly then to his deliverance, and lay prostrate in the dust the traitor who has snatched him from you, and now holds him in chains!"

Merlin ceased with these words, and left to Melissa, the priestess, the charge of more fully instructing the maiden in her future course. "To-morrow," said she, "I will conduct you to the castle on the rock where Rogero is held captive. I will not leave you till I have guided you through this wild wood, and I will direct you on your way so that you shall be in no danger of mistaking it."

The next morning Melissa conducted Bradamante between rocks and precipices, crossing rapid torrents, and traversing intricate passes, employing the time in imparting to her such information as was necessary to enable her to bring her design to a successful issue.

"Not only would the castle, impenetrable by force, and that winged horse of his baffle your efforts, but know that he possesses also a buckler whence flashes a light so brilliant that the eyes of all who look upon it are blinded. Think not to avoid it by shutting your eyes, for how then will you be able to avoid his blows, and make him feel your own? But I will teach you the proper course to pursue.

"Agramant, the Moorish prince, possesses a ring stolen from a queen of India, which has power to render of no avail all enchantments. Agramant, knowing that Rogero is of more importance to him than any one of his warriors, is desirous of rescuing him from the power of the enchanter, and has sent for that purpose Brunello, the most crafty and sagacious of his servants, provided with his wonderful ring, and he is even now at hand, bent on this enterprise. But, beautiful Bradamante, as I desire that no one but yourself shall have the glory of delivering from thraldom your future spouse, listen while I disclose the means of success. Following this path which leads by the seashore, you will come ere long to a hostelry, where the Saracen Brunello will arrive shortly before you. You will readily know him by his stature, under four feet, his great disproportioned head, his squint eyes, his livid hue, his thick eyebrows joining his tufted beard. His dress, moreover, that of a courier, will point him out to you.

"It will be easy for you to enter into conversation with him, announcing yourself as a knight seeking combat with the enchanter, but let not the knave suspect that you know anything about the ring. I doubt not that he will be your guide to the castle of the enchanter. Accept his offer, but take care to keep behind him till you come in sight of the brilliant dome of the castle. Then hesitate not to strike him dead, for the wretch deserves no pity, and take from him the ring. But let him not suspect your intention, for by putting the ring into his mouth he will instantly become invisible, and disappear from your eyes."

Saying thus, the sage Melissa and the fair Bradamante arrived near the city of Bordeaux, where the rich and wide river Garonne pours the tribute of its waves into the sea. They parted with tender embraces. Bradamante, intent wholly on her purpose, hastened to arrive at the hostelry, where Brunello had preceded her a few moments only. The young heroine knew him without difficulty. She accosted him, and put to him some slight questions, to which he replied with adroit falsehoods. Bradamante, on her part, concealed from him her sex, her religion, her country, and the blood from whence she sprung. While they talk together, sudden cries are heard from all parts of the hostelry. "O queen of heaven!" exclaimed Bradamante, "what can be the cause of this sudden alarm?" She soon learned the cause. Host, children, domestics, all, with upturned eyes, as if they saw a comet or a great eclipse, were gazing on a prodigy which seemed to pass the bounds of possibility. She beheld distinctly a winged horse, mounted with a cavalier in rich armor, cleaving the air with rapid flight. The wings of this strange courser were wide extended, and covered with feathers of various colors. The polished armor of the knight made them shine with rainbow tints. In a short time the horse and rider disappeared behind the summits of the mountains.

"It is an enchanter," said the host, "a magician who often is seen traversing the air in that way. Sometimes he flies aloft as if among the stars, and at others skims along the land. He possesses a wonderful castle on the top of the Pyrenees. Many knights have shown their courage by going to attack him, but none have ever returned, from which it is to be feared they have lost either their life or their liberty."

Bradamante, addressing the host, said, "Could you furnish me a guide to conduct me to the castle of this enchanter?" "By my faith," said Brunello, interrupting, "that you shall not seek in vain; I have it all in writing, and I will myself conduct you." Bradamante, with thanks, accepted him for her guide.

The host had a tolerable horse to dispose of, which Bradamante bargained for, and the next day, at the first dawn of morning, she took her route by a narrow valley, taking care to have the Saracen Brunello lead the way.

They reached the summit of the Pyrenees, whence one may look down on France, Spain, and the two seas. From this height they descended again by a fatiguing road into a deep valley. From the middle of this valley an isolated mountain rose, composed of rough and perpendicular rock, on whose summit was the castle, surrounded with a wall of brass. Brunello said, "Yonder is the stronghold where the enchanter keeps his prisoners; one must have wings to mount thither; it is easy to see that the aid of a flying horse must be necessary for the master of this castle, which he uses for his prison and for his abode."

Bradamante, sufficiently instructed, saw that the time had now come to possess herself of the ring; but she could not resolve to slay a defenceless man. She seized Brunello before he was aware, bound him to a tree, and took from him the ring which he wore on one of his fingers. The cries and entreaties of the perfidious Saracen moved her not. She advanced to the foot of the rock whereon the castle stood, and, to draw the magician to the combat, sounded her horn, adding to it cries of defiance.

The enchanter delayed not to present himself, mounted on his winged horse. Bradamante was struck with surprise mixed with joy when she saw that this person, described as so formidable, bore no lance nor club, nor any other deadly weapon. He had only on his arm a buckler, covered with a cloth, and in his hand an open book. As to the winged horse, there was no enchantment about him. He was a natural animal, of a species which exists in the Riphaean mountains. Like a griffin, he had the head of an eagle, claws armed with talons, and wings covered with feathers, the rest of his body being that of a horse. This strange animal is called a Hippogriff.

The heroine attacked the enchanter on his approach, striking on this side and on that, with all the energy of a violent combat, but wounding only the wind; and after this pretended attack had lasted some time dismounted from her horse, as if hoping to do battle more effectually on foot. The enchanter now prepares to employ his sole weapon, by uncovering the magic buckler which never failed to subdue an enemy by depriving him of his senses. Bradamante, confiding in her ring, observed all the motions of her adversary, and, at the unveiling of the shield, cast herself on the ground, pretending that the splendor of the shield had overcome her, but in reality to induce the enchanter to dismount and approach her.

It happened according to her wish. When the enchanter saw her prostrate he made his horse alight on the ground, and, dismounting, fixed the shield on the pommel of his saddle, and approached in order to secure the fallen warrior. Bradamante, who watched him intently, as soon as she saw him near at hand, sprang up, seized him vigorously, threw him down, and, with the same chain which the enchanter had prepared for herself, bound him fast, without his being able to make any effectual resistance.

The enchanter, with the accents of despair, exclaimed, "Take my life, young man!" but Bradamante was far from complying with such a wish. Desirous of knowing the name of the enchanter, and for what purpose he had formed with so much art this impregnable fortress, she commanded him to inform her.

Figure 116: "The Enchantress Vivien" by Howard Pyle

"Alas!" replied the magician, while tears flowed down his cheeks, "it is not to conceal booty, nor for any culpable design that I have built this castle; it was only to guard the life of a young knight, the object of my tenderest affection, my art having taught me that he is destined to become a Christian, and to perish, shortly after, by the blackest of treasons.

"This youth, named Rogero, is the most beautiful and most accomplished of knights. It is I, the unhappy Atlantes, who have reared him from his childhood. The call of honor and the desire of glory led him from me to follow Agramant, his prince, in his invasion of France, and I, more devoted to Rogero than the tenderest of parents, have sought the means of bringing him back to this abode, in the hope of saving him from the cruel fate that menaces him.

"For this purpose I have got him in my possession by the same means as I attempted to employ against you; and by which I have succeeded in collecting a great many knights and ladies in my castle. My purpose was to render my beloved pupil's captivity light, by affording him society to amuse him, and keep his thoughts from running on subjects of war and glory. Alas! my cares have been in vain! Yet, take, I beseech you, whatever else I have, but spare me my beloved pupil. Take this shield, take this winged courser, deliver such of your friends as you may find among my prisoners, deliver them all if you will, but leave me my beloved Rogero; or if you will snatch him too from me, take also my life, which will cease then to be to me worth preserving."

Bradamante replied: "Old man, hope not to move me by your vain entreaties. It is precisely the liberty of Rogero that I require. You would keep him here in bondage and in slothful pleasure, to save him from a fate which you foresee. Vain old man! how can you foresee his fate when you could not foresee your own? You desire me to take your life. No, my aim and my soul refuse the request." This said, she required the magician to go before, and guide her to the castle. The prisoners were set at liberty, though some, in their secret hearts, regretted the voluptuous life which was thus brought to an end. Bradamante and Rogero met one another with transports of joy.

They descended from the mountain to the spot where the encounter had taken place. There they found the Hippogriff, with the magic buckler in its wrapper, hanging to his saddle-bow. Bradamante advanced to seize the bridle; the Hippogriff seemed to wait her approach, but before she reached him he spread his wings and flew away to a neighboring hill, and in the same manner, a second time, eluded her efforts. Rogero and the other liberated knights dispersed over the plain and hilltops to secure him, and at last the animal allowed Rogero to seize his rein. The fearless Rogero hesitated not to vault upon his back, and let him feel his spurs, which so roused his mettle that, after galloping a short distance, he suddenly spread his wings, and soared into the air. Bradamante had the grief to see her lover snatched away from her at the very moment of reunion. Rogero, who knew not the art of directing the horse, was unable to control his flight. He found himself carried over the tops of the mountains, so far above them that he could hardly distinguish what was land and what water. The Hippogriff directed his flight to the west, and cleaved the air as swiftly as a new-rigged vessel cuts the waves, impelled by the freshest and most favorable gales.

ASTOLPHO AND THE ENCHANTRESS

In the long flight which Rogero took on the back of the Hippogriff he was carried over land and sea, unknowing whither. As soon as he had gained some control over the animal he made him alight on the nearest land. When he came near enough to earth Rogero leapt lightly from his back, and tied the animal to a myrtle-tree. Near the spot flowed the pure waters of a fountain, surrounded by cedars and palm-trees. Rogero laid aside his shield, and, removing his helmet, breathed with delight the fresh air, and cooled his lips with the waters of the fountain. For we cannot wonder that he was excessively fatigued, considering the ride he had taken. He was preparing to taste the sweets of repose when he perceived that the Hippogriff, which he had tied by the bridle to a myrtle-tree, frightened at something, was making violent efforts to disengage himself. His struggle shook the myrtle-tree so that many of its beautiful leaves were torn off, and strewed the ground.

A sound like that which issues from burning wood seemed to come from the myrtle-tree, at first faint and indistinct, but growing stronger by degrees, and at length was audible as a voice which spoke in this manner: "O knight, if the tenderness of your heart corresponds to the beauty of your person, relieve me, I pray you, from this tormenting animal. I suffer enough inwardly without having outward evils added to my lot."

Rogero, at the first accents of this voice, turned his eyes promptly on the myrtle, hastened to it, and stood fixed in astonishment when he perceived that the voice issued from the tree itself. He immediately untied his horse, and, flushed with surprise and regret, exclaimed, "Whoever thou art, whether mortal or the goddess of these woods, forgive me, I beseech you, my involuntary fault. Had I imagined that this hard bark covered a being possessed of feeling, could I have exposed such a beautiful myrtle to the insults of this steed? May the sweet influences of the sky and air speedily repair the injury I have done! For my part, I promise by the sovereign lady of my heart to do everything you wish in order to merit your forgiveness."

At these words the myrtle seemed to tremble from root to stem, and Rogero remarked that a moisture as of tears trickled down its bark, like that which exudes from a log placed on the fire. It then spoke:

"The kindness which inspires your words compels me to disclose to you who I once was, and by what fatality I have been changed into this shape. My name was Astolpho, cousin of Orlando and Rinaldo, whose fame has filled the earth. I was myself reckoned among the bravest paladins of France, and was by birth entitled to reign over England, after Otho, my father. Returning from the distant East, with Rinaldo and many other brave knights, called home to aid with our arms the great Emperor of France, we reached a spot where the powerful enchantress Alcina possessed a castle on the borders of the sea. She had gone to the water-side to amuse herself with fishing, and we paused to see how, by her art, without hook or line, she drew from the water whatever she would.

"Not far from the shore an enormous whale showed a back so broad and motionless that it looked like an island. Alcina had fixed her eyes on me, and planned to get me into her power. Addressing us, she said: 'This is the hour when the prettiest mermaid in the sea comes regularly every day to the shore of yonder island. She sings so sweetly that the very waves flow smoother at the sound. If you wish to hear her come with me to her resort.' So saying, Alcina pointed to the fish, which we all supposed to be an island. I, who was rash, did not hesitate to follow her; but swam my horse over, and mounted on the back of the fish. In vain Rinaldo and Dudon made signs to me to beware; Alcina, smiling, took me in charge, and led the way. No sooner were we mounted upon him than the whale moved off, spreading his great fins, and cleft rapidly the waters. I then saw my folly, but it was too late to repent. Alcina soothed my anger, and professed that what she had done was for love of me. Ere long we arrived at this island, where at first everything was done to reconcile me to my lot, and to make my days pass happily away. But soon Alcina, sated with her conquest, grew indifferent, then weary of me, and at last, to get rid of me, changed me into this form, as she had done to many lovers before me, making some of them olives, some palms, some cedars, changing others into fountains, rocks, or even into wild beasts. And thou, courteous knight, whom accident has brought to this enchanted isle, beware that she get not the power over thee, or thou shalt haply be made like us, a tree, a fountain, or a rock."

Rogero expressed his astonishment at this recital. Astolpho added that the island was in great part subject to the sway of Alcina. By the aid of her sister Morgana, she had succeeded in dispossessing a third sister, Logestilla, of nearly the whole of her patrimony, for the whole isle was hers originally by her father's bequest. But Logestilla was temperate and sage, while the other sisters were false and voluptuous. Her empire was divided from theirs by a gulf and chain of mountains, which alone had thus far prevented her sister from usurping it.

Astolpho here ended his tale, and Rogero, who knew that he was the cousin of Bradamante, would gladly have devised some way for his relief; but, as that was out of his power, he consoled him as well as he could, and then begged to be told the way to the palace of Logestilla, and how to avoid that of Alcina. Astolpho directed him to take the road to the left, though rough and full of rocks. He warned him that this road would present serious obstacles; that troops of monsters would oppose his passage, employed by the art of Alcina to prevent her subjects from escaping from her dominion. Rogero thanked the myrtle, and prepared to set out on his way.

He at first thought he would mount the winged horse, and scale the mountain on his back; but he was too uncertain of his power to control him to wish to encounter the hazard of another flight through the air, besides that he was almost famished for the want of food. So he led the horse after him, and took the road on foot, which for some distance led equally to the dominions of both the sisters.

He had not advanced more than two miles when he saw before him the superb city of Alcina. It was surrounded with a wall of gold, which seemed to reach the skies. I know that some think that this wall was not of real gold, but only the work of alchemy; it matters not; I prefer to think it gold, for it certainly shone like gold.

A broad and level road led to the gates of the city, and from this another branched off, narrow and rough, which led to the mountain region. Rogero took without hesitation the narrow road; but he had no sooner entered upon it than he was assailed by a numerous troop which opposed his passage.

You never have seen anything so ridiculous, so extraordinary, as this host of hobgoblins were. Some of them bore the human form from the neck to the feet, but had the head of a monkey or a cat; others had the legs and the ears of a horse; old men and women, bald and hideous, ran hither and thither as if out of their senses, half clad in the shaggy skins of beasts; one rode full speed on a horse without a bridle, another jogged along mounted on an ass or a cow; others, full of agility, skipped about, and clung to the tails and manes of the animals which their companions rode. Some blew horns, others brandished drinking-cups; some were armed with spits, and some with pitchforks. One, who appeared to be the captain, had an enormous belly and a gross fat head; he was mounted on a tortoise, that waddled, now this way, now that, without keeping any one direction.

One of these monsters, who had something approaching the human form, though he had the neck, ears, and muzzle of a dog, set himself to bark furiously at Rogero, to make him turn off to the right, and reenter upon the road to the gay city; but the brave chevalier exclaimed, "That will I not, so long as I can use this sword,"—and he thrust the point directly at his face. The monster tried to strike him with a lance, but Rogero was too quick for him, and thrust his sword through his body, so that it appeared a hand's breadth behind his back. The paladin, now giving full vent to his rage, laid about him vigorously among the rabble, cleaving one to the teeth, another to the girdle; but the troop were so numerous, and in spite of his blows pressed around him so close, that, to clear his way, he must have had as many arms as Briareus.

If Rogero had uncovered the shield of the enchanter, which hung at his saddle-bow, he might easily have vanquished this monstrous rout; but perhaps he did not think of it, and perhaps he preferred to seek his defence nowhere but in his good sword. At that moment, when his perplexity was at its height, he saw issue from the city gate two young beauties, whose air and dress proclaimed their rank and gentle nurture. Each of them was mounted on a unicorn, whose whiteness surpassed that of ermine. They advanced to the meadow where Rogero was contending so valiantly against the hobgoblins, who all retired at their approach. They drew near, they extended their hands to the young warrior, whose cheeks glowed with the flush of exercise and modesty. Grateful for their assistance, he expressed his thanks, and, having no heart to refuse them, followed their guidance to the gate of the city.

This grand and beautiful entrance was adorned by a portico of four vast columns, all of diamond. Whether they were real diamond or artificial I cannot say. What matter is it, so long as they appeared to the eye like diamond, and nothing could be more gay and splendid.

On the threshold, and between the columns, was seen a bevy of charming young women, who played and frolicked together. They all ran to receive Rogero, and conducted him into the palace, which appeared like a paradise.

We might well call by that name this abode, where the hours flew by, without account, in ever-new delights. The bare idea of satiety, want, and, above all, of age, never entered the minds of the inhabitants. They experienced no sensations except those of luxury and gayety; the cup of happiness seemed for them ever- flowing and exhaustless. The two young damsels to whom Rogero owed his deliverance from the hobgoblins conducted him to the apartment of their mistress. The beautiful Alcina advanced, and greeted him with an air at once dignified and courteous. All her court surrounded the paladin, and rendered him the most flattering attentions. The castle was less admirable for its magnificence than for the charms of those who inhabited it. They were of either sex, well matched in beauty, youth, and grace; but among this charming group the brilliant Alcina shone, as the sun outshines the stars. The young warrior was fascinated. All that he had heard from the myrtle-tree appeared to him but a vile calumny. How could he suspect that falsehood and treason veiled themselves under smiles and the ingenuous air of truth? He doubted not that Astolpho had deserved his fate, and perhaps a punishment more severe; he regarded all his stories as dictated by a disappointed spirit, and a thirst for revenge. But we must not condemn Rogero too harshly, for he was the victim of magic power.

They seated themselves at table, and immediately harmonious lyres and harps waked the air with the most ravishing notes. The charms of poetry were added in entertaining recitals; the magnificence of the feast would have done credit to a royal board. The traitress forgot nothing which might charm the paladin, and attach him to the spot, meaning, when she should grow tired of him, to metamorphose him as she had done others. In the same manner passed each succeeding day. Games of pleasant exercise, the chase, the dance, or rural sports, made the hours pass quickly; while they gave zest to the refreshment of the bath, or sleep.

Thus, Rogero led a life of ease and luxury, while Charlemagne and Agramant were struggling for empire. But I cannot linger with him while the amiable and courageous Bradamante is night and day directing her uncertain steps to every spot where the slightest chance invites her, in the hope of recovering Rogero.

I will therefore say that, having sought him in vain in fields and in cities, she knew not whither next to direct her steps. She did not apprehend the death of Rogero. The fall of such a hero would have reechoed from the Hydaspes to the farthest river of the West; but, not knowing whether he was on the earth or in the air, she concluded, as a last resource, to return to the cavern which contained the tomb of Merlin, to ask of him some sure direction to the object of her search.

While this thought occupied her mind, Melissa, the sage enchantress, suddenly appeared before her. This virtuous and beneficent magician had discovered by her spells that Rogero was passing his time in pleasure and idleness, forgetful of his honor and his sovereign. Not able to endure the thought that one who was born to be a hero should waste his years in base repose, and leave a sullied reputation in the memory of survivors, she saw that vigorous measures must be employed to draw him forth into the paths of virtue. Melissa was not blinded by her affection for the amiable paladin, like Atlantes, who, intent only on preserving Rogero's life, cared nothing for his fame. It was that old enchanter whose arts had guided the Hippogriff to the isle of the too charming Alcina, where he hoped his favorite would learn to forget honor, and lose the love of glory.

At the sight of Melissa joy lighted up the countenance of Bradamante, and hope animated her breast. Melissa concealed nothing from her, but told her how Rogero was in the toils of Alcina. Bradamante was plunged in grief and terror; but the kind enchantress calmed her, dispelled her fears, and promised that before many days she would lead back the paladin to her feet.

"My daughter," she said, "give me the ring which you wear, and which possesses the power to overcome enchantments. By means of it I doubt not but that I may enter the stronghold where the false Alcina holds Rogero in durance, and may succeed in vanquishing her and liberating him." Bradamante unhesitatingly delivered her the ring, recommending Rogero to her best efforts. Melissa then summoned by her art a huge palfrey, black as jet, excepting one foot, which was bay. Mounted upon this animal, she rode with such speed that by the next morning she had reached the abode of Alcina.

She here transformed herself into the perfect resemblance of the old magician Atlantes, adding a palm-breadth to her height, and enlarging her whole figure. Her chin she covered with a long beard, and seamed her whole visage well with wrinkles. She assumed also his voice and manner, and watched her chance to find Rogero alone. At last she found him, dressed in a rich tunic of silk and gold, a collar of precious stones about his neck, and his arms, once so rough with exercise, decorated with bracelets. His air and his every motion indicated effeminacy, and he seemed to retain nothing of Rogero but the name; such power had the enchantress obtained over him.

Melissa, under the form of his old instructor, presented herself before him, wearing a stern and serious visage. "Is this, then," she said, "the fruit of all my labors? Is it for this that I fed you on the marrow of bears and lions, that I taught you to subdue dragons, and, like Hercules, strangle serpents in your youthful grasp, only to make you, by all my cares, a feeble Adonis? My nightly watchings of the stars, of the yet warm fibres of animals, the lots I have cast, the points of nativity that I have calculated, have they all falsely indicated that you were born for greatness? Who could have believed that you would become the slave of a base enchantress? O Rogero, learn to know this Alcina, learn to understand her arts and to countervail them. Take this ring, place it on your finger, return to her presence, and see for yourself what are her real charms."

At these words, Rogero, confused, abashed, cast his eyes upon the ground, and knew not what to answer. Melissa seized the moment, slipped the ring on his finger, and the paladin was himself again. What a thunderclap to him! Overcome by shame, he dared not to encounter the looks of his instructor. When at last he raised his eyes he beheld not that venerable form, but the priestess Melissa, who in virtue of the ring now appeared in her true person. She told him of the motives which had led her to come to his rescue, of the griefs and regrets of Bradamante, and of her unwearied search for him. "That charming Amazon," she said, "sends you this ring, which is a sovereign antidote to all enchantments. She would have sent you her heart in my hands, if it would have had greater power to serve you."

It was needless for Melissa to say more. Rogero's love for Alcina, being but the work of enchantment, vanished as soon as the enchantment was withdrawn, and he now hated her with an equal intensity, seeing no longer anything in her but her vices, and feeling only resentment for the shame that she had put upon him.

His surprise when he again beheld Alcina was no less than his indignation. Fortified by his ring from her enchantments, he saw her as she was, a monster of ugliness. All her charms were artificial, and, truly viewed, were rather deformities. She was, in fact, older than Hecuba or the Sibyl of Cumae; but an art, which it is to be regretted our times have lost, enabled her to appear charming, and to clothe herself in all the attractions of youth. Rogero now saw all this, but, governed by the counsels of Melissa, he concealed his surprise, assumed under some pretext his armor, long neglected, and bound to his side Belisarda, his trusty sword, taking also the buckler of Atlantes, covered with its veil.

He then selected a horse from the stables of Alcina, without exciting her suspicions; but he left the Hippogriff, by the advice of Melissa, who promised to take him in charge, and train him to a more manageable state. The horse he took was Rabican, which belonged to Astolpho. He restored the ring to Melissa.

Rogero had not ridden far when he met one of the huntsmen of Alcina, bearing a falcon on his wrist, and followed by a dog. The huntsman was mounted on a powerful horse, and came boldly up to the paladin, demanding, in a somewhat imperious manner, whither he was going so rapidly. Rogero disdained to stop or to reply; whereupon the huntsman, not doubting that he was about making his escape, said, "What if I, with my falcon, stop your ride?" So saying, he threw off the bird, which even Rabican could not equal in speed. The huntsman then leapt from his horse, and the animal, open-mouthed, darted after Rogero with the swiftness of an arrow. The huntsman also ran as if the wind or fire bore him, and the dog was equal to Rabican in swiftness. Rogero, finding flight impossible, stopped and faced his pursuers; but his sword was useless against such foes. The insolent huntsman assailed him with words, and struck him with his whip, the only weapon he had; the dog bit his feet, and the horse drove at him with his hoofs. At the same time the falcon flew over his head and over Rabican's and attacked them with claws and wings, so that the horse in his fright began to be unmanageable. At that moment the sound of trumpets and cymbals was heard in the valley, and it was evident that Alcina had ordered out all her array to go in pursuit. Rogero felt that there was no time to be lost, and luckily remembered the shield of Atlantes, which he bore suspended from his neck. He unveiled it, and the charm worked wonderfully. The huntsman, the dog, the horse, fell flat; the trembling wings of the falcon could no longer sustain her, and she fell senseless to the ground. Rogero, rid of their annoyances, left them in their trance, and rode away.

Meanwhile Alcina, with all the force she could muster, sallied forth from her palace in pursuit. Melissa, left behind, took advantage of the opportunity to ransack all the rooms, protected by the ring. She undid one by one all the talismans and spells which she found, broke the seals, burned the images, and untied the hagknots. Thence, hurrying through the fields, she disenchanted the victims changed into trees, fountains, stones, or brutes; all of whom recovered their liberty, and vowed eternal gratitude to their deliverer. They made their escape, with all possible despatch, to the realms of the good Logestilla, whence they departed to their several homes.

Astolpho was the first whom Melissa liberated, for Rogero had particularly recommended him to her care. She aided him to recover his arms, and particularly that precious golden-headed lance which once was Argalia's. The enchantress mounted with him upon the winged horse, and in a short time arrived through the air at the castle of Logestilla, where Rogero joined them soon after.

In this abode the friends passed a short period of delightful and improving intercourse with the sage Logestilla and her virtuous court; and then each departed, Rogero with the Hippogriff, ring, and buckler; Astolpho with his golden lance, and mounted on Rabican, the fleetest of steeds. To Rogero Logestilla gave a bit and bridle suited to govern the Hippogriff; and to Astolpho a horn of marvellous powers, to be sounded only when all other weapons were unavailing.

THE ORC

We left the charming Angelica at the moment when, in her flight from her contending lovers, Sacripant and Rinaldo, she met an aged hermit. We have seen that her request to the hermit was to furnish her the means of gaining the sea-coast, eager to avoid Rinaldo, whom she hated, by leaving France and Europe itself. The pretended hermit, who was no other than a vile magician, knowing well that it would not be agreeable to his false gods to aid Angelica in this undertaking, feigned to comply with her desire. He supplied her a horse, into which he had by his arts caused a subtle devil to enter, and, having mounted Angelica on the animal, directed her what course to take to reach the sea.

Angelica rode on her way without suspicion, but when arrived at the shore, the demon urged the animal headlong into the water. Angelica in vain attempted to turn him back to the land; he continued his course till, as night approached, he landed with his burden on a sandy headland.

Angelica, finding herself alone, abandoned in this frightful solitude, remained without movement, as if stupefied, with hands joined and eyes turned towards

Figure 117: "Victory Kiss" by Henry Justice Ford

heaven, till at last, pouring forth a torrent of tears, she exclaimed: "Cruel fortune, have you not yet exhausted your rage against me? To what new miseries do you doom me? Alas! then finish your work! Deliver me a prey to some ferocious beast, or by whatever fate you choose bring me to an end. I will be thankful to you for terminating my life and my misery." At last, exhausted by her sorrows, she fell asleep, and sunk prostrate on the sand.

Before recounting what next befell, we must declare what place it was upon which the unhappy lady was now thrown. In the sea that washes the coast of Ireland there is an island called Ebuda, whose inhabitants, once numerous, had been wasted by the anger of Proteus till there were now but few left. This deity was incensed by some neglect of the usual honors which he had in old times received from the inhabitants of the land, and, to execute his vengeance, had sent a horrid sea-monster, called an Orc, to devour them. Such were the terrors of his ravages that the whole people of the isle had shut themselves up in the principal town, and relied on their walls alone to protect them. In this distress they applied to the Oracle for advice, and were directed to appease the wrath of the sea-monster by offering to him the fairest virgin that the country could produce.

Now it so happened that the very day when this dreadful oracle was announced, and when the fatal mandate had gone forth to seek among the fairest maidens of the land one to be offered to the monster, some sailors, landing on the beach where Angelica was, beheld that beauty as she lay asleep.

O blind Chance! whose power in human affairs is but too great, canst thou then abandon to the teeth of a horrible monster those charms which different sovereigns took arms against one another to possess? Alas! the lovely Angelica is destined to be the victim of those cruel islanders.

Still asleep, she was bound by the Ebudians, and it was not until she was carried on board the vessel that she came to a knowledge of her situation. The wind filled the sails and wafted the ship swiftly to the port, where all that beheld her agreed that she was unquestionably the victim selected by Proteus himself to be his prey. Who can tell the screams, the mortal anguish of this unhappy maiden, the reproaches she addressed even to the heavens themselves, when the dreadful information of her cruel fate was made known to her? I cannot; let me rather turn to a happier part of my story.

Rogero left the palace of Logestilla, careering on his flying courser far above the tops of the mountains, and borne westward by the Hippogriff, which he guided with ease, by means of the bridle that Melissa had given him. Anxious as he was to recover Bradamante, he could not fail to be delighted at the view his rapid flight presented of so many vast regions and populous countries as he passed over in his career. At last he approached the shores of England, and perceived an immense army in all the splendor of military pomp, as if about to go forth flushed with hopes of victory. He caused the Hippogriff to alight not far from the scene, and found himself immediately surrounded by admiring spectators, knights and soldiers, who could not enough indulge their curiosity and wonder. Rogero learned, in reply to his questions, that the fine array of troops before him was the army destined to go to the aid of the French Emperor, in compliance with the request presented by the illustrious Rinaldo, as ambassador of King Charles, his uncle.

By this time the curiosity of the English chevaliers was partly gratified in beholding the Hippogriff at rest, and Rogero, to renew their surprise and delight, remounted the animal, and, slapping spurs to his sides, made him launch into the air with the rapidity of a meteor, and directed his flight still westwardly, till he came within sight of the coasts of Ireland. Here he descried what seemed to be a fair damsel, alone, fast chained to a rock which projected into the sea. What was his astonishment when, drawing nigh, he beheld the beautiful princess Angelica! That day she had been led forth and bound to the rock, there to wait till the sea-monster should come to devour her. Rogero exclaimed as he came near, "What cruel hands, what barbarous soul, what fatal chance can have loaded thee with those chains?" Angelica replied by a torrent of tears, at first her only response; then, in a trembling voice, she disclosed to him the horrible destiny for which she was there exposed. While she spoke, a terrible roaring was heard far off on the sea. The huge monster soon came in sight, part of his body appearing above the waves and part concealed. Angelica, half dead with fear, abandoned herself to despair.

Rogero, lance in rest, spurred his Hippogriff toward the Orc, and gave him a thrust. The horrible monster was like nothing that nature produces. It was but one mass of tossing and twisting body, with nothing of the animal but head, eyes, and mouth, the last furnished with tusks like those of the wild boar. Rogero's lance had struck him between the eyes; but rock and iron are not more impenetrable than were his scales. The knight, seeing the fruitlessness of the first blow, prepared to give a second. The animal, beholding upon the water the shadow of the great wings of the Hippogriff, abandoned his prey, and turned to seize what seemed nearer. Rogero took the opportunity, and dealt him furious blows on various parts of his body, taking care to keep clear of his murderous teeth; but the scales resisted every attack. The Orc beat the water with his tail till he raised a foam which enveloped Rogero and his steed, so that the knight hardly knew whether he was in the water or the air. He began to fear that the wings of the Hippogriff would be so drenched with water that they would cease to sustain him. At that moment Rogero bethought him of the magic shield which hung at his saddle-bow; but the fear that Angelica would also be blinded by its glare discouraged him from employing it. Then he remembered the ring which Melissa had given him, the power of which he had so lately proved. He hastened to Angelica and placed it on her finger. Then, uncovering the buckler, he turned its bright disk full in the face of the detestable Orc. The effect was instantaneous. The monster, deprived of sense and motion, rolled over on the sea, and lay floating on his back. Rogero would fain have tried the effect of his lance on the now exposed parts, but Angelica implored him to lose no time in delivering her from her chains before the monster should revive. Rogero, moved with her entreaties, hastened to do so, and, having unbound her, made her mount behind him on the Hippogriff. The animal, spurning the earth, shot up into the air, and rapidly sped his way through it. Rogero, to give time to the princess to rest after her cruel agitations, soon sought the earth again, alighting on the shore of Brittany. Near the shore a thick wood presented itself, which resounded with the songs of birds. In the midst, a fountain of transparent water bathed the turf of a little meadow. A gentle hill rose near by. Rogero, making the Hippogriff alight in the meadow, dismounted, and took Angelica from the horse.

When the first tumults of emotion had subsided Angelica, casting her eyes downward, beheld the precious ring upon her finger, whose virtues she was well acquainted with, for it was the very ring which the Saracen Brunello had robbed her of. She drew it from her finger and placed it in her mouth, and, quicker than we can tell it, disappeared from the sight of the paladin.

Rogero looked around him on all sides, like one frantic, but soon remembered the ring which he had so lately placed on her finger. Struck with the ingratitude which could thus recompense his services, he exclaimed: "Thankless beauty, is this then the reward you make me? Do you prefer to rob me of my ring rather than receive it as a gift? Willingly would I have given it to you, had you but asked it." Thus he said, searching on all sides with arms extended like a blind man, hoping to recover by the touch what was lost to sight; but he sought in vain. The cruel beauty was already far away.

Though sensible of her obligations to her deliverer, her first necessity was for clothing, food, and repose. She soon reached a shepherd's hut, where, entering unseen, she found what sufficed for her present relief. An old herdsman inhabited the hut, whose charges consisted of a drove of mares. When recruited by repose Angelica selected one of the mares from the flock, and, mounting the animal, felt the desire revive in her mind of returning to her home in the East, and for that purpose would gladly have accepted the protection of Orlando or of Sacripant across those wide regions which divided her from her own country. In hopes of meeting with one or the other of them she pursued her way.

Meanwhile Rogero, despairing of seeing Angelica again, returned to the tree where he had left his winged horse, but had the mortification to find that the animal had broken his bridle and escaped. This loss, added to his previous disappointment, overwhelmed him with vexation. Sadly he gathered up his arms, threw his buckler over his shoulders, and, taking the first path that offered, soon found himself within the verge of a dense and widespread forest.

He had proceeded for some distance when he heard a noise on his right, and, listening attentively, distinguished the clash of arms. He made his way toward the place whence the sound proceeded, and found two warriors engaged in mortal combat. One of them was a knight of a noble and manly bearing, the other a fierce giant. The knight appeared to exert consummate address in defending herself against the massive club of the giant, evading his strokes, or parrying them with sword or shield. Rogero stood spectator of the combat, for he did not allow himself to interfere in it, though a secret sentiment inclined him strongly to take part with the knight. At length he saw with grief the massive club fall directly on the head of the knight, who yielded to the blow, and fell prostrate. The giant sprang forward to despatch him, and for that purpose unlaced his helmet, when Rogero, with dismay, recognized the face of Bradamante. He cried aloud, "Hold, miscreant!" and sprang forward with drawn sword. Whereupon the giant, as if he cared not to enter upon another combat, lifted Bradamante on his shoulders, and ran with her into the forest.

Rogero plunged after him, but the long legs of the giant carried him forward so fast that the paladin could hardly keep him in sight. At length they issued from the wood, and Rogero perceived before him a rich palace, built of marble, and adorned with sculptures executed by a master hand. Into this edifice, through a golden door, the giant passed, and Rogero followed; but, on looking round, saw nowhere either the giant or Bradamante. He ran from room to room, calling aloud on his cowardly foe to turn and meet him; but got no response, nor caught another glimpse of the giant or his prey. In his vain pursuit he met, without knowing them, Ferrau, Florismart, King Gradasso, Orlando, and many others, all of whom had been entrapped like himself into this enchanted castle. It was a new stratagem of the magician Atlantes to draw Rogero into his power, and to secure also those who might by any chance endanger his safety. What Rogero had taken for Bradamante was a mere phantom. That charming lady was far away, full of anxiety for her Rogero, whose coming she had long expected.

The Emperor had committed to her charge the city and garrison of Marseilles, and she held the post against the infidels with valor and discretion. One day Melissa suddenly presented herself before her. Anticipating her questions, she said, "Fear not for Rogero; he lives, and is as ever true to you; but he has lost his liberty. The fell enchanter has again succeeded in making him a prisoner. If you would deliver him, mount your horse and follow me." She told her in what manner Atlantes had deceived Rogero, in deluding his eyes with the phantom of herself in peril. "Such," she continued, "will be his arts in your own case, if you penetrate the forest and approach that castle. You will think you behold Rogero, when, in fact, you see only the enchanter himself. Be not deceived, plunge your sword into his body, and trust me when I tell you that, in slaying him, you will restore not only Rogero, but with him many of the bravest knights of France, whom the wizard's arts have withdrawn from the camp of their sovereign."

Bradamante promptly armed herself, and mounted her horse. Melissa led her by forced journeys, by field and forest, beguiling the way with conversation on the theme which interested her hearer most. When at last they reached the forest, she repeated once more her instructions, and then took her leave, for fear the enchanter might espy her, and be put on his guard.

Bradamante rode on about two miles when suddenly she beheld Rogero, as it appeared to her, hard pressed by two fierce giants. While she hesitated she heard his voice calling on her for help. At once the cautions of Melissa lost their weight. A sudden doubt of the faith and truth of her kind monitress flashed across her mind. "Shall I not believe my own eyes and ears?" she said, and rushed forward to his defence. Rogero fled, pursued by the giants, and Bradamante followed, passing with them through the castle gate. When there, Bradamante was undeceived, for neither giant nor knight was to be seen. She found herself a prisoner, but had not the consolation of knowing that she shared the imprisonment of her beloved. She saw various forms of men and women, but could recognize none of them; and their lot was the same with respect to her. Each viewed the others under some illusion of the fancy, wearing the semblance of giants, dwarfs, or even four-footed animals, so that there was no companionship or communication between them.

ASTOLPHO'S ADVENTURES CONTINUED AND ISABELLA'S BEGUN

When Astolpho escaped from the cruel Alcina, after a short abode in the realm of the virtuous Logestilla, he desired to return to his native country. Logestilla lent him the best vessel of her fleet to convey him to the mainland. She gave him at parting a wonderful book, which taught the secret of overcoming all manners of enchantments, and begged him to carry it always with him, out of regard for her. She also gave him another gift, which surpassed everything of the kind that mortal workmanship can frame; yet it was nothing in appearance but a simple horn.

Astolpho, protected by these gifts, thanked the good fairy, took leave of her, and set out on his return to France. His voyage was prosperous, and on reaching the desired port he took leave of the faithful mariners, and continued his journey by land. As he proceeded over mountains and through valleys he often met with bands of robbers, wild beasts, and venomous serpents, but he had only to sound his horn to put them all to flight.

Having landed in France, and traversed many provinces on his way to the army, he one day, in crossing a forest, arrived beside a fountain, and alighted to drink. While he stooped at the fountain a young rustic sprang from the copse, mounted Rabican, and rode away. It was a new trick of the enchanter Atlantes. Astolpho, hearing the noise, turned his head just in time to see his loss; and, starting up, pursued the thief, who, on his part, did not press the horse to his full speed, but just kept in sight of his pursuer till they both issued from the forest; and then Rabican and his rider took shelter in a castle which stood near. Astolpho followed, and penetrated without difficulty within the court-yard of the castle, where he looked around for the rider and his horse, but could see no trace of either, nor any person of whom he could make inquiry. Suspecting that enchantment was employed to embarrass him, he bethought him of his book, and on consulting it discovered that his suspicions were well founded. He also learned what course to pursue. He was directed to raise the stone which served as a threshold, under which a spirit lay pent, who would willingly escape, and leave the castle free of access. Astolpho applied his strength to lift aside the stone. Thereupon the magician put his arts in force. The castle was full of prisoners, and the magician caused that to all of them Astolpho should appear in some false guise—to some a wild beast, to others a giant, to others a bird of prey. Thus all assailed him, and would quickly have made an end of him, if he had not bethought him of his horn. No sooner had he blown a blast than, at the horrid larum, fled the cavaliers and the necromancer with them, like a flock of pigeons at the sound of the fowler's gun. Astolpho then renewed his efforts on the stone, and turned it over. The under face was all inscribed with magical characters, which the knight defaced, as directed by his book; and no sooner had he done so, than the castle, with its walls and turrets, vanished into smoke.

The knights and ladies set at liberty were, besides Rogero and Bradamante, Orlando, Gradasso, Florismart, and many more. At the sound of the horn they fled, one and all, men and steeds, except Rabican, which Astolpho secured, in spite of his terror. As soon as the sound had ceased Rogero recognized Bradamante, whom he had daily met during their imprisonment, but had been prevented from knowing by the enchanter's arts. No words can tell the delight with which they recognized each other, and recounted mutually all that had happened to each since they were parted. Rogero took advantage of the opportunity to press his suit, and found Bradamante as propitious as he could wish, were it not for a single obstacle, the difference of their faiths. "If he would obtain her in marriage," she said, "he must in due form demand her of her father, Duke Aymon, and must abandon his false prophet, and become a Christian." The latter step was one which Rogero had for some time intended taking, for reasons of his own. He therefore gladly accepted the terms, and proposed that they should at once repair to the abbey of Vallombrosa, whose towers were visible at no great distance. Thither they turned their horses' heads, and we will leave them to find their way without our company.

I know not if my readers recollect that at the moment when Rogero had just delivered Angelica from the voracious Orc that scornful beauty placed her ring in her mouth, and vanished out of sight. At the same time the Hippogriff shook off his bridle, soared away, and flew to rejoin his former master, very naturally returning to his accustomed stable. Here Astolpho found him, to his very great delight. He knew the animal's powers, having seen Rogero ride him, and he longed to fly abroad over all the earth, and see various nations and peoples from his airy course. He had heard Logestilla's directions how to guide the animal, and saw her fit a bridle to his head. He therefore was able, out of all the bridles he found in the stable, to select one suitable, and, placing Rabican's saddle on the Hippogriff's back, nothing seemed to prevent his immediate departure. Yet before he went he bethought him of placing Rabican in hands where he would be safe, and whence he might recover him in time of need. While he stood deliberating where he should find a messenger, he saw Bradamante approach. That fair warrior had been parted from Rogero on their way to the abbey of Vallombrosa, by an inopportune adventure which had called the knight away. She was now returning to Montalban, having arranged with Rogero to join her there. To Bradamante, therefore, his fair cousin, Astolpho committed Rabican, and also the lance of gold, which would only be an incumbrance in his aerial excursion. Bradamante took charge of both; and Astolpho, bidding her farewell, soared in air.

Among those delivered by Astolpho from the magician's castle was Orlando. Following the guide of chance, the paladin found himself at the close of day in a forest, and stopped at the foot of a mountain. Surprised to discern a light which came from a cleft in the rock, he approached, guided by the ray, and discovered a narrow passage in the mountain-side, which led into a deep grotto.

Orlando fastened his horse, and then, putting aside the bushes that resisted his passage, stepped down from rock to rock till he reached a sort of cavern. Entering it, he perceived a lady, young and handsome, as well as he could discover through the signs of distress which agitated her countenance. Her only companion was an old woman, who seemed to be regarded by her young partner with terror and indignation. The courteous paladin saluted the women respectfully, and begged to know by whose barbarity they had been subjected to such imprisonment.

The younger lady replied, in a voice often broken with sobs:

"Though I know well that my recital will subject me to worse treatment by the barbarous man who keeps me here, to whom this woman will not fail to report it, yet I will not hide from you the facts. Ah! why should I fear his rage? If he should take my life, I know not what better boon than death I can ask.

"My name is Isabella. I am the daughter of the king of Galicia, or rather I should say misfortune and grief are my parents. Young, rich, modest, and of tranquil temper, all things appeared to combine to render my lot happy. Alas! I see myself to-day poor, humbled, miserable, and destined perhaps to yet further afflictions. It is a year since, my father having given notice that he would open the lists for a tournament at Bayonne, a great number of chevaliers from all quarters came together at our court. Among these Zerbino, son of the king of Scotland, victorious in all combats, eclipsed by his beauty and his valor all the rest. Before departing from the court of Galicia he testified the wish to espouse me, and I consented that he should demand my hand of the king, my father. But I was a Mahometan, and Zerbino a Christian, and my father refused his consent. The prince, called home by his father to take command of the forces destined to the assistance of the French Emperor, prevailed on me to be married to him secretly, and to follow him to Scotland. He caused a galley to be prepared to receive me, and placed in command of it the chevalier Oderic, a Biscayan, famous for his exploits both by land and sea. On the day appointed, Oderic brought his vessel to a seaside resort of my father's, where I embarked. Some of my domestics accompanied me, and thus I departed from my native land.

"Sailing with a fair wind, after some hours we were assailed by a violent tempest. It was to no purpose that we took in all sail; we were driven before the wind directly upon the rocky shore. Seeing no other hopes of safety,

Oderic placed me in a boat, followed himself with a few of his men, and made for land. We reached it through infinite peril, and I no sooner felt the firm land beneath my feet, than I knelt down and poured out heartfelt thanks to the Providence that had preserved me.

"The shore where we landed appeared to be uninhabited. We saw no dwelling to shelter us, no road to lead us to a more hospitable spot. A high mountain rose before us, whose base stretched into the sea. It was here the infamous Oderic, in spite of my tears and entreaties, sold me to a band of pirates, who fancied I might be an acceptable present to their prince, the Sultan of Morocco. This cavern is their den, and here they keep me under the guard of this woman, until it shall suit their convenience to carry me away."

Isabella had hardly finished her recital when a troop of armed men began to enter the cavern. Seeing the prince Orlando, one said to the rest, "What bird is this we have caught, without even setting a snare for him?" Then addressing Orlando, "It was truly civil in you, friend, to come hither with that handsome coat of armor and vest, the very things I want." "You shall pay for them, then," said Orlando; and seizing a half-burnt brand from the fire, he hurled it at him, striking his head, and stretching him lifeless on the floor.

There was a massy table in the middle of the cavern, used for the pirates' repasts. Orlando lifted it and hurled it at the robbers as they stood clustered in a group toward the entrance. Half the gang were laid prostrate, with broken heads and limbs; the rest got away as nimbly as they could.

Leaving the den and its inmates to their fate, Orlando, taking Isabella under his protection, pursued his way for some days, without meeting with any adventure.

One day they saw a band of men advancing, who seemed to be guarding a prisoner, bound hand and foot, as if being carried to execution. The prisoner was a youthful cavalier, of a noble and ingenuous appearance. The band bore the ensigns of Count Anselm, head of the treacherous house of Maganza. Orlando desired Isabella to wait, while he rode forward to inquire the meaning of this array. Approaching, he demanded of the leader who his prisoner was, and of what crime he had been guilty. The man replied that the prisoner was a murderer, by whose hand Pinabel, the son of Count Anselm, had been treacherously slain. At these words the prisoner exclaimed, "I am no murderer, nor have I been in any way the cause of the young man's death." Orlando, knowing the cruel and ferocious character of the chiefs of the house of Maganza, needed no more to satisfy him that the youth was the victim of injustice. He commanded the leader of the troop to release his victim, and, receiving an insolent reply, dashed him to the earth with a stroke of his lance; then by a few vigorous blows dispersed the band, leaving deadly marks on those who were slowest to quit the field.

Orlando then hastened to unbind the prisoner, and to assist him to reclothe himself in his armor, which the false Magencian had dared to assume. He then led him to Isabella, who now approached the scene of action. How can we picture the joy, the astonishment, with which Isabella recognized in him Zerbino, her husband, and the prince discovered her whom he had believed overwhelmed in the waves! They embraced one another, and wept for joy. Orlando, sharing in their happiness, congratulated himself in having been the instrument of it. The princess recounted to Zerbino what the illustrious paladin had done for her, and the prince threw himself at Orlando's feet, and thanked him as having twice preserved his life.

While these exchanges of congratulation and thankfulness were going on, a sound in the underwood attracted their attention, and caused the two knights to brace their helmets and stand on their guard. What the cause of the interruption was we shall record in another chapter.

MEDORO

France was at this time the theatre of dreadful events. The Saracens and the Christians, in numerous encounters, slew one another. On one occasion Rinaldo led an attack on the infidel columns, broke and scattered them, till he found himself opposite to a knight whose armor (whether by accident or by choice, it matters not) bore the blazon of Orlando. It was Dardinel, the young and brave prince of Zumara, and Rinaldo remarked him by the slaughter he spread all around. "Ah," said he to himself, "let us pluck up this dangerous plant before it has grown to its full height."

As Rinaldo advanced, the crowd opened before him, the Christians to let his sword have free course, the Pagans to escape its sweep. Dardinel and he stood face to face. Rinaldo exclaimed, fiercely, "Young man, whoever gave you that noble buckler to bear made you a dangerous gift; I should like to see how you are able to defend those quarterings, red and white. If you cannot defend them against me, how pray will you do so when Orlando challenges them?" Dardinel replied: "Thou shalt learn that I can defend the arms I bear, and shed new glory upon them. No one shall rend them from me but with life." Saying these words, Dardinel rushed upon Rinaldo with sword uplifted. The chill of mortal terror filled the souls of the Saracens when they beheld Rinaldo advance to attack the prince, like a lion against a young bull. The first blow came from the hand of Dardinel, and the weapon rebounded from Mambrino's helmet without effect. Rinaldo smiled, and said, "I will now show you if my strokes are more effectual." At these words he thrust the unfortunate Dardinel in the middle of his breast. The blow was so violent that the cruel weapon pierced the body, and came out a palm-breadth behind his back. Through this wound the life of Dardinel issued with his blood, and his body fell helpless to the ground.

As a flower which the passing plough has uprooted languishes, and droops its head, so Dardinel, his visage covered with the paleness of death, expires, and the hopes of an illustrious race perish with him.

Like waters kept back by a dike, which, when the dike is broken, spread abroad through all the country, so the Moors, no longer kept in column by the example of Dardinel, fled in all directions. Rinaldo despised too much such easy victories to pursue them; he wished for no

Figure 118: "Angelica and Medoro" by Simone Peterzano

combats but with brave men. At the same time, the other paladins made terrible slaughter of the Moors. Charles himself, Oliver, Guido, and Ogier the Dane, carried death into their ranks on all sides.

The infidels seemed doomed to perish to a man on that dreadful day; but the wise king, Marsilius, at last put some slight degree of method into the general rout. He collected the remnant of the troops, formed them into a battalion, and retreated in tolerable order to his camp. That camp was well fortified by intrenchments and a broad ditch. Thither the fugitives hastened, and by degrees all that remained of the Moorish army was brought together there.

The Emperor might perhaps that night have crushed his enemy entirely; but not thinking it prudent to expose his troops, fatigued as they were, to an attack upon a camp so well fortified, he contented himself with encompassing the enemy with his troops, prepared to make a regular siege. During the night the Moors had time to see the extent of their loss. Their tents resounded with lamentations. This warrior had to mourn a brother, that a friend; many suffered with grievous wounds, all trembled at the fate in store for them.

There were two young Moors, both of humble rank, who gave proof at that time of attachment and fidelity rare in the history of man. Cloridan and Medoro had followed their prince, Dardinel, to the wars of France. Cloridan, a bold huntsman, combined strength with activity. Medoro was a mere youth, his cheeks yet fair and blooming. Of all the Saracens, no one united so much grace and beauty. His light hair was set off by his black and sparkling eyes. The two friends were together on guard at the rampart. About midnight they gazed on the scene in deep dejection. Medoro, with tears in his eyes, spoke of the good prince Dardinel, and could not endure the thought that his body should be cast out on the plain, deprived of funeral honors. "O my friend," said he, "must then the body of our prince be the prey of wolves and ravens? Alas! when I remember how he loved me, I feel that if I should sacrifice my life to do him honor, I should not do more than my duty. I wish, dear friend, to seek out his body on the battlefield, and give it burial, and I hope to be able to pass through King Charles's camp without discovery, as they are probably all asleep. You, Cloridan, will be able to say for me, if I should die in the adventure, that gratitude and fidelity to my prince were my inducements."

Cloridan was both surprised and touched with this proof of the young man's devotion. He loved him tenderly, and tried for a long time every effort to dissuade him from his design; but he found Medoro determined to accomplish his object or die in the endeavor.

Cloridan, unable to change his purpose, said, "I will go with you, Medoro, and help you in this generous enterprise. I value not life compared with honor, and if I did, do you suppose, dear friend, that I could live without you? I would rather fall by the arms of our enemies than die of grief for the loss of you."

When the two friends were relieved from their guard duty they went without any followers into the camp of the Christians. All there was still; the fires were dying out; there was no fear of any attempt on the part of the Saracens, and the soldiers, overcome by fatigue or wine, slept secure, lying upon the ground in the midst of their arms and equipage. Cloridan stopped, and said, "Medoro, I am not going to quit this camp without taking vengeance for the death of our prince. Keep watch, be on your guard that no one shall surprise us; I mean to mark a road with my sword through the ranks of our enemies." So saying, he entered the tent where Alpheus slept, who a year before had joined the camp of Charles, and pretended to be a great physician and astrologer. But his science had deceived him, if it gave him hope of dying peacefully in his bed at a good old age; his lot was to die with little warning. Cloridan ran his sword through his heart. A Greek and a German followed, who had been playing late at dice: fortunate if they had continued their game a little longer; but they never reckoned a throw like this among their chances. Cloridan next came to the unlucky Grillon, whose head lay softly on his pillow. He dreamed probably of the feast from which he had but just retired; for when Cloridan cut off his head wine flowed forth with the blood.

The two young Moors might have penetrated even to the tent of Charlemagne; but knowing that the paladins encamped around him kept watch by turns, and judging that it was impossible they should all be asleep, they were afraid to go too near. They might also have obtained rich booty; but, intent only on their object, they crossed the camp, and arrived at length at the bloody field, where bucklers, lances, and swords lay scattered in the midst of corpses of poor and rich, common soldier and prince, horses and pools of blood. This terrible scene of carnage would have destroyed all hope of finding what they were in search of until dawn of day, were it not that the moon lent the aid of her uncertain rays.

Medoro raised his eyes to the planet, and exclaimed, "O holy goddess, whom our fathers have adored under three different forms,—thou who displayest thy power in heaven, on earth, and in the underworld,—thou who art seen foremost among the nymphs chasing the beasts of the forest,—cause me to see, I implore thee, the spot where my dear master lies, and make me all my life long follow the example which thou dost exhibit of works of charity and love."

Either by accident, or that the moon was sensible of the prayer of Medoro, the cloud broke away, and the moonlight burst forth as bright as day. The rays seemed especially to gild the spot where lay the body of Prince Dardinel; and Medoro, bathed in tears and with bleeding heart, recognized him by the quarterings of red and white on his shield.

With groans stifled by his tears, and lamentations in accents suppressed, not from any fear for himself, for he cared not for life, but lest any one should be roused to interrupt their pious duty while yet incomplete, he proposed to his companion that they should together bear Dardinel on their shoulders, sharing the burden of the beloved remains.

Marching with rapid strides under their precious load, they perceived that the stars began to grow pale, and that the shades of night would soon be dispersed by the dawn. Just then Zerbino, whose extreme valor had urged him far from the camp in pursuit of the fugitives, returning, entered the wood in which they were. Some knights in his train perceived at a distance the two brothers-in-arms. Cloridan saw the troop, and, observing that they dispersed themselves over the plain as if in search of booty, told Medoro to lay down the body, and let each save himself by flight. He dropped his part, thinking that Medoro would do the same; but the good youth loved his prince too well to abandon him, and continued to carry his load singly as well as he might, while Cloridan made his escape. Near by there was a part of the wood tufted as if nothing but wild animals had ever penetrated it. The unfortunate youth, loaded with the weight of his dead master, plunged into its recesses.

Cloridan, when he perceived that he had evaded his foes, discovered that Medoro was not with him. "Ah!" exclaimed he, "how could I, dear Medoro, so forget myself as to consult my own safety without heeding yours?" So saying, he retraced the tangled passes of the wood toward the place from whence he had fled. As he approached he heard the noise of horses, and the menacing voices of armed men. Soon he perceived Medoro, on foot, with the cavaliers surrounding him. Zerbino, their commander, bade them seize him. The unhappy Medoro turned now this way, now that, trying to conceal himself behind an oak or a rock, still bearing the body, which he would by no means leave. Cloridan not knowing how to help him, but resolved to perish with him, if he must perish, takes an arrow, fits it to his bow, discharges it, and pierces the breast of a Christian knight, who falls helpless from his horse. The others look this way and that, to discover whence the fatal bolt was sped. One, while demanding of his comrades in what direction the arrow came, received a second in his throat, which stopped his words, and soon closed his eyes to the scene.

Zerbino, furious at the death of his two comrades, ran upon Medoro, seized his golden hair, and dragged him forward to slay him. But the sight of so much youth and beauty commanded pity. He stayed his arm. The young man spoke in suppliant tones. "Ah! signor," said he, "I conjure you by the God whom you serve, deprive me not of life until I shall have buried the body of the prince, my master. Fear not that I will ask you any other favor; life is not dear to me; I desire death as soon as I shall have performed this sacred duty. Do with me then as you please. Give my limbs a prey to the birds and beasts; only let me first bury my prince." Medoro pronounced these words with an air so sweet and tender that a heart of stone would have been moved by them. Zerbino was so to the bottom of his soul. He was on the point of uttering words of mercy, when a cruel subaltern, forgetting all respect to his commander, plunged his lance into the breast of the young Moor. Zerbino, enraged at his brutality, turned upon the wretch to take vengeance, but he saved himself by a precipitate flight.

Cloridan, who saw Medoro fall, could contain himself no longer. He rushed from his concealment, threw down his bow, and, sword in hand, seemed only desirous of vengeance for Medoro, and to die with him. In a moment, pierced through and through with many wounds, he exerts the last remnant of his strength in dragging himself to Medoro, to die embracing him. The cavaliers left them thus to rejoin Zerbino, whose rage against the murderer of Medoro had drawn him away from the spot.

Cloridan died; and Medoro, bleeding copiously, was drawing near his end when help arrived.

A young maiden approached the fallen knights at this critical moment. Her dress was that of a peasant-girl, but her air was noble, and her beauty celestial; sweetness and goodness reigned in her lovely countenance. It was no other than Angelica, the Princess of Cathay.

When she had recovered that precious ring, as we have before related, Angelica, knowing its value, felt proud in the power it conferred, travelled alone without fear, not without a secret shame that she had ever been obliged to seek protection in her wanderings of the Count Orlando and of Sacripant. She reproached herself too as with a weakness that she had ever thought of marrying Rinaldo; in fine, her pride grew so high as to persuade her that no man living was worthy to aspire to her hand.

Moved with pity at the sight of the young man wounded, and melted to tears at hearing the cause, she quickly recalled to remembrance the knowledge she had acquired in India, where the virtues of plants and the art of healing formed part of the education even of princesses. The beautiful queen ran into the adjoining meadow to gather plants of virtue to staunch the flow of blood. Meeting on her way a countryman on horseback seeking a strayed heifer, she begged him to come to her assistance, and endeavor to remove the wounded man to a more secure asylum.

Angelica, having prepared the plants by bruising them between two stones, laid them with her fair hand on Medoro's wound. The remedy soon restored in some degree the strength of the wounded man, who, before he would quit the spot, made them cover with earth and turf the bodies of his friend and of the prince. Then surrendering himself to the pity of his deliverers, he allowed them to place him on the horse of the shepherd, and conduct him to his cottage. It was a pleasant farmhouse on the borders of the wood, bearing marks of comfort and competency. There the shepherd lived with his wife and children. There Angelica tended Medoro, and there, by the devoted care of the beautiful queen, his sad wound closed over, and he recovered his perfect health.

O Count Rinaldo, O King Sacripant! what availed it you to possess so many virtues and such fame? What advantage have you derived from all your high deserts? O hapless king, great Agrican! if you could return to life, how would you endure to see yourself rejected by one who will bow to the yoke of Hymen in favor of a young soldier of humble birth? And thou, Ferrau, and ye numerous others who a hundred times have put your lives at hazard for this cruel beauty, how bitter will it be to you to see her sacrifice you all to the claims of the humble Medoro!

There, under the low roof of a shepherd, the flame of Hymen was lighted for this haughty queen. She takes the shepherd's wife to serve in place of mother, the shepherd and his children for witnesses, and marries the happy Medoro.

Angelica, after her marriage, wishing to endow Medoro with the sovereignty of the countries which yet remained to her, took with him the road to the East. She had preserved through all her adventures a bracelet of gold enriched with precious stones, the present of the Count Orlando. Having nothing else wherewith to reward the good shepherd and his wife, who had served her with so much care and fidelity, she took the bracelet from her arm and gave it to them, and then the newly-married couple directed their steps toward those mountains which separate France and Spain, intending to wait at Barcelona a vessel which should take them on their way to the East.

ORLANDO MAD

Orlando, on the loss of Angelica, laid aside his crest and arms, and arrayed himself in a suit of black armor expressive of his despair. In this guise he carried such slaughter among the ranks of the infidels that both armies were astonished at the achievements of the stranger knight. Mandricardo, who had been absent from the battle, heard the report of these achievements and determined to test for himself the valor of the knight so extolled. He it was who broke in upon the conference of Zerbino and Isabella, and their benefactor Orlando, as they stood occupied in mutual felicitations, after the happy reunion of the lovers by the prowess of the paladin.

Mandricardo, after contemplating the group for a moment, addressed himself to Orlando in these words: "Thou must be the man I seek. For ten days and more I have been on thy track. The fame of thy exploits has brought me hither, that I may measure my strength with thine. Thy crest and shield prove thee the same who spread such slaughter among our troops. But these marks are superfluous, and if I saw thee among a hundred I should know thee by thy martial bearing to be the man I seek."

"I respect thy courage," said Orlando; "such a design could not have sprung up in any but a brave and generous soul. If the desire to see me has brought thee hither, I would, if it were possible, show thee my inmost soul. I will remove my visor, that you may satisfy your curiosity; but when you have done so I hope that you will also try and see if my valor corresponds to my appearance." "Come on," said the Saracen, "my first wish was to see and know thee; I will not gratify my second."

Orlando, observing Mandricardo was surprised to see no sword at his side, nor mace at his saddle-bow. "And what weapon hast thou," said he, "if thy lance fail thee?"

"Do not concern yourself about that," said Mandricardo; "I have made many good knights give ground with no other weapon than you see. Know that I have sworn an oath never to bear a sword until I win back that famous Durindana that Orlando, the paladin, carries. That sword belongs to the suit of armor which I wear; that only is wanting. Without doubt it was stolen, but how it got into the hands of Orlando I know not. But I will make him pay dearly for it when I find him I seek him the more anxiously that I may avenge with his blood the death of King Agrican, my father, whom he treacherously slew. I am sure he must have done it by treachery, for it was not in his power to subdue in fair fight such a warrior as my father."

"Thou liest," cried Orlando; "and all who say so lie. I am Orlando, whom you seek; yes, I am he who slew your father honorably. Hold, here is the sword: you shall have it if your courage avails to merit it. Though it belongs to me by right, I will not use it in this dispute. See, I hang it on this tree; you shall be master of it, if you bereave me of life; not else."

At these words Orlando drew Durindana, and hung it on one of the branches of a tree near by.

Both knights, boiling with equal ardor, rode off in a semicircle; then rushed together with reins thrown loose, and struck one another with their lances. Both kept their seats, immovable. The splinters of their lances flew into the air, and no weapon remained for either but the fragment which he held in his hand. Then those two knights, covered with iron mail, were reduced to the necessity of fighting with staves, in the manner of two rustics, who dispute the boundary of a meadow, or the possession of a spring.

These clubs could not long keep whole in the hands of such sturdy smiters, who were soon reduced to fight with naked fists. Such warfare was more painful to him that gave than to him that received the blows. They next clasped, and strained each his adversary, as Hercules did Antaeus. Mandricardo, more enraged than Orlando, made violent efforts to unseat the paladin, and dropped the rein of his horse. Orlando, more calm, perceived it. With one hand he resisted Mandricardo, with the other he twitched the horse's bridle over the ears of the animal. The Saracen dragged Orlando with all his might, but Orlando's thighs held the saddle like a vise. At last the efforts of the Saracen broke the girths of Orlando's horse; the saddle slipped; the knight, firm in his stirrups, slipped with it, and came to the ground hardly conscious of his fall. The noise of his armor in falling startled Mandricardo's horse, now without a bridle. He started off in full career, heeding neither trees nor rocks nor broken ground. Urged by fright, he ran with furious speed, carrying his master, who, almost distracted with rage, shouted and beat the animal with his fists, and thereby impelled his flight. After running thus three miles or more, a deep ditch opposed their progress. The horse and rider fell headlong into it, and did not find the bottom covered with feather-beds or roses. They got sadly bruised; but were lucky enough to escape without any broken limbs.

Mandricardo, as soon as he gained his feet, seized the horse by his mane with fury; but, having no bridle, could not hold him. He looked round in hopes of finding something that would do for a rein. Just then fortune, who seemed willing to help him at last, brought that way a peasant with a bridle in his hand, who was in search of his farm horse that had strayed away.

Orlando, having speedily repaired his horse's girths, remounted, and waited a good hour for the Saracen to return. Not seeing him, he concluded to go in search of him. He took an affectionate leave of Zerbino and Isabella, who would willingly have followed him; but this the brave paladin would by no means permit. He held it unknightly to go in search of an enemy accompanied by a friend, who might act as a defender. Therefore, desiring them to say to Mandricardo, if they should meet him, that his purpose was to tarry in the neighborhood three days, and then repair to the camp of Charlemagne, he took down Durindana from the tree, and proceeded in the direction which the Saracen's horse had taken. But the animal, having no guide but its terror, had so doubled and confused its traces that Orlando, after two days spent in the search, gave up the attempt.

It was about the middle of the third day when the paladin arrived on the pleasant bank of a stream which wound through a meadow enamelled with flowers. High trees, whose tops met and formed an arbor, overshadowed the fountain; and the breeze which blew through their foliage tempered the heat. Hither the shepherds used to resort to quench their thirst, and to enjoy the shelter from the midday sun. The air, perfumed with the flowers, seemed to breathe fresh strength into their veins. Orlando felt the influence, though covered with his armor. He stopped in this delicious arbor, where everything seemed to invite to repose. But he could not have chosen a more fatal asylum. He there spent the most miserable moments of his life.

He looked around, and noted with pleasure all the charms of the spot. He saw that some of the trees were carved with inscriptions —he drew near, and read them, and what was his surprise to find that they composed the name of Angelica! Farther on he found the name of Medoro mixed with hers. The paladin thought he dreamed. He stood like one amazed—like a bird that, rising to fly, finds its feet caught in a net.

Orlando followed the course of the stream, and came to one of its turns where the rocks of the mountain bent in

Figure 119: "Orlando Furioso" by Gustave Dore

such a way as to form a sort of grotto. The twisted stems of ivy and the wild vine draped the entrance of this recess, scooped by the hand of nature.

The unhappy paladin, on entering the grotto, saw letters which appeared to have been lately carved. They were verses which Medoro had written in honor of his happy nuptials with the beautiful queen. Orlando tried to persuade himself it must be some other Angelica whom those verses celebrated, and as for Medoro, he had never heard his name. The sun was now declining, and Orlando remounted his horse, and went on his way. He soon saw the roof of a cottage whence the smoke ascended; he heard the barking of dogs and the lowing of cattle, and arrived at a humble dwelling which seemed to offer an asylum for the night. The inmates, as soon as they saw him, hastened to tender him service. One took his horse, another his shield and cuirass, another his golden spurs. This cottage was the very same where Medoro had been carried, deeply wounded,—where Angelica had tended him, and afterwards married him. The shepherd who lived in it loved to tell everybody the story of this marriage, and soon related it, with all its details, to the miserable Orlando.

Having finished it, he went away, and returned with the precious bracelet which Angelica, grateful for his services, had given him as a memorial. It was the one which Orlando had himself given her.

This last touch was the finishing stroke to the excited paladin. Frantic, exasperated, he exclaimed against the ungrateful and cruel princess who had disdained him, the most renowned, the most indomitable of all the paladins of France,—him, who had rescued her from the most alarming perils,—him, who had fought the most terrible battles for her sake,—she to prefer to him a young Saracen! The pride of the noble Count was deeply wounded. Indignant, frantic, a victim to ungovernable rage, he rushed into the forest, uttering the most frightful shrieks.

"No, no!" cried he, "I am not the man they take me for! Orlando is dead! I am only the wandering ghost of that unhappy Count, who is now suffering the torments of hell!"

Orlando wandered all night, as chance directed, through the wood, and at sunrise his destiny led him to the fountain where Medoro had engraved the fatal inscription. The frantic paladin saw it a second time with fury, drew his sword, and hacked it from the rock.

Unlucky grotto! you shall no more attract by your shade and coolness, you shall no more shelter with your arch either shepherd or flock. And you, fresh and pure fountain, you may not escape the rage of the furious Orlando! He cast into the fountain branches, trunks of trees which he tore up, pieces of rocks which he broke off, plants uprooted, with the earth adhering, and turf and brushes, so as to choke the fountain, and destroy the purity of its waters. At length, exhausted by his violent exertions, bathed in sweat, breathless, Orlando sunk panting upon the earth, and lay there insensible three days and three nights.

The fourth day he started up and seized his arms. His helmet, his buckler, he cast far from him; his hauberk and his clothes he rent asunder; the fragments were scattered through the wood. In fine, he became a furious madman. His insanity was such that he cared not to retain even his sword. But he had no need of Durindana, nor of other arms, to do wonderful things. His prodigious strength sufficed. At the first wrench of his mighty arm he tore up a pine- tree by the roots. Oaks, beeches, maples, whatever he met in his path, yielded in like manner. The ancient forest soon became as bare as the borders of a morass, where the fowler has cleared away the bushes to spread his nets. The shepherds, hearing the horrible crashing in the forest, abandoned their flocks to run and see the cause of this unwonted uproar. By their evil star, or for their sins, they were led thither. When they saw the furious state the Count was in, and his incredible force, they would fain have fled out of his reach, but in their fears lost their presence of mind. The madman pursued them, seized one and rent him limb from limb, as easily as one would pull ripe apples from a tree. He took another by the feet, and used him as a club to knock down a third. The shepherds fled; but it would have been hard for any to escape, if he had not at that moment left them to throw himself with the same fury upon their flocks. The peasants, abandoning their ploughs and harrows, mounted on the roofs of buildings and pinnacles of the rocks, afraid to trust themselves even to the oaks and pines. From such heights they looked on, trembling at the raging fury of the unhappy Orlando. His fists, his teeth, his nails, his feet, seize, break, and tear cattle, sheep, and swine; the most swift in flight alone being able to escape him.

When at last terror had scattered everything before him, he entered a cottage which was abandoned by its inhabitants, and there found that which served for food. His long fast had caused him to feel the most ravenous hunger. Seizing whatever he found that was eatable, whether roots, acorns, or bread, raw meat or cooked, he gorged it indiscriminately.

Issuing thence again, the frantic Orlando gave chase to whatever living thing he saw, whether men or animals. Sometimes he pursued the deer and hind, sometimes he attacked bears and wolves, and with his naked hands killed and tore them, and devoured their flesh.

Thus he wandered, from place to place, through France, imperilling his life a thousand ways, yet always preserved by some mysterious providence from a fatal result. But here we leave Orlando for a time, that we may record what befell Zerbino and Isabella after their parting with him.

The prince and his fair bride waited, by Orlando's request, near the scene of the battle for three days, that, if Mandricardo should return, they might inform him where Orlando would give him another meeting. At the end of that time their anxiety to know the issue led them to follow Orlando's traces, which led them at last to the wood where the trees were inscribed with the names of Angelica and Medoro. They remarked how all these inscriptions were defaced, and how the grotto was disordered, and the fountain clogged with rubbish. But that which surprised them and distressed them most of all was to find on the grass the cuirass of Orlando, and not far from it his helmet, the same which the renowned Almontes once wore.

Hearing a horse neigh in the forest, Zerbino turned his eyes in that direction, and saw Brigliadoro, with the bridle yet hanging at the saddle-bow. He looked round for Durindana, and found that famous sword, without the scabbard, lying on the grass. He saw also the fragments of Orlando's other arms and clothing scattered on all sides over the plain.

Zerbino and Isabella stood in astonishment and grief, not knowing what to think, but little imagining the true cause. If they had found any marks of blood on the arms or on the fragments of the clothing, they would have supposed him slain, but there were none. While they were in this painful uncertainty they saw a young peasant approach. He, not yet recovered from the terror of the scene, which he had witnessed from the top of a rock, told them the whole of the sad events.

Zerbino, with his eyes full of tears, carefully collected all the scattered arms. Isabella also dismounted to aid him in the sad duty. When they had collected all the pieces of that rich armor they hung them like a trophy on a pine; and to prevent their being violated by any passers-by, Zerbino inscribed on the bark this caution: "These are the arms of the Paladin Orlando."

Having finished this pious work, he remounted his horse, and just then a knight rode up, and requested Zerbino to tell him the meaning of the trophy. The prince related the facts as they had happened; and Mandricardo, for it was that Saracen knight, full of joy, rushed forward, and seized the sword, saying, "No one can censure me for what I do; this sword is mine; I can take my own wherever I find it. It is plain that Orlando, not daring to defend it against me, has counterfeited madness to excuse him in surrendering it."

Zerbino vehemently exclaimed, "Touch not that sword. Think not to possess it without a contest. If it be true that the arms you wear are those of Hector, you must have got them by theft, and not by prowess."

Immediately they attacked one another with the utmost fury. The air resounded with thick-falling blows. Zerbino, skilful and alert, evaded for a time with good success the strokes of Durindana; but at length a terrible blow struck him on the neck. He fell from his horse, and the Tartar king, possessed of the spoils of his victory, rode away.

ZERBINO AND ISABELLA

Zerbino's pain at seeing the Tartar prince go off with the sword surpassed the anguish of his wound; but now the loss of blood so reduced his strength that he could not move from where he fell. Isabella, not knowing whither to resort for help, could only bemoan him, and chide her cruel fate. Zerbino said, "If I could but leave thee, my best beloved, in some secure abode, it would not distress me to die; but to abandon thee so, without protection, is sad indeed." She replied, "Think not to leave me, dearest; our souls shall not be parted; this sword will give me the means to follow thee." Zerbino's last words implored her to banish such a thought, but live, and be true to his memory. Isabella promised, with many tears, to be faithful to him so long as life should last.

When he ceased to breathe, Isabella's cries resounded through the forest, and reached the ears of a reverend hermit, who hastened to the spot. He soothed and calmed her, urging those consolations which the word of God supplies; and at last brought her to wish for nothing else but to devote herself for the rest of life wholly to religion.

As she could not bear the thoughts of leaving her dead lord abandoned, the body was, by the good hermit's aid, placed upon the horse, and taken to the nearest inhabited place, where a chest was made for it, suitable to be carried with them on their way. The hermit's plan was to escort his charge to a monastery, not many days' journey distant, where Isabella resolved to spend the remainder of her days. Thus they travelled day after day, choosing the most retired ways, for the country was full of armed men. One day a cavalier met them, and barred their way. It was no other than Rodomont, king of Algiers, who had just left the camp of Agramant, full of indignation at the treatment he had received from Doralice. At sight of the lovely lady and her reverend attendant, with their horse laden with a burden draped with black, he asked the meaning of their journey. Isabella told him her affliction, and her resolution to renounce the world and devote herself to religion, and to the memory of the friend she had lost. Rodomont laughed scornfully at this, and told her that her project was absurd; that charms like hers were meant to be enjoyed, not buried, and that he himself would more than make amends for her dead lover. The monk, who promptly interposed to rebuke this impious talk, was commanded to hold his peace; and still persisting was seized by the knight and hurled over the edge of the cliff, where he fell into the sea, and was drowned.

Rodomont, when he had got rid of the hermit, again applied to the sad lady, heartless with affright, and, in the language used by lovers, said, "she was his very heart, his life, his light." Having laid aside all violence, he humbly sued that she would accompany him to his retreat, near by. It was a ruined chapel from which the monks had been driven by the disorders of the time, and which Rodomont had taken possession of. Isabella, who had no choice but to obey, followed him, meditating as she went what resource she could find to escape out of his power, and keep her vow to her dead husband, to be faithful to his memory as long as life should last. At length she said, "If, my lord, you will let me go and fulfil my vow, and my intention, as I have already declared it, I will bestow upon you what will be to you of more value than a hundred women's hearts. I know an herb, and I have seen it on our way, which, rightly prepared, affords a juice of such power, that the flesh, if laved with it, becomes impenetrable to sword or fire. This liquor I can make, and will, to-day, if you will accept my offer; and when you have seen its virtue you will value it more than if all Europe were made your own."

Rodomont, at hearing this, readily promised all that was asked, so eager was he to learn a secret that would make him as Achilles was of yore. Isabella, having collected such herbs as she thought proper, and boiled them, with certain mysterious signs and words, at length declared her labor done, and, as a test, offered to try its virtue on herself. She bathed her neck and bosom with the liquor, and then called on Rodomont to smite with all his force, and see whether his sword had power to harm. The pagan, who during the preparations had taken frequent draughts of wine, and scarce knew what he did, drew his sword at the word, and struck across her neck with all his might, and the fair head leapt sundered from the snowy neck and breast.

Rude and unfeeling as he was, the pagan knight lamented bitterly this sad result. To honor her memory he resolved to do a work as unparalleled as her devotion. From all parts round he caused laborers to be brought, and had a tower built to enclose the chapel, within which the remains of Zerbino and Isabella were entombed. Across the stream which flowed near by he built a bridge, scarce two yards wide, and added neither parapet nor rail. On the top of the tower a sentry was placed, who, when any traveller approached the bridge, gave notice to his master. Rodomont thereupon sallied out, and defied the approaching knight to fight him upon the bridge, where any chance step a little aside would plunge the rider headlong in the stream. This bridge he vowed to keep until a thousand suits of armor should be won from conquered knights, wherewith to build a trophy to his victim and her lord.

Within ten days the bridge was built, and the tower was in progress. In a short time many knights, either seeking the shortest route, or tempted by a desire of adventure, had made the attempt to pass the bridge. All, without exception, had lost either arms or life, or both; some falling before Rodomont's lance, others precipitated into the river. One day, as Rodomont stood urging his workmen, it chanced that Orlando in his furious mood came thither, and approached the bridge. Rodomont halloed to him, "Halt, churl; presume not to set foot upon that bridge; it was not made for such as you!" Orlando took no notice, but pressed on. Just then a gentle damsel rode up. It was Flordelis, who was seeking her Florismart. She saw Orlando, and, in spite of his strange appearance, recognized him. Rodomont, not used to have his commands disobeyed, laid hands on the madman, and would have thrown him into the river, but to his astonishment found himself in the gripe of one not so easily disposed of. "How can a fool have such strength?" he growled between his teeth. Flordelis stopped to see the issue, where each of these two puissant warriors strove to throw the other from the bridge. Orlando at last had strength enough to lift his foe with all his armor, and fling him over the side, but had not wit to clear himself from him, so both fell together. High flashed the wave as they together smote its surface. Here Orlando had the advantage; he was naked, and could swim like a fish. He soon reached the bank, and, careless of praise or blame, stopped not to see what came of the adventure. Rodomont, entangled with his armor, escaped with difficulty to the bank. Meantime, Flordelis passed the bridge unchallenged.

After long wandering without success she returned to Paris, and there found the object of her search; for Florismart, after the fall of Albracca, had repaired thither. The joy of meeting was clouded to Florismart by the news which Flordelis brought of Orlando's wretched plight. The last she had seen of him was when he fell with Rodomont into the stream. Florismart, who loved Orlando like a brother, resolved to set out immediately, under the guidance of the lady, to find him, and bring him where he might receive the treatment suited to his case. A few days brought them to the place where they found the Tartar king still guarding the bridge. The usual challenge and defiance was made, and the knights rode to encounter one another on the bridge. At the first encounter both horses were overthrown; and, having no space to regain their footing, fell with their riders into the water. Rodomont, who knew the soundings of the stream, soon recovered the land; but Florismart was carried downward by the current, and landed at last on a bank of mud where his horse could hardly find footing. Flordelis, who watched the battle from the bridge, seeing her lover in this piteous case, exclaimed aloud, "Ah! Rodomont, for love of her whom dead you honor, have pity on me, who love this knight, and slay him not. Let it suffice he yields his armor to the pile, and none more glorious will it bear than his." Her prayer, so well directed, touched the pagan's heart, though hard to move, and he lent his aid to help the knight to land. He kept him a prisoner, however, and added his armor to the pile. Flordelis, with a heavy heart, went her way.

We must now return to Rogero, who, when we parted with him, was engaged in an adventure which arrested his progress to the monastery whither he was bound with the intention of receiving baptism, and thus qualifying himself to demand Bradamante as his bride. On his way he met with Mandricardo, and the quarrel was revived respecting the right to wear the badge of Hector. After a warm discussion both parties agreed to submit the question to King Agramant, and for that purpose took their way to the Saracen camp. Here they met Gradasso, who had his controversy also with Mandricardo. This warrior claimed the sword of Orlando, denying the right of Mandricardo to possess it in virtue of his having found it abandoned by its owner. King Agramant strove in vain to reconcile these quarrels, and was forced at last to consent that the points in dispute should be settled by one combat, in which Mandricardo should meet one of the other champions, to whom should be committed the cause of both. Rogero was chosen by lot to maintain Gradasso's cause and his own. Great preparations were made for this signal contest. On the appointed day it was fought in the presence of Agramant, and of the whole army. Rogero won it; and Mandricardo, the conqueror of Hector's arms, the challenger of Orlando, and the slayer of Zerbino, lost his life. Gradasso received Durindana as his prize, which lost half its value in his eyes, since it was won by another's prowess, not his own.

Rogero, though victorious, was severely wounded, and lay helpless many weeks in the camp of Agramant, while Bradamante, ignorant of the cause of his delay, expected him at Montalban. Thither he had promised to repair in fifteen days, or twenty at furthest, hoping to have obtained by that time an honorable discharge from his obligations to the Saracen commander. The twenty days were passed, and a month more, and still Rogero came not,

Figure 120: "Encounter of Bradamante and Fiordispine" by Guido Reni

nor did any tidings reach Bradamante accounting for his absence. At the end of that time, a wandering knight brought news of the famous combat, and of Rogero's wound. He added, what alarmed still more, that Marphisa, a female warrior, young and fair, was in attendance on the wounded knight. He added that the whole army expected that, as soon as Rogero's wounds were healed, the pair would be united in marriage.

Bradamante, distressed by this news, though she believed it but in part, resolved to go immediately and see for herself. She mounted Rabican, the horse of Astolpho, which he had committed to her care, and took with her the lance of gold, though unaware of its wonderful powers. Thus accoutred, she left the castle, and took the road toward Paris and the camp of the Saracens.

Marphisa, whose devotion to Rogero in his illness had so excited the jealousy of Bradamante, was the twin sister of Rogero. She, with him, had been taken in charge when an infant by Atlantes, the magician, but while yet a child she had been stolen away by an Arab tribe. Adopted by their chief, she had early learned horsemanship and skill in arms, and at this time had come to the camp of Agramant with no other view than to see and test for herself the prowess of the warriors of either camp, whose fame rang through the world. Arriving at the very moment of the late encounter, the name of Rogero, and some few facts of his story which she learned, were enough to suggest the idea that it was her brother whom she saw victorious in the single combat. Inquiry satisfied the two of their near kindred, and from that moment Marphisa devoted herself to the care of her new-found and much-loved brother.

In those moments of seclusion Rogero informed his sister of what he had learned of their parentage from old Atlantes. Rogero, their father, a Christian knight, had won the heart of Galaciella, daughter of the Sultan of Africa, and sister of King Agramant, converted her to the Christian faith, and secretly married her. The Sultan, enraged at his daughter's marriage, drove her husband into exile, and caused her with her infant children, Rogero and Marphisa, to be placed in a boat and committed to the winds and waves, to perish; from which fate they were saved by Atlantes. On hearing this, Marphisa exclaimed, "How can you, brother, leave our parents unavenged so long, and even submit to serve the son of the tyrant who so wronged them?" Rogero replied that it was but lately he had learned the full truth; that when he learned it he was already embarked with Agramant, from whom he had received knighthood, and that he only waited for a suitable opportunity when he might with honor desert his standard, and at the same time return to the faith of his fathers. Marphisa hailed this resolution with joy, and declared her intention to join with him in embracing the Christian faith.

We left Bradamante when, mounted on Rabican and armed with Astolpho's lance, she rode forth, determined to learn the cause of Rogero's long absence. One day, as she rode, she met a damsel, of visage and of manners fair, but overcome with grief. It was Flordelis, who was seeking far and near a champion capable of liberating and avenging her lord. Flordelis marked the approaching warrior, and, judging from appearances, thought she had found the champion she sought. "Are you, Sir Knight," she said, "so daring and so kind as to take up my cause against a fierce and cruel warrior who has made prisoner of my lord, and forced me thus to be a wanderer and a suppliant?" Then she related the events which had happened at the bridge. Bradamante, to whom noble enterprises were always welcome, readily embraced this, and the rather as in her gloomy forebodings she felt as if Rogero was forever lost to her.

Next day the two arrived at the bridge. The sentry descried them approaching, and gave notice to his lord, who thereupon donned his armor and went forth to meet them. Here, as usual, he called on the advancing warrior to yield his horse and arms an oblation to the tomb. Bradamante replied, asking by what right he called on the innocent to do penance for his crime. "Your life and your armor," she added, "are the fittest offering to her tomb, and I, a woman, the fittest champion to take them." With that she couched her spear, spurred her horse, and ran to the encounter. King Rodomont came on with speed. The trampling sounded on the bridge like thunder. It took but a moment to decide the contest. The golden lance did its office, and that fierce Moor, so renowned in tourney, lay extended on the bridge. "Who is the loser now?" said Bradamante; but Rodomont, amazed that a woman's hand should have laid him low, could not or would not answer. Silent and sad, he raised himself, unbound his helm and mail, and flung them against the tomb; then, sullen and on foot, left the ground; but first gave orders to one of his squires to release all his prisoners. They had been sent off to Africa. Besides Florismart, there were Sansonnet and Oliver, who had ridden that way in quest of Orlando, and had both in turn been overthrown in the encounter.

Bradamante after her victory resumed her route, and in due time reached the Christian camp, where she readily learned an explanation of the mystery which had caused her so much anxiety. Rogero and his fair and brave sister, Marphisa, were too illustrious by their station and exploits not to be the frequent topic of discourse even among their adversaries, and all that Bradamante was anxious to know reached her ear, almost without inquiry.

We now return to Gradasso, who by Rogero's victory had been made possessor of Durindana. There now only remained to him to seek the horse of Rinaldo; and the challenge, given and accepted, was yet to be fought with that warrior, for it had been interrupted by the arts of Malagigi. Gradasso now sought another meeting with Rinaldo, and met with no reluctance on his part. As the combat was for the possession of Bayard, the knights dismounted and fought on foot. Long time the battle lasted. Rinaldo, knowing well the deadly stroke of Durindana, used all his art to parry or avoid its blow. Gradasso struck with might and main, but wellnigh all his strokes were spent in air, or if they smote they fell obliquely and did little harm.

Thus had they fought long, glancing at one another's eyes, and seeing naught else, when their attention was arrested perforce by a strange noise. They turned, and beheld the good Bayard attacked by a monstrous bird. Perhaps it was a bird, for such it seemed; but when or where such a bird was ever seen I have nowhere read, except in Turpin; and I am inclined to believe that it was not a bird, but a fiend, evoked from underground by Malagigi, and thither sent on purpose to interrupt the fight. Whether a fiend or a fowl, the monster flew right at Bayard, and clapped his wings in his face. Thereat the steed broke loose, and ran madly across the plain, pursued by the bird, till Bayard plunged into the wood, and was lost to sight.

Rinaldo and Gradasso, seeing Bayard's escape, agreed to suspend their battle till they could recover the horse, the object of contention. Gradasso mounted his steed, and followed the foot- marks of Bayard into the forest. Rinaldo, never more vexed in spirit, remained at the spot, Gradasso having promised to return thither with the horse, if he found him. He did find him, after long search, for he had the good fortune to hear him neigh. Thus he became possessed of both the objects for which he had led an army from his own country, and invaded France. He did not forget his promise to bring Bayard back to the place where he had left Rinaldo, but only muttering, "Now I have got him, he little knows me who expects me to give him up; if Rinaldo wants the horse let him seek him in India, as I have sought him in France,"—he made the best of his way to Arles, where his vessels lay; and in possession of the two objects of his ambition, the horse and the sword, sailed away to his own country.

ASTOLPHO IN ABYSSINIA

When we last parted with the adventurous paladin Astolpho, he was just commencing that flight over the countries of the world from which he promised himself so much gratification. Our readers are aware that the eagle and the falcon have not so swift a flight as the Hippogriff on which Astolpho rode. It was not long, therefore, before the paladin, directing his course toward the southeast, arrived over that part of Africa where the great river Nile has its source. Here he alighted, and found himself in the neighborhood of the capital of Abyssinia, ruled by Senapus, whose riches and power were immense. His palace was of surpassing splendor; the bars of the gates, the hinges and locks, were all of pure gold; in fact, this metal, in that country, is put to all those uses for which we employ iron. It is so common that they prefer for ornamental purposes rock crystal, of which all the columns were made. Precious stones of different kinds, rubies, emeralds, sapphires, and topazes were set in ornamental designs, and the walls and ceilings were adorned with pearls.

It is in this country those famous balms grow of which there are some few plants in that part of Judaea called Gilead. Musk, ambergris, and numerous gums, so precious in Europe, are here in their native climate. It is said the Sultan of Egypt pays a vast tribute to the monarch of this country to hire him not to cut off the source of the Nile, which he might easily do, and cause the river to flow in some other direction, thus depriving Egypt of the source of its fertility.

At the time of Astolpho's arrival in his dominions, this monarch was in great affliction. In spite of his riches and the precious productions of his country, he was in danger of dying of hunger. He was a prey to a flock of obscene birds called Harpies, which attacked him whenever he sat at meat, and with their claws snatched, tore, and scattered everything, overturning the vessels, devouring the food, and infecting what they left with their filthy touch. It was said this punishment was inflicted upon the king because when young, and filled with pride and presumption, he had attempted to invade with an army the terrestrial paradise, which is situated on the top of a mountain whence the Nile draws its source. Nor was this his only punishment. He was struck blind.

Astolpho, on arriving in the dominions of this monarch, hastened to pay him his respects. King Senapus received him graciously, and ordered a splendid repast to be prepared in honor of his arrival. While the guests were seated at table, Astolpho filling the place of dignity at the king's right hand, the horrid scream of the Harpies was heard in the air, and soon they approached, hovering over the tables, seizing the food from the dishes, and overturning everything with the flapping of their broad wings. In vain the guests struck at them with knives and any weapons which they had, and Astolpho drew his sword and gave them repeated blows, which seemed to have no more effect upon them than if their bodies had been made of tow.

At last Astolpho thought of his horn. He first gave warning to the king and his guests to stop their ears; then blew a blast. The Harpies, terrified at the sound, flew away as fast as their wings could carry them. The paladin mounted his Hippogriff, and pursued them, blowing his horn as often as he came near them. They stretched their flight towards the great mountain, at the foot of which there is a cavern, which is thought to be the mouth of the infernal abodes. Hither those horrid birds flew, as if to their home. Having seen them all disappear in the recess, Astolpho cared not to pursue them farther, but alighting, rolled huge stones into the mouth of the cave, and piled branches of trees therein, so that he effectually barred their passage out, and we have no evidence of their ever having been seen since in the outer air.

After this labor Astolpho refreshed himself by bathing in a fountain whose pure waters bubbled from a cleft of the rock. Having rested awhile, an earnest desire seized him of ascending the mountain which towered above him. The Hippogriff bore him swiftly upwards, and landed him on the top of the mountain, which he found to be an extensive plain.

A splendid palace rose in the middle of this plain, whose walls shone with such brilliancy that mortal eyes could hardly bear the sight. Astolpho guided the winged horse towards this edifice, and made him poise himself in the air while he took a leisurely survey of this favored spot and its environs. It seemed as if nature and art had striven with one another to see which could do the most for its embellishment.

Astolpho, on approaching the edifice, saw a venerable man advance to meet him. This personage was clothed in a long vesture as white as snow, while a mantle of purple covered his shoulders, and hung down to the ground. A white beard descended to his middle, and his hair, of the same color, overshadowed his shoulders. His eyes were so brilliant that Astolpho felt persuaded that he was a blessed inhabitant of the heavenly mansions.

The sage, smiling benignantly upon the paladin, who from respect had dismounted from his horse, said to him: "Noble chevalier, know that it is by the Divine will you have been brought to the terrestrial paradise. Your mortal nature could not have borne to scale these heights and reach these seats of bliss if it were not the will of Heaven that you should be instructed in the means to succor Charles, and to sustain the glory of our holy faith. I am prepared to impart the needed counsels; but before I begin let me welcome you to our sojourn. I doubt not your long fast and distant journey have given you a good appetite."

The aspect of the venerable man filled the prince with admiration; but his surprise ceased when he learned from him that he was that one of the Apostles of our Lord to whom he said, "I will that thou tarry till I come."

St. John, conducting Astolpho, rejoined his companions. These were the patriarch Enoch and the prophet Elijah; neither of whom had yet seen his dying day, but, taken from our lower world, were dwelling in a region of peace and joy, in a climate of eternal spring, till the last trumpet shall sound.

The three holy inhabitants of the terrestrial paradise received Astolpho with the greatest kindness, carried him to a pleasant apartment, and took great care of the Hippogriff, to whom they gave such food as suited him, while to the prince they presented fruits so delicious that he felt inclined to excuse our first parents for their sin in eating them without permission.

Astolpho, having recruited his strength, not only by these excellent fruits, but also by sweet sleep, roused himself at the first blush of dawn, and as soon as he left his chamber met the beloved Apostle coming to seek him. St. John took him by the hand, and told him many things relating to the past and the future. Among others, he said, "Son, let me tell you what is now going on in France. Orlando, the illustrious prince who received at his birth the endowment of strength and courage more than mortal, raised up as was Samson of old to be the champion of the true faith, has been guilty of the basest ingratitude in leaving the Christian camp when it most needed the support of his arm, to run after a Saracen princess, whom he would fain marry, though she scorns him. To punish him his reason has been taken away, so that he runs naked through the land, over mountains and through valleys, without a ray of intelligence. The duration of his punishment has been fixed at three months, and that time having nearly expired, you have been brought hither to learn from us the means by which the reason of Orlando may be restored. True, you will be obliged to make a journey with me, and we must even leave the earth, and ascend to the moon, for it is in that planet we are to seek the remedy for the madness of the paladin. I propose to make our journey this evening, as soon as the moon appears over our head."

As soon as the sun sunk beneath the seas, and the moon presented its luminous disk, the holy man had the chariot brought out in which he was accustomed to make excursions among the stars, the same which was employed long ago to convey Elijah up from earth. The saint made Astolpho seat himself beside him, took the reins, and giving the word to the coursers, they bore them upward with astonishing celerity.

At length they reached the great continent of the Moon. Its surface appeared to be of polished steel, with here and there a spot which, like rust, obscured its brightness. The paladin was astonished to see that the earth, with all its seas and rivers, seemed but an insignificant spot in the distance.

The prince discovered in this region so new to him rivers, lakes, plains, hills, and valleys. Many beautiful cities and castles enriched the landscape. He saw also vast forests, and heard in them the sound of horns and the barking of dogs, which led him to conclude that the nymphs were following the chase.

The knight, filled with wonder at all he saw, was conducted by the saint to a valley, where he stood amazed at the riches strewed all around him. Well he might be so, for that valley was the receptacle of things lost on earth, either by men's fault, or by the effect of time and chance. Let no one suppose we speak here of kingdoms or of treasures; they are the toys of Fortune, which she dispenses in turning her wheel; we speak of things which she can neither give nor take away. Such are reputations, which appear at one time so brilliant, and a short time after are heard of no more. Here, also, are countless vows and prayers for unattainable objects, lovers' sighs and tears, time spent in gaming, dressing, and doing nothing, the leisure of the dull and the intentions of the lazy, baseless projects, intrigues, and plots; these and such like things fill all the valley.

Astolpho had a great desire to understand all that he saw, and which appeared to him so extraordinary. Among the rest, he observed a great mountain of blown bladders, from which issued indistinct noises. The saint told him these were the dynasties of Assyrian and Persian kings, once the wonder of the earth, of which now scarce the name remains.

Astolpho could not help laughing when the saint said to him, "All these hooks of silver and gold that you see are the gifts of courtiers to princes, made in the hope of getting something better in return." He also showed him garlands of flowers in which snares were concealed; these were flatteries and adulations, meant to deceive. But nothing was so comical as the sight of numerous grasshoppers which had burst their lungs with chirping. These, he told him, were sonnets, odes, and dedications, addressed by venal poets to great people.

The paladin beheld with wonder what seemed a lake of spilled milk. "It is," said the saint, "the charity done by frightened misers on their death-beds." It would take too long to tell all that the valley contained: meanness, affectations, pretended virtues, and concealed vices were there in abundance.

Among the rest Astolpho perceived many days of his own lost, and many imprudent sallies which he had made, and would have been glad not to have been reminded of. But he also saw among so many lost things a great abundance of one thing which men are apt to think they all possess, and do not think it necessary to pray for,—good sense. This commodity appeared under the form of a liquor, most light and apt to evaporate. It was therefore kept in vials, firmly sealed. One of these was labelled, "The sense of the Paladin Orlando."

All the bottles were ticketed, and the sage placed one in Astolpho's hand, which he found was his own. It was more than half full. He was surprised to find there many other vials which contained almost the whole of the wits of many persons who passed among men for wise. Ah, how easy it is to lose one's reason! Some lose theirs by yielding to the sway of the passions; some in braving tempests and shoals in search of wealth; some by trusting too much to the promises of the great; some by setting their hearts on trifles. As might have been expected, the bottles which held the wits of astrologers, inventors, metaphysicians, and above all, of poets, were in general the best filled of all.

Astolpho took his bottle, put it to his nose, and inhaled it all; and Turpin assures us that he was for a long time afterwards as sage as one could wish; but the Archbishop adds that there was reason to fear that some of the precious fluid afterwards found its way back into the bottle. The paladin took also the bottle which belonged to Orlando. It was a large one, and quite full.

Before quitting the planetary region Astolpho was conducted to an edifice on the borders of a river. He was shown an immense hall full of bundles of silk, linen, cotton, and wool. A thousand different colors, brilliant or dull, some quite black, were among these skeins. In one part of the hall an old woman was busy winding off yarns from all these different bundles. When she had finished a skein another ancient dame took it and placed it with others; a third selected from the fleeces spun, and mingled them in due proportions. The paladin inquired what all this might be. "These old women," said the saint, "are the Fates, who spin, measure, and terminate the lives of mortals. As long as the thread stretches in one of those skeins, so long does the mortal enjoy the light of day; but nature and death are on the alert to shut the eyes of those whose thread is spun."

Each one of the skeins had a label of gold, silver, or iron, bearing the name of the individual to whom it belonged. An old man, who, in spite of the burden of years, seemed brisk and active, ran without ceasing to fill his apron with these labels, and carried them away to throw them into the river, whose name was Lethe. When he reached the shore of the river the old man shook out his apron, and the labels sunk to the bottom. A small number only floated for a time, hardly one in a thousand. Numberless birds, hawks, crows, and vultures hovered over the stream, with clamorous cries, and strove to snatch from the water some of these names; but they were too heavy for them, and after a while the birds were forced to let them drop into the river of oblivion. But two beautiful swans, of snowy whiteness, gathered some few of the names, and returned with them to the shore, where a lovely nymph received them from their beaks, and carried them to a temple placed upon a hill, and suspended them for all time upon a sacred column, on which stood the statue of Immortality.

Astolpho was amazed at all this, and asked his guide to explain it. He replied, "The old man is Time. All the names upon the tickets would be immortal if the old man did not plunge them into the river of oblivion. Those clamorous birds which make vain efforts to save certain of the names are flatterers, pensioners, venal rhymesters, who do their best to rescue from oblivion the unworthy names of their patrons; but all in vain; they may keep them from their fate a little while, but ere long the river of oblivion must swallow them all.

"The swans, that with harmonious strains carry certain names to the temple of Eternal Memory, are the great poets, who save from oblivion worse than death the names of those they judge worthy of immortality. Swans of this kind are rare. Let monarchs know the true breed and fail not to nourish with care such as may chance to appear in their time."

THE WAR IN AFRICA

When Astolpho had descended to the earth with the precious phial, St. John showed him a plant of marvellous virtues, with which he told him he had only to touch the eyes of the king of Abyssinia to restore him to sight. "That important service," said the saint, "added to your having delivered him from the Harpies, will induce him to give you an army wherewith to attack the Africans in their rear, and force them to return from France to defend their own country." The saint also instructed him how to lead his troops in safety across the great deserts, where caravans are often overwhelmed with moving columns of sand. Astolpho, fortified with ample instructions, remounted the Hippogriff, thanked the saint, received his blessing, and took his flight down to the level country.

Keeping the course of the river Nile, he soon arrived at the capital of Abyssinia, and rejoined Senapus. The joy of the king was great when he heard again the voice of the hero who had delivered him from the Harpies. Astolpho touched his eyes with the plant which he had brought from the terrestrial paradise, and restored their sight. The king's gratitude was unbounded. He begged him to name a reward, promising to grant it, whatever it might be. Astolpho asked an army to go to the assistance of Charlemagne, and the king not only granted him a hundred thousand men, but offered to lead them himself.

The night before the day appointed for the departure of the troops Astolpho mounted his winged horse, and directed his flight towards a mountain, whence the fierce South-wind issues, whose blast raises the sands of the Nubian desert, and whirls them onward in overwhelming clouds. The paladin, by the advice of St. John, had prepared himself with a leather bag, which he placed adroitly, with its mouth open, over the vent whence issues this terrible wind. At the first dawn of morning the wind

Figure 121: "Astolpho" by Charles F. Horne

rushed from its cavern to resume its daily course, and was caught in the bag, and securely tied up. Astolpho, delighted with his prize, returned to his army, placed himself at their head, and commenced his march. The Abyssinians traversed without danger or difficulty those vast fields of sand which separate their country from the kingdoms of Northern Africa, for the terrible South-wind, taken completely captive, had not force enough left to blow out a candle.

Senapus was distressed that he could not furnish any cavalry, for his country, rich in camels and elephants, was destitute of horses. This difficulty the saint had foreseen, and had taught Astolpho the means of remedying. He now put those means in operation. Having reached a place whence he beheld a vast plain and the sea, he chose from his troops those who appeared to be the best made and the most intelligent. These he caused to be arranged in squadrons at the foot of a lofty mountain which bordered the plain, and he himself mounted to the summit to carry into effect his great design. Here he found vast quantities of fragments of rock and pebbles. These he set rolling down the mountain's side, and, wonderful to relate, as they rolled they grew in size, made themselves bodies, legs, necks, and long faces. Next they began to neigh, to curvet, to scamper on all sides over the plain. Some were bay, some roan, some dapple, some chestnut. The troops at the foot of the mountain exerted themselves to catch these new-created horses, which they easily did, for the miracle had been so considerate as to provide all the horses with bridles and saddles. Astolpho thus suddenly found himself supplied with an excellent corps of cavalry, not fewer (as Archbishop Turpin asserts) than eighty thousand strong. With these troops Astolpho reduced all the country to subjection, and at last arrived before the walls of Agramant's capital city, Biserta, to which he laid siege.

We must now return to the camp of the Christians, which lay before Arles, to which city the Saracens had retired after being defeated in a night attack led on by Rinaldo. Agramant here received the tidings of the invasion of his country by a fresh enemy, the Abyssinians, and learned that Biserta was in danger of falling into their hands. He took counsel of his officers, and decided to send an embassy to Charles, proposing that the whole quarrel should be submitted to the combat of two warriors, one from each side, according to the issue of which it should be decided which party should pay tribute to the other, and the war should cease. Charlemagne, who had not heard of the favorable turn which affairs had taken in Africa, readily agreed to this proposal, and Rinaldo was selected on the part of the Christians to sustain the combat.

The Saracens selected Rogero for their champion. Rogero was still in the Saracen camp, kept there by honor alone, for his mind had been opened to the truth of the Christian faith by the arguments of Bradamante, and he had resolved to leave the party of the infidels on the first favorable opportunity, and to join the Christian side. But his honor forbade him to do this while his former friends were in distress; and thus he waited for what time might bring forth, when he was startled by the announcement that he had been selected to uphold the cause of the Saracens against the Christians, and that his foe was to be Rinaldo, the brother of Bradamante.

While Rogero was overwhelmed with this intelligence Bradamante on her side felt the deepest distress at hearing of the proposed combat. If Rogero should fall she felt that no other man living was worthy of her love; and if, on the other hand, Heaven should resolve to punish France by the death of her chosen champion, Bradamante would have to deplore her brother, so dear to her, and be no less completely severed from the object of her affections.

While the fair lady gave herself up to these sad thoughts, the sage enchantress, Melissa, suddenly appeared before her. "Fear not, my daughter," said she, "I shall find a way to interrupt this combat which so distresses you."

Meanwhile Rinaldo and Rogero prepared their weapons for the conflict. Rinaldo had the choice, and decided that it should be on foot, and with no weapons but the battle-axe and poniard. The place assigned was a plain between the camp of Charlemagne and the walls of Arles.

Hardly had the dawn announced the day appointed for this memorable combat, when heralds proceeded from both sides to mark the lists. Erelong the African troops were seen to advance from the city, Agramant at their head; his brilliant arms adorned in the Moorish fashion, his horse a bay, with a white star on his forehead. Rogero marched at his side, and some of the greatest warriors of the Saracen camp attended him, bearing the various parts of his armor and weapons. Charlemagne, on his part, proceeded from his intrenchments, ranged his troops in semicircle, and stood surrounded by his peers and paladins. Some of them bore portions of the armor of Rinaldo, the celebrated Ogier, the Dane, bearing the helmet which Rinaldo took from Mambrino. Duke Namo of Bavaria and Salomon of Bretagne bore two axes, of equal weight, prepared for the occasion.

The terms of the combat were then sworn to with the utmost solemnity by all parties. It was agreed that if from either part any attempt was made to interrupt the battle both combatants should turn their arms against the party which should be guilty of the interruption; and both monarchs assented to the condition that in such case the champion of the offending party should be discharged from his allegiance, and at liberty to transfer his arms to the other side.

When all the preparations were concluded the monarchs and their attendants retired each to his own side, and the champions were left alone. The two warriors advanced with measured steps towards each other, and met in the middle of the space. They attacked one another at the same moment, and the air resounded with the blows they gave. Sparks flew from their battle-axes, while the velocity with which they managed their weapons astonished the beholders. Rogero, always remembering that his antagonist was the brother of his betrothed, could not aim a deadly wound; he strove only to ward off those levelled against himself. Rinaldo, on the other hand, much as he esteemed Rogero, spared not his blows, for he eagerly desired victory for his own sake, and for the sake of his country and his faith.

The Saracens soon perceived that their champion fought feebly, and gave not to Rinaldo such blows as he received from him. His disadvantage was so marked that anxiety and shame were manifest on the countenance of Agramant. Melissa, one of the most acute enchantresses that ever lived, seized this moment to disguise herself under the form of Rodomont, that rude and impetuous warrior, who had now for some time been absent from the Saracen camp. Approaching Agramant, she said, "How could you, my lord, have the imprudence of selecting a young man without experience to oppose the most redoubtable warrior of France? Surely you must have been regardless of the honor of your arms, and of the fate of your empire! But it is not too late. Break without delay the agreement which is sure to result in your ruin." So saying, she addressed the troops who stood near, "Friends," said she, "follow me; under my guidance every one of you will be a match for a score of those feeble Christians." Agramant, delighted at seeing Rodomont once more at his side, gave his consent, and the Saracens, at the instant, couched their lances, set spurs to their steeds, and swept down upon the French. Melissa, when she saw her work successful, disappeared.

Rinaldo and Rogero, seeing the truce broken, and the two armies engaged in general conflict, stopped their battle; their martial fury ceased at once, they joined hands, and resolved to act no more on either side until it should be clearly ascertained which party had failed to observe its oath. Both renewed their promise to abandon forever the party which had been thus false and perjured.

Meanwhile, the Christians, after the first moment of surprise, met the Saracens with courage redoubled by rage at the treachery of their foes. Guido the Wild, brother and rival of Rinaldo, Griffon and Aquilant, sons of Oliver, and numerous others whose names have already been celebrated in our recitals, beat back the assailants, and at last, after prodigious slaughter, forced them to take shelter within the walls of Arles.

We will now return to Orlando, whom we last heard of as furiously mad, and doing a thousand acts of violence in his senseless rage. One day he came to the borders of a stream which intercepted his course. He swam across it, for he could swim like an otter, and on the other side saw a peasant watering his horse. He seized the animal, in spite of the resistance of the peasant, and rode it with furious speed till he arrived at the sea-coast, where Spain is divided from Africa by only a narrow strait. At the moment of his arrival a vessel had just put off to cross the strait. She was full of people who, with glass in hand, seemed to be taking a merry farewell of the land, wafted by a favorable breeze.

The frantic Orlando cried out to them to stop and take him in; but they, having no desire to admit a madman to their company, paid him no attention. The paladin thought this behavior very uncivil; and by force of blows made his horse carry him into the water in pursuit of the ship. The wretched animal soon had only his head above water; but as Orlando urged him forward, nothing was left for the poor beast but either to die or swim over to Africa.

Already Orlando had lost sight of the bark; distance and the swell of the sea completely hid it from his sight. He continued to press his horse forward, till at last it could struggle no more, and sunk beneath him. Orlando, nowise concerned, stretched out his nervous arms, puffing the salt water from before his mouth, and carried his head above the waves. Fortunately they were not rough, scarce a breath of wind agitated the surface; otherwise, the invincible Orlando would then have met his death. But fortune, which it is said favors fools, delivered him from this danger, and landed him safe on the shore of Ceuta. Here he rambled along the shore till he came to where the black army of Astolpho held its camp.

Now it happened, just before this time, that a vessel filled with prisoners which Rodomont had taken at the bridge had arrived, and, not knowing of the presence of the Abyssinian army, had sailed right into port, where of course the prisoners and their captors changed places, the former being set at liberty and received with all joy, the latter sent to serve in the galleys. Astolpho thus found himself surrounded with Christian knights, and he and his friends were exchanging greetings and felicitations, when a noise was heard in the camp, and seemed to increase every moment.

Astolpho and his friends seized their weapons, mounted their horses, and rode to the quarter whence the noise proceeded. Imagine their astonishment when they saw that the tumult was caused by a single man, perfectly naked, and browned with dirt and exposure, but of a force and fury so terrible that he overturned all that offered to lay hands on him.

Astolpho, Dudon, Oliver, and Florimart gazed at him with amazement. It was with difficulty they knew him. Astolpho, who had been warned of his condition by his holy monitor, was the first to recognize him. As the paladins closed round Orlando, the madman dealt one and another a blow of his fist, which, if they had not been in armor, or he had had any weapon, would probably have despatched them; as it was, Dudon and Astolpho measured their length on the sand. But Florimart seized him from behind, Sansonnet and another grasped his legs, and at last they succeeded in securing him with ropes. They took him to the water-side and washed him well, and then Astolpho, having first bandaged his mouth so that he could not breathe except through his nose, brought the precious phial, uncorked it, and placed it adroitly under his nostrils, when the good Orlando took it all up in one breath. O marvellous prodigy! The paladin recovered in an instant all his intelligence. He felt like one who had awakened from a painful dream, in which he had believed that monsters were about to tear him to pieces. He seemed prostrated, silent, and abashed. Florismart, Oliver, and Astolpho stood gazing upon him, while he turned his eyes around and on himself. He seemed surprised to find himself naked, bound, and stretched on the sea-shore. After a few moments he recognized his friends, and spoke to them in a tone so tender that they hastened to unbind him, and to supply him with garments. Then they exerted themselves to console him, to diminish the weight with which his spirits were oppressed, and to make him forget the wretched condition into which he had been sunk.

Orlando, in recovering his reason, found himself also delivered from his insane attachment to the queen of Cathay. His heart felt now no further influenced by the recollection of her than to be moved with an ardent desire to retrieve his fame by some distinguished exploit. Astolpho would gladly have yielded to him the chief command of the army, but Orlando would not take from the friend to whom he owed so much the glory of the campaign; but in everything the two paladins acted in concert, and united their counsels. They proposed to make a general assault on the city of Biserta, and were only waiting a favorable moment, when their plan was interrupted by new events.

Agramant, after the bloody battle which followed the infraction of the truce, found himself so weak that he saw it was in vain to attempt to remain in France. So, in concert with Sobrino, the bravest and most trusted of his chiefs, he embarked to return to his own country, having previously sent off his few remaining troops in the same direction. The vessel which carried Agramant and Sobrino approached the shore where the army of Astolpho lay encamped before Biserta, and having discovered this fact before it was too late, the king commanded the pilot to steer eastward, with a view to seek protection of the King of Egypt. But the weather becoming rough, he consented to the advice of his companions, and sought harbor in an island which lies between Sicily and Africa. There he found Gradasso, the warlike king of Sericane, who had come to France to possess himself of the horse Bayard and the sword Durindana; and having procured both these prizes was returning to his own country.

The two kings, who had been companions in arms under the walls of Paris, embraced one another affectionately. Gradasso learned with regret the reverses of Agramant, and offered him his troops and his person. He strongly deprecated resorting to Egypt for aid. "Remember the great Pompey," said he, "and shun that fatal shore. My plan," he continued, "is this: I mean to challenge Orlando to single combat. Possessed of such a sword and steed as mine, if he were made of steel or bronze, he could not escape me. He being removed, there will be no difficulty in driving back the Abyssinians. We will rouse against them the Moslem nations from the other side of the Nile, the Arabians, Persians, and Chaldeans, who will soon make Senapus recall his army to defend his own territories."

Agramant approved this advice except in one particular. "It is for me," said he, "to combat Orlando; I cannot with honor devolve that duty on another."

"Let us adopt a third course," said the aged warrior Sobrino. "I would not willingly remain a simple spectator of such a contest. Let us send three squires to the shore of Africa to challenge Orlando and any two of his companions in arms to meet us three in this island of Lampedusa."

This counsel was adopted; the three squires sped on their way; and now presented themselves, and rehearsed their message to the Christian knights.

Orlando was delighted, and rewarded the squires with rich gifts. He had already resolved to seek Gradasso and compel him to restore Durindana, which he had learned was in his possession. For his two companions the Count chose his faithful friend Florismart and his cousin Oliver.

The three warriors embarked, and sailing with a favorable wind, the second morning showed them, on their right, the island where this important battle was to be fought. Orlando and his two companions, having landed, pitched their tent. Agramant had placed his opposite.

Next morning, as soon as Aurora brightened the edges of the horizon, the warriors of both parties armed themselves and mounted their horses. They took their positions, face to face, lowered their lances, placed them in rest, clapped spurs to their horses, and flew to the charge. Orlando met the charge of Gradasso. The paladin was unmoved, but his horse could not sustain the terrible shock of Bayard. He recoiled, staggered, and fell some paces behind. Orlando tried to raise him, but, finding his efforts unavailing, seized his shield, and drew his famous Balisardo. Meanwhile Agramant and the brave Oliver gained no advantage, one or the other; but Florismart unhorsed the King Sobrino. Having brought his foe to the ground, he would not pursue his victory, but hastened to attack Gradasso, who had overthrown Orlando. Seeing him thus engaged, Orlando would not interfere, but ran with sword upraised upon Sobrino, and with one blow deprived him of sense and motion. Believing him dead, he next turned to aid his beloved Florismart. That brave paladin, neither in horse nor arms equal to his antagonist, could but parry and evade the blows of the terrible Durindana. Orlando, eager to succor him, was delayed for a moment in securing and mounting the horse of the King Sobrino. It was but an instant, and with sword upraised, he rushed upon Gradasso who, noways disconcerted at the onset of this second foe, shouted his defiance, and thrust at him with his sword, but, having miscalculated the distance, scarcely reached him, and failed to pierce his mail. Orlando, in return, dealt him a blow with Balisardo, which wounded as it fell face, breast, and thigh, and, if he had been a little nearer, would have cleft him in twain. Sobrino, by this time recovered from his swoon, though severely wounded, raised himself on his legs, and looked to see how he might aid his friends. Observing Agramant hard pressed by Oliver, he thrust his sword into the bowels of the latter's horse, which fell, and bore down his master, entangling his leg as he fell, so that Oliver could not extricate himself. Florismart saw the danger of his friend, and ran upon Sobrino with his horse, overthrew him, and then turned to defend himself from Agramant. They were not unequally matched, for though Agramant, mounted on Brigliadoro, had an advantage over Florismart, whose horse was but indifferent, yet Agramant had received a serious wound in his encounter with Oliver.

Nothing could exceed the fury of the encounter between Orlando and Gradasso. Durindana, in the hands of Gradasso, clove asunder whatever it struck; but such was the skill of Orlando, who perfectly knew the danger to which he was exposed from a stroke of that weapon, it had not yet struck him in such a way as to inflict a wound. Meanwhile, Gradasso was bleeding from many wounds, and his rage and incaution increased every moment. In his desperation he lifted Durindana with both hands, and struck so terrible a blow full on the helmet of Orlando, that for a moment it stunned the paladin. He dropped the reins, and his frightened horse scoured with him over the plain. Gradasso turned to pursue him, but at that moment saw Florismart in the very act of striking a fatal blow at Agramant, whom he had unhorsed. While Florismart was wholly intent upon completing his victory, Gradasso plunged his sword into his side. Florismart fell from his horse, and bathed the plain with his blood.

Orlando recovered himself just in time to see the deed. Whether rage or grief predominated in his breast, I cannot tell; but, seizing Balisardo with fury, his first blow fell upon Agramant, who was nearest to him, and smote his head from his shoulders. At this sight Gradasso for the first time felt his courage sink, and a dark presentiment of death came over him. He hardly stood on his defence when Orlando cast himself upon him, and gave him a fatal thrust. The sword penetrated his ribs, and came out a palm's breadth on the other side of his body.

Thus fell beneath the sword of the most illustrious paladin of France the bravest warrior of the Saracen host. Orlando then, as if despising his victory, leaped lightly to the ground, and ran to his dear friend Florismart, embraced him, and bathed him with his tears. Florismart still breathed. He could even command his voice to utter a few parting words: "Dear friend, do not forget me,— give me your prayers,—and oh! be a brother to Flordelis." He died in uttering her name.

After a few moments given to grief Orlando turned to look for his other companion and his late foes. Oliver lay oppressed with the weight of his horse, from which he had in vain struggled to liberate himself. Orlando extricated him with difficulty; he then raised Sobrino from the earth, and committed him to his squire, treating him as gently as if he had been his own brother. For this terrible warrior was the most generous of men to a fallen foe. He took Bayard and Brigliadoro, with the arms of the conquered knights; their bodies and their other spoils he remitted to their attendants.

But who can tell the grief of Flordelis when she saw the warriors return, and found not Florismart as usual after absence hasten to her side. She knew by the aspect of the others that her lord was slain. At the thought, and before the question could pass her lips, she fell senseless upon the ground. When life returned, and she learned the truth of her worst fears, she bitterly upbraided herself that she had let him depart without her. "I might have saved him by a single cry when his enemy dealt him that treacherous blow, or I might have thrown myself between and given my worthless life for his. Or if no more, I might have heard his last words, I might have given him a last kiss." So she lamented, and could not be comforted.

ROGERO AND BRADAMANTE

After the interruption of the combat with Rinaldo, as we have related, Rogero was perplexed with doubts what course to take. The terms of the treaty required him to abandon Agramant, who had broken it, and to transfer his allegiance to Charlemagne; and his love for Bradamante called him in the same direction; but unwillingness to desert his prince and leader in the hour of distress forbade this course. Embarking, therefore, for Africa, he took his way to rejoin the Saracen army; but was arrested midway by a storm which drove the vessel on a rock. The crew took to their boat, but that was quickly swamped in the waves, and Rogero with the rest were compelled to swim for their lives. Then while buffeting the waves Rogero bethought him of his sin in so long delaying his Christian profession, and vowed in his heart that, if he should live to reach the land, he would no longer delay to be baptized. His vows were heard and answered; he succeeded in reaching the shore, and was aided and relieved on landing by a pious hermit, whose cell overlooked the sea. From him he received baptism, having first passed some days with him, partaking his humble fare, and receiving instruction in the doctrines of the Christian faith.

While these things were going on, Rinaldo, who had set out on his way to seek Gradasso and recover Bayard from him, hearing on his way of the great things which were doing in Africa, repaired thither to bear his part in them. He arrived too late to do more than join his friends in lamenting the loss of Florismart, and to rejoice with them in their victory over the Pagan knights. On the death of their king the Africans gave up the contest, Biserta submitted, and the Christian knights had only to dismiss their forces, and return home. Astolpho took leave of his Abyssinian army, and sent them back laden with spoil to their own country, not forgetting to intrust to them the bag

Figure 122 "Roger Borne Away from Bradamante" by Henry Justice Ford

which held the winds, by means of which they were enabled to cross the sandy desert again without danger, and did not untie it till they reached their own country.

Orlando now, with Oliver, who much needed the surgeon's care, and Sobrino, to whom equal attention was shown, sailed in a swift vessel to Sicily, bearing with him the body of Florismart, to be laid in Christian earth. Rinaldo accompanied them, as did Sansonnet and the other Christian leaders. Arrived at Sicily, the funeral was solemnized with all the rites of religion, and with the profound grief of those who had known Florismart, or had heard of his fame. Then they resumed their course, steering for Marseilles. But Oliver's wound grew worse instead of better, and his sufferings so distressed his friends that they conferred together, not knowing what to do. Then said the pilot, "We are not far from an isle where a holy hermit dwells alone in the midst of the sea. It is said none seek his counsel or his aid in vain. He hath wrought marvellous cures, and if you resort to that holy man without doubt he can heal the knight." Orlando bade him steer thither, and soon the bark was laid safely beside the lonely rock; the wounded man was lowered into their boat, and carried by the crew to the hermit's cell. It was the same hermit with whom Rogero had taken refuge after his shipwreck, by whom he had been baptized, and with whom he was now staying, absorbed in sacred studies and meditations.

The holy man received Orlando and the rest with kindness, and inquired their errand; and being told that they had come for help for one who, warring for the Christian faith, was brought to perilous pass by a sad wound, he straightway undertook the cure. His applications were simple, but they were seconded by his prayers. The paladin was soon relieved from pain, and in a few days his foot was perfectly restored to soundness. Sobrino, as soon as he perceived the holy monk perform that wonder, cast aside his false prophet, and with contrite heart owned the true God, and demanded baptism at his hands. The hermit granted his request, and also by his prayers restored him to health, while all the Christian knights rejoiced in his conversion almost as much as at the restoration of Oliver. More than all Rogero felt joy and gratitude, and daily grew in grace and faith.

Rogero was known by fame to all the Christian knights, but not even Rinaldo knew him by sight, though he had proved his prowess in combat. Sobrino made him known to them, and great was the joy of all when they found one whose valor and courtesy were renowned through the world no longer an enemy and unbeliever, but a convert and champion of the true faith. All press about the knight; one grasps his hand, another locks him fast in his embrace; but more than all the rest, Rinaldo cherished him, for he more than any knew his worth.

It was not long before Rogero confided to his friend the hopes he entertained of a union with his sister, and Rinaldo frankly gave his sanction to the proposal. But causes unknown to the paladin were at that very time interposing obstacles to its success.

The fame of the beauty and worth of Bradamante had reached the ears of the Grecian Emperor, Constantine, and he had sent to Charlemagne to demand the hand of his niece for Leo, his son, and the heir to his dominions. Duke Aymon, her father, had only reserved his consent until he should first have spoken with his son Rinaldo, now absent.

The warriors now prepared to resume their voyage. Rogero took a tender farewell of the good hermit who had taught him the true faith. Orlando restored to him the horse and arms which were rightly his, not even asserting his claim to Balisarda, that sword which he himself had won from the enchantress.

The hermit gave his blessing to the band, and they reembarked. The passage was speedy, and very soon they arrived in the harbor of Marseilles.

Astolpho, when he had dismissed his troops, mounted the Hippogriff, and at one flight shot over to Sardinia, thence to Corsica, thence, turning slightly to the left, hovered over Provence, and alighted in the neighborhood of Marseilles. There he did what he had been commanded to do by the holy saint; he unbridled the Hippogriff, and turned him loose to seek his own retreats, never more to be galled with saddle or bit. The horn had lost its marvellous power ever since the visit to the moon.

Astolpho reached Marseilles the very day when Orlando, Rinaldo, Oliver, Sobrino, and Rogero arrived there. Charles had already heard the news of the defeat of the Saracen kings, and all the accompanying events. On learning the approach of the gallant knights, he sent forward some of his most illustrious nobles to receive them, and himself, with the rest of his court, kings, dukes, and peers, the queen, and a fair and gorgeous band of ladies, set forward from Arles to meet them.

No sooner were the mutual greetings interchanged, than Orlando and his friends led forward Rogero, and presented him to the Emperor. They vouch him son of Rogero, Duke of Risa, one of the most renowned of Christian warriors, by adverse fortune stolen in his infancy, and brought up by Saracens in the false faith, now by a kind Providence converted, and restored to fill the place his father once held among the foremost champions of the throne and Church.

Rogero had alighted from his horse, and stood respectfully before the Emperor. Charlemagne bade him remount and ride beside him; and omitted nothing which might do him honor in sight of his martial train. With pomp triumphal and with festive cheer the troop returned to the city; the streets were decorated with garlands, the houses hung with rich tapestry, and flowers fell like rain upon the conquering host from the hands of fair dames and damsels, from every balcony and window. So welcomed, the mighty Emperor passed on till he reached the royal palace, where many days he feasted, high in hall, with his lords, amid tourney, revel, dance, and song.

When Rinaldo told his father, Duke Aymon, how he had promised his sister to Rogero, his father heard him with indignation, having set his heart on seeing her united to the Grecian Emperor's son. The Lady Beatrice, her mother, also appealed to Bradamante herself to reject a knight who had neither title nor lands, and give the preference to one who would make her Empress of the wide Levant. But Bradamante, though respect forbade her to refuse her mother's entreaty, would not promise to do what her heart repelled, and answered only with a sigh, until she was alone, and then gave a loose to tears.

Meanwhile Rogero, indignant that a stranger should presume to rob him of his bride, determined to seek the Prince of Greece, and defy him to mortal combat. With this design he donned his armor, but exchanged his crest and emblazonment, and bore instead a white unicorn upon a crimson field. He chose a trusty squire, and, commanding him not to address him as Rogero, rode on his quest. Having crossed the Rhine and the Austrian countries into Hungary, he followed the course of the Danube till he reached Belgrade. There he saw the imperial ensigns spread, and white pavilions, thronged with troops, before the town. For the Emperor Constantine was laying siege to the city to recover it from the Bulgarians, who had taken it from him not long before.

A river flowed between the camp of the Emperor and the Bulgarians, and at the moment when Rogero approached, a skirmish had begun between the parties from either camp, who had approached the stream for the purpose of watering. The Greeks in that affray were four to one, and drove back the Bulgarians in precipitate rout. Rogero, seeing this, and animated only by his hatred of the Grecian prince, dashed into the middle of the flying mass, calling aloud on the fugitives to turn. He encountered first a leader of the Grecian host in splendid armor, a nephew of the Emperor, as dear to him as a son. Rogero's lance pierced shield and armor, and stretched the warrior breathless on the plain. Another and another fell before him, and astonishment and terror arrested the advance of the Greeks, while the Bulgarians, catching courage from the cavalier, rally, change front, and chase the Grecian troops, who fly in their turn. Leo, the prince, was at a distance when this sudden skirmish rose, but not so far but that he could see distinctly, from an elevated position which he held, how the changed battle was all the work of one man, and could not choose but admire the bravery and prowess with which it was done. He knew by the blazonry displayed that the champion was not of the Bulgarian army, though he furnished aid to them. Although he suffered by his valor, the prince could not wish him ill, for his admiration surpassed his resentment. By this time the Greeks had regained the river, and crossing it by fording or swimming, some made their escape, leaving many more prisoners in the hands of the Bulgarians. Rogero, learning from some of the captives that Leo was at a point some distance down the river, rode thither with a view to meet him, but arrived not before the Greek prince had retired beyond the stream, and broken up the bridge. Day was spent, and Rogero, wearied, looked round for a shelter for the night. He found it in a cottage, where he soon yielded himself to repose. It so happened, a knight who had narrowly escaped Rogero's sword in the late battle also found shelter in the same cottage, and, recognizing the armor of the unknown knight, easily found means of securing him as he slept, and next morning carried him in chains and delivered him to the Emperor. By him he was in turn delivered to his sister Theodora, mother of the young knight, the first victim of Rogero's spear. By her he was cast into a dungeon, till her ingenuity could devise a death sufficiently painful to satiate her revenge.

Bradamante, meanwhile, to escape her father's and mother's importunity, had begged a boon of Charlemagne, which the monarch pledged his royal word to grant; it was that she should not be compelled to marry any one unless he should first vanquish her in single combat. The Emperor therefore proclaimed a tournament in these words: "He that would wed Duke Aymon's daughter must contend with the sword against that dame, from the sun's rise to his setting; and if, in that time, he is not overcome the lady shall be his."

Duke Aymon and the Lady Beatrice, though much incensed at the course things had taken, brought their daughter to court, to await the day appointed for the tournament. Bradamante, not finding there him whom her heart required, distressed herself with doubts what could be the cause of his absence. Of all fancies, the most painful one was that he had gone away to learn to forget her, knowing her father's and her mother's opposition to their union, and despairing to contend against them. But oh, how much worse would be the maiden's woe, if it were known to her what her betrothed was then enduring!

He was plunged in a dungeon where no ray of daylight ever penetrated, loaded with chains, and scantily supplied with the coarsest food. No wonder despair took possession of his heart, and he longed for death as a relief, when one night (or one day, for both were equally dark to him) he was roused with the glare of a torch and saw two men enter his cell. It was the Prince Leo, with an attendant, who had come as soon as he had learned the wretched fate of the brave knight whose valor he had seen and admired on the field of battle. "Cavalier," said he, "I am one whom thy valor hath so bound to thee, that I willingly peril my own safety to lend thee aid." "Infinite thanks I owe you," replied Rogero, "and the life you give me I promise faithfully to render back upon your call, and promptly to stake it at all times for your service." The prince then told Rogero his name and rank, at hearing which a tide of contending emotions almost overwhelmed Rogero. He was set at liberty, and had his horse and arms restored to him.

Meanwhile, tidings arrived of King Charles' decree that whoever aspired to the hand of Bradamante must first encounter her with sword and lance. This news made the Grecian prince turn pale, for he knew he was no match for her in fight. Communing with himself, he sees how he may make his wit supply the place of valor, and employ the French knight, whose name was still unknown to him, to fight the battle for him. Rogero heard the proposal with extreme distress; yet it seemed worse than death to deny the first request of one to whom he owed his life. Hastily he gave his assent "to do in all things that which Leo should command." Afterward, bitter repentance came over him; yet, rather than confess his change of mind, death itself would be welcome. Death seems his only remedy; but how to die? Sometimes he thinks to make none but a feigned resistance, and allow her sword a ready access, for never can death come more happily than if her hand guide the weapon. Yet this will not avail, for, unless he wins the maid for the Greek prince, his debt remains unpaid. He had promised to maintain a real, not a feigned encounter. He will then keep his word, and banish every thought from his bosom except that which moved him to maintain his truth.

The young prince, richly attended, set out, and with him Rogero. They arrived at Paris, but Leo preferred not to enter the city, and pitched his tents without the walls, making known his arrival to Charlemagne by an embassy. The monarch was pleased, and testified his courtesy by visits and gifts. The prince set forth the purpose of his coming, and prayed the Emperor to dispatch his suit—"to send forth the damsel who refused ever to take in wedlock any lord inferior to herself in fight; for she should be his bride, or he would perish beneath her sword."

Rogero passed the night before the day assigned for the battle like that which the felon spends, condemned to pay the forfeit of his life on the ensuing day. He chose to fight with sword only, and on foot, for he would not let her see Frontino, knowing that she would recognize the steed. Nor would he use Balisarda, for against that enchanted blade all armor would be of no avail, and the sword that he did take he hammered well upon the edge to abate its sharpness. He wore the surcoat of Prince Leo, and his shield, emblazoned with a golden, double-headed eagle. The prince took care to let himself be seen by none.

Bradamante, meanwhile, prepared herself for the combat far differently. Instead of blunting the edge of her falchion she whets the steel, and would fain infuse into it her own acerbity. As the moment approached she seemed to have fire within her veins, and waited impatiently for the trumpet's sound. At the signal she drew her sword, and fell with fury upon her Rogero. But as a well- built wall or aged rock stands unmoved the fury of the storm, so Rogero, clad in those arms which Trojan Hector once wore, withstood the strokes which stormed about his head and breast and flank. Sparks flew from his shield, his helm, his cuirass; from direct and back strokes, aimed now high, now low, falling thick and fast, like hailstones on a cottage roof; but Rogero, with skilful ward, turns them aside, or receives them where his armor is a sure protection, careful only to protect himself, and with no thought of striking in return. Thus the hours passed away, and, as the sun approached the west, the damsel began to despair. But so much the more her anger increases, and she redoubles her efforts, like the craftsman who sees his work unfinished while the day is wellnigh spent. O miserable damsel! didst thou know whom thou wouldst kill,—if, in that cavalier matched against thee thou didst but know Rogero, on whom thy very life-threads hang, rather than kill him thou wouldst kill thyself, for he is dearer to thee than life.

King Charles and the peers, who thought the cavalier to be the Grecian prince, viewing such force and skill exhibited, and how without assaulting her the knight defended himself, were filled with admiration, and declared the champions well matched, and worthy of each other.

When the sun was set Charlemagne gave the signal for terminating the contest, and Bradamante was awarded to Prince Leo as a bride. Rogero, in deep distress, returned to his tent. There Leo unlaced his helmet, and kissed him on both cheeks. "Henceforth," said he, "do with me as you please, for you cannot exhaust my gratitude." Rogero replied little, laid aside the ensigns he had worn, and resumed the unicorn, then hasted to withdraw himself from all eyes. When it was midnight he rose, saddled Frontino, and sallied from his tent, taking that direction which pleased his steed. All night he rode absorbed in bitter woe, and called on Death as alone capable of relieving his sufferings. At last he entered a forest, and penetrated into its deepest recesses. There he unharnessed Frontino, and suffered him to wander where he would. Then he threw himself down on the ground, and poured forth such bitter wailings that the birds and beasts, for none else heard him, were moved to pity with his cries.

Not less was the distress of the lady Bradamante, who, rather than wed any one but Rogero, resolved to break her word, and defy kindred, court, and Charlemagne himself; and, if nothing else would do, to die. But relief came from an unexpected quarter. Marphisa, sister of Rogero, was a heroine of warlike prowess equal to Bradamante. She had been the confidante of their loves, and felt hardly less distress than themselves at seeing the perils which threatened their union. "They are already united by mutual vows," she said, "and in the sight of Heaven what more is necessary?" Full of this thought she presented herself before Charlemagne, and declared that she herself was witness that the maiden had spoken to Rogero those words which they who marry swear; and that the compact was so sealed between the pair that they were no longer free, nor could forsake the one the other to take another spouse. This her assertion she offered to prove, in single combat, against Prince Leo, or any one else.

Charlemagne, sadly perplexed at this, commanded Bradamante to be called, and told her what the bold Marphisa had declared. Bradamante neither denied nor confirmed the statement, but hung her head, and kept silence. Duke Aymon was enraged, and would fain have set aside the pretended contract on the ground that, if made at all, it must have been made before Rogero was baptized, and therefore void. But not so thought Rinaldo, nor the good Orlando, and Charlemagne knew not which way to decide, when Marphisa spoke thus:

"Since no one else can marry the maiden while my brother lives, let the prince meet Rogero in mortal combat, and let him who survives take her for his bride."

This saying pleased the Emperor, and was accepted by the prince, for he thought that, by the aid of his unknown champion, he should surely triumph in the fight. Proclamation was therefore made for Rogero to appear and defend his suit; and Leo, on his part, caused search to be made on all sides for the knight of the Unicorn.

Meanwhile Rogero, overwhelmed with despair, lay stretched on the ground in the forest night and day without food, courting death. Here he was discovered by one of Leo's people, who, finding him resist all attempts to remove him, hastened to his master, who was not far off, and brought him to the spot. As he approached he heard words which convinced him that love was the cause of the knight's despair; but no clew was given to guide him to the object of that love. Stooping down, the prince embraced the weeping warrior, and, in the tenderest accents, said: "Spare not, I entreat you, to disclose the cause of your distress, for few such desperate evils betide mankind as are wholly past cure. It grieves me much that you would hide your grief from me, for I am bound to you by ties that nothing can undo. Tell me, then, your grief, and leave me to try if wealth, art, cunning, force, or persuasion cannot relieve you. If not, it will be time enough after all has been tried in vain to die."

He spoke in such moving accents that Rogero could not choose but yield. It was some time before he could command utterance; at last he said, "My lord, when you shall know me for what I am, I doubt not you, like myself, will be content that I should die. Know, then, I am that Rogero whom you have so much cause to hate, and who so hated you that, intent on putting you to death, he went to seek you at your father's court. This I did because I could not submit to see my promised bride borne off by you. But, as man proposes and God disposes, your great courtesy, well tried in time of sore need, so moved my fixed resolve, that I not only laid aside the hate I bore, but purposed to be your friend forever. You then asked of me to win for you the lady Bradamante, which was all one as to demand of me my heart and soul. You know whether I served you faithfully or not. Yours is the lady; possess her in peace; but ask me not to live to see it. Be content rather that I die; for vows have passed between myself and her which forbid that while I live she can lawfully wive with another."

So filled was gentle Leo with astonishment at these words that for a while he stood silent, with lips unmoved and steadfast gaze, like a statue. And the discovery that the stranger was Rogero not only abated not the good will he bore him, but increased it, so that his distress for what Rogero suffered seemed equal to his own. For this, and because he would appear deservedly an Emperor's son, and, though in other things outdone, would not be surpassed in courtesy, he says: "Rogero, had I known that day when your matchless valor routed my troops that you were Rogero, your virtue would have made me your own, as then it made me while I knew not my foe, and I should have no less gladly rescued you from Theodora's dungeon. And if I would willingly have done so then, how much more gladly will I now restore the gift of which you would rob yourself to confer it upon me. The damsel is more due to you than to me, and though I know her worth, I would forego not only her, but life itself, rather than distress a knight like you."

This and much more he said to the same intent; till at last Rogero replied, "I yield, and am content to live, and thus a second time owe my life to you."

Figure 123: Untitled from Orlando Furioso by Gustave Dore

But several days elapsed before Rogero was so far restored as to return to the royal residence, where an embassy had arrived from the Bulgarian princes to seek the knight of the unicorn, and tender to him the crown of that country, in place of their king, fallen in battle.

Thus were things situated when Prince Leo, leading by the hand Rogero, clad in the battered armor in which he had sustained the conflict with Bradamante, presented himself before the king. "Behold," he said "the champion who maintained from dawn to setting sun the arduous contest; he comes to claim the guerdon of the fight." King Charlemagne, with all his peerage, stood amazed; for all believed that the Grecian prince himself had fought with Bradamante. Then stepped forth Marphisa, and said, "Since Rogero is not here to assert his rights, I, his sister, undertake his cause, and will maintain it against whoever shall dare dispute his claim." She said this with so much anger and disdain that the prince deemed it no longer wise to feign, and withdrew Rogero's helmet from his brow, saying, "Behold him here!" Who can describe the astonishment and joy of Marphisa! She ran and threw her arms about her brother's neck, nor would give way to let

Charlemagne and Rinaldo, Orlando, Dudon, and the rest, who crowded round, embrace him, and press friendly kisses on his brow. The joyful tidings flew fast by many a messenger to Bradamante, who in her secret chamber lay lamenting. The blood that stagnated about her heart flowed at that notice so fast, that she had wellnigh died for joy. Duke Aymon and the Lady Beatrice no longer withheld their consent, and pledged their daughter to the brave Rogero before all that gallant company.

Now came the Bulgarian ambassadors, and, kneeling at the feet of Rogero, besought him to return with them to their country, where, in Adrianople, the crown and sceptre were awaiting his acceptance. Prince Leo united his persuasions to theirs, and promised, in his royal father's name, that peace should be restored on their part. Rogero gave his consent, and it was surmised that none of the virtues which shone so conspicuously in him so availed to recommend Rogero to the Lady Beatrice as the hearing her future son-in-law saluted as a sovereign prince.

THE BATTLE OF RONCESVALLES

After the expulsion of the Saracens from France Charlemagne led his army into Spain, to punish Marsilius, the king of that country, for having sided with the African Saracens in the late war. Charlemagne succeeded in all his attempts, and compelled Marsilius to submit, and pay tribute to France. Our readers will remember Gano, otherwise called Gan, or Ganelon, whom we mentioned in one of our early chapters as an old courtier of Charlemagne, and a deadly enemy of Orlando, Rinaldo, and all their friends. He had great influence over Charles, from equality of age and long intimacy; and he was not without good qualities: he was brave and sagacious, but envious, false, and treacherous. Gan prevailed on Charles to send him as ambassador to Marsilius, to arrange the tribute. He embraced Orlando over and over again at taking leave, using such pains to seem loving and sincere, that his hypocrisy was manifest to every one but the old monarch. He fastened with equal tenderness on Oliver, who smiled contemptuously in his face, and thought to himself, "You may make as many fair speeches as you choose, but you lie." All the other paladins who were present thought the same, and they said as much to the Emperor, adding that Gan should on no account be sent ambassador to the Spaniards. But Charles was infatuated.

Gan was received with great honor by Marsilius. The king, attended by his lords, came fifteen miles out of Saragossa to meet him, and then conducted him into the city with acclamations. There was nothing for several days but balls, games, and exhibitions of chivalry, the ladies throwing flowers on the heads of the French knights, and the people shouting, "France! Mountjoy and St. Denis!"

After the ceremonies of the first reception the king and the ambassador began to understand one another. One day they sat together in a garden on the border of a fountain. The water was so clear and smooth it reflected every object around, and the spot was encircled with fruit-trees which quivered with the fresh air. As they sat and talked, as if without restraint, Gan, without looking the king in the face, was enabled to see the expression of his countenance in the water, and governed his speech accordingly. Marsilius was equally adroit, and watched the face of Gan while he addressed him. Marsilius began by lamenting, not as to the ambassador, but as to the friend, the injuries which Charles had done him by invading his dominions, charging him with wishing to take his kingdom from him and give it to Orlando; till at length he plainly uttered his belief that if that ambitious paladin were but dead good men would get their rights.

Gan heaved a sigh, as if he was unwillingly compelled to allow the force of what the king said; but unable to contain himself long he lifted up his face, radiant with triumphant wickedness, and exclaimed: "Every word you utter is truth; die he must, and die also must Oliver, who struck me that foul blow at court. Is it treachery to punish affronts like these? I have planned everything,—I have settled everything already with their besotted master. Orlando will come to your borders—to Roncesvalles—for the purpose of receiving the tribute. Charles will await him at the foot of the mountains. Orlando will bring but a small band with him: you, when you meet him, will have secretly your whole army at your back. You surround him, and who receives tribute then?"

The new Judas had scarcely uttered these words when his exultation was interrupted by a change in the face of nature. The sky was suddenly overcast, there was thunder and lightning, a laurel was split in two from head to foot, and the Carob-tree under which Gan was sitting, which is said to be the species of tree on which Judas Iscariot hung himself, dropped one of its pods on his head.

Marsilius, as well as Gan, was appalled at this omen; but on assembling his soothsayers they came to the conclusion that the laurel-tree turned the omen against the Emperor, the successor of the Caesars, though one of them renewed the consternation of Gan by saying that he did not understand the meaning of the tree of Judas, and intimating that perhaps the ambassador could explain it. Gan relieved his vexation by anger; the habit of wickedness prevailed over all other considerations; and the king prepared to march to Roncesvalles at the head of all his forces.

Gan wrote to Charlemagne to say how humbly and submissively Marsilius was coming to pay the tribute into the hands of Orlando, and how handsome it would be of the Emperor to meet him half-way, and so be ready to receive him after the payment at his camp. He added a brilliant account of the tribute, and the accompanying presents. The good Emperor wrote in turn to say how pleased he was with the ambassador's diligence, and that matters were arranged precisely as he wished. His court, however, had its suspicion still, though they little thought Gan's object in bringing Charles into the neighborhood of Roncesvalles was to deliver him into the hands of Marsilius, after Orlando should have been destroyed by him.

Orlando, however, did as his lord and sovereign desired. He went to Roncesvalles, accompanied by a moderate train of warriors, not dreaming of the atrocity that awaited him. Gan, meanwhile, had hastened back to France, in order to show himself free and easy in the presence of Charles, and secure the success of his plot; while Marsilius, to make assurance doubly sure, brought into the passes of Roncesvalles no less than three armies, which were successively to fall on the paladin in case of the worst, and so extinguish him with numbers. He had also, by Gan's advice, brought heaps of wine and good cheer to be set before his victims in the first instance; "for that," said the traitor, "will render the onset the more effective, the feasters being unarmed. One thing, however, I must not forget," added he; "my son Baldwin is sure to be with Orlando; you must take care of his life for my sake."

"I give him this vesture off my own body," said the king; "let him wear it in the battle, and have no fear. My soldiers shall be directed not to touch him."

Gan went away rejoicing to France. He embraced the sovereign and the court all round with the air of a man who had brought them nothing but blessings, and the old king wept for very tenderness and delight.

"Something is going on wrong, and looks very black," thought Malagigi, the good wizard; "Rinaldo is not here, and it is indispensably necessary that he should be. I must find out where he is, and Ricciardetto too, and send for them with all speed."

Malagigi called up by his art a wise, terrible, and cruel spirit, named Ashtaroth. "Tell me, and tell me truly, of Rinaldo," said Malagigi to the spirit. The demon looked hard at the paladin, and said nothing. His aspect was clouded and violent.

The enchanter, with an aspect still cloudier, bade Ashtaroth lay down that look, and made signs as if he would resort to angrier compulsion; and the devil, alarmed, loosened his tongue, and said, "You have not told me what you desire to know of Rinaldo."

"I desire to know what he has been doing, and where he is."

"He has been conquering and baptizing the world, east and west," said the demon, "and is now in Egypt with Ricciardetto."

"And what has Gan been plotting with Marsilius?" inquired
Malagigi; "and what is to come of it?"

"I know not," said the devil. "I was not attending to Gan at the time, and we fallen spirits know not the future. All I discern is that by the signs and comets in the heavens something dreadful is about to happen—something very strange, treacherous, and bloody; and that Gan has a seat ready prepared for him in hell."

"Within three days," cried the enchanter, loudly, "bring Rinaldo and Ricciardetto into the pass of Ronces-Valles. Do it, and I hereby undertake to summon thee no more."

"Suppose they will not trust themselves with me?" said the spirit.

"Enter Rinaldo's horse, and bring him, whether he trust thee or not."

"It shall be done," returned the demon.

There was an earthquake, and Ashtaroth disappeared.

Marsilius now made his first movement towards the destruction of Orlando, by sending before him his vassal, King Blanchardin, with his presents of wines and other luxuries. The temperate but courteous hero took them in good part, and distributed them as the traitor wished; and then Blanchardin, on pretence of going forward to salute Charlemagne, returned, and put himself at the head of the second army, which was the post assigned him by his liege- lord. King Falseron, whose son Orlando had slain in battle, headed the first army, and King Balugante the third. Marsilius made a speech to them, in which he let them into his design, and concluded by recommending to their good will the son of his friend Gan, whom they would know by the vest he had sent him, and who was the only soul amongst the Christian they were to spare.

This son of Gan, meanwhile, and several of the paladins, who distrusted the misbelievers, and were anxious at all events to be with Orlando, had joined the hero in the fatal valley; so that the little Christian host, considering the tremendous valor of their lord and his friends, were not to be sold for nothing. Rinaldo, alas! the second thunderbolt of Christendom, was destined not to be there in time to meet the issue. The paladins in vain begged Orlando to be on his guard against treachery, and send for a more numerous body of men. The great heart of the Champion of the Faith was unwilling to harbor suspicion as long as he could help it. He refused to summon aid which might be superfluous; neither would he do anything but what his liege-lord had directed. And yet he could not wholly repress a misgiving. A shadow had fallen on his heart, great and cheerful as it was. The anticipations of his friends disturbed him, in spite of the face with which he met them. Perhaps by a certain foresight he felt his death approaching; but he felt bound not to encourage the impression. Besides, time pressed; the moment of the looked-for tribute was at hand, and little combinations of circumstances determine often the greatest events.

King Marsilius was to arrive early next day with the tribute, and Oliver, with the morning sun, rode forth to reconnoitre, and see if he could discover the peaceful pomp of the Spanish court in the distance. He rode up the nearest height, and from the top of it beheld the first army of Marsilius already forming in the passes. "O devil Gan," he exclaimed, "this then is the consummation of thy labors!" Oliver put spurs to his horse, and galloped back down the mountain to Orlando.

"Well," cried the hero, "what news?"

"Bad news," said his cousin, "such as you would not hear of yesterday. Marsilius is here in arms, and all the world is with him."

The paladins pressed round Orlando, and entreated him to sound his horn, in token that he needed help. His only answer was to mount his horse, and ride up the mountain with Sansonetto.

As soon, however, as he cast forth his eyes, and beheld what was round about him, he turned in sorrow, and looked down into Roncesvalles, and said, "O miserable valley! the blood shed in thee this day will color thy name forever."

Orlando's little camp were furious against the Saracens. They armed themselves with the greatest impatience. There was nothing but lacing of helmets and mounting of horses, while good Archbishop Turpin went from rank to rank exhorting and encouraging the warriors of Christ. Orlando and his captains withdrew for a moment to consultation. He fairly groaned for sorrow, and at first had not a word to say, so wretched he felt at having brought his people to die in Roncesvalles. Then he said: "If it had entered into my heart to conceive the king of Spain to be such a villain never would you have seen this day. He has exchanged with me a thousand courtesies and good words; and I thought that the worse enemies we had been before, the better friends we had become now. I fancied every human being capable of this kind of virtue on a good opportunity, saving, indeed, such base-hearted wretches as can never forgive their very forgivers; and of these I did not suppose him to be one. Let us die, if die we must, like honest and gallant men, so that it shall be said of us it was only our bodies that died. The reason why I did not sound the horn was partly because I thought it did not become us, and partly because our liege lord could hardly save us, even if he heard it." And with these words Orlando sprang to his horse, crying, "Aways against the Saracens!" But he had no sooner turned his face than he wept bitterly, and said, "O Holy Virgin, think not of me, the sinner Orlando, but have pity on these thy servants!"

And now with a mighty dust, and an infinite sound of horns and tambours, which came filling the valley, the first army of the infidels made its appearance, horses neighing, and a thousand pennons flying in the air. King Falseron led them on, saying to his officers: "Let nobody dare to lay a finger on Orlando. He belongs to myself. The revenge of my son's death is mine. I will cut the man down that comes between us." "Now, friends," said Orlando, "every man for himself, and St. Michael for us all! There is not one here that is not a perfect knight." And he might well say it, for the flower of all France was there, except Rinaldo and Ricciardetto—every man a picked man, all friends and constant companions of Orlando.

So the captains of the little troop and of the great army sat looking at one another, and singling one another out as the latter came on, and then the knights put spear in rest, and ran for a while two and two in succession, one against the other.

Astolpho was the first to move. He ran against Arlotto of Sorio, and thrust his antagonist's body out of the saddle, and his soul into the other world. Oliver encountered Malprimo, and, though he received a thrust which hurt him, sent his lance right through the heart of Malprimo.

Falseron was daunted at this blow. "Truly," thought he, "this is a marvel." Oliver did not press on among the Saracens, his wound was too painful; but Orlando now put himself and his whole band in motion, and you may guess what an uproar ensued. The sound of the rattling of blows and helmets was as if the forge of Vulcan had been thrown open. Falseron beheld Orlando coming so furiously, that he thought him a Lucifer who had burst his chain, and was quite of another mind than when he purposed to have him all to himself. On the contrary, he recommended himself to his gods, and turned away, meaning to wait for a more auspicious season of revenge. But Orlando hailed him with a terrible voice, saying, "O thou traitor! was this the end to which old quarrels were made up?" Then he dashed at Falseron with a fury so swift, and at the same time with a mastery of his lance so marvellous, that, though he plunged it in the man's body so as instantly to kill him, and then withdrew it, the body did not move in the saddle. The hero himself, as he rushed onwards, was fain to see the end of a stroke so perfect, and turning his horse back, touched the carcass with his sword, and it fell on the instant!

When the infidels beheld their leader dead such fear fell upon them that they were for leaving the field to the paladins, but they were unable. Marsilius had drawn the rest of his forces round the valley like a net, so that their shoulders were turned in vain. Orlando rode into the thick of them, and wherever he went thunderbolts fell upon helmets. Oliver was again in the fray, with Walter and Baldwin, Avino and Avolio, while Arch-bishop Turpin had changed his crosier for a lance, and chased a new flock before him to the mountains.

Yet what could be done against foes without number? Marsilius constantly pours them in. The paladins are as units to thousands. Why tarry the horses of Rinaldo and Ricciardetto?

The horses did not tarry, but fate had been quicker than enchantment. Ashtaroth had presented himself to Rinaldo in Egypt, and, after telling his errand, he and Foul-mouth, his servant, entered the horses of Rinaldo and Ricciardetto, which began to neigh, and snort, and leap with the fiends within them, till off they flew through the air over the pyramids and across the desert, and reached Spain and the scene of action just as Marsilius brought up his third army. The two paladins on their horses dropped right into the midst of the Saracens, and began making such havoc among them that Marsilius, who overlooked the fight from a mountain, thought his soldiers had turned against one another. Orlando beheld it, and guessed it could be no other but his cousins, and pressed to meet them. Oliver coming up at the same moment, the rapture of the whole party is not to be expressed. After a few hasty words of explanation they were forced to turn again upon the enemy, whose numbers seemed perfectly without limit.

Orlando, making a bloody passage towards Marsilius, struck a youth on the head, whose helmet was so strong as to resist the blow, but at the same time flew off, Orlando prepared to strike a second blow, when the youth exclaimed, "Hold! you loved my father; I am Bujaforte!" The paladin had never seen Bujaforte, but he saw the likeness to the good old man, his father, and he dropped his sword. "O Bujaforte," said he, "I loved him indeed; but what does his son do here fighting against his friends?"

Bujaforte could not at once speak for weeping. At length he said: "I am forced to be here by my lord and master, Marsilius; and I have made a show of fighting, but have not hurt a single Christian. Treachery is on every side of you. Baldwin himself has a vest given him by Marsilius, that everybody may know the son of his friend Gan, and do him no harm."

"Put your helmet on again," said Orlando, "and behave just as you have done. Never will your father's friend be an enemy to the son."

The hero then turned in fury to look for Baldwin, who was hastening towards him at that moment, with friendliness in his looks.

"'Tis strange," said Baldwin, "I have done my duty as well as I could, yet nobody will come against me. I have slain right and left, and cannot comprehend what it is that makes the stoutest infidels avoid me."

"Take off your vest," said Orlando, contemptuously, "and you will soon discover the secret, if you wish to know it. Your father has sold us to Marsilius, all but his honorable son."

"If my father," said Baldwin, impetuously tearing off the vest, "has been such a villain, and I escape dying, I will plunge this sword through his heart. But I am no traitor, Orlando, and you do me wrong to say it. Think not I can live with dishonor."

Baldwin spurred off into the fight, not waiting to hear another word from Orlando, who was very sorry for what he had said, for he perceived that the youth was in despair.

And now the fight raged beyond all it had done before; twenty pagans went down for one paladin, but still the paladins fell. Sansonetto was beaten to earth by the club of Grandonio, Walter d'Amulion had his shoulder broken, Berlinghieri and Ottone were slain, and at last Astolpho fell, in revenge of whose death Orlando turned the spot where he died into a lake of Saracen blood. The luckless Bujaforte met Rinaldo, and before he could explain how he seemed to be fighting on the Saracen side received such a blow upon the head that he fell, unable to utter a word. Orlando, cutting his way to a spot where there was a great struggle and uproar, found the poor youth Baldwin, the son of Gan, with two spears in his breast. "I am no traitor now," said Baldwin, and those were the last words he said. Orlando was bitterly sorry to have been the cause of his death, and tears streamed from his eyes. At length down went Oliver himself. He had become blinded with his own blood, and smitten Orlando without knowing him. "How now, cousin," cried Orlando, "have you too gone over to the enemy?" "O my lord and master," cried the other, "I ask your pardon. I can see nothing; I am dying. Some traitor has stabbed me in the back. If you love me, lead my horse into the thick of them, so that I may not die unavenged."

"I shall die myself before long," said Orlando, "out of very toil and grief; so we will go together."

Orlando led his cousin's horse where the press was thickest, and dreadful was the strength of the dying man and his tired companion. They made a street through which they passed out of the battle, and Orlando led his cousin away to his tent, and said, "Wait a little till I return, for I will go and sound the horn on the hill yonder."

"'Tis of no use," said Oliver, "my spirit is fast going and desires to be with its Lord and Saviour."

He would have said more, but his words came from him imperfectly, like those of a man in a dream, and so he expired.

When Orlando saw him dead he felt as if he was alone on the earth, and he was quite willing to leave it, only he wished that King Charles, at the foot of the mountains, should know how the case stood before he went. So he took up the horn and blew it three times, with such force that the blood burst out of his nose and mouth. Turpin says that at the third blast the horn broke in two.

In spite of all the noise of the battle, the sound of the horn broke over it like a voice out of the other world. They say that birds fell dead at it, and that the whole Saracen army drew back in terror. Charlemagne was sitting in the midst of his court when the sound reached him, and Gan was there. The Emperor was the first to hear it.

"Do you hear that?" said he to his nobles. "Did you hear the horn as I heard it?"

Upon this they all listened, and Gan felt his heart misgive him. The horn sounded a second time.

"What is the meaning of this?" said Charles.

"Orlando is hunting," observed Gan, "and the stag is killed."

But when the horn sounded yet a third time, and the blast was one of so dreadful a vehemence, everybody looked at the other, and then they all looked at Gan in a fury. Charles rose from his seat.

"This is no hunting of the stag," said he. "The sound goes to my very heart. O Gan! O Gan! Not for thee do I blush, but for myself. O foul and monstrous villain! Take him, gentleman, and keep him in close prison. Would to God I had not lived to see this day!"

But it was no time for words. They put the traitor in prison and then Charles, with all his court, took his way to Roncesvalles, grieving and praying.

It was afternoon when the horn sounded, and half an hour after it when the Emperor set out; and meantime Orlando had returned to the fight that he might do his duty, however hopeless, as long as he could sit his horse. At length he found his end approaching, for toil and fever, and rode all alone to a fountain where he had before quenched his thirst. His horse was wearier than he, and no sooner had his master alighted than the beast, kneeling down as if to take leave, and to say, "I have brought you to a place of rest," fell dead at his feet. Orlando cast water on him from the fountain, not wishing to believe him dead; but when he found it to no purpose, he grieved for him as if he had been a human being, and addressed him by name with tears, and asked forgiveness if he had ever done him wrong. They say that the horse, at these words, opened his eyes a little, and looked kindly at his master, and then stirred never more. They say also that Orlando then summoning all his strength, smote a rock near him with his beautiful sword Durindana, thinking to shiver the steel in pieces, and so prevent its falling into the hands of the enemy, but though the rock split like a slate, and a great cleft remained ever after to astonish the eyes of pilgrims, the sword remained uninjured.

And now Rinaldo and Ricciardetto came up, with Turpin, having driven back the Saracens, and told Orlando that the battle was won. Then Orlando knelt before Turpin and begged remission of his sins, and Turpin gave him absolution. Orlando fixed his eyes on the hilt of his sword as on a crucifix, and embraced it, and he raised his eyes and appeared like a creature seraphical and transfigured, and bowing his head, he breathed out his pure soul.

And now King Charles and his nobles came up. The Emperor, at sight of the dead Orlando, threw himself, as if he had been a reckless youth, from his horse, and embraced and kissed the body, and said: "I bless thee, Orlando; I bless thy whole life, and all that thou wast, and all that thou ever didst, and the father that begat thee; and I ask pardon of thee for believing those who brought thee to thine end. They shall have their reward, O thou beloved one! But indeed it is thou that livest, and I who am worse than dead."

Horrible to the Emperor's eyes was the sight of the field of Roncesvalles. The Saracens indeed had fled, conquered; but all his paladins but two were left on it dead, and the whole valley looked like a great slaughter-house, trampled into blood and dirt, and reeking to the heat. Charles trembled to his heart's core for wonder and agony. After gazing dumbly on the place he cursed it with a solemn curse, and wished that never grass might grow in it again, nor seed of any kind, neither within it nor on any of its mountains around, but the anger of Heaven abide over it forever.

Charles and his warriors went after the Saracens into Spain. They took and fired Saragossa, and Marsilius was hung to the carob-tree under which he had planned his villainy with Gan; and Gan was hung and drawn and quartered in Roncesvalles, amidst the execrations of the country.

RINALDO AND BAYARD

CHARLEMAGNE was overwhelmed with grief at the loss of so many of his bravest warriors at the disaster of Roncesvalles, and bitterly reproached himself for his credulity in resigning himself so completely to the counsels of the treacherous Count Gan. Yet he soon fell into a similar snare when he suffered his unworthy son, Charlot, to acquire such an influence over him, that he constantly led him into acts of cruelty and injustice that in his right mind he would have scorned to commit. Rinaldo and his brothers, for some slight offence to the imperious young prince, were forced to fly from Paris, and to take shelter in their castle of Montalban; for Charles had publicly said, if he could take them he would hang them all. He sent numbers of his bravest knights to arrest them, but all without success. Either Rinaldo foiled their efforts and sent them back, stripped of their armor and of their glory, or, after meeting and conferring with him, they came back and told the king they could not be his instruments for such a work.

At last Charles himself raised a great army, and went in person to compel the paladin to submit. He ravaged all the country round about Montalban, so that supplies of food should be cut off, and he threatened death to any who should attempt to issue forth, hoping to compel the garrison to submit for want of food.

Rinaldo's resources had been brought so low that it seemed useless to contend any longer. His brothers had been taken prisoners in a skirmish, and his only hope of saving their lives was in making terms with the king.

So he sent a messenger, offering to yield himself and his castle if the king would spare his and his brothers' lives. While the messenger was gone Rinaldo, impatient to learn what tidings he might bring, rode out to meet him. When he had ridden as far as he thought prudent he stopped in a wood, and alighting, tied Bayard to a tree. Then he sat down, and, as he waited, he fell asleep. Bayard meanwhile got loose, and strayed away where the grass tempted him. Just then came along some country people, who said to one another, "Look, is not that the great horse Bayard that Rinaldo rides? Let us take him, and carry him to King Charles, who will pay us well for our trouble." They did so, and the king was delighted with his prize, and gave them a present that made them rich to their dying day.

When Rinaldo woke he looked round for his horse, and, finding him not, he groaned, and said, "O unlucky hour that I was born! how fortune persecutes me!" So desperate was he that he took off his armor and his spurs, saying, "What need have I of these, since Bayard is lost?" While he stood thus lamenting, a man came from the thicket, seemingly bent with age. He had a long beard hanging over his breast, and eyebrows that almost covered his eyes. He bade Rinaldo good day. Rinaldo thanked him, and said, "A good day I have hardly had since I was born." Then said the old man, "Signor Rinaldo, you must not despair, for God will make all things turn to the best." Rinaldo answered, "My trouble is too heavy for me to hope relief. The king has taken my brothers, and means to put them to death. I thought to rescue them by means of my horse Bayard, but while I slept some thief has stolen him." The old man replied, "I will remember you and your brothers in my prayers. I am a poor man, have you not something to give me?" Rinaldo said, "I have nothing to give," but then he recollected his spurs. He gave them to the beggar, and said, "Here, take my spurs. They are the first present my mother gave me when my father, Count Aymon, dubbed me knight. They ought to bring you ten pounds."

The old man took the spurs, and put them into his sack, and said, "Noble sir, have you nothing else you can give me?" Rinaldo replied, "Are you making sport of me? I tell you truly if it were not for shame to beat one so helpless, I would teach you better manners." The old man said, "Of a truth, sir, if you did so you would do a great sin. If all had beaten me of whom I have begged I should have been killed long ago, for I ask alms in churches and convents, and wherever I can." "You say true," replied Rinaldo, "if you did not ask, none would relieve you." The old man said, "True, noble sir, therefore I pray if you have anything more to spare, give it me." Rinaldo gave him his mantle, and said, "Take it, pilgrim. I give it you for the love of Christ, that God would save my brothers from a shameful death, and help me to escape out of King Charles's power."

The pilgrim took the mantle, folded it up, and put it into his bag. Then a third time he said to Rinaldo, "Sir, have you nothing left to give me that I may remember you in my prayers?" "Wretch!" exclaimed Rinaldo, "do you make me your sport?" and he drew his sword, and struck at him; but the old man warded off the blow with his staff, and said, "Rinaldo, would you slay your cousin, Malagigi?" When Rinaldo heard that he stayed his hand, and gazed doubtingly on the old man, who now threw aside his disguise, and appeared to be indeed Malagigi. "Dear cousin," said Rinaldo, "pray forgive me. I did not know you. Next to God, my trust is in you. Help my brothers to escape out of prison, I entreat you. I have lost my horse, and therefore cannot render them any assistance." Malagigi answered, "Cousin Rinaldo, I will enable you to recover your horse. Meanwhile, you must do as I say."

Then Malagigi took from his sack a gown, and gave it to Rinaldo to put on over his armor, and a hat that was full of holes, and an old pair of shoes to put on. They looked like two pilgrims, very old and poor. Then they went forth from the wood, and after a little while saw four monks riding along the road. Malagigi said to Rinaldo, "I will go meet the monks, and see what news I can learn."

Malagigi learned from the monks that on the approaching festival there would be a great crowd of people at court, for the prince was going to show the ladies the famous horse Bayard that used to belong to Rinaldo. "What!" said the pilgrim; "is Bayard there?" "Yes," answered the monks; "the king has given him to Charlot, and, after the prince has ridden him the king means to pass sentence on the brothers of Rinaldo, and have them hanged." Then Malagigi asked alms of the monks, but they would give him none, till he threw aside his pilgrim garb, and let them see his armor, when, partly for charity and partly for terror, they gave him a golden cup, adorned with precious stones that sparkled in the sunshine.

Malagigi then hastened back to Rinaldo, and told him what he had learned.

The morning of the feast-day Rinaldo and Malagigi came to the place where the sports were to be held. Malagigi gave Rinaldo his spurs back again, and said, "Cousin, put on your spurs, for you will need them." "How shall I need them," said Rinaldo, "since I have lost my horse?" Yet he did as Malagigi directed him.

When the two had taken their stand on the border of the field among the crowd the princes and ladies of the court began to assemble. When they were all assembled the king came also, and Charlot with him, near whom the horse Bayard was led, in the charge of grooms, who were expressly enjoined to guard him safely. The king, looking round on the circle of spectators, saw Malagigi and Rinaldo, and observed the splendid cup that they had, and said to Charlot, "See, my son, what a brilliant cup those two pilgrims have got. It seems to be worth a hundred ducats." "That is true," said Charlot; "Let us go and ask where they got it." So they rode to the place where the pilgrims stood, and Charlot stopped Bayard close to them.

The horse snuffed at the pilgrims, knew Rinaldo, and caressed his master. The king said to Malagigi, "Friend, where did you get that beautiful cup?" Malagigi replied, "Honorable sir, I paid for it all the money I have saved from eleven years' begging in churches and convents. The Pope himself has blessed it, and given it the power that whosoever eats or drinks out of it shall be pardoned of all his sins." Then said the king to Charlot, "My son, these are right holy men; see how the dumb beast worships them."

Then the king said to Malagigi, "Give me a morsel from your cup, that I may be cleared of my sins." Malagigi answered, "Illustrious lord, I dare not do it, unless you will forgive all who have at any time offended you. You know that Christ forgave all those who had betrayed and crucified him." The king replied, "Friend, that is true; but Rinaldo has so grievously offended me, that I cannot forgive him, nor that other man, Malagigi, the magician. These two shall never live in my kingdom again. If I catch them I will certainly have them hanged. But tell me, pilgrim, who is that man who stands beside you?" "He is deaf, dumb, and blind," said Malagigi. Then the king said again, "Give me to drink of your cup, to take away my sins." Malagigi answered, "My lord king, here is my poor brother, who for fifty days has not heard, spoken, nor seen. This misfortune befell him in a house where we found shelter, and the day before yesterday we met with a wise woman, who told him the only hope of a cure for him was to come to some place where Bayard was to be ridden, and to mount and ride him; that would do him more good than anything else." Then said the king, "Friend, you have come to the right place, for Bayard is to be ridden here to-day. Give me a draught from your cup, and your companion shall ride upon Bayard." Malagigi, hearing these words, said, "Be it so." Then the king, with great devotion, took a spoon, and dipped a portion from the pilgrim's cup, believing that his sins should be thereby forgiven.

When this was done, the king said to Charlot, "Son, I request that you will let this sick pilgrim sit on your horse, and ride if he can, for by so doing he will be healed of all his infirmities." Charlot replied, "That will I gladly do." So saying, he dismounted, and the servants took the pilgrim in their arms, and helped him on the horse.

Wher Rinaldo was mounted, he put his feet in the stirrups, and said, "I would like to ride a little." Malagigi, hearing him speak, seemed delighted, and asked him whether he could see and hear also. "Yes," said Rinaldo, "I am healed of all my infirmities." When the king heard it he said to Bishop Turpin, "My lord bishop, we must celebrate this with a procession, with crosses and banners, for it is a great miracle."

When Rinaldo remarked that he was not carefully watched, he spoke to the horse, and touched him with the spurs. Bayard knew that his master was upon him, and he started off upon a rapid pace, and in a few moments was a good way off. Malagigi pretended to be in great alarm. "O noble king and master," he cried, "my poor companion is run away with; he will fall and break his neck." The king ordered his knights to ride after the pilgrim, and bring him back, or help him if need were. They did so, but it was in vain. Rinaldo left them all behind him, and kept on his way till he reached Montalban. Malagigi was suffered to depart, unsuspected, and he went his way, making sad lamentation for the fate of his comrade, who he pretended to think must surely be dashed to pieces.

Malagigi did not go far, but having changed his disguise, returned to where the king was, and employed his best art in getting the brothers of Rinaldo out of prison. He succeeded; and all three got safely to Montalban, where Rinaldo's joy at the rescue of his brothers and the recovery of Bayard was more than tongue can tell.

DEATH OF RINALDO

THE distress in Rinaldo's castle for want of food grew more severe every day, under the pressure of the siege. The garrison were forced to kill their horses, both to save the provision they would consume, and to make food of their flesh. At last all the horses were killed except Bayard, and Rinaldo said to his brothers, "Bayard must die, for we have nothing else to eat." So they went to the stable and brought out Bayard to kill him. But Alardo said, "Brother, let Bayard live a little longer; who knows what God may do for us?"

Bayard heard these words, and understood them as if he was a man, and fell on his knees, as if he would beg for mercy. When Rinaldo saw the distress of his horse his heart failed him, and he let him live.

Just at this time Aya, Rinaldo's mother, who was the sister of the Emperor, came to the camp, attended by knights and ladies, to intercede for her sons. She fell on her knees before the king, and besought him that he would pardon Rinaldo and his brothers: and all the peers and knights took her side, and entreated the king to grant her prayer. Then said the king, "Dear sister, you act the part of a good mother, and I respect your tender heart, and yield to your entreaties. I will spare your sons their lives if they submit implicitly to my will."

When Charlot heard this he approached the king and whispered in his ear. And the king turned to his sister and said, "Charlot must have Bayard, because I have given the horse to him. Now go, my sister, and tell Rinaldo what I have said."

When the Lady Aya heard these words she was delighted, thanked God in her heart, and said, "Worthy king and brother, I will do as you bid me." So she went into the castle, where her sons received her most joyfully and affectionately, and she told them the king's offer. Then Alardo said, "Brother, I would rather have the king's enmity than give Bayard to Charlot, for I believe he will kill him." Likewise said all the brothers. When Rinaldo heard them he said, "Dear brothers, if we may win our forgiveness by giving up the horse, so be it. Let us make our peace, for we cannot stand against the king's power." Then he went to his mother, and told her they would give the horse to Charlot, and more, too, if the king would pardon them, and forgive all that they had done against his crown and dignity. The lady returned to Charles and told him the answer of her sons.

When the peace was thus made between the king and the sons of Aymon, the brothers came forth from the castle, bringing Bayard with them, and, falling at the king's feet, begged his forgiveness. The king bade them rise, and received them into favor in the sight of all his noble knights and counsellors, to the great joy of all, especially of the Lady Aya, their mother. Then Rinaldo took the horse Bayard, gave him to Charlot, and said, "My lord and prince, this horse I give to you; do with him as to you seems good." Charlot took him, as had been agreed on. Then he made the servants take him to the bridge, and throw him into the water. Bayard sank to the bottom, but soon came to the surface again and swam, saw Rinaldo looking at him, came to land, ran to his old master, and stood by him as proudly as if he had understanding, and would say, "Why did you treat me so?" When the prince saw that he said, "Rinaldo, give me the horse again, for he must die." Rinaldo replied, "My lord and prince, he is yours without dispute," and gave him to him. The prince then had a millstone tied to each foot, and two to his neck, and made them throw him again into the water. Bayard struggled in the water, looked up to his master, threw off the stones, and came back to Rinaldo.

When Alardo saw that, he said, "Now must thou be disgraced forever, brother, if thou give up the horse again." But Rinaldo answered, "Brother, be still. Shall I for the horse's life provoke the anger of the king again?" Then Alardo said, "Ah, Bayard! what a return do we make for all thy true love and service!" Rinaldo gave the horse to the prince again, and said, "My lord, if the horse comes out again I cannot return him to you any more, for it wrings my heart too much." Then Chariot had Bayard loaded with the stones as before, and thrown into the water; and commanded Rinaldo that he should not stand where the horse would see him. When Bayard rose to the surface he stretched his neck out of the water and looked round for his master, but saw him not. Then he sunk to the bottom.

Rinaldo was so distressed for the loss of Bayard that he made a vow to ride no horse again all his life long, nor to bind a sword to his side, but to become a hermit. He resolved to betake himself to some wild wood, but first to return to his castle, to see his children, and to appoint to each his share of his estate.

So he took leave of the king and of his brothers, and returned to Montalban, and his brothers remained with the king. Rinaldo called his children to him, and he made his eldest born, Aymeric, a knight, and made him lord of his castle and of his land. He gave to the rest what other goods he had, and kissed and embraced them all, commended them to God, and then departed from them with a heavy heart.

He had not travelled far when he entered a wood, and there met with a hermit, who had long been retired from the world. Rinaldo greeted him, and the hermit replied courteously, and asked him who he was and what was his purpose. Rinaldo replied, "Sir, I have led a sinful life; many deeds of violence have I done, and many men have I slain, not always in a good cause, but often under the impulse of my own headstrong passions. I have also been the cause of the death of many of my friends, who took my part, not because they thought me in the right, but only for love of me. And now I come to make confession of all my sins, and to do penance for the rest of my life, if perhaps the mercy of God will forgive me." The hermit said, "Friend, I perceive you have fallen into great sins, and have broken the commandments of God, but his mercy is greater than your sins; and if you repent from your heart, and lead a new life, there is yet hope for you that he will forgive you what is past." So Rinaldo was comforted, and said, "Master, I will stay with you, and what you bid ane I will do." The hermit replied, "Roots and vegetables will be your food; shirt or shoes you may not wear; your lot must be poverty and want if you stay with me." Rinaldo replied, "I will cheerfully bear all this, and more." So he remained three whole years with the hermit, and after that his strength failed, and it seemed as if he was like to die.

One night the hermit had a dream, and heard a voice from heaven, which commanded him to say to his companion that he must without delay go to the Holy Land, and fight against the heathen. The hermit, when he heard that voice, was glad, and calling Rinaldo, he said, "Friend, God's angel has commanded me to say to you that you must without delay go to Jerusalem, and help our fellow- Christians in their struggle with the Infidels." Then said Rinaldo, "Ah! master, how can I do that? It is over three years since I made a vow no more to ride a horse, nor take a sword or spear in my hand." The hermit answered, "Dear friend, obey God, and do what the angel commanded." "I will do so," said Rinaldo, "and pray for me, my master, that God may guide me right." Then he departed, and went to the seaside, and took ship and came to Tripoli in Syria.

And as he went on his way his strength returned to him, till it was equal to what it was in his best days. And though he never mounted a horse, nor took a sword in his hand, yet with his pilgrim's staff he did good service in the armies of the Christians; and it pleased God that he escaped unhurt, though he was present in many battles, and his courage inspired the men with the same. At last a truce was made with the Saracens, and Rinaldo, now old and infirm, wishing to see his native land again before he died, took ship and sailed for France. When he arrived he shunned to go to the resorts of the great, and preferred to live among the humble folk, where he was unknown. He did country work, and lived on milk and bread, drank water, and was therewith content. While he so lived he heard that the city of Cologne was the holiest and best of cities, on account of the relics and bodies of saints who had there poured out their blood for the faith. This induced him to betake himself thither. When the pious hero arrived at Cologne he went to the monastery of St. Peter, and lived a holy life, occupied night and day in devotion. It so happened that at that time in the next town to Cologne there raged a dreadful pestilence. Many people came to Rinaldo, to beg him to pray for them, that the plague might be stayed. The holy man prayed fervently, and besought the Lord to take away the plague from the people, and his prayer was heard. The stroke of the pestilence was arrested, and all the people thanked the holy man and praised God.

Now there was at this time at Cologne a bishop, called Agilolphus, who was a wise and understanding man, who led a pure and secluded life, and set a good example to others. This bishop undertook to build the Church of St. Peter, and gave notice to all stonemasons and other workmen round about to come to Cologne, where they should find work and wages. Among others came Rinaldo; and he worked among the laborers and did more than four or five common workmen. When they went to dinner he brought stone and mortar so that they had enough for the whole day. When the others went to bed he stretched himself out on the stones. He ate bread only, and drank nothing but water; and had for his wages but a penny a day. The head workman asked him his name, and where he belonged. He would not tell, but said nothing and pursued his work. They called him St. Peter's workman, because he was so devoted to his work.

When the overseer saw the diligence of this holy man he chid the laziness of the other workmen, and said, "You receive more pay than this good man, but do not do half as much work." For this reason the other workmen hated Rinaldo, and made a secret agreement to kill him. They knew that he made it a practice to go every night to a certain church to pray and give alms. So they agreed to lay wait for him, with the purpose to kill him. When he came to the spot, they seized him, and beat him over the head till he was dead. Then they put his body into a sack, and stones with it, and cast it into the Rhine, in the hope the sack would sink to the bottom, and be there concealed. But God willed not that it should be so, but caused the sack to float on the surface, and be thrown upon the bank. And the soul of the holy martyr was carried by angels, with songs of praise, up to the heavens.

Now at that time the people of Dortmund had become converted to the Christian faith; and they sent to the Bishop of Cologne, and desired him to give them some of the holy relics that are in such abundance in that city. So the Bishop called together his clergy to deliberate what answer they should give to this request. And it was determined to give to the people of Dortmund the body of the holy man who had just suffered martyrdom.

When now the body with the coffin was put on the cart, the cart began to move toward Dortmund without horses or help of men, and stopped not till it reached the place where the church of St. Rinaldo now stands. The Bishop and his clergy followed the holy man to do him honor, with singing of hymns, for a space of three miles. And St. Rinaldo has ever since been the patron of that place, and many wonderful works has God done through him, as may be seen in the legends.

HUON OF BORDEAUX

WHEN Charlemagne grew old he felt the burden of government become heavier year by year, till at last he called together his high barons and peers to propose to abdicate the empire and the throne of France in favor of his sons, Charlot and Lewis.

The Emperor was unreasonably partial to his eldest son; he would have been glad to have had the barons and peers demand Charlot for their only sovereign; but that prince was so infamous, for his falsehood and cruelty, that the council strenuously opposed the Emperor's proposal of abdicating, and implored him to continue to hold a sceptre which he wielded with so much glory.

Amaury of Hauteville, cousin of Ganelon, and now head of the wicked branch of the house of Maganza, was the secret partisan of Charlot, whom he resembled in his loose morals and bad dispositions. Amaury nourished the most bitter resentment against the house of Guienne, of which the former Duke, Sevinus, had often rebuked his misdeeds. He took advantage of this occasion to do an injury to the two young children whom the Duke Sevinus had left under the charge of the Duchess Alice, their mother; and at the same time, to advance his interest with Charlot by increasing his wealth and power. With this view he suggested to the prince a new idea.

He pretended to agree with the opinion of the barons; he said that it would be best to try Charlot's capacity for government by giving him some rich provinces before placing him upon the throne; and that the Emperor, without depriving himself of any part of his realm, might give Charlot the investiture of Guienne. For although seven years had passed since the death of Sevinus, the

Figure 124: "Rinaldo and Armida" by Anthony van Dyck

young Duke, his son, had not yet repaired to the court of Charlemagne to render the homage due to his lawful sovereign.

We have often had occasion to admire the justice and wisdom of the advice which on all occasions the Duke Namo of Bavaria gave to Charlemagne, and he now discountenanced, with indignation, the selfish advice of Amaury. He represented to the Emperor the early age of the children of Sevinus, and the useful and glorious services of their late father, and proposed to Charlemagne to send two knights to the Duchess at Bordeaux, to summon her two sons to the court of the Emperor, to pay their respects and render homage.

Charlemagne approved this advice, and sent two chevaliers to demand the two young princes of their mother. No sooner had the Duchess learned the approach of the two knights, than she sent distinguished persons to receive them; and as soon as they entered the palace she presented herself before them, with her elder and younger sons, Huon and Girard.

The deputies, delighted with the honors and caresses they received, accompanied with rich presents, left Bordeaux with regret and on their return represented to Charlemagne that the young Duke Huon seemed born to tread in the footsteps of his brave father, informing him that in three months the young princes of Guienne would present themselves at his court.

The Duchess employed the short interval in giving her sons her last instructions. Huon received them in his heart, and Girard gave as much heed to them as could be expected from one so young.

The preparations for their departure having been made, the Duchess embraced them tenderly, commending them to the care of Heaven, and charged them to call, on their way, at the celebrated monastery of Cluny, to visit the Abbot, the brother of their father. This Abbot, worthy of his high dignity, had never lost an opportunity of doing good, setting an example of every excellence, and making virtue attractive by his example.

He received his nephews with the greatest magnificence; and, aware how useful his presence might be to them with Charlemagne, whose valued counsellor he was, he took with them the road to Paris.

When Amaury learned what reception the two deputies of Charlemagne had received at Bordeaux, and the arrangements made for the visit of the young princes to the Emperor's court, he suggested to Charlot to give him a troop of his guards, with which he proposed to lay wait for the young men in the wood of Montlery, put them to death, and thereby give the prince Charlot possession of the duchy of Guienne.

A plan of treachery and violence agreed but too well with Charlot's disposition. He not only adopted the suggestion of Amaury, but insisted upon taking a part in it. They went out secretly, by night, followed by a great number of attendants, all armed in black, to lie in ambuscade in the wood where the brothers were to pass.

Girard, the younger of the two, having amused himself as he rode by flying his hawk at such game as presented itself, had ridden in advance of his brother and the Abbot of Cluny. Charlot, who saw him coming, alone and unarmed, went forth to meet him, sought a quarrel with him, and threw him from his horse with a stroke of his lance. Girard uttered a cry as he fell; Huon heard it, and flew to his defence, with no other weapon than his sword. He came up with him, and saw the blood flowing from his wound. "What has this child done to you, wretch!" he exclaimed to Charlot. "How cowardly to attack him when unprepared to defend himself!" "By my faith," said Charlot, "I mean to do the same by you. Know that I am the son of Duke Thierry of Ardennes, from whom your father, Sevinus, took three castles; I have sworn to avenge him, and I defy you." "Coward," answered Huon, "I know well the baseness that dwells in your race; worthy son of Thierry, use the advantage that your armor gives you; but know that I fear you not." At these words Charlot had the wickedness to put his lance in rest, and to run upon Huon, who had barely time to wrap his arm in his mantle. With this feeble buckler he received the thrust of the lance. It penetrated the mantle, but missed his body. Then, rising upon his stirrups, Sir Huon struck Charlot so terrible a blow with his sword that the helmet was cleft asunder, and his head too. The dastardly prince fell dead upon the ground.

Huon now perceived that the wood was full of armed men. He called the men of his suite, and they hastily put themselves in order, but nobody issued from the wood to attack him. Amaury, who saw Charlot's fall, had no desire to compromit himself; and, feeling sure that Charlemagne would avenge the death of his son, he saw no occasion for his doing anything more at present. He left Huon and the Abbot of Cluny to bind up the wound of Girard, and, having seen them depart and resume their way to Paris, he took up the body of Charlot, and, placing it across a horse, had it carried to Paris, where he arrived four hours after Huon.

The Abbot of Cluny presented his nephew to Charlemagne, but Huon refrained from paying his obeisance, complaining grievously of the ambush which had been set for him, which he said could not have been without the Emperor's permission. Charlemagne, surprised at a charge which his magnanimous soul was incapable of meriting, asked eagerly of the Abbot what were the grounds of the complaints of his nephew. The Abbot told him faithfully all that had happened, informing him that a coward knight, who called himself the son of Thierry of Ardennes, had wounded Girard, and run upon Huon, who was unarmed; but by his force and valor he had overcome the traitor, and left him dead upon the plain.

Charlemagne indignantly disavowed any connection with the action of the infamous Thierry, congratulated the young Duke upon his victory, himself conducted the two brothers to a rich apartment, stayed to see the first dressing applied to the wound of Girard, and left the brothers in charge of Duke Namo of Bavaria, who, having been a companion in arms of the Duke Sevinus, regarded the young men almost as if they were his own sons.

Charlemagne had hardly quitted them when, returning to his chamber, he heard cries, and saw through the window a party of armed men just arrived. He recognized Amaury, who bore a dead knight stretched across a horse;

and the name of Charlot was heard among the exclamations of the people assembled in the court-yard.

Charles's partiality for this unworthy son was one of his weaknesses. He descended in trepidation to the court-yard, ran to Amaury, and uttered a cry of grief on recognizing Charlot. "It is Huon of Bordeaux," said the traitor Amaury, "who has massacred your son before it was in my power to defend him." Charlemagne, furious at these words, seized a sword, and flew to the apartment of the two brothers to plunge it into the heart of the murderer of his son. Duke Namo stopped his hand for an instant, while Charles told him the crime of which Huon was accused. "He is a peer of the realm," said Namo, "and if he is guilty, is he not here in your power, and are not we peers the proper judges to condemn him to death? Let not your hand be stained with his blood." The Emperor, calmed by the wisdom of Duke Namo, summoned Amaury to his presence. The peers assembled to hear his testimony, and the traitor accused Huon of Bordeaux of having struck the fatal blow without allowing Charlot an opportunity to defend himself, and though he knew that his opponent was the Emperor's eldest son.

The Abbot of Cluny, indignant at the false accusation of Amaury, advanced, and said, "By Saint Benedict, sire, the traitor lies in his throat. If my nephew has slain Charlot it was in his own defence, and after having seen his brother wounded by him, and also in ignorance that his adversary was the prince. Though I am a son of the Church," added the good Abbot, "I forget not that I am a knight by birth. I offer to prove with my body the lie upon Amaury, if he dares sustain it, and I shall feel that I am doing a better work to punish a disloyal traitor, than to sing lauds and matins."

Huon to this time had kept silent, amazed at the black calumny of Amaury; but now he stepped forth, and, addressing Amaury, said: "Traitor! darest thou maintain in arms the lie thou hast uttered?" Amaury, a knight of great prowess, despising the youth and slight figure of Huon, hesitated not to offer his glove, which Huon seized; then, turning again to the peers, he said: "I pray you let the combat be allowed me, for never was there a more legitimate cause." The Duke Namo and the rest, deciding that the question should be remitted to the judgment of Heaven, the combat was ordained, to which Charlemagne unwillingly consented. The young Duke was restored to the charge of Duke Namo, who the next morning invested him with the honors of knighthood, and gave him armor of proof, with a white shield. The Abbot of Cluny, delighted to find in his nephew sentiments worthy of his birth, embraced him, gave him his blessing, and hastened to the church of St. Germains to pray for him, while the officers of the king prepared the lists for the combat.

The battle was long and obstinate. The address and agility of Huon enabled him to avoid the terrible blows which the ferocious Amaury aimed at him. But Huon had more than once drawn blood from his antagonist. The effect began to be perceived in the failing strength of the traitor; at last he threw himself from his horse, and kneeling, begged for mercy. "Spare me," he said, "and I will confess all. Aid me to rise, and lead me to Charlemagne." The brave and loyal Huon, at these words, put his sword under his left arm, and stretched out his right to raise the prostrate man, who seized the opportunity to give him a thrust in the side. The hauberk of Huon resisted the blow, and he was wounded but slightly. Transported with rage at this act of baseness, he forgot how necessary for his complete acquittal the confession of Amaury was, and without delay dealt him the fatal blow.

Duke Namo and the other peers approached, had the body of Amaury dragged forth from the lists, and conducted Huon to Charlemagne. The Emperor, however, listening to nothing but his resentment and grief for the death of his son, refused to be satisfied; and under the plea that Huon had not succeeded in making his accuser retract his charge seemed resolved to confiscate his estates and to banish him forever from France. It was not till after long entreaties on the part of Duke Namo and the rest that he consented to grant Huon his pardon, under conditions which he should impose.

Huon approached, and knelt before the Emperor, rendered his homage, and cried him mercy for the involuntary killing of his son. Charlemagne would not receive the hands of Huon in his own, but touched him with his sceptre, saying, "I receive thy homage, and pardon thee the death of my son, but only on one condition. You shall go immediately to the court of the Sultan Gaudisso; you shall present yourself before him as he sits at meat; you shall cut off the head of the most illustrious guest whom you shall find sitting nearest to him; you shall kiss three times on the mouth the fair princess, his daughter, and you shall demand of the Sultan, as token of tribute to me, a handful of the white hair of his beard, and four grinders from his mouth."

These conditions caused a murmur from all the assembly. "What!" said the Abbot of Cluny; "slaughter a Saracen prince without first offering him baptism?" "The second condition is not so hard," said the young peers, "but the demand that Huon is bound to make of the old Sultan is very uncivil, and will be hard to obtain."

The Emperor's obstinacy when he had once resolved upon a thing is well known. To the courage of Huon nothing seemed impossible. "I accept the conditions," said he, silencing the intercessions of the old Duke of Bavaria; "my liege, I accept my pardon at this price. I go to execute your commands, as your vassal and a peer of France."

The Duke Namo and Abbot of Cluny, being unable to obtain any relaxation of the sentence passed by Charlemagne, led forth the young Duke, who determined to set out at once on his expedition. All that the good Abbot could obtain of him was, that he should prepare for this perilous undertaking by going first to Rome, to pay his homage to the Pope, who was the brother of the Duchess Alice, Huon's mother, and from him demand absolution and his blessing. Huon promised it, and forthwith set out on his way to Rome.

HUON OF BORDEAUX (CONTINUED)

HUON, having traversed the Apennines and Italy, arrived at the environs of Rome, where, laying aside his armor, he assumed the dress of a pilgrim. In this attire he presented himself before the Pope, and not till after he had made a full confession of his sins did he announce himself as his nephew. "Ah! my dear nephew," exclaimed the Holy Father, "what harder penance could I impose than the Emperor has already done? Go in peace, my son," he added, absolving him, "I go to intercede for you with the Most High." Then he led his nephew into his palace, and introduced him to all the Cardinals and Princes of Rome as the Duke of Guienne, son of the Duchess Alice, his sister.

Huon, at setting out, had made a vow not to stop more than three days in a place. The Holy Father took advantage of this time to inspire him with zeal for the glory of Christianity, and with confidence in the protection of the Most High. He advised him to embark for Palestine, to visit the Holy Sepulchre, and to depart thence for the interior of Asia.

Loaded with the blessings of the Holy Father, Huon, obeying his counsels, embarked for Palestine, arrived, and visited with the greatest reverence the holy places. He then departed, and took his way toward the east.

But, ignorant of the country and of the language, he lost himself in a forest, and remained three days without seeing a human creature, living on honey and wild fruits which he found on the trees. The third day, seeking a passage through a rocky defile, he beheld a man in tattered clothing, whose beard and hair covered his breast and shoulders. This man stopped on seeing him, observed him, and recognized the arms and bearing of a French knight. He immediately approached, and exclaimed, in the language of the South of France, "God be praised! Do I indeed behold a chevalier of my own country, after fifteen years passed in this desert without seeing the face of a fellow-countryman?"

Huon, to gratify him still more, unlaced his helmet, and came towards him with a smiling countenance. The other regarded him with more surprise than at first. "Good Heaven!" he exclaimed, "was there ever such a resemblance? Ah, noble sir," he added, "tell me, I beseech you, of what country and race you come?" "I require," replied Huon, "before telling you mine, that you first reveal your own; let it suffice you at present to know that I am a Christian, and that in Guienne I was born." "Ah! Heaven grant that my eyes and my heart do not deceive me," exclaimed the unknown; "my name is Sherasmin; I am brother to Guire, the Mayor of Bordeaux. I was taken prisoner in the battle where my dear and illustrious master, Sevinus, lost his life. For three years I endured the miseries of slavery; at length I broke my chains and escaped to this desert, where I have sustained myself in solitude ever since. Your features recall to me my beloved sovereign, in whose service I was from my infancy till his death." Huon made no reply but by embracing the old man, with tears in his eyes. Then Sherasmin learned that his arms enfolded the son of the Duke Sevinus. He led him to his cabin, and spread before him the dry fruits and honey which formed his only aliment.

Huon recounted his adventures to Sherasmin, who was moved to tears at the recital. He then consulted him on means of conducting his enterprise. Sherasmin hesitated not to confess that success seemed impossible; nevertheless he swore a solemn oath never to abandon him. The Saracen language, which he was master of, would be serviceable to them when they should leave the desert, and mingle with men.

They took the route of the Red Sea, and entered Arabia. Their way lay through a region which Sherasmin described as full of terrors. It was inhabited by Oberon, King of the Fairies, who made captive such knights as were rash enough to penetrate into it, and transformed them into Hobgoblins. It was possible to avoid this district at the expense of somewhat lengthening their route; but no dangers could deter Huon of Bordeaux; and the brave Sherasmin, who had now resumed the armor of a knight, reluctantly consented to share with him the dangers of the shorter route.

They entered a wood, and arrived at a spot whence alleys branched off in various directions. One of them seemed to be terminated by a superb palace, whose gilded roofs were adorned with brilliant weathercocks covered with diamonds. A superb chariot issued from the gate of the palace, and drove toward Huon and his companion, as if to meet them half-way. The prince saw no one in the chariot but a child apparently about five years old, very beautiful, and clad in a robe which glittered with precious stones. At the sight of him, Sherasmin's terror was extreme. He seized the reins of Huon's horse, and turned him about, hurrying the prince away, and assuring him that they were lost if they stopped to parley with the mischievous dwarf, who, though he appeared a child, was full of years and of treachery. Huon was sorry to lose sight of the beautiful dwarf, whose aspect had nothing in it to alarm; yet he followed his friend, who urged on his horse with all possible speed. Presently a storm began to roar through the forest, the daylight grew dim, and they found their way with difficulty. From time to time they seemed to hear an infantine voice, which said, "Stop, Duke Huon; listen to me: it is in vain you fly me!"

Sherasmin only fled the faster, and stopped not until he had reached the gate of a monastery of monks and nuns, the two communities of which were assembled at that time in a religious procession. Sherasmin, feeling safe from the malice of the dwarf in the presence of so many holy persons and the sacred banners, stopped to ask an asylum, and made Huon dismount also. But at that moment they were joined by the dwarf, who blew a blast upon an ivory horn which hung from his neck. Immediately the good Sherasmin, in spite of himself, began to dance like a young collegian, and seizing the hand of an aged nun, who felt as if it would be her death, they footed it briskly over the grass, and were imitated by all the other monks and nuns, mingled together, forming the strangest dancing-party ever beheld. Huron alone felt no disposition to dance; but he came near dying of laughter at seeing the ridiculous postures and leaps of the others.

The dwarf, approaching Huon, said, in a sweet voice, and in Huon's own language, "Duke of Guienne, why do you shun me? I conjure you, in Heaven's name, speak to me." Huon, hearing himself addressed in this serious manner, and knowing that no evil spirit would dare to use the holy name in aid of his schemes, replied, "Sir, whoever you are, I am ready to hear and answer you." "Huon, my friend," continued the dwarf, "I always loved your race, and you have been dear to me ever since your birth. The gracious state of conscience in which you were when you entered my wood has protected you from all enchantments, even if I had intended to practise any upon you. If these monks, these nuns, and even your friend Sherasmin, had had a conscience as pure as yours, my horn would not have set them dancing; but where is the monk or the nun who can always be deaf to the voice of the tempter, and Sherasmin in the desert has often doubted the power of Providence."

At these words Huon saw the dancers overcome with exertion. He begged mercy for them, the dwarf granted it, and the effect of the horn ceased at once; the nuns got rid of their partners, smoothed their dresses, and hastened to resume their places in the procession. Sherasmin, overcome with heat, panting, and unable to stand on his legs, threw himself upon the grass, and began, "Did not I tell you"—He was going on in an angry tone, but the dwarf, approaching, said, "Sherasmin, why have you murmured against Providence? Why have you thought evil of me? You deserved this light punishment; but I know you to be good and loyal; I mean to show myself your friend, as you shall soon see." At these words he presented him a rich goblet. "Make the sign of the cross on this cup," said he, "and then believe that I hold my power from the God you adore, whose faithful servant I am, as well as you." Sherasmin obeyed, and on the instant the cup was filled with delicious wine, a draught of which restored vigor to his limbs, and made him feel young again. Overcome with gratitude, he threw himself on his knees, but the dwarf raised him, and bade him sit beside him, and thus commenced his history:

"Julius Caesar, going by sea to join his army, was driven by a storm to take shelter in the island of Celea, where dwelt the fairy Glorianda. From this renowned pair I draw my birth. I am the inheritor of that which was most admirable in each of my parents: my father's heroic qualities, and my mother's beauty and magic art. But a malicious sister of my mother's, in revenge for some slight offence, touched me with her wand when I was only five years old, and forbade me to grow any bigger; and my mother, with all her power, was unable to annul the sentence. I have thus continued infantile in appearance, though full of years and experience. The power which I derive from my mother I use sometimes for my own diversion, but always to promote justice and to reward virtue. I am able and willing to assist you, Duke of Guienne, for I know the errand on which you come hither. I presage for you, if you follow my counsels, complete success; and the beautiful Clarimunda for a wife."

When he had thus spoken he presented to Huon the precious and useful cup, which had the faculty of filling itself when a good man took it in his hand. He gave him also his beautiful horn of ivory, saying to him, "Huon, when you sound this gently, you will make the hearers dance, as you have seen; but if you sound it forcibly, fear not that I shall hear it, though at a hundred leagues' distance, and will fly to your relief; but be careful not to sound it in that way, unless upon the most urgent occasion."

Oberon directed Huon what course he should take to reach the country of the Sultan Gaudisso. "You will encounter great perils," said he, "before arriving there, and I fear me," he added, with tears in his eyes, "that you will not in everything obey my directions, and in that case you will suffer much calamity." Then he embraced Huon and Sherasmin, and left them.

Huon and his follower travelled many days through the desert before they reached any inhabited place, and all this while the wonderful cup sustained them, furnishing them not only wine, but food also. At last they came to a great city. As day was declining, they entered its suburbs, and Sherasmin, who spoke the Saracen language perfectly, inquired for an inn where they could pass the night. A person who appeared to be one of the principal inhabitants, seeing two strangers of respectable appearance making this inquiry, stepped forward and begged them to accept the shelter of his mansion. They entered, and their host did the honors of his abode with a politeness which they were astonished to see in a Saracen. He had them served with coffee and sherbet, and all was conducted with great decorum, till one of the servants awkwardly overturned a cup of hot coffee on the host's legs, when he started up, exclaiming in very good Gascon, "Blood and thunder! you blockhead, you deserve to be thrown over the mosque!"

Huon could not help laughing to see the vivacity and the language of his country thus break out unawares. The host, who had no idea that his guests understood his words, was astonished when Huon addressed him in the dialect of his country. Immediately confidence was established between them; especially when the domestics had retired. The host, seeing that he was discovered, and that the two pretended Saracens were from the borders of the Garonne, embraced them, and disclosed that he was a Christian. Huon, who had learned prudence from the advice of Oberon, to test his host's sincerity, drew from his robe the cup which the Fairy- king had given him, and presented it empty to the host. "A fair cup," said he, "but I should like it better if it was full." Immediately it was so. The host, astonished, dared not put it to his lips. "Drink boldly, my dear fellow-countryman," said Huon; "your truth is proved by this cup, which only fills itself in the hands of an honest man." The host did not hesitate longer; the cup passed freely from hand to hand; their mutual cordiality increased as it passed, and each recounted his adventures. Those of Huon redoubled his host's respect; for he recognized in him his legitimate sovereign: while the host's narrative was in these words:

"My name is Floriac; this great and strong city, you will hear with surprise and grief, is governed by a brother of Duke Sevinus, and your uncle. You have no doubt heard that a young brother of the Duke of Guienne was stolen away from the sea-shore, with his companions, by some corsairs. I was then his page, and we were carried by those corsairs to Barbary, where we were sold for slaves. The Barbary prince sent us as part of the tribute which he yearly paid to his sovereign, the Sultan Gaudisso. Your uncle, who had been somewhat puffed up by the flattery of his attendants, thought to increase his importance with his new master by telling him his rank. The Sultan, who, like a true Mussulman, detested all Christian princes, exerted himself from that moment to bring him over to the Saracen faith. He succeeded but too well. Your uncle, seduced by the arts of the Santons, and by the pleasures and indulgences which the Sultan allowed him, committed the horrid crime of apostasy; he renounced his baptism, and embraced Mahometanism. Gaudisso then loaded him with honors, made him espouse one of his nieces, and sent him to reign over this city and adjoining country. Your uncle preserved for me the same friendship which he had had when a boy; but all his caresses and efforts could not make me renounce my faith. Perhaps he respected me in his heart for my resistance to his persuasions, perhaps he had hopes of inducing me in time to imitate him. He made me accompany him to this city, of which he was master, he gave me his confidence, and permits me to keep in my service some Christians, whom I protect for the sake of their faith."

"Ah!" exclaimed Huon, "take me to this guilty uncle. A prince of the house of Guienne, must he not blush at the cowardly abandonment of the faith of his fathers?"

"Alas!" replied Floriac, "I fear he will neither be sensible of shame at your reproaches, nor of pleasure at the sight of a nephew so worthy of his lineage. Brutified by sensuality, jealous of his power, which he often exercises with cruelty, he will more probably restrain you by force or put you to death."

"Be it so," said the brave and fervent Huon, "I could not die in a better cause; and I demand of you to conduct me to him to-morrow, after having told him of my arrival and my birth." Floriac still objected, but Huon would take no denial, and he promised obedience.

Next morning Floriac waited upon the Governor and told him of the arrival of his nephew, Huon of Bordeaux; and of the intention of the prince to present himself at his court that very day. The Governor, surprised, did not immediately answer; though he at once made up his mind what to do. He knew that Floriac loved Christians and the princes of his native land too well to aid in any treason to one of them; he therefore feigned great pleasure at hearing of the arrival of the eldest born of his family at his court. He immediately sent Floriac to find him; he caused his palace to be put in festal array, his divan to be assembled, and after giving some secret orders, went himself to meet his nephew, whom he introduced under his proper name and title to all the great officers of his court.

Huon burned with indignation at seeing his uncle with forehead encircled with a rich turban, surmounted with a crescent of precious stones. His natural candor made him receive with pain the embraces which the treacherous Governor lavished upon him. Meanwhile the hope of finding a suitable moment to reproach him for his apostasy made him submit to those honors which his uncle caused to be rendered to him. The Governor evaded with address the chance of being alone with Huon and spent all the morning in taking him through his gardens and palace. At last, when the hour of dinner approached, and the Governor took him by the hand to lead him into the dining-hall, Huon seized the opportunity and said to him in a low voice, "O my uncle! O Prince, brother of the Duke Sevinus! in what condition have I the grief and shame of seeing you!" The Governor pretended to be moved, pressed his hand, and whispered in his ear, "Silence! my dear nephew; to-morrow morning I will hear you fully."

Huon, comforted a little by these words, took his seat at the table by the side of the Governor. The Mufti, some Cadis, Agas, and Santons, filled the other places. Sherasmin sat down with them; but Floriac, who would not lose sight of his guests, remained standing, and passed in and out to observe what was going on within the palace. He soon perceived a number of armed men gliding through the passages and antechambers connected with the dining-hall. He was about to enter to give his guests notice of what he had seen when he heard a violent noise and commotion in the hall. The cause was this.

Huon and Sherasmin were well enough suited with the first course and ate with good appetite; but the people of their country not being accustomed to drink only water at their meals, Huon and Sherasmin looked at one another, not very well pleased at such a regimen. Huon laughed outright at the impatience of Sherasmin, but soon, experiencing the same want himself, he drew forth Oberon's cup and made the sign of the cross. The cup filled and he drank it off, and handed it to Sherasmin, who followed his example. The Governor and his officers, seeing this abhorred sign, contracted their brows and sat in silent consternation. Huon pretended not to observe it, and having filled the cup again handed it to his uncle, saying, "Pray, join us, dear uncle; it is excellent Bordeaux wine, the drink that will be to you like mother's milk." The Governor, who often drank in secret with his own favorite Sultanas the wines of Greece and Shiraz, never in public drank anything but water. He had not for a long time tasted the excellent wines of his native land; he was sorely tempted to drink what was now handed to him, it looked so bright in the cup, outshining the gold itself. He stretched forth his hand, took the brimming goblet, and raised it to his lips, when immediately it dried up and disappeared. Huon and Sherasmin, like Gascons as they were, laughed at his astonishment. "Christian dogs!" he exclaimed, "do you dare to insult me at my own table? But I will soon be revenged." At these words he threw the cup at the head of his nephew, who caught it with his left hand, while with the other he snatched the turban, with its crescent, from the Governor's head and threw it on the floor. All the Saracens started up from table, with loud outcries, and prepared to avenge the insult. Huon and Sherasmin put themselves on their defence, and met with their swords the scimitars directed against them. At this moment the doors of the hall opened and a crowd of soldiers and armed eunuchs rushed in, who joined in the attack upon Huon and Sherasmin. The Prince and his followers took refuge on a broad shelf or side- board, where they kept at bay the crowd of assailants, making the most forward of them smart for their audacity. But more troops came pressing in and the brave Huon, inspired by the wine of Bordeaux, and not angry enough to lose his relish for a joke, blew a gentle note on his horn, and no sooner was it heard than it quelled the rage of the combatants and set them to dancing. Huon and Sherasmin, no longer attacked, looked down from their elevated position on a scene the most singular and amusing. Very soon the Sultanas, hearing the sound of the dance and finding their guards withdrawn, came into the hall and mixed with the dancers. The favorite Sultana seized upon a young Santon, who performed jumps two feet high; but soon the long dresses of this couple got intermingled and threw them down. The Santon's beard was caught in the Sultana's necklace, and they could not disentangle them. The Governor by no means approved this familiarity, and took two steps forward to get at the Santon, but he stumbled over a prostrate Dervise and measured his length on the floor. The dancing continued till the strength of the performers was exhausted, and they fell, one after the other, and lay helpless. The Governor at length made signs to Huon that he would yield everything if he would but allow him to rest. The bargain was ratified; the Governor allowed Huon and Sherasmin to depart on their way, and even gave them a ring which would procure them safe passage through his country and access to the Sultan Gaudisso. The two friends hastened to avail themselves of this favorable turn, and taking leave of Floriac, pursued their journey.

HUON OF BORDEAUX (CONTINUED)

HUON had seen many beauties at his mother's court, but his heart had never been touched with love. Honor had been his mistress, and in pursuit of that he had never found time to give a thought to softer cares. Strange that a heart so insensible should first be touched by something so unsubstantial as a dream; but so it was.

The day after the adventure with his uncle night overtook the travellers as they passed through a forest. A grotto offered them shelter from the night dews. The magic cup supplied their evening meal; for such was its virtue that it afforded not only wine, but more solid fare when desired. Fatigue soon threw them into profound repose. Lulled by the murmur of the foliage, and breathing the fragrance of the flowers, Huon dreamed that a lady more beautiful than he had ever before seen hung over him and imprinted a kiss upon his lips. As he stretched out his arms to embrace her a sudden gust of wind swept her away.

Huon awoke in an agony of regret. A few moments sufficed to afford some consolation in showing him that what had passed was but a dream; but his perplexity and sadness could not escape the notice of Sherasmin. Huon hesitated not to inform his faithful follower of the reason of his pensiveness; and got nothing in return but his rallyings for allowing himself to be disturbed by such a cause. He recommended a draught from the fairy goblet, and Huon tried it with good effect.

At early dawn they resumed their way. They travelled till high noon, but said little to one another. Huon was musing on his dream, and Sherasmin's thoughts flew back to his early days on the banks of the flowery Garonne.

On a sudden they were startled by the cry of distress, and turning an angle of the wood, came where a knight hard pressed was fighting with a furious lion. The knight's horse lay dead, and it seemed as if another moment would end the combat, for terror and fatigue had quite disabled the knight for further resistance. He fell, and the lion's paw was raised over him, when a blow from Huon's sword turned the monster's rage upon a new enemy. His roar shook the forest, and he crouched in act to spring, when, with the rapidity of lightning, Huon plunged his sword into his side. He rolled over on the plain in the agonies of death.

They raised the knight from the ground, and Sherasmin hastened to offer him a draught from the fairy cup. The wine sparkled to the brim, and the warrior put forth his lips to quaff it, but it shrunk away, and did not even wet his lips. He dashed the goblet angrily on the ground, with an exclamation of resentment. This incident did not tend to make either party more acceptable to the other; and what followed was worse. For when Huon said, "Sir knight, thank God for your deliverance,"—"Thank Mahomet, rather, yourself," said he, "for he has led you this day to render service to no less a personage than the Prince of Hyrcania."

At the sound of this blasphemy Huon drew his sword and turned upon the miscreant, who, little disposed to encounter the prowess of which he had so lately seen proof, betook himself to flight. He ran to Huon's horse,

Figure 125: "Giant Drinking a Stream" by John Dickson Batten

and lightly vaulting on his back, clapped spurs to his side, and galloped out of sight.

The adventure was vexatious, yet there was no remedy. The prince and Sherasmin continued their journey with the aid of the remaining horse as they best might. At length, as evening set in, they descried the pinnacles and towers of a great city full before them, which they knew to be the famous city of Bagdad.

They were well-nigh exhausted with fatigue when they arrived at its precincts, and in the darkness, not knowing what course to take, were glad to meet an aged woman, who, in reply to their inquiries, offered them such accommodations as her cottage could supply. They thankfully accepted the offer, and entered the low door. The good dame busily prepared the best fare her stores supplied,—milk, figs, and peaches,—deeply regretting that the bleak winds had nipped her almond-trees.

Sir Huon thought he had never in his life tasted any fare so good. The old lady talked while her guests ate. She doubted not, she said, they had come to be present at the great feast in honor of the marriage of the Sultan's daughter, which was to take place on the morrow. They asked who the bridegroom was to be, and the old lady answered, "The Prince of Hyrcania," but added, "Our princess hates him, and would rather wed a dragon than him." "How know you that?" asked Huon; and the dame informed him that she had it from the princess herself, who was her foster-child. Huon inquired the reason of the princess's aversion; and the woman pleased to find her chat excite so much interest, replied that it was all in consequence of a dream. "A dream!" exclaimed Huon. "Yes! a dream. She dreamed that she was a hind, and that the Prince, as a hunter, was pursuing her, and had almost overtaken her, when a beautiful dwarf appeared in view, drawn in a golden car, having by his side a young man of yellow hair and fair complexion, like one from a foreign land. She dreamed that the car stopped where she stood, and that, having resumed her own form, she was about to ascend it, when suddenly it faded from her view, and with it the dwarf and the fair-haired youth. But from her heart that vision did not fade, and from that time her affianced bridegroom, the Hyrcanian prince, had become odious to her sight. Yet the Sultan, her father, by no means regarding such a cause as sufficient to prevent the marriage, had named the morrow as the time when it should be solemnized, in presence of his court and many princes of the neighboring countries, whom the fame of the princess's beauty and the bridegroom's splendor had brought to the scene."

We may suppose this conversation woke a tumult of thoughts in the breast of Huon. Was it not clear that Providence led him on, and cleared the way for his happy success? Sleep did not early visit the eyes of Huon that night; but, with the sanguine temper of youth, he indulged his fancy in imagining the sequel of his strange experience.

The next day, which he could not but regard as the decisive day of his fate, he prepared to deliver the message of Charlemagne. Clad in his armor, fortified with his ivory horn and his ring, he reached the palace of Gaudisso when the guests were assembled at the banquet. As he approached the gate a voice called on all true believers to enter; and Huon, the brave and faithful Huon, in his impatience passed in under that false pretention. He had no sooner passed the barrier than he felt ashamed of his baseness, and was overwhelmed with regret. To make amends for his fault he ran forward to the second gate, and cried to the porter, "Dog of a misbeliever, I command you in the name of Him who died on the cross, open to me!" The points of a hundred weapons immediately opposed his passage. Huon then remembered for the first time the ring he had received from his uncle, the Governor. He produced it, and demanded to be led to the Sultan's presence. The officer of the guard recognized the ring, made a respectful obeisance, and allowed him free entrance. In the same way he passed the other doors to the rich saloon where the great Sultan was at dinner with his tributary princes. At sight of the ring the chief attendant led Huon to the head of the hall, and introduced him to the Sultan and his princes as the ambassador of Charlemagne. A seat was provided for him near the royal party.

The Prince of Hyrcania, the same whom Huon had rescued from the lion, and who was the destined bridegroom of the beautiful Clarimunda, sat on the Sultan's right hand, and the princess herself on his left. It chanced that Huon found himself near the seat of the princess, and hardly were the ceremonies of reception over before he made haste to fulfill the commands of Charlemagne by imprinting a kiss upon her rosy lips, and after that a second, not by command, but by good will. The Prince of Hyrcania cried out, "Audacious infidel! take the reward of thy insolence!" and aimed a blow at Huon, which, if it had reached him, would have brought his embassy to a speedy termination. But the ingrate failed of his aim, and Huon punished his blasphemy and ingratitude at once by a blow which severed his head from his body.

So suddenly had all this happened that no hand had been raised to arrest it; but now Gaudisso cried out, "Seize the murderer!" Huon was hemmed in on all sides, but his redoubtable sword kept the crowd of courtiers at bay. But he saw new combatants enter, and could not hope to maintain his ground against so many. He recollected his horn, and raising it to his lips, blew a blast almost as loud as that of Roland at Roncesvalles. It was in vain. Oberon heard it; but the sin of which Huon had been guilty in bearing, though but for a moment, the character of a believer in the false prophet, had put it out of Oberon's power to help him. Huon, finding himself deserted, and conscious of the cause, lost his strength and energy, was seized, loaded with chains, and plunged into a dungeon.

His life was spared for the time, merely that he might be reserved for a more painful death. The Sultan meant that, after being made to feel all the torments of hunger and despair, he should be flayed alive.

But an enchanter more ancient and more powerful than Oberon himself interested himself for the brave Huon. The enchanter was Love. The Princess Clarimunda learned with horror the fate to which the young prince was destined. By the aid of her governante she gained over the keeper of the prison, and went herself to lighten the chains of her beloved. It was her hand that removed his fetters, from her he received supplies of food to sustain a life which he devoted from thenceforth wholly to her. After the most tender explanations the princess departed, promising to repeat her visit on the morrow.

The next day she came according to promise, and again brought supplies of food. These visits were continued during a whole month. Huon was too good a son of the Church to forget that the amiable princess was a Saracen, and he availed himself of these interviews to instruct her in the true faith. How easy it is to believe the truth when uttered by the lips of those we love! Clarimunda ere long professed her entire belief in the Christian doctrines, and desired to be baptized.

Meanwhile the Sultan had repeatedly inquired of the jailer how his prisoner bore the pains of famine, and learned to his surprise that he was not yet much reduced thereby. On his repeating the inquiry, after a short interval, the keeper replied that the prisoner had died suddenly, and had been buried in the cavern. The Sultan could only regret that he had not sooner ordered the execution of the sentence.

While these things were going on the faithful Sherasmin, who had not accompanied Huon in his last adventure, but had learned by common rumor the result of it, came to the court in hopes of doing something for the rescue of his master. He presented himself to the Sultan as Solario, his nephew. Guadisso received him with kindness, and all the courtiers loaded him with attentions. He soon found means to inform himself how the Princess regarded the brave but unfortunate Huon, and having made himself known to her, confidence was soon established between them. Clarimunda readily consented to assist in the escape of Huon, and to quit with him her father's court to repair to that of Charlemagne. Their united efforts had nearly perfected their arrangement, a vessel was secretly prepared, and all things in forwardness for the flight, when an unlooked-for obstacle presented itself. Huon himself positively refused to go leaving the orders of Charlemagne unexecuted.

Sherasmin was in despair. Bitterly he complained of the fickleness and cruelty of Oberon in withdrawing his aid at the very crisis when it was most necessary. Earnestly he urged every argument to satisfy the prince that he had done enough for honor, and could not be held bound to achieve impossibilities. But all was of no avail, and he knew not which way to turn, when one of those events occurred which are so frequent under Turkish despotisms. A courier arrived at the court of the Sultan, bearing the ring of his sovereign, the mighty Agrapard, Caliph of Arabia, and bringing the bow-string for the neck of Gaudisso. No reason was assigned; none but the pleasure of the Caliph is ever required in such cases; but it was suspected that the bearer of the bow-string had persuaded the Caliph that Gaudisso, whose rapacity was well known, had accumulated immense treasures, which he had not duly shared with his sovereign, and thus had obtained an order to supersede him in his Emirship.

The body of Gaudisso would have been cast out a prey to dogs and vultures, had not Sherasmin, under the character of nephew of the deceased, been permitted to receive it, and give it decent burial, which he did, but not till he had taken possession of the beard and grinders, agreeably to the orders of Charlemagne.

No obstacle now stood in the way of the lovers and their faithful follower in returning to France. They sailed, taking Rome in their way, where the Holy Father himself blessed the union of his nephew, Duke Huon of Bordeaux, with the Princess Clarimunda.

Soon afterward they arrived in France, where Huon laid his trophies at the feet of Charlemagne, and, being restored to the favor of the Emperor, hastened to present himself and his bride to the Duchess, his mother, and to the faithful liegemen of his province of Guienne and his city of Bordeaux, where the pair were received with transports of joy.

OGIER, THE DANE

OGIER, the Dane, was the son of Geoffrey, who wrested Denmark from the Pagans, and reigned the first Christian king of that country. When Ogier was born, and before he was baptized, six ladies of ravishing beauty appeared all at once in the chamber of the infant. They encircled him, and she who appeared the eldest took him in her arms, kissed him, and laid her hand upon his heart. "I give you," said she, "to be the bravest warrior of your times." She delivered the infant to her sister, who said, "I give you abundant opportunities to display your valor." "Sister," said the third lady, "you have given him a dangerous boon; I give him that he shall never be vanquished." The fourth sister added, as she laid her hand upon his eyes and his mouth, "I give you the gift of pleasing." The fifth said, "Lest all these gifts serve only to betray, I give you sensibility to return the love you inspire." Then spoke Morgana, the youngest and handsomest of the group. "Charming creature, I claim you for my own; and I give you not to die till you shall have come to pay me a visit in my isle of Avalon." Then she kissed the child and departed with her sisters.

After this the king had the child carried to the font and baptized with the name of Ogier.

In his education nothing was neglected to elevate him to the standard of a perfect knight, and render him accomplished in all the arts necessary to make him a hero.

He had hardly reached the age of sixteen years when Charlemagne, whose power was established over all the sovereigns of his time, recollected that Geoffroy, Ogier's father, had omitted to render the homage due to him as Emperor, and sovereign lord of Denmark, one of the grand fiefs of the empire. He accordingly sent an embassy to demand of the king of Denmark this homage, and on receiving a refusal, couched in haughty terms, sent an army to enforce the demand. Geoffroy, after an unsuccessful resistance, was forced to comply, and as a pledge of his sincerity delivered Ogier, his eldest son, a hostage to Charles, to be brought up at his court. He was placed in charge of the Duke Namo of Bavaria, the friend of his father, who treated him like his own son.

Ogier grew up more and more handsome and amiable every day. He surpassed in form, strength, and address all the noble youths his companions; he failed not to be present at all tourneys; he was attentive to the elder knights, and burned with impatience to imitate them. Yet his heart rose sometimes in secret against his condition as a hostage, and as one apparently forgotten by his father.

The King of Denmark, in fact, was at this time occupied with new loves. Ogier's mother having died, he had married a second wife, and had a son named Guyon. The new queen had absolute power over her husband, and fearing that, if he should see Ogier again, he would give him the preference over Guyon, she had adroitly persuaded him to delay rendering his homage to Charlemagne, till now four years had passed away since the last renewal of that ceremony. Charlemagne, irritated at this delinquency, drew closer the bonds of Ogier's captivity until he should receive a response from the king of Denmark to a fresh summons which he caused to be sent to him.

The answer of Geoffroy was insulting and defiant, and the rage of Charlemagne was roused in the highest degree. He was at first disposed to wreak his vengeance upon Ogier, his hostage; but at the entreaties of Duke Namo, who felt towards his pupil like a father, consented to spare his life, if Ogier would swear fidelity to him as his liege-lord, and promise not to quit his court without his permission. Ogier accepted these terms, and was allowed to retain all the freedom he had before enjoyed.

The Emperor would have immediately taken arms to reduce his disobedient vassal, if he had not been called off in another direction by a message from Pope Leo, imploring his assistance. The Saracens had landed in the neighborhood of Rome, occupied Mount Janiculum, and prepared to pass the Tiber and carry fire and sword to the capital of the Christian world. Charlemagne hesitated not to yield to the entreaties of the Pope. He speedily assembled an army, crossed the Alps, traversed Italy, and arrived at Spoleto, a strong place to which the Pope had retired. Leo, at the head of his Cardinals, advanced to meet him, and rendered him homage, as to the son of Pepin, the illustrious protector of the Holy See, coming, as his father had done, to defend it in the hour of need.

Charlemagne stopped but two days at Spoleto, and learning that the Infidels, having rendered themselves masters of Rome, were besieging the Capitol, which could not long hold out against them, marched promptly to attack them.

The advanced posts of the army were commanded by Duke Namo, on whom Ogier waited as his squire. He did not yet bear arms, not having received the order of knighthood. The Oriflamme, the royal standard, was borne by a knight named Alory, who showed himself unworthy of the honor.

Duke Namo, seeing a strong body of the Infidels advancing to attack him, gave the word to charge them. Ogier remained in the rear, with the other youths, grieving much that he was not permitted to fight. Very soon he saw Alory lower the Oriflamme, and turn his horse in flight. Ogier pointed him out to the young men, and seizing a club, rushed upon Alory and struck him from his horse. Then, with his companions, he disarmed him, clothed himself in his armor, raised the Oriflamme, and mounting the horse of the unworthy knight, flew to the front rank, where he joined Duke Namo, drove back the Infidels, and carried the Oriflamme quite through their broken ranks. The Duke, thinking it was Alory, whom he had not held in high esteem, was astonished at his strength and valor. Ogier's young companions imitated him, supplying themselves with armor from the bodies of the slain; they followed Ogier and carried death into the ranks of the Saracens, who fell back in confusion upon their main body.

Duke Namo now ordered a retreat, and Ogier obeyed with reluctance, when they perceived Charlemagne advancing to their assistance. The combat now became general, and was more terrible than ever. Charlemagne had overthrown Corsuble, the commander of the Saracens, and had drawn his famous sword, Joyeuse, to cut off his head, when two Saracen knights set upon him at once, one of whom slew his horse, and the other overthrew the Emperor on the sand. Perceiving by the eagle on his casque who he was, they dismounted in haste to give him his deathblow. Never was the life of the Emperor in such peril. But Ogier, who saw him fall, flew to his rescue. Though embarrassed with the Oriflamme, he pushed his horse against one of the Saracens and knocked him down; and with his sword dealt the other so vigorous a blow that he fell stunned to the earth. Then helping the Emperor to rise, he remounted him on the horse of one of the fallen knights. "Brave and generous Alory!" Charles exclaimed, "I owe to you my honor and my life!" Ogier made no answer; but, leaving Charlemagne surrounded by a great many of the knights who had flown to his succor, he plunged into the thickest ranks of the enemy, and carried the Oriflamme, followed by a gallant train of youthful warriors, till the standard of Mahomet turned in retreat, and the Infidels sought safety in their intrenchments.

Then the good Archbishop Turpin laid aside his helmet and his bloody sword (for he always felt that he was clearly in the line of his duty while slaying Infidels), took his mitre and his crosier, and intoned Te Deum.

At this moment Ogier, covered with blood and dust, came to lay the Oriflamme at the feet of the Emperor. He was followed by a train of warriors of short stature, who walked ill at ease loaded with armor too heavy for them. Ogier knelt at the feet of Charlemagne, who embraced him, calling him Alory, while Turpin from the height of the altar, blessed him with all his might. Then young Orlando, son of the Count Milone, and nephew of Charlemagne, no longer able to endure this misapprehension, threw down his helmet, and ran to unlace Ogier's, while the other young men laid aside theirs. Our author says he cannot express the surprise, the admiration, and the tenderness of the Emperor and his peers. Charles folded Ogier in his arms, and the happy fathers of those brave youths embraced them with tears of joy. The good Duke Namo stepped forward, and Charlemagne yielded Ogier to his embrace. "How much do I owe you," he said, "good and wise friend, for having restrained my anger! My dear Ogier! I owe you my life! My sword leaps to touch your shoulder, yours and those of your brave young friends." At these words he drew that famous sword, Joyeuse, and while Ogier and the rest knelt before him, gave them the accolade conferring on them the order of knighthood. The young Orlando and his cousin Oliver could not refrain, even in the presence of the Emperor, from falling upon Ogier's neck, and pledging with him that brotherhood in arms, so dear and so sacred to the knights of old times; but Charlot, the Emperor's son, at the sight of the glory with which Ogier had covered himself, conceived the blackest jealousy and hate.

The rest of the day and the next were spent in the rejoicings of the army. Turpin in a solemn service implored the favor of Heaven upon the youthful knights, and blessed the white armor which was prepared for them. Duke Namo presented them with golden spurs, Charles himself girded on their swords. But what was his astonishment when he examined that intended for Ogier! The loving Fairy, Morgana, had had the art to change it, and to substitute one of her own procuring, and when Charles drew it out of the scabbard, these words appeared written on the steel: "My name is Cortana, of the same steel and temper as Joyeuse and Durindana." Charles saw that a superior power watched over the destinies of Ogier; he vowed to love him as a father would, and Ogier promised him the devotion of a son. Happy had it been for both if they had always continued mindful of their promises.

The Saracen army had hardly recovered from its dismay when Carahue, King of Mauritania, who was one of the knights overthrown by Ogier at the time of the rescue of Charlemagne, determined to challenge him to single combat. With that view he assumed the dress of a herald, resolved to carry his own message. The French knights admired his air, and said to one another that he seemed more fit to be a knight than a bearer of messages.

Carahue began by passing the warmest eulogium upon the knight who bore the Oriflamme on the day of the battle, and concluded by saying that Carahue, King of Mauritania, respected that knight so much that he challenged him to the combat.

Ogier had risen to reply, when he was interrupted by Charlot, who said that the gage of the King of Mauritania could not fitly be received by a vassal, living in captivity; by which he meant Ogier, who was at that time serving as hostage for his father. Fire flashed from the eyes of Ogier, but the presence of the Emperor restrained his speech, and he was calmed by the kind looks of Charlemagne, who said, with an angry voice, "Silence, Charlot! By the life of Bertha, my queen, he who has saved my life is as dear to me as yourself. Ogier," he continued, "you are no longer a hostage. Herald! report my answer to your master, that never does knight of my court refuse a challenge on equal terms. Ogier, the Dane, accepts of his, and I myself am his security."

Carahue, profoundly bowing, replied, "My lord, I was sure that the sentiments of so great a sovereign as yourself would be worthy of your high and brilliant fame; I shall report your answer to my master, who I know admires you, and unwillingly takes arms against you." Then, turning to Charlot, whom he did not know as the son of the Emperor, he continued, "As for you, Sir Knight, if the desire of battle inflames you, I have it in charge from Sadon, cousin of the King of Mauritania, to give the like defiance to any French knights who will grant him the honor of the combat."

Charlot, inflamed with rage and vexation at the public reproof which he had just received, hesitated not to deliver his gage. Carahue received it with Ogier's, and it was agreed that the combat should be on the next day in a meadow environed by woods and equally distant from both armies.

The perfidious Charlot meditated the blackest treason. During the night he collected some knights unworthy of the name, and like himself in their ferocious manners; he made them swear to avenge his injuries, armed them in black armor, and sent them to lie in ambush in the wood, with orders to make a pretended attack upon the whole party, but in fact, to lay heavy hands upon Ogier and the two Saracens.

At the dawn of day Sadon and Carahue, attended tonly by two pagesto carry their spears, took their way to the appointed meadow; andCharlot and Ogier repaired thither also, but by different paths.Ogier advanced with a calm air, saluted courteously the twoSaracen knights, and joined them in arranging the terms of combat.

While this was going on the perfidious Charlot remained behind and gave his men the signal to advance. That cowardly troop issued from the wood and encompassed the three knights. All three were equally surprised at the attack, but neither of them suspected the other to have any hand in the treason. Seeing the attack made equally upon them all, they united their efforts to resist it, and made the most forward of the assailants bite the dust. Cortana fell on no one without inflicting a mortal wound, but the sword of Carahue was not of equal temper and broke in his hands. At the same instant his horse was slain, and Carahue fell, without a weapon, and entangled with his prostrate horse. Ogier, who saw it, ran to his defence, and leaping to the ground covered the prince with his shield, supplied him with the sword of one of the fallen ruffians, and would have him mount his own horse. At that moment Charlot, inflamed with rage, pushed his horse upon Ogier, knocked him down, and would have run him through with his lance if Sadon, who saw the treason, had not sprung upon him and thrust him back. Carahue leapt lightly upon the horse which Ogier presented him, and had time only to exclaim, "Brave Ogier, I am no longer your enemy, I pledge to you an eternal friendship," when numerous Saracen knights were seen approaching, having discovered the treachery, and Charlot with his followers took refuge in the wood.

The troop which advanced was commanded by Dannemont, the exiled king of Denmark, whom Geoffroy, Ogier's father, had driven from his throne and compelled to take refuge with the Saracens. Learning who Ogier was, he instantly declared him his prisoner, in spite of the urgent remonstrances and even threats of Carahue and Sadon, and carried him under a strong guard to the Saracen camp. Here he was at first subjected to the most rigorous captivity, but Carahue and Sadon insisted so vehemently on his release, threatening to turn their arms against their own party if it was not granted, while Dannemont as eagerly opposed the measure, that Corsuble, the Saracen commander, consented to a middle course, and allowed Ogier the freedom of his camp, upon his promise not to leave it without permission.

Carahue was not satisfied with this partial concession. He left the city next morning, proceeded to the camp of Charlemagne, and demanded to be led to the Emperor. When he reached his presence he dismounted from his horse, took off his helmet, drew his sword, and holding it by the blade presented it to Charlemagne as he knelt before him.

"Illustrious prince," he said, "behold before you the herald who brought the challenge to your knights from the King of Mauritania. The cowardly old King Dannemont has made the brave Ogier prisoner, and has prevailed on our general to refuse to give him up. I come to make amends for this ungenerous conduct by yielding myself, Carahue, King of Mauritania, your prisoner."

Charlemagne, with all his peers, admired the magnanimity of Carahue; he raised him, embraced him, and restored to him his sword. "Prince," said he, "your presence and the bright example you afford my knights consoles me for the loss of Ogier. Would to God you might receive our holy faith, and be wholly united with us." All the lords of the court, led by Duke Namo, paid their respects to the King of Mauritania. Charlot only failed to appear, fearing to be recognized as a traitor; but the heart of Carahue was too noble to pierce that of Charlemagne by telling him the treachery of his son.

Meanwhile the Saracen army was rent by discord. The troops of Carahue clamored against the commander-in-chief because their king was left in captivity. They even threatened to desert the cause and turn their arms against their allies. Charlemagne pressed the siege vigorously, till at length the Saracen leaders found themselves compelled to abandon the city and betake themselves to their ships. A truce was made; Ogier was exchanged for Carahue, and the two friends embraced one another with vows of perpetual brotherhood. The Pope was reestablished in his dominions, and Italy being tranquil, Charlemagne returned with his peers and their followers to France.

OGIER, THE DANE (CONTINUED)

CHARLEMAGNE had not forgotten the offence of Geoffroy, the King of Denmark, in withholding homage, and now prepared to enforce submission. But at this crisis he was waited upon by an embassy from Geoffroy, acknowledging his fault, and craving assistance against an army of invaders who had attacked his states with a force which he was unable to repel. The soul of Charlemagne was too great to be implacable, and he took this opportunity to test that of Ogier, who had felt acutely the unkindness of his father, in leaving him, without regard or notice, fifteen years in captivity. Charles asked Ogier whether, in spite of his father's neglect, he was disposed to lead an army to his assistance. He replied, "A son can never be excused from helping his father by any cause short of death." Charlemagne placed an army of a thousand knights under the command of Ogier, and great numbers more volunteered to march under so distinguished a leader. He flew to the succor of his father, repelled the invaders, and drove them in confusion to their vessels. Ogier then hastened to the capital, but as he drew near the city he heard all the bells sounding a knell. He soon learned the cause; it was the obsequies of Geoffroy, the King. Ogier felt keenly the grief of not having been permitted to embrace his father once more, and to learn his latest commands; but he found that his father had declared him heir to his throne. He hastened to the church where the body lay; he knelt and bathed the lifeless form with his tears. At that moment a celestial light beamed all around, and a voice of an angel said, "Ogier, leave thy crown to Guyon, thy brother, and bear no other title than that of 'The Dane.' Thy destiny is glorious, and other kingdoms are reserved for thee." Ogier obeyed the divine behest. He saluted his stepmother respectfully, and embracing his brother, told him that he was content with his lot in being reckoned among the paladins of Charlemagne, and resigned all claims to the crown of Denmark.

Ogier returned covered with glory to the court of Charlemagne, and the Emperor, touched with this proof of his attachment, loaded him with caresses, and treated him almost as an equal.

We pass in silence the adventures of Ogier for several ensuing years, in which the fairy-gifts of his infancy showed their force in making him successful in all enterprises, both of love and war. He married the charming Belicene, and became the father of young Baldwin, a youth who seemed to inherit in full measure the strength and courage of his father and the beauty of his mother. When the lad was old enough to be separated from his mother, Ogier took him to court and presented him to Charlemagne, who embraced him and took him into his service. It seemed to Duke Namo, and all the elder knights, as if they saw in him Ogier himself, as he was when a youth; and this resemblance won for the lad their kind regards. Even Charlot at first seemed to be fond of him, though after a while the resemblance to Ogier which he noticed had the effect to excite his hatred.

Baldwin was attentive to Charlot, and lost no occasion to be serviceable. The Prince loved to play chess, and Baldwin, who played well, often made a party with him.

One day Charlot was nettled at losing two pieces in succession; he thought he could, by taking a piece from Baldwin, get some amends for his loss; but Baldwin, seeing him fall into a trap which he had set for him, could not help a slight laugh, as he said, "Check-mate." Chariot rose in a fury, seized the rich and heavy chess-board, and dashed it with all his strength on the head of Baldwin, who fell, and died where he fell.

Frightened at his own crime, and fearing the vengeance of the terrible Ogier, Charlot concealed himself in the interior of the palace. A young companion of Baldwin hastened and informed Ogier of the event. He ran to the chamber, and beheld the body of his child bathed in blood, and it could not be concealed from him that Charlot gave the blow. Transported with rage, Ogier sought Charlot through the palace, and Charlot, feeling safe nowhere else, took refuge in the hall of Charlemagne, where he seated himself at table with Duke Namo and Salomon, Duke of Brittany. Ogier, with sword drawn, followed him to the very table of the Emperor. When a cupbearer attempted to bar his way he struck the cup from his hand and dashed the contents in the Emperor's face. Charles rose in a passion, seized a knife, and would have plunged it into his breast, had not Salomon and another baron thrown themselves between, while Namo, who had retained his ancient influence over Ogier, drew him out of the room. Foreseeing the consequence of this violence, pitying Ogier, and in his heart excusing him, Namo hurried him away before the guards of the palace could arrest him, made him mount his horse, and leave Paris.

Charlemagne called together his peers, and made them take an oath to do all in their power to arrest Ogier, and bring him to condign punishment. Ogier on his part sent messages to the Emperor, offering to give himself up on condition that Charlot should be punished for his atrocious crime. The Emperor would listen to no conditions, and went in pursuit of Ogier at the head of a large body of soldiers. Ogier, on the other hand, was warmly supported by many knights, who pledged themselves in his defence. The contest raged long, with no decisive results. Ogier more than once had the Emperor in his power, but declined to avail himself of his advantage, and released him without conditions. He even implored pardon for himself, but demanded at the same time the punishment of Charlot. But Charlemagne was too blindly fond of his unworthy son to subject him to punishment for

Figure 126: "Ogier the Dane, or Holger Danske" by Unknown Artist

the sake of conciliating one who had been so deeply injured.

At length, distressed at the blood which his friends had lost in his cause, Ogier dismissed his little army, and slipping away from those who wished to attend him, took his course to rejoin the Duke Guyon, his brother. On his way, having reached the forest of Ardennes, weary with long travel, the freshness of a retired valley tempted him to lie down to take some repose. He unsaddled Beiffror, relieved himself of his helmet, lay down on the turf, rested his head on his shield, and slept.

It so happened that Turpin, who occasionally recalled to mind that he was Archbishop of Rheins, was at that time in the vicinity, making a pastoral visit to the churches under his jurisdiction. But his dignity of peer of France, and his martial spirit, which caused him to be reckoned among the "preux chevaliers" of his time, forbade him to travel without as large a retinue of knights as he had of clergymen. One of these was thirsty, and knowing the fountain on the borders of which Ogier was reposing, he rode to it, and was struck by the sight of a knight stretched on the ground. He hastened back, and let the Archbishop know, who approached the fountain, and recognized Ogier.

The first impulse of the good and generous Turpin was to save his friend, for whom he felt the warmest attachment; but his archdeacons and knights, who also recognized Ogier, reminded the Archbishop of the oath which the Emperor had exacted of them all. Turpin could not be false to his oath; but it was not without a groan that he permitted his followers to bind the sleeping knight. The Archbishop's attendants secured the horse and arms of Ogier, and conducted their prisoner to the Emperor at Soissons.

The Emperor had become so much embittered by Ogier's obstinate resistance, added to his original fault, that he was disposed to order him to instant death. But Turpin, seconded by the good Dukes Namo and Salomon, prayed so hard for him that Charlemagne consented to remit a violent death, but sentenced him to close imprisonment, under the charge of the Archbishop, strictly limiting his food to one quarter of a loaf of bread per day, with one piece of meat, and a quarter of a cup of wine. In this way he hoped to quickly put an end to his life without bringing on himself the hostility of the King of Denmark, and other powerful friends of Ogier. He exacted a new oath of Turpin to obey his order strictly.

The good Archbishop loved Ogier too well not to cast about for some means of saving his life, which he foresaw he would soon lose if subjected to such scanty fare, for Ogier was seven feet tall, and had an appetite in proportion. Turpin remembered, moreover, that Ogier was a true son of the Church, always zealous to propagate the faith and subdue unbelievers; so he felt justified in practising on this occasion what in later times has been entitled "mental reservation," without swerving from the letter of the oath which he had taken. This is the method he hit upon.

Every morning he had his prisoner supplied with a quarter of a loaf of bread, made of two bushels of flour, to this he added a quarter of a sheep or a fat calf, and he had a cup made which held forty pints of wine, and allowed Ogier a quarter of it daily.

Ogier's imprisonment lasted long; Charlemagne was astonished to hear, from time to time, that he still held out; and when he inquired more particularly of Turpin, the good Archbishop, relying on his own understanding of the words, did not hesitate to affirm positively that he allowed his prisoner no more than the permitted ration.

We forgot to say that, when Ogier was led prisoner to Soissons, the Abbot of Saint Faron, observing the fine horse Beiffror, and not having at the time any other favor to ask of Charlemagne, begged the Emperor to give him the horse, and had him taken to his abbey. He was impatient to try his new acquisition, and when he had arrived in his litter at the foot of the mountain where the horse had been brought to meet him mounted him and rode onward. The horse, accustomed to bear the enormous weight of Ogier in his armor, when he perceived nothing on his back but the light weight of the Abbot, whose long robes fluttered against his sides, ran away, making prodigious leaps over the steep acclivities of the mountain till he reached the convent of Jouaire, where, in sight of the Abbess and her nuns, he threw the Abbot, already half dead with fright, to the ground. The Abbot, bruised and mortified, revenged himself on poor Beiffror, whom he condemned, in his wrath, to be given to the workmen to drag stones for a chapel that he was building near the abbey. Thus, ill-fed, hard-worked, and often beaten, the noble horse Beiffror passed the time while his master's imprisonment lasted.

That imprisonment would have been as long as his life if it had not been for some important events which forced the Emperor to set Ogier at liberty.

The Emperor learned at the same time that Carahue, King of Mauritania, was assembling an army to come and demand the liberation of Ogier; that Guyon, King of Denmark, was prepared to second the enterprise with all his forces; and, worse than all, that the Saracens, under Bruhier, Sultan of Arabia, had landed in Gascony, taken Bordeaux, and were marching with all speed for Paris.

Charlemagne now felt how necessary the aid of Ogier was to him. But, in spite of the representations of Turpin, Namo, and Salomon, he could not bring himself to consent to surrender Charlot to such punishment as Ogier should see fit to impose. Besides, he believed that Ogier was without strength and vigor, weakened by imprisonment and long abstinence.

At this crisis he received a message from Bruhier, proposing to put the issue upon the result of a combat between himself and the Emperor or his champion; promising, if defeated, to withdraw his army. Charlemagne would willingly have accepted the challenge, but his counsellors all opposed it. The herald was therefore told that the Emperor would take time to consider his proposition, and give his answer the next day.

It was during this interval that the three Dukes succeeded in prevailing upon Charlemagne to pardon Ogier, and to send for him to combat the puissant enemy who now defied him; but it was no easy task to persuade Ogier. The idea of his long imprisonment and the recollection of his son, bleeding and dying in his arms by the blow of the ferocious Charlot, made him long resist the urgency of his friends. Though glory called him to encounter Bruhier, and the safety of Christendom demanded the destruction of this proud enemy of the faith, Ogier only yielded at last on condition that Charlot should be delivered into his hands to be dealt with as he should see fit.

The terms were hard, but the danger was pressing, and Charlemagne, with a returning sense of justice, and a strong confidence in the generous though passionate soul of Ogier, at last consented to them.

Ogier was led into the presence of Charlemagne by the three peers. The Emperor, faithful to his word, had caused Charlot to be brought into the hall where the high barons were assembled, his hands tied, and his head uncovered. When the Emperor saw Ogier approach he took Charlot by the arm, led him towards Ogier, and said these words: "I surrender the criminal; do with him as you think fit." Ogier, without replying, seized Charlot by the hair, forced him on his knees, and lifted with the other hand his irresistible sword. Charlemagne, who expected to see the head of his son rolling at his feet, shut his eyes and uttered a cry of horror.

Ogier had done enough. The next moment he raised Charlot, cut his bonds, kissed him on the mouth, and hastened to throw himself at the feet of the Emperor.

Nothing can exceed the surprise and joy of Charlemagne at seeing his son unharmed and Ogier kneeling at his feet. He folded him in his arms, bathed him with tears, and exclaimed to his barons, "I feel at this moment that Ogier is greater than I." As for Charlot, his base soul felt nothing but the joy of having escaped death; he remained such as he had been, and it was not till some years afterwards he received the punishment he deserved, from the hands of Huon of Bordeaux, as we have seen in a former chapter.

OGIER, THE DANE (CONTINUED)

WHEN Charlemagne had somewhat recovered his composure he was surprised to observe that Ogier appeared in good case, and had a healthy color in his cheeks. He turned to the Archbishop, who could not help blushing as he met his eye. "By the head of Bertha, my queen," said Charlemagne, "Ogier has had good quarters in your castle, my Lord Archbishop; but so much the more am I indebted to you." All the barons laughed and jested with Turpin, who only said, "Laugh as much as you please, my lords; but for my part I am not sorry to see the arm in full vigor that is to avenge us on the proud Saracen."

Charlemagne immediately despatched his herald, accepting the challenge, and appointing the next day but one for the encounter. The proud and crafty Bruhier laughed scornfully when he heard the reply accepting his challenge, for he had a reliance on certain resources besides his natural strength and skill. However, he swore by Mahomet to observe the conditions as proposed and agreed upon.

Ogier now demanded his armor, and it was brought to him in excellent condition, for the good Turpin had kept it faithfully; but it was not easy to provide a horse for the occasion. Charlemagne had the best horses of his stables brought out, except Blanchard, his own charger; but all in vain, the weight of Ogier bent their backs to the ground. In this embarrassment the Archbishop remembered that the Emperor had given Beiffror to the Abbot of St. Faron, and sent off a courier in haste to re-demand him.

Monks are hard masters, and the one who directed the laborers at the abbey had but too faithfully obeyed the orders of the Abbot. Poor Beiffror was brought back, lean, spiritless, and chafed with the harness of the vile cart that he had had to draw so long. He carried his head down, and trod heavily before Charlemagne; but when he heard the voice of Ogier he raised his head, he neighed, his eyes flashed, his former ardor showed itself by the force with which he pawed the ground. Ogier caressed him, and the good steed seemed to return his caresses; Ogier mounted him, and Beiffror, proud of carrying his master again, leapt and curvetted with all his youthful vigor.

Nothing being now wanted, Charlemagne, at the head of his army, marched forth from the city of Paris, and occupied the hill of Montmartre, whence the view extended over the plain of St. Denis, where the battle was to be fought.

When the appointed day came the Dukes Namo and Salomon, as seconds of Ogier, accompanied him to the place marked out for the lists, and Bruhier, with two distinguished Emirs, presented himself on the other side.

Bruhier was in high spirits, and jested with his friends, as he advanced, upon the appearance of Beiffror. "Is that the horse they presume to match with Marchevallee, the best steed that ever fed in the vales of Mount Atlas?" But now the combatants, having met and saluted each other, ride apart to come together in full career. Beiffror flew over the plain, and met the adversary more than half-way. The lances of the two combatants were shivered at the shock, and Bruhier was astonished to see almost at the same instant the sword of Ogier gleaming above his head. He parried it with his buckler, and gave Ogier a blow on his helmet, who returned it with another, better aimed or better seconded by the temper of his blade, for it cut away part of Bruhier's helmet, and with it his ear and part of his cheek. Ogier, seeing the blood, did not immediately repeat his blow, and Bruhier seized the moment to gallop off at one side. As he rode he took a vase of gold which hung at his saddle-bow, and bathed with its contents the wounded part. The blood instantly ceased to flow, the ear and the flesh were restored quite whole, and the Dane was astonished to see his antagonist return to the ground as sound as ever.

Bruhier laughed at his amazement. "Know," said he, "that I possess the precious balm that Joseph of Arimathea used upon the body of the crucified one, whom you worship. If I should lose an arm I could restore it with a few drops of this. It is useless for you to contend with me. Yield yourself, and, as you appear to be a strong fellow, I will make you first oarsman in one of my galleys."

Ogier, though boiling with rage, forgot not to implore the assistance of Heaven. "O Lord!" he exclaimed, "suffer not the enemy of thy name to profit by the powerful help of that which owes all its virtue to thy divine blood." At these words he attacked Bruhier again with more vigor than ever; both struck terrible blows, and made grievous wounds; but the blood flowed from those of Ogier, while Bruhier stanched his by the application of his balm. Ogier, desperate at the unequal contest, grasped Cortana with both hands, and struck his enemy such a blow that it cleft his buckler, and cut off his arm with it; but Bruhier at the same time launched one at Ogier, which, missing him, struck the head of Beiffror, and the good horse fell, and drew down his master in his fall.

Bruhier had time to leap to the ground, to pick up his arm and apply his balsam; then, before Ogier had recovered his footing, he rushed forward with sword uplifted to complete his destruction.

Charlemagne, from the height of Montmartre, seeing the brave Ogier in this situation, groaned, and was ready to murmur against Providence; but the good Turpin, raising his arms, with a faith like that of Moses, drew down upon the Christian warrior the favor of Heaven.

Ogier, promptly disengaging himself, pressed Bruhier with so much impetuosity that he drove him to a distance from his horse, to whose saddle-bow the precious balm was suspended; and very soon Charlemagne saw Ogier, now completely in the advantage, bring his enemy to his knees, tear off his helmet, and, with a sweep of his sword, strike his head from his body.

After the victory, Ogier seized Marchevallee, leaped upon his back, and became possessed of the precious flask, a few drops from which closed his wounds and restored his strength. The French knights who had been Bruhier's captives, now released, pressed round Ogier to thank him for their deliverance.

Charlemagne and his nobles, as soon as their attention was relieved from the single combat, perceived from their elevated position an unusual agitation in the enemy's camp. They attributed it at first to the death of their general, but soon the noise of arms, the cries of combatants, and new standards which advanced, disclosed to them the fact that Bruhier's army was attacked by a new enemy.

The Emperor was right; it was the brave Carahue of Mauritania, who, with an army, had arrived in France, resolved to attempt the liberation of Ogier, his brother in arms. Learning on his arrival the changed aspect of affairs, he hesitated not to render a signal service to the Emperor, by attacking the army of Bruhier in the midst of the consternation occasioned by the loss of its commander.

Ogier recognized the standard of his friend, and leaping upon Marchevallee, flew to aid his attack. Charlemagne followed with his army; and the Saracen host, after an obstinate conflict, was forced to surrender unconditionally.

The interview of Ogier and Carahue was such as might be anticipated of two such attached friends and accomplished knights. Charlemagne went to meet them, embraced them, and putting the King of Mauritania on his right and Ogier on his left, returned with triumph to Paris. There the Empress Bertha and the ladies of her court crowned them with laurels, and the sage and gallant Eginhard, chamberlain and secretary of the Emperor, wrote all these great events in his history.

A few days after Guyon, King of Denmark, arrived in France with a chosen band of knights, and sent an ambassador to Charlemagne, to say that he came, not as an enemy, but to render homage to him as the best knight of the time and the head of the Christian world. Charlemagne gave the ambassador a cordial reception, and mounting his horse, rode forward to meet the King of Denmark.

These great princes, being assembled at the court of Charles, held council together, and the ancient and sage barons were called to join it.

It was decided that the united Danish and Mauritanian armies should cross the sea and carry the war to the country of the Saracens, and that a thousand French knights should range themselves under the banner of Ogier, the Dane, who, though not a king, should have equal rank with the two others.

We have not space to record all the illustrious actions performed by Ogier and his allies in this war. Suffice it to say, they subdued the Saracens of Ptolemais and Judaea, and, erecting those regions into a kingdom, placed the crown upon the head of Ogier. Guyon and Carahue then left him, to return to their respective dominions. Ogier adopted Walter, the son of Guyon of Denmark, to be his successor in his kingdom. He superintended his education, and saw the young prince grow up worthy of his cares. But Ogier, in spite of all the honors of his rank, often regretted the court of Charlemagne, the Duke Namo, and Salomon of Brittany, for whom he had the respect and attachment of a son. At last, finding Walter old enough to sustain the weight of government, Ogier caused a vessel to be prepared secretly, and, attended only by one squire, left his palace by night, and embarked to return to France.

The vessel, driven by a fair wind, cut the sea with the swiftness of a bird; but on a sudden it deviated from its course, no longer obeyed the helm, and sped fast towards a black promontory which stretched into the sea. This was a mountain of loadstone, and, its attractive power increasing as the distance diminished, the vessel at last flew with the swiftness of an arrow towards it, and was dashed to pieces on its rocky base. Ogier alone saved himself, and reached the shore on a fragment of the wreck.

Ogier advanced into the country, looking for some marks of inhabitancy, but found none. On a sudden he encountered two monstrous animals, covered with glittering scales, accompanied by a horse breathing fire. Ogier drew his sword and prepared to defend himself; but the monsters, terrific as they appeared, made no attempt to assail him, and the horse, Papillon, knelt down, and appeared to court Ogier to mount upon his back. Ogier hesitated not to see the adventure through; he mounted Papillon, who ran with speed, and soon cleared the rocks and precipices which hemmed in and concealed a beautiful landscape. He continued his course till he reached a magnificent palace, and, without allowing Ogier time to admire it, crossed a grand court-yard adorned with colonnades, and entered a garden, where, making his way through alleys of myrtle, he checked his course, and knelt down on the enamelled turf of a fountain.

Ogier dismounted and took some steps along the margin of the stream, but was soon stopped by meeting a young beauty, such as they paint the Graces, and almost as lightly attired as they. At the same moment, to his amazement, his armor fell off of its own accord. The young beauty advanced with a tender air, and placed upon his head a crown of flowers. At that instant the Danish hero lost his memory; his combats, his glory, Charlemagne and his court, all vanished from his mind; he saw only Morgana, he desired nothing but to sigh forever at her feet.

We abridge the narrative of all the delights which Ogier enjoyed for more than a hundred years. Time flew by, leaving no impression of its flight. Morgana's youthful charms did not decay, and Ogier had none of those warnings of increasing years which less favored mortals never fail to receive. There is no knowing how long this blissful state might have lasted, if it had not been for an accident, by which Morgana one day, in a sportive moment, snatched the crown from his head. That moment Ogier regained his memory, and lost his contentment. The recollection of Charlemagne, and of his own relatives and friends, saddened the hours which he passed with Morgana. The fairy saw with grief the changed looks of her lover. At last she drew from him the acknowledgment that he wished to go, at least for a time, to revisit Charles's court. She consented with reluctance, and with her own hands helped to reinvest him with his armor. Papillon was led forth, Ogier mounted him, and, taking a tender adieu of the tearful Morgana, crossed at rapid speed the rocky belt which separated Morgana's palace from the borders of the sea. The sea-goblins which had received him at his coming awaited him on the shore. One of them took Ogier on his back, and the other placing himself under Papillon, they spread their broad fins, and in a short time traversed the wide space that separates the isle of Avalon from France. They landed Ogier on the coast of Languedoc, and then plunged into the sea and disappeared.

Ogier remounted on Papillon, who carried him across the kingdom almost as fast as he had passed the sea. He

Figure 127: "The Love Potion" by Evelyn de Morgan

arrived under the walls of Paris, which he would scarcely have recognized if the high towers of St. Genevieve had not caught his eye. He went straight to the palace of Charlemagne, which seemed to him to have been entirely rebuilt. His surprise was extreme, and increased still more on finding that he understood with difficulty the language of the guards and attendants in replying to his questions; and seeing them smile as they tried to explain to one another the language in which he addressed them. Presently the attention of some of the barons who were going to court was attracted to the scene, and Ogier, who recognized the badges of their rank, addressed them, and inquired if the Dukes Namo and Salomon were still residing at the Emperor's court. At this question the barons looked at one another in amazement; and one of the eldest said to the rest, "How much this knight resembles the portrait of my grand-uncle, Ogier the Dane." "Ah! my dear nephew, I am Ogier the Dane," said he; and he remembered that Morgana had told him that he was little aware of the flight of time during his abode with her.

The barons, more astonished than ever, concluded to conduct him to the monarch who then reigned, the great Hugh Capet.

The brave Ogier entered the palace without hesitation; but when, on reaching the royal hall, the barons directed him to make his obeisance to the King of France, he was astonished to see a man of short stature and large head, whose air, nevertheless, was noble and martial, seated upon the throne on which he had so often seen Charlemagne, the tallest and handsomest sovereign of his time.

Ogier recounted his adventures with simplicity and affectedness. Hugh Capet was slow to believe him; but Ogier recalled so many proofs and circumstances, that at last he was forced to recognize the aged warrior to be the famous Ogier the Dane.

The king informed Ogier of the events which had taken place during his long absence; that the line of Charlemagne was extinct; that a new dynasty had commenced; that the old enemies of the kingdom, the Saracens, were still troublesome; and that at that very time an army of those miscreants was besieging the city of Chartres, to which he was about to repair in a few days to its relief. Ogier, always inflamed with the love of glory, offered the service of his arm, which the illustrious monarch accepted graciously, and conducted him to the queen. The astonishment of Ogier was redoubled when he saw the new ornaments and head-dresses of the ladies; still, the beautiful hair which they built up on their foreheads, and the feathers interwoven, which waved with so much grace, gave them a noble air that delighted him. His admiration increased when, instead of the old Empress Bertha, he saw a young queen who combined a majestic mien with the graces of her time of life, and manners candid and charming, suited to attach all hearts. Ogier saluted the youthful queen with a respect so profound that many of the courtiers took him for a foreigner, or at least for some nobleman brought up at a distance from Paris, who retained the manners of what they called the old court.

When the queen was informed by her husband that it was the celebrated Ogier the Dane whom he presented to her, whose memorable exploits she had often read in the chronicles of antiquity, her surprise was extreme, which was increased when she remarked the dignity of his address, the animation and even the youthfulness of his countenance. This queen had too much intelligence to believe hastily; proof alone could compel her assent; and she asked him many questions about the old court of Charlemagne, and received such instructive and appropriate answers as removed every doubt. It is to the corrections which Ogier was at that time enabled to make to the popular narratives of his exploits that we are indebted for the perfect accuracy and trustworthiness of all the details of our own history.

King Hugh Capet, having received that same evening couriers from the inhabitants of Chartres, informing him that they were hard pressed by the besiegers, resolved to hasten with Ogier to their relief.

Ogier terminated this affair as expeditiously as he had so often done others. The Saracens having dared to offer battle, he bore the Oriflamme through the thickest of their ranks; Papillon, breathing fire from his nostrils, threw them into disorder, and Cortana, wielded by his invincible arm, soon finished their overthrow.

The king, victorious over the Saracens, led back the Danish hero to Paris, where the deliverer of France received the honors due to his valor. Ogier continued some time at the court, detained by the favor of the king and queen; but erelong he had the pain to witness the death of the king. Then it was that, impressed with all the perfections which he had discerned in the queen, he could not withhold the tender homage of the offer of his hand. The queen would perhaps have accepted it, she had even called a meeting of her great barons to deliberate on the proposition, when, the day before the meeting was to be held, at the moment when Ogier was kneeling at her feet, she perceived a crown of gold which an invisible hand had placed on his brow, and in an instant a cloud enveloped Ogier, and he disappeared forever from her sight. It was Morgana, the fairy, whose jealousy was awakened at what she beheld, who now resumed her power, and took him away to dwell with her in the island of Avalon. There, in company with the great King Arthur of Britain, he still lives, and when his illustrious friend shall return to resume his ancient reign he will doubtless return with him, and share his triumph.

Figure 128: Untitled from Orlando Furioso by Gustave Dore

Glossary

A

ABDALRAHMAN, founder of the independent Ommiad (Saracenic) power in Spain, conquered at Tours by Charles Martel

ABERFRAW, scene of nuptials of Branwen and Matholch

ABSYRTUS, younger brother of Medea

ABYDOS, a town on the Hellespont, nearly opposite to Sestos

ABYLA, Mount, or Columna, a mountain in Morocco, near Ceuta, now called Jebel Musa or Ape's Hill, forming the Northwestern extremity of the African coast opposite Gibraltar (See Pillars of Hercules)

ACESTES, son of a Trojan woman who was sent by her father to Sicily, that she might not be devoured by the monsters which infested the territory of Troy

ACETES, Bacchanal captured by Pentheus

ACHATES, faithful friend and companion of Aeneas

ACHELOUS, river-god of the largest river in Greece—his Horn of Plenty

ACHILLES, the hero of the Iliad, son of Peleus and of the Nereid Thetis, slain by Paris

ACIS, youth loved by Galatea and slain by Polyphemus

ACONTIUS, a beautiful youth, who fell in love with Cydippe, the daughter of a noble Athenian.

ACRISIUS, son of Abas, king of Argos, grandson of Lynceus, the great-grandson of Danaus.

ACTAEON, a celebrated huntsman, son of Aristaeus and Autonoe, who, having seen Diana bathing, was changed by her to a stag and killed by his own dogs.

ADMETA, daughter of Eurystheus, covets Hippolyta's girdle.

ADMETUS, king of Thessaly, saved from death by Alcestis

ADONIS, a youth beloved by Aphrodite (Venus), and Proserpine; killed by a boar.

ADRASTUS, a king of Argos.

AEACUS, son of Zeus (Jupiter) and Aegina, renowned in all Greece for his justice and piety.

AEAEA, Circe's island, visited by Ulysses.

AEETES, or Aeeta, son of Helios (the Sun) and Perseis, and father of Medea and Absyrtus.

AEGEUS, king of Athens.

AEGINA, a rocky island in the middle of the Saronic gulf.

AEGIS, shield or breastplate of Jupiter and Minerva.

AEGISTHUS, murderer of Agamemnon, slain by Orestes.

AENEAS, Trojan hero, son of Anchises and Aphrodite (Venus), and born on Mount Ida, reputed first settler of Rome,

AENEID, poem by Virgil, relating the wanderings of Aeneas from Troy to Italy,

AE'OLUS, son of Hellen and the nymph Orseis, represented in Homer as the happy ruler of the Aeolian Islands, to whom Zeus had given dominion over the winds,

AESCULAPIUS, god of the medical art,

AESON, father of Jason, made young again by Medea,

AETHIOPIANS, inhabitants of the country south of Egypt,

AETHRA, mother of Theseus by Aegeus,

AETNA, volcano in Sicily,

AGAMEDES, brother of Trophonius, distinguished as an architect,

AGAMEMNON, son of Plisthenis and grandson of Atreus, king of Mycenae, although the chief commander of the Greeks, is not the hero of the Iliad, and in chivalrous spirit altogether inferior to Achilles,

AGAVE, daughter of Cadmus, wife of Echion, and mother of Pentheus,

AGENOR, father of Europa, Cadmus, Cilix, and Phoenix,

AGLAIA, one of the Graces,

AGNI, Hindu god of fire,

AGRAMANT, a king in Africa,

AGRICAN, fabled king of Tartary, pursuing Angelica, finally killed by Orlando,

AGRIVAIN, one of Arthur's knights,

AHRIMAN, the Evil Spirit in the dual system of Zoroaster, See Ormuzd

AJAX, son of Telamon, king of Salamis, and grandson of Aeacus, represented in the Iliad as second only to Achilles in bravery,

ALBA, the river where King Arthur fought the Romans,

ALBA LONGA, city in Italy founded by son of Aeneas,

ALBERICH, dwarf guardian of Rhine gold treasure of the Nibelungs

ALBRACCA, siege of,

ALCESTIS, wife of Admetus, offered herself as sacrifice to spare her husband, but rescued by Hercules,

ALCIDES (Hercules),

ALCINA, enchantress,

ALCINOUS, Phaeacian king,

Glossary

ALCIPPE, daughter of Mars, carried off by Halirrhothrus,

ALCMENA, wife of Jupiter, and mother of Hercules,

ALCUIN, English prelate and scholar,

ALDROVANDUS, dwarf guardian of treasure,

ALECTO, one of the Furies,

ALEXANDER THE GREAT, king of Macedonia, conqueror of Greece, Egypt, Persia, Babylonia, and India,

ALFADUR, a name for Odin,

ALFHEIM, abode of the elves of light,

ALICE, mother of Huon and Girard, sons of Duke Sevinus,

ALPHENOR, son of Niobe,

ALPHEUS, river god pursuing Arethusa, who escaped by being changed to a fountain,

ALTHAEA, mother of Meleager, whom she slew because he had in a quarrel killed her brothers, thus disgracing "the house of Thestius," her father,

AMALTHEA, nurse of the infant Jupiter in Crete,

AMATA, wife of Latinus, driven mad by Alecto,

AMAURY OF HAUTEVILLE, false hearted Knight of Charlemagne,

AMAZONS, mythical race of warlike women,

AMBROSIA, celestial food used by the gods,

AMMON, Egyptian god of life identified by Romans with phases of Jupiter, the father of gods,

AMPHIARAUS, a great prophet and hero at Argos,

AMPHION, a musician, son of Jupiter and Antiope (See Dirce),

AMPHITRITE, wife of Neptune,

AMPHYRSOS, a small river in Thessaly,

AMPYX, assailant of Perseus, turned to stone by seeing Gorgon's head,

AMRITA, nectar giving immortality,

AMUN, See Ammon

AMYMONE, one of the fifty daughters of Danaus, and mother by Poseidon (Neptune) of Nauplius, the father of Palamedes,

ANAXARETE, a maiden of Cyprus, who treated her lover Iphis with such haughtiness that he hanged himself at her door,

ANBESSA, Saracenic governor of Spain (725 AD),

ANCEUS, one of the Argonauts,

ANCHISES, beloved by Aphrodite (Venus), by whom he became the father of Aeneas,

ANDRAEMON, husband of Dryope, saw her changed into a tree,

ANDRET, a cowardly knight, spy upon Tristram,

ANDROMACHE, wife of Hector

ANDROMEDA, daughter of King Cephas, delivered from monster by Perseus

ANEURIN, Welsh bard

ANGELICA, Princess of Cathay

ANEMONE, short lived wind flower, created by Venus from the blood of the slain Adonis

ANGERBODE, giant prophetess, mother of Fenris, Hela and the Midgard Serpent

ANGLESEY, a Northern British island, refuge of Druids fleeing from Romans

ANTAEUS, giant wrestler of Libya, killed by Hercules, who, finding him stronger when thrown to the earth, lifted him into the air and strangled him

ANTEA, wife of jealous Proetus

ANTENOR, descendants of, in Italy

ANTEROS, deity avenging unrequited love, brother of Eros (Cupid)

ANTHOR, a Greek

ANTIGONE, daughter of Aedipus, Greek ideal of filial and sisterly fidelity

ANTILOCHUS, son of Nestor

ANTIOPE, Amazonian queen. See Dirce

ANUBIS, Egyptian god, conductor of the dead to judgment

APENNINES

APHRODITE See Venus, Dione, etc.

APIS, Egyptian bull god of Memphis

APOLLO, god of music and song

APOLLO BELVEDERE, famous antique statue in Vatican at Rome

APPLES OF THE HESPERIDES, wedding gifts to Juno, guarded by daughters of Atlas and Hesperis, stolen by Atlas for Hercules,

AQUILO, or Boreas, the North Wind,

AQUITAINE, ancient province of Southwestern France,

ARACHNE, a maiden skilled in weaving, changed to a spider by Minerva for daring to compete with her,

ARCADIA, a country in the middle of Peloponnesus, surrounded on all sides by mountains,

ARCADY, star of, the Pole star,

ARCAS, son of Jupiter and Callisto,

ARCHER, constellation of the,

AREOPAGUS, court of the, at Athens,

ARES, called Mars by the Romans, the Greek god of war, and one of the great Olympian gods,

ARETHUSA, nymph of Diana, changed to a fountain,

ARGIUS king of Ireland, father of Isoude the Fair,

ARGO, builder of the vessel of Jason for the Argonautic expedition,

ARGOLIS, city of the Nemean games,

ARGONAUTS, Jason's crew seeking the Golden Fleece,

ARGOS, a kingdom in Greece,

ARGUS, of the hundred eyes, guardian of Io,

ARIADNE, daughter of King Minos, who helped Theseus slay the Minotaur,

ARIMANES SEE Ahriman.

ARIMASPIANS, one-eyed people of Syria,

ARION, famous musician, whom sailors cast into the sea to rob him, but whose lyric song charmed the dolphins, one of which bore him safely to land,

ARISTAEUS, the bee keeper, in love with Eurydice,

ARMORICA, another name for Britain,

ARRIDANO, a magical ruffian, slain by Orlando,

ARTEMIS SEE Diana

ARTHGALLO, brother of Elidure, British king,

ARTHUR, king in Britain about the 6th century,

ARUNS, an Etruscan who killed Camilla,

ASGARD, home of the Northern gods,

ASHTAROTH, a cruel spirit, called by enchantment to bring Rinaldo to death,

ASKE, the first man, made from an ash tree,

ASTOLPHO OF ENGLAND, one of Charlemagne's knights,

ASTRAEA, goddess of justice, daughter of Astraeus and Eos,

ASTYAGES, an assailant of Perseus,

ASTYANAX, son of Hector of Troy, established kingdom of Messina in Italy,

ASUIAS, opponents of the Braminical gods,

ATALANTA, beautiful daughter of King of Icaria, loved and won in a foot race by Hippomenes,

ATE, the goddess of infatuation, mischief and guilt,

ATHAMAS, son of Aeolus and Enarete, and king of Orchomenus, in Boeotia, SEE Ino

ATHENE, tutelary goddess of Athens, the same as Minerva,

ATHENS, the capital of Attica, about four miles from the sea, between the small rivers Cephissus and Ilissus,

ATHOR, Egyptian deity, progenitor of Isis and Osiris,

ATHOS, the mountainous peninsula, also called Acte, which projects from Chalcidice in Macedonia,

ATLANTES, foster father of Rogero, a powerful magician,

ATLANTIS, according to an ancient tradition, a great island west of the Pillars of Hercules, in the ocean, opposite Mount Atlas,

ATLAS, a Titan, who bore the heavens on his shoulders, as punishment for opposing the gods, one of the sons of Iapetus,

ATLAS, Mount, general name for range in northern Africa,

ATROPOS, one of the Fates

ATTICA, a state in ancient Greece,

AUDHUMBLA, the cow from which the giant Ymir was nursed. Her milk was frost melted into raindrops,

AUGEAN STABLES, cleansed by Hercules,

AUGEAS, king of Elis,

AUGUSTAN AGE, reign of Roman Emperor Augustus Caesar, famed for many great authors,

AUGUSTUS, the first imperial Caesar, who ruled the Roman Empire 31 BC—14 AD,

AULIS, port in Boeotia, meeting place of Greek expedition against Troy,

AURORA, identical with Eos, goddess of the dawn,

AURORA BOREALIS, splendid nocturnal luminosity in northern sky, called Northern Lights, probably electrical,

AUTUMN, attendant of Phoebus, the Sun,

AVALON, land of the Blessed, an earthly paradise in the Western Seas, burial place of King Arthur,

AVATAR, name for any of the earthly incarnations of Vishnu, the Preserver (Hindu god),

AVENTINE, Mount, one of the Seven Hills of Rome,

AVERNUS, a miasmatic lake close to the promontory between Cumae and Puteoli, filling the crater of an extinct volcano, by the ancients thought to be the entrance to the infernal regions,

AVICENNA, celebrated Arabian physician and philosopher,

AYA, mother of Rinaldo,

AYMON, Duke, father of Rinaldo and Bradamante,

B

BAAL, king of Tyre,

BABYLONIAN RIVER, dried up when Phaeton drove the sun chariot,

BACCHANALI A, a feast to Bacchus that was permitted to occur but once in three years, attended by most shameless orgies,

BACCHANALS, devotees and festal dancers of Bacchus,

BACCHUS (Dionysus), god of wine and revelry,

BADON, battle of, Arthur's final victory over the Saxons,

BAGDEMAGUS, King, a knight of Arthur's time,

BALDUR, son of Odin, and representing in Norse mythology the sun god,

BALISARDO, Orlando's sword,

BAN, King of Brittany, ally of Arthur, father of Launcelot,

BARDS, minstrels of Welsh Druids,

BASILISK SEE Cockatrice

BAUCIS, wife of Philemon, visited by Jupiter and Mercury,

BAYARD, wild horse subdued by Rinaldo,

BEAL, Druids' god of life,

BEDIVERE, Arthur's knight,

BEDVER, King Arthur's butler, made governor of Normandy,

BEDWYR, knightly comrade of Geraint,

BELISARDA, Rogero's sword,

BELLEROPHON, demigod, conqueror of the Chimaera,

BELLONA, the Roman goddess of war, represented as the sister or wife of Mars,

BELTANE, Druidical fire festival,

BELUS, son of Poseidon (Neptune) and Libya or Eurynome, twin brother of Agenor,

BENDIGEID VRAN, King of Britain,

BEOWULF, hero and king of the Swedish Geats,

BEROE, nurse of Semele,

BERTHA, mother of Orlando,

BIFROST, rainbow bridge between the earth and Asgard

BLADUD, inventor, builder of the city of Bath,

BLAMOR, a knight of Arthur,

BLEOBERIS, a knight of Arthur,

BOEOTIA, state in ancient Greece, capital city Thebes,

BOHORT, King, a knight of Arthur,

BONA DEA, a Roman divinity of fertility,

BOOTES, also called Areas, son of Jupiter and Calisto, changed to constellation of Ursa Major,

BOREAS, North wind, son of Aeolus and Aurora,

BOSPORUS (Bosphorus), the Cow-ford, named for Io, when as a heifer she crossed that strait,

BRADAMANTE, sister to Rinaldo, a female warrior,

BRADEMAGUS, King, father of Sir Maleagans,

BRAGI, Norse god of poetry,

BRAHMA, the Creator, chief god of Hindu religion,

BRANWEN, daughter of Llyr, King of Britain, wife of Mathclch,

BRECILIANDE, forest of, where Vivian enticed Merlin,

BRENGWAIN, maid of Isoude the Fair

BRENNUS, son of Molmutius, went to Gaul, became King of the Allobroges,

BREUSE, the Pitiless, a caitiff knight,

BRIAREUS, hundred armed giant,

BRICE, Bishop, sustainer of Arthur when elected king,

BRIGLIADORO, Orlando's horse,

BRISEIS, captive maid belonging to Achilles,

BRITTO, reputed ancestor of British people,

BRUHIER, Sultan of Arabia,

BRUNELLO, dwarf, thief, and king

BRUNHILD, leader of the Valkyrie,

BRUTUS, great grandson of Aeneas, and founder of city of New Troy (London), SEE Pandrasus

BRYAN, Sir, a knight of Arthur,

BUDDHA, called The Enlightened, reformer of Brahmanism, deified teacher of self abnegation, virtue, reincarnation, Karma (inevitable sequence of every act), and Nirvana (beatific absorption into the Divine), lived about

BYBLOS, in Egypt,

BYRSA, original site of Carthage,

C

CACUS, gigantic son of Vulcan, slain by Hercules, whose captured cattle he stole,

CADMUS, son of Agenor, king of Phoenicia, and of Telephassa, and brother of Europa, who, seeking his sister, carried off by Jupiter, had strange adventures—sowing in the ground teeth of a dragon he had killed, which sprang up armed men who slew each other, all but five, who helped Cadmus to found the city of Thebes,

CADUCEUS, Mercury's staff,

CADWALLO, King of Venedotia (North Wales),

CAERLEON, traditional seat of Arthur's court,

CAESAR, Julius, Roman lawyer, general, statesman and author, conquered and consolidated Roman territory, making possible the Empire,

CAICUS, a Greek river,

CAIRNS, Druidical store piles,

CALAIS, French town facing England,

CALCHAS, wisest soothsayer among the Greeks at Troy,

CALIBURN, a sword of Arthur,

CALLIOPE, one of the nine Muses

CALLISTO, an Arcadian nymph, mother of Arcas (SEE Bootes), changed by Jupiter to constellation Ursa Minor,

CALPE, a mountain in the south of Spain, on the strait between the Atlantic and Mediterranean, now Rock of Gibraltar,

CALYDON, home of Meleager,

CALYPSO, queen of Island of Ogyia, where Ulysses was wrecked and held seven years,

CAMBER, son of Brutus, governor of West Albion (Wales),

CAMELOT, legendary place in England where Arthur's court and palace were located,

CAMENAE, prophetic nymphs, belonging to the religion of ancient Italy,

CAMILLA, Volscian maiden, huntress and Amazonian warrior, favorite of Diana,

CAMLAN, battle of, where Arthur was mortally wounded,

CANTERBURY, English city,

CAPANEUS, husband of Evadne, slain by Jupiter for disobedience,

CAPET, Hugh, King of France (987-996 AD),

CARADOC BRIEFBRAS, Sir, great nephew of King Arthur,

CARAHUE, King of Mauretania,

CARTHAGE, African city, home of Dido

CASSANDRA, daughter of Priam and Hecuba, and twin sister of Helenus, a prophetess, who foretold the coming of the Greeks but was not believed,

CASSIBELLAUNUS, British chieftain, fought but not conquered by Caesar,

CASSIOPEIA, mother of Andromeda,

CASTALIA, fountain of Parnassus, giving inspiration to Oracular priestess named Pythia,

CASTALIAN CAVE, oracle of Apollo,

CASTES (India),

CASTOR AND POLLUX—the Dioscuri, sons of Jupiter and Leda,—Castor a horseman, Pollux a boxer (SEE Gemini),

CAUCASUS, Mount

CAVALL, Arthur's favorite dog,

CAYSTER, ancient river,

CEBRIONES, Hector's charioteer,

CECROPS, first king of Athens,

CELESTIALS, gods of classic mythology,

CELEUS, shepherd who sheltered Ceres, seeking Proserpine, and whose infant son Triptolemus was in gratitude made great by Ceres,

CELLINI, Benvenuto, famous Italian sculptor and artificer in metals,

CELTIC NATIONS, ancient Gauls and Britons, modern Bretons, Welsh, Irish and Gaelic Scotch,

CENTAURS, originally an ancient race, inhabiting Mount Pelion in Thessaly, in later accounts represented as half horses and half men, and said to have been the offspring of Ixion and a cloud,

CEPHALUS, husband of beautiful but jealous Procris,

CEPHEUS, King of Ethiopians, father of Andromeda,

CEPHISUS, a Grecian stream,

CERBERUS, three-headed dog that guarded the entrance to Hades, called a son of Typhaon and Echidna

CERES (See Demeter)

CESTUS, the girdle of Venus

CEYX, King of Thessaly (See Halcyone)

CHAOS, original Confusion, personified by Greeks as most ancient of the gods

CHARLEMAGNE, king of the Franks and emperor of the Romans

CHARLES MARTEL', king of the Franks, grandfather of Charlemagne, called Martel (the Hammer) from his defeat of the Saracens at Tours

CHARLOT, son of Charlemagne

CHARON, son of Erebos, conveyed in his boat the shades of the dead across the rivers of the lower world

CHARYB'DIS, whirlpool near the coast of Sicily, See Scylla

CHIMAERA, a fire breathing monster, the fore part of whose body was that of a lion, the hind part that of a dragon, and the middle that of a goat, slain by Bellerophon

CHINA, Lamas (priests) of

CHOS, island in the Grecian archipelago

CHIRON, wisest of all the Centaurs, son of Cronos (Saturn) and Philyra, lived on Mount Pelion, instructor of Grecian heroes

CHRYSEIS, Trojan maid, taken by Agamemnon

CHRYSES, priest of Apollo, father of Chryseis

CICONIANS, inhabitants of Ismarus, visited by Ulysses

CIMBRI, an ancient people of Central Europe

CIMMERIA, a land of darkness

CIMON, Athenian general

CIRCE, sorceress, sister of Aeetes

CITHAERON, Mount, scene of Bacchic worship

CLARIMUNDA, wife of Huon

CLIO, one of the Muses

CLORIDAN, a Moor

CLOTHO, one of the Fates

CLYMENE, an ocean nymph

CLYTEMNESTRA, wife of Agamemnon, killed by Orestes

CLYTIE, a water nymph, in love with Apollo

CNIDOS, ancient city of Asia Minor, seat of worship of Aphrodite (Venus)

COCKATRICE (or Basilisk), called King of Serpents, supposed to kill with its look

COCYTUS, a river of Hades

COLCHIS, a kingdom east of the Black Sea

COLOPHON, one of the seven cities claiming the birth of Homer

COLUMBA, St, an Irish Christian missionary to Druidical parts of Scotland

CONAN, Welsh king

CONSTANTINE, Greek emperor

CORDEILLA, daughter of the mythical King Leir

CORINEUS, a Trojan warrior in Albion

CORNWALL, southwest part of Britain

CORTANA, Ogier's sword

CORYBANTES, priests of Cybele, or Rhea, in Phrygia, who celebrated her worship with dances, to the sound of the drum and the cymbal, 143

CRAB, constellation

CRANES AND THEIR ENEMIES, the Pygmies, of Ibycus

CREON, king of Thebes

CRETE, one of the largest islands of the Mediterranean Sea, lying south of the Cyclades

CREUSA, daughter of Priam, wife of Aeneas

CROCALE, a nymph of Diana

CROMLECH, Druidical altar

CRONOS, See Saturn

CROTONA, city of Italy

CUCHULAIN, Irish hero, called the "Hound of Ireland,"

CULDEES', followers of St. Columba, Cumaean Sibyl, seeress of Cumae, consulted by Aeneas, sold Sibylline books to Tarquin

CUPID, child of Venus and god of love

CUROI OF KERRY, wise man

CYANE, river, opposed Pluto's passage to Hades

CYBELE (Rhea)

CYCLOPES, creatures with circular eyes, of whom Homer speaks as a gigantic and lawless race of shepherds in Sicily, who devoured human beings, they helped Vulcan to forge the thunderbolts of Zeus under Aetna

CYMBELINE, king of ancient Britain

CYNOSURE (Dog's tail), the Pole star, at tail of Constellation Ursa Minor

CYNTHIAN mountain top, birthplace of Artemis (Diana) and Apollo

CYPRUS, island off the coast of Syria, sacred to Aphrodite

CYRENE, a nymph, mother of Aristaeus

D

DAEDALUS, architect of the Cretan Labyrinth, inventor of sails

DAGUENET, King Arthur's fool

DALAI LAMA, chief pontiff of Tibet

DANAE, mother of Perseus by Jupiter

DANAIDES, the fifty daughters of Danaus, king of Argos, who were betrothed to the fifty sons of Aegyptus, but were commanded by their father to slay each her own husband on the marriage night

DANAUS (See Danaides)

DAPHNE, maiden loved by Apollo, and changed into a laurel tree

DARDANELLES, ancient Hellespont

DARDANUS, progenitor of the Trojan kings

DARDINEL, prince of Zumara

DAWN, See Aurora

DAY, an attendant on Phoebus, the Sun

DAY STAR (Hesperus)

DEATH, See Hela

DEIPHOBUS, son of Priam and Hecuba, the bravest brother of Paris

DEJANIRA, wife of Hercules

DELOS, floating island, birthplace of Apollo and Diana

DELPHI, shrine of Apollo, famed for its oracles

DEMETER, Greek goddess of marriage and human fertility, identified by Romans with Ceres

DEMEHA, South Wales

DEMODOCUS, bard of Alomous, king of the Phaeaeians

DEUCALION, king of Thessaly, who with his wife Pyrrha were the only pair surviving a deluge sent by Zeus

DIA, island of

DIANA (Artemis), goddess of the moon and of the chase, daughter of Jupiter and Latona

DIANA OF THE HIND, antique sculpture in the Louvre, Paris

DIANA, temple of

DICTYS, a sailor

DIDIER, king of the Lombards

DIDO, queen of Tyre and Carthage, entertained the shipwrecked Aeneas

DIOMEDE, Greek hero during Trojan War

DIONE, female Titan, mother of Zeus, of Aphrodite (Venus)

DIONYSUS See Bacchus

DIOSCURI, the Twins (See Castor and Pollux)

DIRCE, wife of Lycus, king of Thebes, who ordered Amphion and Zethus to tie Antiope to a wild bull, but they, learning Antiope to be their mother, so treated Dirce herself

DIS See Pluto

DISCORD, apple of, See Eris.

DISCORDIA, See Eris.

DODONA, site of an oracle of Zeus (Jupiter)

DORCEUS, a dog of Diana

DORIS, wife of Nereus

DRAGON'S TEETH sown by Cadmus

DRUIDS, ancient Celtic priests

DRYADES (or Dryads), See Wood nymphs

DRYOPE, changed to a lotus plant, for plucking a lotus—enchanted form of the nymph Lotis

DUBRICIUS, bishop of Caerleon,

DUDON, a knight, comrade of Astolpho,

DUNWALLO MOLMUTIUS, British king and lawgiver

DURINDANA, sword of Orlando or Rinaldo

DWARFS IN WAGNER'S NIBELUNGEN RING

E

EARTH (Gaea); goddess of the

EBUDIANS, the

ECHO, nymph of Diana, shunned by Narcissus, faded to nothing but a voice

ECKLENLIED, the

EDDAS, Norse mythological records,

EDERYN, son of Nudd

EGENA, nymph of the Fountain

EISTEDDFOD, session of Welsh bards and minstrels

ELECTRA, the lost one of the Pleiades, also, sister of Orestes

ELEUSIAN Mysteries, instituted by Ceres, and calculated to awaken feelings of piety and a cheerful hope of better life in the future

ELEUSIS, Grecian city

ELGIN Marbles, Greek sculptures from the Parthenon of Athens, now in British Museum, London, placed there by Lord Elgin

ELIAURES, enchanter

ELIDURE, a king of Britain

ELIS, ancient Greek city

ELLI, old age; the one successful wrestler against Thor

ELPHIN, son of Gwyddiro

ELVES, spiritual beings, of many powers and dispositions—some evil, some good

ELVIDNIR, the ball of Hela

ELYSIAN FIELDS, the land of the blest

ELYSIAN PLAIN, whither the favored of the gods were taken without death

ELYSIUM, a happy land, where there is neither snow, nor cold, nor ram. Hither favored heroes, like Menelaus, pass without dying, and live happy under the rule of Rhadamanthus. In the Latin poets Elysium is part of the lower world, and the residence of the shades of the blessed

EMBLA, the first woman

ENSELADUS, giant defeated by Jupiter

ENDYMION, a beautiful youth beloved by Diana

ENID, wife of Geraint

ENNA, vale of home of Proserpine

ENOCH, the patriarch

EPIDAURUS, a town in Argolis, on the Saronic gulf, chief seat of the worship of Aeculapius, whose temple was situated near the town

EPIMETHEUS, son of Iapetus, husband of Pandora, with his brother Prometheus took part in creation of man

EPIRUS, country to the west of Thessaly, lying along the Adriatic Sea

EPOPEUS, a sailor

ERATO, one of the Muses

ERBIN OF CORNWALL, father of Geraint

EREBUS, son of Chaos, region of darkness, entrance to Hades

ERIDANUS, river

ERINYS, one of the Furies

ERIPHYLE, sister of Polynices, bribed to decide on war, in which her husband was slain

ERIS (Discordia), goddess of discord. At the wedding of Peleus and Thetis, Eris being uninvited threw into the gathering an apple "For the Fairest," which was claimed by Hera (Juno), Aphrodite (Venus) and Athena (Minerva) Paris, being called upon for judgment, awarded it to Aphrodite

ERISICHTHON, an unbeliever, punished by famine

EROS See Cupid

ERYTHEIA, island

ERYX, a mount, haunt of Venus

ESEPUS, river in Paphlagonia

ESTRILDIS, wife of Locrine, supplanting divorced Guendolen

ETEOCLES, son of Oeipus and Jocasta

ETRUSCANS, ancient people of Italy,

ETZEL, king of the Huns

EUBOIC Sea, where Hercules threw Lichas, who brought him the poisoned shirt of Nessus

EUDE, king of Aquitaine, ally of Charles Martel

EUMAEUS, swineherd of Aeeas

EUMENIDES, also called Erinnyes, and by the Romans Furiae or Diraae, the Avenging Deities, See Furies

EUPHORBUS, a Trojan, killed by Menelaus

EUPHROS'YNE, one of the Graces

EUROPA, daughter of the Phoenician king Agenor, by Zeus the mother of Minos, Rhadamanthus, and Sarpedon

EURUS, the East wind

EUYALUS, a gallant Trojan soldier, who with Nisus entered the Grecian camp, both being slain,

EURYDICE, wife of Orpheus, who, fleeing from an admirer, was killed by a snake and borne to Tartarus, where Orpheus sought her and was permitted to bring her to earth if he would not look back at her following him, but he did, and she returned to the Shades,

EURYLOCHUS, a companion of Ulysses,

EURYNOME, female Titan, wife of Ophlon

EURYSTHEUS, taskmaster of Hercules,

EURYTION, a Centaur (See Hippodamia),

EUTERPE, Muse who presided over music,

EVADNE, wife of Capaneus, who flung herself upon his funeral pile and perished with him

EVANDER, Arcadian chief, befriending Aeneas in Italy,

EVNISSYEN, quarrelsome brother of Branwen,

EXCALIBAR, sword of King Arthur,

F

FAFNER, a giant turned dragon, treasure stealer, by the Solar Theory simply the Darkness who steals the day,

FALERINA, an enchantress,

FASOLT, a giant, brother of Fafner, and killed by him,

"**FASTI**," Ovid's, a mythological poetic calendar,

FATA MORGANA, a mirage

FATES, the three, described as daughters of Night—to indicate the darkness and obscurity of human destiny—or of Zeus and Themis, that is, "daughters of the just heavens" they were Clo'tho, who spun the thread of life, Lach'esis, who held the thread and fixed its length and At'ropos, who cut it off

FAUNS, cheerful sylvan deities, represented in human form, with small horns, pointed ears, and sometimes goat's tail

FAUNUS, son of Picus, grandson of Saturnus, and father of Latinus, worshipped as the protecting deity of agriculture and of shepherds, and also as a giver of oracles

FAVONIUS, the West wind

FEAR

FENRIS, a wolf, the son of Loki the Evil Principle of Scandinavia, supposed to have personated the element of fire, destructive except when chained

FENSALIR, Freya's palace, called the Hall of the Sea, where were brought together lovers, husbands, and wives who had been separated by death

FERRAGUS, a giant, opponent of Orlando

FERRAU, one of Charlemagne's knights

FERREX. brother of Porrex, the two sons of Leir

FIRE WORSHIPPERS, of ancient Persia, See Parsees

FLOLLO, Roman tribune in Gaul

FLORA, Roman goddess of flowers and spring

FLORDELIS, fair maiden beloved by Florismart

FLORISMART, Sir, a brave knight,

FLOSSHILDA, one of the Rhine daughters

FORTUNATE FIELDS

FORTUNATE ISLANDS (See Elysian Plain)

FORUM, market place and open square for public meetings in Rome, surrounded by court houses, palaces, temples, etc

FRANCUS, son of Histion, grandson of Japhet, great grandson of Noah, legendary ancestor of the Franks, or French

FREKI, one of Odin's two wolves

FREY, or Freyr, god of the sun

FREYA, Norse goddess of music, spring, and flowers

FRICKA, goddess of marriage

FRIGGA, goddess who presided over smiling nature, sending sunshine, rain, and harvest

FROH, one of the Norse gods

FRONTI'NO, Rogero's horse

FURIES (Erinnyes), the three retributive spirits who punished crime, represented as snaky haired old woman, named Alecto, Megaeira, and Tisiphone

FUSBERTA, Rinaldo's sword

G

GAEA, or Ge, called Tellus by the Romans, the personification of the earth, described as the first being that sprang from Chaos, and gave birth to Uranus (Heaven) and Pontus (Sea)

GAHARIET, knight of Arthur's court

GAHERIS, knight

GALAFRON, King of Cathay, father of Angelica

GALAHAD, Sir, the pure knight of Arthur's Round Table, who safely took the Siege Perilous (which See)

GALATEA, a Nereid or sea nymph

GALATEA, statue carved and beloved by Pygmalion

GALEN, Greek physician and philosophical writer

GALLEHANT, King of the Marches

GAMES, national athletic contests in Greece—Olympian, at Olympia, Pythian, near Delphi, seat of Apollo's oracle, Isthmian, on the Corinthian Isthmus, Nemean, at Nemea in Argolis

GAN, treacherous Duke of Maganza

GANELON of Mayence, one of Charlemagne's knights

GANGES, river in India

GANO, a peer of Charlemagne

GANYMEDE, the most beautiful of all mortals, carried off to Olympus that he might fill the cup of Zeus and live among the immortal gods

GARETH, Arthur's knight

GAUDISSO, Sultan

GAUL, ancient France

GAUTAMA, Prince, the Buddha

GAWAIN, Arthur's knight

GAWL, son of Clud, suitor for Rhiannon

GEMINI (See Castor), constellation created by Jupiter from the twin brothers after death, 158

GENGHIS Khan, Tartar conqueror

GENIUS, in Roman belief, the protective Spirit of each individual man, See Juno

GEOFFREY OF MON'MOUTH, translator into Latin of the Welsh History of the Kings of Britain (1150)

GERAINT, a knight of King Arthur

GERDA, wife of Frey

GERI, one of Odin's two wolves

GERYON, a three bodied monster

GESNES, navigator sent for Isoude the Fair

GIALLAR HORN, the trumpet that Heimdal will blow at the judgment day

GIANTS, beings of monstrous size and of fearful countenances, represented as in constant opposition to the gods, in Wagner's Nibelungen Ring

GIBICHUNG RACE, ancestors of Alberich

GIBRALTAR, great rock and town at southwest corner of Spain (See Pillars of Hercules)

GILDAS, a scholar of Arthur's court

GIRARD, son of Duke Sevinus

GLASTONBURY, where Arthur died

GLAUCUS, a fisherman, loving Scylla

GLEIPNIR, magical chain on the wolf Fenris

GLEWLWYD, Arthur's porter

GOLDEN FLEECE, of ram used for escape of children of Athamas, named Helle and Phryxus (which See), after sacrifice of ram to Jupiter, fleece was guarded by sleepless dragon and gained by Jason and Argonauts (which See, also Helle)

GONERIL, daughter of Leir

GORDIAN KNOT, tying up in temple the wagon of Gordius, he who could untie it being destined to be lord of Asia, it was cut by Alexander the Great, 48

GORDIUS, a countryman who, arriving in Phrygia in a wagon, was made king by the people, thus interpreting an oracle, 48

GORGONS, three monstrous females, with huge teeth, brazen claws and snakes for hair, sight of whom turned beholders to stone, Medusa, the most famous, slain by Perseus

GORLOIS, Duke of Tintadel

GOUVERNAIL, squire of Isabella, queen of Lionesse, protector of her son Tristram while young, and his squire in knighthood

GRAAL, the Holy, cup from which the Saviour drank at Last Supper, taken by Joseph of Arimathea to Europe, and lost, its recovery becoming a sacred quest for Arthur's knights

GRACES, three goddesses who enhanced the enjoyments of life by refinement and gentleness; they were Aglaia (brilliance), Euphrosyne (joy), and Thalia (bloom)

GRADAS'SO, king of Sericane

GRAEAE, three gray haired female watchers for the Gorgons, with one movable eye and one tooth between the three

GRAND LAMA, Buddhist pontiff in Tibet

GRENDEL, monster slain by Beowulf

GRYPHON (griffin), a fabulous animal, with the body of a lion and the head and wings of an eagle, dwelling in the Rhipaean mountains, between the Hyperboreans and the one eyed Arimaspians, and guarding the gold of the North,

GUEBERS, Persian fire worshippers,

GUENDOLEN, wife of Locrine,

GUENEVERE, wife of King Arthur, beloved by Launcelot,

GUERIN, lord of Vienne, father of Oliver,

GUIDERIUS, son of Cymbeline,

GUILLAMURIUS, king in Ireland,

GUIMIER, betrothed of Caradoc,

GULLINBURSTI, the boar drawing Frey's car,

GULLTOPP, Heimdell's horse,

GUNFASIUS, King of the Orkneys,

GANTHER, Burgundian king, brother of Kriemhild,

GUTRUNE, half sister to Hagen,

GWERN son of Matholch and Branwen,

GWERNACH THE Giant,

GWIFFERT Petit, ally of Geraint,

GWYDDNO, Garanhir, King of Gwaelod,

GWYR, judge in the court of Arthur,

GYOLL, river,

H

HADES, originally the god of the nether world—the name later used to designate the gloomy subterranean land of the dead,

HAEMON, son of Creon of Thebes, and lover of Antigone,

HAEMONIAN city,

HAEMUS, Mount, northern boundary of Thrace,

HAGAN, a principal character in the Nibelungen Lied, slayer of Siegfried,

HALCYONE, daughter of Aeneas, and the beloved wife of Ceyx, who, when he was drowned, flew to his floating body, and the pitying gods changed them both to birds (kingfishers), who nest at sea during a certain calm week in winter ("halcyon weather")

HAMADRYADS, tree-nymphs or wood-nymphs, See Nymphs

HARMONIA, daughter of Mars and Venus, wife of Cadmus

HAROUN AL RASCHID, Caliph of Arabia, contemporary of Charlemagne

HARPIES, monsters, with head and bust of woman, but wings, legs and tail of birds, seizing souls of the wicked, or punishing evildoers by greedily snatching or defiling their food

HARPOCRATES, Egyptian god, Horus

HEBE, daughter of Juno, cupbearer to the gods

HEBRUS, ancient name of river Maritzka

HECATE, a mighty and formidable divinity, supposed to send at night all kinds of demons and terrible phantoms from the lower world

HECTOR, son of Priam and champion of Troy

HECTOR, one of Arthur's knights

HECTOR DE MARYS', a knight

HECUBA, wife of Priam, king of Troy, to whom she bore Hector, Paris, and many other children

HEGIRA, flight of Mahomet from Mecca to Medina (622 AD), era from which Mahometans reckon time, as we do from the birth of Christ

HEIDRUN, she goat, furnishing mead for slain heroes in Valhalla

HEIMDALL, watchman of the gods

HEL, the lower world of Scandinavia, to which were consigned those who had not died in battle

HELA (Death), the daughter of Loki and the mistress of the Scandinavian Hel

HELEN, daughter of Jupiter and Leda, wife of Menelaus, carried off by Paris and cause of the Trojan War

HELENUS, son of Priam and Hecuba, celebrated for his prophetic powers

HELIADES, sisters of Phaeton

HELICON, Mount, in Greece, residence of Apollo and the Muses, with fountains of poetic inspiration, Aganippe and Hippocrene

HELIOOPOLIS, city of the Sun, in Egypt

HELLAS, Gieece

HELLE, daughter of Thessalian King Athamas, who, escaping from cruel father with her brother Phryxus, on ram with golden fleece, fell into the sea strait since named for her (See Golden Fleece)

HELLESPONT, narrow strait between Europe and Asia Minor, named for Helle

HENGIST, Saxon invader of Britain, 449 AD

HEPHAESTOS, See VULCAN

HERA, called Juno by the Romans, a daughter of Cronos (Saturn) and Rhea, and sister and wife of Jupiter, See JUNO

HERCULES, athletic hero, son of Jupiter and Alcmena, achieved twelve vast labors and many famous deeds

HEREWARD THE WAKE, hero of the Saxons

HERMES (Mercury), messenger of the gods, deity of commerce, science, eloquence, trickery, theft, and skill generally

HERMIONE, daughter of Menelaus and Helen

HERMOD, the nimble, son of Odin

HERO, a priestess of Venus, beloved of Leander

HERODOTUS, Greek historian

HESIOD, Greek poet

HESPERIA, ancient name for Italy

HESPERIDES (See Apples of the Hesperides)

HESPERUS, the evening star (also called Day Star)

HESTIA, called Vesta by the Romans, the goddess of the hearth

HILDEBRAND, German magician and champion

HINDU TRIAD, Brahma, Vishnu, and Siva

HIPPOCRENE (See Helicon)

HIPPODAMIA, wife of Pirithous, at whose wedding the Centaurs offered violence to the bride, causing a great battle

HIPPOGRIFF, winged horse, with eagle's head and claws

HIPPOLYTA, Queen of the Amazons

HIPPOLYTUS, son of Thesus

HIPPOMENES, who won Atalanta in foot race, beguiling her with golden apples thrown for her to

HISTION, son of Japhet

HODUR, blind man, who, fooled by Loki, threw a mistletoe twig at Baldur, killing him

HOEL, king of Brittany

HOMER, the blind poet of Greece, about 850 B C

HOPE (See PANDORA)

HORAE See HOURS

HORSA, with Hengist, invader of Britain

HORUS, Egyptian god of the sun

HOUDAIN, Tristram's dog

HRINGHAM, Baldur's ship

HROTHGAR, king of Denmark

HUGI, who beat Thialfi in foot races

HUGIN, one of Odin's two ravens

HUNDING, husband of Sieglinda

HUON, son of Duke Sevinus

HYACINTHUS, a youth beloved by Apollo, and accidentally killed by him, changed in death to the flower, hyacinth

HYADES, Nysaean nymphs, nurses of infant Bacchus, rewarded by being placed as cluster of stars in the heavens

HYALE, a nymph of Diana

HYDRA, nine headed monster slain by Hercules

HYGEIA, goddess of health, daughter of Aesculapius

HYLAS, a youth detained by nymphs of spring where he sought water

HYMEN, the god of marriage, imagined as a handsome youth and invoked in bridal songs

HYMETTUS, mountain in Attica, near Athens, celebrated for its marble and its honey

HYPERBOREANS, people of the far North

HYPERION, a Titan, son of Uranus and Ge, and father of Helios, Selene, and Eos, cattle of,

HYRCANIA, Prince of, betrothed to Clarimunda

HYRIEUS, king in Greece,

I

IAPETUS, a Titan, son of Uranus and Ge, and father of Atlas, Prometheus, Epimetheus, and Menoetius,

IASIUS, father of Atalanta

IBYCUS, a poet, story of, and the cranes

ICARIA, island of the Aegean Sea, one of the Sporades

ICARIUS, Spartan prince, father of Penelope

ICARUS, son of Daedalus, he flew too near the sun with artificial wings, and, the wax melting, he fell into the sea

ICELOS, attendant of Morpheus

ICOLUMKILL SEE Iona

IDA, Mount, a Trojan hill

IDAEUS, a Trojan herald

IDAS, son of Aphareus and Arene, and brother of Lynceus Idu'na, wife of Bragi

IGERNE, wife of Gorlois, and mother, by Uther, of Arthur

ILIAD, epic poem of the Trojan War, by Homer

ILIOHEUS, a son of Niobe

ILIUM SEE Troy

ILLYRIA, Adriatic countries north of Greece

IMOGEN, daughter of Pandrasus, wife of Trojan Brutus

INACHUS, son of Oceanus and Tethys, and father of Phoroneus and Io, also first king of Argos, and said to have given his name to the river Inachus

INCUBUS, an evil spirit, supposed to lie upon persons in their sleep

INDRA, Hindu god of heaven, thunder, lightning, storm and rain

INO, wife of Athamas, fleeing from whom with infant son she sprang into the sea and was changed to Leucothea

IO, changed to a heifer by Jupiter

IOBATES, King of Lycia

IOLAUS, servant of Hercules

IOLE, sister of Dryope

IONA, or Icolmkill, a small northern island near Scotland, where St Columba founded a missionary monastery (563 AD)

IONIA, coast of Asia Minor

IPHIGENIA, daughter of Agamemnon, offered as a sacrifice but carried away by Diana

IPHIS, died for love of Anaxarete, 78

IPHITAS, friend of Hercules, killed by him

IRIS, goddess of the rainbow, messenger of Juno and Zeus

IRONSIDE, Arthur's knight

ISABELLA, daughter of king of Galicia

ISIS, wife of Osiris, described as the giver of death

ISLES OF THE BLESSED

ISMARUS, first stop of Ulysses, returning from Trojan War

ISME'NOS, a son of Niobe, slain by Apollo

ISOLIER, friend of Rinaldo

ISOUDE THE FAIR, beloved of Tristram

ISOUDE OF THE WHITE HANDS, married to Tristram

ISTHMIAN GAMES, See GAMES

ITHACA, home of Ulysses and Penelope

IULUS, son of Aeneas

IVO, Saracen king, befriending Rinaldo

IXION, once a sovereign of Thessaly, sentenced in Tartarus to be lashed with serpents to a wheel which a strong wind drove continually around

J

JANICULUM, Roman fortress on the Janiculus, a hill on the other side of the Tiber

JANUS, a deity from the earliest times held in high estimation by the Romans, temple of

JAPHET (Iapetus)

JASON, leader of the Argonauts, seeking the Golden Fleece

JOSEPH OF ARIMATHEA, who bore the Holy Graal to Europe

JOTUNHEIM, home of the giants in Northern mythology

JOVE (Zeus), chief god of Roman and Grecian mythology, See JUPITER

JOYOUS GARDE, residence of Sir Launcelot of the Lake

JUGGERNAUT, Hindu deity

JUNO, the particular guardian spirit of each woman (See Genius)

JUNO, wife of Jupiter, queen of the gods

JUPITER, JOVIS PATER, FATHER JOVE, JUPITER and JOVE used interchangeably, at Dodona, statue of the Olympian

JUPITER AMMON (See Ammon)

JUPITER CAPITOLINUS, temple of, preserving the Sibylline books

JUSTICE, See THEMIS

K

KADYRIATH, advises King Arthur

KAI, son of Kyner

KALKI, tenth avatar of Vishnu

KAY, Arthur's steward and a knight

KEDALION, guide of Orion

KERMAN, desert of

KICVA, daughter of Gwynn Gloy

KILWICH, son of Kilydd

KILYDD, son of Prince Kelyddon, of Wales

KNEPH, spirit or breath

KNIGHTS, training and life of

KRIEMHILD, wife of Siegfried

KRISHNA, eighth avatar of Vishnu, Hindu deity of fertility in nature and mankind

KYNER, father of Kav

KYNON, son of Clydno

L

LABYRINTH, the enclosed maze of passageways where roamed the Minotaur of Crete, killed by Theseus with aid of Ariadne

LACHESIS, one of the Fates (which See)

LADY OF THE FOUNTAIN, tale told by Kynon

LAERTES, father of Ulysses

LAESTRYGONIANS, savages attacking Ulysses

LAIUS, King of Thebes

LAMA, holy man of Tibet

LAMPETIA, daughter of Hyperion LAOC'OON, a priest of Neptune, in Troy, who warned the Trojans against the Wooden Horse (which See), but when two serpents came out of the sea and strangled him and his two sons, the people listened to the Greek spy Sinon, and brought the fatal Horse into the town

LAODAMIA, daughter of Acastus and wife of Protesilaus

LAODEGAN, King of Carmalide, helped by Arthur and Merlin

LAOMEDON, King of Troy

LAPITHAE, Thessalonians, whose king had invited the Centaurs to his daughter's wedding but who attacked them for offering violence to the bride

LARES, household deities

LARKSPUR, flower from the blood of Ajax

LATINUS, ruler of Latium, where Aeneas landed in Italy

LATMOS, Mount, where Diana fell in love with Endymion

LATONA, mother of Apollo

LAUNCELOT, the most famous knight of the Round Table

LAUSUS, son of Mezentius, killed by Aeneas

LAVINIA, daughter of Latinus and wife of Aeneas

LAVINIUM, Italian city named for Lavinia

LAW, See THEMIS

LEANDER, a youth of Abydos, who, swimming the Hellespont to see Hero, his love, was drowned

LEBADEA, site of the oracle of Trophomus

LEBYNTHOS, Aegean island

LEDA, Queen of Sparta, wooed by Jupiter in the form of a swan

LEIR, mythical King of Britain, original of Shakespeare's Lear

LELAPS, dog of Cephalus

LEMNOS, large island in the Aegean Sea, sacred to Vulcan

LEMURES, the spectres or spirits of the dead

LEO, Roman emperor, Greek prince

LETHE, river of Hades, drinking whose water caused forgetfulness

LEUCADIA, a promontory, whence Sappho, disappointed in love, was said to have thrown herself into the sea

LEUCOTHEA, a sea goddess, invoked by sailors for protection (See Ino)

LEWIS, son of Charlemagne

LIBER, ancient god of fruitfulness

LIBETHRA, burial place of Orpheus

LIBYA, Greek name for continent of Africa in general

LIBYAN DESERT, in Africa

LIBYAN OASIS

LICHAS, who brought the shirt of Nessus to Hercules

LIMOURS, Earl of

LINUS, musical instructor of Hercules

LIONEL, knight of the Round Table

LLYR, King of Britain

LOCRINE, son of Brutus in Albion, king of Central England

LOEGRIA, kingdom of (England)

LOGESTILLA, a wise lady, who entertained Rogero and his friends

LOGI, who vanquished Loki in an eating contest

LOKI, the Satan of Norse mythology, son of the giant Farbanti

LOT, King, a rebel chief, subdued by King Arthur, then a loyal knight

LOTIS, a nymph, changed to a lotus-plant and in that form plucked by Dryope

LOTUS EATERS, soothed to indolence, companions of Ulysses landing among them lost all memory of home and had to be dragged away before they would continue their voyage

LOVE (Eros) issued from egg of Night, and with arrows and torch produced life and joy

LUCAN, one of Arthur's knights

LUCIUS TIBERIUS, Roman procurator in Britain demanding tribute from Arthur

LUD, British king, whose capital was called Lud's Town (London)

LUDGATE, city gate where Lud was buried, 387

LUNED, maiden who guided Owain to the Lady of the Fountain

LYCAHAS, a turbulent sailor

LYCAON, son of Priam

LYCIA, a district in Southern Asia Minor

LYCOMODES, king of the Dolopians, who treacherously slew Theseus

LYCUS, usurping King of Thebes

LYNCEUS, one of the sons of Aegyptus

M

MABINOGEON, plural of Mabinogi, fairy tales and romances of the Welsh

MABON, son of Modron

MACHAON, son of Aesculapius

MADAN, son of Guendolen

MADOC, a forester of King Arthur

MADOR, Scottish knight

MAELGAN, king who imprisoned Elphin

MAEONIA, ancient Lydia

MAGI, Persian priests

MAHADEVA, same as Siva

MAHOMET, great prophet of Arabia, born in Mecca, 571 AD, proclaimed worship of God instead of idols, spread his religion through disciples and then by force till it prevailed, with Arabian dominion, over vast regions in Asia, Africa, and Spain in Europe

MAIA, daughter of Atlas and Pleione, eldest and most beautiful of the Pleiades

MALAGIGI the Enchanter, one of Charlemagne's knights

MALEAGANS, false knight

MALVASIUS, King of Iceland

MAMBRINO, with invisible helmet

MANAWYD DAN, brother of King Vran, of London

MANDRICARDO, son of Agrican

MANTUA, in Italy, birthplace of Virgil

MANU, ancestor of mankind

MARATHON, where Theseus and Pirithous met

MARK, King of Cornwall, husband of Isoude the Fair

MARO See VIRGIL

MARPHISA, sister of Rogero

MARSILIUS, Spanish king, treacherous foe of Charlemagne

MARSYAS, inventor of the flute, who challenged Apollo to musical competition, and, defeated, was flayed alive

MATSYA, the Fish, first avatar of Vishnu

MEANDER, Grecian river

MEDE, A, princess and sorceress who aided Jason

MEDORO, a young Moor, who wins Angelica

MEDUSA, one of the Gorgons

MEGAERA, one of the Furies

MELAMPUS, a Spartan dog, the first mortal endowed with prophetic powers

MELANTHUS, steersman for Bacchus

MELEAGER, one of the Argonauts (See Althaea)

MELIADUS, King of Lionesse, near Cornwall

MELICERTES, infant son of Ino. changed to Palaemon (See Ino, Leucothea, and Palasmon)

MELISSA, priestess at Merlin's tomb

MELISSEUS, a Cretan king

MELPOMENE, one of the Muses

MEMNON, the beautiful son of Tithonus and Eos (Aurora), and king of the Ethiopians, slain in Trojan War

MEMPHIS, Egyptian city

MENELAUS, son of King of Sparta, husband of Helen

MENOECEUS, son of Creon, voluntary victim in war to gain success for his father

MENTOR, son of Alcimus and a faithful friend of Ulysses

MERCURY (See HERMES)

MERLIN, enchanter

MEROPE, daughter of King of Chios, beloved by Orion

MESMERISM, likened to curative oracle of Aesculapius at Epidaurus

METABUS, father of Camilla

METAMORPHOSES, Ovid's poetical legends of mythical transformations, a large source of our knowledge of classic mythology

METANIRA, a mother, kind to Ceres seeking Proserpine

METEMPSYCHOSIS, transmigration of souls—rebirth of dying men and women in forms of animals or human beings

METIS, Prudence, a spouse of Jupiter

MEZENTIUS, a brave but cruel soldier, opposing Aeneas in Italy

MIDAS

MIDGARD, the middle world of the Norsemen

MIDGARD SERPENT, a sea monster, child of Loki

MILKY WAY, starred path across the sky, believed to be road to palace of the gods

MILO, a great athlete

MLON, father of Orlando

MILTON, John, great English poet, whose History of England is here largely used

MIME, one of the chief dwarfs of ancient German mythology

MINERVA (Athene), daughter of Jupiter, patroness of health, learning, and wisdom

MINOS, King of Crete

MINO TAUR, monster killed by Theseus

MISTLETOE, fatal to Baldur

MNEMOSYNE, one of the Muses

MODESTY, statue to

MODRED, nephew of King Arthur

MOLY, plant, powerful against sorcery

MOMUS, a deity whose delight was to jeer bitterly at gods and men

MONAD, the "unit" of Pythagoras

MONSTERS, unnatural beings, evilly disposed to men

MONTALBAN, Rinaldo's castle

MONTH, the, attendant upon the Sun

MOON, goddess of, see DIANA

MORAUNT, knight, an Irish champion

MORGANA, enchantress, the Lady of the Lake in "Orlando Furioso," same as Morgane Le Fay in tales of Arthur

MORGANE LE FAY, Queen of Norway, King Arthur's sister, an enchantress

MORGAN TUD, Arthur's chief physician

MORPHEUS, son of Sleep and god of dreams

MORTE D'ARTHUR, romance, by Sir Thomas Mallory

MULCIBER, Latin name of Vulcan

MULL, Island of

MUNIN, one of Odin's two ravens

MUSAEUS, sacred poet, son of Orpheus

MUSES, The, nine goddesses presiding over poetry, etc—Calliope, epic poetry, Clio, history, Erato, love poetry, Euterpe, lyric poetry; Melpomene, tragedy, Polyhymnia, oratory and sacred song Terpsichore, choral song and dance, Thalia, comedy and idyls, Urania, astronomy

MUSPELHEIM, the fire world of the Norsemen

MYCENAS, ancient Grecian city, of which Agamemnon was king

MYRDDIN (Merlin)

MYRMIDONS, bold soldiers of Achilles

MYSIA, Greek district on northwest coast of Asia Minor

MYTHOLOGY, origin of, collected myths, describing gods of early peoples

N

NAIADS, water nymphs

NAMO, Duke of Bavaria, one of Charlemagne's knights

NANNA, wife of Baldur

NANTERS, British king

NANTES, site of Caradoc's castle

NAPE, a dog of Diana

NARCISSUS, who died of unsatisfied love for his own image in the water

NAUSICAA, daughter of King Alcinous, who befriended Ulysses

NAUSITHOUS, king of Phaeacians

NAXOS, Island of

NEGUS, King of Abyssinia

NEMEA, forest devastated by a lion killed by Hercules

NEMEAN GAMES, held in honor of Jupiter and Hercules

NEMEAN LION, killed by Hercules

NEMESIS, goddess of vengeance

NENNIUS, British combatant of Caesar

NEOPTOLEMUS, son of Achilles

NEPENTHE, ancient drug to cause forgetfulness of pain or distress

NEPHELE, mother of Phryxus and Helle

NEPHTHYS, Egyptian goddess

NEPTUNE, identical with Poseidon, god of the sea

NEREIDS, sea nymphs, daughters of Nereus and Doris

NEREUS, a sea god

NESSUS, a centaur killed by Hercules, whose jealous wife sent him a robe or shirt steeped in the blood of Nessus, which poisoned him

NESTOR, king of Pylos, renowned for his wisdom, justice, and knowledge of war

NIBELUNGEN HOARD, treasure seized by Siegfried from the Nibelungs, buried in the Rhine by Hagan after killing Siegfried, and lost when Hagan was killed by Kriemhild, theme of Wagner's four music dramas, "The Ring of the Nibelungen,"

NIBELUNGEN LIED, German epic, giving the same nature myth as the Norse Volsunga Saga, concerning the Hoard

NIBELUNGEN RING, Wagner's music dramas

NIBELUNGS, the, a race of Northern dwarfs

NIDHOGGE, a serpent in the lower world that lives on the dead

NIFFLEHEIM, mist world of the Norsemen, the Hades of absent spirits

NILE, Egyptian river

NIOBE, daughter of Tantalus, proud Queen of Thebes, whose seven sons and seven daughters were killed by Apollo and Diana, at which Amphion, her husband, killed himself, and Niobe wept until she was turned to stone

NISUS, King of Megara

NOAH, as legendary ancestor of French, Roman, German, and British peoples

NOMAN, name assumed by Ulysses

NORNS, the three Scandinavian Fates, Urdur (the past), Verdandi (the present), and Skuld (the future)

NOTHUNG, magic sword

NOTUS, southwest wind

NOX, daughter of Chaos and sister of Erebus, personification of night

NUMA, second king of Rome

NYMPHS, beautiful maidens, lesser divinities of nature Dryads and Hamadryads, tree nymphs, Naiads, spring, brook, and river nymphs, Nereids, sea nymphs Oreads, mountain nymphs or hill nymphs

O

OCEANUS, a Titan, ruling watery elements

OCYROE, a prophetess, daughter of Chiron

ODERIC

ODIN, chief of the Norse gods

ODYAR, famous Biscayan hero

ODYSSEUS See ULYSSES

ODYSSEY, Homer's poem, relating the wanderings of Odysseus (Ulysses) on returning from Trojan War

OEDIPUS, Theban hero, who guessed the riddle of the Sphinx (which See), becoming King of Thebes

OENEUS, King of Calydon

OENONE, nymph, married by Paris in his youth, and abandoned for Helen

OENOPION, King of Chios

OETA, Mount, scene of Hercules' death

OGIER, the Dane, one of the paladins of Charlemagne

OLIVER, companion of Orlando

OLWEN, wife of Kilwich

OLYMPIA, a small plain in Elis, where the Olympic games were celebrated

OLYMPIADS, periods between Olympic games (four years)

OLYMPIAN GAMES, See GAMES

OLYMPUS, dwelling place of the dynasty of gods of which Zeus was the head

OMPHALE, queen of Lydia, daughter of Iardanus and wife of Tmolus

OPHION, king of the Titans, who ruled Olympus till dethroned by the gods Saturn and Rhea

OPS See RHEA

ORACLES, answers from the gods to questions from seekers for knowledge or advice for the future, usually in equivocal form, so as to fit any event, also places where such answers were given forth usually by a priest or priestess

ORC, a sea monster, foiled by Rogero when about to devour Angelica

OREADS, nymphs of mountains and hills

ORESTES, son of Agamemnon and Clytemnestra, because of his crime in killing his mother, he was pursued by the Furies until purified by Minerva

ORION, youthful giant, loved by Diana, Constellation

ORITHYIA, a nymph, seized by Boreas

ORLANDO, a famous knight and nephew of Charlemagne

ORMUZD (Greek, Oromasdes), son of Supreme Being, source of good as his brother Ahriman (Arimanes) was of evil, in Persian or Zoroastrian religion

ORPHEUS, musician, son of Apollo and Calliope, See EURYDICE

OSIRIS, the most beneficent of the Egyptian gods

OSSA, mountain of Thessaly

OSSIAN, Celtic poet of the second or third century

OVID, Latin poet (See Metamorphoses)

OWAIN, knight at King Arthur's court

OZANNA, a knight of Arthur

P

PACTOLUS, river whose sands were changed to gold by Midas

PAEON, a name for both Apollo and Aesculapius, gods of medicine,

PAGANS, heathen

PALADINS or peers, knights errant

PALAEMON, son of Athamas and Ino

PALAMEDES, messenger sent to call Ulysses to the Trojan War

PALAMEDES, Saracen prince at Arthur's court

PALATINE, one of Rome's Seven Hills

PALES, goddess presiding over cattle and pastures

PALINURUS, faithful steersman of Aeeas

PALLADIUM, properly any image of Pallas Athene, but specially applied to an image at Troy, which was stolen by Ulysses and Diomedes

PALLAS, son of Evander

PALLAS A THE'NE (Minerva)

PAMPHA GUS, a dog of Diana

PAN, god of nature and the universe

PANATHENAEA, festival in honor of Pallas Athene (Minerva)

PANDEAN PIPES, musical instrument of reeds, made by Pan in memory of Syrinx

PANDORA (all gifted), first woman, dowered with gifts by every god, yet entrusted with a box she was cautioned not to open, but, curious, she opened it, and out flew all the ills of humanity, leaving behind only Hope, which remained

PANDRASUS, a king in Greece, who persecuted Trojan exiles under Brutus, great grandson of Aeneas, until they fought, captured him, and, with his daughter Imogen as Brutus' wife, emigrated to Albion (later called Britain)

PANOPE, plain of

PANTHUS, alleged earlier incarnation of Pythagoras

PAPHLAGNIA, ancient country in Asia Minor, south of Black Sea

PAPHOS, daughter of Pygmalion and Galatea (both of which, See)

PARCAE See FATES

PARIAHS, lowest caste of Hindus

PARIS, son of Priam and Hecuba, who eloped with Helen (which. See)

PARNASSIAN LAUREl, wreath from Parnassus, crown awarded to successful poets

PARNASSUS, mountain near Delphi, sacred to Apollo and the Muses

PARSEES, Persian fire worshippers (Zoroastrians), of whom there are still thousands in Persia and India

PARTHENON, the temple of Athene Parthenos ("the Virgin") on the Acropolis of Athens

PASSEBREUL, Tristram's horse

PATROCLUS, friend of Achilles, killed by Hector

PECHEUR, King, uncle of Perceval

PEERS, the

PEGASUS, winged horse, born from the sea foam and the blood of Medusa

PELEUS, king of the Myrmidons, father of Achilles by Thetis

PELIAS, usurping uncle of Jason

PELION, mountain

PELLEAS, knight of Arthur

PENATES, protective household deities of the Romans

PENDRAGON, King of Britain, elder brother of Uther Pendragon, who succeeded him

PENELOPE, wife of Ulysses, who, waiting twenty years for his return from the Trojan War, put off the suitors for her hand by promising to choose one when her weaving was done, but unravelled at night what she had woven by day

PENEUS, river god, river

PENTHESILEA, queen of Amazons

PENTHEUS, king of Thebes, having resisted the introduction of the worship of Bacchus into his kingdom, was driven mad by the god

PENUS, Roman house pantry, giving name to the Penates

PEPIN, father of Charlemagne

PEPLUS, sacred robe of Minerva

PERCEVAL, a great knight of Arthur

PERDIX, inventor of saw and compasses

PERIANDER, King of Corinuh, friend of Arion

PERIPHETES, son of Vulcan, killed by Theseus

PERSEPHONE, goddess of vegetation, 8 See Pioserpine

PERSEUS, son of Jupiter and Danae, slayer of the Gorgon Medusa, deliverer of Andromeda from a sea monster, 116 122, 124, 202

PHAEACIANS, people who entertained Ulysses

PHAEDRA, faithless and cruel wife of Theseus

PHAETHUSA, sister of Phaeton, 244

PHAETON, son of Phoebus, who dared attempt to drive his father's sun chariot

PHANTASOS, a son of Somnus, bringing strange images to sleeping men

PHAON, beloved by Sappho

PHELOT, knight of Wales

PHEREDIN, friend of Tristram, unhappy lover of Isoude

PHIDIAS, famous Greek sculptor

PHILEMON, husband of Baucis

PHILOCTETES, warrior who lighted the fatal pyre of Hercules

PHILOE, burial place of Osiris

PHINEUS, betrothed to Andromeda

PHLEGETHON, fiery river of Hades

PHOCIS

PHOEBE, one of the sisters of Phaeton

PHOEBUS (Apollo), god of music, prophecy, and archery, the sun god

PHOENIX, a messenger to Achilles, also, a miraculous bird dying in fire by its own act and springing up alive from its own ashes

PHORBAS, a companion of Aeneas, whose form was assumed by Neptune in luring Palinuras the helmsman from his roost

PHRYXUS, brother of Helle

PINABEL, knight

PILLARS OF HERCULES, two mountains—Calpe, now the Rock of Gibraltar, southwest corner of Spain in Europe, and Abyla, facing it in Africa across the strait

PINDAR, famous Greek poet

PINDUS, Grecian mountain

PIRENE, celebrated fountain at Corinth

PIRITHOUS, king of the Lapithae in Thessaly, and friend of Theseus, husband of Hippodamia

PLEASURE, daughter of Cupid and Psyche

PLEIADES, seven of Diana's nymphs, changed into stars, one being lost

PLENTY, the Horn of

PLEXIPPUS, brother of Althea

PLINY, Roman naturalist

PLUTO, the same as Hades, Dis, etc. god of the Infernal Regions

PLUTUS, god of wealth

PO, Italian river

POLE STAR

POLITES, youngest son of Priam of Troy

POLLUX, Castor and (Dioscuri, the Twins) (See Castor)

POLYDECTES, king of Seriphus

POLYDORE, slain kinsman of Aeneas, whose blood nourished a bush that bled when broken

POLYHYMNIA, Muse of oratory and sacred song

POLYIDUS, soothsayer

POLYNICES, King of Thebes

POLYPHEMUS, giant son of Neptune

POLYXENA, daughter of King Priam of Troy

POMONA, goddess of fruit trees (See VERTUMNUS)

PORREX and FER'REX, sons of Leir, King of Britain

PORTUNUS, Roman name for Palaemon

POSEIDON (Neptune), ruler of the ocean

PRECIPICE, threshold of Helas hall

PRESTER JOHN, a rumored priest or presbyter, a Christian pontiff in Upper Asia, believed in but never found

PRIAM, king of Troy

PRIWEN, Arthur's shield

PROCRIS, beloved but jealous wife of Cephalus

PROCRUSTES, who seized travellers and bound them on his iron bed, stretching the short ones and cutting short the tall, thus also himself served by Theseus

PROETUS, jealous of Bellerophon

PROMETHEUS, creator of man, who stole fire from heaven for man's use

PROSERPINE, the same as Persephone, goddess of all growing things, daughter of Ceres, carried off by Pluto

PROTESILAUS, slain by Hector the Trojan, allowed by the gods to return for three hours' talk with his widow Laodomia

PROTEUS, the old man of the sea

PRUDENCE (Metis), spouse of Jupiter

PRYDERI, son of Pwyll

PSYCHE, a beautiful maiden, personification of the human soul, sought by Cupid (Love), to whom she responded, lost him by curiosity to see him (as he came to her only by night), but finally through his prayers was made immortal and restored to him, a symbol of immortality

PURANAS, Hindu Scriptures

PWYLL, Prince of Dyved

PYGMALION, sculptor in love with a statue he had made, brought to life by Venus, brother of Queen Dido

PYGMIES, nation of dwarfs, at war with the Cranes

PYLADES, son of Straphius, friend of Orestes

PYRAMUS, who loved Thisbe, next door neighbor, and, their parents opposing, they talked through cracks in the house wall, agreeing to meet in the near by woods, where Pyramus, finding a bloody veil and thinking Thisbe slain, killed himself, and she, seeing his body, killed herself (Burlesqued in Shakespeare's "Midsummer Night's Dream")

PYRRHA, wife of Deucalion

PYRRHUS (Neoptolemus), son of Achilles

PYTHAGORAS, Greek philosopher (540 BC), who thought numbers to be the essence and principle of all things, and taught transmigration of souls of the dead into new life as human or animal beings

PYTHIA, priestess of Apollo at Delphi

PYTHIAN GAMES

PYTHIAN ORACLE

PYTHON, serpent springing from Deluge slum, destroyed by Apollo

QUIRINUS (from quiris, a lance or spear), a war god, said to be Romulus, founder of Rome

R

RABICAN, noted horse

RAGNAROK, the twilight (or ending) of the gods

RAJPUTS, minor Hindu caste

REGAN, daughter of Leir

REGILLUS, lake in Latium, noted for battle fought near by between the Romans and the Latins

REGGIO, family from which Rogero sprang

REMUS, brother of Romulus, founder of Rome

RHADAMANTHUS, son of Jupiter and Europa after his death one of the judges in the lower world

RHAPSODIST, professional reciter of poems among the Greeks

RHEA, female Titan, wife of Saturn (Cronos), mother of the chief gods, worshipped in Greece and Rome

RHINE, river

RHINE MAIDENS, OR DAUGHTERS, three water nymphs, Flosshilda, Woglinda, and Wellgunda, set to guard the Nibelungen Hoard, buried in the Rhine

RHODES, one of the seven cities claiming to be Homer's birthplace

RHODOPE, mountain in Thrace

RHONGOMYANT, Arthur's lance

RHOECUS, a youth, beloved by a Dryad, but who brushed away a bee sent by her to call him to her, and she punished him with blindness

RHIANNON, wife of Pwyll

RINALDO, one of the bravest knights of Charlemagne

RIVER OCEAN, flowing around the earth

ROBERT DE BEAUVAIS', Norman poet (1257)

ROBIN HOOD, famous outlaw in English legend, about time of Richard Coeur de Lion

ROCKINGHAM, forest of

RODOMONT, king of Algiers

ROGERO, noted Saracen knight

ROLAND (Orlando), See Orlando

ROMANCES

ROMANUS, legendary great grandson of Noah

ROME

ROMULUS, founder of Rome

RON, Arthur's lance

RONCES VALLES', battle of

ROUND TABLE King Arthur's instituted by Merlin the Sage for Pendragon, Arthur's father, as a knightly order, continued and made famous by Arthur and his knights

RUNIC CHARACTERS, or runes, alphabetic signs used by early Teutonic peoples, written or graved on metal or stone

RUTULIANS, an ancient people in Italy, subdued at an early period by the Romans

RYENCE, king in Ireland

S

SABRA, maiden for whom Severn River was named, daughter of Locrine and Estrildis thrown into river Severn by Locrine's wife, transformed to a river nymph, poetically named Sabrina

SACRIPANT, king of Circassia

SAFFIRE, Sir, knight of Arthur

SAGAS, Norse tales of heroism, composed by the Skalds

SAGRAMOUR, knight of Arthur

ST. MICHAEL'S MOUNT, precipitous pointed rock hill on the coast of Brittany, opposite Cornwall

SAKYASINHA, the Lion, epithet applied to Buddha

SALAMANDER, a lizard like animal, fabled to be able to live in fire

SALAMIS, Grecian city

SALMONEUS, son of Aeolus and Enarete and brother of Sisyphus

SALOMON, king of Brittany, at Charlemagne's court

SAMHIN, or "fire of peace," a Druidical festival

SAMIAN SAGE (Pythagoras)

SAMOS, island in the Aegean Sea

SAMOTHRACIAN GODS, a group of agricultural divinities, worshipped in Samothrace

SAMSON, Hebrew hero, thought by some to be original of Hercules

SAN GREAL (See Graal, the Holy)

SAPPHO, Greek poetess, who leaped into the sea from promontory of
Leucadia in disappointed love for Phaon

SARACENS, followers of Mahomet

SARPEDON, son of Jupiter and Europa, killed by Patroclus

SATURN (Cronos)

SATURNALIA, a annual festival held by Romans in honor of Saturn

SATURNIA, an ancient name of Italy

SATYRS, male divinities of the forest, half man, half goat

SCALIGER, famous German scholar of 16th century

SCANDINAVIA, mythology of, giving account of Northern gods, heroes, etc

SCHERIA, mythical island, abode of the Phaeacians

SCHRIMNIR, the boar, cooked nightly for the heroes of Valhalla becoming whole every morning

SCIO, one of the island cities claiming to be Homer's birthplace

SCOPAS, King of Thessaly

SCORPION, constellation

SCYLLA, sea nymph beloved by Glaucus, but changed by jealous Circe to a monster and finally to a dangerous rock on the Sicilian coast, facing the whirlpool Charybdis, many mariners being wrecked between the two, also, daughter of King Nisus of Megara, who loved Minos, besieging her father's city, but he disliked her disloyalty and drowned her, also, a fair virgin of Sicily, friend of sea nymph Galatea

SCYROS, where Theseus was slain

SCYTHIA, country lying north of Euxine Sea

SEMELE, daughter of Cadmus and, by Jupiter, mother of Bacchus

SEMIRAMIS, with Ninus the mythical founder of the Assyrian empire of Nineveh

SENAPUS, King of Abyssinia, who entertained Astolpho

SERAPIS, or Hermes, Egyptian divinity of Tartarus and of medicine

SERFS, slaves of the land

SERIPHUS, island in the Aegean Sea, one of the Cyclades

SERPENT (Northern constellation)

SESTOS, dwelling of Hero (which See also Leander)

"SEVEN AGAINST THEBES," famous Greek expedition

SEVERN RIVER, in England

SEVINUS, Duke of Guienne

SHALOTT, THE LADY OF

SHATRIYA, Hindu warrior caste

SHERASMIN, French chevalier

SIBYL, prophetess of Cumae

SICHAEUS, husband of Dido

SEIGE PERILOUS, the chair of purity at Arthur's Round Table, fatal to any but him who was destined to achieve the quest of the Sangreal (See Galahad)

SIEGFRIED, young King of the Netherlands, husband of Kriemhild, she boasted to Brunhild that Siegfried had aided Gunther to beat her in athletic contests, thus winning her as wife, and Brunhild, in anger, employed Hagan to murder Siegfried. As hero of Wagner's "Valkyrie," he wins the Nibelungen treasure ring, loves and deserts Brunhild, and is slain by Hagan

SIEGLINDA, wife of Hunding, mother of Siegfried by Siegmund

SIEGMUND, father of Siegfried

SIGTRYG, Prince, betrothed of King Alef's daughter, aided by Hereward

SIGUNA, wife of Loki

SILENUS, a Satyr, school master of Bacchus

SILURES (South Wales)

SILVIA, daughter of Latin shepherd

SILVIUS, grandson of Aeneas, accidentally killed in the chase by his son Brutus

SIMONIDES, an early poet of Greece

SINON, a Greek spy, who persuaded the Trojans to take the Wooden Horse into their city

SIRENS, sea nymphs, whose singing charmed mariners to leap into the sea, passing their island, Ulysses stopped the ears of his sailors with wax, and had himself bound to the mast so that he could hear but not yield to their music

SIRIUS, the dog of Orion, changed to the Dog star

SISYPHUS, condemned in Tartarus to perpetually roll up hill a big rock which, when the top was reached, rolled down again

SIVA, the Destroyer, third person of the Hindu triad of gods

SKALDS, Norse bards and poets

SKIDBLADNIR, Freyr's ship

SKIRNIR, Frey's messenger, who won the god's magic sword by getting him Gerda for his wife

SKRYMIR, a giant, Utgard Loki in disguise, who fooled Thor in athletic feats

SKULD, the Norn of the Future

SLEEP, twin brother of Death

SLEIPNIR, Odin's horse

SOBRINO, councillor to Agramant

SOMNUS, child of Nox, twin brother of Mors, god of sleep

SOPHOCLES, Greek tragic dramatist

SOUTH WIND See Notus

SPAR'TA, capital of Lacedaemon

SPHINX, a monster, waylaying the road to Thebes and propounding riddles to all passers, on pain of death, for wrong guessing, who killed herself in rage when Aedipus guessed aright

SPRING

STONEHENGE, circle of huge upright stones, fabled to be sepulchre of Pendragon

STROPHIUS, father of Pylades

STYGIAN REALM, Hades

STYGIAN SLEEP, escaped from the beauty box sent from Hades to Venus by hand of Psyche, who curiously opened the box and was plunged into unconsciousness

STYX, river, bordering Hades, to be crossed by all the dead

SUDRAS, Hindu laboring caste

SURTUR, leader of giants against the gods in the day of their destruction (Norse mythology)

SURYA, Hindu god of the sun, corresponding to the Greek Helios

SUTRI, Orlando's birthplace

SVADILFARI, giant's horse

SWAN, LEDA AND

SYBARIS, Greek city in Southern Italy, famed for luxury

SYLVANUS, Latin divinity identified with Pan

SYMPLEGADES, floating rocks passed by the Argonauts

SYRINX, nymph, pursued by Pan, but escaping by being changed to a bunch of reeds (See Pandean pipes)

T

TACITUS, Roman historian

TAENARUS, Greek entrance to lower regions

TAGUS, river in Spain and Portugal

TALIESIN, Welsh bard

TANAIS, ancient name of river Don

TANTALUS, wicked king, punished in Hades by standing in water that retired when he would drink, under fruit trees that withdrew when he would eat

TARCHON, Etruscan chief

TARENTUM, Italian city

TARPEIAN ROCK, in Rome, from which condemned criminals were hurled

TARQUINS, a ruling family in early Roman legend

TAURIS, Grecian city, site of temple of Diana (See Iphigenia)

TAURUS, a mountain

TARTARUS, place of confinement of Titans, etc, originally a black abyss below Hades later, represented as place where the wicked were punished, and sometimes the name used as synonymous with Hades

TEIRTU, the harp of

TELAMON, Greek hero and adventurer, father of Ajax

TELEMACHUS, son of Ulysses and Penelope

TELLUS, another name for Rhea

TENEDOS, an island in Aegean Sea

TERMINUS, Roman divinity presiding over boundaries and frontiers

TERPSICHORE, Muse of dancing

TERRA, goddess of the earth

TETHYS, goddess of the sea

TEUCER, ancient king of the Trojans

THALIA, one of the three Graces

THAMYRIS, Thracian bard, who challenged the Muses to competition in singing, and, defeated, was blinded

THAUKT, Loki disguised as a hag

THEBES, city founded by Cadmus and capital of Boeotia

THEMIS, female Titan, law counsellor of Jove

THEODORA, sister of Prince Leo

THERON, one of Diana's dogs

THERSITES, a brawler, killed by Achilles

THESCELUS, foe of Perseus, turned to stone by sight of Gorgon's head

THESEUM, Athenian temple in honor of Theseus

THESEUS, son of Aegeus and Aethra, King of Athens, a great hero of many adventures

THESSALY

THESTIUS, father of Althea

THETIS, mother of Achilles

THIALFI, Thor's servant

THIS'BE, Babylonian maiden beloved by Pyramus

THOR, the thunderer, of Norse mythology, most popular of the gods

THRACE

THRINA'KIA, island pasturing Hyperion's cattle, where Ulysses landed, but, his men killing some cattle for food, their ship was wrecked by lightning

THRYM, giant, who buried Thor's hammer

THUCYDIDES, Greek historian

TIBER, river flowing through Rome

TIBER, FATHER, god of the river

TIGRIS, river

TINTADEL, castle of, residence of King Mark of Cornwall

TIRESIAS, a Greek soothsayer

TISIPHONE, one of the Furies

TITANS, the sons and daughters of Uranus (Heaven) and Gaea (Earth), enemies of the gods and overcome by them

TITHONUS, Trojan prince

TITYUS, giant in Tartarus

TMOLUS, a mountain god

TORTOISE, second avatar of Vishnu

TOURS, battle of (See Abdalrahman and Charles Martel)

TOXEUS, brother of Melauger's mother, who snatched from Atalanta her hunting trophy, and was slain by Melauger, who had awarded it to her

TRIAD, the Hindu

TRIADS, Welsh poems

TRIMURTI, Hindu Triad

TRIPTOL'EMUS, son of Celeus , and who, made great by Ceres, founded her worship in Eleusis

TRISTRAM, one of Arthur's knights, husband of Isoude of the White Hands, lover of Isoude the Fair,

TRITON, a demi god of the sea, son of Poseidon (Neptune) and Amphitrite

TROEZEN, Greek city of Argolis

TROJAN WAR

TROJANOVA, New Troy, City founded in Britain (See Brutus, and Lud)

TROPHONIUS, oracle of, in Boeotia

TROUBADOURS, poets and minstrels of Provence, in Southern France

TROUVERS', poets and minstrels of Northern France

TROY, city in Asia Minor, ruled by King Priam, whose son, Paris, stole away Helen, wife of Menelaus the Greek, resulting in the Trojan War and the destruction of Troy

TROY, fall of

TURNUS, chief of the Rutulianes in Italy, unsuccessful rival of Aeneas for Lavinia

TURPIN, Archbishop of Rheims

TURQUINE, Sir, a great knight, foe of Arthur, slain by Sir Launcelot

TYPHON, one of the giants who attacked the gods, were defeated, and imprisoned under Mt. Aetna

TYR, Norse god of battles

TYRE, Phoenician city governed by Dido

TYRIANS

TYRRHEUS, herdsman of King Turnus in Italy, the slaying of whose daughter's stag aroused war upon Aeneas and his companions

U

UBERTO, son of Galafron

ULYSSES (Greek, Odysseus), hero of the Odyssey

UNICORN, fabled animal with a single horn

URANIA, one of the Muses, a daughter of Zeus by Mnemosyne

URDUR, one of the Norns or Fates of Scandinavia, representing the Past

USK, British river

UTGARD, abode of the giant Utgard Loki

UTGARD LO'KI, King of the Giants (See Skrymir)

UTHER (Uther Pendragon), king of Britain and father of Arthur,

UWAINE, knight of Arthur's court

V

VAISSYAS, Hindu caste of agriculturists and traders

VALHALLA, hall of Odin, heavenly residence of slain heroes

VALKYRIE, armed and mounted warlike virgins, daughters of the gods (Norse), Odin's messengers, who select slain heroes for Valhalla and serve them at their feasts

VE, brother of Odin

VEDAS, Hindu sacred Scriptures

VENEDOTIA, ancient name for North Wales

VENUS (Aphrodite), goddess of beauty

VENUS DE MEDICI, famous antique statue in Uffizi Gallery, Florence, Italy

VERDANDI, the Present, one of the Norns

VERTUMNUS, god of the changing seasons, whose varied appearances won the love of Pomona

VESTA, daughter of Cronos and Rhea, goddess of the homefire, or hearth

VESTALS, virgin priestesses in temple of Vesta

VESUVIUS, Mount, volcano near Naples

VILLAINS, peasants in the feudal scheme

VIGRID, final battle-field, with destruction of the gods ind their enemies, the sun, the earth, and time itself

VILI, brother of Odin and Ve

VIRGIL, celebrated Latin poet (See Aeneid)

VIRGO, constellation of the Virgin, representing Astraea, goddess of innocence and purity

VISHNU, the Preserver, second of the three chief Hindu gods

VIVIANE, lady of magical powers, who allured the sage Merlin and imprisoned him in an enchanted wood

VOLSCENS, Rutulian troop leader who killed Nisus and Euryalus

VOLSUNG, A SAGA, an Icelandic poem, giving about the same legends as the Nibelungen Lied

VORTIGERN, usurping King of Britain, defeated by Pendragon 390, 397

VULCAN (Greek, Haephestus), god of fire and metal working, with forges under Aetna, husband of Venus

VYA'SA, Hindu sage

WAIN, the, constellation

WELLGUNDA, one of the Rhine-daughters

WELSH LANGUAGE

WESTERN OCEAN

WINDS, THE

WINTER

WODEN, chief god in the Norse mythology, Anglo Saxon for Odin

WOGLINDA, one of the Rhine-daughters

WOMAN, creation of

WOODEN HORSE, the, filled with armed men, but left outside of Troy as a pretended offering to Minerva when the Greeks feigned to sail away, accepted by the Trojans (See Sinon, and Laocoon), brought into the city, and at night emptied of the hidden Greek soldiers, who destroyed the town

WOOD NYMPHS

WOTAN, Old High German form of Odin

XANTHUS, river of Asia Minor

YAMA, Hindu god of the Infernal Regions

YEAR, THE

YGDRASIL, great ash-tree, supposed by Norse mythology to support the universe

YMIR, giant, slain by Odin

YNYWL, Earl, host of Geraint, father of Enid

YORK, Britain

YSERONE, niece of Arthur, mother of Caradoc

YSPA DA DEN PEN'KAWR, father of Olwen

Z

ZENDAVESTA, Persian sacred Scriptures

ZEPHYRUS, god of the South wind,

ZERBINO, a knight, son of the king of Scotland

ZETES, winged warrior, companion of Theseus

ZETHUS, son of Jupiter and Antiope, brother of Amphion. See Dirce

ZEUS, See JUPITER

ZOROASTER, founder of the Persian religion, which was dominant in Western Asia from about 550 BC to about 650 AD, and is still held by many thousands in Persia and in India

Index of Figures

Index of Figures

www.ingramcontent.com/pod-product-compliance
Lightning Source LLC
Chambersburg PA
CBHW081330090726
47907CB00011B/2440

* 9 7 8 1 6 4 4 5 0 1 2 4 5 *